Copyright © 2021 Des Burkinshaw
All rights reserved.
No part of this book may be reproduced in any form or by any electronic or mechanical means, including information storage and retrieval systems, without permission in writing from the publisher, except by reviewers, who may quote brief passages in a review.
Published by magnificent!
www.desburkinshaw.com

Paperback version ISBN 978-1-9160664-8-9
E-book version   ISBN 978-1-9160664-9-6

Dedication

To Jean Louise Franklin - my dear mother, who died weeks from publication.
Also, to my late cousin David Yea for his generosity.
You are both missed.

I would also like to thank Nasima Ansary for her help, knowledge and encouragement during many transatlantic calls.

Chapter 1

October 3rd, 1967
Riding House Street, London

The blonde in the red-plastic mac dodged as many puddles and stares as was possible in a crowded London lunchtime. At least her tears were camouflaged by the rain, downgrading her look from despair to sad. No-one in London thought sad was unusual. Besides, they were too busy looking for shelter themselves.

Scrunching the damp letter back into her pocket, she stopped under the awning of The Yorkshire Grey. She barely registered the two men in the doorway. She jumped when the shorter of the two, in a camp theatrical voice yelled, "Look, Dougie darling, this bird has nicked Twiggy's coat!" Stepping towards her, arms out like Frankenstein's monster, he joked, "Saw her in it last night - we can't tolerate this! Thief! Scoundrel! Call the cops!"

Dougie laughed. The shocked girl realised she was looking at one of the DJs from the new Radio 1 station, Kenny Everett. Without a word she pulled up her collar and ran down the side of the pub, putting the nearby BBC to her back.

"I told you she nicked it," joked Everett, as he and his friend ran to the curb, flagging down a black cab, instantly forgetting the dolly bird with the running mascara.

Getting a drenching, bumbling through the backstreets to her flat in Soho, the blonde in the red-plastic mac chewed the letter's contents over. The case was effectively closed. They'd given up looking. She'd never see her friend again. And it was all her fault. Of course, it was. She must be dead. The police had given up. What now? Go to someone in the government? And say, what?

More tears. She wiped her nose on the sleeve of her mac. The plastic smeared the snot, the tears, the mascara. The beautiful girl felt uglier than ever.

Blinking away the rainwater, she was decided. She'd tell her flatmate their dreams and the Summer of Love were over. The Swinging Sixties were dead, three years ahead of time. It was time go home to boring old Bristol.

"You'll be safe there," she muttered, "Home."

Chapter 2

October 15th, 2017
St-John-at-Hackney churchyard, London

Porter was leaning against the iron railings of the burial plot, whistling suspiciously, trying to avoid the gaze of a couple with a pair of pampered rat-dogs. He watched their tiny noses pointing arrogantly towards the sky, the swagger of their pert little arses, which seemed to proclaim, "Sniff my butt: I own this place." And that was just the owners.

"I hate cemeteries. They're so damn noisy," said Porter, once the pack had passed. "Not this one. Not a sound. It's almost like there's no-one buried here."

His spirit guide, The Gliss, tutted. "Most of these graves are from the 19th century. It's *because* the dead from that far back are so difficult to pick up that we're here…in training."

"Yes, yes, I know," said Porter. "The Recession: the longer someone's been dead the harder it is for me to get a vision of their last moments."

"If you know that, and you know why you're in this specific yard, what on earth are you complaining about, *mon ami*?" said The Gliss.

"Because I look like an idiot hopping from grave to grave like this. I appear to be either doing performance art or scoping the place out for a dig. Both carry mandatory life sentences. Or they should, anyway." Porter shuddered, remembering a fringe production called My Life as a Beetroot that one of his friends staged at The Hen & Chickens.

"Porter, I doubt very much anyone has even noticed you," said The Gliss, dismissively. "It is Hackney, after all."

"Oi! You! What do you think you're doing?" An outraged council worker strode towards them, leaf-blower rampant.

"Ah, touché," said The Gliss, casually. "It appears I was wrong. Don't just gawp. What's that thing you say? Hop it?"

"Hop it. Yeah."

"Well, off you go then: hop it. Unless you want to be charged with grave robbing?"

With a sigh, Porter jumped the black railings, landing like a drunk ninja. He put his trainer back on and took off towards Morning Lane. The park attendant made a lame effort to follow but the weight of the leaf-blower, and lack of desire to get a punch-up the throat, held him back. Instead, he contented himself with a hearty bellow. "Bloody vandal!"

Sitting in the back garden of Brew for Two five minutes later, Porter picked at a plate of toast and homemade baked beans. The Gliss hovered.

"You'd think that discovering I wasn't cursed would have cheered me up a bit," said Porter, "but honestly, after all the excitement of the summer, I feel a bit down."

"You're an adrenaline junkie," said The Gliss. "You're missing all the bombs, bullets and evil ghosts from World War 1."

"That's not it," shuddered Porter, remembering the case that nearly killed him. "I'm missing the sense of purpose clearing those soldiers' reputations gave me."

"Your overall mission isn't over. You just have to be patient. Sooner or later, a new case will come up."

"I just hope this one involves less maiming," said Porter, massaging his arm. His cuts had healed, but the still-mending breakages throbbed occasionally.

"I'm sure your next case will be suitably fluffy," said The Gliss, tarter than lemon eyewash. "Perhaps, let me see, we could try and clear the name of a woman accused of making bad cookies?"

Double-checking to make sure no-one was watching him speak to his invisible spirit guide, Porter stuck two fingers up and said, "Sod off."

Earlier that year, plagued by personal and professional problems, weighed down by the Norton family curse which had seen four generations of men before him commit suicide, Porter had tried to kill himself too. He'd woken up, socks on fire, to discover he wasn't allowed to become the fifth Norton to top himself. The Gliss had manifested into his life with all the joy of an unexpected fart, telling him he'd triggered a Quincunx - a sort of community service sentence from the Fates.

Now he had to make up for all the suffering caused by the suicides in his family. He'd been given the gift - if you could call it that - of being able to see and hear the last moments of the unhappy dead - providing he was close enough to their remains. His unwanted mission: right historical wrongs until the scales are re-balanced - some annoyingly indeterminate time later.

His first case - clearing a private executed for spying in World War I - led to a messy confrontation with the evil spirit of the man who'd framed the soldier in Flanders. The sadistic ghost had blown-up half the buried shells left in Belgium, damn near killing Porter and his companions, Namita, Karin and Feng. Between them, the group defeated the Profugus with Saevita (literal translation - the outsider with the rage). Its defeat quietened the graves of Cartwright and Porter's ancestor, Harry Norton. Quiet meant the soldiers' spirits were finally at rest. This was a good thing.

It had been dangerous and, for someone who hadn't believed in the supernatural, quite absurd. But the wounds were their own proof. Despite his annoyance at being made into a psychic Sherlock, the lack of a case since had left him edgy and impatient.

"Have you spoken to Karin this week?" asked The Gliss. "How's she feeling?"

"She won't be flying planes anytime soon with her eye gone, but she's ok in herself," said Porter. "Amazing woman. Tougher than my old school beef." He plunged a forkful of pallid beans into his mouth. "The eye-patch is a funny thing," he said, hankering for the full-fat Heinz experience. "I can't stop staring at it. And it's not just me. She'll spend the rest of her life feeling that life is happening a couple of inches to her right. Everyone stares at her patch."

"Feng okay?"

"What is this? The Spanish Inquisition? They can all see you; you can talk to them. Surely you know how they are?"

"It's called making conversation, old fruit," said The Gliss. "Yes, I know how they all are. Not that I should, of course."

Ah. That screw-up. The gang's VW camper van had been destroyed in a bomb blast in Flanders. Porter pulled all three of his friends from its wreckage. Sliced and diced himself, his blood had mingled with theirs. All three were now also able to see The Gliss, much to the spirit's annoyance. He'd been in a perpetual huff ever since. Porter put metaphorical hands-on-hips and glared. "Well?"

The Gliss tutted. "Ok, they're all fine. Feng is in a meeting, Karin is filming, and Namita is in the bathroom and she's…"

"Stop! Alright, alright. I'll call them."

October 15th, 2017
Riverview Nursing Home, Oxford

If The Gliss had been allowed go into more detail, Porter would have been surprised to hear who Feng Tian was meeting. The gay, Chinese, sceptical ghost-hunter (Feng considered all four labels to be shiny badges of pride) was sitting in a care home in Oxford, having tea with retired occultist, Peregrine Zouche.

Their first meetings hadn't gone well. Yes, Zouche had provided Feng with the details they'd eventually used to defeat the Profugus with the Saevita, but he was old, antagonistic, and racist. Feng, in a rare show of conformity with the general public, disliked him intently. But Zouche had his uses. He was wise and knowledgeable. More importantly, he didn't question the existence of the supernatural.

You had the essential Feng/Zouche clash right there. Feng, a retired and rich ex-City broker, had spent years actively seeking to prove the supernatural did not exist. Despite everything he'd seen in Flanders, despite occasionally having conversations with The Gliss, converting to acceptance, let alone hardcore belief, was not coming easy to him.

Zouche, whose voluminous, white eyebrows could be seen from the Moon, was wrapped in a gaudy robe, a blanket across his legs. He was in the social room of his care home, pasting cuttings into a scrapbook.

Feng sat opposite Zouche, looking around. He was mesmerised by an old lady with a stick moving like a tortoise in lead trousers. She'd set out for breakfast but at this rate, might just make dinner. It was poignant, sad, moving.

"Stupid old bag peed herself last week," said Zouche, following Feng's gaze. "We had to wait half an hour for breakfast while they cleaned up the dining room."

It was precisely this sort of comment which left Feng wondering why he bothered with these visits. "Don't be like that. She can't help it. You're not exactly ready for the 100-yard dash. How's the scrapbook coming along?" Feng peered over the miscellaneous cuttings on paranormal activity from around the world.

"It's an A-Z of weirdness and utterly pointless," said Zouche. "But, let's be honest, I've got nothing better to do. You're the one who's travelled 50 miles to sit with someone you can't stand. What's up? Why are you here, Fu Manchu?"

Feng sighed. "I'll ignore that. Again. Look, I'm having a hard time processing the Profugus, the ghosts, and everything I saw over the summer. For 50 years I believed the supernatural was nonsense. Now, I've seen more of it than most people alive. I thought I was more agile intellectually, but, honestly, I can't bring myself to believe - even now."

"I'm your confessor, now? You're not as intellectually agile as you think you are, are you Mr Wang?" said Zouche.

"Tian."

"Wang. Tian. You say tomato."

Zouche put down his glue stick. "Look, I didn't like olives when I was young. Conkers wrapped in rubber. Got to Cambridge and all the posh bastards ate them. I wanted to fit in, so I started eating them."

"And you grew to like them?"

"God, no. I force-fed myself for three years, every mouthful a green, pitted turd."

"The moral is?"

"I like them now. Didn't touch one for 40 years. Just to check they still made me vomit, I tried one at my retirement soiree. I didn't like the host, you see. Been eating the damn things ever since. If you jumped on my guts, I'd pop 'em out like machine gun bullets."

Feng, who'd had enough of machine gun bullets over the summer, said, "I don't get the moral. Could you be a bit less obscure for the intellectually in-agile among us?"

"Obtuse. Simple enough: some things are an acquired taste." Zouche gave a tut.

"Which applied to me, means...?" Feng was nothing if not persistent.

"Which means, my not-so-agile friend, that you need to have some friggin' patience. A deeply held prejudice is not easily overturned." He thought for a moment and decided to give conciliatory a try. "You spoke to dead soldiers, correct?"

Feng nodded. "Yes, and they gave me buttons to bury in their parents' graves back in England."

"There you go, you buffoon. What other proof do you need?"

"Yes, but…I don't know…what if they were actors or something?"

"Which is how likely?"

"Not at all."

"You're like a bloody hamster going round-and-round on its wheel, aren't you, me old mucker? Sooner or later, Hong Kong Phooey, you're gonna have to jump off."

"Stop talking like that. It's racist."

"It's affectionate. I'm older than you, my terms of reference are different. You lot all bang on about diversity, but it's a mean sort of definition if you can't cope with diverse ways of talking."

"What do you mean, *you lot*? I'm not particularly woke, but even I find it offensive," said Feng.

"So what? To me, an inability to accept diversity of language is offensive. Stalemate."

"I don't know why I come here."

"You don't like the taste, but you want to fit in," said Zouche.

"Touché," said Feng. He was about to move on to other topics but realised Zouche had plunged off a cliff into sudden sleep. "I'll take that as a win," said Feng.

Chapter 3

October 13th, 2017
Namita's flat, Holloway Road, London

Namita Menon was also feeling uncomfortable. As well as the physical injuries she'd picked up in Flanders, she'd been mentally tortured by the Profugus. The malicious spirit took over her mind, making her suicidally reckless. Her arm had been in a cast for most of the summer, so she'd taken the time to consider her professional position. She'd been a lawyer at Quendell's for almost 10 years. She'd constantly discussed going solo and setting up a consultancy with her bitchy friend, Seema. To her surprise, as soon as Namita announced her intention to do exactly that, Seema rejected the idea outright.

"If we set up an agency, there'll be too much paperwork, too much networking, and not enough cash to go around," said Seema. That was the end of that. Seema stayed on at Quendell's, Namita quit. Namita accepted her friend's good-luck, goodbye kisses on both cheeks. *You big, fat, lily-livered coward.*

Flanders had changed her, and Namita had no choice but to break free and go solo. No-one's idea of a wuss, she'd been outraged by the Profugus' intrusion into her mind. It left her feeling violated but also questioning her inner strength. *Karin hadn't let the bloody Profugus in, had she?*

Namita had resolved to become stronger, a process which had brought out all her teddy-bear qualities - albeit a black-market, knock-off teddy-bear from the Soviet era, full of springs and lethal metal pins. She had a new reality, only slightly preferable to the old one: the fruitless check-ins with old clients; unwelcome economising; losing her spare room to a home office.

She'd gained her independence four weeks ago. There hadn't been a single job come in since then. She thought about cutting her budget further but hadn't had a drink for three weeks, was making a packet of fags last three days, and was living on beans on toast.

"Sod it," she said aloud, lighting cigarette number four. Three left for today. Peering from her Victorian flat opposite the Odeon cinema, wondering what to do next, the phone rang. As hopeful as she was desperate for divine intervention, she dived for the mobile, the lit fag bouncing from her fingers. It cartwheeled away across the rug, shedding ash and sparks. *A job won't be much use if you let your flat burn down.* Finally, phone and fag in hand, she answered.

"Namita? It's Karin Pelenot. How are you?"

Oh great. Thank you, God, you stingy bastard. Severely disappointed, Namita managed a choked, "Fine. How are you?"

"I'm on location in Italy, having a quite divine risotto," said Karin, unaware Namita was down to her last pack of dried pasta. "I'm just doing a call around to see who's still available for the meet-up next week."

Namita knew perfectly well she was free but pretended to check her diary. "Fine, fine. For now, anyway. Depends on work."

"God, yes, I forgot. Brilliant. How's the new consultancy going? Hope the work's rolling in? I'm sure it is, knowing you!"

Every time you big me up, you make me feel small. She sighed. "Yes, I've been surprised." This was true, just not in the way she'd hoped, and in a way she'd never admit to.

"That's great. My ex-eye's not too sore now," said Karin, trying to be chatty. "The make-up girl loves it. She used to spend 20 minutes each side of my face getting an old girl like me ready for the cameras. Now all she has to do is curl my eyelashes on one side and buff my patch on the other."

Karin expected a laugh, but her self-deprecation flopped into the void. "You okay? Not having a blue day, I hope?"

"Not at all. Why'd you say that?"

"Okay, okay, I get it. Look forward to seeing you next week," said Karin, taking the hint and ringing off.

Namita was instantly regretful and hoped she hadn't pissed off her friend. She liked Karin now they'd gotten to know each other a bit. Karin had been a bit too patrician, too posh, too white English, at first. But Namita stayed on in Flanders to represent Karin's legal interests in the wake of her eye injury. Their chats during the surge of publicity that accompanied it had broken the impasse. They got on fine, now. *I wish she'd give me a bit more work though.*

She was certainly in a place to do so. Karin was Britain's most famous female TV presenter. A classical historian, she'd been presenting History/ThisStory for a decade and it was the most watched popular history show in the UK. Thanks to streaming it was also becoming popular worldwide. One snippet from the show, the one where Karin's team uncovered a Saxon burial mound, had 4 million hits on YouTube. Karin had lost an eye, stoned in Flanders by the same spirit who'd sexually assaulted and brutalised Namita. Splashed over front pages everywhere, though no-one had the real story, the loss of an eye made Karin even more famous. Namita sighed. She'd been in all the same fights as Karin, but it had done nothing for *her* career.

The phone rang again.

"Can I speak to Namita Menon, please?" It was a Cockney accent so ferocious she thought her neighbour's Rottweiler with the big balls had learned to speak.

"Speaking."

"My name's Gary Stormont. I'm looking for a lawyer. Some bloke at Quendell's suggested I call you?"

She didn't want to seem ungrateful to her former employers, but it was clear from his voice that Big Balls wasn't about to ask her to fight over the Koh-i-Noor. More likely, it was grunt work that Quendell's couldn't be arsed to do themselves.

"I need a lawyer," said Stormont. "Do you do wills and stuff?"

"You want to write a will?" It was worse than she thought: £200 if she was lucky.

"Nah, none of that bollocks, I've been cut out of one, haven't I?"

Hmmm. Better. Sometimes the bills for people ill-advisedly contesting wills ran into the tens of thousands.

Jumping to her feet, Namita went to her office and pulled out a pad. "Tell me a bit about it, Mr Stormont, and I'll let you know if I can help you, and how much it would cost."

"You can call me Gary - or Gaz. What are you? Indian? Funny name."

"Mr Stormont," said Namita with a growl, unwilling to risk losing a client by admonishing further, "please tell me about this will. Whose was it? What happened?" For her own dignity, she mouthed, "Strike one."

"It's my aunt Florence, innit? Florence Prideaux - are you writing this down? P. R. I. D. E. A. U. X. I've been going up to Bristol for years to see the ungrateful bitch. Now she's snuffed it, I hear she's gone and left it all to some old tosser in America no-one's ever heard of."

Bitch/tosser. Strike two.

"Your aunt Florence in Bristol died and left you nothing?"

"Yeah, that's what I said, innit? It's fishy. A few years back, she told me she'd left me the whole hog." Stormont sounded like someone tipping a sack of marbles into a grinder. "Now? Nuffin'."

Namita, feeling as posh as the Queen on gak, asked, "Do you know if there was a will in which you were left everything? Or did you just hear her say it?"

"Oh yeah - there was a bloody will alright. I got a copy, ain't I? The old bag had no-one else, did she? She was in her 90s, knocking a ton."

"Who's the executor of the will?" said Namita, scribbling furiously.

"TSP Bank in Bristol. Some muppet called Dan Little."

"Did TSP tell you who this man in America was? Did she meet him online? Do they think it's a scam?"

"Online? Oh, that's funny. Florence couldn't use a frickin' remote, let alone a PC. The dementia didn't help. Half the time she was as batty as a mouse in a biscuit tin. Nah, some old friend, or summat. They wouldn't say. But I looked him up, it can't be him. No way. Some coloured geezer in California. She never got further than the Isle of friggin' Wight!"

Come on, Namita. Strike three. Coloured? In 2017?

"Well, thanks for all that, Mr Stormont. But honestly? I'm not sure I'm the right person to help you. May I refer you to a friend of mine who specialises in this kind of thing? It's better to have a specialist."

Stormont sounded annoyed. "You're a solicitor, aren't ya? What you playin' at? You said you could help?"

"I said I'd let you know *if* I could help. Would you like a referral or not?"

"No, fanks." He rang off.

"And stuff you, Gary Stormont," said Namita, chucking her phone on the table. "Oh shit." Her precious cigarette had burnt to ashes, unsmoked, while she'd been forced to speak with that idiot.

She looked at her notes. Stormont probably thought because his aunt had dementia the courts would declare incapacity. In her experience that was a risky argument. Plenty of people with dementia had provable capacity at the time of making their will. Judging from the phonecall, his aunt probably just couldn't stand the little... she sought the *mot juste*: Tosser.

Don't worry about it. Something will come up.

When Namita was six, her twin, Sangita, had died of leukaemia. Ever since, Sangita had been a second voice in Namita's head, part-counsellor, part-advisor. Sangita chose this moment to speak up.

"We're so rich we're turning down cases now, are we?"

"He was an arse."

"You can't pick and choose like that. I wonder what it was all about. Aren't you curious?"

"He was an arse. I'd have cut him out of my will."

"In favour of a stranger in America?"

"If I had to."

"Get over it. Stormont's an arse, but he's right: it sounds a bit fishy. Call the executors. It's not too late to save it."

Namita looked at her notes and her dwindling supply of fags. *Dan Little. TSP. Why not?*

Twenty minutes later, Namita put the phone down, intrigued. Prideaux had left everything to Samuel Brownlees - a man living east of Hollywood in Los Angeles. He was in his 90s and had been Florence's friend for more than 70 years. Her estate wasn't big, £300,000 tops, but she had indeed made a second will in the past year. It cut Gary out in favour of Brownlees. Dan Little confirmed the new will was kosher and doubted Stormont would be successful if he challenged it.

She googled Brownlees. Not much. A few old cuttings from his local paper - all from 20+ years ago. He'd been an active charity fundraiser well into his 70s. He was indeed Afro-American and a World War II veteran. There was a photo of him in the 1960s standing outside a strange bakery with a windmill on top. His last address was in Glendale, near Los Feliz.

"He looks like a kindly uncle," said Sangita.

She made a few calls and tracked Brownlees to a private residential care home, not far from Glendale, in Atwater Village.

"What are you going to do now?" asked Sangita. "Hassle him?"

"No. I've never cold-called a client in my life," admitted Namita. She looked at one of the cuttings. "There's something warm and avuncular about his face. It's very honest. I'd like to speak to him. If it turns out I get a bad vibe, I'll call Stormont back, ok? But if he needs help, who knows, I might offer to represent Brownlees."

"You've already spoken to Stormont. Won't that be a conflict of interest?"

"I probably shouldn't, but if I learnt anything from this summer - listen to your gut."

She put in a call or two. Three hours after she'd rejected Gary Stormont she was waiting to be put on the line to Brownlees.

October 13th, 2017
Figaro's, Victoria, London

Karin was mopping up the last of her minestrone, while Angela Bluebottle, factual commissioning editor for Channel 4, read version 11 of Karin's Flanders' script.

"Good. Good. Good," said the executive.

Uh-oh. Now I'm in trouble. She normally spits out great-great-great like a bullet train.

"I do like this draft, but Norton... are you sure you still want to include him as co-presenter?"

Ah. Porter. I should have guessed. He's been the worm in the egg since Draft 1.

But Karin held most of the cards. She was the second highest-paid presenter on Channel 4 (that male newsreader - *quelle surprise* - got more). All her programmes did very well for the network - series or standalone. It would be a brave exec who risked Karin taking her project elsewhere. Her golden-handcuffs deal was supposed to ensure this never happened, but the lick-spittles all knew Karin could leave any time.

"Angela, I'm a fairly experienced presenter and producer, right?"

"The best."

"Well then." Why present a case for others to pick holes in? Let them present their case and she could do the hole-picking.

Bluebottle was no lightweight. "He's not very experienced, is he? And all that publicity about the little girl he killed negligently; he's not exactly sympathetic. Or am I missing something?"

"Angela, you know perfectly well he was cleared of all that. Our Flanders story is about the intimate connections between my family and his. My family does not come out of it well. The viewers will naturally sympathise with Porter and his great grandfather. Are you saying it's not an interesting film?"

"Not at all. I saw the rough cut of Draft 8. I think there's plenty of good stuff in there... I just wasn't sure about Norton." Bluebottle was a commissioner who'd worked her way up through the ranks. She was tough as steel kippers but still found aristocratic haughtiness unsettling.

Karin knew better than to incriminate herself. Make the (expensive) problem Bluebottle's. "It's your money, Angela."

They both knew this wasn't true. Angela was only a custodian, with several layers of vigilant management above her. They were the type of managers who would happily throw Bluebottle's babies to the eagles if she peed off Karin. The conversation could only end one way.

"Great, great. Fine," said Bluebottle.

Resisting to the last: that should have been three greats. Karin was hard-nosed, not evil. Time to throw a bone. "You won't regret it, Angela. His story is very moving. I like to think you and I will be hitting the champagne at BAFTA over this one. I really appreciate your input."

She didn't. Draft 3 had been absolutely fine, but commissioners had become all-powerful. Karin was disgusted they now demanded credits on the programmes they wrote cheques for. The poor old runners, who kept productions going and needed onscreen credits to advance their careers, rarely got them.

"I'd like that, Karin," said Bluebottle. "Anything else on the horizon?"

"It's been a bit quiet actually - between the series commitments, the Flanders doc - and my recovery," Karin said, pointing at her patch in case Bluebottle had missed it. "Look, don't worry about Porter. He's a lawyer, not a presenter. He'll give this film its human face. He's not about to become my full-time presenting partner, okay? Lunch?"

October 13th, 2017
Namita's flat, Holloway Road, London

Namita introduced herself neutrally. "I'm a solicitor in London. I heard about Florence's will. It's probably going to be contested. Would you answer a few questions before I decide whether to represent the other side, please?"

Brownlees, recovering from an institutional breakfast straight from the menu card at Bedlam, said that was fine. "Call me Sam," he said. "What do you want to know, hon?"

Namita, pen at the ready, asked, "How did you know Florence?"

Sam sighed. "It's a long, long story, Miss." Usually, Namita always corrected Miss to Ms but decided not to antagonise Sam - not just yet, anyway.

"I was a GI, stationed in Bristol during World War II," he said. His voice was as slow as honey flowing from a freshly-broken honeycomb. "She was my sweetheart, can you believe?"

"Goodness. Was Florence white? That must have caused a stir in the 40s?"

Sam laughed. "Flo, I called her. You could say that. We met at a jive. Cos of the war, there was a shortage of men, but damn no shortage of women. Black or white, them gals liked to jive with us."

Namita stated the obvious: "But you didn't stay together?"

Sam said, "No. No. You've seen the films, right? You just didn't in those days. I came home, got married to Celia, had my daughter, Cicely. It took some time to get back to normal after the war. I did my best. If it was hard for a white veteran to get work, it weren't no easier being black, let's put it that way. And I landed in the wrong vicinity. Everything here was run by gangs of Latino hoods. I weren't no hophead and I still don't like burritos."

"But it's extraordinary she should remember you in her will so many decades later," said Namita.

"We always stayed in touch." There was a long pause. "Miss, can I trust you?"

"Yes, you can. I mean that."

"I'm old, stupid and gullible, but I believe you. Don't let me down. Not many people know what I'm about to say. Goddam, if you get to my age and can't tell the truth, what's the point? About a year after I got home to the States, I got word from Flo she'd had a baby. Never said a word to me about it till that moment."

"Uh-oh."

"Right! Well, Flo had that little girl, Rose, and as far as I could ever tell, she brought her up real good. What could I do? I was still in shock from the war. I'd seen bad things. I done some things I ain't too proud of.

"Traumatised and out of control, that about covers it. I met and married Celia within five months of getting home. There was no way I could go back to Bristol now I was married and Celia already with child herself. Flo understood. I sent her what money I could. We wrote to each other every month."

"For how long?"

"All our damn lives. She sent me photos. But, and you'll forgive an old man his regrets, I never got to meet my Rose."

"Surely, it's not too late to meet her. Times are different." Before Namita had time to wonder why Florence hadn't left her estate to her daughter, Sam jumped back in.

"I daresay they are, Miss, I daresay they are. But that ain't no good to old Sam Brownlees. First of all, Rose grew up thinking that Lester, Flo's husband, was her daddy. Flo only told her about me when she was 18. She was a bit shocked and refused to speak to me. By then, of course, I expected nothing better. We never had time to repair things before Rose disappeared. Don't you think she'd have left her home to her daughter if she was still alive?"

"I didn't even know she had a daughter, but yes, of course. When did she disappear?"

"I ain't gonna forget that date - January 5th, 1967. Flo and I had an arrangement. She wrote me at a mailbox. Never spoke on the phone. But that day she called me at home in the middle of the night, and she didn't say but two words before I knew something bad, real bad, had gone down. Flo was all broke up. Rose had gone missing in Berlin, Germany, and she didn't know what to do. She was wilder than a trapped polecat."

"Berlin?"

"That's what I said. You see, Rose was an actress. She travelled a lot. Rose told Flo she'd call her to tell her how the audition went, but you know a mother's intuition, right?" Namita, unmarried, childless, and no fan of her own mother, didn't.

"Flo knew something was up when Rose didn't call like she'd promised. I didn't know what to do. I told Flo to be patient, said that Rose'd turn up eventually. But, damn, she never did. She never did. I knew there was dirty business right there.

"Then, one day, Flo got a letter from Rose saying she'd met someone in Germany. Damn handwriting was nothing like Rose's. But your famous London cops? They didn't do a damn thing for our little girl, not one damn thing, Miss. German cops were no better. It took us a long, long time to face the truth. Our little girl must be dead. Bad days, Miss. Bad days."

Namita chewed the end of her pen. "Did Celia ever find out about Rose?"

There was a pregnant pause before Sam replied. "Well, I'm not sayin' I would never have told her, because she was a good woman. If any wife would've understood her husband had a past, it was Celia. But, goddamit, she never lived long enough, either. 1967, the so-called Summer of Love. Cicely had a part-time cleaning gig up on some mansion on Mulholland. One day, Celia was driving her to work. Some hopped-up hippies - hooch, weed, acid - I don't know - drove into them head-on. Both cars went over the bank. I lost them both too, Miss. 1967. What a year."

"I'm so sorry to hear that. I didn't mean to upset you." Namita cursed herself.

"It's ok, Miss. I thinks about 'em every day anyways. The first 20 years were the worst. I can deal with it now. But you know, it was kinda easier to accept what happened with them. There were bodies, coffins, mourners. It was real, physical, you know? I still put a rose on their grave twice a year. That was Celia's favourite - red, red roses. But every damn time I put that rose down, I thought of my other Rose, the child I ain't never gonna see. I sometimes think I've only been kept alive this long to pay for my sins." His voice wavered. "I couldn't help, Miss. I couldn't do nothin' for Flo. Even when I paid for that PI, it went down the Swannee."

"PI?" said Namita, eyebrows raised.

"Sure, I tried to do summat. Once I realised the cops were deadbeats, I paid a guy in London, Alex - yeah, that was him: Alex Harding. I paid him to look into Rose's disappearance. Must have been about December, maybe two months after my wife died. A few weeks later his body was found floating in the London river…what's it called again, Miss?"

"The Thames?"

"Thank you, Miss. Yeah, The Thames. Some son of a bitch had cut his head off."

"What?"

"Yeah, you heard right. Incredible story, huh? Well, it was all real, right enough. I think Flo and I realised there was nothin' more we could do. She'd been happily married to Lester for 15 years at that point. He'd brought Rose up like she was his own. Poor guy went to pieces. I was still here getting over my wife and daughter. There weren't nothing that bound me and Flo but memories of the war and the dying hope that our daughter would turn up safe one day. Well, you can dream all you like, but dreams don't always come true, Miss."

The phone went silent for a bit. Namita picked up the baton.

"And you stayed in touch with Flo? Did you know she'd left everything to you?"

"I gotta kinda inkling she might if she went first. She stopped writing two years back. She was sick and got tired easily. She called me one day, what? - 'bout a year ago? She said it would be the last time we would talk. She had dementia. She told me she still loved me, thanked me for everything, and told me she was leaving her house to me.

"I didn't know there was anyone else. I forgot about all about her nephew. Tell the truth, Miss? What the hell am I gonna do with a house in Bristol at my age?" He started laughing, slow rumbling laughs that didn't suit the conversation.

Namita had been doing the calculations. She didn't doubt what Sam said was true. She didn't doubt he deserved to be in Florence's will. She didn't doubt Gary Stormont was a complete shit who deserved nothing.

"Sam," she said finally, "I would like to take care of this for you. That's a very moving story. Do you have a solicitor?"

"That's right up there with the house in Bristol. What the hell would I want a solicitor for? Miss, I been straight wit you. Time to be straight wit me. Say I took you on. What's it gonna cost?"

"Nothing, Sam," said Namita, making her mind up. "Just expenses. These will be hundreds of dollars, not thousands, and you can pay me those when the estate money comes in. You deserve a break. I can fax you my details to your home. Just sign and date it and get the home to send it back, and I'll get started."

Sangita, watching from inside Namita's head, exploded. "*Pro Bono*? Are you nuts?" Namita ignored the screaming voice.

"Miss? You have a deal, but not for free. Let's say your fee is 5% of the estate if you secure it."

"Don't you dare turn that down," hollered Sangita.

"Ok, deal. Thank you, Sam."

"Tell me, you ever been to Bristol?"

"Once, I think."

"Should've known from the start it would go bad. Nine generations back, my ancestors were shipped there as slaves, before being sold on to the Americas."

"Really?"

Sam coughed and spluttered for a few seconds, before getting his breath back. "Yeah, that's right. My ancestor, Samwell, was the first of the Brownlees to be shipped to Bristol and then over here. Course, when I got to Bristol, I almost expected to still be seeing chains. Weren't nothing left of that, but I went to check out the places where all the trading had been transacted. Guess we never really break free of our history, do we? Ironically, the only name that came down through the centuries, was the Christmas Steps."

"What's that?"

"It's a famous old street in Bristol. When I saw it in 1944 it looked summin' like old Charlie Dickens would have written about. Apparently, Samwell remembered it as he was marched from the market to a shop that wanted a slave. But he wasn't sold, so came to America anyways. Strange it should be in my story too."

Namita paused for a second. "How? Why was it ironic?"

Sam took his time. She suspected it wasn't because he was struggling to remember, but that remembering was causing him to struggle with his past. "After I met Flo at the jive, we used to meet at a pub right there on the Steps," sighed Sam. "That innkeeper welcomed everyone, black or white, so long as they paid for their beer. It was kinda fantastic back then - like heaven for a negro like me and all the others stationed there.

"We got treated so well, many of us came back demanding the same treatment in America. Truth is, if that innkeeper hadn't provided refuge and beer, maybe our love wouldn't have grown; maybe Rose would never have been born; maybe I wouldn't have been a slave myself. I've been chained to regret and sorrow my whole damn life, as sure as Samwell was all those years ago."

Namita was typing up her notes when her sister decided to make her presence felt. Sangita was furious. "What's the bloody point of going solo if you're going to keep turning down cases or offering to work for free?"

"You heard. I'm not working for free, he's going to pay me," said Namita, animatedly typing up a contract. "I'd better tell Porter and the others about Rose on Monday. Sounds right up his street."

"Oh, no. Not them," said Sangita. This time, Namita ignored her. Her guts were sending out flares, telegrams, and morse code. She was listening.

Chapter 4

October 15th, 2017
Porter's flat, Sylvester Path, Hackney

"And you think we should look into it?" asked Porter, pouring a glass of Bordeaux for Namita, who was stuffing her face with Pringles.

"It can't hurt, can it?" she replied.

Feng reached over and speared an olive. "Just one problem, Namita: Porter is supposed to stand over the remains of dead people. That's how he starts his cases. There's no dead body here. The girl went missing."

Porter nodded, Namita shrugged, but Karin waved a fork at them all, rejecting the idea.

"What about the PI? Alex Harding? Samuel Brownlees thinks his murder was linked to his daughter's disappearance. And the girl's mother, Florence? That's two graves for a start. Assuming the PI was buried with his head. Do you need a head to get a reading, Porter?"

The Gliss, hovering over the dinner table, sighed. He was in his usual form of a translucent, ceramic robot head, a shape he'd decided on before manifesting to Porter. He'd thought this form would be neutral and comforting: a way to introduce himself to Porter without disconcerting him. It hadn't worked. It was like being stalked by an Imperial Stormtrooper. He followed up his doorbell of a sigh, with, "As you know, I'm only…"

He was interrupted by all four humans, who chimed together, "…a messenger." It was The Gliss' perpetual excuse for pretending he had less knowledge than he patently possessed. He gave them a scornful look and continued through their giggles. Feng and Namita high-fived.

"…I'm only a messenger, true," he said, mustering his dignity, "but this one gives me a tingle. Porter, why not take a look?"

The four friends ducked the issue for the moment as Porter was pulling dinner from the oven. Feng had brought immaculate, virgin oven-gloves and apron, ready to help. He looked like a contestant on the first day of Bake-Off. But as Porter's dinner consisted of cottage pie and broccoli, not a lot of help was needed. Any apron work - and who needs an apron when you're chopping carrots and tipping frozen peas into a casserole dish of mince? - had taken place hours before.

"How's your sister?" said Feng, camply waving the oven-mitts about in distress, wincing as Porter wrestled the heavy casserole dish with just one tea towel. Feng could smell the coming thumb-burn a mile off.

"Difficult as ever," said Porter, momentarily losing control of the dish. "I told you, she's arguing with me about Ida's estate now. Our grandmother didn't leave a will and, like a madman, I let Cherry apply for probate. Instead of splitting everything 50/50, she's now arguing she should get more because she's got two children. Her ever-so-slightly self-serving rationale is that Ida would have wanted to leave something for them too. Ouch. I've burnt my thumb."

"Cold water - quick! She's a piece of work, that sister of yours," said Feng as Porter iced his thumb. "What do you think?"

"I love Ruby and Scott, but I could do with the money," said Porter, this time almost dropping the dish, which prompted a little cascade of *oohs* and waving hand movements from be-gloved Feng. Plopping the dish down safely at last, Porter added: "It's the principle really. I never thought my sister would try and stiff me over money."

"She had no problem trying to get you locked up in the loony bin. I'm surprised you cut her that much slack."

"Fair point," said Porter. "But, you know, it's depressing to fight over it. Ida would have slapped her down."

"Cherry got the probate, though?"

"Yes."

"Which means she can distribute as she sees fit, right?"

"Yes."

"You're screwed."

"Yes. Well, no, actually. She keeps ringing me, asking me for permission to allocate it on her 3/1 terms. "

"She knows it's wrong but wants your benediction?"

"Yep."

"And you're not inclined to give it her?"

"Nope."

"Good for you. Give me the ladle. I can't watch anymore."

Five minutes later they were all tucking in. The Gliss watched them absentmindedly. He was either in spiritual standby or had come down with a heavy case of ponder. There was no way to tell. His mouth and eyes only moved when he was talking or reacting. Plastic has many admirable qualities but emoting is not one of them

The four all had individual reasons - and the scars to prove it - not to wish for a repeat of the summer's exertions. But they were all hooked on the buzz the investigation had given them. The Gliss hovered, waiting to see if they could stop themselves from joining the fight once they'd cleared their plates.

Sure enough, within five minutes of the dishes being thrown in the sink, all four were busy researching Florence and Harding's last resting places using their phones.

"You look like teenagers at a family wedding," said The Gliss. They ignored him.

"Looks like Harding was cremated," said Feng. "That's a shame. Ashes don't give you a reading, right? Presumably the last thing he saw was his killer/killers. Could have solved that one pretty fast."

"Florence is buried in Bristol," said Karin. "Perhaps you could check her grave?"

"He could, but what would he get?" said Namita. "Flo had dementia and no-one's suggesting she knew what happened to her daughter. Quite the opposite."

"It might rule out some things," said Feng. "A new husband in the house? Lester? A young girl who's not his? Maybe Flo suspected him all along and that might show up in her deathbed thoughts."

"Well, that's a cheery thought," said Karin.

Porter said he had no problem going to Bristol - if only to put his mind at rest by ruling out that possibility. "But she went missing in Berlin, not Bristol. Not likely to be Lester."

Feng said he'd like to keep him company. Namita said she was going up anyway; she had to meet Flo's executors. Karin said, "If we're going to keep the band together, I suppose I'd better come as well then. When's good?"

Namita's trip was already planned for tomorrow. Feng, a financially secure man-about-town with no real-life commitments, gave a *fine-by-me* gesture. Karin wasn't due to start editing again until Thursday. "Well, Porter," said Feng, "you free too?"

Even before his attempted suicide, Porter had been fed up with the domestic and small-fry disputes that were his bread and butter. He'd gotten far more pleasure from working on Karin's film. Karin had advanced him enough to delay his return to practice a few months longer. Upshot? He was free too.

Feng said, "Looks like Alex Harding was cremated in London. There's an Evening Standard story about it. It quotes his sister, Francine, who lived in Elephant & Castle back then."

"What did his sister say" queried Porter.

"The usual: *Who would do a thing like this? Hanging's too good for them.*"

"That's settled then," said Karin. "Bristol tomorrow and let's see if we can track down Harding's sister and see her later this week."

"It'll all probably turn out to be nothing," said Namita. Turning to The Gliss, she asked, "Are you getting any vibes?"

The Gliss looked around, as if to say, "Was someone talking to me?"

"Oh God, you're not still annoyed they can see you?" said Porter. "Just answer - don't be an idiot."

The Gliss harrumphed. Deciding resistance was futile, but only addressing Porter, he said, "I'm not sure I'd call it *vibes* - because it's not 1967 - but yes, I do feel this is worth looking into."

Within weeks, all four had racked up more air miles than Neil Armstrong and were looking back with fondness on those halcyon Flanders days of bombs, broken limbs and blood-loss.

Chapter 5

March 15th, 1965
American Sector, West Berlin

The group were risking everything to meet together like this. If discovered, they faced arrest and global disgrace.

It was early days. Unsure of where they stood with each other, there was apprehension and undertones of fear in the air. Some suspected not all the group were as dedicated to the cause as others. This was too dangerous a game to have doubters. If there were any recalcitrants hiding in their midst, now was the time to find them out before they could do any harm to the committed.

A gentleman in a Merino roll-neck, sweated despite the cold. He'd just been to see the new James Bond, Goldfinger - and he didn't want to end up in a car-crusher.

He checked out the gathering company. Culled from an international elite, they were bound by a dark secret. Today was the day they would vote to move their plan forward.

All but one had agreed Berlin was the place to incorporate the group. But after some wrangling, the single dissenter from New York acceded. Following the first taste of success in Italy, the group were ready to hammer out the rules and etiquette. Despite the danger, there was a frisson too. Who wouldn't be excited?

Merino man relaxed a little. Their initial encounter in Venice last year had led to several months of feeling each other out: Who would take care of what? Who was in charge of security? Who was to be central point of contact? The aims of the group were clear. Surely if there were any doubters, they'd have pulled out by now?

Merino man needn't have worried. There was no doubt everyone was still interested. The car-crusher would not be needed today.

The man from London passed around photos of potential marks. Each man examined the photos. A few nods of approval. A couple of questions.

In the end, the decision was unanimous. London said, "I will begin arranging it. Gentlemen, I propose a toast."

A chorus of voices: *Prost. Cheers. Le Club. Saluti. Salut.*

Chapter 6

October 16th, 2017
TSP Office, Rupert Street, Bristol

"Thank you for coming, Ms Menon," said Dan Little. "Please take a seat."

Namita looked around the grotty office. The carpet had been there since the old King died. It still had burns from the days when you could smoke at work. Little looked like he'd been around to choose the carpet. A streak of vampire-destroying sunlight had somehow fought its way through the murky window. It illuminated the man's dust orbit, which whizzed about him like flies around a horse's arse. *If it's from the room, it's mites; if it's from him, it's dandruff.* Namita shuddered, pressing her hand against her mouth and nostrils. It would be like inhaling porridge oats.

"This really is an open and shut affair," said Little. "Mrs Prideaux not only wrote a will, which was formally witnessed by her doctor and one of her neighbours, but she wrote a side letter explaining why she'd changed it. Incontrovertible. I'm afraid your client is most unlikely to overturn it. It is only my opinion, of course," he said, pompously, "but if I were you, I would advise him accordingly."

His comment took her by surprise. "There's been some mistake. My client is Samuel Brownlees, the new sole beneficiary," she said.

Little's turn to look confused. "Dear me, that is most extraordinary. Mr Stormont, who has called me more times than I care to remember, ahem, mentioned your name as the solicitor he was going to use. You'll have to forgive me. I'm retiring next year. I hope I haven't got things muddled?"

That fills me with confidence. "Yes, he did approach me, but I didn't like him," Namita countered. "I looked into the case, which ended with Mr Brownlees instructing me instead."

"Is that not slightly irregular, Ms Menon?"

"I never met Mr Stormont, just discussed rates etc on the phone. I didn't like his tone."

"Ah yes," said Little, with some sympathy. "Neither did Mrs Prideaux apparently. Here is her side letter."

> *15th August, 2016*
> *To whom it may concern,*
> *I, Florence Prideaux, want to explain why I have re-written my will. For many years, my only surviving relative, my sister's son, Gary Stormont, was the sole beneficiary of my will dated 11th June, 1986. Prior to that, until my sister's death (Gary's mother) in 1986, she had been the sole beneficiary.*
>
> *In his thirties, Gary was a regular visitor to my house from London and was good company, often buying my shopping and pushing me around the park in my wheelchair.*
>
> *I had no reason to doubt he was doing this for any other reason than affection. Besides, ever since our seaside visits when Gary was a toddler, we always got on well.*
>
> *However, as my 80s threw up severe medical problems and my situation became ever-more demanding, Gary visited less often. On one of those rare visits, he demanded to know if he was still in my will. Not wanting to cause a fuss, I showed him the will I'd made. He took one of the copies for safekeeping. I did not see him after that day for five years, confirming my growing suspicion he was more concerned with the money than me.*
>
> *I got the impression he just wanted me out of the way so he could sell my house and be done with it. In total, I think I've only seen him on three occasions in the past 15 years, each visit shorter than the last.*

Luckily, my local council provided me with great carers, and my GP, Dr Alice Harwell, came to visit me every week. My neighbour, Joyce, also helped with cooking for a long time, but, sadly, she passed away last year. It's the curse of the very old to watch all one's friends and family fall one-by-one.

The only other friend I've had, through thick and thin, through smiles and tragedy, is my dear Samuel Brownlees. We've been writing to each other since we were wartime sweethearts, and although we were unable to be man and wife after the war, we both have many happy memories of our time together.

I will never forget the kindness and support he gave me when our daughter, Rose, disappeared in 1967. Samuel co-ordinated the search for her in Berlin, funding everything himself, despite having a family of his own to feed. When he lost his own family in a car accident that same year, it only deepened my love for him. My dear husband, Lester, died in 1983, aware that Samuel was Rose's natural father, but Lester was as much Rose's father as anyone. God rest his soul. Lester was a wonderful man.

Now Gary has written himself out of my affections there is only Samuel left. Who knew that 72 years after we met we would be the only thing left to each other? In spite of all the heartbreak that has been a miracle in itself.

I have good days and bad days with the dementia, but we have waited for this break in the clouds so that my witnesses were able to sign this off as my true intent.

Yours sincerely,
Florence Prideaux (née Appleton)

Witnessed by:
Dr Alice Harwell 17.08.16
Henbury Surgery

Susan Greene 17.08.16
(Neighbour) 32 Meadowland Hill, Bristol

Namita thanked Little for showing her the letter. *I knew it. Stormont's a piece of shit.* Next, she read a copy of the will. *Yep, that all looks legit too.*

"Ok then, Mr Little, leave it with me. Have you heard from Mr Stormont? Do you know who will be representing him?"

"No. As I said, I thought you were."

"Ok, put us in touch when you do hear from anyone, please."

"Most certainly, Ms Menon. At the first opportunity afforded."

Namita raised an eyebrow. *Jesus H Christ. If Trumpton had a banker...*

October 16th, 2017
Canford Cemetery & Crematorium, Westbury-on-Trym, Bristol

Porter, Feng and Karin, watched over by The Gliss, stood in the centre of the long tarmac road leading to the chapel.

The distance gave Porter some protection. "I'm not going anywhere until you find her grave," he said. "This place is home to some seriously unhappy dead people It's louder than a circus."

"What's it feel like, Porter?" asked Karin.

"Like my head's stuck in a Kerplunk! jar and everyone's jabbing it with cocktail sticks. If I stand out here, at least it's only background noise."

"Hence, my insistence on training," said The Gliss. "But, oh-no, Mr Smarty-pants here thinks he knows best."

"I'll go take a looksie," said Feng. "Florence's grave is supposed to be over there somewhere, close to the path. And it's a new monument, so should stand out."

Ten minutes later, they manoeuvred Porter to within spitting distance of a grave marked with a small black headstone.

Here lies Lester Prideaux 1922-1986, also his loving wife, Florence Prideaux 1923-2017. May your eternal sleep be in piece.

"Oh my God," said Feng. "There's a typo: piece instead of peace."

"Yes, and it's a very small headstone," said Karin. "Either she had no money, or the person who organised her funeral didn't want to spend any." She recalled Namita's description of Gary Stormont.

"Well, let's see if the old lady's up for talking," said Porter. He stepped forward like a novice high-diver, scrunched his face, and jumped onto the grass in front of the headstone.

Porter plunged into the Quincunx world before his feet hit the gravel. Blinding lights, screeching noise, electric shocks: everything blurred, even the audio. In a finger-snap, the chaos disappeared, as he emerged like a plane from cloud to eavesdrop the last moments of Florence's life.

He could see *and* hear her. Her soul wasn't at rest. Unhappy experience had taught him only the regretful and sad left voices and images.

A dingy living room: flock wallpaper, faded photos of people in black and white, an old lady dying on a bed, a nurse checking her vitals. The old lady, open-mouthed, eyes-closed, spluttering terrible, laboured breaths. Her skin was as transparent as brown paper stained with oil. Deep blue veins tattooed across her arms made him wonder what the tube map would look like if all the lines were Victoria. He could hear her essence, her doily-holed thoughts. She was beyond speech, but her body and mind radiated words to him alone: *Rose. Darling. Rose. Rose. Baby. Rose.*

No more words, but he saw what she saw: a pretty Mod-ish young lady, innocent in a sunny dress, laughing over a birthday cake with 20 iced on it. This was how Florence had remembered Rose: young and beautiful.

Then something strange. Porter was about to pull out, when Rose turned, lifted her head and almost, but not quite, looked at him. She gave a simple nod.

Porter pulled himself free. The others were expectant. Gasping, Porter shook his head. "Nothing much. Florence on her death bed. Her last thoughts were for her daughter. No clues from her."

"Damn," said Feng. "I don't know why I always hope for easy answers."

"One thing," said Porter, interrupting. "I got a vision of the daughter too. Slightly frizzy, jet-black hair. Sixties-style dress - Quantish A-line - and black, knee-length boots. She looked like something out of Blow Up."

"The film?" queried Karin. "That's one of my favourites."

"Who doesn't love a good murder in the park?" said Feng.

"It's what she looked like," said Porter.

"Was it a waste of time coming?" asked Karin.

"Not at all," said Porter, who was now back on the relative safety of the tarmac. "I think we all knew I wouldn't get much from Florence. But I've got the feeling - actually it's more like a certainty - this has to be my next mission. I'm sure I have to put Florence and Rose's spirits to rest."

"Why do you say that?" said Feng.

"Rose nodded at me. A tiny gesture, but it was not part of Florence's memory. It was independent of that. Rose was saying *find me*. I know it."

"Woah. That's new," said Feng, scrabbling for his notebook.

"Not quite - do you remember how I sensed that Soraya Adair was showing me her email password last time? And my gran, Ida, literally died and spoke to me. The Quincunx is quite interesting that way."

"Porter," said Karin, "if Rose was trying to talk to you, doesn't that mean she's dead?"

Porter nodded, "Sadly, I think it does."

Karin blew her cheeks out and asked, "We're in on this one then?"

Porter said, "Yep. Buckle up. We're back in business."

There was a brief silence.

Feng spoke first. "No broken bones this time, right?"

October 16th, 2017
Rupert Street, Bristol

Namita left the oppressive TSP office and turned onto Rupert Street. Unsure of her location, she walked along the main road hoping to spot a Starbucks. A sense of emptiness to her left tugged on her. She swivelled to look.

A gated, stone archway. Incongruous in the post-war urban landscape, she stepped towards it. Above the archway was an Elizabethan-looking plaster and timber structure. She put her hands on the iron gate, staring inside. The traffic behind her seemed to fade away. She could picture medieval monks and tradesmen drifting around the courtyard inside. *God, you've spent too long with Porter and his cronies. You'll be seeing goblins next.* A synapse sparked. *Oh my God. You are one of his cronies.*

Withdrawing her hands, turning to her left, she saw an Elizabethan pub. It was painted black. On the side, was a vertical board with gold lettering. The sign read: Christmas Steps. Underneath was a standard street sign. It too read: Christmas Steps.

How funny, she thought. *This is where Sam and Flo used to meet during the war.* She walked 30ft to the pub. A building between her and the pub had hidden the actual thoroughfare from sight until now. Ascending at a very steep angle, she saw a pleasing Dickensian parade of wonky shop fronts and Victorian gas lights, long ago converted to electricity.

At the bottom of the street, directly in front of her, was a cafe, Snakes & Ladders, which boasted it had every board game you could think of. She was thirsty. A coffee appealed, but Brownlees' story had touched her, and curious, she began walking up the hill, to try and see what he had seen.

The shops were boutique and independent: a place to do yoga, a DVD shop run by obvious aficionados, a stamp and postcard shop. It reminded her of The Shambles in York.

Cursing her cigarette habit, she edged up the hill, gravity pulling at her calves, clogs pulling at her lungs. She got to the top and admired the view. To her right was a small chapel. There were three statues in alcoves on its exterior. They looked like the Three Wise Men. Another Christmas link?

"This is beautiful," Namita said out loud, snapping a few pics on her phone. No wonder Sam and Flo fell in love. Christmas Steps had the kind of charm that gave Richard Curtis ideas. *Four Lattes and a Muffin. No need to thank me come the Oscars, Dicky boy.*

"Go on – stick her on Insta," sneered a girl in vacuum-packed, leopard-skin leggings, to a mate with a gold puffa jacket.

"Piss off back to borstal," said Namita. "By the way, your leggings are covered in dog shit."

She walked back down, leaving the girls to inspect each other's butts. *I hope the games cafe does good coffee. I'm gasping.* Her phone rang. She didn't recognise the number.

"Hello, Namita Menon. How may I help?"

"What you fuckin' playing' at, bitch?"

Strike four. Namita pushed the cafe door open, awaiting her doom at the hands of a very pissed-off Gary Stormont.

Chapter 7

October 16th, 2017
Bristol Central Library, College Green, Bristol

"You can't beat the local library for local research," said Karin.
"It's more Cathedral than library," said Feng.
"Both of which buildings are generally considered to be at their best when there's no talking in them," shushed Porter.

We sometimes say *so-and-so feels no shame*. Porter was literally the opposite. He felt little else. He scoped every building or space he entered for rules - written and unwritten. *No smoking. No eating. No talking. No loitering.* He sensed obligation before crossing any threshold.

Feng and Karin were not so tight-arsed. Few people were. It brought a little dissonant awkwardness to some of their group transactions. Porter provided all the stiff you could want, Karin dripped with upper, and Feng provided the lip.

Being caught talking in a library was a childhood anxiety he'd never lost, so Porter held a briefing session on College Green before entering. "Please don't do anything to draw attention," he pleaded. "Every cutting, every reference to Rose's disappearance - that's the goal," he said. "With three of us searching, it shouldn't take long."

"The librarians will love us," said Karin, a professional researcher for 30+ years. "Three people demanding microfiche at once."

A few hours later they were back on College Green comparing notes.

Porter had photocopied cuttings. There weren't many. Feng had saved about £5 on photocopying by yanking books from the Local History section and furtively snapping pages on his iPhone. Karin, thinking ahead, knew her cuttings were basic to the point of useless, and had expanded her research to some of the other names mentioned in them.

"What did you all find? Can we wrap the case today?" teased The Gliss.

"Be quiet you," said Karin, without malice. "If you're not going to manifest and help, leave us to it."

"Yeah, you useless lunkhead, keep schtum," said Feng.

"There were only three cuttings I could find," said Porter, "and only two of them relate directly to Rose's disappearance."

> *Bristol Post: Friday 13th January 1967*
> *Families and friends are becoming increasingly concerned for a Bristol woman who has gone missing in Soviet-occupied East Germany.*
> *Rose Prideaux, 22, travelled to Berlin on Monday, January 3rd, but has not been in touch with her family since.*
> *Her mother, Mrs Florence Prideaux of Okebourne Road, Westbury-on-Trym, said her daughter had promised to call her on January 5th, but the call never came.*
> *The aspiring actress told her family she was visiting the American Sector for an audition. The film company said she attended the audition early on January 4th, but had been unsuccessful, Witnesses say she left, along with the other actors and actresses, after her audition. She was last seen near Checkpoint Charlie, one of the border crossing points.*
> *Police have made enquiries at her German lodging house. Her landlady said Rose's bill was paid and nothing suspicious happened. DCI Barry Rutland said enquiries were ongoing, but at this stage police believed it to be a Missing Persons case and nothing more sinister. "As long as she didn't cross into the Russian sector, it is quite possible she will turn up soon."*
> *Mrs Prideaux said, "I just want my girl to come home safe and sound."*

"Friday the 13th," said Porter.

"Let's not add superstition to the supernatural, eh? Apart from the John Le Carré overtones, it's pretty skimpy," said Feng. "Anything else?"

> *Bristol Post: Tuesday 3rd October 1967*
>
> *Detectives investigating the disappearance of a young Bristolian actress in Berlin, have suspended their enquiries.*
>
> *Police say no new leads have emerged since Rose Prideaux, 22, of Okebourne Road, Westbury-on-Trym, went missing on January 4th following an audition for a film part.*
>
> *Her mother, Mrs Florence Prideaux said she received a letter from her daughter in March claiming she had met someone in West Germany and was staying there. However, her mother claimed the handwriting was nothing like her daughter's and she now suspects foul play.*
>
> *DCI Barry Rutland, who has been leading the investigation, said, "We had a look at the letter. It doesn't look exactly like Rose's handwriting but may have been written under duress or under the influence of alcohol. No other clues have turned up. I have personally spoken to the Chief of Police in West Berlin. He has assured me no-one resembling this young lady has turned up alive or dead. We have no other option but to close the case, pending new evidence."*
>
> *Mrs Prideaux said, "As long as I'm alive, I will keep looking for her. There's no way she would have just upped and left like that."*
>
> *Pressed whether Rose might have defected to the Soviet sector, Mrs Prideaux said, "I can't imagine anyone less interested in politics than my daughter."*

"All this really says is that the police didn't spend long looking for her," said Porter. "Young girl runs away from home, leaves parents behind. That's the lyrics of The Beatles' She's Leaving Home right there - and Sergeant Pepper came out around then."

"Samuel Brownlees' PI turned up without a head in the Thames," said Feng. "Goff. Wasn't that enough to make the police suspicious?" said Feng. A staunch atheist, Feng refused to say the word *God*.

Porter checked his notes. "They didn't employ Alex Harding until almost a year later in December '67. His body was found in January '68. She went missing in Berlin, he was killed in London. It's not obvious there's a connection."

The Gliss chipped in. "You said there were three cuttings?" Porter nodded and pulled out a third printout, but it was a cutting, culled from an entry on a local history blog.

"I can't tell when it was written exactly," said Porter, "but the writer mentions Tony Blair as Prime Minister, so it's sometime between 1997 and 2007."

> *A career in crime: DCI Barry Rutland*
>
> *Former Detective Chief Inspector Barry Rutland is in good form over biscuits and tea at his comfy home in Redcliffe.*
>
> *After serving 35 years in the police force, Barry retired five years ago but has fond memories of his time serving the citizens of Bristol and Somerset. How has Bristol changed?*
>
> *"It's unrecognisable, isn't it?" he says, pouring us both a cup of Earl Grey. "In my day, there were no guns, drugs or internet fraud. People say it's idealising the past, but it's not: It really was safer back then."*
>
> *What do you think has caused that?*
>
> *"Politicians, politics and policies. Same old story. When I first started, a murderer knew he faced the death penalty. It didn't stop everyone, but it stopped many. Now he - and it nearly always is a he - knows he'll get a slapped wrist, seven years or so in prison, and all the help in the world to rehabilitate for free. Meanwhile, honest, hard-working folk have to pay for their children to go to University. It's all wrong."*
>
> *Who can disagree with that? What was a typical crime back then? Barry sinks back in his armchair and thinks for a minute.*
>
> *"There's always been burglaries. In spite of what I just said, there's always been murders - just not so many of them. Of course, after the war we had the Cold War, and that led to a few interesting cases even in Bristol."*
>
> *I must have raised my eyebrows, because Barry was quick to put me straight.*

> "*I arrested a Russian, Gregor Sharapov in 1971. He was a professor at Bristol University, but we got a tip-off he was a double agent. Supposedly advising MI6, he was also sending reports back to the Soviet Union. Nothing big, just summaries of the mood amongst the people, that kind of thing.*"
>
> *I suggest that's not exactly Burgess and MacLean, but he cuts me short.*
>
> "*And there was that other case. We had a young girl go missing in Berlin in the 60s. Rose Prideaux. I'll never forget her. She was an actress from a poor background who moved from Bristol to London to pursue her career. I tried to get Interpol to help me trace her. We found she'd been all over the place, including LA and Rome, before going missing in Berlin. No-one could afford air travel those days. Yet here was some 'poor' girl from Bristol, supposedly auditioning for parts she never got, going missing in Spy Central, in the midst of the Cold War. Highly suspicious.*"
>
> *Did you ever find any proof she was a spy?*
>
> "*I didn't need to. Guess who she'd been hanging out with in Soho? Mandy Rice-Davies and Christine Keeler - you remember them, of course? The John Profumo scandal in 1963? That was enough evidence for me. And when her mother received a dodgy letter a few months later saying she'd taken up with a German lad, I knew right away the poor girl had gotten in over her head. Probably still at the bottom of the Rhine now.*"
>
> *A tragic end if true. Luckily, there's not much spying going on today.*
>
> "*Don't kid yourself. The Chinese have got people everywhere, we let our guard down at our peril. I was saying the other day...*"

"He sounds like a completely paranoid nutcase," said Feng.

"Yes," said Karin, cautiously, "but let's be honest, if she did hang around in those kinds of circles in London in the 60s, anything is possible."

"Maybe. He sounds like a nut to me too," said Porter.

"Well, let's find out for ourselves, shall we?" said Karin, pulling out a photocopied sheet of her own. "I checked to see if Rutland was still alive. He is. He's nearly 80 and still in Redcliffe."

Feng, impatient to show his research, said it was a good idea, pulling out his phone. He opened his camera roll. "I didn't find anything in particular, but I did find this, which moved me, I must say."

Feng showed the cover of a book, Bristol Under Siege by Helen Reid. It was a popular history book and was chock full of atmospheric black and white photos. He tapped on a high-contrast, grainy shot of a black American G.I. chatting up a white girl at a dance hall, somewhere in Bristol.

"It's like a classic jazz photo," he said, "all that smoke and blurry depth of field. Gorgeous. Make you think of anyone?"

"Florence and Sam, obviously," said Porter. "Wait, it's not them is it?"

"I'm not a betting man, but I should think the odds are pretty much against it, don't you think?"

"So, that's it," sighed Karin. "A few minor details, a retired cop and a possible link to either/both London spy rings/high-class prostitution."

With nothing else to do, they called Namita to see if she'd finished her meetings. They could all meet for dinner, perhaps. But she wasn't answering her phone.

October 16th, 2017
Snakes & Ladders, Christmas Steps, Bristol

Namita ordered herself a smoothie and a wrap, found the darkest corner and prepared for Stormont. He came into her speaker like a firework igniting in a shed. She told him she wouldn't chat until he calmed down. She said call back in five minutes. She hung up.

For a few minutes her phone repeatedly buzzed and lit up as he tried to get through. Thank God for Silent Mode.

Rearranging herself, she took a breath and called back.

"I'm gonna fuckin' do you," said Stormont. "What kind of shit's that? Tellin' me you don't do will-shit, then speakin' to the other fucker?"

"Mr Stormont don't threaten me, and please stop swearing. As I told you the other day, I can't represent you. I didn't say I can't represent someone else."

"But…"

"Wait. Listen, please. I was intrigued that's all. I looked into it and Mr Brownlees asked me if I wanted to represent him."

"That's against the law, that is," fumed Stormont.

"If it's against anything, it would be against the Solicitors Regulation Authority's Code of Conduct. But I assure you, as I hadn't received instructions from you - and explicitly told you I couldn't represent you - I haven't broken any Code of Conduct."

She wasn't as certain of this as she made out. However, she always said her basic job description was bluffing, more bluffing, and bluffing with cream on top. She decided it was time to pull out her patented Bluff and Muff technique. Speak slowly, sensuously even. No raised voice. It seemed to appease idiot men. Stormont began to abate from a Force 9 to a Force 8 gale. *But that's still one helluva wind.*

Stormont said, "Well, me solicitor - me actual solicitor - says it's not on. He's gonna call you - so watch out, you bitch." Before she had time to warn him again, Stormont was gone.

Her voicemail pinged. It was Karin. It pinged again. A number she didn't recognise. *Ten quid it's that burke's solicitor.*

It was. She called back.

"Martin Skelling of Skelling Associates. It's good to speak to you, Ms Menon," said the solicitor. Unlike his client, he sounded quite reasonable. He had a posh, hyper-English, Hugh Grant-ish lilt - something she found repulsive, exclusive and - alright - a bit sexy. "I gather Mr Stormont has given you both barrels?"

She admitted he had.

"Honestly, don't you think he was a tiny bit justified, Ms Menon? It was a pretty low-trick, what?"

He's straight from Wodehouse. "You've spoken to Mr Stormont? I'm sure you fully understand the reasons why I don't want him as a client?"

"I don't know what you mean," he said. And, to her surprise, let out a laugh like mud bubbles popping. Not exactly professional, but it put her at ease.

Establishing she was in Bristol, Skelling suggested dinner - his treat - to discuss and clear things up. Namita, who'd already texted the others to say she was on her way to join them, declined. He sounded a bit deflated. *Throw him a bone.* "I'm in town until tomorrow afternoon at least, and could do lunch before I go?"

Details agreed, Namita put the phone down.

For the first time, she looked around her. Every inch of shelf space in the cafe was stacked with games for hire. She was pretty sure Monopoly must be in here somewhere, but most of the boxes were obscure board games: Throw, Throw Burrito, Cosmic Encounter, Carcassonne, The Mushroom Eaters, Top Trumps… *Top Trumps!?* Running her fingers along the spines of the games, she thought: "Who the hell would hire a pack of Top Trumps? Didn't they only cost a fiver to buy?" She continued browsing, fascinated. Feed the Ducks, Pointless: The Board Game… hundreds more.

"What a strange place," Namita said to herself, but out loud by mistake.

A tetchy barista responded. "We couldn't keep going without strange customers, eh?" He stared at her coldly.

It was only back out on the Christmas Steps Namita twigged who she'd probably offended. What were the odds he was the owner? Someone who had ploughed his life savings and hobby into a business - just so she could walk in and insult the entire project. *Oh well.* She remembered seeing a shop in Brick Lane which only served cereals - at £5 a bowl.

"If someone's prepared to hire a pack of bloody Top Trumps instead of buying one, good luck to him."

October 16th, 2017
L'Escargot, Clifton, Bristol

The gang reunited at a French bistro near Isambard Kingdom Brunel's Suspension Bridge for dinner. Feng told her about DCI Rutland. They were staying over to interview him tomorrow.

Karin said, "I tried ringing earlier to see if I could get you a room. I pencilled one for you."

Namita, flustered, told them she'd assumed they were all going home, so had already booked a room. She had to stay for meetings about the will. She decided not to tell them about her confrontation with Stormont or the pending lunch with Skelling.

"That's no problem, of course," said Karin, with a suggestion of the opposite. "Let me call and cancel."

Namita listened with interest as Feng outlined Rutland's spy theory, but she thought it was ridiculous. "Come on, what's the chance of a young girl in her 20s getting involved in Cold War spy circles?"

"Ordinarily," said Karin, "I'd say zero. But then I'm sure most girls in the 60's didn't know high class escorts or go missing in Berlin at the height of the Cold War. Oh, and let's not forget, the PI sent to find her ends up in the Thames with his head missing. It would be premature to rule it out entirely at this stage."

"When you put it like that…" said Namita. She had nothing to add from her meeting with Dan Little. They moved on to more important things - who was having what for dessert and who would pay the bill. Karin and Feng were both rich and liked tussling over who bankrolled the gang's jaunts.

"Come on, it's only one dinner. Can't everyone just pay for their own this time?" said Namita, regretting it as soon as she said it. *Damn, no fags tomorrow at all.*

Luckily, Feng wouldn't take no for an answer. "No, it's my turn, but you can all pay me back by joining me on a tour of old Bristol tomorrow morning before we go to see Rutland." There were a few groans. "It'll be fun! We should get to know the old areas while we're here - some of it may even date back to the times when Samuel's ancestor turned up in Bristol as a slave."

Everyone agreed.

Namita sighed with relief. Four cigarettes tomorrow after all.

Chapter 8

October 17th, 2017
Cafe Revival, St Nicholas Markets, Bristol

"They've been serving coffee here continuously since 1788," said Feng, gesturing at the cafe sign.
"Well, they must be looking forward to going home then," said Porter.
"Funny. Come on, let's grab a latte."
The four were mid-way through Feng's imposition of a tour. This was historic Bristol, the four original streets dating back to Saxon times: Broad Street, Wine Street, Corn Street, and the High Street. As true as of anywhere, the churches were the oldest buildings. They had been providing prayer since the town was called Brightstowe, and even Brycgstow, before that. These ancient buildings were surrounded by impressive 18th century guilds and offices. The narrow alleyways spoke of the medieval layout before that.
"You probably all know this, bearing in mind Sam's testimony, but this is one of those English cities that got rich from the slave trade," said Feng, reading from a guidebook. "By 1750, it was the main clearing house for African slaves *en route* to America and the West Indies."

Over the years, the ever-inquisitive Feng had picked up more guidebooks than the Kardashians had facelifts. Not for him, wandering around in a witless fug, hoping for minor illumination from a blue plaque. A professor-that-never-was, Feng had brought the same diligence to 20 years researching the supernatural. Once he scooped up new knowledge, he liked nothing better than to dish it straight back out.

"About a third of the slave trade came through Bristol," he said. "But, weirdly, Bristol was also in the forefront of the abolition movement. It says here that abolitionists reduced the volume of trade so fast, only 23 ships were engaged in 1771. By 1780, even the public was actively engaged in ending it, thanks to vocal locals like John Weekes and John Wesley, who both publicly condemned slavery."

"So Bristol had an evil start and redeemed itself in the end," said Porter. "I love that Sam was able to have a drink here in the 40s, protected by the locals, in supposedly un-enlightened times."

"I'm weird about all that stuff," said Namita. "I had a big row with Seema once over reparations etc. She was banging on about how the British Empire was entirely evil etc. Her basic argument was that Porter and Karin here, should cough up because 10 generations ago there were slaves that they had nothing to do with."

"They're welcome to try and get money out of me," said Porter. "No-one else has had any luck. But the Empire was evil, wasn't it, Namita? And not just Africa: look at India. We asset-stripped it and God knows how many people died. Reparations are about taxing the benefits later generations accrued through evil, not directly punishing the guilty who are all long since dead."

"I understand that, of course," said Namita. "Show me an Empire that wasn't evil. But the first rule of justice is punishing the guilty. Imagine if every time we sent someone down for murder, we sent their mum and dad down too?"

She glugged at her takeaway coffee, fuelling herself for a row. "You might as well say, I owe India money because I'm British too. The people who did it 250 years ago were the guilty ones: evil, no question. But nothing is entirely evil. If there hadn't been an Empire, there would have been no Commonwealth. Without the Commonwealth I doubt my parents could have made their home here. Not everything evil has only evil repercussions. I've been nursed, educated and work here. I only know Britain."

"And that, of course, has been nothing but good for us all," smiled Feng. Even when he meant to compliment, he had a tendency to sound arch. Namita shot him a look that could have frozen a side of pork. Feng the naif looked about as if he was unsure to whom she was giving the evil eye.

"That's an unusual take for a second generation Indian, Namita," said Karin.

"Not really, I'm proud to be British," she said. "I've only been to India for a wedding. I hated it. That's not the problem. I think of myself as British. I just need all the white British to accept I'm British too."

"So, you're not Asian at all then?" said Porter, wary of provoking her. He didn't like the evil eye she pulled out on special occasions.

"Of course, I am - but that's only a bit of my cultural make-up. Sure, it's 100% of my genetics, but culture should be what defines you. If it's only about genes, then the Nazis were right to say Jews who'd been in Germany for 300 years weren't really German. Or the National Front are right saying black Britons should be repatriated. I don't think that's a route civilised society should go down. Look at bloody Trump and his campaign against the Mexicans. It's horrible."

"Who do you support when the cricket's on," said Feng, poking his finger in the cage.

"India," snapped Namita. "I said British, not English."

"Aren't the two ideas contradictory?" said Feng.

"Only if you have a comparatively small brain and can't handle two concurrent streams of thought at once," said Namita.

"Alright, I was only checking." Feng asked if she encountered much racism.

"Have you?" she replied.

"Not really," he admitted. "A bit from the posh City boys when I was a broker. But posh City boys rarely have redeeming features. I probably encountered more homophobia than racism. Besides, I'm in London. London is a special case."

"I've been on the end of exactly one racist incident since I was 20," said Namita. "Some idiot called me a Paki bitch from her car after she nearly run me over. Of course, I believe others who say they've had worse. They used to stick dog turds through our letterbox in the 70s. But the 70s isn't now. Not in London, anyway. As you point out, we're protected in the London bubble."

Karin nodded. "The only trouble is, Namita, this is not the prevailing opinion amongst the sensitive residents of Woke-on-the-Wold. If you were a public figure, they'd lynch you on Twitter for saying that."

"If you're stupid enough to go on Twitter, you deserve it."

Karin, ever the historian, couldn't resist having an opinion. "I agree things are better than they were generally, but they're not perfect. I mean, they've still got a statue up to Edward Colston in Bristol - a prominent slave trader. That should be taken down, yes?"

"Of course," said Namita. "There are plenty of people to celebrate with a statue who didn't kill or enslave people. Strange that the city that produced Tricky and Massive Attack has tolerated that."

"As long as we all live in perfect harmony," said Porter.

"Oh lord, why don't we!" Feng sang at the top of his voice.

Porter looked around, embarrassed, and shushed him. "Look, I don't mind people overhearing us talk about race, religion and slavery, but I don't want them to hear us singing Ebony and Ivory."

The four sipped their drinks, people-watching. The market has been here for centuries, Karin noted

"So has that," said Feng, pointing to a manky box of carrots on one of the stalls.

"They're organic," said Porter. "Like you, they're rough at the edges, but probably tastier as a result."

"Ooh, you tease," camped Feng.

"So, what's the plan?" sighed Namita.

"Rutland in two hours," said Porter. "He's very flattered Karin the Celebrity wants to see him. First, we're going to walk up these famous Christmas Steps of yours and then get an Uber to Portishead. What about you?"

Namita cursed. "I've got to go and fight fires. The little shit I originally spoke to about Florence's will is contesting it. I stayed on to make peace with his solicitor." She saw the time on the large clock tower and started. "Oh damn. Call me later."

Twenty minutes later, Feng, Porter and Karin passed the games cafe and trudged up the steps.

"My lungs feel like a sun-baked chammy," said Feng. "Not as bad as Montmartre, I suppose."

"It's nowhere near that bad," said Karin. "Stop smoking, Feng."

"I don't really understand alcohol and I don't understand cigarettes," said The Gliss. "It appears that with every cigarette you're putting a weight on your legs. One might call it a Jacob Marlboro chain." He stifled a titter.

"You might - if you're writing Christmas cracker jokes," said Porter.

"But what is the purpose?" said The Gliss, ignoring the jibe.

"From chocolate to coffee, wine to fags, virtually every damn thing in this life that's enjoyable, comes with a downside," explained Feng.

"But smoking - surely it's just sucking in pollution?"

"That's the downside," admitted Feng. "Not forgetting heart attacks and lung cancer. The upside is feeling calm, having something to do with my fingers, and giving me a reason to take a few minute's break. Heavier legs is a compromise I can live with. I wouldn't expect a creature with no legs to understand."

"Creature? And who says I haven't got legs?" said The Gliss.

To be fair, it wasn't an unreasonable assumption. Most of the time he presented as a disembodied head, though disembodied hands occasionally appeared too.

"Legs?" said Porter. "What would you need legs for?"

"Why do humans have an appendix? Need is only ever a partial explanation for anything."

"Show us your pins then, honey," said Feng, who looked ready to pounce with a wolf-whistle if the request was granted.

"I think not," said The Gliss, "Suffice it to say, should my legs ever be required to make an appearance, I'll let the fan club know in advance."

"And wear stockings," said Feng. "I'll pre-book Snappy Snaps for the prints."

Karin, who tended to duck out of banter, surveyed the location from the top of the climb: the Christmas Steps rolled out like a carpet before them, the picaresque alms house next door - "Good lord, it looks like Willy Wonka designed it!" - the Three Kings Chapel, and the graceful terrace spreading out to their left. A large white office building on the main road below obscured everything in the distance, although the top of a church spire could just be seen.

"It's beautiful," she said. "I wonder how all this survived. Everything else here looks like Lego."

The Georgian crescent filled with small shops gave a clue. "The redevelopment only runs along the bottom," said Porter, pointing. "Up here feels old and unmolested, thank God." Porter had a particular hatred of 60s/70s office buildings.

"You have to cut them a bit of slack," said Karin. "Bristol was heavily bombed during the war. I suspect most of where we were down there used to be bomb sites. Bristol's a port, and the RAF had a base at Filton. The fact that almost 300,000 Americans were based around Bristol, in preparation for the D-Day landings, drew enemy fire too."

"Three hundred thousand?" queried Feng. "Surely not?"

"Oh, yes, I looked it up before we came. About a tenth of the Yanks were black too. That was after the Blitz, though. I think the first Americans got here in '42."

"Here," said Feng, flipping through his guide. "On September 25th, 1940, 58 Heinkel bombers, with a Messerschmitt fighter escort, bombed the flip out of the airfield at Filton. Over 200 people were killed. Goff."

"I always think of the Blitz as a London thing," admitted Porter.

"Typical Londoner… me, me, me," laughed Karin. "What about Coventry? Glasgow? Leicester? Plymouth? Liverpool?"

"It's so much fun travelling with a historian," Porter grimaced.

"The thing is," said Feng, "as beautiful as these streets are, they were all made on the back of slave trade profits. It gives them a melancholic air once you know, don't you think? I wonder if any of this was here when Samwell Brownlees was here in the 1800s?"

"Not much. Some of the guilds and the churches. But most of the slaves wouldn't have seen the town, whatever it looked like," said Karin. "Bristol was a stopping-off point. A place to change ships, a tick in a ledger somewhere. I think Samwell might have been the exception. Didn't Sam say he was only taken out of the docks for a potential local sale? But, yes, he must have been here for the story to have passed to Sam. It's quite something to think of it."

Feng showed them a picture of a gravestone in Henbury, ironically, very close to Florence Prideaux's home. It was the marker for a man called Scipio Africans, a slave who was later a servant of the Earl of Suffolk. It read:

I who was born a PAGAN and a SLAVE now sweetly sleep a CHRISTIAN in my grave. What tho' my hue was dark my SAVIOR'S sight shall change this darkness into radiant light.

"Very nice," said Karin. "It's almost like blacks can't go to Heaven without the support of a rich, white landowner."

"Yes," said Feng, "but the Earl of Suffolk obviously wasn't entirely a shit, was he?"

"When he wasn't forcing his religion onto his slave," said Karin.

"One thing puzzles me though," said Porter. "Presumably Samwell had no English in the 1700s. How would he have known this was called the Christmas Steps, even if he'd lived here for a month rather than just passing through?"

"He could have described it later on," said Karin. "It's pretty distinctive. In the intervening centuries, maybe someone looked it up. Who knows? I'd really like to speak to Sam Brownlees. He sounds fascinating."

"Get you," said Feng, turning to Porter. "Ms Pelenot's switched her camera on already." Karin punched him on the shoulder.

"Ow. Was that supposed to be playful?" said Feng.

"Not at all," said Karin with a smile. "Not at all."

October 17th, 2017
The Hatchet Inn, Bristol

A few streets away, Namita took a deep breath and walked into the saloon of The Hatchet Inn. Scrawl on the outside wall proclaimed it Bristol's oldest pub, established around 1500. It was quite busy. A mix of tourists and men in suits. Martin Skelling could be literally any one of these…

"Ms Menon?"

She turned to face a handsome, tall, expensive suit. *He looks a bit like Hugh Grant too - floppy hair and all.* "Mr Skelling?"

"Martin, please." He gestured to his table, where a laptop and purple silk-lined overcoat both lay open. The coat had been shrugged off, retaining its owner's shape, creating the impression the Invisible Man was sat there typing.

She pulled up a chair, observing as he sat down. He was smoothing the creases in his trousers. *He's scared of bagging his knees. Doesn't love himself, does he?* She remembered her own fastidiousness and decided to cut him some slack. He, in turn, remembered his manners and immediately jumped back up, ready to head to the bar.

"So, how do you find Bristol?" Skelling talked down to her in her seat, twirling a coaster in one hand as he stood at the bar, trying to catch the attention of the server.

"You turn off the M42 and there it is," she quipped.

"Ha! I love Bristol. I was born and brought up in Bath, but it was a bit too parochial for me. After Cambridge, I decided to move here. It's been good to me. Very cosmopolitan."

Was it? She realised with a start, he'd had no problem spotting her because she was the only brown person in the pub. Coming from London, where every bar looked like the business end of a billiards table, she found it unfamiliar and slightly strange.

"It's lovely to meet you, Namita." The barman turned to Skelling, who realised he still hadn't taken Namita's order. "Beer? Wine? Whiskey?"

"Just a coffee please," said Namita, noting his half-empty glass of red.

"You don't drink?"

"Not at lunchtime."

"We should have met for dinner then. Coffee it is."

Namita watched him as he ordered her coffee. She surprised herself. *Yes, dinner might have been nice.*

Chapter 9

October 17th, 2017
Nore Road, Portishead, Bristol

The former Detective Chief Inspector fussed and wobbled while making his guests tea. Watching the old man dodder like a Weeble made them all nervous. In his shaky paws, a teapot of steaming water looked more like a watering can, ready to sprinkle the delicate flowers of their laps.

"Don't fuss! You're worse than my carer!" he half-joked, half-snapped, as they all did their best to make themselves comfortable.

A bunch of notebooks and folders were dumped on Rutland's table. The expensive wood hadn't been waxed for years. They all noticed the cigarette burns and stains on its surface.

"Love your show, Karin," said Rutland. "That one where you dug up the Saxon hill fort… brilliant."

"Thanks," she said. "We got into trouble with that one. The farmer had to let it go fallow for two years while it was excavated. Sued us for loss of earnings."

"Cheeky bastard."

"Indeed. He lost. The only crop he grew was grass."

"Sheep eat too."

"They do. But he didn't have any sheep."

"Or cows?"

"Not even one."

"Cheeky bastard."

"Indeed," said Karin, laughing.

Pleasantries over, Rutland got straight to the point. "I hope you're doing a show on Rose Prideaux. Killed by the Russians - I'm sure of it."

Eyebrows raised, Porter said they'd seen all the original cuttings. Did Rutland really still believe that?

"I don't know what the hell she got mixed up in down in London, but nothing else ever made sense to me," he said. This was his cue to fan out his papers. "Maybe I've read too many spy novels, but I was there at the time, and it stood out like a sore thumb from your average missing persons case. Especially with everything that happened after."

Karin, who was the most experienced at teasing out details, led the enquiries. Rutland was focused and intelligent but was so keen to tell his story he jumped in and out of sequence, shuffling his papers in a continual search for supporting evidence. Keeping track was like trying to do a jigsaw puzzle on a rollercoaster.

After comparing notes and straightening out the inconsistencies, Feng, Porter and Karin came to understand the following from Rutland's account.

> *I first heard about Rose Prideaux in early January 1967. One of the boys said a mum had come in to report her daughter missing. Jackson, I think it was, said the girl was living in London but had disappeared in Berlin. He wasn't best pleased. I remember him shouting, "What the hell are we supposed to do about it from Bristol?"*
>
> *He was right, of course. If she'd actually gone missing through foul play - and a lot of missing people turn out to be just runaways - it was a case for the cops in Berlin or London.*
>
> *But my dad fought the Nazis and I probably got it stuck in my head that nothing good can come from hanging around with the Germans. A prejudice, I know. I don't honestly remember how I felt. I'm pro-Europe these days. What I do know is, I was the one who spoke to her mum, Florence. I picked up enough of a Bristol connection to keep me interested.*

She was proper beside herself. Her daughter still had a room in Okebourne Road, even though Rose moved to London in September '65. Don't most parents secretly hope their child will come back one day? But Rose was too independent for that, by the sounds of it. She was sharing a flat with her friends in Soho in Wardour Street and had been travelling and what not. I suspect Bristol seemed too small for her. It wasn't as cosmopolitan as it is now.

As you must know, the investigation in Germany got nowhere. However, Florence would stop by occasionally to see if I knew anything. I got to know her a bit over the next year or so. She was a nice lady, and we didn't have so much paperwork to do in those days. She didn't make a nuisance of herself. I enjoyed our infrequent chats, which stopped when I transferred to Somerset for a few years. Our little chats were always strictly 'have-a-cuppa-and-listen' on my part. Rose's disappearance never fell within my jurisdiction. It just fascinated me.

As far as I could tell, Rose, who dreamt of becoming an actress, was offered an audition in Berlin on January 4th, 1967. It was freezing that winter. She flew from London Airport to Berlin on January 3rd and called her mum to say she'd got to her lodgings okay. Rose promised she would call Florence straight after the audition on January 4th.

Florence waited patiently by the phone all day the whole of the 4th and the 5th. Silence. Now that I'm talking about it, Florence must have first come to see us on the 6th. Only two days. That's not really long enough to justify opening a missing persons case; not now, not then. You should never underestimate how inconsiderate people can be - especially young people.

Feng said, "If a person has actually gone missing, isn't two days a long time *not* to open a case. I watch Without a Trace. Don't they say the first 48 hours are the most crucial in an investigation?"

Rutland agreed, adding, "If abduction and murder cases are rare now, they were even rarer then. All the odds were that Rose had just forgotten to keep her mum updated and was off partying somewhere.

"Any of you parents? No? Well, you've heard what it's like, at least. It's all true: if anything happens to your kids, a sixth sense kicks in. Florence told me, 'I know the worst has happened, I just know it.'

"I still had no evidence to believe the worst yet. It was the letter that changed my mind."

Referring to a notebook, Rutland told of the day in late January when Florence came in with a letter from Rose. He had a faded xerox copy of it in his folder. "I mean, just look at it. The letter's very short and untidy. It simply says, 'Sorry mum, have met a nice German lad. Don't worry will be in touch soon, all the best, Rose.' It's dated the 5th of January. Sending address was 43d, Emdener Strasse. Well, you don't have to be a detective to be suspicious about that: why not just call as promised? The formality of the letter was a giveaway. It wasn't the kind of relationship the mother and daughter had. That was easily proved.

"Florence brought in a box of her letters. The girl liked to write. She always signed off, "Love you mum, Rose xxx." The handwriting was a bit iffy too. It *sorta* looked like Rose's, but something was off, like she was drunk or drugged. Or someone else had tried to copy her handwriting."

Karin chipped in. "If the letter was a hoax, it was a pretty flimsy gambit. How long would a casual letter like that stop a parent from looking for their child if they heard nothing more?"

"Well, exactly," said Rutland. "It might buy the abductor a week or two at most. In fact, Florence knew it was hokey and brought it straight to me. The letter tipped my interest into genuine concern. It's what made me start my notebooks."

The gang worked their way through the whole gamut of non-verbal communication, nodding and jigging enough eyebrows to encourage a hermit, let alone a prattling pro like Rutland.

"I still had no jurisdiction. I wondered what I could do, but eventually made a few discreet enquiries to colleagues in the Met. I couldn't have been more surprised. Rose Prideaux was on a watchlist held by Special Branch."

The jig of eyebrow-raising turned into a full-scale production by the Bolshoi.

Rutland, grinning at their reaction, said, "You've got to remember... despite the Cold War, there were only hundreds of Special Branch officers in the UK at that time. Since 9/11 that's become thousands: espionage and terrorism. Of course, the news did nothing to calm my suspicions.

"Maybe Rose was involved in prostitution and/or blackmail? It had only been three years or so since the John Profumo affair - you all know about that, presumably?"

They all nodded. Rutland detailed his thinking. "The upper echelons were still edgy about it happening again. One of the escorts involved with Profumo, Mandy Rice-Davies, had become something of a celebrity, even putting a record out. It's conceivable a young girl might think doing something similar could lead to a bit of fame and fortune - you see it now with X-Factor, don't you? Instant celebrity - as quick and un-nutritious as a Pot Noodle. I'd seen enough of Vice, even in a quiet town like Bristol, to know how easily young girls could get sucked into that world. Maybe she tried to blackmail someone and got killed for her trouble?

"But, to start with, it was all niggling suspicions. I was stuck in Bristol, a long way from London, pre-internet. Special Branch didn't start setting up regional offices until 1968.

"I only had one contact: an old mate from training days. He wasn't helpful, in fact, he was quite stiff with me. He warned me in no uncertain terms to just leave it alone. He said there were fears a Russian-London spy ring was operating out of Berlin. He made it perfectly clear I wasn't to ask any awkward questions. Made me feel like a yokel plod. You have to remember Berlin was the home of the Iron Curtain, where East and West met during the Cold War. Until CCTV came along, it was probably the most surveilled city on the planet. My contact warned that if Rose *was* mixed up in espionage (and he wouldn't confirm or deny), my investigations might jeopardise other agents working in the field.

"Well, I'm a cop. Did you get the key word in all that? *Other*. He said I might jeopardise *other* agents. There was no way I could let that go."

By now, the team's eyebrows were indistinguishable from their hairlines.

"I spoke with my equivalent in Berlin. He said they'd fully investigated Rose's disappearance. They concluded there was nothing to it and treated it as a simple runaway case. He detailed enough to convince me they really had looked for Rose. There had been some sort of investigation, probably not much different than we'd have done. In essence, they found a whole bunch of girls auditioned for the same part as Rose that day. All had signed in and out of the studio on January 4th, including Rose. Whatever happened to her, happened after the audition."

The gang all nodded. He was making sense.

"I got the address of her lodgings in Mitti. Rose's landlady, Mutti Dietrich, confirmed Rose had stayed with her for two nights only, January 3rd/4th.

"She remembered Rose because her husband, Gustav, had offered to drive her to the film studio. Rose was happy and excited. Nothing out of the ordinary to report at all. I double-checked with the Berlin cops that no-one else had ever been reported missing from that address before - just to rule out the Dietrich's as Fred and Rose West goose-steppers. But there had never been a complaint linked to that address and the Dietrich's had taken lodgers without trouble since the mid-50s."

Porter watched Rutland. It was like watching someone ill-advisedly going into fifth gear approaching a hill in a jalopy. Rutland's energy was fading as he approached the end of his story.

"There the trail ended," said Rutland, summing up. "I got in touch with Interpol, who were based in Saint Cloud in Paris. I put in a formal request for info, but they came back with next-to-nothing. They had a note of the Berlin cops' case number - don't forget, Rose was presumed missing in Europe making it an international case - but sod all else.

"I met with Florence regularly that year. Not a peep from Rose. No calls, no postcards. By late '68 both of us guessed, well, knew really, that Rose must be dead."

"We saw your blog interview," said Feng. "You said she was probably at the bottom of the Rhine."

The cop shook his head. "I meant it figuratively. Her body could be anywhere."

"But you carried on making enquiries, I presume?" said Karin, fascinated. "You don't look like the kind of man who accepts no for an answer?"

Rutland nodded, sitting back now. He steepled his hands, clearly relishing his few moments of glory as Bristol's Sherlock. "Indeed, Karin. My enquiries were all speculative, but they had an unexpected result - one that made me think I'd been on the right track from the beginning.

"I had an old friend on Vice in London. I spoke to him and he said that they had been keeping a low-level watch on Mandy Rice-Davies and Christine Keeler since the Profumo affair. They had a growing list of all their acquaintances. Guess who was on it? Rose Prideaux."

Porter, who'd been drifting a bit, was pulled back by this info. He looked at the retired cop. *He's super-enjoying this. He wants this to be a big case as much I need it to be.*

"As you can imagine," said Rutland, "I immediately called my Special Branch guy back and presented this new fact to him. I thought it might loosen him up a bit. It certainly made the swing-o-meter go from Spy back towards Escort. But I was wrong. He didn't loosen up: he was livid. He shouted at me, made all kinds of threats, and made it perfectly clear my questions represented a security hazard."

Porter, an avid spy-fiction fan, looked at Rutland. Had the cop stumbled onto something? Even if there was any truth to the cop's version, how would he and the gang be able to investigate it? *This is always going to be our problem, isn't it? We have no official standing. All I can do is stand on graves and look stuff up in the library.*

Feng took up the mantle of chief inquisitor. "So, you shut up?"

"Of course not," said Rutland. "It just made me think the pendulum had swung heavily back to Spy! I wasn't convinced Special Branch's anger was about Rose, as such. I think Berlin was just so sensitive, so full of dodgy activities on all sides, they didn't want a clueless plod from Bristol poking about dislodging anything."

Porter thought he'd better jump in. "Thanks for telling us all this. It's fascinating. What happened next?"

"Sometime around October '67, we were told by the Berlin cops the case was still open, but active investigation had stopped. I wasn't surprised. Police resourcing issues are the best friends of crooks everywhere."

"Nothing changes, right?" said Porter.

"Definitely," said Rutland, bitterly. "But, of course, my news deeply upset Florence. Then she told me Rose's father - an American gentleman, ahem - had paid for a private eye to look into it. Do you know about that?"

He's a closet racist, thought Porter. *That ahem. Some things never change.*

"We know about Alex Harding, yes," said Karin. "What was your reaction when you heard Harding had been killed?"

"Well, it confirmed it all, didn't it? Turning up dead with his head missing. They're still doing it now."

"Who is? Doing what?" asked Porter, looking over Rutland's scruffy handwriting all over a yellow notepad, but deciphering nothing.

"The Russians! The FSB! Killing people! Look at Salisbury! Look at Litvinenko!"

Up and until now, Rutland had mostly impressed them with his detached professionalism. As soon as he mentioned the Russians, however, a fanatical look came into his eyes. "Did you see Rose's flight schedule? She'd been to Paris and Berlin after moving to London. She probably got recruited in the capital and it all went tits up for her. In over her head."

"Yes, we heard about the flights, said Karin, ignoring the comment about recruitment and the crudity. "Flights were expensive then. We've been wondering about that. With just a few minor acting jobs, it's hard to see how she could afford them…"

"She couldn't - not with a bit of acting and shift work in cafes and bars washing up," barked Rutland. "I was a bloody DCI with a decent salary, and I could just about afford to go to Spain every three years on the ferry. You lot are so used to Easyjet-ing off to Venice for the weekend, you've forgotten that only the rich flew then."

Karin, as lead investigator, was trying to think of something else to ask Rutland, when he shocked them all.

"Of course, I probably would have let it all go if it weren't for Ursa and Bella. By the time Bella went missing and Ursa killed herself, that was it: there was no way that could have all been a coincidence."

All three looked at each other in bewilderment.

"I'm sorry," said Karin, "who are Ursa and Bella?"

Rutland eyed them suspiciously. "I thought you said you'd looked into this?"

"We've just started," said Karin, sheepishly.

"Bella and Ursa were her friends from Bristol? The ones she went to London with - the actresses?"

"Ah, we don't know about them," admitted Karin.

Rutland shook his head at the amateurs and started the long process of standing up, finding a second wind. "Time for another cuppa then. This is gonna take some time."

October 17th, 2017
The Hatchet Inn, Bristol

Martin Skelling was clearly a professional flirt, but Namita was in no doubt about it: he'd principally come to give her a good ticking off for taking Sam Brownlees' brief.

The assault began three sips into her coffee. "Now, look Namita, I'm a broadminded sort of chap, but you've put us in a bit of claggy swamp here," he said.

She immediately thought: *public school*. He had that enviable ability to nervelessly maintain eye contact which only came from having joined the debating society in kindergarten.

"You know perfectly well what the Law Society would say if I flagged this up with them."

"Tell me," she said. Namita was more *hard-knocks* than *public*, but her schooling hadn't left her weaponless. He blinked first. *One-nil to hard-knocks*.

"Are you really going to make me do this?" He looked down and pulled out a document. It was the Solicitors Regulation Authority's Code of Conduct. He plonked it down so aggressively, the waft wobbled her froth.

"Paragraphs 6.1 and 6.2," said Skelling. "Guidance on conflicts of interest."

"I know this stuff by heart. There's nothing in it."

"Au contraire, Namita. It makes it perfectly clear that having spoken to my client, having heard his side of the story, you're in breach by representing Brownlees."

Still staring him out, she went on the attack. "Rubbish. It explicitly says - and I quote - *Although you should not normally act for two or more clients in these scenarios, this does not mean that you can never do so.*"

She didn't honestly think it would shut him up, but she hoped her stare and obvious deep knowledge would show she was no kitten.

It made no difference. Re-attaching himself to her stare, he showed off his deep knowledge too. "Namita, that is possibly the most selective interpretation I've ever seen anyone apply to the Code of Conduct. You quote guidance which specifically relates to a situation where two clients are already agreed on all the terms, where there's no row going on."

He quickly thumbed through the document, found the passage confirming this and showed it to her. She didn't look down. She knew what it said.

"As you know, I've never had Gary Stormont as a client," countered Namita. "We did nothing more than have a quick chat on the phone, along the lines of *how much you gonna cost, bitch?* Scarcely more than that."

"But is that true? You got enough info out of him to get Samuel Brownlees' name, the name of the executor, and an outline of my charming client's position," said Skelling. "That you shouldn't have done it, is beyond doubt. The question is: what are we going to do about it now?"

You bastard. You're going to make me have a glass of wine after all, aren't you?

October 17th, 2017
Nore Road, Portishead, Bristol

Four cups of tea and 20 splashes later, Rutland continued. "Don't you lot wimp out on me now. Look at the evidence: attractive girl moves to London, starts travelling between the major cities of the world - with no reliable source of income - becomes friends with notorious, well-connected call girls, goes missing in the spy capital of the world, at the height of the Cold War. Then the PI sent to find her has his bloody head chopped off and dumped in the Thames. Her flatmate goes missing a few months later in similar circumstances. Their other flatmate 'commits suicide' a few months after that. Use your noggin."

Rutland, in his eighties, had finally worn himself out with this last blast. The others looked at him, unsure what to say next. As keen as Rutland was to help, they had to wind this down for his sake.

Porter sought to clarify. "Let me get this straight: the two girls Rose moved to London with ended up missing and dead too?"

Rutland nodded: "Yes, that's what I said. Bella went missing in America in the summer of '68. Ursa killed herself at home in Bristol a few months later in August. It's all here."

He pushed over a piece of paper which had a hand-drawn timeline on it. The retired DCI leaned back in his chair. "Look. I know I sound a bit mad, but this case *has* driven me mad. Let's take Rose. If it was just, say, a domestic gone wrong in Berlin, how come the PI ended up headless in London?

"To me, it's obvious: The PI's death and location speaks of a cross-border conspiracy. Given the times, that probably means espionage. It's a misnomer to think the security services only use public schoolboys to spy. Many a businessman has snooped for their country."

Porter was the first to brave speaking up. "But a struggling actress? How do we know the PI's death was even linked to Rose's disappearance? This girl, Bella - she went missing in LA, correct? Not Berlin. It could be a three-way coincidence?"

Rutland looked at Porter like he was mad. "Three-way coincidence? You're having me on, right? Let's take Harding. I made calls about him. Do you know how many jobs he had? One. He was living on air! The only investigation on his books between the summer of '67 and his death in Jan '68, was the disappearance of Rose Prideaux. That tells me he wasn't any good or was a plant. As soon as he started asking careless questions about Rose, whoosh - off with his head."

"In London, not Berlin," said Porter.

While the gang were still examining the timeline, Rutland continued. With every minute, the ex-cop's mania escalated. "Alright, let's say you're right. So, you're telling me that two friends from Bristol, both actresses, both living in Soho, both knowing spies, both visiting Berlin, go missing within a year - and there's no connection? It's impossible."

Karin, transfixed by Rutland's testimony, had barely moved since she sat down. She leant forward now, putting a patronising hand on Rutland's knee. "And you told The Met about your suspicions again when Bella - Tompkinson? - went missing? I presume they were interested in Harding, at least? They had a murder on home turf to investigate."

Rutland, staring at the celebrity hand on his knee, calmed slightly. "Sure. They investigated the hell out of Harding. Nothing - just like you suggested, Porter. They found no links between Harding and Rose other than that her dad had hired the PI. But I knew, oh yes, I knew alright."

"You knew what?" said Karin, puzzled.

"It's obvious, isn't it?" said Rutland. "The girls were either being used as a conduit by MI6 or they were blackmailing someone high-up: someone in government, maybe. Foolishly inspired by the Profumo scandal? Who knows? The only other plausible explanation? They had their covers blown. Or, worse, they dipped into John Le Carré territory and turned double agents for the Soviets. Then they did something stupid and got bumped off."

Rutland's obsession was mesmerising. The gang sat like three less-than-wise monkeys; all staring, all mute. Rutland knew how to fill a vacuum.

"We have to assume that Ursa was in on it too," he added. "She'd been to some of the same places as Rose and Bella – so let's assume their auditions were cover for intelligence drops. Presumably, she felt guilty or trapped by her friends' disappearances. She hanged herself in her family home in Bristol. Let me see… 23 Pyecroft Avenue in Henleaze. Her mum refused to talk to me about it. She said her daughter had been depressed since coming back from London."

He checked his notes. "Yep. Ursa got a letter from the police confirming the Berlin investigation had ended. She quit London and came home in late October '67. Locked herself in her room and cried a lot. Wouldn't talk to her parents. Conspiracy. Guilt. Murder. Espionage. That's all I see."

The Gliss, safe in the knowledge Rutland could neither see nor hear him, spoke for the group when he said, "I think this gentleman may have forgotten to take his pills this morning."

Feng looked up to hear The Gliss speak. The sudden movement prompted Rutland to follow Feng's gaze, making him wonder what the batty Chinese guy was looking at. "Seen something?"

Feng stammered, "Er, no. I was just thinking what lovely coving you have."

Rutland looked positively Snape-like, screwing his eyes up as if to say, "Did you just say that?" Shaking his head, he gestured at the table. "Do you want to copy this lot? Any good to you?" They all nodded.

"And now you'll have to listen to him rant on for another half hour while you snap all his documents," said The Gliss. "Excuse me, while I retreat for a bit."

Porter responded to both Rutland and The Gliss, with, "Thank you very much for the sarcasm." Unfortunately, he couldn't help looking at The Gliss either.

Rutland watched Porter's response, gazing up at the same area of ceiling that Feng found so fascinating, and said, "I suppose you like my coving too?"

"It's lovely," said Porter, as Rutland shuffled off to the kitchen, shaking his head even more.

"He's gonna crick his neck if he's not careful," said Feng.

October 17th, 2017
The Hatchet Inn, Bristol

Namita's third dart landed and she cheered.

"Well, that's not a big score to be honest," said Martin, cracking up with a startling, horsey laugh.

"But I got a 20, I thought you said a 20 was good?"

"You got 20, which is good, but your other darts are on the floor."

"You do better then."

Martin accepted the challenge threw treble 20, treble 20, double 20 and shouted, "160!"

"You can have my 20 if you like. 180! Come on let's sit down, Martin. The room's wobbling." She could handle her drink, but a bottle of wine on an empty stomach hadn't been a good idea.

They moved back to their table, checked no-one had stolen anything, and Namita leaned back into the padded seat, exclaiming, "Whoof. I'm knackered."

Martin laughed and asked how long before she had to meet her friends. A snort at the word *friends*. An hour and a half.

Martin brightened. "Do you fancy some food?"

Namita suggested it was a bit early for dinner. Martin said he was thinking of something more portable, like a kebab.

"I'd love a kebab," said Namita. *Yay for me. I feel like a one-woman hen party.*

They tottered from the pub, arm in arm, Namita laughing, as Martin told her his favourite rugby joke.

Sangita chose this moment to pipe up. "What are you doing? You're all over him like baby oil. Get your kebab if you have to - but get some coffee as well. How many fags have you two had?"

Namita, to the bemusement of Martin, replied out loud: "A whole packet, thank God. Now bugger off and let me enjoy myself for once." Turning to Martin she said, "I'm not all over you like baby oil, am I? What a rude thing to say."

Martin widened his eyes. "Namita Menon, you are one crazy woman. Will you be back in Bristol soon? It's always good to have a new partner in crime."

"Wasn't talking to you, posh boy. But, yeah, I might be back. Now where's that kebab? Oh look, a wine bar."

Chapter 10

September 15th, 1965
Flat 6, 47 Wardour Street, London, W1

"Hey, Mr Tangerine Man…" sang Ursa.

Rose, laughing, threw a rolled-up sock at her best friend. "Don't be silly - it's Tambourine and you know it."

"Yeah," said Bella, "it was, like, funny the first 200 times."

"This sock better be clean," said Ursa, dangling it.

"I've only worn it twice. Besides, my Athlete's Foot has nearly cleared up," said Rose.

Ursa screamed, dropping the sock. "You're disgusting!"

Bella tutted, took out a tiny stuffed teddy bear and put it with a few other bits and pieces from home already tarting up the mantelpiece. "Anyone got any smokes?"

Ursa pulled a packet of Chesterfields and they all took one. Rose let hers dangle from her mouth while she knelt, starting up the Dansette and dropping the needle on side one of Help!.

Nodding along, taking a drag, she said, "I can't believe we're finally here! London!"

"Not just London…Soho!" said Ursa. "It's gear."

"And we haven't even partied yet," said Bella. She pulled brightly coloured beakers from her box. Unscrewing the top of a cheap bottle of vodka, she poured a slug for them all. "To the Bristol Girls," she toasted, holding her beaker aloft. The others followed her cue.

"The Bristol Girls!"

"Not sure what mum would say about me drinking vodka at two in the afternoon," said Rose.

"Well, we're here so our mums can't tell us what to do, right?" said Ursa.

"Here's to that," said Bella.

But as soon as the cups touched their lips, the singular melancholy that is homesickness filled the room. John Lennon serenaded. Help me if you can I'm feeling down.

Rose toasted her friends again and talk-sang, "I do appreciate you being round."

Bella, always the best singer among them, went next. "Help me get my feet back on the ground."

Ursa took her turn a beat too late. She gabbled, "Won't you please, please help me."

Ensemble time. "Help me, help me." And with a final discordant bellow, "Wooh!"

They collapsed laughing. Just three crazy girls from Bristol celebrating their first night as wannabe actresses in the coolest, friendliest, swinging-iest city in the world.

Chapter 11

October 17th, 2017
The M4 - Bristol to London

Namita was still pissed when the others picked her up outside the dodgy wine bar ready for the drive home.

"My God, said Feng, "you're all bendy. Where's your slipper, Cinderella?"

Namita laughed, pulled a shoe from her bag and showed where the short, but crucial, heel had snapped off.

"It's easier to go barefoot than hobble, Feng," she said.

"But you are hobbling?"

The sobers stared in disbelief. None of the four was a particularly heavy drinker. Barring the reunion meal a couple of nights back, none had ever had more than a glass of wine in each other's company. This was new.

Let's be honest: picturing Feng pissed was easy. No problem there. Porter, not so much. Maybe if he forgot where he was and got carried away with a couple of mates down the pub? Definitely a once-every-two-years kind of event. Karin? Only at a stretch, and only if the others imagined her in the right environment: an awards dinner after winning yet more glass and steel monstrosities for her mantelpiece, perhaps? However, none could imagine the sometimes-gnarly Namita as a lush. Blotto, shoeless and floppy-bodied, hair from her bob stuck to the side of her mouth - in Bristol on a weekday afternoon at that - was a leap of imagination none of them were capable of. Until now, confronted with this vision made real.

"Kebab?" she offered, layers of doner meat flapping from the pitta like the raggedy trousers of Dickensian orphans.

"What on earth happened?" asked Karin. "Are you having an allergic reaction?"

"Yeah, you alright?" said Porter. "You're dropping onion everywhere."

"What? I'm pissed, you twats," said Namita. "Isn't it soddin' obvious? Damage limitation. Get me in the car. I've had a lucky escape."

Karin was driving, so Porter and Feng looked at each other, paused, and then sprinted for the front passenger seat door, tussling over the handle like two kids trying to get the last doughnut from a box. Feng won.

"Ah come on, Feng…don't make me sit in the back with her…"

"I've ruined enough suits working with you," laughed Feng. "Your turn."

"Porter?"

"Yes, Karin?"

"If you let her be sick in the back of my car, I'm going to make you clean it and pay for the valet. Understood?"

"Yes, Miss." Porter held the door open for Namita. "Come on, chuck the kebab away."

"Good idea," said Namita. "I don't feel that great to be honest."

Namita wouldn't be drawn on the reason for the drinking. "I screwed up on something. I was making amends."

"Well, it sounds like you had fun to me," said Porter.

"You know what? I did! I'm shit at darts, though." She didn't reveal she'd promised to go for dinner with Martin next time she was in Bristol. It was nothing to do with them. "How cos the wop? Splorry, how was the cop?"

"Splorry? My Goff, you're blotto," said Feng. "How amusing."

"He was a bit mad," said Porter, skillfully swerving at the last, avoiding adding *too* to the end of his sentence. "Rutland genuinely thinks Rose was a spy or messed up in a blackmail sting gone wrong. He's been watching too much Line of Duty."

"And Rose isn't the only girl who went missing," said Feng, grinning in the front seat. "Rose moved to London from Bristol with two friends. Within three years, they were all gone: two went missing in LA and Berlin, one moved back to Bristol and committed suicide."

"What?" Sloshing with wine, Namita upgraded to a treble-take.

"Rutland has a point, doesn't he?" said Karin, keeping a watchful eye on Namita in the rear-view. "That's a hell of a lot of weird coincidences."

"Coincidence is a dangerous thing," said Feng. "I once got caught with my trousers down by a jealous boyfriend in a young artist's flat, at 3am, drinks and glasses everywhere. He went berserk, thinking something was going on."

"Was there?"

"No. I'd just spilled wine down my trousers and was simply cleaning up."

"So - nothing happened between you?"

"I didn't say that. But we'd already cleared up and were just having a social drink, all innocent. Then I spilt the wine."

"That's not a coincidence," said Porter, "that's being caught red-handed."

"Not at all, it was white wine."

Through many *Oh-my-Gods!* and *No ways!* they updated Namita.

"Well, what now?" she said. Porter and Feng shrugged.

"I've got an idea, but you'll probably laugh," said Karin. "I want to go to LA and interview Sam Brownlees. Yes, about this case of course, but Feng was right: I also feel a documentary coming on. There's no point waiting. I need to get material now. While I'm there I can look into the last known movements of this Bella girl."

"Great idea!" said Feng. "I love LA!"

"What a cheek," slurred Namita. "He's my client."

"Well, you come too," said Karin. "I'll pay for your flight. I've got a fund for speculative research."

"I'm definitely coming," said Feng. "I can pay for myself."

"I can't afford it!" said Porter.

"I'll get your ticket," said Feng. "I've got a feeling this is gonna be a big one."

"Well, let's make sure we get comprehensive medical insurance this time," said Porter. "You know what our last 'holiday abroad' was like."

They all shuddered, remembering their extensive experience of Belgian hospitals.

Chapter 12

October 22nd, 2017
The Highland Gardens Hotel, Franklin Avenue, LA

It took four days to get their ducks in a row after Sam agreed to see them.
There was a lot to organise. Karin charmed her way into a meeting with a cold case detective in the LAPD; the team got their ESTAs sorted; they booked accommodation; they arranged a hire-car - to be picked-up Downtown the day after arrival.
After a bumpy flight and a bad-tempered fight to get a cab to Hollywood, they were finally sitting by the hotel pool waiting for a cab.

Check-in was fun. Porter read that Janis Joplin had died in this hotel. He asked the receptionist if he could be placed as far away as possible from the Joplin room. He had enough on his plate without adding a famous singer to his client list.
The assistant nodded, but as soon as Porter walked into his 'safe' room, he picked up the all-too-familiar hum of unhappy death. The Gliss said, "Uh-oh." Porter was back in reception within seconds.
"Excuse me again. Which room did Janis Joplin die in?" he asked.
"Your room, 105."

"I don't want that room. I said, any room but that room."

"Oh sorry… your accent. We're full at the moment, hang on let me see… Sorry, completely full. It's that room or nothing."

"Can I swap with one of my friends?"

"Sure, if they'll let you."

Feng was the most flexible of the group but was knackered. When Porter barged in, Feng was already ironing his beachwear. He reluctantly agreed to move on condition Porter helped him fold and re-pack.

"Sorry about this Feng, but I'm guaranteed headaches for the entire trip if I stay in there."

"I get it. Did you get a reading off Janis?" said Feng.

"No, it's too long ago and there's no trace of her remains in there. It's just a vibe thing. I don't fancy migraine for a week."

"That's a shame. I have my EMF meter with me. Wouldn't it be great if I got a reading?"

Porter, who had zero faith in Feng's gadgets, but anxious to complete the room-swap, said, "Sure, sure. That would be great."

The Gliss appeared. "It's too long ago. Janis is long gone. Put away your meter, Feng."

"I definitely got a vibe from something," said Porter.

"It's an old hotel in Hollywood. I imagine someone has died in every room over the years," The Gliss said.

"Well, I won't be booking you as a tour guide," said Feng. "Focus on life, old chap. Focus on life."

"You are already knee deep in death, and now scouting for more. Forgive me if I've left my rose-tints back in London."

"I prefer these," said Feng, waving a brand-new pair of Ray Bans. "The trouble with you, me old China, is that you can't tell the difference between sarcasm and realising that you're in the world's funkiest city, in glorious sunshine, the best food waiting on every corner. Let's go."

They met by the pool. A stranger observing would have been surprised to find they were a group. It takes a few goes to gauge your clothing on arrival in LA - temperature control and style, equal hurdles to fitting in. Karin, Porter and Namita looked out of place, still dressed for England's gloom amid the shock of LA's glare.

Only Feng looked at home. He was overdressed and loving it. He wore a black Paul Smith suit, a white tee, and Armani shades. "It's like having a hot water bottle strapped to your face. Love it. It certainly makes a change from the good old British autumn," he said.

"It's my first time in California," said Porter, blowing his cheeks out, whipping off his jumper. "Funny, LA's never been on my radar. I've only ever fancied New York. This weather's something."

"They don't have weather here - it's sunny all the time," laughed Feng. "You'll love it. The food is great, and the people are friendly as hell."

"I thought they were supposed to be insincere?" said Namita, undoing a top button for ventilation. "Christ, it's hot."

"Insincere? That's the Brits hating on the Yanks," said Feng. "You'll see."

"I don't care if they nick my watch shaking my hand, I can handle this for a few days," she said, laying back, remembering the lair of Dracula her flat had become since going solo.

Karin, blasé about travel and listless from the flight, said nothing, staring into the distance.

"You're quiet," said Porter.

"I was just looking at that palm tree," she replied.

Porter followed the direction of her gaze and saw a huge palm tree outside the hotel grounds which cast a shadow over the back of the 50s hotel. "Never thought I'd see a palm tree," he said.

"I was wondering what it would look like in 3D," said Karin, before closing her remaining eye and letting the sun bask on her face too.

They squashed into a booth at Mel's Drive-In, ordering Sunset Burgers and fries, and a round of malts on Feng's recommendation. They stuck quarters in the table-top 50s style jukeboxes and took the obligatory iPhone shots of enormous plates of food. Only Feng had an Instagram account, but he made up for it by posting enough to compete with, let's say, Kim Kardashian documenting a frock shop.

It was time to get down to business.

"Namita, I think it's best you lead the discussions with Sam," said Karin. "He is, after all, your client. Hopefully that conversation will get us into something deeper. If things go well, I might bring up the subject of a film."

Porter, sucking on the cherry from his malt, looked worried. "Won't he wonder why we've all turned up mob-handed like this? Probably better to be honest and tell him the different reasons we're all here."

Namita shook her head. "I don't think that's necessary, Porter. I've spoken to him. I've told him who Karin is. I've prepped him for the idea that going public on TV might also be a way to shake things loose in the search for Rose."

"It's good he doesn't think we're just here for the contested will," said Porter. "We don't want to shock him."

"He's intrigued I think," said Namita. "He's quite spunky for someone in his 90s. He's been on TV before, talking about his wartime experiences."

Karin was relieved. "I've also spoken to Arnie Flax from LA's Cold Case team. He's going to run the three girls' names, see if anything comes up. There should be some paperwork on Bella as she went missing here. We might as well get him to check the other two anyway."

A middle-aged waitress in a white uniform came over for the fifth time in 20 minutes to ask if everything was okay, offering to top up their coffees.

"If she's angling for a tip, I'd offer - *leave your customers alone to talk*," said Porter, testily, but swigging his free coffee nonetheless.

Roy Orbison's Pretty Woman was playing on the jukebox. The Gliss was mumbling along. "I wish you wouldn't do that," said Porter. "It's very distracting."

"Yes, said Karin. Could you leave us to it? I'm sure Porter will be safe with us for 10 minutes." The other three tended to view The Gliss as Porter's supremely annoying guardian angel.

The Gliss looked down on the four of them, figuratively and literally, and disappeared without another word. Just as they all looked away, he jumped back in, shouting along with Orbison on the song's coda: "Pretty Woman!" before disappearing again.

"Great. He turns into a frat boy the second he gets to America," said Porter. "At least that was singing. He tried Hip-Hop once. Drove me mad."

"Well, I don't know about you guys, but I feel pregnant and jet-lagged," said Namita, patting her stomach, which looked like a ceramic tile to the others. "I need to crash."

Within the hour, jet lag and carbs catching up with them, they were all tucked up in bed, sleeping. Bar Feng.

"Thanks, Porter," he muttered. "I keep hearing Janis singing Me and Bobby McGee on a loop." He looked around the room, nervously. His EMF meter blinked silently by his bedside.

October 23rd, 2017
Robbery Homicide Division, West First Street, LA

Karin left the others to sightsee, agreeing to meet them at Sam Brownlee's care home at 3pm. Right now, fresh from breakfast, she was jumping from her Uber, surveying the HQ of LAPD's famous Robbery Homicide Division. The department had investigated every notorious LA case - from the Manson Family murders to the death of Michael Jackson.

It also housed the city's Cold Case team. Det Arnie Flax was ready and waiting for her.

"Welcome to LA, Miss Pelenot," he said warmly, offering his hand.

"Nice to meet you too, detective."

"Arnie, please."

"And please, call me Karin."

"What the hell happened to your eye?" he said, pointing at her patch. "You bang it or something? Looks pretty damn sore."

"It's not sore now," said Karin, who'd told the same story at least 50 times since the summer. "I'm afraid I lost it. We were making a documentary about World War 1 in Flanders earlier this year and some unexploded munitions went off."

"Jesus H. Christ," said Arnie. "I think I saw that. It was on Fox News. Didn't realise it was you. That's rough. I'm sorry to hear it."

She laughed. "I'm sorry to hear it too. Fox News doesn't have much of a reputation in the UK. It's fine. Impressive building you have here," she said, moving on.

No stranger to cameras, she sometimes felt like her whole life was one giant tracking shot in a documentary directed by God. This was definitely one of those occasions. They walked into a large office and Karin was amazed how accurately TV cop shows had nailed it. It was eerily familiar.

As they walked down the aisle, middle-aged men with bald patches, moustaches and sweaty armpits, barked three-word banter at Arnie. Tough-looking female cops with tied-back hair and overloaded belts pulling trousers low on their hips, wheeled away from their desks with purpose.

"This is amazing," said Karin. "It's like Kojak, NYPD Blue and CSI all rolled into one."

"Well, if they weren't filmed here, they built sets to look like this. Although I wouldn't mention the NYPD round here. East Coast/West Coast beefs. It's not just the rappers who hate each other. Here we are." He pulled a chair away from someone else's desk and gestured for Karin to sit.

"What were you hoping for from us, Karin?"

"A missing person's report for Bella Tompkinson? Maybe a miracle? Some kind of record for Rose or Ursa? But I'm fishing there."

He nodded. "Sorry. There's nothing on those other two ladies, but we do have a few bits for Bella. But don't get your hopes up. Just a parking citation and a very small missing person's file."

"You keep parking records that long?" said Karin, astonished.

"Not usually. Someone obviously saw it and snuck it in her file back in the day. They only had paper files then. Odds are, clerical staff were amalgamating files, saw the ticket and stuck it in the folder. It's all been computerised since the 80s."

He showed her the ticket: June 20th, 1968, routed through her car hire company - a fine for overstaying on a meter outside 4999 Wilshire Boulevard. The fine was paid in cash, Downtown the next morning.

"Any use?"

"I don't know," said Karin. "I didn't even know she drove."

"Everyone drives here," said Flax.

"That's not what really intrigues me. For a start, it's odd that Bella was in the States at all. Flights were staggeringly expensive then. She was poor in London. Yet she had enough money to fly and hire a car too? Odd. Do you know what 4999 Wilshire is?"

"Not now, not in '68 either. Sorry. She may have just parked there and walked somewhere else. Doesn't mean she visited the building."

"Of course, okay. And the missing person report?"

Arnie opened the bent manila file. One sheet of paper and a black and white photo. "As I said, not much." He handed the photo to Karin. "It wasn't really an investigation, more an acknowledgement that the cops in Great Britain had logged her as missing: last known location, Los Angeles."

Karin turned the photo over. It was stamped with an LA case number. A separate stamp showed its origination with the Met in London. She scanned the document. It was bare bones but had a summary of the Met's concerns and a two-line report from LAPD.

> *Bella Jane Tompkinson. Born 10.15.45. Reported missing 06.28.68 by her father, John Tompkinson at Bristol police station, GB. Immigration records shows she arrived in NY on 06.14.68, before traveling on to LA. Her return tickets were bought but unused, according to PanAm (LA to NY 06.23.66) and BOAC (NY to London 06.25.66). She was looking for film roles. She was booked into the Century Plaza Hotel, 2025 Avenue of the Stars, on 06.15.68 - room 1914. (No record of where she stayed for the overnight in NY). She checked out, fully paid up, 06.22.66.*

"What's that pencil note there?" asked Karin, pointing at a faded couple of words, underlined next to the hotel name.

"You've got good eyesight," said Flax, unthinkingly, screwing his eyes up and trying to read it. "Well, I'll be…"

"What is it?" said Karin.

"Someone had a nerve," said Flax, angrily. "It says *kept woman! Ha ha.*" His annoyance at the lack of respect was clear. "I apologise. That shouldn't be there. Some chauvinist joker. We've come a long way - I hope. I'm sure that's probably a reference to the fact that Century Plaza was a very famous hotel and quite expensive. Still is. I hear they're doing a billion-dollar refurbishment right now."

Karin googled the hotel. "Yes, it was quite the landmark. First hotel in LA with a colour TV in every room. It would have been expensive back then? Nineteen floors - the tallest building in Century City at the time."

"Nineteen, you say? And her room was on the 19th. You know what they usually put on the top floors of posh hotels, right?"

"Penthouse suites," said Karin, who'd stayed in dozens of them around the world.

"Right. The piece of shit who scribbled that, knew it too and made assumptions. Doesn't mean anything."

Karin shrugged it off. "As far as we know she was cleaning dishes in London. Doesn't make any sense. The hotel only opened two years before she got here. It would still have been novel, as well as expensive."

"Hard to get a room, you mean?" said Flax.

Karin thought over Rutland's conspiracy theories. "Hard to afford a room - unless she was working for someone, or, as your rather sexist colleague from the 60s pointed out, was a kept woman."

"Who was she working for?" asked Flax.

"Well, that's the question, isn't it?"

They continued reading.

> Bella told her father she had two or three auditions lined-up, but he doesn't know who for. He couldn't reach her by telephone to arrange, but he knew what flight home she was on. He turned up at London Airport to collect her. She wasn't on the plane. He hoped she had been delayed after successful auditions but heard nothing. He finally contacted the police on 06.28.66.
>
> Bristol police referred the case to the Metropolitan Police in London as Bella had been living in Soho district since 1965. Flat 6, 47 Wardour Street, W1.
>
> According to Mr Tompkinson, his daughter flew from London Airport to John F Kennedy, NY, via BOAC on 06.14.68. She flew to Los Angeles next day via PanAm on 06.15.68.

The file ended.

"Is that it?" said Karin.

"Not quite," said Flax. He pointed to a little box at the bottom of the sheet. There was a faint X in it. The box was labelled *NFA*. "I'm sorry. It was designated *No Further Action*. And you say she never turned up? Gee, that's terrible. Let's hope she just overstayed her visa, moved to Arizona and made a family there. Plenty did. Plenty still do."

"I doubt it. Her family never heard from her again. The British police were pretty flippant about it too," said Karin. "It's almost as if no-one cared what happened to Bella apart from her mum and dad."

"Well, when somebody goes missing, it's usually a toss-up between two things, isn't it, Karin? They don't wanna be found, or somebody don't want them found."

October 23rd, 2017
Sunset Boulevard, LA

"Not more food," said Namita.

"Have a coffee then," said Porter, as they stepped into one of the 9 million coffee shops in LA. "It's bloody hot for October, isn't it?" he said, taking off his denim jacket.

The trio were wandering around waiting for Karin. Even Namita found the sun-baked, cracked and faded streets and houses of Hollywood undeniably fascinating. With almost as many signs and billboards as coffee shops, Porter wondered how any advertising message could cut through. He was particularly taken with the plethora of billboards advertising lawyers.

"Hey, Namita. You should move out here. I can just see you splashed over the top of a doughnut store - *Accident at work? Call Menon and Partners.*"

"No thanks," she said. "I don't even take selfies - imagine my ugly mug up there frightening the kids."

"You're so not ugly, darling," said Feng. "She's not ugly, is she Porter?"

Porter, who thought she was stunning, but scary, said, "Oh, er, well, I. Well. No."

"Oh, thanks. That fills me with warmth, love and confidence," said Namita.

On a terrace with coffee #18, Porter called on The Gliss to join them. "We need a proper chat. Would you mind putting your prejudices aside and actually talk to the three of us, please?"

The Gliss nodded.

"Well, that's a start," said Porter. Feng stuck his tongue out at the spirit. Porter continued. "I've been thinking. All that stuff with Pelenot was very *ad hoc*, right? We just made it up as we went along. Here we are again, and we still haven't got a game plan. It's time to talk methodology."

Namita sighed. "It was *ad hoc* because that's what it was - unplanned. What are you proposing? That we form a committee and have formal job titles?"

Feng put his hand up and said, "Can I be Chief Investigator? Please!"

"That's not what I meant," said Porter. "Namita and I are both very grateful to you and Karin for paying for us to come out here, but it's not sustainable long term, is it?"

"Right," said Namita, who was embarrassed she'd gone from rationed fags at home to overdosing on coffee in LA at someone else's expense. "Are we here because of a contested will? Or because Karin wants to make a documentary? Or because Porter and The Gliss are trying to track down a missing girl? It's a bit of a mess."

"Bravo, Namita. My thoughts exactly," said The Gliss. "I'm supposed to be helping Porter atone for his family's sins, not doing Five Go Mad in Hollywood."

"Ah, but, the streams have already crossed," said Feng, batting away their concerns. "After we've been to see Samuel, we'll have a better idea of how to proceed with the investigation. But let's face it: you can dish out as many missions as you like, but a fat lot of good that is, if penniless Porter needs to buy a plane ticket. I'm happy to help."

Porter was about to protest his dignity, but Feng cut him off. "Don't anyone dare patronise me. I've been doing this for 20 years. I've funded all sorts of nutters – no offence. Remember the Doves, my amazingly credulous gaggle of ghost hunters from Dalston? We're still mates, of course, but now I'm working with Porter & The Gliss - a direct line to other worlds..." He sat back in his chair. "You can try and get rid of me, but I'm here, I'm happy, and I'm staying - however much it dents my wallet."

Namita sighed. "As long as I can be of some help, I'm staying too. When Pelenot attacked me in Flanders, I was frightened, yes, but I also learnt something about myself: I'm damned if I'm gonna stand by and let the bullies win - real or ghost. Rose and Bella. They didn't disappear. Someone disappeared them."

Porter looked at The Gliss and shrugged. The Gliss looked at Namita. She shrugged too. Porter looked at Namita. Feng watched them all, slurping his coffee. With everyone now staring at her, she said, "What?" The Gliss turned to Feng. Feng stuck his tongue out again.

"Oh rapture," said The Gliss. "Five Go Mad in Hollywood it is."

Chapter 13

October 23rd, 2017
Grey's Nursing Home, Atwater Village, LA

Reunited at 3pm, the Famous Five finished yet another coffee. Dodging a zoo's worth of yappy rat-dogs which seemed to be this year's Los Feliz fashion accessory, they scooted past the Out of the Closet thrift store and turned onto Sam Brownlee's road.

"Namita, it's probably best you lead things," said Karin. "Get your business sorted, and then I'll introduce myself properly and get chatting about the past, if that's okay?"

Namita agreed. "I haven't got much to say to him. It's a fairly straightforward case."

Karin suggested Feng and Porter act the part of researchers for her production company. They agreed.

"This is what I meant," said Porter. "We're making it up as we go along."

"You don't even know how to spell spontaneous, do you?" Feng tutted and patted Porter on the back.

More collectively nervous than they'd been for a while, they were buzzed into Grey's. An assistant said Sam was in the garden and guided them through.

Porter-the-music-buff's first impression was good. Brownlees was wearing massive headphones, eyes closed, tapping his foot.

The assistant gently touched his shoulder. Sam didn't jump but turned like a tranquilised bear. Removing the headphones, he surprised them all by saying, "Stevie Wonder. Songs in the Key of Life. What an album."

They introduced themselves and found places to sit.

"It's so nice to meet you in person, Sam," said Namita, sweetly. That was a first for the others. To see her smiling in client-mode was a shock.

"Glad you could all make it, Miss. How you finding California?" He was trying to stow the headphones but tangled the curly lead.

"It's great, Sam," said Porter. "It's my first time - loving the sun."

"Sun. Sun. Sun. Always sun," said Sam, as if it was a bad thing. For four anaemic Brits, it was a pleasant change - once they'd ditched the jumpers. "When God wants to mix it up a little, we get one day of rain every two years, usually when there's a wedding or something important on. Not like when I was back in Bristol. Rain. Rain. Rain. More like one day of sun every two years." He laughed a rumbling basso.

Namita updated him on the contested will but could see Karin was impatient to get started on the real business. Sam was no fool and saw that Namita had nothing to really say. "All sounds good," he said. "Now then. Let's talk about my daughter."

Karin was grateful for the reins. "Sam, we've been looking into Rose's case," said the historian. "We were all in Bristol last week. We even went to the Christmas Steps."

"Did you now, Miss. Don't suppose you took any photos?"

Karin borrowed Feng's phone and showed him a few snaps.

"Well, I'll be…it hasn't changed much," said Sam. "Lord, that takes me back." He pointed to an area of the photo taken from the top of the Steps, on the right. "There used to be a cafe there. Hokey ration food. Bread fried in pig fat. Wartime belly fodder. Flo and I used to meet there."

"When was that?" asked Porter.

"I was there from '43 until we went to Normandy for D-Day," said Sam. "I went there a lot in '43 with Flo. But as we got closer to the invasion, there were so many of us damned Yanks there, you couldn't get in. Took to strolling in the park instead." He looked at the photo again. "Would you look at that. I can see it all like it was yesterday."

Feng chipped in. "We've been talking about that. Bristol's a big university town now, lots of young people, and folks from all over. But it must have been a sight for the locals seeing you two together?"

"Cos I'm black, you mean? Not as much as you'd think. By '44 there were 30,000 black GIs based in and around Bristol. I remember the innkeeper in the pub telling a couple of mouthy white guys to leave the pub because they didn't like having negroes in the place."

"How did that make you feel?" asked Karin.

"Well, we were used to the white guys' reaction. America was still segregated, right? It was the white innkeeper standing up for us that was shocking. Yes, indeed. They was different times, different times."

Feng pulled up a photo of a page in one of the Bristol books. "It wasn't all good though, right? I read this story about a vicar's wife in Somerset who gave advice to local women on how to deal with black American servicemen. It's pretty shocking: cross the street if you see one approach; move if one sits next to you in the cinema; don't let coloured troops visit the home of white women. Goff, the language."

Sam laughed. "Well, weren't no different than home. I remember that story, sir. She was some damn fool woman, but my white friends in Bristol were angry when they heard about it, you know? Day to day, we didn't get anything like that. We played with children, gave them gum, talked to the women, hung out with the British soldiers. No, the only trouble we had was with the white American soldiers. They acted just the same as at home. Damn Yankees."

Feng nodded. "There's a story here about about a confrontation between a black soldier and a white U.S. military policeman. The black soldier said, 'We ain't no slaves; This is England.'"

"Sounds about right, sounds about right," said Sam, nodding.

"If it was all so nice, Sam," said Namita, and the others could see she was going to ask the awkward question they'd all been contemplating during this conversation, "how come you and Flo didn't make a go of it? Sorry, if that's a personal question."

Sam laughed, a low, muffled sort of laugh, but they could tell he wasn't offended. "You came a long way to ask your questions. No point being shy now, Miss." He closed his eyes to tell his story, and none of them had any doubt he was reliving his days in Bristol as he spoke.

"We had to have music. We had to dance. Man, it was dull being stationed in a cold, wet place like England - waitin' for action. Like I said, all the problems were with the whites from our side. The negroes got all the crap duties, got paid less. But we was young and itchin'. Know what I mean?

"There was a dance hall, and there were enough white and black musicians to put little bands together. Musos never had no colour problem. Must have been wild for the Brits - proper jazz cats, wailin' on them horns. The girls were lonely, most of their able-bodied were already servin' in Europe. There was a hole and we jumped at the chance to fill it. Them Bristol girls never did know if their man was coming home.

"You ever hear that saying about us GIs? Overpaid, Oversexed, Over here?" Sam chuckled. "That was us. Well, I had my laughs and a bit of a fun, just like all the rest. Then one night I saw Flo across the room. Man, she was a glorious sight back then. Lipstick red as a fire truck. A figure-hugging dress all patterned up with flowers. I swear to God, I fell in love first sight.

"With death hanging like a buzzard over everybody, life was for the livin' - so I plucked up the courage and asked her to dance. Who could have guessed 70 years of tragedy lay ahead? Would I still have done it if I'd known? Sure. She was one of the two loves of my life."

Karin asked how their relationship developed.

"It was fine. Easy. She fell for me too. Oh boy, sure we canoodled, but what I remember most is laying in the parks, just gassing. Bristol sure had some fine parks back then. We was just talking, holding hands, talking about our childhoods. You know, ain't nothing changed on that front. Y'all done the same thing."

There was quiet in the room. All four of the gang were single and not overly lucky in love. Picking up the vibe, Sam said awkwardly, "Well, you know. Oh sure, there were looks. And bar the one fight, everything was ok. But we always knew, were always certain, that the acceptance came from the knowledge that it was all temporary. Them Bristol folks all thought, *this is just for the war. Have your fun but go home after*."

"Sorry, Sam," said Karin, backtracking. "What fight?"

"Oh, that wasn't good. One night, Flo and I was walking, talking and laughing, just minding our own business, when a gang of local white boys jumped us. I took the worst of it, but I was young, had boxed a bit and was fit for action. What upset me was seeing Flo booted in the stomach and called a nigger-lover."

"I'm sorry to hear that," said Porter.

"What the Sam Hill has it got to do with you? You ever kicked a woman in the gut and called her a nigger-lover, son?"

"No, sir," said Porter, deferentially.

"No need to apologise then," said Sam. "I was laid up for a week and Flo's mother wouldn't let her out for a bit. By the time I met up with her again, her belly was one giant yellow bruise. I kissed it and swore I'd never let it happen again."

"Did you ever see the boys who did it again?" asked Namita.

"I did. I'm not right proud of it, either. Me, Jess and Fontaine went looking for them. We found them. Let's just leave it at that. Bet they still got the bruises to show for it." He rumble-laughed again.

Karin brought up the Steps again. "You said your ancestor, Samwell, saw the Christmas Steps? We were wondering how he knew what it was called?"

"I don't understand, Miss?"

"Presumably, he didn't speak English when he first stepped off the slave ship?"

"Well, that's an interesting story too. Did you ever read Roots?"

"I saw it on TV when I was a kid," said Porter. "Kunte Kinte, Miss Kizzy."

"Right," said Sam. "Well, didn't you ever wonder how Alex Haley managed to find out about his folks? It should be obvious, but I better educate you. Africans are storytellers. Always have been. There weren't much else to do around the fires in Africa at night!

"Samwell learnt some English on the boat over. He was lucky, amid the misfortune of being sold into slavery by his so-called leaders in Africa. There were a lot more deaths on his ship than usual, and a couple of Africans were trained up as seamen. Did you know sailors were some of the biggest opponents of slavery? They soon realised we were all humans together. A lot of them testified when abolition came up. You damn Brits. You're so strange. You were the biggest slave traders of them all, and then damn it, if you weren't the ones who pushed hardest for abolition! Contrary, I call it!" he said.

It was clearly a subject he knew a bit about. "Yeah, you Brits were contrary, alright. Once you changed tack, your government sent gunships to Africa and the West Indies to enforce no slavery. Slave traders became the new pirates."

Sam took a sip of water. He was enjoying his story, but it was clearly taking it out of him too. "That smattering of English and being the favourite of the captain, probably saved Samwell's life. Later, he told his family many negroes died in chains on his ship. Some of the sick ones were thrown overboard to drown, God rest their poor souls. But Samwell, he got extra rations and could walk about."

"I see," said Karin. "Is that how he came to be put up for sale in Bristol?"

"I guess so. A bit of English and healthy-looking would have been a big plus, right? And as for the Steps? You have to remember: Bristol was the first place he ever saw that wasn't the bush or sea. It went over big with him. He talked all the time about the Christmas Steps because the captain bought him a hot drink there."

"Do you know when this was?" asked Karin.

"Not sure of the dates, but I know Samwell was my great great great great great grandfather. 5Gs!"

"Did you know his story when you were in Bristol?" Porter asked.

"Sure I did, son. Can you imagine how I felt? Being abroad as a young man myself, and then seeing the very street my ancestor saw? I've already said this to Miss here," indicating Namita, "but in a way, that street… it links my family to slavery over seven generations if you count me and my Rose. I took Flo there often, I was drawn to it, I guess. But that relationship with Flo and Rose, the child I was desperate to see, but never got to… that's a life of slavery too. You ever wanted somethin' so bad you can taste it, but never reach it, no matter what? It takes the spine out of a man."

The four of them rushed to assure him he was still quite a character and had been brave.

"I don't need that," he said, waving them away. "No need to talk to me like I'm an old man. I got hollowed out and there ain't nothing that can fill that hole. That's my story. We all got a story. I got used to mine a long time ago."

Sam closed his eyes. The four sat patiently waiting for him to continue. The Gliss, who hadn't said a word, said, "Ah, I believe the gentleman has nodded off. In the parlance of Cockney, you've tuckered him out."

Chapter 14

October 23rd, 2017
Highland Gardens Hotel, Franklin Avenue, LA

Back at the hotel they compared notes and discussed what to do next.

"We're flying home tomorrow afternoon," said Namita. "Shall we try Sam again in the morning?"

"I'm not flying home," said Karin. "I can see Sam tomorrow."

"Why aren't you coming home?" said Feng. "You decided you'd be better off with a house in the Hills?"

"No, but there could be a great documentary about Sam's life in there. I'm going to double-check with Sam and then book a crew and start interviewing him. Better to interview people in their 90s while you can. It might turn out to be nothing. However, while I'm doing it, I can get all the extra info we need from him. Staying on also gives me a chance to spend some time with the Cold Case team. Detective Flax has invited me to see their work. I think he's angling for an HBO doc too."

"Is there one?" said Porter.

"On him? God no. His team's just a load of cooped-up middle-aged men and women going through old paperwork, resubmitting DNA samples, the whole team wondering why they all buy each other soap for Christmas. But there may be other links yet. I want him on my side."

"What are you proposing to Sam?" asked Namita.

"I want his family story. The whole Christmas Steps link. It's so circular. A sad but perfect story arc: The Steps enslaving him as much as they did his ancestor. I'll think of other angles as I go."

"You think that'll get commissioned?" said Porter.

"You forget who I am," laughed Karin, remembering her last meeting with Bluebottle. "And when I pitch it and chuck in slavery, guilt, murder and transatlantic connections, the commissioners will wet themselves. Those people can smell a BAFTA a mile off. And you know me, Justice is my middle name. It's a story that *should* be told."

Off the hook, the four decided they could afford to round off their trip with dinner on the Venice Beach boardwalk. Porter was particularly excited - wasn't that where they shot Baywatch? Karin and Namita gave him contemptuous stares, while Feng, whose own middle name was Kitsch, gave him a wink.

"This is gorgeous," said Porter staring at what seemed like 100 miles of wide, clean beach. The Pacific washed in quietly, the moon reflecting on the dead centre of the horizon. A couple of kids on skateboards flipped skilfully in front of them.

"This is the LA I had in my head," said Porter. To his distant right he saw the Santa Monica pier. "Oh my God… that's the ferris wheel from The Lost Boys!"

"Porter," said Feng, "this is all very strange. I thought you were lost in ancient musicals and Broadway. Where did this love of tacky TV and films suddenly come from?"

"I do love musicals," said Porter, "but that doesn't make me immune to everything else. There's only one thing I hate - EDM."

"Oh yes, the four-on-the-floor so beloved of your ex - Tania. Oops. Sorry."

But Feng was pleasantly surprised. Earlier that year, a mention of Tania, who'd dumped him because he wasn't exciting enough, could provoke deflation and handwringing on a biblical scale. All the way through the adventure in Flanders, it seemed like Porter was hanging onto hopes of a reconciliation. She'd repeatedly made it clear that was never going to happen. Her message had taken a long time to sink in, but even Feng found this new nonchalance surprising. Instead of deflating, Porter punched back: "Well, Tania never had much taste. Sod her."

Karin and Namita, who had been on the periphery of the Porter-Tania drama, were oblivious. But Feng nodded at his friend. *Good for you.*

The Gliss appeared. "I suppose you call this work, Porter? Not a lot of atoning going on here. Or am I missing something?"

"We're just chilling for once," Porter replied. "If that's ok with you?"

"Be my guest," said The Gliss, with enough chill of his own to turn Dubai into Lapland.

"This is all so weird, isn't it?" said Namita, a glass of Chablis in her hand. "A year ago, I didn't know any of you. Here we all are, four misfits having seafood salad by the Pacific."

"*Misfits?*" said Porter and Feng at the same time.

"That's life," said Karin. "I'm very privileged, of course. Being a film-maker I get to travel a lot and meet new people all the time. But yes, as a bunch of misfits, it has been an interesting ride."

"There they go with *misfits* again," said Feng. "Who are they talking about?"

"I'm not the easiest person to get on with, I know," said Namita, "but meeting you all, being attacked by Georges Pelenot… it's changed my life. I may be poor and have no clients right now, but I'd been meaning to go solo for a long time. Watching you all nearly die, busting my arm, gave me the courage to do it."

"What do you mean - *haven't got any clients?*" said Karin. "You said things were going well?"

Two glasses of Chablis empowered, Namita finally told the truth. "Not really. Sam's my only client. Phone didn't ring for a month before that little shit Gary Stormont called. I'm broke for now. But I'm determined to make it work."

"But why didn't you say?" said Karin. "I could have given you a bit of work. There are people I can recommend you to. I thought you did a great job in Flanders."

Namita blushed. "Yes, but you'll notice all those invoices came through Quendell's. I was still working for them in Flanders."

"I never looked. I've got a woman who does the book-keeping. This cannot be. Let's chat when I get back to England. If we're going to be tied together doing these investigations, we'd better learn to help each other out. This isn't a cheap business."

"*These*? Don't you mean, *this*?" said Porter.

"I meant *these*," said Karin. "While you have these powers, we have to make the most of them. I see many investigations - and documentaries - ahead."

Porter baulked. "Oh, come on. It was fun doing the Flanders film with you, but we're not going to make it a habit, surely? It's not really my thing."

"Don't underestimate yourself or your powers. Hey, Gliss, how long do you think he'll have them?"

The Gliss let out a weary sigh. "It's *The* Gliss."

"But you can't say, 'Hey, *The* Gliss.' It offends my carefully honed grammatical sensibilities."

"Well, no-one is asking you to converse with me. I'm supposed to be Porter's secret guide, a messenger, not doing crowd control with a loudhailer."

"My goodness," said Feng. "Why don't you chillax? None of us asked to have you creeping around on our shoulders, either. But we're diverse. We're tolerant. We've accepted you. How about a bit of reciprocation?"

"Bully for you," The Gliss replied, before returning to Karin's original question. "Ms Pelenot, I do not know how long Porter will have his powers. I'm only a messenger, as you know." Sighs all round. "However," he pre-empted before they could start, "his mission is to atone for all the pain the men in his family caused with their suicides. Think about that. Four generations of men with wives, children, friends, cousins…the ripples must have affected hundreds, if not thousands. How many people do you think you've put to rest so far, Porter?"

They did a quick count: the four Nortons - Harry, Geraint, Owen, Mortimer; Maximilian Cartwright; another private, Graham Smith; a couple of MPs who gave Feng their buttons; Soraya Adair; Porter's grandmother, Ida…

"It's been a good start," said The Gliss, "but it's not hundreds, is it?"

"It's eye for an eye, is it?" queried Namita.

"I don't know. There's probably some sort of scale out there that needs to be balanced," said The Gliss.

"You make this extraordinary, supernatural, once in a lifetime experience, sound like it's being managed by the Health and Safety Executive," said Feng.

"Well…"

"Don't start," said Porter, cutting The Gliss off. "I for one am happy to have met you all, glad we're doing something useful, and well - you're all good company." He lifted his glass and clinked Karin's, giving her a smile. Namita, noticing the glance, clinked too. "Chin Chin," she said.

"Chin Chin," said Feng. He paused for a second. "What does Chin Chin actually mean?"

Chapter 15

October 26th, 2017
Porter's Flat, Sylvester Path, Hackney

"Wakey, wakey, rise and shine," said The Gliss, as Porter covered his head with a pillow and told him to go away.

"I won't go away. You're supposed to be meeting Feng in two hours."

"I've got jet lag, leave me alone."

"No."

Getting no further response, The Gliss broke his cardinal rule - never do anything corporeal. Porter, his head still under the pillow, suddenly sat up. A muffled Bing Crosby was singing Moonlight Becomes You. The crackles suggested a 78rpm was playing. He sat bolt upright.

"Hey! Did you put that on? How did you do that?"

"Moi?"

"Yes, you! Oh my God, I knew it! You can do physical. The burning sock wasn't just a one-off!"

"I've no idea what you're talking about," said The Gliss.

"Well, go and put the bloody kettle on then," said Porter. "Earn your keep."

"You know I can't do that."

Grousing, Porter put his feet on the floor. "I feel like someone's turned my brain into sofa stuffing," he said. "What time am I meeting Feng?"

"Oh, I'm your secretary now, am I?"

"I'm going to knock your block off if you don't give it a rest," said Porter.

"Two hours. In Elephant and Castle. Interview with Francine Harding."

"Thank you," said Porter, lifting the needle and its heavy arm off the Crosby record. "I love a bit of Bing, but not with a head on."

October 26th, 2017
Henbury Surgery, Bristol

Sod it. Namita was at the surgery for a scheduled appointment with Dr Alice Harwell. Florence Prideaux's GP had been very co-operative and agreed to give Namita a statement and a copy of all the entries in her appointment diary. The GP visited Florence every week at home for two years before her death. That record, along with the statement, would show, beyond reasonable doubt, Florence had the capacity to make her final will. *Harwell could wipe out Stormont's claim right there.*

Except Harwell wasn't here.

The GP had asked Namita to come in person as she wasn't happy emailing confidential information. Namita, who'd spend the whole of the previous day in bed recovering from the flight home, had dragged herself to Paddington, got a train, then an Uber, only to find Dr Harwell had been called away on urgent family business. She wouldn't be back till tomorrow.

The surgery receptionist, sensing trouble from the agitated solicitor, promised Dr Harwell would be in tomorrow. "I'll put you down for a 10am. Is that okay, my love?" she asked in her Bristol burr, pen hovering in hopeful anticipation of a *yes*.

"Screw it. I'll have to stay overnight now," said Namita, ungraciously, as if it was the receptionist's fault.

"I'm so sorry, my love. It must have been urgent for her to not come in. First time in 10 years."

Namita walked away like she was clenching nettles between her butt cheeks. "Fat lot of good that does me," she muttered.

The receptionist sighed as if it was going to be one of those days.

Outside the surgery, waiting for another expensive cab back into town, Namita unexpectedly remembered Martin. She was tempted to call and see if dinner was still on offer. She hesitated. She knew he would grill her about this sudden visit. Screw him too. *No need to lay your cards on the table until you have a decent hand.*

"You know, you really are an idiot," said Sangita. "Professionally, you're already in trouble - if that posh knobhead decides to make a fuss about you taking on Brownlees. Why make it messier?"

"It's only dinner," said Namita.

"You know I'm inside your body, right? You can lie to yourself but not to me."

"I think I've got better control than that. Anyway, when was my last date? I'm hardly Katie Price, am I?"

"What would Mum say? Posh? White? Christian? Bristolian?"

"Oh my God. Sangita, back off. You're my sister, not my mother."

"Stupid *and* reckless. Your sister died a long time ago. I'm you. Your sensible half."

"Bollocks are you. I honestly don't care if he's any of those things. It's only dinner."

"You're in denial."

Thank God, the Uber arrived and Namita uncharacteristically chatted to the female driver all the way back into Bristol city centre. It was her way of putting Sangita on mute.

As soon as she shut the door on the cab, alongside College Green, she dialled Martin. *Screw you, Sangita.*

October 26th, 2017
Gaywood Street, Elephant & Castle, London

Francine Harding, sister of the murdered PI, Alex, had lived in the same flat since 1962. Feng took 20 minutes to find her on the electoral register. On her doorstep, they were nervous. They hadn't spoken to her. This was a cold call. Porter ruefully noted he and Feng looked like Jehovah's Witnesses in their suits. It might not go well.

"Relax, leave it to me," said Feng. "I'll charm her."

"Oh God no…sorry, didn't mean it like that. Let me. She might be an old racist or something."

"If you're sure…"

"I'm sure."

They pressed her buzzer.

"Allo?"

"Francine Harding?" said Porter in his calmest voice.

"If you're trying to get me to vote, sell me double glazing, or give me a pamphlet on Jesus, you can fuck off," a raspy voice said over the intercom.

"No, nothing like that, I assure you. My name's Porter and I wondered if we could talk to you about your brother?"

Silence.

"Who the fuck are you?" Suspicion wafted from the speaker like green pantomime smoke.

"We're looking into the disappearance of a young girl. Your brother was investigating it when he was murdered. I'm sorry if I've upset you, but…"

"Are you the fuckin' cops?"

"No."

"What are you then?"

"I'm a solicitor. We're just looking at the case again on behalf of the family. Please, Mrs Harding…"

"I'm not a Mrs anymore, thank God. Divorced the bastard years ago. You'd better come up. I've got anti-rape spray…"

"You won't need it. If we could just have a minute…"

"I said come up, didn't I?" The buzzer sounded. Porter looked round in relief, only to see Feng grinning and giving him two big thumbs-up.

"Calm down, Feng. She's going to need the gentle touch. I'm expecting Alf Garnett in a bloody frock."

Alf Garnett wasn't in. Zelda from Terrahawks was. "Who's he?" she asked, suspicion crawling across her face like geckos.

"This is my partner, Feng Tian. We're looking into it together."

"Partners, eh? Like that is it? Come in, come in."

They stepped in, Feng pinching Porter's arse to mock Zelda's insinuation. Porter gave Feng a cut-it-out look. Zelda, oblivious, slammed the door behind them, locking and chaining it. She had a fag in one hand, an aerosol in the other. Both men flinched when they saw the can.

"Nice place you have here," said Feng.

"It's a shithole."

"I like it. You could do a lot with a place like this," said Feng.

"I've been here 55 bloody years. Don't you think I'd have done something with it by now if it had fuckin' potential? I don't need any Grand Designs from you, sonny boy. Tea?"

"Yes, please." Porter and Feng stood like naughty schoolboys, taken aback by her aggression, which filled the flat like a runaway train.

"Would you like us to take our shoes off?" asked Porter.

"What? And stink the 'ouse out with your dirty great plates of meat? I think not. Go on. Go in there. How d'you 'ave it?"

"Sorry?"

"Your tea. How d'you 'ave it, Brains of Britain?" she repeated. She gave the impression she was dealing with the two stupidest people on earth. It was certainly how they felt.

"Milk and one sugar, please," said Porter.

"Me too," said Feng.

"Well, you'll have to have it black. Won't get milk till Betty comes over later. And sugar rots me teeth. Gave it up years ago."

"Black's fine," said Porter.

"Well, go on then… in you go. Mind Mendelssohn. He doesn't like strangers."

Porter and Feng moved a few old papers and a 1976 Marshall Ward catalogue to one side and sat either end of a sofa. The middle cushion was occupied by a ginger moggy, which appeared to be weighing up which of them to eat first.

"Mendelssohn, I presume. Is it purring?" said Feng.

"Growling. Don't look at it."

There they sat, like ancient Buddha statues, waiting for Francine to rescue them. She appeared in the doorway like heavy machinery. Her legs moved like they were worked by two uncoordinated winch operators. The tea-tray wobbled and rattled accordingly.

"Can I help with that?" said Porter, attempting to stand. Either Harding or the cat growled, but the sound was enough to make him sit back down.

"Now what the fuck is this all about?" she said. "Why are you interested in Alex? God rest his soul."

Porter did his best. He told her about Florence and Sam, how they'd given up on the cops, and employed Alex to look into Rose's disappearance in 1967.

"Well, I know all that. The cops were useless. I mean, the poor sod had his fuckin' 'ead chopped off, and they were treating it like he topped himself. Backhanders."

"Backhanders?" said Porter.

"Yeah, must have been. Someone didn't want the cops looking into it or they'd have investigated it like a proper murder. Stands to reason."

"How did you find out about it? Back in '68?" asked Feng.

A look, which might have been fleeting sentimentality, crossed her face. "What you have to understand is," said Harding, "is that my dear departed brother, God bless him, was a fuckin' idiot. He'd been doing alright as a barrow boy, flogging dodgy goods up Petticoat Lane, right? It was a job. I mean, it don't make you rich, but it don't make you poor? You understand?"

The men nodded.

"Then the pillock went and got one of the first colour tellies. Obsessed he was. Started watching shows like The Avengers, Department S - even Dixon of Dock bleedin' Green - and the idiot got it into his head he should be a detective." She waggled a spoon aggressively in the teapot. It clanged like Quasimodo's last peal.

"Course, the cops took one look at his misdemeanours - all petty - don't get me wrong, he weren't a bad lad - and told him to sling his hook. So, what's the bloody idiot do? Prints up some business card, puts an ad in the phone book, and starts telling all and sundry he's a private friggin' detective."

"Did he get much work?" asked Feng.

"Course he bloody didn't. He was so poor he had to sell the telly to pay his rent one month. He soon nicked another one, to be fair. What kind of friggin' detective nicks a telly? Prat."

"Do you know how he came to be working for Sam Brownlees?" asked Feng.

"He got a call from America. Some coloured bloke looking for his daughter. No offence," she said, tipping her saucer at Feng. "I says to him, how the fuck you gonna find her? We're in London, not a soddin' village in the Cotswolds. He said, 'Don't you worry, Franny, I'll just ask around up West. She was working in the clubs in Soho.' I says to him, don't you go messing with all those bloody gangsters, they'll nail your effin' foot to the floor. Do you know what he said? 'You watch too much telly, Franny.' Well, that was a bloody laugh, weren't it? It was telly what got him in the pickle in the first place. Fuckin' clueless."

Porter and Feng sat open-mouthed as she reeled it all out.

"What you staring at? Come and get your tea. I'm not a fuckin' waitress."

She sat back down and the boys noticed a greasy scum floating on the top of their drink. She hadn't rinsed the cups. For all they knew, they'd been in a cupboard since 1967. They both suspected she didn't get many visitors.

"Did Alex say anything to you once he started looking?" asked Porter.

"Not much. He was busy. He did come over for Christmas dinner. I don't know who the bloke in America was, but he obviously had cash to burn cos Alex brought me an electric teas-maid instead of a box of Milk Tray. Made tea that tasted like piss. What's wrong with a kettle?"

"And he didn't say anything?" asked Feng.

"He didn't shut up. Full of it he was. Started comparing himself to John bloody Steed. Said he'd seen all kinds of weird stuff."

"Like what?"

"Do you like The Beatles?" she asked.

"Some of it, yeah," said Porter.

"So you know what 1967 looked like? Sergeant fuckin' Pepper lookalikes everywhere. Bloody hippies in Victorian military uniforms. Those that weren't looking like a bunch of nancies, wore godawful clothes - tie-die, crocheted waistcoats, smelly sandals, and jeans with holes in. Greasy, long hair, smoking weed all the bloody time. I was in my 20s, a bit of a looker you might say, but all those technicolour kids made me feel like a Victorian scrubber. My wanker of a husband - pardon my French - gave me about a £2 a week. I had to make my own clothes."

"And what, your brother was a hippy?" asked Porter, not sure where she was going with this.

"Don't be bloody stupid. No, but he had to go to a lot of clubs and stuff asking after this Rose girl. I'll never forget it. He's stuffing his face with my turkey - both legs, would you believe, half the brussels, and not a shilling towards it - and he starts going on about all the freaks. 'Franny, you wouldn't believe what's going on in Soho and Mayfair. Drink, drugs, orgies - every other club is filled with pop stars, homos, spies, tarts, gangsters.' He saw Judy Garland getting pissed once. Said she was puking up on the carpet. Disgusting. Haven't been able to listen to Somewhere Over the Rainbow since without seeing her bring her guts up." Porter grimaced. Nor would he now.

"He thought Rose was mixed up in all that?" asked Feng. "We met a cop in Bristol who thought she might have got mixed up with spy rings or blackmail. We thought he was being a bit silly."

"Oh God. Another one watching too much telly. Well, to be honest, Alex never said nuffin' like that. He was just telling us how the other 'alf lived. I remember he was looking forward to going to Berlin in the January. Got his 'ead chopped off, so never made it, of course. Do you want to see my box?"

Startled, the pair said, "Box?"

"Oh, don't get your hopes up. Alex left about a tenner, his stolen colour TV and a few letters and postcards. You know the kind of thing. I think his notebook's in there too."

Unable to control their excitement, the pair nodded eagerly.

"Alright, Tweedledum, Tweedledee. Let me see if I can find it. Don't stroke the mog. He doesn't like strangers."

"Yes, you told us," said Feng.

"Well, I told the last person that too, but he didn't listen. Cheeky sod made me pay for his tetanus shot. And his trousers." She waddled off, little farts popping off as she went. "Bloody cat," she muttered, passing the buck to Mendelssohn.

The box was, they both agreed, completely awesome.

It was filled with everything from pools coupons to IOUs, ID cards to letters. There were a couple of photos of Alex Harding. There was one black and white of him and Franny. Her forehead was smooth and there was a sparkle in her eye. Porter looked at her now. Unrecognisable. You could park a bike in the lines on her face and Voldemort would covet those eyes. Alex looked like a proper Cockney wide-boy - he even had a spiv moustache. He didn't look like a PI. Not at all.

"He said he wanted to look like John Steed," said Franny, dismissively. "But he couldn't pull that off. Course not. He looked a right pranny. He wore a bowler hat for a day, but some kids threw a pebble at it. Little fuckers, but you could see their point."

Rummaging, they found the black notebook. It was 3" by 2", had gilt-edged thin pages, and had a small black pencil with a white plastic top stored in the spine.

Porter grabbed the book. The second he touched it he got the familiar glow of the Quincunx at work. There wasn't enough of Alex's grease and DNA left to give him visions. However, the background hum told him the notebook's owner died an unhappy death - not that decapitation left much room for doubt on that score. "Great," he thought. "Another one I've got to solve."

They examined the book carefully. It was a sort of diary/cum notebook. It had plain pages, so Alex had written dates in by hand. First entry was in 1966 and full of useless dates and notes including a disturbing entry for 16th February which said, "Haemorrhoid cream."

Moving on to late '67 they found an entry for November 2nd. It simply said: Samwell Brownlees. Underneath was an address in Glendale, California, and a phone number. Below that were a few scribbled notes.

> *Rose Prideaux. Missing in Berlin Jan 4-6th 1967. London: 47 Wardour Street. Mum: Florence, in Bristol, 0272 67532. <u>£35pm plus expenses.</u>*

That last sentence was heavily underlined.

> *Nov 10. Spoke to flatmates. Ursa Fielding, Bella Tompkinson. Rose had an audition in Berlin. Sometimes worked at Joe's, Old Compton, shift work. Did a few TV commercials. Bit parts, soap powder. Only two big movie auditions - one in London, one in Berlin.*
> *Nov 12. Interview. Jimmy Farr. 3pm Bag O'Nails*
> *Nov 14. Brinjle Johnson 7pm The Lord Dellafield*
> *Nov 15. Ryan Bradley 9pm Kitty Kitty*
> *Nov 17. Artie Mosser 1pm Joe's*

Then there was a gap until Dec 13th.

> *Dec 13. Angie Grew, Scarlet Club*
>   *Bert Rossi 4pm Wardour Street*
> *Dec 14. DCI Anderson Berwick St Cafe.*
> *Dec 19. Jimmy Farr. 4pm Red Hart*
> *Dec 20. Bradley. 11pm Kitty Kitty.*

Another gap until January.

Jan 8. Artie Mosser. 3pm. Joe's.
Jan 9. Jimmy Farr. 9pm. Red Hart.
Jan 11. Boris 2pm Dellafield.
Jan 19. Artie Mosser. 1pm. Joe's.

Harding never made that final meeting. Digging deeper in the box they found a newspaper cutting from January 15th, 1968. The police had found his headless corpse in the Thames the previous day.

"We didn't know it was Alex then," said Francine. "It took a couple of days to identify him. I was beside meself when they told me. One of the coppers gave me the cutting. I think the daft cow thought I was gonna start a scrapbook. Still, I kept it, didn't I?" She allowed them to photograph what they wanted. "Any good to ya?" she asked.

"Yes, very useful, thank you," said Porter. "Certainly gives us something to think about. I wish the entries said a bit more."

"They tell us he had leads, though" said Feng. "That's a lot of names, and he interviewed some of them twice."

"They're probably all dead, love," said Francine. "Most people from then are. It's only Mick Jagger who's still up there prancing about like a demented fairy. Fuck knows what they put in his Horlicks."

October 27th, 2017
The Hazlemere Hotel, Bristol

Namita opened her eyes and immediately wished her hangover an early death. She hadn't drunk that much for 10 years. Bloody good night though. She vaguely remembered oysters and more darts.

The blinds were down, and much as she dreaded the light, she felt like a bit of sun, plus coffee, plus somehow getting outside for a fag, were the inevitable steps she had to take if she was ever going to feel human again.

The room was very warm. Her head was as dry as a camel's foot. *Air. I need air.* She wobbled naked and unsteady to the window. With some trepidation, she moved the blinds millimetre by millimetre to let in just enough light to warm a daisy.

"Ah. You up at last, sleepyhead?"

Shocked, she spun on her heels, instinctively covering herself up. A towel wrapped around his waist, freshly showered, Martin Skelling grinned. "Bit late to cover your beautiful body up now."

Oh my God. Oh my God. Oh my God.

Through the muzziness of her pickled head, she dimly heard Sangita shout, "Now look what you've done."

Coming alive at last, she threw herself to the floor, crawled to the bed, pulled off the sheet, wrapping herself as fast as her shaking hands would allow.

"Martin," she said, quietly. "Did we, um… we didn't, did we? Oh my God, did we?"

"Someone's got a bit confused," he said. "Yeah, baby, we did. You were wonderful."

Oh my God. Oh my God. Oh my God.

"I was just going to wake you," said Martin, walking towards her, confidently. "You said you had an appointment at ten?"

Backing away, she saw the hotel alarm clock. 9am. "Oh shit, it's not in town. Can I use the shower, please?"

"I'm all done," said Martin. "No time for Round Four then?"

Round Four? She didn't even remember getting in the ring.

Chapter 16

October 27th, 2017
The British Library, Euston Road, London

While Namita was scrambling to make her appointment with Dr Harwell, Feng and Porter were registering at the British Library. They knew the spartan list of entries from Alex's notebook wasn't likely to yield much, but they wanted to research the few lines they did have. Who were these people he went to see? Were they connected to Rose? Were they connected to his haemorrhoids?

"Well, one of them's definitely dead," said Porter. "Bert Rossi - I saw his obit in The Guardian a couple of months ago. He was something to do with the Mafia in London. Which means Francine was right - the fool went talking to gangsters."

"Ooh, yes. That's an exciting start. The trouble with Alex - he was an amateur," said Feng. "We know who he went to see, but we don't know who they are, or what came of the meetings. You'd think he'd have used his expenses to buy a proper notebook to write down a record of his convos."

"Maybe he did," said Porter, "but I imagine whoever cut his head off would have looked for anything like that and destroyed it."

"I suppose. At least the little notebook got through."

"That's something."

They began with the buildings, which yielded a few photos and a couple of irrelevant stories. Then they searched for, and found, The Lord Dellafield, a pub on Greek Street, Soho.

They found a few references and called up the archives. Feng couldn't help himself. "Oh. My. Goff."

> *The Times*
> *July 8th, 1963*
>
> *As the fallout from Kim Philby's defection continues, The Times has learnt that he used a public house in London's Soho as a rendezvous for dropping off messages to Soviet agents.*
>
> *The Lord Dellafield on Wardour Street was codenamed The Barn. Philby regularly drank there from 1951, through his increasingly rare visits to London, until his flight to Russia from Beirut last week.*
>
> *Philby, whose defection has shocked the Western powers, resigned from the Secret Service under a cloud in 1951, but had been re-employed by MI6 since the late 1950s while working as a Middle East correspondent for The Economist and The Observer. In 1955 he was publicly exonerated by then prime minister, Harold Macmillan.*
>
> *Harry Brown, the landlord of The Lord Dellafield, said he was shocked by the revelation.*
>
> *"I've been here since 1950 so well remember Philby," said Brown. "I always thought he was a homosexual, because he always seemed to meet men here. I'm even more disgusted to learn they were Russian spies."*

> Brown said he hadn't seen Philby recently, but recognised him when the news broke that Philby had been unmasked as "The Third Man," following the previous defections of double-agents, Guy Burgess and Donald Maclean in 1951.
> "Hanging's too good for them," said Brown.

Feng snorted. "Hang them for being gay or for being spies?"

Porter ruffled his hair, thinking. "We've got to find out if it's just a coincidence that Harding was interviewing - let me see, Brinjle Johnson and someone called Boris at The Dellafield. My God - Boris. Could there be a more Russian name?"

Feng said, "Probably was a coincidence though. I mean, it was a pub, in Soho. Not everyone who drank there was a famous double-agent. And if Philby was busted in '63 you'd think that the Russians might have found another pub to meet their spies after that?"

"I'm sure you're right," said Porter.

"Still… did you get shivers?"

"I bloody well did."

The discovery pushed them on to check for similar connections with the other buildings.

"There's quite a few Red Harts in London," said Porter, "but presumably it was this one in Frith Street, Soho." He pointed to a Time Out article about the history of gay sex in London. Apparently, the Soho Red Hart was one of the pubs where gay men could go and be relatively open about their sexuality in the Sixties.

"Of course, homosexuality was illegal until 1967," said Feng. "I've never been an activist, but I know '67 is pretty much Year Zero for progress. That's when the recommendations of the Wolfenden Report became law."

"And look at this," said Porter. "In the mid-60s, vice officers were still often raiding the place, but the raids stopped when they found most of the clientele were from the Home Office."

"More government stuff. Hmmm."

They moved onto people. There was no way of knowing who Boris was, but the peculiarly named Brinjle Johnson, pulled up a Who's Who entry.

> JOHNSON, Brinjle, UK ambassador to Washington, 1959-1970; b. Calcutta, India, July 11, 1904; closed academic ed. under Nathaniel Peabody, writer on international law. Served, Somerset Light Infantry, 1941-46, Died, Aug 13, 1976; m. Dec 26, 1932, Mary Louise Du Bois of Canterbury, Kent.

"Ambassador to Washington?" said Porter. "What the hell was he doing in a well-known spy pub in Soho in 1967, then?"

"Curiouser and curiouser," replied Feng. "Well, he's dead, so not much use to us."

They looked for Jimmy Farr next. It turned out that both Porter and Feng had seen him on TV under his more famous moniker, Jimmy the Shanker. Like the late Mad Frankie Fraser, Shanker often cropped up in crime documentaries about the Sixties. Shanker had served 33 years for violent offences, but now eked a living talking about The Krays and The Richardsons on low-rent cable shows.

"Harding saw him three times," said Porter. "That suggests Jimmy knew something."

"Francine said her brother was a spiv. Maybe they were just friends? You know, birds of a feather…"

"It's the way the names are ordered," countered Porter. "Like he's ticking them off on a list. I'd put money on it being part of his investigation."

"Well, Jimmy the Shanker is still alive," said Feng, showing Porter a recent article. "We've got a live one at last."

There was nothing on Artie Mosser, Angie Grew or DCI Anderson.

"Anderson was probably in Vice or something. Bob Crawley might be able to help us work out who he was," suggested Porter. DCI Bob Crawley had been a reluctant ally on their last adventure.

"Ok," said Feng. "You'd better call him. He doesn't trust me."

"Will do."

That just left Ryan Bradley. There wasn't much on him. He'd been a TV director for Redifusion. He died in 1985. Porter put a small bundle of cuttings back on the table.

"Harding's notes said Rose did a few commercials. Redifusion was an independent, it later became Thames TV. He may have used Rose in an advert. Or she auditioned for him. He seems to have done a bit of news, a bit of drama, some adverts. No awards that I can see."

"He was a hack then," said Feng. "but no good to us, whatever he was. Another dead one."

Using IMDB and a bit of lateral thinking, they eventually tracked down Pete Dennehey, a journalist on the Willesden Chronicle, who claimed to represent Jimmy the Shanker.

Three phone calls and the promise of a £200 tip-fee for Dennehey later, they had a number for Jimmy.

"This is exciting," said Feng. "Do old gangsters still bite?"

"Let's just hope he remembers something," said Porter. "Our entire cast list has zimmer frames, Alzheimer's or a grave."

"At least they're not mad ghosts, dripping green fire, hoping to take over the world," said Feng, remembering the Profugus with a shudder.

October 27th, 2017
Henbury Surgery, Bristol

Dr Alice Harwell photocopied the last of the appointment book pages and then sat down to run a black marker through anything irrelevant.

Namita asked if she doubted Florence Prideaux's capacity to change her will.

"Not really. We'd been discussing it for a long time," said the GP, "Two years at least. She had plenty of lucid moments. We actually waited for one of those gaps before we did it formally. She must have made five or six drafts first. I saw them all. They all said the same thing - her nephew to get nothing; Samuel Brownlees to get everything."

"And you think her nephew deserved that?" asked Namita.

"From what I could tell he was pretty horrible. It's one of the reasons I'm so keen to help. I know that final will is what Florence really wanted. No question."

Dr Harwell gave Namita a letter outlining her connection to the case and her professional opinion on Florence's capacity. Coupled with the appointment sheets, Namita pretty much had the case sewn up. All she had to do now was hope Martin could talk some sense into Stormont.

"What was Florence like?" she asked. Before the GP could answer, Namita's phone pinged. Suspecting it was Martin, she blushed and ignored it.

Dr Harwell stopped marking out data for a second. "You know about her daughter, Rose? Well, she was exactly like you'd expect a woman who'd no idea what happened to her daughter to be like: hollow, sad, distracted."

"I read that people with Alzheimer's sometimes have hallucinations. Did Florence suffer from those?"

"One or two. I prescribed anti-psychotics only twice," said the GP.

"What did she hallucinate?" The phone pinged again. This time she put it on silent. She maintained eye contact with the GP hoping it expressed annoyance with the caller.

"She got very frightened, like she was seeing figures in the dark," said Dr Harwell. "Not surprising perhaps with what she'd been through. I wouldn't have wanted her nightmares. All in all, nothing major. Virtually every Alzheimer's patient I've ever treated had worse hallucinations than Florence. Here you go. Hope it all helps. What next?"

"The executor is meeting me at Florence's house. I just want to get a sense of her," said Namita.

"Well, it's tidy, but it's a sad house. You'll see."

As soon as she was clear of the surgery, Namita checked the texts. She was right: both from Martin.

I can still taste you on my lips.

She grimaced, hardly daring to read the second.

I can't wait for you to come back. Unfinished business. X.

Now she felt sick.

There was no avoiding her now. Walking the half mile to Florence's house, Sangita pounced. "What were you thinking? You don't know anything about Skelling."

Namita double-checked no-one was watching her talk to herself. "Look, I'm a grown woman. If I want to sleep with someone, that's my call, not yours."

"Yes, but did you want to sleep with him? That's the question. I didn't pick up much of that from you up here?"

Namita who vacillated between thinking of Sangita as her real sister or her conscience, thought maybe she had a point. "The funny thing... I was so drunk I don't remember what happened. Reading his texts made me shake. Fear? Regret? Lust? I honestly don't know."

"And you don't remember any of it? You think he spiked you? Are you pregnant? Do you have herpes?"

In the intervening hours, flashes of memory had come back to Namita - she had been too busy with Dr Harwell to process them. She was pretty sure he hadn't spiked her - he hadn't needed to. She could remember the third bottle of wine turning up at the table. That she helped drink it meant one of only three things: she needed courage, she needed anaesthetising, or she was indulging her wild child. Probably the latter, she admitted. It was her who had called him, after all.

"No, nothing like that," she answered her sister. "Look, I had fun. I don't remember much, but I do remember a condom. Stop being mortified on my behalf. He said we got to Round 3. To be honest, I wish I could remember all of it. It's been a while."

A woman was waving at her from Florence's front porch. Namita was glad the executor had sent someone else. Dandruff Dan made her feel a bit icky. Her phone pinged again as she walked the path. *God, go away!*

The house was tidy and - yes, Dr Harwell was right - *sad*. The dominant colours were grey and white. Dozens of photos in gaudy frames were anchored to every surface. There were pictures which Namita assumed were of Florence's parents and sister, and a few with her arm around a man who was probably her husband, Lester. There were a couple of more recent ones: Florence on a picnic with other old people; an excited wave to the camera on a bus trip through Italy in the early 80s. There were those. Then there was the Rose collection.

Namita started counting but got to 50 before quitting. Rose as a baby. Rose as a schoolgirl, squinting in the backyard sun. Rose with some friends on a beach. Rose in a server's uniform. Rose and a boyfriend? No wait, the boy was 10 years younger than the girl. Might be her cousin. Could that be Gary Stormont as a young man? Namita had never met him, but something about the child's face suggested aggression awaiting maturation.

And still there were more: Rose made-up. Rose in a cool 60s dress. Rose and two girls gurning for the camera in London. Was that Ursa and Bella? Rose dressed up as a pirate for a school play. Every photo was in its own frame. The collective impact was overpowering.

"I wonder what it's like to love someone this much," said Namita.

Rebecca, the woman from the bank looked at her, surprised. "Don't you know?"

If Feng or Porter had made that remark, she'd have dug into their ribs and made light of it. Coming from this ordinary woman, it stung surprisingly hard.

"Er. Yes. Of course," said Namita. "It's just, I don't have children."

"I've got three. Breaks my heart every time I come here."

Namita changed the subject. "What's going to happen to this lot, Rebecca?"

"We've had the contents valued for tax purposes. Everything saleable we'll auction off. Everything else will go in the house clearance. Landfill probably. I don't think she has anyone else who might care about the photos."

Namita surprised herself. "I care. Not only am I handling Samuel Brownlee's legal affairs, we're trying to find out what happened to Rose."

"For Mr Brownlees?"

"Yes, but also to put the record straight. The cops did a terrible job of looking for her when she went missing. If these photos are worthless to the estate, may I take a few? I'm sure Mr Brownlees would like them."

"Be my guest," said Rebecca. "Better than seeing them burned."

The pair spent 10 minutes prising Rose pictures from their frames. Namita began looking in cupboards, unsure what she was looking for. It was clear Florence had led a spartan life. There was very little clutter, barring the swarm of photo frames. Their preponderance in a vacuum heightened their impact.

Between the living room and the kitchen was a very small room with a table and glass-fronted cabinet. A faded, embroidered cloth was draped over two sides of the table. On it was a battered metal biscuit tin. It had once been shiny silver with colourful wooden soldiers painted on the side, but most of the paint had come off, and the exposed patches of metal, were tarnished and rusting.

Namita guessed it would either contain buttons or letters. She was wrong. It contained both. She nearly snapped a nail trying to get the lid off.

"Anything interesting?" asked Rebecca.

Namita, feeling like a Scene of Crime Officer examining entrails, said, "I don't know. Help me."

The pair sifted the letters; most were from her husband, Lester. He wrote from a surprisingly large number of towns across the UK. "He must have travelled for work," said Rebecca.

They skimmed a few. He was a man of few words.

> *Hi, I'm in Preston. B&B is nice. Raining a lot. Miss you, Lester.*

That was one of the long ones.

"He was sending texts 30 years before smartphones," said Rebecca.

Namita found one 1999 letter from Sam Brownlees. She felt awkward opening it, but it was pure vanilla. He was simply catching up, wishing Flo a Happy Christmas and New Year. It was full of fluffy nonsense. No mention of Rose whatsoever.

> *Somehow we made it to a new Millennium, Flo.*
> *Best wishes, your old friend, Sam.*

Namita could picture Sam saying this. He wasn't the sort to blow kisses and declare eternal love by saying it directly. However, she suspected all the love in the world was disguised by that innocuous sign-off. After all, Flo was a married woman, discretion and secrecy had been their watchwords for decades. Sam probably thought Christmas cards were sufficiently neutral to protect Lester. Both Sam and Flo sounded decent enough to have considered that.

At the bottom of the pile was a mess of rumpled plastic. An old Co-op bag, folded and scrunched. Namita withdrew the papers within. Top of the pile was a classic actor's headshot: black and white, contact number at the bottom.

It was unremarkable except for one thing: the face had been horribly scratched out and disfigured. If Jack the Ripper had been given kitchen scissors and told to "really mess this photo up," it would have looked tidier than the maniacal destruction wrought on this one. There was no-way to tell whose photo it was. It must be Rose. Of course it was. Flo couldn't even throw this one out.

Was the defacing done out of vindictive hatred for Rose? Or did she do it herself out of self-hatred? Namita, who unnecessarily viewed her own mirror as an agent of reprimand, concluded it was done by Rose. But why?

"That's horrible," said Rebecca. "Who would want to keep that?"

Now who doesn't understand a mother's love? Namita continued sorting and picked up an envelope. A well-thumbed letter inside. It was from Rose in LA. *What? Rose went to LA? No-one's told us that.*

The letter was headed 2122 South Gramercy Place, Griffiths Park, LA. It wasn't clear whether the address was a house or a hotel. Namita would have to look it up later.

> *3rd Dec 1966*
> *Dear Mum,*
> *Oh my! Hollywood! Can you believe I'm actually here? It's incredible really. I've already had a hamburger - it was so big! - and I walked down Sunset Boulevard. It all feels like one giant movie set - and the sun! Mum - it's like God forgot to turn out the lights. It's hot all day, all night.*

Namita skimmed the rest. It was banal but conveyed Rose's excitement. It revealed she had an audition for a film part, that she was safe and well, and was very excited to spot a few actors in the clubs she visited.

> *The film company have treated me very well, Mum. I've got an apartment all to myself, and I can see the Hollywood sign every time I walk down the street. Tomorrow I'm going to Burbank for my first audition. I'm very nervous but determined to do my best. It's for a Steve McQueen film. I wonder if he'll be there?! I don't know what I'll do if he is. I've learnt my lines and been practising in the flat. It's all very different from doing the Pirates of Penzance at school. And the men are all gentlemen, you'll be glad to hear! Ursa told me that when she was out here, there were a few straying hands, but I've seen nothing like that. But if I see Steve McQueen, I might let him stray a bit. Sorry Mum!*

Namita put this letter to one side and scanned the next. It was the letter from Berlin sent on January 5th, 1967.

Namita's first reaction was anger. What were the cops playing at? Anyone with eyes could see the same person didn't write both these notes. The handwriting and signatures were way off, but the obvious difference was tone. Rose was clearly fun and sounded relaxed in the way she wrote to her mother from LA. The letter from Berlin was terse and to the point.

Rutland had allowed them to snap a pic of his Xerox copy, but this was different: the real thing.

Sorry, have met a nice German lad. Don't worry will be in touch soon, all the best, Rose. 43d Emdener Strasse, Berlin.

She was astonished anyone ever considered this to be anything other than a forgery or, at the very least, written under massive duress.

One hour later, having gone through as much of Flo's stuff as she could stomach, Namita was back on the front porch, saying goodbye to Rebecca. The woman from the bank, far friendlier and chatty than most Londoners are comfortable with, jabbered away on the doorstep. Namita let the words wash over her.

"I need to call Karin," thought Namita as she grinned and nodded and prayed for a fast getaway.

Chapter 17

October 27th, 2017
Atwater Village, LA.

Karin was watching American football and eating rattlesnake and rabbit sausage at the Link 'n' Hops bar when Namita called. Karin was astonished. "I can't believe Rose was here too. I drove past Gramercy Place the other day. I remember it because the Uber driver told me it's where Marvin Gaye was killed. It's only five minutes from here. When was that?"

Namita checked her notes. "Dec 2nd to Dec 7th, 1966."

Karin, who had been spending time with Sam, was heartbroken on his behalf. "So, the daughter he always wanted to see was once on his doorstep? That's so sad. Not sure he could have met her even if he'd known. It doesn't sound like Rose knew much about her biological father, and Sam's wife and daughter were still alive then. But, well, it's just sad."

Namita said, "You think that's sad? You should visit Florence's house in Bristol. It was a shrine to her daughter."

After a quick recap, Namita asked Karin for an update.

"Things are ok," said Karin. "Sam is getting into the spirit of it. I hired a local crew and we've done two basic interviews with him. I'm going to send transcripts of those over in the next couple of days."

"Anything I should know about?"

"Not really. His experiences living through the Civil Rights Movement and more on his family history. He has some good old photos going back to early 1900s. But that's all my end of the deal, the documentary.

"He knew about Bella and Ursa. Florence kept him updated, but the other girls were beyond his thoughts really. The poor man was dealing with so much at the time. And obviously, he didn't pay for a PI to investigate their fates as well. He said that by the beginning of '69 he had accepted in his heart that Rose was dead. He did add that Flo never really accepted it, only said she did, so as not to upset Sam."

"That much was clear from her house. Did he have anything to say about Ursa and Bella?"

"No. Only that he knew their fates. I think he only communicated with Flo occasionally in those days."

"Anything on Harding?"

"A little something, perhaps. Harding was working on the case for a few weeks. He called Sam once, to encourage him to wire some money, but also to say he thought Rose had got caught up in something."

"What?"

"Apparently, Harding wasn't the best communicator," said Karin. "He wouldn't be drawn. He said he had to be sure of his facts first. Sam wasn't convinced Harding was any good and was thinking about handing the case over to someone else."

"How did he find out about Alex's death?" asked Namita.

"From Flo, but not for well over a month after Flo saw Harding identified in the papers. Sam was resigned when Harding stopped calling. He assumed he was being flaky."

Namita suggested Karin pass on the details of Rose's trip to LA to her detective.

"Yes, I'll do that, of course," said Karin. "There's definitely no file on Rose - we've already checked - but with specific dates there's maybe other sources they can check - immigration, for example."

117

October 27th, 2017
LAPD Robbery Homicide Division, West First Street, LA

"I found out what 4999 Wilshire was," said Detective Arnie Flax, sharing coffee and doughnuts at his desk with Karin. "It was Stephen Kellerman's HQ back in 1966."

"Should I know Stephen Kellerman?" said Karin, brushing sugar from her lap.

"He was a big tycoon who tried to create a market for cheap air travel. Quite famous here."

"What about this address in South Gramercy Place?"

Flax typed a few queries into his computer. He moved the screen around so Karin could see. "It was a nice place. Marvin Gaye used to live a few doors down in the 80s."

Karin nodded smugly. *Tell me something I don't know.* She looked at the photo. It wasn't a hotel. It wasn't an office. It was a solidly middle-class, 4-5 bedroom house.

"It was owned in 1966 by Morrie Crystal. You probably don't know him, either? He's the Reverend Crystal now, but back then he was PA to the film director, Don Lascelles."

"I don't know that director. What did he do?"

"He's just one of those directors you know the name of… hang on." He pulled up IMDB and showed her Lascelles' CV. "He worked with stars but none of the films are what you'd call classics, right?"

Morrie Crystal showed up in IMDB's *people also searched for box*. He was listed as a producer.

"He has a nice face. Producer to priest - that's a route few choose," laughed Karin.

"I don't know what he was like back then, but I can vouch for him now. His shelter on Griffiths Park has saved dozens of punks from prison."

"I must go see him at some point," said Karin. "Rose was over here for at least one audition. Maybe it was for Lascelles?"

"Makes sense," agreed Flax. "Especially if they were putting her up. They must have really rated her to do that. Hollywood's that place where you walk through a door stuffed full of hope, only to find someone's pickpocketed your heart and soul when you leave."

Karin, a TV veteran and no stranger to other people's broken dreams, nodded. "Sadly, Rose never got any big parts as far as we can tell, so the Hollywood dream certainly didn't work out for her. Story of her life. She went missing after another audition in Berlin."

"Well, that's every actor's story, right? A million of them and only 10 new famous ones a year. My daughter did acting-classes, but soon realised it was futile and became an accountant."

Forewarned, Flax had thrown a general information request out on Rose. All he'd got back was confirmation she'd arrived in New York and flown out of LA on the dates Namita found.

"Sorry about that," he said. "She was obviously a good girl who came over, caused no trouble and left again. Morrie and Lascelles are your best bets. At least they met her. But can you imagine how many actors they dealt with? What's the chance of them remembering Rose from all that time ago?"

As it turned out, Don Lascelles probably didn't remember his mum, let alone Rose. Karin read on Google that he'd been suffering from dementia for 10 years. Now in his mid-80s, he was being cared for in his Beverly Hills mansion. She found an old picture in the LA Times of Lascelles and Kirk Douglas, both in wheelchairs, at some awards show.

The Reverend Morrie Crystal was easily reached by phone but wasn't much use either. He didn't remember Rose and said he would have been surprised if she stayed at his house. "My Lord, we auditioned a thousand actors a year back then."

Karin asked if he knew why Rose had given his address?

"You've heard about film people, I'm sure," he said, sounding slightly ashamed. "I was no saint back then, I admit it, but I don't remember ever having anyone stay - that's why the Devil invented hotels. But you know how tough US Customs have always been. Maybe they demanded an address before approving her visa? If my secretary was organising her work visa, I suppose she might have given my address. But then, why not give our office address? I'm sorry, it doesn't make much sense to me."

They chatted for a bit and he told her how he'd tired of the showbiz life and turned to religion in the 80s. "I tell you, Miss, my only regret in life is not starting The Mission much earlier. I'd have been far happier, for far longer. I quit the hedonism, the *me, me, me,* and locked my ego away. Only then did I start doing some small good. It's the only way to have a meaningful life, I think."

Karin thanked him and told him about her documentary.

"I didn't realise I was talking to a famous person!" he joked. "It's been a while. If you come through my doors, you're more likely to be infamous. If you have time, please do come over and see me. I'd love to show you The Mission and introduce you to some of our boys."

"If I've got time. I'm fairly tied up with the documentary," she said, politely but dismissively.

"Ah! You don't think an old Jew turned Anglican helping deprived American black boys is relevant to your story about a black man and his multi-generational attempt to put slavery behind him?" He laughed. "Don't you think it's all part of the healing?"

Not simply chastened, but also converted, Karin promised to visit. Leaning back in her chair, she looked out of her hotel window at the palm trees and the Hollywood Hills. *So alluring. So full of promise. So full of dead ends.*

Karin was enjoying her trip fully aware that her celebrity status and privilege were not shared by the majority of visitors. She tried to picture Rose, pop-eyed in awe, wandering around 60s LA. But she struggled to form an image.

Karin shook her head. She was up against the oldest delusion of all; the desire for fame continued to send young people into the arms of pimps, abusers and charlatans. What on earth made a provincial girl from the UK think she could make it in Tinseltown? She probably had bad teeth. Everyone in England had bad teeth in the 60s.

It was the teeth that cracked it. Finally, a fantasy picture of Rose came to Karin: a young woman, Cathy McGowan hair, an A-line dress, firetruck red lipstick being badly applied in front of a mirror surrounded by lightbulbs. A crumb of lippy, resting on a slightly wonky front tooth.

Damn. Rose disappeared so long ago. There's nothing to go on. I'm wasting my time here, aren't I?

Chapter 18

October 29th, 2017
Britannia Leisure Centre, Hackney

Wham! Wham! Wham!

Feng was smacking the hell out of Porter who hadn't played squash since he was at school. Porter dripped like broken guttering. Feng took it in his stride. Feng's sweat, if you could call it that, resembled nothing but a dab from a wet flannel. Porter looked like he'd been dunked in a tub of glue, his clothes clinging, his hair matted, his calf muscles bulging like a condom full of marbles.

"Soddin' hell, Feng, this is torture," said Porter, waving away Feng's ready? "I can't carry on."

"I win then!" said Feng. "Squash is good for sweating the toxins out."

"A gentle sweat is one thing," said an incredulous Porter. "But this? My toxins are dangling from my pores like worms. I don't think I'll ever breathe normally again."

"Well, this is why you need to do it. Fag break?"

"God, yes."

Alternating between cigarette and Coca Cola, Porter was still looking distressed 20 minutes later. "I'm shaking all over. I feel like I've been strapped to a tumble dryer for the weekend."

Feng shrugged. "I've been thinking about it. We need to go to Berlin."

"Feng, I can't let you pay for me again."

"Nonsense, couple of hundred quid at most."

"I feel like Alan Whicker, all this travelling. It's not sustainable, is it?"

"I think it's exciting. You can still visit Checkpoint Charlie - did you know that?"

"You like the spy angle, don't you?"

"From what I've read about Rose, I doubt she was a Master Spy," said Feng. "But it's not difficult to imagine actual spies using Rose and her friends as pawns. Just like drug mules now. It's not that far-fetched. It's hard to explain her travel otherwise."

Porter understood, but still couldn't see what they'd gain from the trip. "What would we look at when we got there? There are no graves for me to test."

Feng opened Dropbox on his phone. "We have Rose's address in Berlin. I don't suppose we'll have any luck finding her landlady, but we can at least rule out Rose being buried in the garden. Just in case her hosts were twisted murderers."

"Porter Norton, the human metal detector," said The Gliss, appearing from nowhere.

"Hey you," said Porter.

Feng asked The Gliss, "What do you think? Is it worth a shot? Going to Berlin?"

The Gliss, unused to Feng addressing him without rancour, said he thought it was. "You should definitely find out who she auditioned for. The police said that whatever happened to Rose, happened after her audition. That seems reasonable, but it is of course possible, probable even, that she met her killer/abductor *at* the audition, bearing in mind she was only in Berlin for a couple of days."

Feng nodded. "Yes, that's true. Mingling with actors is always a tricky business. I know a couple, and, my Goff, they're bitches. And that's just the boys. Give them a bad review - or do better than them at an audition, for example - and you'd better watch your back."

"Do you ever have anything good to say about your friends?" laughed Porter. "What on earth do you say about me when I'm not here?"

Rhetorical questions whizzed over Feng's head like unannounced frisbees. "I tell people I met a troubled but kindly man who puts his life on the line for others, despite going through a lot of personal pain. I skip all the stuff about ghosts and The Gliss, of course. I don't want people thinking me mad as well."

"Wait. Who's mad?"

"Oh, you know, people in general," said Feng.

"Liar. You mean me," Porter smiled.

"No, no, no. No, no."

"You liar!"

October 29th, 2017
Highland Gardens Hotel, Franklin Avenue, LA

Karin was surprised to hear from Arnie Flax so soon after their last visit. Her first random thought: Oh God, don't ask me on a date. He didn't.

"So, I was thinking about Rose and Bella," he said. "I know we don't have much on either of them, so I thought I'd reduce them to types. *Young women, involved in film, reported murdered or missing in LA since the 60s.*"

Karin's ears pricked up. "Anything interesting?"

"Actually, it's something I should do more often," said Flax. "Often with Cold Cases, we're responding to new evidence that comes in from somewhere in relation to a specific case. Could be a belated confession or new DNA evidence. Rarely, it could be discovery of remains. But one of the things computers allow us to do is run cross-checking algorithms and look for patterns the human eye would miss."

"Sure," said Karin, "I understand."

"Well, you can probably guess what the problem is here? If you go back to the 60s and 70s, a lot of those cases are still on paper. They don't show up in computer searches. There's no incentive or resources to digitise them, either. There are so many unsolved cases from the 80s onwards, no amount of staffing could cover the research if we just kept going back."

"Does this story have a happy ending?" laughed Karin. "Sounds like you're saying it's an impossible job."

"It is. But here's the thing. I went to see Perdita in Records," said Flax. "She ticked me off for not going to her before. Apparently, one of my predecessors, Captain Melville Wright, manually sorted through all the cases of young missing women between 1960 and 1980. Unfortunately, he didn't narrow it down by any other factors. It's only an index."

"Do a lot of people go missing in LA?"

"Staggering numbers. These days the Missing Persons Unit investigates about 3,900 cases a year, though 80% of those people turn up again after a couple of days. But that still leaves about 800 which take longer to resolve."

Karin was trying to jot these figures down. "That's a lot."

"It's too many. And investigate them all? Can't be done. A good few of those 800 will turn up anyway over the long haul, but you're still talking several hundred who don't. Some eventually become murder cases. Most, we just never know what the hell happened."

Karin said, "So this Captain Wright… what did he discover?"

"He took all the unresolved cases and broke them down into demographics. So, yes, he had a file on young women. As I say, it's just an index, referencing the actual case files. But wait for it: 2,100 young women went missing in LA between 1960 and 1980 and are still registered as missing."

Karin whistled.

Flax nodded. "Scary, right? These 2,100 aren't connected to Bella Tompkinson in any way, though of course her name's on the list. I sweet-talked my boss into it, and she's allocated funds to digitise this document. Once it's in, we'll run some cross-checks. There's no way of knowing if the details of any of these cases have been digitised until we run the cross-check, but thought I'd let you know. There may be similarities between Bella's disappearance and other women that point us in a new direction. But it's only an index. Don't expect too much."

"Thank you, Arnie," said Karin. "I owe you dinner some time."

"How about tonight?" said Flax.

Karin stuttered and stumbled like the posh English fool she suddenly felt. "Oh, I can't… not tonight, I'm, er, filming."

"Understood. Another time then."

Chapter 19

October 31st, 2017
Brandenburg Gate, Berlin

"Ich bin ein Berliner," said The Gliss.

"No," said Feng. "You should have said, 'Ich bin ein messenger.'"

Porter laughed, shaded his eyes, and took a photo of the Brandenburg Gate. "Do you ever think about aesthetics, Feng?"

"Only when I'm dating or buying a suit. Why?"

Porter pulled up a photo of the Brandenburg Gate draped in Nazi flags, Hitler driving through huge crowds. The shot was blurry, grainy, black and white. "For example, take a gander at this. When we look at the past, our perceptions are determined by the medium it was captured on. It's almost impossible to correlate this photo with what we're looking at now. Real life is 3D, full-colour, people move at the correct speed, and the audio is 5.1 surround.

"Look at this photo again. Because of their clothes, their hair, but most of all the type of photograph it is, we can barely imagine that a real, 3D, colour, 5.1 Hitler drove through that gate, cheered on by exactly the same sort of people who are here today. The colours would have dazzled, the air filled with vehicle fumes. People stamped and shouted. Next to impossible to imagine."

Feng looked puzzled. "What's your point?"

"My point," said Porter, "is that even the people who experienced the past, don't see it as it was, but as an amalgam of memory and other cues. I went to Live Aid with a friend's family when I was about 12. When I remember it now, all I see is Freddie Mercury and David Bowie. I don't see my girlfriend or the toilets. My actual memory has been overwritten by seeing the video footage a few times. I don't see the 80s clothes and haircuts of the people who were around me. Not only that, but because of the technical format, even the colours in my head are artificial Beta SP video colours, not real colours."

The Gliss said, "All very interesting, but I don't get your point either."

Porter put his phone away and gestured around him. "Our cases involve looking at the past, right? But the past is hard to visualise. When we've talked about Rose in 1967, we're all thinking Super 8 footage of Carnaby Street, hippies, Sergeant Pepper etc. But Rose walked about these streets and she was the same as any of these people here. Maybe she had dry skin on her heels? Fluff on her top. An itchy butt. She was real. We're in danger of being seduced by half a century of images of the Swinging Sixties. The itchy butt? Real life - not the wide shot of a girl in 60s' fashion we're probably all picturing. We need to try and imagine the real young woman who came here looking for something. What was going through her head? Was she excited? Nervous?"

The Gliss said, "I'm pretty sure you could have just said that last sentence and we'd all have got your meaning."

Porter said The Gliss was wrong. "No, it's a real prejudice we have to overcome. It's the same with the old music I remaster. Captured on one-track mono and played back on a 78rpm, an orchestra sounds quite small. Play the same piece of music, recorded by the same musicians, in the same hall, but with modern mics and processed into 5.1 surround, not only do the recordings sound different, but the listener approaches them differently because of the character of the medium. The 5.1 mix would probably sound more professional, dynamic, modern, serious.

"But in essence, it's not true: whatever the medium, the recordings originated with the same type of event - a proficient orchestra playing in a room: the medium is what changes your perception. Real life doesn't look like a Polaroid snap. Polaroids have their own aesthetic as distinctive as Picasso's painting style. I don't want us all to confuse our images of the 60s with what life was actually like."

Feng addressed The Gliss, "I think the last sentence of that one probably just about covers it too. Well, thank you, Porter for that advice. I thought that's what we were doing?"

"Are we though? We're here and the first place we've come to is the Brandenburg Gate. Yes, it's magnificent, but it suggests mid-20th century war and geopolitics to me."

"You mean we're indulging in a form of confirmation bias; we're pre-loading our investigation to be about the Cold War?" said Feng.

"Right. This is a tourist destination. We should have gone straight to the house she stayed in. We should have started clean, looking at the very street she stayed in, the corner shop she might have bought fags from."

"I hear what you're saying, but honestly, I couldn't finally make it to Berlin and not look at the Gate," Feng replied. "And I tell you something else, when Rose was here, mid-20th century war and geopolitics *were* in the background. Anyone who flew into Berlin knew they were coming into a protected enclave within the Soviet Empire. It would have been part of the thrill."

"I'm just saying," said Porter.

"I think what he's trying to say, in the most roundabout way imaginable," sighed The Gliss, "is that he's impatient to see where Rose stayed."

October 31st, 2017
Emdener Strasse, Mitte, Berlin

If Porter hoped to find a two-up, two-down with a potential grave site in the back garden, he was to be severely disappointed.

43d Emdener Strasse, the 1967 home of Mutti and Gustav Dietrich, the posting address on Rose's letter to her mother, was a grey block of flats that looked like it might have been pre-war. It had one wooden door with glass panels. Most of the door surround was covered in graffiti.

"Oh shit," said Porter, turning to The Gliss, "what a waste of…"

"Guten tag, sprechen sie Englisch, bitte?"

Porter turned back to see Feng with his finger jammed on the intercom.

A croaky voice said, "Ja. Wer ist das, bitte?"

Feng reminded the voice, "Englisch, bitte." He explained slowly who he was and why they were here. He mentioned Mutti and Gustav Dietrich. No reply. But the buzzer rang, and Feng pushed the door open. "Well," he said to Porter, "what are you standing there for?"

As soon as they stepped into the flat, they realised the magnitude of their luck. The decor, the furniture and the occupant all looked like they hadn't changed since the 50s. Mutti Dietrich was in a wheelchair and was rather large for a woman in her 90s. Not that they could tell immediately. The cigarette smoke was so dense, Mutti could have kept a pet elephant and they wouldn't have known till they tripped on its trunk.

"I don't get the visitors so much," she said in broken, heavily accented English.

I'm not surprised, thought Porter. It was the kind of place Hazmat would sponsor. A small, cheap plasma TV was blaring out a daytime quiz show. Feng pointed at it and the painfully loud German voices sounding like a throat-clearing convention.

"You want it off?" Flicking ash on the carpet, Mutti gestured for Feng to help himself. He picked up her sticky remote and muted the TV.

"Fräulein Dietrich," said Porter. "We are looking into the disappearance of Rose Prideaux. She stayed with you and your husband for a few days in 1967."

"Ja. The girl who went missing. Mein Gott! Have they found her?" She crossed herself.

"No. We're just taking a fresh look at it. We had no idea you still lived here. We were just looking at the building."

"The missing fräulein, ja, ja," said Mutti, crossing herself. "The polizei - police, ja? - came. But we had many visitors. Ja. Hundreds. *Thousands*. After the war, my husband…" She made a gesture which suggested illness or incompetence - they couldn't tell which. "You understand, ja? Naturlich, we made use of our home to survive." She waved her hand, inviting them to survey the grandeur of her palace.

Both Porter and Feng hoped it had been a tad brighter back in the day, for the sake of Rose and the *thousands*. "What do you remember?" asked Porter.

"Zigarette?" she offered. Porter and Feng both smoked occasionally, and they looked at each other. Feng gave a slight nod, which Porter took to mean, "I will if you will in the cause of creating empathy with her." He was either saying that or: Go ahead, but the next squash session will really hurt.

They both accepted the offer with badly pronounced *danke schön*'s. Mutti used her foot to push a packet of Marlboro's at them.

"The girl stayed here two nights. Neujahr. Es was eiskalt."

"Eiskalt?" said Porter.

"She means it was freezing," said The Gliss. "Don't stop her after every word, even I will have died of lung cancer by the time she's finished. I'll translate. Don't react to me, bitte."

Porter and Feng held Mutti's gaze, listening and watching as she mimed shuddering from the cold.

"Ah, eiskalt," said Feng, to show her he understood.

"Ja. A pretty junges mädchen. Movie star. Tsch." She said it with derision.

"Yes, she was an actress," said Porter.

"Ja. Pretty but…" she tapped her temple.

"Mad?"

"Nein. Nicht sehr klug… er… how you say in the Englisch… clever not?"

It took some time of criss-crossed meanings, translated by The Gliss, before they got a full un-muddled account.

According to Mutti, Rose was just like any of the other young men and women who stayed there over the years. The Dietrichs had signs in local shops offering accommodation, but also took out paid adverts in the local newspapers. The first thing the couple asked every guest was how they'd heard about the accommodation. If it was from the postcards in the shops, they charged a budget fee: if it was from the press ads, they felt they could charge more.

Rose was different. She'd been pre-booked by the film company. Mutti had charged them double the normal rate.

Her husband liked all their guests but used to joke the actresses were either stupid or spies. Even in those days, actresses had to be good looking. Over the years they hosted dozens from Rome, Paris, London, Sweden etc, and they were often very pretty indeed, much to Herr Dietrich's pleasure. None of the many actresses Mutti hosted ever became famous which made her husband suspicious. Were they even actresses? Half his family were trapped in East Berlin, the other side of the Wall. He was paranoid with good reason. He'd heard his brother now worked for The Stasi. When quizzed on her own opinion, she repeated her remark about most of them not being so bright.

She said her husband was kind as well as occasionally flirty. On the day of Rose's audition, it was snowing. He offered to drive her to SpellenGross Studios. He didn't say much about it until a few weeks later when the police called. They told them she had gone missing after the audition. Luckily for Herr Dietrich, several witnesses gave statements showing Rose made it to the film studios in one piece. Otherwise, perhaps the Dietrichs would have been the last to see her alive? Never a good label in a potential murder investigation.

Her husband told the police that Rose seemed happy and excited, although he also got the sense that she was nervous and thought this audition might be her last big chance.

Mutti admitted she never understood how Rose would get the role if it was a speaking part: the only German she had was *danke schön*. Mutti didn't know what part Rose auditioned for.

"We minded ourselves," she said.

Rose returned to Endemer Strasse that evening, said it went well, had dinner, went to bed and checked out next morning. As far as Mutti and her husband were concerned, everything was fine. She was a good guest and they'd been paid already by the film studio. Rose booked a taxi, presumably to the airport, and left. It wasn't until the police came asking questions that her visit became something memorably out of the ordinary. Mutti had thought of the girl many times over the years.

"And that's it?" asked Porter. "Nothing else?"

"Nein," said Mutti, hacking at her lungs, which sounded like a box of pissed-off snakes.

Feng thanked her, offering 40 Euros for her trouble. She waved the offer away.

Mutti called them back as they reached the door. She had just remembered a tiny detail. On arrival, Rose asked for permission to use the phone to update her mother in England after the audition. After returning from the studio, Mutti asked if she was ready to make her call. The landlady was surprised when Rose said it was too soon. She said she'd call her mother later. Mr Dietrich offered to drive her to the airport but she said she didn't need a lift.

"Was it still snowing?" asked Porter.

"Nein. The snow had stopped. But eiskald, ja. Eiskald."

"I wonder why she didn't accept the lift?" wondered Feng.

Mutti tapped her head. Not very bright.

"She walked from the door, and with that, she was gone. Yes, she was gone," Mutti sighed, looking away from them, into her past.

Standing outside, wondering if they would ever feel clean again, Porter said the only new info was that Rose auditioned for a production company called SpellenGross. They could look into that.

Feng agreed, adding, "If I don't get a change of clothes in the next half an hour, my threads are going to start disintegrating."

Chapter 20

October 31st, 2017
Grey's Nursing Home, Atwater Village, LA

While Feng and Porter were deciding what to do next in Berlin, Karin was finishing her breakfast, ready for the 20-minute drive to Atwater Village.

Sam was pleased to see her. "Make yourself at home, Karin. How you doin' today?"

"Fine, Sam. Hope you're ok?"

"All good, Miss. Spoke to your boys yet?"

Karin, laughing at the thought of Porter and Feng being her boys, put her bag down and said, "Yes. We spoke on the phone just now."

"Any news?"

Karin told them what she knew of their visit to Mutti Dietrich.

"We're all so old," he said. "Have you noticed that? Rose and her friend were so young. All us survivors are so damn old. It's like we've borrowed all those stolen years from them."

As if he needs another reason to feel guilty. Karin said although they started out looking for Rose, they were shocked about Bella also going missing. Feeling everything must be connected, they were also now counting Ursa as a victim. The three girls roomed together and when the second went missing, the third killed herself. Whoever was responsible for Rose and Bella had Ursa on their conscience too.

"Conscience? Miss, whoever did this never had one. They know perfectly well what they did. They left us all hanging. For eternity. No-one with a conscience does that." He clearly wanted to talk about something else. "What's your plan for today?"

Karin discussed questions, explained logistics, but his words rang in her ears. *They were so young.*

October 31st, 2017
Pyecroft Avenue, Henleaze, Bristol

Namita took a deep breath and rapped on the door of Lenny Fielding, Ursa's mum. A frail old lady answered the door, looking as suspicious as a serial killer signing for a package.

"Hello, Mrs Fielding?" asked Namita.

"Who the hell are you?"

"My name's Namita Menon. I'm a lawyer." She showed her some ID. Not that it meant anything. "I'm representing the estate of a woman called Florence Prideaux…"

As soon as she got the name out, Fielding's face scrunched ominously. "Them! What do you want?"

Namita got her explanation out quickly. The family had asked her to take one last look at the disappearance of her daughter's friends, Bella and Rose. "I understand if you don't want to talk to me. It was tragic, what happened to them all," said Namita, "but there are very few people left alive to talk about it. Could you spare me a few minutes?"

"What bloody good will that do me?" said Fielding. "She's gone. They're all gone. I don't want to bring it all up again."

"Lenny, isn't it?"

"Leonora. No-one's called me Lenny for 30 years."

"Could we have a cup of tea? I'll tell you what I think: I think whoever is responsible for Bella and Rose's disappearance, was responsible for what happened to your daughter too. If there's anyone left alive to bring to justice, we will."

Leonora stared at her for a minute, fighting some internal battles, and gave in. "Come in. Ten minutes."

As Namita stepped over the threshold her phone pinged. It was a text from Martin.

Hello sexy.

She blushed and shoved the phone back in her pocket. In contrast to Florence's poignant shrine, Namita could only see one photo of Ursa. The colours had faded and the pretty teenager who stared out of it smiled like the Charlie Brown's sister at a prizegiving. It brought a lump to Namita's throat. Memories fade. So do photos. So do people. Namita looked at the old lady, lowering herself into her comfy chair, and realised, for the first time, that they were in a race against time. The witnesses were all ancient.

She hadn't experienced it often, but Namita got the sense Leonora was suspicious of having a *foreigner* in the house. The defensiveness and reticence were more than just not wanting to bring up the past.

Namita told her how she got involved. It would be very helpful if Leonora could tell her a bit about the three friends.

"I told them not to go," said Leonora. "I told them it would be dangerous. I didn't blame her friends, but that wasn't the point. They were all too young to just up-sticks and move to London. It's a dangerous place for young women, isn't it?"

Namita, who could easily identify with the problem of strict parents and defiant children - she was that child - merely nodded.

But Leonora wasn't finished. "Do you know what Ursa said? 'I'm old enough to get married, I'm old enough to pay my own rent. Try and stop me.' I couldn't stop her, of course. But there were tears and arguments."

Namita nodded. "But you made it up?"

"Of course we bloody well made up," said Leonora, appalled. "She was my daughter. To start with, I had to eat my own words. Ursa was doing brilliantly. They got their tiny dosshole and skivvy jobs, but all three wanted to be actresses and, to my amazement, they got things moving. They mostly got bit parts and stuff, a little bit of theatre, an advert on the telly… you know how it is. She was a good-looking girl."

Namita looked at the portrait on the wall. *She is. She was.*

"One day she rang to tell me she was auditioning for a big film in London. She was so excited because Alan Bates and Susannah York were in it. She didn't get the part. But the producer was so interested in her work he recommended Ursa for a role in a Hollywood film. The Americans paid for her to go to LA.

"I don't know if you can understand this, but… in the 60s? Going to LA! Even I was excited. She had a great time in LA and stopped off in New York on the way home. She didn't get the parts but it felt like progress. She got to know various actors and producers. They'd recommend her for parts. She went all over Europe - Germany, Italy and France. Dad said she was a lucky cow."

In the re-telling there was a tiny glimpse of the proud mum still poking through the misery. "That must have been so exciting," said Namita. "I haven't been to all those places yet."

"France was the one. You must have heard of Oli Caron? The famous director? He auditioned her for a part in a Brigitte Bardot film. I have a picture of her with Bardot somewhere. I remember thinking how amazing it was my daughter could sit next to the most famous film star in the world and not look out of place. Ursa's dad, bless him, spoke to her on the phone and said, 'Give Brigitte a hug from me.' Cheeky sod."

"But she didn't get the role?" asked Namita.

"No. She came home and was still upbeat. She got on really well with Caron, but of course, he was murdered by the Mafia soon after. That didn't help her mood. She said he was the person most likely to have helped her career along. I believe they kept in touch once she got back to England. She took it hard when he was murdered. But the trouble started before that. I could sense something was wrong with her generally. I guess getting all those rejections hurt. It started to dent her confidence."

"Was this after Rose disappeared?"

"Oh no. She got back from Paris in autumn of '66. All her travelling was done earlier that year. A few months later, Rose went missing. We were all upset, of course. It seemed to affect Ursa really badly. She carried on living in the same flat with Bella in London. I think Bella's career started to take off, while hers seemed to have stalled. Things got very dark when the police stopped looking for Rose. She would sit in her room for hours. No music. No books. Just brooding. Eventually, she asked if she could move back here. I said yes, of course."

"When was that?"

"Halloween 1967. Never forget it."

"How was she when she got home?" asked Namita, scribbling down as much as she could.

"It was like she had a split personality. She'd be happy for a bit, and then… the black dog would take her. She got a job as a secretary and that seemed to be going okay. But I could tell she wasn't well. Without warning, she'd start to cry and cuddle up with me on the sofa. 'What's the matter, baby?' I used to ask. 'Nothing, Mum. Just down.' Next day she'd be right as rain again. I even started wondering if she'd been taking drugs. In the end we put it down to the combination of Rose's disappearance and the lack of acting work. She was headstrong, but a lovely, sensitive girl."

Leonora's hands shook. Her teacup caused a tiny peal of china bells as she rattled it against its saucer.

Namita checked her notes. "And then Bella went missing on June 23rd, 1968?"

"Sounds about right. Bella's mum came over to tell us. After what happened to Rose, we were all worried."

"How did Ursa handle it?"

"How do you think? Rose and Bella had been her best friends since school. She was devastated. She seemed to blame herself for some reason."

Leonora suddenly became earnest and begging. "Look love, I know what you're going to ask me now, but don't. I can't. Don't you see? Yes, it was me who found her. My own daughter, hanging herself in our home. August 15th, 1968. Don't make me talk about it. Don't make me picture it. It's all you need to know. Twenty-four. That's no age at all, is it?"

Namita leaned over and squeezed Leonora's hand. "Ok. Thank you. Do you need a tissue?" Namita pulled a pack of Handy Andies from her bag and passed it over. "I'm only going to ask one more thing - did she leave a note?"

"No, love. We put her in the ground at Canford and we had no idea what had changed her - apart from grief and disappointment. Isn't that enough? But I admit, I always thought there might be more to it than that. My husband never got over it. He was dead three years later from a broken heart. It's hard not to feel like we brought some kind of curse down on us. I wish I knew what we'd done wrong."

"You did nothing wrong," said Namita. She stopped staring at her pad and looked at Leonora. "We're really going to try and find out what happened," she said as firmly as she could, but couldn't stop her voice from wavering.

Leonora caught the waver. Grateful, it gave her the power to unburden. "You know something else, my love? I hate myself. I hate that I didn't stop her from going to London. I hate that I couldn't cure her split personality. I hate that my husband died of a broken heart. And me still here. I must be a cold, callous old bitch to have survived it all."

"Don't be silly," said Namita. "Survivors always feel guilt. I lost my twin sister when I was six. I'm the same. Whose suffering has been the longest? Yours. And mine. Your girl and my sister have been sleeping a long time."

"Suffering? No more than I deserve. What kind of mum lets her baby die like that?"

Namita realised there was nothing more to be said. The guillotine had fallen. She changed subject, asking if Leonora kept cards or letters from Ursa's travels. Without reply, Leonora straining to get up, tucked the tissue into her cardie and shuffled over to a cabinet. She brought back a bashed and beaten blue cardboard box, which had once housed expensive soap, to show Namita.

There were a few postcards, a couple of playbills, a pile of snaps, and a few airmail letters.

"I don't want to look. You go in the kitchen, sit at the table and take your time," said Leonora. "Do me a favour, love? Turn the telly on for me and pass the remote."

As Namita carried the box into the kitchen she was embarrassed she'd overstated and over-lived her own grief to gain empathy. Losing Sangita at six was a blow, but children are resilient. They find a way through most things. She could barely remember the real Sangita. The voice in her head was a concoction of fantasy and personal conscience. By contrast, poor Leonora was so traumatised she couldn't even look at photos. Namita, glancing back as she left the room, saw the one picture of Ursa was on the wall behind Leonora's TV chair. It was in the one place Leonora wouldn't see very often.

To an incongruous soundtrack of daytime-TV sofa-laughs, Namita sifted the box, sorting its contents into piles. Ephemera. Photos. Letters. Postcards.

Her first quick scan removed three quarters of the content. School stuff and friendly but inconsequential letters. She was left with what appeared to be material from 1965 up to her death.

Ephemera. A cheaply made handbill for a production of a Pinter play in 1965 at the Hampstead Theatre. Ursa and Bella were both on the cast list, but at the bottom. Not leading roles then? A photo ad for soap powder with Ursa grinning in a perfect 60s kitchen. A page torn from a directory of actors and actresses. Ursa's entry listed a few more small productions. Nothing major. *Her acting career seems to be small scale, but she's being jetted all over the world for film parts. Very odd.*

Photos. A few atmospheric black and white snaps of Ursa with Bella, Ursa with Rose, Ursa with both of them. The photo that struck her most looked like it had been taken against her will at a party. Wine glasses everywhere. Ursa sported a gorgeous mini-skirt and blouse, looking sexy and fresh. Yet, she had her hand up as if asking the photographer to leave her alone. A copy of The Beatles' Revolver was visible. Namita checked on her phone. The album came out in August '66. Checking her notes, she saw that Ursa got back from her final trip in September '66. There were no signs of Christmas, so it was probably a party somewhere between September '66 and Ursa returning home to Bristol on October 31st, 1967. Wherever the party had been, it wasn't in this house.

She found the picture of Ursa and Brigitte Bardot. They were smoking and laughing. Two beautiful blondes. An attractive man - Caron? - had his arm around Bardot. Leonora was right: Ursa had held her own against the biggest pin-up of all time.

Letters. There was a letter from Los Angeles in 1966. She couldn't make out the date on the faded envelope.

> *Dear Mum and Dad,*
>
> *I feel like I'm in a Beach Boys' song! I travelled up The Strip today in Don's T-Bird, top down, sun in my hair, singing along to Mr Tambourine Man on the radio. It's like a dream come true. We had burgers and shakes at a diner. Oh my God. You haven't had a burger till you've had an American one! I couldn't even fit it into my mouth! Had to squash it flat. It tasted amazing. I'm not sure what they make the burgers from over here, but it's not the same meat we get at the Co-op.*

All the people at the film studio are amazing. I've met lots of girls and boys here who are also trying to break into films. I don't know what will happen with the audition, but they certainly know how to look after people. They give you amazing salads and fruit juices while you're waiting. I could live here!

The only bad thing so far were the flights! Oh my God - the one to New York wasn't too bad, but I was sure the propellor was going to fall off on the way to Los Angeles. Maybe I shouldn't become famous because the famous fly all the time, don't they?

But don't worry - I feel perfectly safe and so happy to be here. Will write properly, soon.

Lots of love,

Ursa

(Can you please give each other a hug and pretend it's from me)

There was another letter from New York. This time she could just make out the date. March 28th, 1966. She was posting from the Wolcott Hotel.

Dear Mum and Dad,

Still waiting to hear how my audition turned out in LA. It went ok, I think. The director said that if I was going back through New York, I should meet a buddy of his (see I'm turning into an American - don't think I'd have said 'buddy' before this trip). But in this case, it literally was a 'buddy' - Buddy Demsky, who directs movies from New York. He took me out to dinner and said I had a real interesting look. He doesn't have a movie to cast right now, but said if I had time, to come to the studios tomorrow and they would do a screen test with me. So who knows, in future, I might get to star in one of his films. He's made films with Gregory Peck, James Coburn and Rosemary Clooney! Can you imagine? All those people seem so far away to us over in the UK. Here they talk about them as if they are the same as the man who works down the sweet shop. I guess I'll have to get used to it!

I thought of you, Dad, as soon as I saw the Empire State Building. You cannot believe how tall it is. It made me feel sick just looking up at it from the base. One of Buddy's assistant, a lovely woman called Ruth, took me to the top! I thought I was going to die I was so scared. My legs were shaking. But the views were incredible. I so wish you could see it, Dad.

And Mum, wait for it… guess who stayed in this hotel? Buddy Holly. Can you believe it?

Well, the rest of my American trip beckons. Yep, the food is good here too. I will probably be back before this letter reaches you and will struggle to get into my favourite miniskirt.

Lots of love, missing you more than I can say.
Ursa.

There was also a letter from Berlin dated July 9th, 1966. It didn't say where she was staying.

Dear Mum and Dad,
After all the excitement of LA, New York and Rome, Berlin is the first place I've been to that I don't like.

Maybe I'm not cut out to be a traveller after all? My hotel is ok, but the city is in an even worse state than London. There are still bombsites everywhere. It gives me chills sometimes to see walls that are covered in huge holes left by bullets in the war. How anyone can have survived at all is beyond me. It's a bleak place and a bit scary. I walked over to where the American Sector ends and saw Checkpoint Charlie, and a soldier pointed his rifle at me! I was so frightened. My legs were still shaking when I got back to the hotel and had a bath.

German sausages are horrible. Really tight, and they pop when you bite into them - not to mention all the horrible boiled cabbage called sauerkraut they put on them.

I'm beginning to wonder if I'll actually ever get a role in a movie, though I guess it's the film crew's job to encourage me and make me feel like it went really well. Heinrich the director is ok. What do I have to do? Never mind. At least I got to travel a bit.

See you soon.
Ursa.

Ursa's change of tone was striking. New York and LA were obviously great for her, but in her sign-off to her parents, Namita picked up a more weary, jaded tone.

Postcards. There was a few, but none had anything special written on the back. They looked like the equivalent of whatsapp messages. She did her best to decipher the date stamps and put them in chronological order.

March 25th, 1966 - Sunset Boulevard, LA
To Mum and Dad…
Had to send this…I'm getting bugged driving up the same old strip?
I don't think so!
Love you, Ursa.

March 29th, 1966 - The Empire State Building, NYC
I can see for miles! Wish you were here! Love, Ursa xxx

May 1st, 1966 - The Trevi Fountain, Rome
I threw a coin in and wished you both the longest, happiest lives of anyone on Earth.
Love you both, Ursa. X

May 5th, 1966 - Trafalgar Square, London
We've been feeding the pigeons all day and thought we should send you a picture!
Love from Ursa (and Bella and Rose).

Sept 4th, 1966 - Eiffel Tower, Paris
Pretty!
Love you both.

Sept 6th, 1966 - La Follies Bergere, Paris
Paris is so pretty. Brigitte is so pretty!
Can't wait to get home to England and see you both again.
Save a hug for me,
Your loving daughter,
Ursa

Namita snapped some photos and batch uploaded them to Dropbox. When she got back to the front room, Leonora was fast asleep, gently snoring. She didn't want to wake her, so Namita returned the box, took the cups and saucers and washed them. Leonora was still out, so Namita wrote a note, attached her phone number and told her she could call anytime - even if it was just to chat.

Namita closed the door as gently as she could and dialled for a cab. Where to now? To stay or not to stay? To see Martin again or not to see Martin again? As Martin Skelling's phone rang, Namita could feel a warmth inside her, she hadn't felt since her student days.

Chapter 21

October 31st, 2017
Kaffee Schwarzer, Wilhelmshavener Strasse, Berlin

Porter and Feng didn't waste a second. They immediately found a coffee shop and ordered drinks.

Namita called and told them about Ursa's visit to Berlin in 1966. Huddled in a corner on speakerphone, Feng and Porter agreed with Namita: Ursa presumably came for an audition too - her letter dated July 9th, 1966, mentioned film crew. They also agreed it probably wasn't that important - Ursa was in Berlin but made it home in one piece, not dying until two years later, at her own hand. But the city and film were something Rose and Ursa had in common. Worth looking at.

Once Namita had gone, they googled over muffins. After a bit of research, they found SpellenGross Studios was long since defunct as both physical and creative entity. It had been entirely owned and managed by the controversial German director, Heinrich Becker. When he died in the mid-80s, the studios closed with him. The chances of finding staff or paperwork to shed light on Rose and Ursa's experiences auditioning now gone, they went to the library to see what they had on Becker. Answer: plenty. However, it was all in German and way beyond the scope of Feng's *Good morning - can I have a latte* handle on der Wortschatz Deutsche.

Resorting to Google, they were relieved that a recent biography, Das Licht, had also been published in English as The Light. Porter bought it and opened it on his Kindle app. By the time they'd read the foreword, they were excited again. The author lived in Berlin. Biographers have access to documents, papers, records. The foreword confirmed Max Fascher knew Becker and curated his estate. He might be able to help. Besides, his pretentious foreword had them giggling.

> *When things turn dark, when the shutters are down, we crave The Light to re-imagine the world. Without illumination we are all cave animals, sheltering from our predators, unsure what lies around the corner. Never-ending dark brings fear, uncertainty and pain. We humans need The Light. We need it as sure as the plants if we are to grow.*
>
> *But what is The Light? The literal should abandon ship now, for the sun has little to do with The Light.*
>
> *To find it we must look to the Humanities, the Social Sciences, the Arts.*
>
> *What makes a great artist, great? Mozart, Da Vinci, Shakespeare, Sartre - even Bob Dylan. The answer, of course, is that they bring The Light to us all. They expose the corners and holes of the psyche and push us out of our caves into a bigger, brighter world.*
>
> *And so, at last to my friend and mentor, Heinrich Becker. Did any German filmmaker ever produce a richer body of work designed to illuminate? His work ranged from grand failed experiments to the heights of sublime, but his worth and contribution cannot be measured piece by piece, by box office receipts, or by 5-star reviews.*

His best work is quoted by intelligent Germans everywhere, not just as words, but as a mode of living, a way of approaching the world and its conundrums.

Despite the unfounded mutually exclusive allegations of a Nazi and Communist past, Becker was a key part in re-shaping pre-war sensibilities to those of the modern era. Audiences saw that his shame for Germany's sins was their shame too. His dialogue with himself, through film, became Germany's dialogue with itself.

Although Becker died in 1986, his work lives on. I worked with him from 1982-86, when I was a very young man, and he was a very old man. I was just starting out as a writer; he had all but completed his life's work. We became close and he allowed me to interview him many times. I have managed his estate, represented his interests, protected his reputation, and been instrumental in the development of the forthcoming Becker Haus - a publicly funded museum, located in his final residence in Charlottenburg, Berlin.

2017 marks the 35th anniversary of our meeting. Some may think this is too long to spend in the shadow of one artist. Say it not. For the darkness he banished, for the holes he filled, for the wisdom he gave, I, for one, am proud to still be sharing The Light of one of Germany's greatest artists.

*Max Fascher,
Berlin. Jan. 2017*

"*For the holes he filled?* I'm Jules, this is my friend, Sandy," said Feng, impersonating the camp character from the old BBC radio show, Round the Horne. "Pompous old windbag. This won't be a biography; it'll be a hagiography."

"I'm not reading the whole bloody thing," said Porter. "It'll be a waste of time. Let's just do searches for *SpellenGross, Rose, missing, 1967, audition,* etc and see what comes up."

"I'm surprised you two haven't been triggered by the words *Nazi* and *Communist*," said The Gliss.

"Alright, add *Nazi* and *Communist*," said Porter.

There were plenty of references to SpellenGross because it was the studio Becker set up in 1952. It was his creative workshop as well as the administrative hub for his film company. SpeleenGross had generated plenty of hits and quite a lot more misses. Bar 1964's staple of Western cinema, Die Schwachen und Die Gauche (The Feeble and The Gauche), neither Feng nor Porter recognised a single title.

"That's a terrible film," said Porter, shuddering. "My art teacher at VI Form seemed to think it was the best film ever made."

"It can't be that bad," said Feng, "It won Best Film at the 1964 Venice Film Festival."

"So? More often than not The Oscars pick the tamest of the year," said The Gliss.

"Oh no, here he comes - Leonard Maltin reincarnated," said Porter.

"Well, I'm a messenger, not a Blockbuster customer, but of course, I can now see everything you four have seen. That's a lot of films. Thanks to Porter, I know every line of Home Alone and the lyrics to every musical since talkies began. Yes, I feel very cultured. Mr Tian, in particular, has a very, shall we say, broad range of filmic interests. Stallions Volume 7, if I remember correctly?"

"Yes, well, thank you for your wisdom and insight," said Porter, as Feng scowled. "The Feeble and The Gauche was a truly terrible film in which a young man creeps around Berlin in the dark, staring at women he fancies, until they realise they're being stalked, then he loses interest. Awful, pretentious shit."

"Yes, I saw it too," said Feng. "Wasn't it a parable about the perils of putting one's faith in a consumerist society that discards you as soon as you cannot afford to consume? I think that's what I was told?"

"No, it was an unbelievable tale of a willy-twitcher who harasses women," said Porter.

"Gentlemen," said The Gliss, "having now concluded that Herr Becker was no Speilberg, perhaps we could move on to more important things?"

They learned that the studios, built from the remnants of a factory in Voltastraße, Mitte, were knocked down the year Becker died and replaced by housing in 1988. It was Becker's house in Charlottenburg that Fascher was turning into a museum.

References to 1967 included Becker's bust for smoking marijuana, a whole bunch of anecdotes about a movie filmed in Munich, Schweinefleisch, but nothing about auditions. The only time the word even came up was in an anecdote about a row between Becker and Marlene Dietrich. Unsurprisingly, neither the words Rose nor Ursa cropped up.

Searching the words Nazi and Communist, however, brought up whole chapters.

"Oh no, we've got the Cold War and now we've got World War II," groaned Porter.

Feng and Porter read that 45-year-old Heinrich Becker came into some money in 1947 and decided to invest in his long-term hobby of making film.

He funded, produced and directed his first film himself. Becker could only afford two prints for distribution. One he kept for screening in Berlin, the other he gave to a picture house in Munich. To his, and everyone's amazement, Die Längste Nacht, became a hit. The cinema in Munich, realising it was selling more tickets for this film than any other, paid to have more copies made. Word of mouth spread. Soon it was showing all over Germany. Its two stars, Irene Scoll and Hugo Felix, became household names in West Germany overnight.

Then the trouble began. In June 1949, a survivor of Flossenbürg Concentration Camp, Helene Hirsch, alleged that Heinrich Becker was in fact, a Nazi war criminal, **SS Obergruppenführer Heinz Hartmann**. Becker was shocked and appalled by the accusation and said he'd been a clerical assistant, drafted into the army against his wishes, and was never a member of the Nazi Party, let alone the SS.

Intrigued, the German newspapers tried to source Becker's army records. These had been destroyed with millions of others during the final days of the war when the Russians assaulted Berlin. However, photographs of Heinz Hartmann were easily found and published with comparison photos of Becker. The pictures split public opinion because there were clear similarities, but also clear differences. Hirsch said the differences were nothing that could not be explained by plastic surgery during the two years after the war when both Hartmann and Becker seemed to generate no records.

Hartmann had been a top-level Nazi. During the whole of the Nazi era, only 106 men ever held the position of Obergruppenführer including such notorious figures as Reinhard Heydrich, Rudolf Hess and Theodor Eicke. Hartmann held the title within the Waffen-SS, the military branch of the SS. During the Nuremberg Trials which followed Germany's defeat, the Waffen-SS was declared a criminal organisation. Its 38 divisions took part in many atrocities and many of its members were denied the rights of other military personnel and prosecuted.

Helene Hirsch said she'd witnessed Hartmann shoot Jews in the head for fun at Flossenbürg, one of Germany's six domestic concentration camps, tucked away on the Czech border.

Unfortunately, Hartmann was never found, closing off the quickest means for Becker to clear his name and reputation. There were rumours the Nazi had fled to Argentina. Hartmann remains on the Most Wanted list to this day, though would be 112 if still alive.

No decisive physical evidence that Becker was Hartmann was ever uncovered, and the German public ultimately recognised this, enjoying his films and celebrating his work for the remainder of his life. Fascher's book dwelt on Becker's response.

"It was bad during the witch-hunt," said Becker. "But when I look back on it, the mistaken identity led to a certain amount of valuable publicity which would have been hard to find otherwise. I prefer it had not happened, but that it did held no detriment in the long haul."

The controversy didn't stop there. During the 1960s, Becker was accused of being a spy for the Russians. Becker, who despised Communists, brushed it off as muckraking by factions in the Jewish community who could not/would not let go of the Nazi allegation.

"I have no problem with any group or religion," he told me, "but that specific group of Jews who were after me made my life hell, and I have no love for them."

SpellenGross Studios were targeted several times by Jewish activists who pasted notices and leaflets exposing Becker's alleged connections with the Russians on its walls. At one point, it is believed an assassination attempt by rifle was attempted. Becker heard the shot as he walked around the courtyard, but no trace of bullet was ever found.

"It's ridiculous," he said in 1981. "What was I? A Communist or a Fascist? I couldn't possibly be both, could I? They even said Die Schwachen und Die Gauche was Communist propaganda. Insane! I admit to being only one type of *ist*: an art*ist*. It is the only designation I will accept."

"Interesting, but we're not getting very far," said Porter. "We need to contact this Fascher bloke and see if he'll talk to us. It'd be great to see what paperwork he has. Which I doubt he'll show us."

"Are you serious?" said Feng. "Every line, every word, every letter of this doo-doo of a book says the author is so up his own arse, that his head is hanging out his mouth. Tell him you want to do a documentary on his book, on Becker. He'll tell you everything."

"What are we looking for?" asked The Gliss.

"Well, if he's curated Becker's estate, maybe there's not just paperwork but diaries, screen test footage…"

"If I might butt in?" said The Gliss. "Becker's probably buried in Berlin too. Porter could visit the grave."

They looked it up. Becker was buried in Städtischer Friedhof III, just south of the Stadtring. Ironically, it was also where Marlene Dietrich was buried. Whatever beef they had in real life they were partnered together in death.

They fired off an email to Fascher, hopeful rather than expectant, and decided to head to the grave.

October 31st, 2017
Städtischer Friedhof III Cemetery, Berlin

"I don't like cemeteries anymore," said Porter. They used to be quiet places of reflection, somewhere I could go to work out where I was going wrong, maybe even begin to work out solutions."

"And now?" asked Feng.

"Now, it's like living inside the Ministry of Sound's PA system whilst being slowly grilled. I've been learning how to deflect the unnecessary voices, honing-in on whoever it is I'm focusing on, but it's still very painful."

The Gliss coughed. "You may have treated my requests to train like a teenage boy responds to parental demands to take a shower, but there was a reason for my endeavours."

"Whatever," said Porter, sounding, indeed, like a teenager.

In common with all German cemeteries and their strict rules about upkeep, Städtischer Friedhof III was both beautifully landscaped and yet, fuelled by an abundance of nutrients in the soil, bordered on unkempt. The trees and plants flourished faster than they could be maintained.

As they walked down the aisles, Porter's phone rang. It was his sister, Cherry. "Where the hell have you been?," she cursed. "I've got to get this bloody will sorted out."

Porter mouthed *Cherry* to Feng, who rolled his eyes. Taking a deep breath, he said, "Cherry, I'm in Berlin, working and..."

"Berlin? I thought you were in America?"

"That was last week. How are you?"

"Trying to sort a will out, handling all the paperwork, while my brother, who apparently has no money, is galavanting around the world, sightseeing and leaving it all to me to make sure he gets some."

"And Scott and Ruby are ok?"

"Sod them… yes, yes, of course they're ok…question is, when are you going to get back to me on my offer?"

Porter thought for a second and said, "I'm not going to say anything else about this. You know the right thing to do. You disagree with me about what that is. Do what you have to, but I'm not condoning the choice. Whatever you want to do, do it. You can make your own peace with your conscience." He added, sarcastically,"I'm sure Ida would say the same thing."

There was a silence only the dead knew while Cherry considered her option. "Twat," she said, and ended the call.

"Oh dear," said Feng. "No movement on that then?"

"I'm not moving on that, no." He looked at the map and pointed. "Becker's grave should be three rows back, two to the left over there."

The Gliss, following like a leashless dog, said, "It's a bit desperate this, I know, but we're not getting very far with the investigation at the moment, are we?"

"No, we're not," said Porter. "But SpellenGross was the pet project of Becker. It doesn't look as though any other film producers worked there, which means Rose, and maybe Ursa, auditioned for him. We know they left there safe, but with so few leads…"

Feng agreed. "It's been lovely visiting Berlin, but I do think we're wasting our time until we get some concrete leads on Rose."

They got to the curb leading to the gravel path adjacent to Becker's row. Feng and The Gliss were familiar with the ritual now. Porter would stand, blow out his cheeks in trepidation, step close to the grave and then hop in. Usually, while Porter sunk into the Quincunx world, Feng and The Gliss would watch as he lost consciousness of them, wriggling and twitching like a catfish on a pole.

The three of them took up their usual positions. Porter gave them a wish-me-luck look, blew his cheeks out and walked past the graves surrounding Becker's. He had to concentrate hard not to be distracted by the voices coming from them. The German-speaking voices dragged at him like quicksand. He got to Becker's headstone, took a breath, and hopped on and in.

Porter was in a hospital ward. A very old man was laying on a bed. He was being given oxygen via a nose tube. A cannula on his left hand was connected to saline, a cannula on his right was connected to something smaller with valves. Morphine probably. His eyes were closed, and the machines emitted hums and pings. So far, so ER. A young black nurse was pottering at the end of the bed, making notes. Porter knew he was looking at Becker's last few seconds and was disappointed they were inert and told him nothing.

Then Becker opened his eyes. He scarcely had any voice left. He reedily whispered, "Komm her, bitte." The nurse looked up and smiled, but her face suggested she hadn't heard properly, because she didn't immediately respond. He repeated it. "Komm her, bitte." She still did not move.

Becker's eyes opened as wide as plates and said, so spitefully that Porter thought he was hissing, "Komm her, du kleine nigger-hure!" Porter didn't speak German but was in no doubt about the hatred in the words. The nurse, in shock, stepped forward. Becker's arm reached out and fumbled for the fork on his plate. He tried to hold it like a dagger, but it slipped and fell.

The nurse, finding her voice, shouted, "Herr Becker! Rede nicht so…!" Incensed at losing his grip on the fork, he reached further, grabbed a tray and flung its contents at the poor nurse. Faeces and urine hit her face and tunic. "Heil Hitler, nigger-hure!" His back arched, his eyes popped a little wider, he flopped back, dead. The scene looped back to the beginning. Porter forced himself to watch again. And again. He wanted to make sure he could remember the insult.

Porter tried to stand up. It was like someone had placed a cartoon 1-ton barbell on his back. He pushed, he strained, but was halfway through the loop's fifth play before he was able to break out of the Quincunx back into the real world.

He opened his eyes to find Feng and The Gliss staring at him expectantly. Catching his breath was long enough for The Gliss to read his mind. The Gliss said, "Oh!"

Feng cried out, "What is it? What happened? What did you see?"

Massaging his chin for a comfort he couldn't readily achieve, Porter said, "That was horrible. Just horrible. This guy is on our radar."

Feng looked at him amazed. "He said something about Rose?"

Porter shook his head. "But I'd put money on one thing: he wasn't a bloody Communist. Becker was a murderous, racist, seriously unrepentant, full-bodied, Nazi." He shook his head, sickened by what he'd seen. "Heinrich Becker bloody well was Heinz Hartmann. Becker was the guy who shot Jews in the head for fun. And if he was capable of that…"

Chapter 22

October 31st, 2017
LA Central Library, LA

Karin was nine hours behind the boys. They were about to go for an evening meal; she was still an hour from lunch after her early start with Sam. Her phone pinged. It was Feng saying he had updated Dropbox.

She read the content, eyes-wide and gawping. That was another documentary right there: the murdering Nazi who hid in plain sight in Germany. Snapping out of it, Karin, who was more of a critical thinker than the others, wondered if there was likely to be a connection between their case and Becker. Re-reading the digests Feng and Namita had been uploading. She drew a little timeline.

Jan 3	Jan 4	Jan 5
Rose arrives in Berlin	Auditions at SpellenGross	Checks out. 8pm flight unused. **Fake letter sent**
	<u>OVERNIGHT @ DIETRICHS</u>	<u>OVERNIGHT @ DIETRICHS</u>
	Mr Dietrich drives her	Turns down lift offer to airport
	Witnesses see her leave	Doesn't call mum
	Arrives back at Dietrichs	Leaves Dietrichs
	Doesn't call her mum	

So, we don't know what was going through her mind when she arrived, she did what she was supposed to on January 4th. It's the final day that's the mystery. Karin sat back and sighed. It was time to call in Rekka.

Rekka was Karin's abstract-thinking trick. While it's crucial to gather hard evidence to corroborate theories, that very requirement often held researchers and journalists from committing to a testable theory in the first place. Karin got around it by imagining herself as Rekka Laslow, a horrible schoolfriend she hadn't seen for 30 years. Rekka was a bitch who gathered girls around her and speculated on their crimes and misdemeanours. She was vicious, but she was often accurate because she had an innate handle on human psychology.

Picking up the timeline, Karin let herself go. *Time to be a bitch*.

Of course, her fancy man paid for the flight and board. She was just a skivvy. She couldn't afford it. She probably spent the night at the landlady's rehearsing her lines, right? She must have learnt from her failed experience in LA. She knew the score now. No mistakes this time. Typical struggling actor - never understanding when it's time to quit. Unless she really was a spy like crazy Rutland thought?

Karin shook her head. *I can't see it. She's too ordinary.* She decided to assume Rose really was what she looked like: a desperate actress.

The weather was bad, so of course she accepted a lift to the studio. Lazy cow, true. but probably saved her from looking bedraggled when she got to the audition - just another little edge. And listen to her talk to her mum on that postcard - <u>there were lots of nice girls and boys there</u>, *she said - so the audition went normally, might even have gone well. But she left and went back to her lodgings. Why didn't she go drinking with all the nice girls and boys then? She was young, she was British; surely she'd naturally want to network with other actors. If she was a spy, wouldn't she have gone out and done some spying?*

If she didn't party or spy and just went home, well, she obviously didn't meet the love of her life either! The fake letter on Jan 5th? There wasn't time!

And why didn't she call her mum with news? Because she didn't have news. During the audition she got a "we'll let you know" just like all the other lame actors. Unless the dirty old man director asked her to come back for a second audition next day, when the studio was empty?

Why didn't she accept Dietrich's second offer of a lift to the airport? The weather was still bad. Why wouldn't she want a lift like before? Had Mr Dietrich hit on her the previous day? But if he had, wouldn't she have said something to Mrs Dietrich? She couldn't walk to the airport. She'd have had to get a cab.

However, she wouldn't need a lift to the studios though. It wasn't that long a walk; just a cold one. And this time she maybe didn't mind looking a bit bedraggled?

What if she'd met a boy the previous day and arranged to meet him before going to the airport? No way. If it was a boy, she'd have made the most of her time and met him the previous night, surely?

It was freezing cold, she didn't have to leave Berlin until the evening, but she checked out early and refused a lift. She took her luggage with her. She was either meeting one of the actors from the day before, or the only other person she knew in Berlin: the man who could make her famous, the film director.

Karin sat back. It didn't mean it happened that way. But there weren't many options.

1. A stranger abducted her.
2. She met someone and ran off with them.
3. She had some kind of follow-up to her audition the previous day.
4. She was involved in some kind of accident that was covered up.
5. The Russians bumped her off for spying.

Karin read and re-read her list. Rose came for a very short trip to audition. What was the most likely of those options? Number 3. Every time. And the director turns out to have been a former Nazi who murdered people for fun.

October 31st, 2017
Big Al's, Bristol

Namita refused to dress up in Halloween costume for anyone, let alone a man she hardly knew taking her out for a supposed romantic dinner.

"Just put a witch's hat on… it'll be a laugh. You can take it off while we eat," Martin had said.

"No, chance. Can we eat early?" Namita reasoned a light meal, then a hotel as early as possible, equalled the most fun. *You're going to screw him again? Why the hell not.*

"Ok, I'll book us a table at 6.30pm at Big Al's," he said, without asking her what kind of food she fancied.

When she got to the rough and ready bistro, she was shocked to find Martin already laughing and drinking with a group of boisterous men in suits. Martin wasn't in fancy dress. *Well, wouldn't you have looked stupid?* Disconcerted, she stared at Martin's back, not knowing what to do. One of the men nudged Martin.

He turned, saw her and beamed. "Namita!" He walked over, pecked her on the cheek and put his arm over her shoulder. "Here she is! Isn't she beautiful?"

A cold chill ran through Namita. *Here she is.* He had been talking about her. Another chill. She knew immediately the men had been told she'd done the dirty. His arm over her shoulder said it all. He was marking his territory. *This one's mine, lads.*

She remembered something the actress Meera Syal once said about her white boyfriends: they wore her like an exotic charm bracelet. She instantly knew what Syal meant. It was only one step to supposing he'd boasted about his prowess, or worse, hers. Drunk, she could easily picture him saying, "She's got great tits."

One look at the pack confirmed it. Martin's friends were gawping like lions sizing up a gazelle. Every pack of men has a diffident one. Namita sought him out. As soon as she caught his shifty eye, he looked away, unable to cope with her X-ray vision. He was ashamed.

These thoughts took seconds, during which time Martin had manoeuvred her in front of the gaggle. Almost against her will, she found herself shaking hands with Biffo, Tim, Klaus, Herring and Balders.

Sangita piped up. "I hate to say I told you so..."

Namita smiled at the men. She nodded for Sangita's benefit. But the speech in her head was directed at Martin. "As soon as I get Florence's will locked down, you're toast, mate."

Chapter 23

October 18th, 1965
The Coach and Horses, Greek Street, Soho.

Ursa pushed her bob back behind her ears, took the fag out of her mouth, and passed it to Rose. "Be a pet and hold this for me," she laughed, before bending and blowing out the candles on Bella's homemade seedcake.

The pub's raucous clientele broke into a spirited version of Happy Birthday making a cacophonous racket during the "dear Ursa" bit as none knew her name. A single-toothed, Peter Cushing-cheeked old man, led the drunken singalong.

"Cheers me darlings!" shouted Ursa to the strangers in the pub. Taking her fag back from Rose, she pulled the candles out and chopped the cake into three. "Well, it's not going too bad is it? Who'd have thought I'd be celebrating my 22nd in London?"

"Not too bad? I wish we could afford a few more shillings for the meter," said Bella. "That flat's colder than a snowman's arse."

"Miniskirts are murder, aren't they?" said Rose. "My legs are like ice-pops."

"Yeah, and if you bend over in the street the workmen can see what you had for breakfast," laughed Ursa. "If I ever meet Mary Quant, I'm going to punch her face in."

"Too right," said Bella. "I mean, I love the colours, and they're cool, right? But these things were designed for men, not women."

"Well, if we all end up with legs like our mums it's probably better to enjoy 'em while we can," said Rose. "Ice-pops or not."

"Yeah, me mum's legs look an A-Z map of Venice there are so many blue lines," said Ursa.

"Disgusting," said Rose. "I miss my mum - legs 'n' all."

For a few sentimental seconds they ate their cake in silence. The barman sidled over.

"Can I treat you ladies to a birthday drink on the house?" He whipped three small bottles of Babycham and a bottle opener from behind his back.

"Ooh! Ta, Johnny!" clapped Ursa.

"I owe you one," said Johnny. It can get a bit dingy in here, right? You three always bring a bit of colour in. You look like a pop group. Wait, I'll get the glasses."

The three friends sniggered. "So funny," said Rose, "imagine us three in a group! We can't sing to save our lives... well, you two can't anyway!"

Johnny put the glasses down and poured the drinks. "To my favourite customers…"

A drunk with Brylcreemed hair shouted, "Oi! We are 'ere you know."

Speaking over the good-natured jeering, Johnny said, "Alright Chas, calm down. To my new favourite customers then... in a pub full of old favourite customers. Happy birthday, young lady!"

Johnny, Ursa, Bella and Rose clinked glasses.

"Do you mind me asking what you girls do?" said Johnny. "You don't sound from around these parts?"

"We're from Bristol," said Ursa, turning up the burr. "Can't you tell, my love?"

"We're actresses," said Bella. A few of the older customers laughed. "We are," she protested. "The critics said my Cleopatra was sublime."

"Well, you should see my Anthony," leered one man with a Bobby Charlton comb-over. A couple of his mates laughed and letched with him.

"Ignore them," said Johnny. In a quieter voice, he said, "You're ok though, right? It's hard getting work round here." Their three glum faces spoke the collective truth. "Look, my mate Clem runs a few bars in Soho. He's always looking for pretty girls - hostesses, dancers, you know." Off their look, he quickly added, "Nothing smutty. But I can put you in touch if you like? He pays well. You must have heard about Rock Hudson and people like that drinking up West? Well, it's Clem's bars they go to."

The Bristol Girls looked to each other for reactions, none daring to take the lead. But Ursa, whose nose was just in front, said, "We could speak to him. Wouldn't do any harm, would it, girls?"

"That's right," said Johnny. "We've all got to put shillings in the meter."

Whether it was Ursa's tentative yes, or Johnny unconsciously resonating their biggest fear - the heating going off - Rose and Bella nodded too.

"Right," said Johnny. "Let me give him a tinkle… you stay there, enjoy your cake and bubbly."

Chapter 24

October 31st, 2017
The Scheiner Inn, Kreutzburg, Berlin

By midnight, Porter and Feng were a bit piddly.

After leaving the cemetery, Porter refused to talk more until he had a litre of beer in front of him. He told Feng and The Gliss everything he'd seen. They jotted down Becker's last words; useless in a court of law, but 100% useful to them. Feng had uploaded the notes to Dropbox.

Karin had read them, found their account chimed with her own conclusions, and called for a stuttery video chat from LA. They all agreed it was worth pursuing the Becker lead. She offered to research him from the States. Feng told her he'd already been contacted by Max Fascher. The conversation had gone exactly as Feng had predicted. *A documentary, you say? For the BBC? How can I help?* They'd arranged to meet Fascher at Becker Haus first thing tomorrow before they flew home.

After the day's work, Porter and Feng both wanted to relax. It had been the longest Halloween Porter could ever remember - and one of the most unpleasant. He gulped on a third bierkrug. Feng was still on his second. "Good stuff," he said, foam giving his top lip a white David Niven tache.

"Interesting place, Berlin," said Feng. "Nothing seems to open until midnight. That's what I call nightlife."

"Let's not overdo it, gentlemen," advised The Gliss, "We've got a guided tour of Becker's house tomorrow. We don't want the tour to start with the toilet bowl, do we?"

"There are two things about that vision I don't think I'll ever get out of my head," said Porter, toasting The Gliss as if to say, "Bugger off." He looked at Feng. "The hatred. I have never seen anything like it. If Pelenot had been behind those eyes, I could have believed it." Feng shuddered.

"The other thing was the look of shock and hurt on the black nurse's face. There she was doing her job, not the most pleasant job either, and this vile man calls her a 'nigger bitch' and flings shit and piss all over her. She actually stood still for a few seconds, blinking as the liquid ran down her face. It was disgusting. I wanted to step out of my vision and punch him."

Feng looked the incident up in Fascher's book. There was no mention of it. Despite Becker's fame in Germany, the deathbed horror obviously hadn't leaked.

"It was the hospital," murmured a man sitting next to Porter, angled away from him until now. Turning, he said, more confidently, "You think the hospital would allow something like that to get out? They bought their own member of staff off." He saw their *who-the-hell* looks and said, "Efrayim Davidov, pleased to meet you. Drink?"

Porter and Feng were so surprised, they just nodded.

"So, my friends, you are looking into that disgusting creature, Heinrich Becker?" Davidov said. "What are you trying to find out about him, may I ask?"

"Er, who's asking?" Porter finally found the gumption to say. "I mean, I know your name. Where are you from. What's it got to do with you?"

"Let's just say I represent the interests of some of the thousands this vile monster murdered," said the man.

"Thousands?" said Feng.

"Thousands - at Flossenbürg and beyond."

"And you represent their interests?" reiterated Feng. "I presume you're Jewish?"

"Efrayim Davidov? What do I need? A badge?" He started laughing. "A poor joke in Berlin, perhaps. Tell me what you're trying to find out. I may be able to help you."

Porter was on the verge of replying, when Feng took control. "You know he's been dead since 1986, right? We can't help you find him. What can you do to help his victims now? And how did you know we were looking for him? Answer those questions first, please."

Davidov nodded and considered the request. "Ok. Deal." He shook hands with them both.

Davidov said he worked for a group of Israeli financiers who'd set up a small working group to track down former Nazis never brought to justice.

"They are nearly all dead, yes," he said, "but their descendants are often living on the spoils of war. My job is to correct the historical record and prosecute for the return of assets - money, jewellery, artwork, property. These are either recovered or liquidated and returned to the descendants of their original owners. By this way we have funded doctors, scientists, humanitarians who otherwise might have lost their opportunities."

"Oh God," said Porter. "I'm glad Namita's not here: we'd be having that whole conversation about slavery and reparations again."

"I don't know what you mean by that," said Davidov, "but surely you do not think it right that people should profit off the misery of others - especially if these were Holocaust victims - killed, tortured, separated from families? This is a stain that money alone cannot cleanse. But there is natural justice too."

Feng said, "You know, I think I agree. Everyone agrees crime victims should be compensated. But isn't the other side of that argument that those who profited from the spoils of war should be uncompensated?"

"Not politics," said Porter, "anything but politics."

"It needs a political solution, agreed," said Davidov. "But surely what we are talking about here is ethics?"

"Well, Mr Davidov," said Porter, "You may have a point. I can't tell you how we know, but you were right - Becker was Heinz Hartmann. I'm 100% certain of that."

"How can this be?" said Davidov, astonished. "Can it be that you have new witnesses after all this time? Tell me more, please."

"We do have a new eye-witness - of a sort," said Porter, cautiously. "But we haven't finished investigating yet. If it suits us all, we can stay in touch, if you like. But first, tell me something. Becker was accused of being both Nazi and a Communist. What do you know? Do you think he was also a spy for the Soviets? As cover maybe?"

Davidov simply laughed. "Why would he have done that? He jettisoned his true political views after the war. Any political position he held on the left was for show. That's not what this man's - how say you? - bag was. The German authorities did very little in the 60s or 70s to find and prosecute Nazi war criminals. Their job was to rebuild Germany and move on. Becker became famous and feted. He successfully covered up his transition from Hartmann to Becker.

"In truth, only the Simon Wiesenthal Institute actively pursued people like him during the 60s and 70s. By the time official investigations began in the 80s, many Nazi origin stories were well hidden."

The Gliss, hovering in silence all this time, whispered to Feng and Porter, "He's telling the truth. Confide a little. It may help."

Feng nodded and opened up. "We're looking into the case of a British girl who went missing in Berlin in 1967. Her name was Rose Prideaux. One of the last people to see her alive was Becker. He auditioned her and she may have gone for a second meeting the following day. Either way, she was never seen again. We're just hoping to get a breakthrough while we're here."

Porter added, "We heard Hartmann killed people for fun. That's our worry, right now."

Davidov nodded. "Yes, he was a terrible monster. But you interest me. As far as we know he did not kill anyone after the war. It wasn't in his interests. He was rich and famous. But the leopard does not change its spots, no? Either way, you will need proof. 1967. That is a long time ago."

Davidov pushed over new beers for them, though he was only drinking iced water. Porter and Feng toasted him. Feng said, "The other question was - how did you find out about us?"

"Anyone who researches people like Hartmann/Becker will eventually come to our notice. But if I may let you in on a secret?" Porter and Feng nodded eagerly. "The biographer. Fascher. He's a fool who chooses to ignore the mountain of evidence about Becker's past. But, of course, we have long since hacked and monitored his email. We were alerted you are meeting tomorrow."

The admission temporarily quietened Feng and Porter. Neither was a fan of Big Brother tactics, despite having hacked a few accounts themselves.

Feng broke the silence. "Fascher only confirmed three or four hours ago. You act fast."

"I work all over the world, but I am based in Berlin. It was not so hard to find you. We have resources."

The Gliss said Davidov was principled but clearly ruthless. "It's probably best to go along with whatever he suggests. If nothing else, it will probably speed things up, don't you think?"

Feng and Porter nodded assent. "How can we help you?" said Porter. "We're not detectives, just keen amateurs."

"Perhaps you could say the same of me," said Davidov. "Our interests are aligned in any case."

"Would you like to join us tomorrow?" asked Porter.

"No. I think not. There may come a time when I have to act against Becker's estate. I would not like to prejudice those proceedings by giving Fascher a heads-up or giving him any ammunition in any court action to follow. But I would, of course, love to know how you get on with your investigation."

Porter asked what was in it for them. After all, he was just a stranger, piggybacking their work.

"Are you asking for money?" said Davidov. He answered his own question. "No, I think not. I think you are working to find justice, and that is your reward. Am I right in this?"

Both Feng and Porter nodded.

"I have a proposal," said Davidov. "If there are any specific expenses relating to the Becker enquiry, I will reimburse you. I understand you are looking wider than Becker's Nazi past, but where our investigations cross, I can help you. I can see you are both honourable men." He took a card from his pocket. "You can reach me any time."

"Do you want our numbers?" asked Porter.

"I already have them."

"Of course, you do," said Feng. "I presume at one point you were Mossad?"

"Every Israeli has to serve their country at some point. But do not get confused: this is not an issue about Israel, Zionism or Judaism. This is about justice. Nothing more, nothing less."

Porter doubted it but shook Davidov's hand. "I guess you could say the same about us. It's justice that drives us. I'm a solicitor by trade, but I seem to have been sidetracked into it. I have to put things right. My life depends upon it, I think."

The statement shocked Feng. Although he had been there since almost the beginning, he hadn't quite realised the extent of mission the Quincunx had instilled in his friend. For Feng, it was about solving mysteries, and exploring the strange phenomena that happened around Porter. He was delighted to discover that Porter, a reluctant hero at best, was possessed of a purity of purpose that was missing in Karin, Namita and himself. He was impressed enough to pat Porter on the back. Porter spluttered with the force of the blow.

"We're looking around Becker Haus tomorrow. Is there anything specific you think we should look for?" said Porter, mopping froth from his chest.

Davidov said it was a matter of understanding Becker's psychology. "I believe he was an unrepentant racist and Nazi to the last. Ten years ago, we spoke to the nurse who suffered at his bedside. I know what happened. Should we think the vile Nazi philosophy was absent from his life from 1945 until that ugly resurgence on his deathbed 41 years later? No, that is impossible."

Davidov leant in. "He was a serial killer during the War. What do we know about serial killers? They like to repeat themselves; their urges never go away; they keep trophies. As far as we know, he managed to refrain from murder once he was famous. That leaves the urges. They must have resurfaced in some form. Have you seen his film Operation Geknackt Spiegel?"

"I missed that one," said Porter. "What's it about?"

"Operation Geknackt Spiegel - I think it translates as Operation Cracked Mirror in English - is the story of a small town in which in which a spurned young man breaks into houses and smashes all the mirrors as a protest against women's vanity. Eventually, that is not enough, and he takes to murdering the women - by shooting them in the head with a Luger."

Davidov looked the film up on his phone and showed them some images. In one, the protagonist, his face covered in sweat, is raging in front of a street covered in glass.

"Your point?" said Feng.

"Look. Do you not know your German history? Does it not remind you of anything?" said Davidov.

That was enough of a prompt for Porter. "Kristallnacht, right?"

"Correct. And shooting innocent women in the head with a Luger? He was reliving his crimes at Flossenbürg."

Porter and Feng got it. Becker had never moved on.

"Here was a true monster without regret, without soul, without conscience," said Davidov. "That leaves one thing: trophies. Are we to believe he kept no record, no signs, nothing to remind him of his past? Look for those. If you are right that he murdered this Rose woman, look for the trophy, the keepsake. Yes, that is my tip to you."

Chapter 25

November 1st, 2017
Becker Haus, Charlottenburg, Berlin

"And this, gentlemen, is the study," said Max Fascher, ushering Porter and Feng (and The Gliss, though Fascher didn't know that) into a miserably dark room.

It was full of books and boxes and smelled of mouse droppings and mildew. "It is not in its best state yet," he continued. "We are trying to work out how best to preserve it as Becker used it, but also to present a pleasant aspect to visitors when they come. And come, they surely will."

So far, the trip to Becker Haus had given Porter and Feng nothing but a bad case of the creeps. They quickly came to the same conclusion as Davidov: Fascher was a fool with a blind-spot. It happens with acolytes of the rich and famous. Long after their connection has finished, they find themselves unable to cope with life without its former glow. They find increasingly desperate ways to keep touching the flame.

Porter knew a man who worked for Michael Caine for a year. He could turn any conversation, any subject, into an opportunity to throw in an anecdote that usually began, "When I worked for Michael Caine…" And although Porter found it funny-sad, over the years he had seen the power of it. Even in reflected glory, a lot of people responded with an excited, "You worked for Michael Caine?" and his friend owned the conversation from that point on. Fascher clearly had this trait in spades and was perfectly happy to witter on about Becker. It might have meant something to a German film buff but came across as sad and desperate to the few suffering Brits who'd been forced to watch Becker's iffy work as students.

Porter and Feng's biggest problem was the talking at cross-purposes. They were lying their arses off, selling the idea of a celebratory documentary, while trying to find ways of destroying Fascher's hero. There was only one point of contact where the two narratives met. It fell to Porter to bring it up.

"Of course, one of the themes of any documentary on Becker must be the allegations of his Nazi past, and the suggestion he spied for the Soviets." Porter tried to pull his best serious-but-fair documentary-maker face. Not that he had any idea what such a face would look like. "It would be impossible to make a film without discussing these issues."

Fascher nodded. "You have, of course, read my chapters on the subject? I was not happy researching it. If you had known the man as well as I did, you would know how ridiculous either suggestion was. But even if I had somehow been fooled by him, I've had 30 years to analyse this mountain of paperwork and never seen a thing to corroborate either story."

Thank God for that, thought Porter. *At least Fascher knows we have to discuss it*. "Are there any documents from World War II? He was born in 1905, so he was in the prime of life 1936-1947, yet I believe no official documents exist. What about personal ones?"

"Nein, Herr Porter. Not just that period, but even his birth certificate is missing. I admit, it is intriguing the paper trail only begins in 1947 - a coincidence more than enough to trigger myriad conspiracy theories. But it's not so unusual to discover papers missing following such a time of turmoil, nein?"

Feng was wandering about, peering at things on the wall. It was covered in a mass of paintings, photos and notes. "Good lord!" he said, examining one of the paintings. "Is this a Picasso?"

"Yes! Indeed!" Fascher said, preening. "A fine work. Becker knew the artist. It was a personal gift. One artist to another."

"But this must be worth millions?" gasped Feng. "Wouldn't it be easier to auction it? You'd have the funds then to open the museum?"

"Impossible!" said Fascher. "Becker himself considered the painting to be an anchor, the touchstone that gave this room its creative magic."

The magic had done a bunk now as far as Feng and Porter could tell. They nodded politely at Fascher. Both felt it unwise to say anything derogatory out loud, but Feng whispered to Porter, "Why doesn't he just sell the bloody thing and hang a copy?"

They began surveying the room properly. Dotted around the study were objet d'art, knick-knacks and film awards. Three people crammed into this small space made the study feel more like an antiques' shop out of Tales from the Crypt than a place of magic creativity. There were bronze replicas of Grecian statues, African tribal art, stuffed animals, an absolutely hideous plaster statue of a ballerina in a tutu, an equally ugly tableau featuring two warthogs having a fight, some amateurishly carved wooden birds… it was untidy, uncoordinated, and deeply unsettling.

As well as the Picasso, the walls of the study were lined with framed pictures and certificates: Best Foreign Film nominations at Cannes, The Oscars, the Toronto Film Festival, and the Venice Film Festival. There were film posters for several of Becker's films including Operation geknackt Spiegel, **Die Schwachen und Die Gauche**, and his big hit, Die Längste Nacht.

In addition to celebrating his work, there were paintings and photos of Berlin. Becker clearly loved his city. There were two oil paintings of parks, some gorgeous black-and-white Brassaï-esque shots of Berlin at night and by day - ordinary folk, oblivious of the camera, caught au naturel on bridges, in shops, taverns, depots and parks. Feng studied them all, hoping for a Eureka! moment which never came.

Books were piled comically high, tottering like novice stilt-walkers at a sideshow. One careless fart and the lot would fall like ninepins. Then there were the work papers.

Feng and Porter quickly accepted that even if a full confession lay on Becker's desk, they wouldn't discover it; it was all in German. There were a few curled headshots lying around and a few more, male and female, pinned to a board. They were typical actor headshots, and Porter suspected they'd been sent speculatively by struggling actors and agents.

Porter said, "Come and look at this one." It was a young woman, Julie Clark, represented by the Ashworth Agency, Park Street. Her eyes had been lit well. A diamond sparkle in each iris shone as brightly today as when the picture had been taken, sometime - judging from the Farah hair - in the late 70s or early 80s.

"What about it?" said Feng. "She's British? Is that what you mean?"

"Yes, but look, it's embossed - you see? - bottom right."

"VC Soho. So what?" said Feng.

"I dunno," said Porter. "But Soho is where the Bristol girls lived?"

"And where most of the photographers and studios in London were based in the 60s," said Feng. Shrugging, Feng turned to Fascher and said, "You're right, Max; this would make a fantastic museum. May I take a few shots?" Fascher agreed, and Feng set about capturing images of the room's absurdly random collections.

"Don't forget to get Julie Clark," said Porter.

"Done," said Feng. "Can we go soon? Berlin's starting to give me the willies."

Checking in at the airport later, Feng said, "I forgot to ask, Porter - did you get any Quincunx reactions from the room? I managed to turn my EMF meter on, but it showed nothing."

The Gliss and Porter both confirmed they hadn't picked up any vibes. "I was surprised actually," said Porter. "I was sure something would show up, but it was one of the psychically cleanest rooms I've ever been in. Even with Becker's DNA everywhere, I didn't get a repeat of the hospital scene. Not so much as a tingle. If he did kill Rose, it wasn't in his office, that's for sure."

The Gliss, chipped in, "Clearly, Becker was a nasty piece of work, but I wonder if it's all just coincidence insofar as it links to our case?"

Porter shook his head. "You read Karin's timeline and saw her conclusions. I think she's right. Rose was friendless in Berlin. If she went anywhere the day she went missing, it makes sense that, for whatever reason - she left something behind, she was invited back, she went to beg - the person she most likely met up with on Day 2 was the same person she met on Day 1. That was probably Becker. We know he murdered people in the war. That's neither fluff nor coincidence; that's building a case."

The Gliss and Feng bowed to the lawyer in the room. Feng said, "I tell you what - I'm bloody glad to be going home."

Chapter 26

November 1st, 2017
The Mission, Griffiths Park, LA

As soon as Namita, Feng and Porter had jetted home a week earlier, Karin had driven straight to the car hire depot and swapped their Dodge Durango for a Bentley Continental GT V8 soft-top. One eye or not, driving in the sun was one of life's great pleasures. She could afford it, and nothing says *I-am-quite-rich-actually* like a Bentley Continental GT V8 soft-top.

She pulled through the gates of The Mission, top-down, pulling stares from the group of Latinos hanging at the back door. Climbing out, classily dressed in a silk blouse, comfortable trousers, with a stylish leather satchel, she looked very Miss Moneypenny circa 1968. Aware the boys were staring, she took a swallow, striding towards them like a knight into battle. *Could you be any more bloody English? Silk blouse and Bentley? A satchel? In LA?*

One of the boys jumped down off a wall. Instinctively taking a defensive step back, she was first surprised, and then embarrassed, when he said, "Are you here to see Reverend Crystal, Miss?"

"Er, yes, I am. He's expecting me. Karin Pelenot."

"I'll let him know you're here, Miss." And the boy hopped off with a swinging gait that suggested he was carrying two invisible pails of milk on a yoke.

There's a great clip of Bill Withers singing Ain't No Sunshine on the BBC music show, The Old Grey Whistle Test. His hair is receding, he's wearing blue jeans and an orange turtle-neck sweater. He looks impossibly cool. If Withers had been Caucasian, aged 30 years into white-hairdom, and become a vicar, that was the Reverend Morrie Crystal.

The founder of The Mission, in long-flowing black robes and a dog collar, a large outsize silver crucifix on a chain around his neck, strode towards Karin like he was heading to the stage to pick up his Best Album Grammy.

"Ms Pelenot," he said, his hand outstretched, 10ft before she could possibly have shaken it. "Welcome to The Mission! My, that is a nice car!" his attention caught by the striking silver-grey convertible. "Boys, make sure it's left alone while we're gone."

"Yes, sir," the group said as one.

He gave her a quick guided tour of The Mission. A games room, dorms, a kitchen, a cafe area, a small chapel. He explained how their outreach workers targeted boys thought to be at risk of joining gangs. "I'd love to say we rescue kids from gangs, but the truth is once they're in one…"

Karin talked a little about her work, and her plans for the Sam Brownlees documentary.

"It all sounds very admirable," said the Reverend. "Awareness is everything. I'm not sure what Britain is like, but we still have a long way to go in America. Look what happened when Colin Kaepernick began kneeling during the national anthem last year. The poor man was simply protesting racial injustice and can't find a team to play in since."

"I saw that," said Karin. "He made a fair point, and I'm not so sure his story has finished yet. But yes - I do hope our film will shine a deeply personal light into the darkness of the Transatlantic slave trade."

"That is good," said Crystal. Pulling up chairs in the Mission's closed and empty cafe, he asked one of his boys to fetch coffee for them both. The young man, name-tagged, Junior - trotted off obligingly.

"They're certainly well behaved," said Karin.

"Respect. That's all it's about. I respect you; you respect me. I'm not ramming fire and brimstone down their throats - though I warn you, Junior's coffee is a pretty good substitute."

Settled with drinks, Crystal asked Karin to recap. "I've wracked my brains, hoping something would come back to my fading memory. But, sorry, nothing on that girl you mentioned - Rose, was it? I would be very interested to hear what you think happened."

Karin updated him. "We have two girls missing now, Rose and Bella, both from the same town in England. Both went to London to seek fame and fortune as actors. Rose, as you know, gave your address during a trip to LA. She disappeared later on another trip to Berlin."

"And the other young lady?" asked Crystal.

Karin revealed that Bella had stayed at Century Plaza. A third friend of the girls, Ursa, later killed herself. She too visited LA as a struggling actress. Also tying the trio together was their loose connections to people who were famous in the UK for espionage and blackmail. Karin, finding her low-slung armchair uncomfortable, criss-crossed her legs awkwardly. "Oh yes, and one other thing - a private investigator who went looking for one of the girls had his head chopped off and his body was dumped in The Thames."

"Goodness," said Crystal. "But apart from their respective visits, there are no other LA connections?"

"Rose's biological father is American, and he lives here, but she never knew him." She decided not to reveal Sam Brownlee's paternity.

"Well, I know nothing about espionage and spies. That said, after JFK, Vietnam, and the growth of the Civil Rights movement, America became a very political place in the 60s. I was lost in showbiz, I'm afraid. It all passed me by. I only know what I've read."

Crystal paused. "What I do know about is the film-world. It's not very edifying, but I can tell you a bit about the movie biz as it was then - if it's useful?"

He started with himself. He grew up in a Jewish household in Brooklyn, New York. His father sold sheet music for a living. A love of film and the arts dominated his family upbringing. His father got him a job as a song plugger for a publishing company. The young Morrie soon saw a gap in the market - selling songs to film companies.

"I probably wasn't the best plugger in the world," he said. "In those days, you were expected to demonstrate songs to prospective clients. If you can imagine me singing cute songs about puppies and broken hearts? No, well neither could most of my clients." He laughed, a pleasant heh-heh-heh that spoke of inner mischievousness.

"Although Hollywood is the real centre, New York has always had a healthy film industry. I soon realised I enjoyed working with film producers more than I did working with advertisers and popular singers. I got a job as an assistant to Carl Bunning, a busy director in those days, forgotten now. He showed me the ropes."

Karin, nodded encouragingly, wondering if it would be rude to add a third sugar to her sulphuric coffee.

"Sometime in 1963, I met Don Lascelles," said Crystal, and his eyes lit up. "What an interesting time! He'd just had his breakthrough with Paul Newman in Daylight Robbery and was on the up-and-up. The first film we worked on together was Black and Blue. You ever see that one? David Niven and Gregory Peck as two chalk-and-cheese cops. It was a typical shoot-em-up except for the sub-plot about Gregory Peck slightly losing his mind as the film wore on."

"I can't imagine Gregory Peck losing his mind," said Karin.

"Ah. Nor could picture-goers. That was the problem - I didn't say it was a great film. But it got me into Hollywood. I worked there for almost 20 years. But I got more and more uneasy about the sleaze, the drink and drugs. I'd never been a practicing Jew, you understand, but the values were still there. I just ignored them for too long. When I woke up, I went through a few years exploring different belief systems. Anglican seemed the most natural fit for me, so I converted. I ran a small congregation in Los Feliz for a while, but realised that wasn't for me."

"Why not?"

"Prevention versus cure," said Morrie. "All those folk who came to my church were already saved. They were good, decent people who already knew God. I asked myself if I literally wanted to preach to the converted. I guess there's always been a missionary inside me. I thought it would be better to intervene, to improve lives. I got the idea for The Mission, tapped a few old film friends, bought the lease on this place, and here we are."

"If you don't me asking, aren't you old enough to retire?"

"You flatter me. I'm quite clearly 20 years past retirement. I'm like one of those old rock'n'rollers destined to die on stage, except my stage is now the pulpit. What the heck would I do if I didn't have The Mission? But it's in good hands. It will continue after I go."

Karin wanted to get on. She opened her bag and pulled out a little file. "I can show you pictures of the girls, if that's ok?"

She put down photos of Rose, Bella and Ursa. "This is the one who put down your address in Gramercy Place," she said, showing Rose. The Reverend took a long time, examining it from several angles, before shaking his head.

"I honestly don't recognise her," he said. "I'm curious why and how she put my address down. 1967, you say? Well, I was working for Don full-time then." He shook his head.

"Why the head-shake?"

"I know what Don was like. I mean, he wasn't a weirdo or anything, but he sure liked women. She looks just his type. There were so many women in the 60s. I've said before, I was no angel, either. It was my growing disgust with myself that eventually got me out." He gestured around. "As you can see, my penitence and atonement has been a long one."

"When you say he wasn't a weirdo, what do you mean?"

"He loved women. Treated them like Queens: had his fill, said goodbye. But no funny stuff, no whips or chains. I guarantee no woman ever left Don with a bruise, unless it was to her soul."

"He used them?"

"Am I being too kind on us? I think, I am. Yes, Miss Pelenot, we used them. I was no better. Don't ask me for numbers, I'm ashamed enough as it is."

"Don?"

"Over his entire career? Thousands, I'm sorry to say. But I bet none of them went missing. How do I know? On that scale of course, if any had, it would be easy to link them with him. Most of them went home with more money than they arrived with, some went on to be stars, some got a little work, but Don would never have physically hurt anyone. I'm sure of it. Perhaps despite appearances, he liked women."

Karin raised an eyebrow. It really does depend on how you define *hurt*.

"All I'm saying," said Crystal, "is that whatever happened to this poor girl, Rose, she went home in one piece if she met Don."

Karin, thinking of all the women who had come forward in the #MeToo movement, said: "In one piece, physically, maybe."

"Yes, you're right, of course. I'm so very sorry for my part in any of that back then." Morrie looked uncomfortable.

Karin, a skilled interviewer, exploited the silence and said nothing. He broke. "This is not the time for treading gingerly on what's left of my ego," he said. "What we did was horrible. I can only put my hands up, show you how I've tried to make amends. But they were different times. It was almost expected of you."

Karin let that go and put down a copy of the postcard Namita found at Lenny Fielding's house.

> *Dear Mum and Dad,*
> *I feel like I'm in a Beach Boys' song! I travelled up The Strip today in Don's T-Bird, top down, sun in my hair, singing along to Mr Tambourine Man on the radio. It's like a dream come true. We had burgers and shakes at a diner.*

"And this is from the Rose girl, is it?" said Morrie. "I remember that T-Bird. Fabulous car. Red and cream. I used to drive it too."

"No, this is from Ursa."

"The other girl who went missing. Really?"

"No, she's the one who killed herself a couple of years later."

"Show me the picture again?" Karin could see Crystal was getting confused.

Maybe it was the T-Bird reminder, but Karin saw something like recognition briefly flicker in Morrie's eyes. He squinted and looked a few times. "It's so hard to say for sure," he said, "but, yes, possibly I do remember her. And you say she came to LA and had an audition for Don?"

"We don't know who she auditioned for. The only people who could tell us that are the girls themselves, but they're all dead. Here's the thing: they were all poor. There's no way, they could have afforded the flights." She put down the picture of Bella. "Bella stayed at the Century Plaza, all expenses paid."

"I'm getting confused now. Bella is the one who went missing in LA?"

"Correct. Did Don ever pay for girls to come over for auditions?"

"What? No way. Not unknowns anyway. Why would he? You think we had a shortage of wannabe actresses in LA? We would certainly have laid on luxury for famous actors and actresses if we were trying to persuade them to come on board with a film, but unknowns? Never."

Karin accepted the logic but said, "Well, someone or something paid for them to come over."

Morrie said, "Are you sure they didn't just save up and pay for the trips themselves?"

"It really wasn't feasible. The UK was virtually a Third World economy at the time."

"Then I'm at a loss to explain it, Karin. I remember the opening of the Century Plaza well. We had people stay there sometimes. It was very expensive, especially the penthouse suites, but they sure were luxury."

"Guess where Bella stayed."

"The penthouse suites? My God. Well, let me tell you - someone, somewhere thought she was very important then. Are you sure she wasn't working for your government? Or a big advertising agency? I can assure you, we never put anyone up in places like that. Elsa, the production manager, would have crucified us."

He looked around and crossed himself.

November 2nd, 2017
Covent Garden, London

Porter's sister, Cherry, and his ex, Tania Muriskava, were chatting over breadsticks and olives. They were nibbling al fresco, wrapped up like Huskies, braving London's autumn chill.

Despite Tania and Porter's break-up, the two women remained friends. Tania had imposed the condition on Cherry that Porter never found out. When the women did meet up, the unspoken agreement was Porter could only be mentioned once. Briefly. Cherry didn't mind talking about her brother; Tania most certainly did. So, Cherry was taken aback when Tania asked how he was.

"Right now? I could wring the little bastard's neck," said Cherry. "He left me to sort out Ida's estate because the silly cow didn't leave a will. He's done nothing but nitpick."

"Why? What happened?" said Tania, lighting up.

"I spoke to Ida loads of times. She said she had no-one but me and Porter and the kids."

Tania, no stranger to bending logic, spotted the problem immediately. "Ah, so you want to divvy it up 3-to-1 in your favour, and Porter's told you to get lost?"

"Not in my favour - in favour of her grandkids," said Cherry, defiantly.

"You can see his point, though? What's the latest?"

"He says he won't say anything else on the subject and it's up to my conscience."

"Ooh. Clever. And now you're stuck?"

"Annoying little bastard," said Cherry, breaking a breadstick in two.

"Why don't you try and get him locked up again?" Tania laughed, recalling Cherry's attempt to get him sectioned the previous summer.

"I feel like it. I wouldn't mind but since he started working with Karin Pelenot, he's got money coming in."

"What's he still doing with her?" said Tania startled. "Is this something to do with the World War 1 stuff earlier this year? I thought that was all done?"

"They're working on another documentary. They were in LA together last week. I think they were in Berlin till a couple of days ago."

"What about his practice? I thought all that stuff with the little girl was cleared up?"

"Janine Crane. Yes, but he's too busy with Karin to do it."

"Is he now?" said Tania, stubbing her fag out.

November 1st, 2017
Namita's flat, Holloway Road, London

Namita had typed up the email five times so far. Each time she had faltered, cursing herself for mixing business with pleasure. How do you start a business email with someone you've slept with?

Dear Martin. Too informal. *Dear Sir.* Too formal. *Mr Skelling.* Too formal. *Martin.* Way too informal. In the end she thought she would have to go with *Dear Mr Skelling* - strictly by the book - though it made her feel as awkward as a nun on a porno shoot.

In possession of all the evidence she needed, Namita decided to give Martin a way out. She suggested they make a joint *Larke V Nugus* approach to Florence's executors. This would allow both sides to see all the documents the bank was holding. It was a technique designed to give opposing solictors a level playing field, but with the side letter from Florence and Namita's evidence from Dr Harwell confirming Florence's capacity, it should make things clear to Martin. If he was professional, if he was sensible, he would advise Stormont it wasn't worth pursuing. *But is he any of those things?*

With little choice, she pressed send, and turned on the TV. She didn't have much time for the box generally but had become hooked on Miramax's Banshee. She was in the middle of a wildly implausible Season 2. Rough plot: A tough ex-con assumes a dead man's identity. He becomes sheriff of a small town in PA riddled with psychotic Amish butchers and rednecks. He tries to win back the love of his life, now married to the town's DA. It was nonsense but had lots of oddball characters and a ton of sex and violence. "Why should I go to the cinema for sex and violence," the comedian Peter Cook once said. "I can get all that at home." Thanks to Banshee, so could Namita.

Watching a graphic sex scene, beautifully lit and leaving very little to the imagination, Namita found her embers warming up, stoked by memories of her night with Martin. Over the past few days, little snippets had come back to her. With a little distance, she was able to admit that drunk Namita had actually had a good time. Why had it been so long since she'd seen anyone? What was she doing wrong? Was it them – men - or her?

Her mother and father still half-heartedly nudged her now and again about finding a husband, but the wife-life had never been on her radar. She'd known since she was a child that she wasn't going to marry someone her parents found. She didn't want the pressure of expectations that would come from an arranged marriage. She wanted to be successful on her own terms, had never wanted kids, and couldn't face anyone cramping her style. For many years, she'd kidded herself a white Englishman might be a better option. Beautiful though she was, they rarely ever hit on her.

She caught her reflection in the mirror. *You're not that bad.* Did she have the words "Bugger off" tattooed on her forehead?

Looking around her tasteful but spartan flat, she wondered if its clinical tidiness was symptomatic of her problem. She would hate to admit it in public, but her unregretted life decisions also came with a certain amount of loneliness built-in. She had periods where she felt on top of the world and free, but there always came moments like this, when she could picture and hanker for an alternate life - married, hosting dinner parties, maybe even kids. These momentary thoughts scudded across her horizon as quickly as clouds in a storm. Brief and unwanted, they nevertheless came. She acknowledged one dark bugger was crossing the sky right now. It was straight from Mordor, but she pretended to ignore it.

Sangita came to life. "I know I gave you a hard time about Martin, but I just need to check: you know he's not right for you, correct?"

"Yes, Sangita," said Namita. "I know he's not right for you."

"I said *you*."

"So, did I."

"But when you say it, that means, *me*."

"Whatever."

"If you're going to do stupid, white British solicitors, what about Porter?"

"Don't be mad."

"Well, as long as we can have a nice, reasoned discussion about it."

"I'm watching telly." Namita quoted her forehead: "Bugger off."

As things hotted up again in Banshee - a wayward Amish girl was getting serviced by the ex-con up against a pillar - Namita suddenly thought: *Porter? Why on earth would Sang say that? I've never given him a second look. She might as well have said Feng.*

This made her laugh so much, that she spilled red wine over the sofa. Cursing, Namita paused a second as the Amish girl pulled a flimsy dress over her head and walked away without going to the bathroom.

Why does no-one ever take a shower after sex in the movies? She mopped at the wine stains with sheets of kitchen roll.

Chapter 27

November 2nd, 2017
Pellicci's Cafe, Bethnal Green Road, London

"The Krays used to get their bacon sarnies 'ere too," said Jimmy Farr, aka Jimmy the Shanker. "Top notch grub. Everyfin' else round here is fuckin' curry and kebab now."

Porter and Feng tucked into their doorstop sandwiches and swigged from white mugs with the teabag still in. "Did you know the Krays?" asked Porter.

Shanker, a shrunken, with Grand Canyon creases, laughed. "Know 'em? I worked for the fuckers, did'n' I? If you was dodgy back then, you was bound to end up doin' summat for 'em. Either that or get ya fuckin' head nailed to the floor."

It had been Karin's idea. "If you call people and ask them to randomly chat about their experiences in crime, they'll probably tell you to get lost," she explained. "If you use my name to set up a film about vice in 60s Soho, you will probably find nearly everyone agrees to speak."

A bit of finagling with headed notepaper and email address signatures saw Porter and Feng equipped with the tools. The only living person on Harding's list was Jimmy. The promise of a £500 fee (on top of what they'd already paid the journalist) secured a pre-interview over coffee. Karin explained that filmmakers used these to work out what interviewees were likely to say on camera and to build up rapport. But in the presence of an aged and unrepentant murderer and thug, the boys weren't so sure there was a rapport to be built.

Porter and Feng got chapter and verse on how *fings ain't wot they used to be*, a quick run through how he got his nickname - "the trick is to hit the kidney, brown bread in seconds" - his 30 years in prison, and his hatred of foreigners, especially the Muslims.

"No offence, son," he said to Feng.

"I'm not Indian, Pakistani or Bengali. And I'm certainly not a Muslim," was the only thing he could think to say in his shock.

Already unsure how much they could take of Jimmy, Porter pulled out his folder. He showed him Harding's diary. "Alex was investigating Rose's disappearance," said Porter. "Here, look."

Either Jimmy needed his glasses or couldn't read, but he navigated the words like an OAP looking for the last parking space in Tesco's. "Ain't got me glasses. Wossit say?"

Porter read out the entire list.

> *Nov 12. Interview. Jimmy Farr. 3pm Bag O'Nails*
> *Nov 14. Brinjle Johnson 7pm The Lord Dellafield*
> *Nov 15. Ryan Bradley 9pm Kitty Kitty*
> *Nov 17. Artie Mosser 1pm Joe's*
> *Dec 13. Angie Grew, Scarlet Club*
>   *Bert Rossi 4pm Wardour Street*
> *Dec 14. DCI Anderson Berwick St Cafe*
> *Dec 19. Jimmy Farr. 4pm Red Hart*
> *Dec 20. Bradley. 11pm Kitty Kitty*
> *Jan 8. Artie Mosser. 3pm Joe's*
> *Jan 9. Jimmy Farr. 9pm. Red Hart*
> *Jan 11. Boris 2pm Dellafield.*

Porter brandished a photo of Harding. "This was the PI. Remember him?"

"Yeah. I remember him. Twat. The geezer had fuckin' wads of cash. He was an easy mark. Look at that for a start - the Bag O' Nails! That was a top club. Expensive. Paul McCartney met his missus there. Georgie Fame and The Blue Flames were the house band. This muppet Hardin' comes along… 'Can we talk?' he says. I said, 'If you're buying the drinks, course we can fuckin' talk!'"

As if to confirm his mouth was still up for sale, Jimmy toasted Porter and Feng with a corner of white bread, dripping in butter and pig fat. "Don't mean I know nuffin', does it?"

"Do you remember what you chatted about?" asked Feng.

"Yeah. This girl had gone missin', right? She worked in bars around Soho. I knew her by sight. She did a bit of waitressing for Clem too."

"Clem?" asked Feng.

"Gor, fuck me…you done any fuckin' research? Clem fuckin' Rossiter. Him, The Krays, The Richardsons, Rossi's Mafia mob… they were the ones who run everyfin'. Twenny years I got for slicin' up one of his people who dipped his jazz bands in the till. *Owe Rossiter and die*, that's what we used to say. Psycho."

Porter said, "I know who he is. I read." He showed a photo of Rose. "She worked for him? Waitressing? Was it, you know, dodgy?"

"Nah, Clem liked an air of respectability. Wanted to see a Hollywood star slummin' it in London? You'd go to one of Clem's gaffs, like the Kitty, Kitty on Frith Street. All above board. No tits out or nuffin' like that. Your girl probably got a pinched arse, but nuffin' else. I saw punters duffed up for goin' too far with Clem's girls."

"What do you remember about Rose?" asked Porter.

"Nuffin' much, really. When she went missing in Berlin, that was a bit of a thing. Fuckin' Krauts. Two World Wars, millions of dead, and 20 years later, we were all supposed to be pals again? I lost family and friends in the Blitz. Fuck 'em."

"What did you say when she went missing," Feng asked in disgust, eyeing Jimmy chew his food. It was like watching entrails going around a cement mixer.

"Well, we was all worried 'bout her, weren't we? The cops came nosing, but we didn' know nuffin. The fuckin' Krauts topped her. Not us. What the fuck would we know?"

"Why did Harding approach you then, do you think?" asked Porter, yanking the hot teabag out before his drink turned entirely the colour of creosote.

"Clem, obviously. That twat 'Arding got it into his thick numbskull that Clem had been doing blue movies and the girl got caught up in it. But I was right in the fick of it, right? I can tell you now, without troublin' what's left of me conscience, Clem never made no skin flicks. Never! The NW5 gang up in Kentish Town, they might 'ave, but Clem? Not on your Nelly. And you know why? No fuckin' need to! Where do you think all the German, Danish, Swedish porno came when it was smuggled in? Soho. Who owned Soho? Clem fuckin' Rossiter, that's who."

Feng said, "We hadn't really considered that, but thanks." He scribbled down *NW5 gang* in his notebook.

Jimmy, ignoring Feng, said, "Clem had a photographer, right? On Old Compton Street, some poof called Vince, own darkroom and everyfin'. I went there dozens of times - bit of whisky, bit of blow, couple of birds - big parties. I thought - he's Clem's photographer - gonna be a few nudies lying around, right? Got pissed one night and went looking, for a bit of a laugh, right? Nuffin'. I told 'Arding all that. He was well pissed off I couldn't back up his crap theory."

Porter said, "Why do you think a gangster needed his own photographer?"

"Vince was a freelance - know what I mean? Clem gave him a retainer and called him as and when. Nothing smutty - publicity shots of Clem's bars, poster shots, lobby cards, headshots, crap like that. Clem had a pack of playing cards made up once. Tasteful shots of all 13 of his girls with the suits laid over the top, hiding all their bits. Yah, very tasteful."

"When you say *headshots*?"

"For the girls, you know. A couple of girls saw the clubs as a steppin' stone for showbiz - same ol', same ol'. And cos Clem liked the girls and he loved movies, you know, he used to 'elp 'em - get 'em free headshots and that - what do you fink I meant?"

Jimmy was treating them as if they were both idiots. Feng recalled the picture in Becker's study and scrabbled to find the snap of Julie Clark on his phone. Blowing the corner of the picture up, he showed Jimmy the logo - VC Soho.

"Cor fuck me, where'd you get that? That's him - that's his moniker, Vince Chambers."

"Do you recognise this woman?" asked Porter.

"Nah. Never seen 'er before. She missing too?"

"No. We looked her up. She's a retired teacher now. Didn't want to talk to us. Found her on Google."

"What's that?" Jimmy looked at the picture again. "Nah, sorry. Her boat race... never seen it before." Jimmy picked his nose and wiped it on a hanky, before stuffing it back in his pocket. "The fing is, Soho's always been teeming with fillies - still is. Tryin' to remember *one* of 'em... they all look the same, don't they?"

"What do you mean? How do they all look the same?" asked Feng.

"Fuckin' desperate, mate." He looked at Julie Clark again. "Nah, sorry, never seen that one. Judging by her 'aircut, I was probably in pokey then anyway."

"What about all the other names on the list? Ring any bells?" asked Porter.

"Brinjle was a poof. Used to hang out in Soho and pick up gayboys."

"I'm gay, actually," said Feng, hoping his admission would tone down Jimmy's language.

"You don't say. You stink like a perfumed arsehole."

"Look, we're paying you for this interview," said Porter. "I'd appreciate it if you stopped being so offensive."

"Fuck off, mate. I'm too old to worry about all that PC shit - turning Christmas into Winter Festival...It's all bollocks. Anyway, Liberace here don't mind, do you, cock?"

"I do, but whatever," said Feng, determined to get this over and done with as soon as possible. "Any of the other names?"

"DCI Anderson was a bent copper in a turn-a-blind-eye kinda way. Didn't get involved, just took a few backhanders. Sensible. Saved himself from getting duffed up. Angie was a dancer at Kitty, Kitty. That 'Arding prat was probably looking for someone who knew ya gal at work. But she was a good un, Ang. Ended up a doctor, can you believe - from nipple tassels to stethoscopes in 10 years." He looked at the rest of the list. Bradley and Mosser he didn't recognise.

"I'll be honest, guv, not quite sure what 'Ardin' was looking at 'ere. Geezers like me, well, we was working with Clem, right? So he was just getting background. But Brinjle the Poof?" He looked at Feng. "Sorry, guv."

Porter showed him the Who's Who entry. "He was ambassador to the Americans."

"Was he now? Well, like I say - homos, spies, tarts and Nazis. That was Soho."

"We came across a German film director, Heinrich Becker," said Porter, remembering his vision at Becker's grave. "He was definitely a Nazi."

"Sure. There were loads of 'em. How many of the top brass did we hang at Nuremberg? 10? 20? 30? That left several 'undred still wandering about, right?"

"Did you ever meet Becker?" asked Feng.

"Once or twice."

"How?" said Porter.

"He knew Clem. Film stuff. Fuckin' Krauts."

November 2nd. 2017
Old Compton Street, Soho.

"You see people like him on TV and you think it's all made up," said Feng, still recovering from their encounter. "It was like bathing in a sewer."

Porter, sipping on an expensive coffee in a tiny takeaway cup, nodded. "An unrepentant sinner. It goes against the narrative we all hope to see in our pensioners. They're supposed to show remorse and reform, wisdom and compassion; not wallow in their badness."

Faced with the Soho pedestrian nightmare as usual, the duo slalomed their way towards Chambers' 60s address. "When we get back from this recce, I'll try and track down this Rossiter bloke," said Feng. "He must be knocking 90 himself." Feng was ahead of him as usual. He held out his phone. Google confirmed Rossiter was still alive and living in Stansted Mountfichet, Essex.

"That's something," said Porter. "For now, I'm just curious to see where Chambers had his studio."

The Gliss, launching into a cheery optimism that he struggled to pull off: "If you can get in, you might even pick-up vibes."

"Unlikely, but yes, I did mean *see* in the widest possible sense of the word."

They arrived at the black doorway, sandwiched between two open-fronted posh cafes. The buzzer showed the building was divided into four flats. VC Soho, long since folded as a company, had given number 46 as its address. Checking the nameplate, they saw 46 was now subdivided into A, B, C, D.

Peering at the buzzer, Feng exclaimed, "This could be a stroke of luck… 46A, look: V. Chambers."

"What the hell's an old feller like him still doing in a place like Soho? This is a young man's manor," said Porter, sounding like a Cockney villain.

They pressed the buzzer. Nothing happened. Feng pressed it again. Nothing.

"Shall we leave a note?" asked Porter.

"Can't do any harm," said Feng, disappointed.

Porter wrote a short note asking Vince Chambers to give him a call. Feng, for the sake of it pressed the buzzer one last time. A croaky voice yelled, "Go away."

"He's in then," said Porter, stuffing the note in his pocket. He jabbed at the buzzer. "Mr Chambers? Can we talk to you about your photographs?" Silence. They pressed the buzzer a few more times. Nothing.
"Come on, forget it. Poke your note through and…" Feng was cut-off by the door opening. A man dressed as a woman, sporting a Purdey wig and luminous lipstick, stepped out onto the street with yet another rat-dog. After a nuclear holocaust, the only things to survive will be cockroaches and rat-dogs.

"Gents," said the tranny in a voice that bubbled like a kettle at boiling point. He squeezed past.

Porter was transfixed. "That's some wig, Feng. It's not on straight."

"Porter, forget the wig." Feng gestured down to his foot. He'd stretched out his leg and wedged his foot in the door. "If I move, I'm going to fall flat on my face. I'm too old for the splits. Get the door, give me your arm."

Neither Porter nor Feng was particularly girthy, but they had to hunch their shoulders as they squeezed their way along the dingy corridor. It was narrower than a straw. The door closed behind them with a loud click and the growl of Soho was muffled.

The entrance hallway led to stairs, and tucked away in the abyss, door 46A. The whole place needed a good spruce up, but the landlord clearly thought the circa 1975 paint job was good enough.

They knocked. Nothing. They knocked again. Nothing.

"Did we press the wrong buzzer?" Porter wondered.

Feng was scrutinising the door. "If I just give this a little push, it'll open by the looks of it."

"We can't break in!" Porter admonished. "We're not the cops."

"Porter, Porter, Porter," said Feng, pushing pretty hard with his shoulder. The door popped open.

"Mr Chambers are you ok? Have you had a fall?" Feng winked at Porter. "We're here to help."

Porter, shaking his head but complicit in conspiracy, stepped into the smelliest, dirtiest flat to ever shanghai his nostrils. It was physically spartan, but you could have carved a guitar from the odour. The only movement was steam from a cuppa.

"Mr Chambers," repeated Feng. "We're here to help. Are you okay?" He scoped the place out. A living room, a small kitchen, a bedroom and bathroom. No sign of anyone.

The Gliss chimed in. "Porter, play along." He did.

Feng, sounding like the Child Catcher from Chitty Chitty, Bang Bang, said, "Where could Mr Chambers have gone? I'm very worried about him."

Both of them jumped when a voice barked from the empty kitchen, "Who the bloody hell are you? How dare you come into my flat."

They turned to find Vince Chambers appear, as if by magic, from the tiny galley kitchen. It had been completely empty 30 seconds ago.

The wizened, old ape-of-a-man spat words like sparks. "What do you want? I'll call the police."

"The door was open," lied Feng. "We heard you on the intercom and were worried you'd taken a fall." He reasoned it would just about cover the legal basis for their entry if things went bad. The old man ignored him.

"Are you Vince?" Porter offered a hand. It wasn't taken. And looking at the state of the place, Porter was relieved. Vince's hand would have given agar jelly wet dreams.

"What if I am? What's it to do with you?"

"My name's Porter. I want to show you something." He pulled the photograph of Julie Clark from his bag. "Is this one of yours?"

The change was instantaneous. The venom was gone, replaced by fear. Chambers backed away, a dog offering its belly. He made mewling noises and held his hands up as if to ward off blows. He sunk to his knees.

The Gliss said, "Well, he looks about as innocent as Bill Clinton at a dry-cleaners."

Chambers continued to back away. "No. No. Leave me in peace. Never again. I can't. You mustn't."

Porter said, "We're not here to hurt you."

"Please," said Feng, "Please, can we talk?"

"You won't get me! No. All done. All gone. Never! Not again! Leave me in peace. No. No."

"Honestly, we wish you no harm," said Porter, watching in frustration as Chambers backed himself into a corner.

"Yes, Mr Chambers. We really mean you no harm," said Feng. "We were just wondering if you took this picture. She's a teacher now." Feng looked around the room. It was the kind of filthy that Charles Dickens would have made a social issue. Rotting cardboard boxes piled everywhere. Empty cans of beans and dog food stacked in the corner. Flies circled the open tins.

"I don't think he has a dog," said The Gliss. "It's one way to get your protein, I suppose."

"God, you're right," said Porter. He decided to change tack. "Are you ok, Mr Chambers? Is there anything we can do to help?"

"Not now, not ever. I told them. I said - it's all up here. No-one gets me. I'm safe. I'm safe already."

"I'll make us a fresh cup of tea," said Feng, who believed this was the English cure for most ills. "Is this your kitchen?" He reluctantly headed back in. If anything, it was in a worse state than the living room, but he found an old stove-top kettle and rummaged for ingredients in the cupboard. As Feng happened to be right about the English and tea, he soon found teabags and sugar-cubes. There was no milk. He scrubbed brown concrete stains from the chipped china. It was like cleaning up after Chernobyl. He looked around. There was nowhere Chambers could have hidden. Strange.

In the living room, Porter knelt down and offered his hand to Chambers. "Come and sit with me. I won't hurt you. My friend is making the tea."

His calm manner worked. Chambers got back on his feet, his wary eyes still watering with fear. "I need my pills," he said, pointing to a ripped pharmacy bag containing a mountain of white-capped, brown plastic pots.

Porter checked the labels. Diazepam. 10mg. A big dose of tranquiliser and anti-depressant.

"There you go," said Feng. "Is it ok if I sit here?" He moved a pile of yellowing magazines and newspapers and sat in a chair whose seat springs had long since given out. His butt felt like it was being caressed by a metal crab.

"I'm so sorry if we startled you," said Porter, handing Chambers his pills. The old man swallowed two.

Porter got on with it. They were looking for two girls from Soho who went missing in the 60s. He told Chambers his photographs had been mentioned twice - in Berlin and via Jimmy the Shanker. Off another terrified look, Porter confirmed they just wanted to ask him about his time as a photographer in the 60s. "We're not accusing you of anything," said Porter, "Please don't worry. We're just building a picture."

The Gliss asked if Porter could sense anything. Unwilling to reply verbally, Porter shook his head.

Chambers quietened a little. He looked at his unwanted guests. "The 60s, eh? In Soho? Tarts and Spivs with an occasional Russian spy chucked in. What else do you need to know?"

"Everyone tells us that. Jimmy told us you worked for one of the gangsters - Clem Rossiter?"

Chambers winced. "Yes."

"He said Clem had you on a retainer? Must have felt like you were at the centre of the world," said Feng.

"I couldn't say no, could I? You said no to a bastard like Clem and - guess what? – a week later they fished your body out of the Thames." Feng gave Porter a knowing look at the mention of the Thames.

Chambers mumbled to himself. "Don't show your hand. Play it by the book. I had to look after myself."

"Unwilling servant syndrome. Makes sense," said The Gliss.

"What did he want from you?" said Porter, persisting. "Advertising shots?"

A little fire sparked up in Chambers. "Rossiter was a gangster, not a bleedin' detergent salesman."

Feng added, "Jimmy said you used to do headshots for Rossiter? Actors and dancers?"

"Yeah. Jimmy should shut his mouth. Never could keep quiet."

"What's wrong with doing headshots?" said Feng.

"Nothing. Nothing at all. Just helping the girls out. He rarely helped the boys, just the girls."

"Do you think he took advantage of them? Did he ask you to do anything dodgy?" said Porter.

"No, no. Course not. Don't shit on your own doorstep." Chambers waved the suggestion away. He tackled his black tea with a spoon, slurping, spilling, sucking at the freshly boiled water with asbestos lips. Some dripped into Chambers' lap, but the veteran photographer never flinched.

"His bollocks must be made of steel," whispered Feng to The Gliss.

"He's high," was the reply, "or getting there."

Chambers wiped a sleeve across his mouth. "You didn't mess with Clem. Or The Krays. Or The Richardsons. I was young, I had a darkroom. Met Clem, he gave me plenty of legit work."

"And stuff that wasn't legit?" asked Porter.

"Never did no porn. Proper, I was. Proper." He gazed the strung-out gaze of an anaesthetised sentimentalist.

"Is this one of yours?" said Feng, pointing at an artful black-and-white of a worker unloading eggs down the docks.

"Yeah. In the 60s I had a few exhibitions. But once they heard about me and Clem up West... that all dried up."

"Was Clem that bad?" asked Porter.

"That depends, doesn't it? He didn't care what you were - black, gay, a Nazi, a Commie, a tart, a film star... act good, splash out. Fine. If not... his goons had iron whips like car aerials. They'd beat on you pretty good. Look." He pulled his sleeve up and showed them scarred skin healed in ugly lines, criss-crossing his forearm. "Took a year to heal. Just cos I left the lens cap on. The roll came out blank."

"What was the shoot?" asked Feng.

"Nothing. Shots of his club. Lobby cards."

"Do you still have any of your 60s shots? Of Soho?" asked Feng. "If you have more like that one, I'd love to see them. I might even buy one."

Chambers pointed to a couple of heavy looking books on the shelf. "There's the good stuff."

Porter and Feng were genuinely impressed. The photos were beautifully shot and printed, casual scenes of a long-gone Soho. There were tramps, street entertainers, tourists, workers, and sketchy punters craving for vices only Soho could sate.

The pills induced enough docility to enable conversation. Chambers' commentary was slurred. Feng used the chemical calm as cover, checking out some of Chambers' boxes. Contact strips and headshots, male and female: nothing spectacular. Feng snuck in a couple of phone shots after switching it to silent. While they were flipping through the photos, Porter asked the question he had been dying to get someone to answer. "Spies and Nazis - what do you all mean by that?"

Chambers gave him an idiot stare. "Don't you understand? They all came here. To Soho. It's where they could meet in red-tinted darkness. Sex. Benzedrine. Coke. Grass. LSD. Anything. They got their shit, but at a cost. The place was full of blackmailers, rollers, vermin. Soho is where it all collided: homos, TVs, whores by the thousand. Of course, all the spies came here. Philby, Burgess and Maclean - they came for girls and boys, booze and drugs. Nowhere better to swap dirty secrets in the dark. And you think all the Germans stopped being Nazis just because the war ended? Don't make me laugh."

Feng said, "Did you ever hear of a German called Heinrich Becker? A film director? He's the one who had your print of Julie Clark on his wall."

Chambers was calmer, but his reaction was immediate and final. There was no doubting he meant it, when he closed his eyes and said, "No. I told them. I look after myself. Go now. Please, just go."

The audience was over.

Chapter 28

November 2nd, 2017
Porter's flat, Sylvester Path, Hackney

The Gliss watched Feng wiping tears from his eyes. "If onions make you cry, why do you eat them?" he asked.

"They only make you cry when you're cutting them," said Feng, using a tea-towel to dab his eyes. "Curry without onions is unthinkable."

"Well, it seems an odd way to go about things," said The Gliss. "And you like onions too, do you, Porter?"

"Yes, of course," replied Porter, who was busy slicing up some raw chicken.

"Well, I don't get it," said The Gliss.

"That fact that you don't get onions," said Porter, "somewhat lessens your ability to interpret human behaviour. Hey Feng - a couple of months ago he asked me what the point of a gin and tonic was." They both laughed. Namita, de-seeding a pile of chillis, tutted.

The doorbell rang.

"That's odd," said Porter. "No-one ever visits, present company excepted."

Wearing an apron and carrying a sharp knife, he opened the door. He almost dropped the blade.

"Hi, Porter. Someone tell you I was coming?" said Tania Muriskava, eyeing the knife before stepping in uninvited. She was already halfway to the kitchen before Porter snapped out of it and closed the door.

She walked into the kitchen to see Feng in his apron, sniffling and dicing. Namita was chopping her chillis and barely looked up. It had nothing to do with her.

"Er, hello?" said Tania, directing her comments at Feng and Namita as though addressing intruders.

"Hi," said Feng, jovially. "And you are?"

"Tania."

"What? *The* Tania? Pleased to meet you. I'm Feng Tian."

"And I'm Namita. Porter's solicitor."

"He needs a solicitor to see me now?"

"From what I've heard, it's good to cover all bases."

Porter returned to the kitchen, also in his apron. "Namita, Feng, this is Tania. *The* Tania."

"I'm a *The* now, then?" said The Tania. "What's this? Bake off? Since when did you start wearing an apron, Porter?"

"Blame me," said Feng. "I bought a matching set so we could cook together properly." He said it so sweetly, so innocently, he didn't notice Tania's raised eyebrows.

"Something you want to tell me, Porter?" she said.

"What do you mean?"

"I do believe she is wondering if you two are an item," said The Gliss. Feng, Porter and Namita, looked at The Gliss, then each other, then Tania, and cracked up.

"*I* am gay, darling," Feng told Tania, "but Porter and I are just good friends."

"And I, as I've already said, am his solicitor," said Namita.

"Not that it's any of your business, Tania," said Porter, still laughing. "What on earth are you doing here?"

Tania, whose humourlessness proved something of a stimulant to the gang, was not amused. "Porter, could we have a chat in private, please?"

"Feng, you okay with the chicken?" asked Porter.

"Sure, if you're okay with the hen," Feng giggled.

After washing his hands and taking off the apron, Porter found himself alone with his ex for the first time in eight months. His heart was pounding like a tart's mattress. He asked her what she wanted, gloves up in a defensive position.

"Porter, I've missed you."

If someone had taken a broadsword and swept his legs off at the knees, Porter could not have been more surprised. Where he might have once reacted with at least an *ah,* his aura now radiated a visible *aargh.*

"What are you talking about? You haven't said a nice word to me for months."

"Absence makes the heart grow fonder, right?"

"Does it." Porter didn't even pose it as a question. "Honestly? I'm not sure it does. Not in my case, anyway."

"Are you saying you don't love me anymore?" said Tania, splitting her own aura between offended, annoyed, and coquette.

"I'm saying I stopped trying when you made it clear you had no time for me. In the meantime, I've made new friends, like Feng and Namita, and moved on."

"And I hear you're working with Karin Pelenot, now?"

"Yes, we've…"

"And you've been to LA together?"

"Yes, but I don't…"

"So, you've just given up on us, and got back in the saddle? Is that it?"

"What the hell are you going on about?" said Porter, mystified. "I'm not seeing anyone, if that's what you mean."

"Good, because I was…"

Porter decided to head this one off before it got too uncomfortable. "Listen, Tania. I've no idea what's come over you, but for a whole year you've made it plain I was a giant dog turd of a boyfriend. It devastated me. But you refused to talk, cut me off, and insisted I leave the house when you came over to get your belongings. I don't want to be harsh, but you clearly hated me." He waved away nascent signs of protestation. "I use the word *hate* advisedly. I got the message. I've moved on. Sorry."

"To what?" she said, bitterly. "Hanging out with chums? Making curry?"

"Two admirable pursuits. Sorry."

"You really won't discuss this? What I say doesn't matter?"

"It used to - until you crushed my heart into a pulp." He tried to think of something, anything, to mollify her. "You're welcome to stay for curry."

"I don't like curry. You should know that."

"Ah, yes. See - I've even forgotten your quirks."

Tania, tougher than a concrete muffin, was no masochist. She stormed back through the kitchen. "I'll let myself out," she said, reaching for the door handle.

"Wait!" shouted Porter.

She stopped, her attitude visibly softening. "Yes, Porter?"

"The door handle's covered in chicken juice. I offered you curry, not salmonella. Wanna wash your hands?"

With a scowl, Tania stepped out into the street and slammed the door behind her.

"What the hell was that about?" said Feng. "I thought you two were finished?"

"We are. I've no idea. I'd have done anything for her… once upon a time."

"And then you met us," said Namita.

"Yeah, you replaced the asp with bosom buddies," said Feng.

"You haven't replaced her. She replaced herself. She was like a goddess to me. Before she turned into some sort of demon with an arse-poking trident of rejection."

Feng smiled. Namita shook her head, wondering how anyone could have mistaken Tania for a goddess. Porter acknowledged his former pain. "I really would have died for her," he admitted.

"Well, if she doesn't wash the chicken off her hands soon, it's her'll be doing the dying," said Namita.

One hour later, Feng, Porter and The Gliss were gathered around one of the flat's workstations, Skyping Karin. She brought them up to speed. They told her about Chambers and Jimmy the Shanker.

"This is something to do with gangsters and film, not espionage," said Karin. "I'm almost certain of it. I'm inclined to believe the Reverend Crystal when he says he knows nothing, but it's a fact that all three of the Bristol girls ended up in LA. Two of them ended up in Berlin. One disappeared in Berlin, one in LA. It's too much of a coincidence."

"It's all so tenuous," said Feng. "We've established that one of London's biggest gangsters helped girls get headshots. That's it. We've zilch evidence of porn, for example. Everyone we've met so far says there was none of that going on. I found a memoir of the NW5 Gang that Shanker mentioned. Stories of amputation, beatings, shootings and stabbings, but nothing about porn."

"Shanker was adamant there was no homegrown porn," confirmed Porter.

"Just because that scumbag says so, doesn't mean there wasn't any," said Namita. "But, from what you told me, Jimmy would surely have boasted about it if he knew anything sordid. Sounds like he wouldn't have passed up the chance to talk about breasts and pubes."

"Tits and fannies - that's what he'd have said, the disgusting old bastard," said Feng.

"There are so many locations," said Porter, thoughtfully. "You're right about LA, London and Berlin, but we know Ursa went to Paris, Rome and New York too."

"That might be incidental," said Feng. "But maybe the most important thing is they all started their unfortunate journeys in London."

"Rose went to New York, and so did Bella," said Namita. "Whatever they were up to, they travelled a lot. Are we sure they weren't drug mules or something like that? You can carry more than secrets."

"We literally know nothing," said Porter. "Let's face it - we have a pile of geriatric witnesses to things that happened 50 years ago. No-one has a coherent theory yet."

"Despite my own reservations, Morrie Crystal speculated that we look to government or big business," said Karin. "It's obvious someone paid for Bella's trip and he couldn't see anyone in Hollywood doing so. He's on the spy-side of things. It's a theoretical possibility, I grant you, but the chances of it feel remote. Why on earth would the British government fund a green actress to spy? In America? Spy on what? No, I can't see it."

"Nor can I," said Namita. "The postcards and letters I've seen are from nice, boring suburban girls - not Mata Haris."

"If there's a London link, it's probably this guy, Clem Rossiter," said Porter. "If he's the link, from what we've heard, we'd need to look to the sordid, not espionage. I'm sure it'll all turn out to be fairly mundane."

"Where are you up to on Rossiter?" asked Karin.

"The day we found out he and Becker are linked by Vince Chambers, we put an interview request in," said Porter. "This time we're pretending to be your researchers working on a documentary about the 60s club scene in London. I left a message with his daughter."

"If I actually had to make all these films, I'd be fully booked until retirement," laughed Karin. "If he agrees before I get back, interview him as my associate producers. I'll text you the numbers of my camera and sound guys, Daly Johns and John Borrison. They know what they're doing; all you'll need to do is turn up."

"Don't be seduced into thinking this is only a London gangster thing just yet," said Namita. "There's definitely an international dimension. All those film people... Don Lascelles and Morrie Crystal in LA, right, Karin? Ursa mentioned two others, Oli Caron in France, and Buddy Demsky in New York."

"We'll continue to look into them, of course," said Porter. "Film's a small world. I'm just saying, from what we've seen so far, I'm not expecting to find some giant international Cold War conspiracy."

"I've got the list of movie names, Namita," said Feng. "I'm going to look them up tomorrow."

Karin nodded. "It's a capital mistake to theorise without data, correct? We're still early doors with the research. Let me know if you have any luck with Rossiter. Whatever happened, it's clear the girls were caught up in something, and two of them got into the worst kind of trouble - either disappearing or being disappeared. Harding looked into it and was beheaded for his trouble. It's sad, but perfectly understandable, that whatever happened to Rose and Bella lead to Ursa's suicide too. There's clearly something here, we just don't know what it is yet. Let's face it: it could be anything."

"I'm only a messenger," said The Gliss - a collective sigh - "but my spider senses tell me you're on the right track; this is the correct mission. Well done, Porter."

"What about us?" Feng jibed.

"Yes, they're doing okay too," said The Gliss.

Chapter 29

November 3rd, 2017
British Library, Euston Road, London

Researcher Feng came up trumps on a fag-break. He called Porter from the library quadrangle, braving biting winds for a smoke, his jacket foolishly left inside.
"You're not going to believe this," said Feng. "Buddy Demsky and Oli Caron were both murdered weeks after Rose disappeared in Berlin."
"Coincidence."
"I really don't think so. Paolo Agresti was killed the same day."
"And who the hell is he?"
"He was another film bod. Guess where he was based?"

"With that name... Italy?"

"Rome to be exact."

"What did they do? How did they die?"

Suffering a steady shiver, Feng said, "All three were producers or directors - successful in their own countries, but none had much success in Hollywood."

"They all died on the same day? How?"

"Demsky was gunned down in a restaurant in Little Italy - Mob hit because he owed them money. Agresti's Ferrari went over the edge of a mountain in Tuscany, killing him and a young starlet. If he hadn't died the same day as two other film bods, it wouldn't be suspicious at all. Oli Caron was also shot. His live-in lover, Steffi Posano, was jailed for the murder. She died in prison in 1983, still protesting her innocence."

Porter was disappointed. "Maybe it was coincidence? That's three very different ways of dying."

"Coincidence? Are you kidding?" Feng exploded. "All three died on February 3rd, 1967. We know two of them met at least one of our girls."

"Yes, Ursa, but nothing happened to her. She killed herself."

"All three of these guys died less than a month after Rose disappeared in Berlin."

"But Agresti - that's the first time we've heard his name," said Porter, cautiously.

"Sure, but that doesn't mean he's not connected," said Feng. "I don't know what we've got, but we've got something."

"Can you get a little dossier on everyone? We need to find connections between these people - other than the coincidence of the day they died."

Feng corrected Porter. "No, we have three coincidences - they were all film directors in the cities our girls visited. They met at least two of them. They all died on the same day. There's no getting away from it."

"My brain hurts."

"Mine too. Can you meet at mine later? We need to get organised."

"I have some good news too. Clem Rossiter's daughter called. I filled her in. We can interview him the day after tomorrow. I've booked Karin's film crew."

Feng was pleased. "Perhaps you can help me set up the Murder Room before we go see him?"

"Help you set up the *what*?" said Porter.

November 3rd, 2017
Starbucks, Central Bristol.

Martin Skelling took a day to respond to Namita's suggestion of a *Larke V Nugus* - the agreed sharing of documents in the contested will case.

Instead of simply acquiescing, he requested she come to Bristol to discuss. "And who knows? We might be able to squeeze dinner in?"

After being ogled by Martin's odious friends, she was reluctant to commit to that.

"He must be really desperate to get in your pants again," said Sangita. "Mind you, it's not like he's coming to London to serenade you. But you're a good obedient little puppy, aren't you? I'm sure you'll go."

For once, Namita didn't get into a fight with the ghost of her sister. Sangita was right. Namita, who was resolved not to sleep with Skelling again, decided she should still go to Bristol. If there was going to be trouble over Flo's will, the confrontation wasn't far away. No point ducking it.

She was meeting Martin in a bistro near the SS Great Britain. As soon as she walked in, she knew she'd been right. Trouble had come.

Gone was the man who'd died laughing trying to teach her darts. Gone was the man who'd kissed her passionately, despite the smell of kebab. Sitting at the table, sour-faced and business-like, he had transformed into a full-on Doberman of a lawyer. *Shit*. If she hadn't gleaned it from his face, his words left her in no doubt.

"Ms Menon, thank you for coming. Obviously, this is a very serious situation. We have to work out how best to proceed."

Here goes.

"How are you, Martin?" He ignored her, shuffling a few papers, waiting for her to sit. "Come on, what's going on?" she tried again. "Why are you being so formal all of a sudden?" She looked at the papers on the table and her blood curdled. Copies of the Solicitors Regulation Authority Code of Conduct and something from the Law Society.

"Ms Menon, as you know I've been instructed by Gary Stormont in the case of his aunt's will…"

She wasn't going to allow this. "Look, Martin, can you cut this professional lawyer crap. We've already been through this…"

But Skelling was not to be deflected. "It has come to my attention that Mr Stormont instructed you first, however…"

Right. She wasn't having that. "You know perfectly well that I didn't take instruction from Gary Stormont, the little shit…"

"…then, armed with details provided by my client, you contacted one Samuel Brownlees…"

"It's no good trying to reset the clock…"

"…this being a serious breach of the SRA's Code of Conduct…"

"Can you stop being such a jerk, you know…"

"…we have no option but to make a complaint against you…"

"Jesus, Martin - even if you do that…"

Martin continued as though Namita wasn't there. He held up an envelope. "…unless, of course, you agree to stop fighting this case on behalf of Brownlees."

Namita gasped. "Are you seriously trying to blackmail me, you bastard?"

Sangita had to shout, "Do not punch him! Do you hear me? Do not punch him!"

For only the second time ever, Namita took direct instruction from her sister. It was all she could do not to pick up the chair and smash it over his stupid, tousled head. It was her turn to be Hugh Grant. *Fuck, fuck, fucketty-fuck.*

November 3rd, 2017
Feng's house, Church Lane, Walthamstow, London

"You can be quite scary, Feng," said Porter, taking his first astonished look around the Murder Room.

Feng had converted the largest of his spare rooms into something straight from a cheap TV crime series. Photos of the Bristol Girls, Becker, Jimmy, Clem, Harding and co, were pinned to the walls. Pieces of red wool connected the photos. The smell was overpowering.

"Sorry about the stink," explained Feng. "I stuck about 100 tiles up and used enough cork glue to put The Titanic back together again. I've had the windows open day and night, but the whiff is proving persistent. It's like someone swapped my face flannel for a teenager's underpants."

"Besides the fact I can't breathe, what's going on here?"

"I've made an assumption. You can see it obviously?"

"That the girls are all victims - and the perpetrators are all men?"

"Right. Look at it. Three rows. City on top; men from those cities underneath. Below that, our girls. A red thread connects the city to the girls. Another red thread connects the men to the girls. If we don't know who the girls met in a particular city yet, I haven't connected the man and the girls, just the city. And it's very revealing, isn't it?"

Rome	Paris	London	Berlin	LA	New York
Paolo Agresti	Oli Caron	Clem Rossiter	Heinrich Becker	Don Lascelles	Buddy Demsky
		Vince Chambers		Morrie Crystal	

So far, they had the following confirmations.

Rose visited LA, New York, London and Berlin. She met Becker, Rossiter, Chambers.

Ursa visited LA, New York, London, Berlin, Paris, Rome. She met Rossiter, Demsky, Caron, Becker and Lascelles/Crystal.

Bella visited London, New York, LA. She met Rossiter.

"I would bet a million pounds all three girls met all the men from each city they visited," said Feng. "All we have to do is prove it."

"A big assumption and difficult to prove," said Porter. "I get what you are saying, but the person we know most about, Ursa, returned home from all these travels in one piece. If you're constructing some sort of evil masterplan between these guys, how do you explain that?"

"I don't know, it's puzzling me too. The next stage is to fill in the timeline."

"God," said Porter. His face resembled Charlton Heston getting his first gander at the Statue of Liberty on its side. "You know this means we're going to have to go back over everything in the Dropbox, right?"

Feng held up a fistful of take-away menus. "The local Thai's quite good, but the vegetable thali at The Pink Poppadum is fabulous too."

Chapter 30

November 3rd, 2017
LAPD Robbery Homicide Division, West First Street, LA

Eight hours behind in Los Angeles, Karin was standing on the corner of Santa Monica and La Brea, waiting for Arnie Flax to pick her up.

She'd agreed to go for breakfast. He wanted to take her to Alfredo's in WeHo.

"They do a good English breakfast there," he'd said. Karin, who was developing a foodie crush on breakfast burritos, wasn't fussed about tucking into sausage and egg, but let Arnie choose.

He pulled up in a black-and-white and her heart skipped a beat. "I arrest you in the name of the law," he said, in a terrible Cockney accent. "Hop in."

"I've always wanted a ride in one of these," said Karin. "How exciting."

"Yeah? You should try driving in one when you've got a stinking panhandler in the back. The grill is just big enough to strain out the biggest chunks of vomit, but every officer I know has had to dry clean their outfit at some point."

"And the breakfast is nice at Alfredo's, is it?" said Karin, quickly discarding the image.

"Well, they have a thing every Tuesday morning - Brits do LA. Anyone can go, but it's mostly writers, actors, casting agents and directors."

"I'm not really interested in meeting any," laughed Karin. "They're my panhandlers back home."

"Don't worry; that's not why I'm taking you," laughed Flax. "Fifteen bucks and a full English and as much coffee as you can handle. It's cheap and good for my ego. Screenwriters love a chat with a cop. More often than not, it doesn't even cost me 15 bucks. They put it down as research."

They pulled into Alfredo's drive, Flax waiving away the valet, sticking his arm out and tapping the LAPD logo on his door. He reversed into a space. It was warm, but there was a breeze making the in-shadow parking lot a little too cool for Karin.

"I've got to ask about the eye," said Flax. "Did you really get it from an unexploded World War 1 bomb? That's some rough luck."

Karin, stoned by the Profugus in Flanders, had no choice but to trot out the same old cover story. Yes, it was a UXB. Yes, she was filming. Yes, she was, as far as she knew, the last casualty of the battlefields of World War 1. The millions of munitions still buried meant she wouldn't be the last.

"What's going to happen? Will you eventually have an operation and a glass eye?" Flax was typically American. He didn't mean his directness to offend, but Karin was still getting used to the loss. His cavalier question smarted a little.

"I don't know, Arnie." She shrugged. "It's a little too soon to talk about it. Funnily enough, the eye patch has made me a little more famous. Did you ever read about the journalist, Marie Colvin? She was assassinated in Syria a few years back, but before that she lost an eye to shrapnel covering the Sri Lankan civil war. I always admired her so much. Now she's gone, although my work isn't as important as hers, I feel like I'm carrying the mantle for one-eyed, middle-aged, female journalists everywhere."

Missing the sarcasm, Flax nodded. "That's very noble of you. I read about Colvin. Amazing woman. I understand your position. I'll let you in on a secret: you see these cufflinks? They belonged to my mentor, Lionel Footer. He was shot dead confronting some punks down Skid Row in the mid-90s. I asked his widow if I could have them. Worn them ever since. Wanting to feel connected to those who've passed is not uncommon or unhealthy, is it?"

"Sure, but I didn't know Marie Colvin. Mine isn't so much of a remembrance as a club badge," said Karin. "But anyway…" *For God's sake, talk about something else.*

Luckily, Arnie was spun on his heels by Charlie, the man who ran the Brits do LA club. They greeted each other as old friends and Charlie showed them to a table. In keeping with the informal networking vibe, a woman immediately came over and introduced herself.

"Hi, Karin Pelenot? I just wanted to say hello. My name is Sara, I'm a writer from London. I love your work. What are you doing here?"

Irritated by the interruption, but doing her best not to appear rude, Karin made something up. Flax watched on in amusement.

"Can I give you my card?" said Sara, handing one over before Karin had time to react. "I'm sorry about your eye. I saw it on the news."

After Sara came two others. Flax saw he'd made a mistake bringing her here. "I'm sorry, I didn't realise you were *this* well-known."

Karin waved it away, and they tucked into their posh English breakfasts. She told him about the meeting with Reverend Crystal.

"He's a good guy, right? Like I told you?"

"Yes," said Karin, "he's honest, though I think his past might be a little murkier than he's ready to admit to." She summarised Crystal's confession.

"Sure," said Flax, "but Hollywood has always been like that. People think it *used* to be full of douchebags and slime-balls, but they have no idea. It's just as bad now."

"Even with #MeToo?" asked Karin.

"If you ask me, it might have made things worse. Before #MeToo these douchebags could operate in the open, right? They saw the casting couch as just part of the process." Arnie gave her two examples of hugely famous actresses he knew for a fact had been high-class call girls before getting their big breaks.

"But now, the sons-of-bitches will find another way. You can change the rules, but some people will do anything to become famous. Sadly, there are plenty of people who will demand even worse simply because they hold the keys."

"That's very cynical."

"Yeah? Do you know how many young suicides I've dealt with in Hollywood? Some people can divorce themselves from their bodies, their backgrounds, their souls even. Other people absorb the compromises they've made and feel cheated and beaten later on. And not everything's consensual. Far from it. Even now, people assume most rape claims are a woman scorned."

"Crystal said he and Don Lascelles slept with many hundreds of women. Maybe as many as 1,000. You're on the ground. You think some of those women went on to kill themselves?"

"He admitted to that many? Some of those girls would have felt pretty ashamed of what they'd been coerced into. It's a given some of them couldn't live with it."

"It's not all coercion, though?" said Karin, thinking of the era of Free Love.

"Are you kidding?" Flax spluttered. *"Suck my dick or you don't get the job.* That's not coercion, to you? If we were talking about awarding company contracts on that basis, the directors would all go to prison. Or your High School examiner said he'd only give you a good grade if you screwed him? Nope, there's no defence. None."

"I thought Weinstein would change all that," said Karin, daintily wiping egg from her chin. *Bloody over-easy. Why not call it uncooked and be done with it?*

Flax shook his head and leant back, patting his stomach. "The power in Hollywood is still held by-and-large, by white men. The sons-of-bitches just have to be smarter working out which ones will squeal. I hope that bastard Weinstein goes down for life."

Karin nodded. "Crystal said Lascelles wasn't into anything weird, though. What do you think?"

"Depends on your definition of weird. I've never heard anything about his peccadilloes - and Hollywood is nothing if not good for gossip. But this is a man who felt the need to sleep with 1,000 women. That's not weird to you?"

"I think I might be guilty of thinking this is normal in Hollywood. We had a children's TV presenter in England called Jimmy Savile. After he died, hundreds of people came forward to say he'd sexually assaulted them. Cue obvious and deserved public hatred." Arnie was about to reply, when Karin leant forward.

"Yet, there's also a well-known story that David Bowie passed a 13-year-old groupie around the rock aristocracy in the early 70s. But no-one says anything about that because they hero-worshipped Bowie. A lot of today's adults - boys and girls - would have slept with Bowie back then if they'd had the chance, so in a twisted way, they either ignore the 13-year-old or they think she was lucky. No-one fancies Polanski, so the campaign to get him to face justice is decades long."

"Yep. It's a crazy, mixed-up world."

"I'm clear what right and wrong is, I just think the public has double standards," said Karin.

"Hell, I'm American. Some of the things our president has said would get me or you chucked out of church, but people still support him."

Karin told Flax about the London research, and showed him the little chart Feng had made.

"The thing is," she said, "although there are gangsters and spies in the background of this story, I'm concerned at how many film producers/directors are turning up."

"I hear what you're saying, but I've been in LA forever. I've never heard complaints about Lascelles - or Morrie Crystal for that matter. If either had started disappearing people or abusing people, there would be complaints on file - especially if they put it around that much. Don't you think?"

"What about the expensive hotels? Does it suggest anything to you?"

"Ok. So, let's say Lascelles paid for the hotel. But if anyone went missing the paper trail would lead straight to him. Same with Crystal's address turning up. It doesn't make sense. I can't see the connection right now. But you're right: it's worth finding out who paid for your girls' hotels. It's what I'd do. And don't forget the hangers-on. I can't imagine Lascelles being involved. Doesn't mean he didn't have a freak or two working for him."

Karin considered the possibilities. "Couldn't you run Morrie's address and the hotel address against your database of missing women?"

Arnie forked a grilled slice of tomato and said, "If this was an episode of CSI, sure. In real life, no. Only names and case numbers are in that index. It would take forever to go through the files manually."

Karin mused. "Ok, how about you randomly pull 50 files, and I'll manually check them."

Flax said that was a possibility but would take time to organise.

"Well, I'm here for a few more days yet," said Karin, tucking into a tepid field mushroom. "Let's do it."

Flax was as good as his word, but it would be weeks before Karin got a chance to check the files he pulled.

November 2nd, 2017
Holloway Road, London

Namita was chewing her nails, having a fag, and drinking espresso. Three vices, each a symptom of her professional and personal discomfort.

She'd failed to talk Martin Skelling down. He wanted her to ignore Dr Harwell's evidence and advise Sam Brownlee to let Gary Stormont's appeal go through, uncontested. If she refused, he was going to lodge a complaint against her with the SRA. She was pretty sure she was screwed if he did. Her defence was thin.

After pushing her in the snake-pit, the cheeky bastard still had the gall to suggest dinner. "Business is business, but pleasure is pleasure," he'd said.

To her annoyance, she'd been half-tempted, but stayed with the battling-solicitors script and stormed out. He shouted after her, "I'll give you a week."

She couldn't afford to let him cow her. She'd only just gone solo. She had to keep a clean sheet. She had to win Brownlee's case. Only one option. She stubbed out the fag, only half-done, swigged the coffee, and dialled.

"Barry? It's Namita." Barry Hammell was her ex-SAS, clandestine, private investigator. He wasn't cheap and he wasn't scrupulous. "I'm in trouble. I need a favour."

"What's up?" said Barry.

She told him.

"And you want me to dig up some dirt on Skelling? Blackmail the blackmailer?"

"Yep. It's not my preferred way of doing things but…"

"It's not a good idea, Namita. It never works. Just escalates things."

"Even so…"

Hammell wasn't the sort to waste time. "You give me a lot of work. I'll do this as a freebie. Two days for free. Any more than that, it'll cost you. How's that sound?"

"Thanks, Barry. It might not even take that long. He's a dick."

"Well, he's in Bristol, not Chicago, so he's unlikely to have left a trail of corpses behind him but… leave it with me."

"I'll make it up to you," said Namita.

"Promises, promises."

"Don't be cheeky."

"I'll be in touch."

Sangita appeared and told her she was nuts. "You know this won't end well. Skelling's a ruthless little sod. If Hammell screws up…"

"He's good. If there is anything, he'll find it soon enough."

"Alright, if you say so. Don't say I didn't warn you."

Namita knew Sangita was right. She just didn't know what else to do.

Chapter 31

November 5th, 2017
Carol's Chase, Stansted Mountfichet, Essex

Daly Johns and John Borrison watched Feng and Porter get out of the cab.
"Do you know anything about these chumps?" said Johns.
"Karin says they're green as Kermit and have never done a shoot before," said Borrison, stubbing out a fag with his foot.
"I bet she didn't put it like that. Great."
"She's paying. Be on your best behaviour."
"Me? I'm a kitten."
"From Pet Sematary."
"I have claws, but I can retract them for Miss Pelenot." Johns snorted. "That said... she's in LA in the sun, and she sends us to Essex in the cold. She owes us."

"Well, it can't all be Nassau and Tahiti." The pair had travelled the world on the back of Karin's programmes and could easily afford to forgive a few early starts in the cold. But where would be the fun in that?

Porter and Feng advanced towards them, making those awkward gestures Englishmen make when approaching strangers for the first time - a kind of hand-and-eyebrow shuffle which says, "You are, aren't you?"

They were, so they introduced themselves. "What's the score?" asked Johns.

"You've heard of Clem Rossiter?" said Porter.

"Yeah. I've filmed him for Channel 4's Bad Boys."

"Ok. We're looking into the case of a woman who went missing in the 60s. She and her friends worked for Rossiter," said Feng.

"You're not accusing him, are you?" said Borrison, alarmed. "He's a psycho."

"No, we're just doing background research for Karin's film about 60s Soho," said Feng.

"Yeah, well make sure you don't piss him off. He might take it out on all of us," said Borrison.

Grace Rossiter had clearly spent a good chunk of her 55 years in the sun. She was the sort of orange that made people slap the side of their heads to check their eyes were still working. Her hair had been pulled back by a weightlifter and knotted by a sailor. Her dress suit showed off an orange-peel chest, with several gold and silver chains and pendants creating a barbed wire tangle by Faberge.

"Welcome," she said, a ringmaster ushering children into the circus. "Dad's just getting ready. He said to set you up in the study."

The team wheeled in several cases of filming equipment and Johns surveyed the room, assessing it for light. "We'll need to pull the curtains," he said. Grace told them to move anything they wanted, promising to bring her Dad, and tea, in 20 minutes.

The room was as heavy as a Victorian mourning lounge. Mahogany furniture, puffy green-and-white striped cushions on a dark maroon Chesterfield. Tacky ornaments everywhere. Monstrous table lamps clustered like conspiring Daleks, and the main light was provided by a chandelier clearly stolen from Buckingham Palace.

One wall was lined with books bought by the yard. Rossiter presumably hoped the room and library would say something about him. It did: he had no taste.

"God, look," said Feng. "He's got the same awful ballet dancer statue Becker had."

"They must have had a sale on at Steptoe and Sons," said Porter.

"Too classy for them," sniffed Feng. Clem's version was battered and chipped and the tutu was torn and pinned together with a safety pin. "What is that? I mean, it's the ugliest statue I've ever seen."

"Are you sure? What about that one?" said Porter, pointing to a huge bronze figure looking like a skinny brass version of Rodin's Thinker. "This is the home of a troll."

"Nice shag though," said Borrison, moving his feet around the fluffy carpet.

"It would be - if it wasn't purple," said Feng, his impeccable sense of style offended. "I mean, is this guy colourblind or what?"

Johns and Borrison unpacked, setting up tripods and lighting stands.

"I'm a bit nervous," said Porter. "I've never interviewed anyone on camera before."

"It's easy, mate," said Johns. "Just ask *who, why, what, where, when* questions - and if appropriate, add *and why* on the end. *What's your favourite album - and why?* That sort of thing. Forces them to waffle."

"Ah, a whole profession reduced to a one-sentence description," said The Gliss. "Watch out, Emily Maitlis."

"I'm sure there's a bit more to it than that," said Feng, "but we'll manage."

"And only one of you can ask the questions," said Johns. "You'll need to sit next to the camera so that the eyeline's right. If you sit next to each other, he'll swivel his eyes between you - and it'll look shit – like marbles rolling round a tin. If you both want to ask questions, one of you will have to sit on the other's shoulder."

"Like a parrot," confirmed Borrison.

"Aye, aye, cap'n," said Porter.

Grace flounced back in with a Filipino maid carrying a tray. "If you need anything, Dalisay will fetch it for you. I'm off to get Dad. How long before you're ready?"

"Ten minutes, love," said Borrison.

"Excuse me?" said Grace.

"Sorry, Miss Rossiter," he apologised. "Northerner. Can't help myself. I'm all *love this, pet that*."

"Not in this house, you're not," said Grace, turning away dismissively.

Bowing slightly, Dalisay asked how they liked their tea. Orders taken, the four-man team completed their set-up alone and waited for Rossiter to arrive.

Dalisay returned and poured the tea on a tray before dishing the cups out. Feng, who was gasping for refreshment, smiled with gratitude. She didn't smile back, but nodded downwards, her eyes pleading. Feng, puzzled, followed her gaze and saw a tiny slip of paper poking out from under his cup. He nodded gently and slipped the piece of paper into his pocket.

As he did so, Grace reappeared, reprising her ringmaster impression. She gestured to the doorway. Clem Rossiter entered. He looked like the bastard child of Mike Reid and Flava Flav. Big aviator sunglasses, hairy gold-ringed knuckles, and ill-fitting tracksuit. His voice was gruff, rumbling, and still deeply Cockney. "Gents."

The tea in Feng's cup rippled. Even in his 80s, Rossiter was impressive. No gut hung over his jogging bottoms. He looked in better shape than Porter.

Before they could shake, Johns butted in. "Hi, Mr Rossiter. We've worked together before. Bad Boys on Channel 4? Same deal, I'm afraid. You can't wear mirrored shades - we'll see the lights and crew in them."

"Dalisay. Get my other glasses." The maid left with a backwards curtsey that reminded Porter of Imperial China.

"What a charmer," said The Gliss. "No please or thank-yous, eh?"

Porter and Feng stepped forward. Rossiter shook their hands in turn, gripping firmly with sausage fingers. If he hadn't been a gangster, he could have strangled chickens for a living. "And probably enjoyed it," thought Porter.

"Where's Pelenot?"

"I'm Porter, this is Feng. We're Ms Pelenot's assistant producers on the film."

"She couldn't be arsed to come herself, then? Not important enough, eh?" Rossiter rumbled.

"She's in LA," said Feng.

"What the fuck's LA got to do with 60s Soho? The organ grinder's sunning it up in Malibu, eh?"

Daly Johns smirked. Borrison elbowed him to be quiet.

"We're dividing the work up," said Feng, leaving the implied insult unacknowledged. "We've already interviewed a few other people in London."

"Yeah? Like who?"

"Jimmy Farr," said Porter. The pause became a hammy moment of suspense in a 40s' horror movie. Thunder rumbled and lightning flashed.

"That scumbag," growled Rossiter. "What does he know? He was just a gopher. Don't listen to anything he says. He wouldn't have a pension unless people like you bunged him a few quid all the time for trotting out the same old cobblers."

"Didn't he work for you?" said Porter.

"Like I said - fucking gopher. Well, you're talking to me, now. I'm the one with the gen. The organ grinder is here."

Feng and Porter fidgeted while Johns and Borrison did their thing, setting up three-point lighting and putting a lapel mic on. Borrison went to dab a bit of powder, annoying Rossiter.

"Easy tiger. I don't want to look like an iron hoof."

"Pardon?" said Feng.

"Iron hoof - poof."

They were forced to let that one go, too. Dalisay returned with a spectacle case.

Rossiter's temper flared. "Not these ones, you idiot. The brown case." Dalisay hurried from the room again, giving Feng a knowing look.

"Like I said - a real charmer," said The Gliss.

Feng, with the introductions over, and Rossiter and the crew setting up, finally took Dalisay's note from his pocket. It was slightly damp with spilled tea.

They've taken my passport. Please help me get out of here.

Feng looked at Rossiter. Yes. He could believe this grotesque would do that. He vowed to help the maid.

Eventually, with the right glasses, just enough powder to take the shine off his face, and a noisy slurp of tea from the saucer, Rossiter was ready.

Porter led the questions, uncomfortably conscious of the parrots on his shoulder. Trying his best to ignore Feng and The Gliss, Porter began. "Our film's about the seamy side of Soho in the 60s. A lot of people have told us it was a strange time with gangsters, Cold War spies, actors, musicians all mixing together. How do you remember it?"

Rossiter cleared his throat like someone had chucked a mug of marbles in a blender. "Golden times, golden times. Hairy and lairy. Not like now. Fucking Starbucks and Pret. Golden times, just what us Blitz survivors needed."

Off Porter's encouraging look, which was really terror of playing inquisitor, Rossiter added, "It was hard to have a good time in London at the start of the 60s, right? There were bugger all fancy restaurants, for a start. They you had the Lord Chancellor stamping out any show about sex or politics. It was fucking boring - you can bleep that, right? Everything in black and white. Just lots of pissheads in pubs. Every bloke thought he was hard. Every hairy-legged tart thought she was Monroe. Bleedin' horrible."

"But it didn't stay like that?"

"Course not. And you know what changed it? Beyond the fucking Fringe and The Beatles. As soon as Peter Cook took the piss out of Harold MacMillan on stage and The Beatles made everyone want to come to London, it all got going. My first club was on Greek Street in 1961. It did alright but was boring as shit - more pub than club. Loads of old soldiers banging on about the bloody war, old fellers in flat caps reading the Racing Post. I was young, had won a bit of prizefighting dosh in Bethnal Green, and I thought - if The Beatles are making London swing, I'd better swing along with 'em."

"What did you do?"

"I sold The Scarlet and opened Kitty, Kitty. Good times from then on."

"How?"

"I put on little bits of cabaret - risqué but nothing dodgy, know what I mean? I shipped in posh booze from the continent no-one else had and got a proper cocktail scene going." He stopped to slurp more tea.

"They ain't gonna arrest me now are they, ha ha? It's okay now to admit we got a little pill scene going too. I put feelers out to a few TV bods and before you knew it, I had celebs coming down.

"Do you remember Dale Storey? Course you don't. Way before your time. Looked like Dirk Bogarde. Proper fanny magnet and a total pill-head. Once he realised he could come and enjoy himself at the Kitty, they all started coming. I set up a little gaming room out back - invitation only - and we'd have pop stars and TV presenters tossing wads of moolah about."

"I heard Judy Garland came to yours once?"

"Once? Fuck me, it was her second home when she was in London. And, of course, once that got out, there were bunfights to get in. It got crowded and we were turning punters away, so I opened The Scene in Berwick Street. It wasn't as flashy - more of a spillover joint. Almost anyone could get in there if they flashed the cash. Less celebs but the same 'anything goes' vibe. Did pretty well. I miss the fug of that place. Fucking snowflakes banning fags."

Porter gulped. "And you were known as a bit of a hard man?"

Rossiter laughed. "I was a bit more than that, son. I was the hardest bastard in Soho. I owned it. I gave it all up years ago, of course, but yeah, if there was a dodgy pie, sod a finger, I had my whole damn fist in it. I've done my time, so I can talk about it now. Pills, weed, tarts, booze… I went from one club to running an empire."

"Did that cause trouble with the other crime gangs? The Krays and all that lot?"

"There were little mishaps along the way, but we all knew better than to get in each other's way. It was all carved up, know what I mean? I used to go for a night out at The Krays' place occasionally. They came to mine. It could be pretty friendly."

"No violence at all?"

"Course there was! One of Reggie's lads got a bit out of hand at Kitty one night - the fucker tried to rape one of my girls."

"What happened?" said Porter.

"Look, I had the best girls in London, right? I made sure they were safe. I made sure they got paid. I wasn't gonna have some fucking gorilla from Whitechapel mess with them. Jill came in crying one day. She'd been raped.

"It started with some moron from the Kray's mob ripping her gown trying to grab her tits. The spangles scraped all down her arm. When she still didn't play ball, he punched her. He left a rose of a bruise on her upper arm, then gave her one against a pillar. We had to put make-up on it before she could go on."

You're claiming the high ground – but you made a raped and traumatised woman work? Animal. Porter put his disgust aside for a moment, resorting to the weaker weapon of sarcasm, instead. "And you didn't take such an affront lying down, I presume?"

"Too fuckin' right. I had a guy called Browz. Psycho. We took this guy out back and before I could say anything, Browz cut a couple of fucking fingers off with shears. I didn't necessarily agree with that," said Rossiter cautiously, before admitting, "I said to the cunt, 'You won't be hitting any little girls from now on, will you?' The prick was throwing up. We used some string as a tourniquet, wrapped his hand in a towel, and stuck him in a cab. Sending him to hospital seemed like the decent thing to do."

It was more than you did for the girl. "What happened to the fingers?" Porter asked, a tremor in his voice.

"Browz fed 'em to his fucking dog. How should I know. I didn't do it. I didn't order it."

No-one in the room believed that. "How did the Krays take that?" said Feng, blanching.

"Reggie demanded a sit-down. I told him what happened. He told me I should've come to him first."

"Did he get violent?"

Rossiter laughed. "With me? Yeah, right! He took a baseball bat to his bloke though. Sounds brutal, right? Show me one civilian who got that treatment. This was between people in the biz. Best way to avoid all-out war was to make sure we all stuck by the code. Between us we sent out a pretty strong message, right? Don't fuck with each other's territory."

Porter asked, "So what happened to the bloke who lost his fingers?"

"Who cares. Never saw him again. I can tell you this - the dick never played snooker again - not unless he got a bionic hand," Rossiter chuckled. "I can tell you about it now. Browz died in the 80s. Psycho. Absolute fuckin' psycho."

Rossiter's words hung in the air. Porter actually felt a bit sick. Feng took up the slack. "Were you aware of how many Cold War spies were hanging around Soho at that time?"

"You just said it: it was the Cold War. We thought anyone who wasn't an East Ender was probably spying for the Russians. Look - Cockneys, actors and bankers could sort of mingle. But the besuited public schoolboy wankers from Cambridge - they stood out a mile. City people still wore bowler hats and ties. These bastards from government wore top clobber from Mayfair, smoked cheroots and drank cocktails. They didn't fit in with ex-boxers, actors, and tarts." Rossiter coughed up another lungful, lobbed it into a hanky and took another slurp of tea.

"The public schoolboys were all poofters looking for rough trade. Same as now, really. You had to crave excitement and danger to come to my places. Kitty, Kitty, right? Dangerous, illegal and expensive. Not the place for a barrow boy to bring his bird in exchange for a bit of finger pie. Your average public schoolboy ponce knew he was putting himself in danger, but that was the thrill, right? Most of my clients were from the fucked-up end of society - poofters, addicts, thrillseekers - and yeah, probably a spy or two."

"Do you think they used your club as a rendezvous?" asked Porter.

"Maybe. Mostly just adrenalin junkies," said Rossiter. "After Burgess and Maclean, every posh bastard was a spy as far as I was concerned, right? As long as they ponied up, I didn't give a shit."

"Some people said there were former Nazis in your clubs too?" said Porter.

"Well, we were all friends again by then, right? If they had the dosh, I didn't give a shit what they'd done in the bloody war."

"I heard you were friends with the German film director, Heinrich Becker?" The air immediately chilled.

"Who the fuck told you that? Was that Shanker?"

"Several people."

"Yeah. I knew him. They said he was a Commie too. Did you know that? So bloody what if he was? Loads of TV and film bods came to our club. John fuckin' Lennon came to my clubs. Becker was just another director hanging out in London."

Porter decided it was time to go in. "You were into film too, I heard."

"I didn't do porn."

"I never said you did."

"Real films. I liked to put a bit of cash into them."

"What do you mean?"

"You know, like a film producer. There weren't that many films coming out of Britain at the time. Hitchcock was in America. Powell and Pressburger had stopped in the 50s. But there were a few brave bastards who managed to make a few. I invested a bit of a cash every now and again."

"Was it profitable?"

"I broke even over the long run. No classics. But that's not why I did it. I loved film. Look, I was a pretty bad lad, right? No point denying it. But film was something even my mum loved. She got a kick out of seeing my name on the credits. It made me feel legit."

Feng and Porter both immediately thought: money laundering.

Porter rejoined the fray. "And that's how you met Becker?"

"Yeah. I think we met at the Venice Film Festival in 1961. It was my first time out there. Trying to flog a Brit flick I'd put money into - The Hot Week. Had no luck on that, but sure enjoyed myself trying. Becker was just another contact really. We never made a film together. He never did English-speaking stuff. Why the fascination with Becker?" Rossiter eyed them coldly.

"It's just something we were looking into. There was an actress called Rose Prideaux. She worked for you, apparently, but she went missing in Berlin. Another one of your girls, Bella, went missing in LA too."

A cold wind sprinkled with pepper blew through the room. Rossiter shifted ominously. "What the fuck is this? I thought we were talking about 60s Soho - gangsters and shit?"

"Do you remember Rose?" asked Porter.

"Course I fucking remember her. The poor kid worked for me and went missing. We were cut up about it. Same with Bella. What's this got to do with me?"

"The guy who went looking for Rose was found in the Thames with his head missing. He had a diary which said he met you."

"What are you fucking insinuating?"

Feng pictured Browz and his shears. "Nothing. You asked me."

"I know nothing about that. Move on, Sonny." The implied threat was clear.

But there was no point being here unless they pushed it. Feng took up the challenge. "It's just that we found a few connections - you knew Becker, and Rose had an audition with Becker too. Becker used your photographer, Vince Chambers… you both even had the same statue," said Porter, pointing at the ballet dancer.

This was evidently a lame step too far. "You're trying to stitch me up! You're saying Becker killed the Rose girl and I had something to do with it? Just cos we both shopped at Conran? Right, that's it. Interview over. Get the fuck out of here."

"Honestly, we're not saying *that*," said Porter, but he was cut off.

"I said get the fuck out of my house." He ripped the lapel mic off, stood, and then lumbered from the room.

"That went well," said Porter.

"You touched a nerve," said The Gliss. "He clearly knows something."

Johns and Borrison shook their heads; bloody amateurs.

Two minutes later, Grace flew into the room, seething. "What the hell are you guys up to? You can forget the release form. If you use any of this footage, we'll sue your arses from here to Timbuktu. Get the hell out of here." Her hands were by her side but her anger gave them the impression her hands were on her hips.

Johns and Borrison were packing up double-quick time. They'd seen it all before. They were getting paid, whatever, but a quick exit was required.

"What do we do now?" said Porter, sipping a cappuccino an hour later.

"We'd better let Karin know," said Feng. "I doubt she'll be pleased. It was all done in her name." He took the piece of paper from his pocket. "Dalisay slipped me this. She says they're treating her like a slave."

"That's all we need. What are we going to do about that?" said Porter.

"We'll pass it on to our old mate Dan Crawley," said Feng. "It's a police matter. Did you call him about DCI Anderson from Harding's list?"

"God, no. Sorry. I'll call him in a minute."

The Gliss hovered between them. "You'd also better go through that tape. There was plenty in there to chase up, no?"

"Like what?" said Porter. "I thought it was pretty dull stuff - although I'll never look at garden shears the same way again."

"Porter - have you learnt nothing? He admitted he knew Becker. They met at a film festival."

Porter shrugged. "We can look into it."

"Don't sound too disappointed. It was probably all you were ever going to get," said The Gliss. "If he was involved in an unsolved set of disappearances, he wasn't going to admit that on tape, was he?"

November 5th, 2017
Feng's house, Church Lane, Walthamstow

Karin, on Skype, wasn't best pleased. "Jesus. I hope he doesn't make a complaint. I'm your producer. The buck stops with me if he takes it further."

"As The Gliss said," Feng chipped in, "what else could we expect? I've updated the Dropbox. There's an electronic transcription of the interview. See if you get anything from it."

Karin rang off, in a slight huff. Feng and Porter spent some time updating the Murder Room, pinning up the transcription, re-arranging photos, cutting out little bits of card with Bella's travel times etc. It gave them a sense of purpose. Feng said it was good prep for the master timeline he was going to produce. Porter offered to help, but Feng said it would be easier to do it alone.

Porter, repeating his earlier promise to call DCI Dan Crawley, was putting his coat on when Feng's computer started ringing. It was Karin again.

"Look at this," she said, pinging a screengrab through. She obviously hadn't wasted time looking through their material.

The cutting was from Variety magazine, a report about the 1961 Venice Film Festival. The piece was headed, *International Co-operation on Films*. A group of eight men, posing for a photograph, captioned:

International film producers discuss their next project. L-R Paulo Agresti, Simon Bell, Clem Rossiter, Alex Parfitt, Constantine Kryoplous, Heinrich Becker, Morrie Crystal and Karl Lutz.

"Holy crap," said Feng.

"I can think of better ways of expressing it," said Karin, "but, yes, that's what I thought. Four of the people who've cropped up in our investigation in one photo. That's not all."

The machine pinged again. Another screenshot, this time about the 1964 Venice Film Festival, again illustrated with a group photo.

From left to right: Simon Bell, Heinrich Becker, Buddy Demsky, Karl Lutz, Clem Rossiter, Paulo Agresti, Don Lascelles, Morrie Crystal, Oli Caron, Dieter Hamburg, Geoffrey Norris.

The room went quiet.

"Is it ok if I swear?" said The Gliss.

"Be my guest," said Porter.

"Jesus H. Christ," said The Gliss.

"I think that only counts as swearing in Alabama," said Porter, "But yeah, I'll see your *Jesus H. Christ* and raise you a *fuck me*."

"Blow me," said Feng.

"That's just inappropriate," said Porter.

"Let me finish: Blow me down with a feather."

"I'm coming home," said Karin. "This is getting serious."

She hung up. And Porter, Feng and The Gliss all stared at each other.

True staring is an act of concentration which demands silence for full effect. They were concentrating; they were staring; they were quiet. The crash and smash tore through the staring silence like a sword in a pocket.

"What the hell?" said Feng, rushing to his landing. He was just in time to see three men in hoods sprinting up the stairs. He turned to run, but the impetus was with the intruders and he was tripped easily before reaching the Murder Room door. The last thing he saw as he hit the floor was Porter's shocked face in the doorway.

The men in black spent the next five minutes liberally hitting Feng and Porter with wooden sticks. The Gliss watched on, helpless.

Chapter 32

November 7th, 2017
Royal Free Hospital, Hampstead, London

Feng came round two days later to find Namita and Karin staring at him. He was groggy from morphine but instinctively tried to raise an arm and wave hello.

"Ow."

"Ow indeed," said Karin. "I leave you two alone for a week and you're back in hospital."

"Is Porter alive?" said Feng, in slow-motion panic.

"Oh yes. He's alive but he won't be running the marathon anytime soon," said Namita.

"Beat the crap out of us," Feng said, somewhat redundantly. He looked like a loo roll left alone with a puppy.

"Did they say who they were? Why they were doing it?" asked Karin.

"Rossiter, no prize," said Feng, still muggy. "Angry potato."

"Evidently. You guys sure know how to piss people off," said Namita, before whispering to Karin, "He's gibbering."

"Was a warning," said Feng.

"Feng, I have a little surprise for you," said Karin. She stood to one side, revealing a tall man in an overcoat.

"Mr Tian? You really are trouble, aren't you?" said DCI Bob Crawley. The friendly cop, based at Stoke Newington nick, who'd inadvertently got caught up in their last case. Despite the trouble they caused, he'd come to like Porter and Feng.

"DCI Crawley," said Feng, still wading through the morphine penumbra. "I'd shake your hand, but my bones will fall out. Did Porter call you?"

DCI Crawley pulled up a chair. "No, haven't heard from Porter for a while. But you know I'm a cop, right? Reports come in. I saw you and Porter had taken a beating. Thought I'd better come and say hello. See what you've got yourself mixed up in this time. No jurisdiction. Just a friendly call."

"Could you use your inestimable powers of detection to let me know how badly injured I am? I can't move a German sausage at the moment."

Crawley registered Feng's confusion. He pointed at the bedridden sleuth. "You're pretty messed up. Whoever did this, knew what they were doing. Did you insult Mike Tyson's mum? But you're not crippled and you're not dead. Come on, what have you two been poking your noses into this time?"

"Two? There's five of us," snorted Feng. "Me, Porter, Karin, Namita, The…" Karin stuck a hand over Feng's mouth before he could start talking about their supernatural mentor, and Namita was forced to fill in the blanks. Whenever Karin's grip loosened, Feng would try and speak. He mentioned blue elephants. Twice.

By the time Namita had finished, Crawley was appalled. "Clem Rossiter? Are you kidding? That's very stupid of you. He's retired, but his organisation's still running."

"Let me guess... we met his daughter, the satsuma one," said Feng.

"Grace? Yep. She's the top dog now. You're lucky to be alive. You dissed him? In his own home?"

"Apparently so."

"Porter's not even awake yet," said Namita.

"Is he pancakes?" said Feng, alarmed.

"Same as you," she replied. "Nicely duffed up, but he'll live."

Karin confirmed Porter had no breakages but was covered in bruises and had concussion from the repeated blows around the head.

"Yeah, I took a few on the noggin too. I'm glad in a way. I feel muzzy. I don't remember much about the actual beating. Are you going to arrest Rossiter?"

Crawley laughed. "For what? He wasn't there. He'll have been at home gorging on brandy and cigars. Could you ID your assailants?"

"Not without X-ray vision," admitted Feng. "Men in black balaclavas. One second I was thinking of Milk Tray, the next I was getting a good thrashing."

"I have some other bad news," said Karin. "While you were unconscious, some opportunistic little bastard came in through your broken door and nicked your telly and hi-fi."

"What about the Murder Room?" said Feng, alarmed. "They didn't touch that, I hope. I can buy a new telly."

"Murder room?" Crawley frowned.

"It's all still there," Karin confirmed. "Might have been a bit of a giveaway if they'd gone for that. Rossiter has plausible deniability. He's an old pro. Lucky for you, your neighbours called the police when they saw the door kicked in. The ambulance got there before you both melted into puddles."

DCI Crawley said he wanted to know more about the case and invited Karin and Namita out to the canteen for coffee.

After they'd gone, The Gliss appeared.

"Oh, it's you," said Feng.

"I'm sorry about this," said The Gliss. "I wish there was something I could have done."

"You could've set fire to their socks?" said Feng, sarcastically referring to the infamous time The Gliss had physically manifested.

"I really couldn't. I went into Porter's head a minute ago; it was quite scary. Just blackness."

"Will he be ok?"

"I think so, he's just unconscious. Your head was black all day yesterday too."

"You've been inside my head?"

"You can see me; I can see you."

"What's it like being inside my head?"

"You don't know?"

"For you, you great lunk."

"Like being drunk in a hall of mirrors."

Feng laughed despite the bruises. "Ow. God, that hurts."

"Now's not really the time to discuss the case, obviously, but surely it's clear now the girls going missing is something to do with these gangsters. Not spying."

"Gangsters and acting. It certainly feels that way. I need to get up. I can't just lie here."

"The doctor said you're not allowed up until tomorrow at the earliest. And even then, you're going to be sorer than a fat arse on a wicker chair."

"Well, I don't need a doctor to tell me that. I feel like I've been through a mangle. I remember when I had bones. Now I feel like my legs are bags of water. I keep thinking of gazelles. That can't be right. I hope I come back to normal soon."

The Gliss raised his eyebrows. *Normal?*

Half an hour later, Karin, Namita and Crawley returned to see Feng.

"You lot are skating on thin ice," said the detective, now fully up to speed. "Luckily for you, I know just the man who might be able to steer you. DCI Ronnie Phelps. He was my mentor back in Bow Street when I was just a promising young constable."

"What did you promise?" smiled Feng.

"Then? Anything to keep my nose clean. Phelps was in Soho Vice during the 60s and 70s. He hated Rossiter. Ronnie's retired now. Lucky sod."

"Why did he hate him?" asked Karin.

"Cos Rossiter was an evil bastard and he got away with everything. If I remember rightly, they got him on tax evasion - two lousy years behind bars."

"That's how they got Al Capone," said Karin.

"Yeah, but the accountants of the Inland Revenue aren't The Untouchables. Just two short years for a life of violent crime? It's not right. His lieutenants picked up his jail tab. They had to - or get a visit from men in hoods with sticks, presumably."

"Or shears," said Feng. Talking with Phelps sounded like a good idea, but he asked Crawley if any meet-up could wait until he could stand straight again, and all the safari animals had gone.

"He might be dead before then," deadpanned Crawley.

Feng grimaced as he discovered he had laughing bruises too. He wheezed, "Karin, Namita, can you give the DCI access to the Dropbox?" They nodded. "DCI Crawley, there's a folder in there called VC Soho. It's a bunch of snaps I took at Vince Chambers' studio."

"Vince Chambers?"

"Rossiter's photographer in the 60s and 70s. If there is a connection between these girls and Rossiter's crew, maybe some of the names on those headshots will show up in one of your databases."

"I can certainly look," said Crawley, "but we're not Quantico. Don't expect miracles. But I see where you're coming from. Be happy to check."

"Porter was supposed to have already asked you."

"He's been tied up?"

"Tied up and walloped, yes."

November 8th, 2017
Royal Free Hospital, Hampstead, London

When Porter came round the next day, Karin was by his bedside, reading. She couldn't face another psychedelic conversation while Porter emerged from the fug like Feng, so she simply nodded and went off to let the nurse know. Half an hour later she came back, cursing the bad hospital coffee.

"Hey, Karin," said Porter. "Thought you were in LA?"

"I told you I was coming home. You forget?"

"Must have been something to do with being hit around the head 30 times by a bunch of psychos looking like extras from a Gene Kelly routine. I'll remember their black-clad muscles for the rest of my life."

"How are you feeling?"

"Do you have a thesaurus? Look up *sore* and read the entry out. It'll save you time."

"They didn't actually want to kill you. The cops think you were being warned."

"Rossiter?"

"That's the best guess," she agreed. She filled him in on the previous day's convos with Crawley. "Feng is being insufferably smug because he's been up on his feet for 24 hours, while you're still laid up."

"There's nothing like empathy," sighed Porter.

"Porter, I agree with Crawley. If this was Rossiter, it either means he's mightily displeased that you disrespected him, or he's in it up to his eyes."

"I'm going with *eyes*."

"Me too, especially since I saw those Variety pics."

"What now? My God, I'm bashed up. When I try to focus on any particular point of pain to calm it, 10 other points flare up."

"Don't think about it then."

The doors to Porter's room flung open and Feng came in on double crutches, looking like an Asiatic Long John Silver.

"Ahoy there, me hearties," said Porter.

"I hope that's not a joke about my eye patch," said Karin.

"God, no… sorry. Course not," fumbled Porter.

"No empathy."

"Touché."

"I'm teasing, you idiot," said Karin, lightly slapping his thigh. Porter jumped like he'd had a cactus enema.

"Sorry," said Karin. "No empathy."

"We're all quits then," said Porter, breathless with pain.

"Have I missed something?" said Feng, puzzled. "How are you feeling?"

"Like you look," said Porter.

"Oh, not that bad, surely?"

"At least you're hobbling about. I'm still Bedpan Bill."

"Rossiter sure didn't like our interview technique," said Feng, lowering himself into a chair, dropping his crutches. "Do you think Kirsty Wark had to go through this after her first interview?"

"I doubt the BBC would let it through on health and safety grounds," said Porter.

"Ah, but they don't pay the women as much as the men," said Karin. "Who knows how they view working conditions?"

"What do we do now?" said Porter, who liked sparring but was too groggy to climb in the ring.

"DCI Bob Crawley is across the case," said Feng. "He's hoping we can meet an old colleague who tried to bring Rossiter down in the 60s."

"Crawley? My God. Are we in trouble?"

"Yes, you idiot. That's why he's trying to help."

The doors thudded open again. Porter groaned. Tania and Cherry burst into the room.

"Porter! Oh my God. You look like an elephant wiped his feet on you," said Cherry.

"You're purple!" was all that Tania could say.

"What are you two doing here?" said Porter, immediately suspicious. As far he knew, the two most troublesome women in his life hadn't spoken for almost a year.

"You think we don't care?" said Cherry, blushing. She knew perfectly well how it looked.

Tania came to his side and tenderly reached out to take his hand.

"If you touch me, I'll scream," said Porter.

"I'm offended," said Tania, bringing both hands to her chest, reminding Feng of a Victorian corpse laid out in a coffin.

"No, you idiot. I'll scream in pain."

"We'll leave you to it," said Karin, failing her empath entrance exam again.

"No!" said Porter, so emphatically that a flight of Butterflies in the Amazon dropped from the skies with the impact, abandoning their plans to start a tornado in Texas.

"You must be Karin Pelenot?" said Tania. "You like getting him into trouble, don't you? How long's he known you? Less than a year? He's been in and out of hospital ever since."

"I'm not exactly unscathed myself," said Karin, touching her cheek, hoping the eyepatch would shut Tania up.

"My point exactly," said Tania.

"Well, any wounds he's received from working with me will heal," said Karin, dredging up a little upper-class imperiousness.

Tania tried the old gimlet-eye trick, but Karin was used to dealing with TV commissioners and ignored the rank amateur dramatism. "Come on, Feng, let me buy you the foulest cup of coffee you've ever tasted," Karin said, retrieving Long John Silver's crutches from the floor.

"Don't leave me!" said Porter. "These two are more dangerous than Rossiter!"

"You're on your own, buddy," said Feng.

"Well, that's a charming thing to say," said Cherry. "I wouldn't have brought grapes if I'd known you were going to be rude." She plonked a slightly soggy brown paper bag down on the side. "I had a few on the way over. I hope you don't mind."

Porter, his throat still mildly broken, waved the grapes away. He said that as his oesophagus felt like a corkscrew waterslide at Centre Parcs, he wouldn't risk choking himself to death on fruit if that was okay with her. With a suit-yourself shrug, Cherry grabbed the bag and started picking.

"Come on," he demanded, "how do you two just happen to turn up at the same time?"

"She called me," said Tania. "She knows how much I care about you."

"Oh really?" said Porter, bitterly. "Look in the wastebasket. There you can find the broken shards of grey lead that used to be my beating heart before you took a hammer to it."

"That's unfair," said Cherry. "Tania has always said she loves you. She just found it hard to live with you."

"There you go again," said Porter. "Have you two been talking all this time behind my back?"

"Look, we've had coffee once or twice. Just because you couldn't get on with her, didn't mean I couldn't," said his sister, coming clean.

"I got on with her fine," said Porter. "She didn't get on with me. Unbelievable. I'm groggy with morphine but, confronted by you two, frankly, it could be acid."

"We just wanted to check you're okay. There's no need to be so rude," said Tania.

"I need sleep, not nightmares. I'm sorry, but Cherry is trying to stiff me over Ida's will. Tania, you've treated me like you never heard that a dog's for life. I thought I'd made myself clear: I'm done with it; with you. Can I rest, now?"

"But it's ok for Karin to come and talk to you, is that it?" said Tania.

"Karin's got nothing to do with it. Don't take this personally, but I'd rather her and Feng were here. Your timing's not good. Can I rest now? Please?"

There are various etiquettes it is advisable to observe in the world. Not hanging around the hospital bed of someone who doesn't want you there is one of them. Even Tania and Cherry knew this one. Even so, neither was quick to move. "Seriously? Do I have to pull the red cord?" said Porter.

"I'm disappointed in you," said Tania. "I think Pelenot's been a bad influence. You never used to be this rude."

"You mean, I suppose, that I never used to be this non-compliant?"

"Come on, Tania. It's the meds. He's not himself." Cherry stood to go, reality finally winning its battle against expectation.

"It's not the meds," said Porter. "They make me feel better. You two don't. But thanks for the concern."

Tania and Cherry harrumphed and left. Porter turned his head and looked at the half-empty bag of grapes. Little nobbles of green left after Cherry's plucking stared at him like tiny eyes in the dark.

"Well played, sir," said The Gliss.

Porter looked up at the translucent white ceramic robot head manifestation. "Like I said - acid," he muttered, before sliding back into dopey tranquil.

Chapter 33

November 10th, 2017
Feng's house, Church Lane, Walthamstow, London

A few days later, Feng and Porter had been discharged and the gang of four were back at Feng's. For once, they were all punctual. It was a special occasion. DCI Crawley was driving over with his friend, Ronnie Phelps.

Feng's Skype rang. It was Efrayim Davidov.

"I hear you've been attacked," said the Israeli.

"You could say that. How did you find out?" queried Feng. Porter poked his head into shot so Davidov could see his bandage.

"My God," said the Israeli, ignoring the question. "Who did it? Is this something to do with Becker?"

Feng shook his head. "Becker's dead and I can't believe Max Fascher had anything to do with it. No, this was probably one of Becker's buddies, a British criminal called Clem Rossiter."

"They're connected," said Porter. "They knew each other, met up a few times, and had at least some link to the same photographer. Has Vince Chambers ever come up on your radar?"

"No. Who is he? What's the connection?"

They told him what they knew. "Can you look into it your end?" asked Feng.

"Thank you for the information," said Davidov. "It's not unusual for a director like Becker to have headshots of actors around. Probably just a coincidence. I'll do what I can. Be careful."

Five minutes later, Namita answered the door to greet Crawley, who was supporting Phelps on his arm. Tea and biscuits distributed, Feng, Porter, Karin and Namita, recapped. Phelps listened carefully. When they had finished, Crawley broke his news.

"I ran your pictures from Chambers' flat," he explained. "I called in a favour at Scotland Yard and they ran them through some facial recognition software. Only one match I'm afraid." He pulled out a slim manila folder and opened it. "Tonya Hutchins, a wannabe actress from LA. She showed up on the Interpol database because she travelled to London and Paris at one point."

"Let me guess," said Karin. "For auditions?"

"The file is small, but yes. She was reported missing by LAPD in February 1973."

"Thanks, Dan. It's another VC Soho picture. It's too much of a coincidence Chambers took her picture too," said Porter, pointing at the embossed logo. "What the hell is going on here? Does Chambers look like a serial killer to you, Feng?"

"If my gran's a serial killer, so is Chambers."

"I'll send this to Arnie Flax," said Karin. "I'm working with him. He's on cold cases in LA, Robbery and Homicide Division."

"Great," said Crawley, visibly impressed. "So, Ronnie - what's your take?"

All eyes turned to the retired DCI. He was frail and watery-eyed but had a touch of the Yoda about him. "I knew Clem pretty well back then," he said. "Ruthless bastard. Owned most of Soho. I did everything in my power to bring him down. It was no good. Sadly, most of my fellow cops were bent back then. Evidence would get misplaced our side; crimes covered up.

"We only ever had minor successes. His people took the rap on small misdemeanours. Either that or their families caught it. That's how he operated."

Porter thought he might as well doublecheck. "Do you know if Clem was involved in porn?" The group still hadn't dismissed the idea the missing girls were caught up in sex films.

"Not that I know of," admitted Phelps. "I'm sure he distributed plenty of mags from Scandinavia, but I'm sure I'd have heard if he'd been making films himself."

"Maybe he was just supplying girls to filmmakers who did?" said Namita.

"That's possible," said Phelps. "But obviously that would rule out this new girl you've found - Tonya. That would be receiving - not supplying - if she came to London. At the moment, all our obvious girls have left London, not come to it."

"I should have stayed in LA," said Karin. "There's more to uncover out there. Dom Lascelle's assistant, Morrie Crystal, knows more than he's saying. I'd love to run Tonya Hutchins by him."

Phelps continued. "Don't get me wrong; Rossiter was involved in film. He used productions to launder money." Phelps pulled out a folded-up piece of paper. "Dan told me you were interested. I scribbled this down for you. All the films I could remember he was involved in. There will be more."

The writing was virtually illegible, but it was a useful list.

The White Bull
Four Days in London
The Spyglass
Climb the Peak
The Mombassa Conundrum
The Days Become Night
Forage
Crystal Shaman
All You Need is Guns

"I like film," said Porter, "but I've never heard of any of these. They must be terrible."

"Never saw any myself," said Phelps, "but yes, I think he made them as a tax dodge and a way to launder funds. I bet half the crew were villains in his pay."

"He told us he liked his mum to see his name on the credits," said Feng.

"Well, that would have been hard," said Phelps. "She was killed in the Blitz. Rossiter was brought up in an orphanage."

"So, we know he's a liar, at least," said Porter.

Phelps laughed. "The best. But that was the extent of his involvement in film as far as I know. He liked to big-up himself and go to film festivals and stuff like that. I doubt any of his films were ever nominated for anything - unless he leant on the judges. On the other hand, I knew Vince Chambers - he definitely did some dodgy photographic jobs, but I'm sure that was for other clients, not Rossiter."

"What do you mean by dodgy?" asked Karin.

"Page 3 stuff, mostly. But he was a gun for hire; could've been for anyone, private clients, probably. Soho was the UK's porn capital back then."

"How bad was it?" asked Porter, offering the biscuit plate around.

"Pretty bad,' said Phelps. "But on the plus side, it was self-contained and mostly hidden. If you'd passed through Soho during the day, you'd have seen the sex shops etc, but wouldn't have been pestered. Night-time, it was red lights and neon everywhere. Nothing like today, when it's crammed 24/7 with workers and tourists." Phelps dunked a biscuit and continued. "At one time, the hookers used to display red lights in their window. Must have been well confusing after Sergeant Pepper when every bloody student had red lights and patchouli burning." He imitated a dirty old man importuning the wrong person. 'How much for a quickie? Oops. Sorry.'"

"Did you ever meet the German film director, Heinrich Becker?" asked Porter.

"I did," said Phelps, "And I didn't like him one bit."

"Why not?"

"He was a Nazi. People said he wasn't - but he wasn't fooling me. Look, I know you youngsters are cool with the Germans, and that's good. But when I was young, we all had relatives who'd died or been injured in the war. I might have been able to put that aside if Becker had behaved himself in London."

"What do you mean?" asked Porter.

"Do you like jazz?" asked Phelps. Porter nodded. "Do you know Desi Persimmon? The tenor sax player? Becker got pissed after a gig at Ronnie Scott's and beat the crap out of Desi. He stamped on his head, ranting on about how disgusting negroes are."

"His biographer didn't mention that, funnily enough," said Porter, "but, yes, we worked out he was a racist for ourselves." Becker's assault on the nurse crossed his mind again, making him feel newly sick.

Phelps took a sip of tea. "To me, the worst thing was the way the system bent to accommodate these thugs. Even though I knew about the corruption, what could I do? The gangs had a long reach. I'm sure home visits were paid to judges, senior cops etc. The message would have been clear: turn a blind eye or lose one."

"Didn't your stance put you in danger?" asked Namita.

"You'd think - but actually I got on fine with them. Rossiter wasn't very subtle. He'd slip a £50 note on me - just as a present, you understand. I'd hand it back and say, 'I don't drink.' One man can't do much, can he? I wasn't much of a threat. I think The Krays and Rossiter found me amusing.

"He probably wasn't laughing when I just about managed to get the tax evasion charge to stick. But even that helped him. I'm sure he was annoyed to do two year's porridge, but he also knew there was unlikely to be another prosecution for a while after that. It left him clear to carry on, so he was probably happy to take it on the chin. Jail would have been a doddle for someone like him - like Noel Coward in The Italian Job. Porridge, yes, but thick and creamy porridge, dripping with jam. No hardship."

The group struggled, at some cost to his dignity, to wiggle Phelps upstairs to the Murder Room. DCI Crawley was shocked.

"You guys are crazy, you know that? This looks like you're trying to pin the missing girls on Rossiter and his cronies. No wonder he came after you."

Phelps studied it. "Where's your timeline? Without a timeline none of this makes sense."

"I'm working on it," said Feng.

"I've got to be honest; this makes me feel very uncomfortable," said Crawley. "You guys aren't cops. It's admirable trying to find the girls, but you don't want to cross any lines here. I didn't realise you were going this deep."

"Dan," said Phelps softly, "they're the only ones investigating. We had our go."

Crawley's mobile rang and he took the call outside. Phelps used the time to give Feng housekeeping suggestions on how to make the layout more effective.

Crawley returned. He did not look happy. "You guys really have stirred up a hornets' nest. Jimmy the Shanker is dead."

"What?" said Porter. "How?"

"He appears to have committed suicide by jumping in the Thames."

"Oh my Goff," said Feng. "Rossiter was furious we'd spoken to Jimmy."

"Right, I've had enough," said Crawley. "This has to stop. You'll all get killed."

"Why didn't he kill us when he had the chance?" said Porter.

"You're civilians. Shanker was a grass. In Rossiter's eyes there's a difference. What the hell was it Shanker said that made Rossiter so angry? Jimmy has done 100 cheap documentaries without getting himself killed before now."

"Well, that's the thing," said Feng. "He didn't really say anything. He said he'd met Becker once or twice and that Rossiter knew him through film."

Porter added, "Rossiter demanded to know how we'd heard about Becker and guessed it was through Jimmy." He looked deflated. "Are we really responsible?"

"I think so," said Crawley.

Phelps nodded. "Classic Rossiter. More than a few people who'd crossed him turned up in the river."

"What about our PI, Alex Harding?" asked Porter. "He was dumped in the river, decapitated. Rossiter told us about a guy called Browz who chopped some guy's fingers off with a pair of shears."

"If Rossiter was behind that then your PI must have done something really stupid," said Phelps. "He wasn't like Ronnie Kray - a violent psychopath - he was just ruthless and saw violence as a tool. This Harding bloke - was he nosing around asking questions about the girls?"

"Yes," said Porter. "By all accounts, he was a bit of an amateur."

"There you go," said Phelps. "It probably was Rossiter's command. Browz died years ago, so if he was the executioner, you'll only ever find out for certain if Rossiter fesses up, which I have to tell you is never going to happen."

Now Namita's phone rang. She'd been listening quietly for the past half hour, her mind miles away on her own troubles. Her heart jumped. It was Hammell.

"Excuse me," she said, and ducked out into the hallway. She knew before he spoke that it was trouble.

"There's been a bit of a cock-up," confirmed Hammell.

Namita's heart sank. "What kind of cock-up?"

"I did some digging into Martin Skelling, like you asked. He's actually pretty clean, bar one incident five years ago when his girlfriend, Aysha Miah, made a domestic violence report to Bath Police."

"What kind of domestic violence?" asked Namita.

"He beat her. She reported it, but it went no further. A few days later she withdrew the complaint. But they never got back together again. I called her and…"

"You did what?" said Namita, appalled.

"Yeah, I called her. She sounded terrified."

"I bet she did. What on earth did you give as your reason for the call?"

"Here comes the cock-up bit. I thought she might want to help, so I told her Skelling had been making threats against my client…"

"Oh my God! What were you thinking?"

"It gets worse. She had my number on her mobile. About an hour later, I got a call from Martin Skelling, threatening all sorts. Sorry, boss. Mea culpa."

Namita wanted to be sick. "He's not stupid, he'll know this is my doing."

"I know. Hence the head's up. I'm sure you'll be getting a call before long."

"Hammell, you know you've probably just dropped me right in it?"

"Sorry, boss. This one's on me. If he gives you any trouble, I'll sort it."

Namita walked back into the Murder Room. Her head was spinning, her legs shaking. She put her phone on silent.

"You ok, Namita?" said Karin, seeing confusion and distress on her friend's face.

"Yes, yes, fine," snapped Namita, demonstrating to one and all through a loudhailer that she most definitely was not.

Phelps, absorbed by the Rossiter story, bypassed the change in temperature and said they needed to either come to a quick conclusion and pass the info onto the police, or give it up. Crawley was right about that: they were all in danger now.

"Pass on what?" said Porter. "We don't even have a theory, let alone evidence."

Karin leaned forward. "You know, there's not much point in having my celebrity status if I don't use it. I've got a plan. Time to go on the attack."

The others looked at her, expectantly. "How do you propose we go on the offensive against a gangster unafraid to use shears, decapitate and drown people?" said Porter.

"Breakfast TV," said Karin.

Chapter 34

November 10th, 2017
Namita's flat, Holloway Road, London

"You fuckin' bitch," Skelling screamed down the phone. "You dare to try and dig up dirt on me? You'll pay for that."

Namita had dreaded the call but had also steeled herself for it. The bastard was violent. And he had a thing about Indian girls by the sound of it. She wasn't going to let him have his way entirely.

"No, you listen to me, you piece of shit," she said. "You dare to try and blackmail *me*? You dare to try and frighten me off the case? How do I even know you didn't put something in my drink that night in Bristol?"

"I didn't put anything in your fucking drink, you uptight bastard. You put a lot of drink in yourself. Don't blame me for that. Right, the gloves are off. Is that how it is?"

"You mean, you like your Indian girls nice and compliant, is that how it is?"

"Go fuck yourself, you Paki bitch."

Namita was so shocked that Skelling was gone before she could respond.

"Well," said Sangita. "He turned out to be a charmer."

"As he said, the gloves are off now, the racist prick."

"You shouldn't have said that about spiking your drink. You know perfectly well that was all you."

"I know… but I got angry."

"With good reason. But now he's really going to come after us, isn't he?"

"He can try."

"Good girl. Bravado in the face of utter catastrophe. That's just what's needed."

"Screw you, Sangita."

Skelling's final words had left her shaking - with rage. Hadn't she told Feng she rarely encountered racism? But what the hell was that? Where did that come from? The same place that led to him smacking Aysha, obviously. *How could you get involved with someone like that?* She thought she was quizzing Aysha and then saw she was actually questioning herself.

Curled up on her sofa, she took a few seconds to gather herself. She surveyed her living room. Coming from the oblique, she experienced the environment anew: *Jesus, it's so bare in here! Where the hell's the character?*

And with that simple question, a door opened.

Why were you so keen to shag Skelling? You've batted off enough men over the years. You don't need or want a bloody man, especially a prick like Skelling. All you have is your career and that bunch of bloody misfits. Where are your friends, Namita Menon? What happened to all your friends?

Uncomfortable thoughts. Had she used her career as an excuse to isolate herself? She'd certainly used it as a weapon against her family. She recalled showing her degree certificate to her father. Nothing was ever good enough for him, but he did seem pleased just that once. Not as pleased as Namita had been. *I'm independent at last and here's the paperwork to prove it.*

Her life, her self-worth, was built upon the successful career that followed. It became the foundations her family had been incapable of giving. She didn't hate them. She just didn't want to be like them.

She *was* her career. And Skelling was threatening to topple it. *I don't think so, you prick.*

And friends. Another disaster. *The bloody misfits? They aren't real friends. Are they?* She ran through a list of the real people she called friends. *You never actually call them anymore though, do you?*

Everyone she listed had fallen to the wayside because of that evil triumvirate of friend-splitters: marriage, kids, and the move out of London. It sometimes felt like she only graduated last year, but here she was - the only one of her college mates left in London, still slogging it out with millions of the most competitive people in the world.

Sangita thought it was worth reappearing. "At least you know what you don't want: a husband, kids and a sheepdog. That's something. You can't expect everything to be perfect if you choose ambition."

"Am I ambitious?"

"Are you kidding? You know you're the best. You just want the chance to prove it. If you succeed solo, then you'll have ticked that box. Maybe you can move on to the next stage then? Whatever the next stage is."

As usual, her long-dead sister made points Namita could agree on but rarely came up with by herself. "You're saying, in the most patronizing and simplistic way possible, that if I win this case, pick up a slew of clients and win an award or two, my life will suddenly be okay?"

"No, I'm saying there's no end point - only markers along the way. But you haven't reached where you want to be yet."

"Oh, God. Tell me you're not telling me to be patient?"

"I am. You're alright, sister. Now, pep talk over, how are we going to kneecap that bastard, Skelling?"

November 10th, 2017
Karin's house, Chartwell House, Surrey

Karin got off the phone from Zara Goodwin, producer of This is the Morning, Britain's top-rated breakfast TV show. They had a slot tomorrow if she wanted it. She did. Booked

Karin knew full well that Tim and Sophie, the slightly clueless presenters, would want to focus on her eye. She hadn't done a single interview about it yet. It would be a nice exclusive for them. But, as she had felt with Flax, she wasn't ready to talk about it yet. She could, however, cope with saying a few words as cover.

She needed to prepare. She had to sound serious. And she would need an email address to give out.

Karin, despite, and possibly because she worked in TV, rarely watched any. But now, wandering into the living room, she found her grandfather had left his on. She was slightly shocked to see a picture of herself on the screen.

"And tomorrow," boomed the trailer voice, "TV historian, Karin Pelenot, talks for the first time about the accident that cost her an eye."

My God. That was quick. She only spoke to Goodwin an hour ago. She found it deeply uncomfortable. Not least, because she had no intention of talking about her eye for more than 30 seconds.

November 10th, 2017
Feng's house, Church Lane, Walthamstow

Washing-up complete, Feng had been back in the Murder Room for so long, he moved his kettle upstairs to save time. Phelps was right. They needed a timeline. With so much information coming in, his original string-and-card set up had become unnavigable.

He and Porter had made a decent inroad over the Thai curry last week, but they needed a better system.

When Feng was earning a fortune in the City, he was well-known for his exacting attention to detail. The discovery that he had a conscience made him quit high finance, but his ability to focus remained intact. Now he was a semi-pro investigator, that was probably a good thing. He'd always taken refuge in his commitment, curiosity, and consumerism. It was evident in his expensive suits, it was in the bottles and potions arraigned like the Manhattan skyline on his bathroom shelf, and it was in his methodical laying out of facts in the Murder Room.

Feng had enjoyed going to Mothercare to buy a large roll of children's drawing paper. All the yummy mummies were thinking of their little Delilahs and Justins. He'd been thinking of murder and mayhem. It had made him feel oddly superior. *It's good to be different.*

He unrolled a 3m length and pinned it chest-high on the wall. He unwrapped more boxes of coloured cards for the key incidents. Phelps' suggestion of a master timeline, with key moments and analysis - disappearances, deaths etc - laid out as a secondary layer above, made total sense.

He admired his prep work and took out a fat black marker, sniffing the tip. The pen made a satisfying squeak and emitted more fumes than a tramp's sock. The long, black line ran from one end of the paper to the other. Next, vertical lines marking out 1961 to 1973. He used Rossiter and Becker's meeting at the Venice Film Festival as his starting point and Tonya Hutchins going missing in 1973 as the end point. *Arbitrary, but I can change it later if I need to.*

He sighed. It was going to be a long night and he had to meet Porter in the morning. They were going back to Bristol.

November 10th, 2017
Porter's flat, Sylvester Path, Hackney

The Gliss watched Porter hobble around his flat.

"I should have chosen a doctor as my form," said The Gliss. "All your adventures seem to come with broken bones and sore heads."

"Yes, your choice of a robot head hasn't ever been particularly comforting," said Porter, chopping some garlic. "But, let's be honest, there aren't many forms a disembodied head could take that would give comfort. Most of the doctors I've ever seen tended to have bodies."

"Your current condition will make your trip tomorrow uncomfortable."

"The walking around, yes. But then I've got to go all Quincunx and sit on Ursa's grave. That will be a whole heap of laughs too."

"I don't think you'll get much from it," said The Gliss. "She killed herself. Her final thoughts will be about herself, most probably."

"You'd think. If I've learnt anything, the Quincunx is unpredictable."

"It'll be no more than detail, at best," said The Gliss, "but I'm up for you standing on as many graves as possible. It's just that - now that you work so closely with the others," The Gliss emitted a whiff of disdain, "I feel like I'm not as useful."

"*As useful?* When have you ever been useful? Until you start setting my enemies' socks on fire on a regular basis, your usefulness will always be a subject of debate."

"Thank you, very much."

"My pleasure."

"I do shout *duck!* occasionally?"

"Ok, so I'm a few bruises short of a full quota thanks to you, but I've still got plenty of scars."

"You had those before you met me."

"I also had a full complement of limbs and 100% mobility."

"Into every life some rain must fall."

"Can I get on with my curry now, please?"

"Suit yourself. A spicy one?"

"Very."

"So, you're going to make food that burns your mouth, guts and bum. And you think I'm a danger to your health?"

"For God's sake. Isn't there some other poor soul needing your help?"

"I am wedded to you, sir."

"Well, you're a lousy bride."

Chapter 35

November 11th, 2017
This is the Morning Studios, Camden, London

"Welcome, Karin Pelenot," said Tim.
"So great to see you," said Sophie.
"It's great to be here," lied Karin.
"I'm sure all our viewers have been wondering how you've coped after your accident?"
Jesus wept. That wasn't even an attempt at a bridge. Karin nodded for the camera. "Yes, Tim. It's been a trying few months. But that's making documentaries for you. Sometimes they go wrong."
"That was a film about your great grandfather in World War 1? When does that come out?" said Sophie, grinning like someone had jammed a coat-hanger behind her lips.
"Soon. Production was delayed a bit," she said, pointing at her patch. "And I've still got History/ThisStory to make. But on top of that, we've started working on another film."

"Oh really? Can you tell us what it is yet?" said Tim, leaning back a little, one hand on the sofa, groin rampant.

"I've been inspired by the #MeToo movement," said Karin, eye briefly drawn to the groin, unimpressed. *He's got a sock in there.* "In particular, I'm interested in seeing how things have changed in the British film industry over the years."

"Wow! Topical," said Sophie, with the sincerity of an MP kissing a baby.

"I've been wondering how the casting couch situation has changed. I was hoping that by appearing here this morning, I could put out an appeal."

"Er... certainly," said Tim, whose briefing notes only contained info on the "accident" that cost Karin an eye.

Breaking the cardinal rule of all breakfast TV sofas that guests should only converse with the hosts, Karin turned directly to the camera. The live director had nowhere to go. She signalled to the camera operator to hold on Karin. Sophie and Tim did their best not to look uncomfortable. *Thank God for those coat-hangers.*

"Were you a struggling actress in the UK in the 1960s/1970s?" said Karin. "If so, I want to hear from you about your experiences going for auditions. Did anyone ever pressure you into sex? Anything you tell me will be in the strictest confidence, though I would be happy to film you if you have something to say. I'm particularly interested in women who feel like producers and directors tried to exploit them or forced them into having sex to get a part."

Tim looked over his shoulder at some authority offstage as if to say, "Can she say that over breakfast?" A close-up of Tim's look would later appear as a Twitter meme with the caption, *When women accuse men of sexploitation.*

Karin continued. "In particular, I want to hear from anyone who did auditions in London, but also Rome, Paris, Berlin, LA, New York. If anyone ever auditioned for the directors Heinrich Becker, Oli Caron, Buddy Demsky or Paulo Agresti - then I really want to talk to you."

Now Tim and Sophie looked very concerned indeed.

"Karin, I'm not sure you can say that," said Sophie.

"Don't worry, they're all dead: they can't sue me. Or you." Karin turned back to the camera. "Just get in touch with me directly via email: karin@pelenotpictures.com. The emails are coming directly to me and no-one else will see them."

Done, she turned back to her appalled hosts. "Should be an interesting film."

November 11th, 2017
Canford Cemetery & Crematorium, Westbury-on-Trym, Bristol

Porter, Feng and The Gliss stood together, looking over the section housing Ursa Fielding's grave.

"Is your head raging?" asked Feng.

Knocking back a small handful of pills, Porter nodded. "Oh, yes. Though it's hard to tell where Rossiter's bruises end, and the Quincunx starts."

"Remember your training," said The Gliss. "Let the voices bounce off you. Save yourself."

"It's easy for you to say," said Porter. "It's bloody hard. The voices only come into focus when I'm very close to them and quickly disappear again, but you hear terrible things."

"Like what?" said Feng.

"It's depressing I only hear the voices of those who died unhappy. If there was the occasional 'Didn't we have a lovely time the day we went to Bangor?' or 'The weather's nice up here,' I wouldn't mind. But what I get are cries for help, sobs, wails, appeals."

"Do you remember any?" asked Feng.

"I once heard a woman say, 'I love you all…' and then I heard a bang. I think she shot herself. I heard a little girl crying 'Mummy' once. That hurt too. I know they're all dead and I can't help them, but hearing their voices makes me think of people trapped in cages, buried in the soil. It's really horrible. Thank God, I'm not near them long enough for pictures to form."

"Sounds dreadful," said Feng.

"It's not as bad as all that, Porter," said The Gliss, who could hear and see everything Porter experienced. "Everyone has a final moment. They really are dead, not writhing about in their coffins. Eventually, The Recession erases even those voices."

"I know, and truthfully, it's a rare voice I think I could even help. Most of the pain is more like angst. When I heard Max Cartwright earlier this year protesting that he hadn't spied for the Germans and was being unfairly executed, I knew there was something concrete I could do: restore his reputation. If someone basically had a miserable life or died early of cancer, that's just life in all its horror."

"I wish I could take some of the strain away from you," admitted Feng. "I don't suppose you could add that on, could you?" he asked The Gliss.

"No. I couldn't."

"Suit yourself. Two heads are better than one," said Feng, before taunting The Gliss, "Unless you have a brother. In which case, please tell him to stay away."

Porter, ignoring his two bickering companions, stepped forward. He had to take a few deep breaths and steady himself before taking the plunge into the Quincunx world. They had identified Ursa's grave and Porter sighed, seeing he had 50ft to shuffle before reaching it. Plenty of time to be prodded with other voices.

He set off, his injuries prolonging the agony of the voices coming and going.

... you never loved me...

... Aaargh...

... Stanley! No! Please...

He saw the headstone. Ursa's name was carved in golden recessed lettering. He took another glancing blow from another sad voice.

... I don't want to go ...

Muzzy-headed from the chorus, he mis-stepped, tipping and plunging. He fell onto the grave and was left hugging the black granite.

Porter didn't have time to register his discomfort. The second he hit the stone, he was sucked down through white heat, swirling pictures and electric shocks. As the fuzz cleared, he emerged on the other side. He was in a quiet bedroom.

T-Rex was pumping from a Dansette. Ursa was blonde, attractive and... sobbing. She was sat on the floor, arms around her knees, head bowed, crying. A red plastic mac lay across her bed.

Ursa unfurled herself and picked up a photograph. Ursa, Rose and Bella. She kissed it. Porter watched as the young woman spoke to the photo through sniffles and choked cries.

"I'm so sorry. It was all my fault. I should never have let you go. I knew what they were like and I let you go."

She dropped the photo, turned T-Rex up a notch, and stood, bolting her door. To Porter's horror, he saw a short nylon noose hanging from the handle. Ursa tugged the cord.

Get it on, bang a gong, Get it on.

She put her back to the door, dropped the noose over her head and tightened it. Shockingly, without hesitation, she immediately slid heavily down the door to the floor, her bottom just off the floor. Her legs kicked and shook. Her hands went to her neck reflexively, but Ursa made no real attempt to free herself. He couldn't watch anymore. He pulled himself out of the vision.

"Are you ok?" said Feng.

"Anything useful?" asked The Gliss.

Porter fell on all fours and retched up his breakfast.

November 11th, 2017
Namita's flat, Holloway Road, London

Namita was about to leave to link up with Karin. They'd booked in coffee to follow her TV appearance. Namita had watched Karin's slot live on her phone.

She wondered again how she'd managed to get mixed up in this crazy shit. She admitted she was envious. Namita wasn't short on self-assurance, but she marvelled at Karin's innate super-confidence. She never stumbled over words and always spoke in perfectly constructed sentences. Namita had long since noted Karin had to make a conscious decision *not* to dominate a room. Without restraint, Karin ruled any space she was in before she even spoke. Namita had seen this included Sophie and Tim's TV sofa domain. With Karin on the couch, they'd became spectators at their own wedding.

Time to leave. An envelope flopped on the doormat. Shit. It was from the Solicitors Regulation Authority. She couldn't face opening it, though knew it would weigh heavy in her pocket until she did. She admitted she'd prefer to open it with Karin present. If anyone could help with the Skelling problem, it was Karin. *She would suggest something sensible. Wouldn't she?*

This was a long way from the women's first interactions in Flanders earlier that year. Namita had dismissed Karin as a posh snob, while Karin sniffed at Namita's glamour and ambition.

The turning point was Karin saving them all from the evil they faced in Flanders. Namita, Feng and Porter had all been hypnotised by the Profugus. It was steely Karin who had built walls in her mind, refused to submit, and had gone on the offensive.

Namita took a look around her apartment before she closed the door on it. *You're doing ok. Everything will be ok. You just have to take a leaf out of Karin's book.*

November 11th, 2017
Pedro's Cafe, Camden Road, London

The SRA letter lay unopened between their coffee cups.

"You'd better open it," said Karin softly, putting a hand on Namita's arm. "Let's see what the bastard has done."

It was as expected. Complaint received; tribunal being set up to rule on whether Namita had breached the Code of Conduct.

"Crap," was all she could say.

Karin studied the letter's contents. "In practice, he's done worse than what he accuses you of. Wisely, he hasn't mentioned you're trying to blackmail each other. Self-interest, obviously. If he accused you, you'd counterclaim." She waved the letter. "Despicable, yes, but he's playing by the rules. By-the-rules can always be fought by-the-rules *and* other means."

Namita wasn't so sure. "But what do I do now? If I get struck off, that's my career over."

"You're not going to like what I have to say," said Karin.

"Go on."

"You were right to go to your PI. But maybe you didn't go far enough. You're going to have to blackmail Skelling to hell and back. Your best protection is to get the complaint withdrawn."

"You're right: I don't like that idea," said Namita. "That's what got me in this mess in the first place."

"No, it's not. I suspect this Skelling character has done worse before, and probably been on the other end of it too. He's shady. No, what got you into this mess was mundane - breaking your professional rules – taking on Sam's case. Skelling's response has been disproportionate."

"Even if I wanted to blackmail him, I don't have anything on him."

"Find something. As I say, he's shady."

"How?"

"You can't take this attitude. The man is trying to chop your legs off. You need to jump away and swing back at him even harder."

Namita wasn't convinced. "He called me a Paki bitch."

"Jesus. Do you have that on tape?"

"No."

"There you go. Get him to call you it again, and this time tape it."

"How? Why?"

"Oh, come on. You're better than that. I don't think your professional body will take him seriously if you can get his rants on tape. Lie. Set up a meeting. Say you want to broker a solution. Then pull the rug out from under him and provoke him."

"He might hit me," said Namita, "He seems to like hitting Indian women."

"Pathetic, yes, but it can't be worse than being attacked by the Profugus, right? The end justifies the means. Besides, you can always carry a can of Mace. I do."

"So do I, funnily enough. He's not stupid. He'll scent the trap."

"It's all sleight of hand. Your SAS guy owes you one. Get him up to Bristol. Organise something short notice with Skelling. Flirt if you have to. Let Skelling choose the location. Tip Hammell by text. Guys like him will be able to rig something pretty fast."

"Hammell's no problem, but I don't think Skelling will go for it. I think we're past flirting."

Karin sat back in her chair, looking at Namita disapprovingly. "Have you actually looked at yourself, lately? You are gorgeous. One thing I've learned about men - they are clever, ingenious, brilliant and capable."

Namita wondered where this was going.

"But they have their classic fatal weakness. They just can't help themselves when a beautiful woman comes along. We already know he's up for it. God, you could turn me. Look, since we got caught up with Porter, we seem to have become the equivalent of secret agents - so let's see you start acting like one. The Honey Trap is the oldest trick in the book, but, God knows, men fall for it every day."

"I'll think about it," said Namita.

"Now is not the time to be squeamish." Her phone pinged. "That was quick! An email." She read it out. It was from a woman called Lucy Pelling. And Karin said, "Jackpot!"

Hi Karin,

Hope you don't mind me getting in touch. Saw you on TV this morning and had to reach out.

I'm a gran now, but back in the 60s I was a struggling actress.

Was there a casting couch? Oh my God, you have no idea. As for that bastard Buddy Demsky...

I'm not ashamed of what happened back then. I went into it with eyes wide open. Fat lot of good it ever did me. But all the stuff about #MeToo has had me thinking over the last year. It's too late to rectify the damage now, but I'd be happy to tell you about my experiences. I'm not sure about going on camera, but let's talk and see.

She gave her mobile number. The phone pinged again. Another woman: Jane Atkinson.

You're not joking, are you? If I had a pound for every grope and pinch I got in the 80s, I'd be richer than Beyonce. Call me. Love History/ThisStory.

Ping. A man. Presumably. The sender hadn't seen fit to leave a name.

You're a fat, ugly, one-eyed pig. What's it got to do with you what happened? Just because no-one wants to give you one.

"I was wondering how long it would take for that to happen," said Karin. "I've already had to block five people on Twitter this morning."

"What's the matter with people?" said Namita.

"Anonymous bullying. Didn't you know it's all the rage?" laughed Karin. "They're wasting their time trying to troll me."

A few minutes later, another ping.

Karin, you bitch,

How dare you insult the memory of people like Paulo Agresti. I knew him well back in the day and he was a great man. You go on TV and insinuate that he abused women? Shame on you. I shall never watch your programmes again. You are filth for doing this.

It was unsigned and from a clearly made-up Hotmail account. "I doubt they knew Agresti at all," said Karin. "Classic troll. Why does social media make people so vituperative?"

Over coffee, the pings picked up pace. By the time Karin was settling the bill, she had more than 20 emails, including two chancer CVs seeking work experience.

November 11th, 2017
Snakes & Ladders, The Christmas Steps, Bristol

"I haven't played Ludo for a long time?" said Feng. "We used to play it at Christmas."

"It's better with four," said Porter. "How about Dungeons and Dragons?"

"Not if we want to get home before next Christmas," said Feng.

"Harry Potter Top Trumps it is."

The pair had a sandwich and coffee and tried to win each other's cards.

"Dumbledore. Magical powers. 10," said Porter.

"Snape. 8," sighed Feng, handing over his card.

"Hermione Grainger. Flying. 8," said Porter.

"Griphook the Goblin. 1."

"Hand it over."

Two hands later and Porter had won.

"That's a shit game," said Feng. "No skill whatsoever. You just have to read out your biggest number."

"Sore loser," said Porter. "Look at all these grown men playing games. Don't people have jobs to go to?"

"One should take a look at oneself," said The Gliss. "At least most of these chaps haven't got bandages on their head. You look like a Sikh guru."

"That's not a game though, is it?" snapped Porter. "That's real life. This lot should be doing their dissertations. We're trying to solve a real riddle."

"Don't get so uppity," said Feng. "Life is much poorer without games. Just not this one." He tossed the Top Trumps box back on the shelf.

Karin called. She had been getting emails all morning and was quite excited by some of them. Could they meet later?

Feng settled the coffee bill. "Let's get back to Paddington and see what's she's come up with. I hope it's good. You're not the only one still sore as hell from the beating."

Chapter 36

November 11th, 2017
Starbucks, Paddington Station, London

The four, watched over by The Gliss, their annoyingly inseparable companion, sat on comfy sofas watching Japanese tourists trying to juggle coffees with suitcases.

Porter and Feng had little to report but told them about Ursa's final moments.

"I knew what *they* were like and I let you go," said Karin. "*They*: plural. Not, *him*: singular."

"Yes, I picked up on that," said Porter. "Feng, can you remind me of the timeline?"

"Work in progress," said Feng, indicating he was about to rely on memory by tapping his temple, "but Ursa was the one who went to New York etc first."

"So, Ursa had a set of failed auditions and later, Rose and Bella went for theirs?"

"Basically."

"Well, that's interesting, isn't it?" said Namita. "Ursa came home in one piece, though she seems to have done the most travelling. And then she blames herself for letting the other two do the same thing."

"Conclusion: Ursa didn't have good experiences," said Porter.

"Despite the postcards to her family suggesting she did," said Namita.

Feng nodded. "Let's be honest, who tells the truth to their mum and dad?"

Karin told them about the TV response emails. "They're still coming in. I've had almost 200. I think you can discount 99% of them. Most are trolling me or irrelevant virtue signalling. There are four that got me quite excited." She showed them the very first email, from Lucy Pelling, the one mentioning Buddy Demsky.

She read out the next. It was from a woman in Leicester called Sally Graham.

> *Dear Karin*
>
> *I'm sorry about your eye. I hope all is going well. I saw you on TV this morning and had to write in.*
>
> *I feel a bit stupid and gullible writing to you, if I'm honest. You're probably being inundated...*
>
> *I had bit parts in a few feature films and TV shows in the 60s. I was in an episode of The Avengers! Girl in beret. That's all it said on the credits. My character didn't even have a name, and yet it was probably my biggest success. I was full of dreams of Hollywood and stardom in those days. Now I run a small charity shop back home in Leicester. I'm going to retire this year - if you know anyone who wants a shop filled with musty, secondhand cardigans.*
>
> *So, yes, I know all about the casting couch. I probably wouldn't have gotten in touch, but you mentioned someone who has been in my dreams many times over the years - Heinrich Becker. When I say dreams, I mean nightmares, of course.*
>
> *I had been doing a bit of part-time work in Soho at various clubs and bars and there was this guy called Clem Rossiter. You may have seen him on TV? He was a bit of a villain. But he was a lovely boss. He made sure we were all looked after and made sure the guests didn't paw at us.*

He found out I was an actress and said he'd put me in touch with some producers he knew. You know what it's like when you're young. I think I was about 21 and every slender lead felt like an unmissable opportunity. Clem invited me over to meet British film producer, Albert Mayes. The meeting went well!

Later, Clem said Albert needed persuading whether to cast me or not. I asked what I could do to convince him. Such innocence. To my horror, Clem undid his flies, pulled out his you-know-what, and said, "Well, to start with, you could adopt me to push your case."

Let's be honest, I'm not going to tell this story on camera. Sorry. But, yeah, I did what he wanted. Later, we had sex on his office table. I still didn't get the part with Mayes. I felt sick at myself for giving in. Bloody Pill. He was very nice to me on the other occasions I met him, and he never tried it on again. Free love? Right? What a load of horseshit.

About two months later, he called me over for a chat. I was very nervous, as you can imagine. He told me a German director needed an English-speaking girl for one of his films. He was very clever about it. He said he felt bad I hadn't got the job with Mayes after you-know-what. He wanted to make it up to me. "After all, you've already paid, right?" I felt sick that he made me feel like a prostitute by saying that, but he made no attempt to force me to do anything else. Instead, he offered to fly me to Berlin to audition for Becker. He got me some headshots done and off I went. I was actually grateful for the opportunity, can you believe?

Well, guess what? It was like a repeat of the previous occasion. Becker had his way - God, yes, I gave in again - and still I didn't get the job. Where Rossiter had been fairly nice to me, Becker treated me like a slave. Even as he did his business and I stared up at the ceiling, I knew I had no chance of getting that job. He didn't care whether I was there or not. It was horrible. I just stared over his shoulder at the paintings and photos, the ugly statues, and prayed for it all to be over.

I was dumped back at the airport next day and flew back to London. I cried all the way.

Rossiter seemed disappointed I didn't get the role and offered to fly me to New York for another audition. I said no, finally. At no time did he show anything other than care for me - apart from the blow job - but the two of them had squashed the life out of me.

I stayed in London for another year or two without incident, but I knew I was done with an industry more sordid than creative. The funny thing was, I later met an American girl, Shelley Bland, who was in London for an audition for one of Clem's film. Since she was here, she decided to stay a little longer, to see if she could pick up some acting work in London. I think she did better than most of us and ended up in a play at the Royal Court. Good for her.

She was the same age as me, so we hung out a bit. One night, she got a bit pissed and told me she'd had her flight to London paid for by some big shot producer in LA - after she screwed him. That was the night I realised how truly disgusting the industry was.

I opened up about Rossiter and Becker and she told me Rossiter had screwed her in exchange for introducing her to Bob Crowes, who was the casting director at Vosbourgh Films. She failed her audition there too.

We both ranted and raved about how awful it all was. But she was determined to plug away, while I moved back to Leicester. I never got married. Between them they kind of put me off men.

Karin - I'm not sure I want to talk about this on camera, but I wanted you to know that, yes, the casting couch was fully operational in London, in 1965 at least. Feel free to call me if I can be of any further help.

With regards,
Sally Graham

"Oh my God, that's horrible," said Namita. "Well, that confirms that Rossiter and Becker were bastards."

"That's amazing testimony," said Porter. "Thank you, Karin, for finding it."

"I haven't finished," said Karin. "This one came from a woman called Alice Hopper."

Karin! How strange you should make that appeal today! I was only talking about this stuff yesterday with my granddaughter, Regina. She has just signed up at RADA and I was giving her the industry equivalent of the Birds and Bees chat!

Back in 1969, I was trying to break into the film industry. I had a big head full of dreams. I've attached a picture of me, back then.

They opened it. Alice was beautiful. She was wearing a clinging, ribbed polo neck jumper, clearly no bra, and a short skirt. She had a dark brown bob and was leaning against a lamp post somewhere in London. The photo was in black and white and, truly, all four agreed, she was stunning.

"I bet those bastards gobbled her up," said Feng.

"No, they didn't," said Karin, "Listen."

The closest I came to the casting couch was when I met a guy called Clem Rossiter. He scared the pants off me. Everyone knew he was a bit of a gangster, but the girls I knew said he was very kind to actresses and liked to help them. When I got referred to him, I was scared, but not worried. I was about 19 at the time but looked older. I used to say my playing age was 16-30. Although I was pretty confident, I wasn't used to being in the room with gangsters. They were trying to be nice, but you could just see they had all done terrible things. I remember shaking as they sized me up. But the initial meeting went well.

Rossiter asked if I would like to have a headshot done. They were expensive things to do, so of course I said yes. I went to a photographic studio in London with just him and this really creepy photographer called Vince. I'd have forgotten his name probably, but I still have some of the headshots with his company name embossed in the corner.

I needn't have worried. They were both perfect gentlemen! I was dreading, but certain, they were going to ask me to strip or have sex. There was actually a couch in the studio! But I couldn't have been more wrong. Rossiter was a perfect gentleman and said he'd like to keep an eye out for me and hoped I had success.

They gave me a box of headshots, which were very useful, and I did get a few acting parts. I can't remember now if they were through Rossiter directly, but like I say, the photos were very useful.

I did have a theatre director try it on with me once - and I lost count of the number of people who pinched my arse or tried to stick a hand up my skirt - but I never gave in.

Hope this is useful! Happy to talk on camera at some point - I might not have been on the casting couch but I sure as hell knew girls who had.

All my best and good luck!!!

Alice Hopper

"Ah, that's disappointing," said Porter.

"Disappointing in what way?" said Karin. "That the poor girl wasn't molested or raped by Rossiter and his cronies?"

Embarrassed, Porter said, "You know what I mean. If we're building a case against Rossiter…"

"You already have *prima facia* evidence that Rossiter assaulted one actress," admonished Namita.

"Sorry, yes, of course. I hope that's the only case."

Karin decided to let him off the hook. "Alright, I know what you meant. Just don't be so happy to hear about other people's troubles next time."

She turned her iPad around. "And now," she said, "look who the last one's from."

Porter and Feng leaned in to look at the final email. They did a double-take.

"Her?" said Feng. "Really?"

"My God," said Porter.

"Yes, it's her, can you believe," said Namita. "Dame Susan Wills, no less."

Dame Susan Wills. A hundred films to her name. Two Oscars, several Golden Globes, countless other awards, and probably one of the five most famous British women alive, known all over the world.

"What on earth does she say?" said Porter.

Karin,

If it wasn't you, I wouldn't be getting in touch. I have a great respect for your work and was very upset to read about your accident earlier this year.

I doubt many veteran actresses haven't given a lot of thought in the past year or so to your subject. The casting couch has always been an occupational hazard. That's how we saw it back then. The slave accepting its master. What were we thinking? I can't tell you how refreshing, and overdue, it has been to see so many young actresses coming forward and calling men's bad behaviour out. I've often said, in no other industry, bar music and fashion perhaps, could men behave in such a beastly fashion and get away with it.

A caveat. I fully enjoyed the 1960s. You may well have read that I was a bit of a devil in the 60s and 70s. That's absolutely true - I was. I was a fully signed-up feminist who celebrated the arrival of the Pill and threw myself into it. This is all a matter of public record. I had flings with everyone from Roger Moore (my, he was handsome!), to John Lennon (weird) - he sang Yellow Submarine after we made love. It was the times, and I was so happy not to have to live the restricted life of my mother.

But, and here's the important thing, those encounters were my choice and my right. But the freer social mores of the Sixties also led some men to think all women were fair game, whether they wanted it or not.

There were so many incidents, I've forgotten most of them. But, let me tell you, I was never the kind of person to say yes when I meant no. Never. I just liked to say yes - a lot.

I'd be happy to talk on camera about this. My manager will go crazy, but that's why I decided to reach out in person. I'm too old to worry about what people think. I'm in London for two weeks before I head back to Los Angeles, and would love to be interviewed for your film if you can squeeze me in. I'll do my best to recall some specific incidents.

You can reach me....

"Wow," said Porter. "Can I come along to the shoot?"

"And me," said Feng.

"I'm impressed too," said The Gliss. "I've seen some of her films in Porter's head."

"I bet it's better than an IMAX in there," said Feng.

"It's more portable black and white TV," said The Gliss, "but I get the gist."

"We haven't finished," said Namita. "That was her first email."

"She wrote again, an hour later," said Karin.

> *Karin - me again, I know how documentaries work and have just thought of an incident that still makes me laugh. It's not really funny, but it connects to your theme.*
>
> *It must have been late '67 or early '68, when a friend of mine introduced me to The Krays. I hung out with them for a bit - they were very disturbing! - when Reg said I should meet a friend of his, Clem Rossiter. You've probably heard of him, of course, one of London gangland's big shots. He was also a film producer. Reggie set up a meeting and as soon as I got to this photographic studio in Soho somewhere, I knew it was hokey.*
>
> *Clem was on his own, bar a very strange photographer. As soon as I saw the equipment I thought, "Oh great, they're going to try and get me to do nudies." To my surprise, they didn't. Clem ordered the photographer out and chatted to me. Despite myself, I was quite turned on by him. I think, in those early days, I was possibly drawn to the Bad Boys a bit too much. He was well-built and handsome and quite seductive. We chatted about the role he wanted me to audition for and, I'll be honest, I was ready for a bit of fun with him.*
>
> *I was absolutely certain he was going to try and get my knickers off. But then he said something funny. "I don't want to take advantage of you. And you're perhaps a little too old for the role."*
>
> *The part in question was for one of his crap little films. In the script it said, "Anita. 22yo." Well, I was only 23-24 at the time, so that was ridiculous. I just assumed he didn't fancy me or something.*
>
> *The photographer came back, we did some headshots, and that was that. I got home and, to my amazement, got a call from Fellini the same day. The rest of my career is history, I suppose. I've been very lucky.*

I've often wondered what would have happened if I'd stayed at that studio for an hour or two longer. Would I have missed the call that changed my life?

Later that year, I met an Italian actress, Valeria Greco. She told me she was going to London to seek modelling/acting work. I hadn't had a bad experience with Clem, so put her in touch with him. He met her which led to her auditioning for Paolo Agresti - one of the directors you mentioned today. That at least worked out well for her and she starred in his film La Famillia, so she was back in Italy before she knew it.

She had an OK career, I guess. I haven't seen her for many years but I haven't read her obit either, so she's probably still alive. You should speak to her. I hope her auditions with Clem and Agresti were clean ones, but you never know.

Hope that helps. Speak soon.

Susan

"Wow again," said Porter. "Rossiter was a strange one, wasn't he? Imagine turning down Dame Susan in the 60s?"

"Again, Porter," said Karin, "could you moderate your tone? I find it a bit unsettling."

"Is that all of it?" asked Feng. "I'm desperate to update and finish my timeline now. We have quite a few new leads to follow."

"Do you need any help?" said Namita.

"That would be great," said Feng. "Why don't you come over in the morning?"

Namita agreed.

"I've got a hospital appointment," said Porter. "I'll come over in the morning too. In the meantime, I'll have a quick search for those other directors she mentioned."

"Albert Mayes and Bob Crowe," confirmed Karin.

"I'll see what I can find on Shelley Bland and Valeria Greco," said Feng, checking his notes.

"Let me do Shelley Bland. I've got to go back home to do some real work too, but I want to chip in," said Karin, unaware of the slight on the others. "And I'd better get responding to all these emails."

Chapter 37

January 3rd, 1967
Emdener Strasse, Mitte, Berlin

Rose put her cardboard suitcase down on the floral quilt and looked around the bedroom. *God, it was ugly.* And it reeked of cigarette smoke. She pulled a pack out. *If you can't beat 'em…*
She held the fag in her mouth, the smoke burning her eyes. She struggled out of her mac, threw it on the bed, and noted the chill with a sigh. Frau Dietrich said she could put the 3-bar electric heater on if she needed it. That must have been German humour. *A friggin' polar bear would need it.*
Sitting on the floor, her knees pulled up, she saw her gooseflesh legs, the Bible in braille. *Why on earth did you come in a skirt?* Berlin in winter was no better than London. Glamour could be painful.
"This isn't exactly LA, is it, Rose?" Her voice was tremulous from the cold. *Oh, to be back in Hollywood. LA was wonderfully warm.* She laughed, remembering the first time she'd left her hotel room. The receptionist, ogling, told her she wouldn't need a coat. She hadn't believed her. She stepped outside to see the flickering, luminous sapphire of the pool, felt warmth flood over her face, and went straight back to her room to dump her coat.

But Berlin? Tonight? In the dead of winter? There were ice blobs forming on the window. She longed for one of her mum's hot water bottles, a big heavy coat, and a roaring fire. Instead, she looked around at the peculiar room. The door and skirting board were painted a sickly green. A few panels in the door had been painted pink.

"It's a lovely little room," Frau Dietrich had said. "My father used to stay here before he died."

Ever since, Rose had been staring at the bed wondering what the hell the father died from. Was it contagious? Was it the same mattress? Did he leak? She resolved to sleep on top of the sheets, though she guessed she would miss even one thin layer in this hideous cold.

Teeth chattering, she pulled out the letter from Heinrich Becker's production company. The role was a small English-speaking part in his latest movie. The letter contained a brief summary of the audition process and contained a mix of requests. Firstly, he would like to see her deliver lines from the film (attached). Secondly, he would like her to perform a short section of any piece she thought she did well. Thirdly, he would like her to attempt a few words in German. *What's the point of that? The role's for an English speaker.*

She'd settled for a short section of Pinter. She took a second to think of her motivation and began her monologue. *How strange I must look, wandering around this room, talking aloud to myself.*

This was her 20th audition in two years. She'd picked up a couple of small parts, giving her the confidence to keep going. But the juicy roles eluded her. Surely, it was only a matter of time before one of the bigger parts came her way?

She thought back to LA and New York. Taken in the round, neither had been particularly pleasant. She was determined to be strictly professional this time. She either got the part or she didn't. But she wouldn't shag the director again, no matter what he promised.

Chapter 38

November 12th, 2017
Feng's house, Church Lane, Walthamstow, London

The previous evening, Feng had arrived home so tired he'd eaten a can of cold spaghetti hoops and fallen asleep on the sofa. His doorbell rang as painfully as if he'd been Big Ben's clapper, his head bashing from side to side in the giant bell.

"You alright?" said Namita, shivering on his doorstep.

"I'm so sorry. I just woke up. Come in. Excuse the rumple."

"I bought some muffins."

"Sustenance welcome. Coffee coming right up."

The pair were still getting to know each other. They both knew there were rivers to be crossed, bridges to be built, and dinners to be shared before they would truly understand each other. But there was willing on both sides.

Their relationship flaws were down to a mixture of simple difference, but also to their unwillingness to acknowledge the other's strengths. Namita found Feng flippant and casual. She tended to ignore his commitment, diligence and passion. Feng thought Namita temperamental, arrogant and dismissive, ignoring her tenacity and intelligence.

Namita also wasn't fond of Feng's fundamental, discomforting honesty. He said what was on his mind. Like now.

"You don't really like me, do you?"

Shocked again by this uncouth directness, Namita, who liked to dance in the shadows, was reduced to a garbled, "Er? What?"

"You don't really like me. I'm not surprised. We didn't get off to a good start. Haven't I earned a few Brownie points since then?"

"I do like you," lied Namita. She saw his raised eyebrow. "Alright, I find you a bit unsettling."

"Because I'm gay? Because I'm Chinese?"

"Don't be stupid. No, because I don't understand why you spend your entire life looking for something you don't believe exists. And you're a bit sarcastic, of course."

"I'm sarcastic, am I?" said Feng. "Maybe. But I have shifted a bit on my beliefs. After Flanders I could hardly keep saying I don't think the paranormal exists with any conviction. You're right, though. Something in me is still resisting, despite that. I've been chatting with Peregrine Zouche a good deal. He's an expert on the occult and he's opening my mind. But it's still only a crack in the door at the moment. I'm fairly logical. Funny thing is, I thought that would endear me to you - your calculating side."

Namita's turn to raise an eyebrow. "What do you mean *calculating side?*"

The doorbell rang. Feng gave Namita a knowing look and set off to let Porter in.

The newcomer noticed the atmosphere as soon as he sat down at Feng's kitchen table. "Everything alright?"

Namita repeated Feng's accusation. "You don't think I'm calculating, do you?" she asked.

"I…oh…er…," said Porter.

"Oh thanks!"

"No, I mean, well…you know. You can be a bit biting sometimes."

"Calculating *and* biting? Thanks guys."

"I think you sometimes act like everyone's the enemy, that's all," said Porter, inadvertently adding another fault to the list. "But I like you. And so does Feng, don't you Feng?"

"I find you interesting," Feng said, with an unconvincing smile.

"If you have a fault, Porter, it's that you're not particularly precise," said Namita. "I think you get muddled easily."

"And so, the Team Porter Awayday was a great success," said Feng.

"There you go…sarcastic as ever," said Namita.

"Oh, he's definitely sarcastic," said Porter. "It's one of the reasons I like him so much." He toasted Feng with his mug.

"I love you both and wish I could have your children," said Feng, a comment that did nothing to lift the mood.

"Your problem, if I may so," said The Gliss, popping into startling view without warning, "is that you haven't learned to accept each other's foibles. I did my best to stop Porter from taking any of you into his confidence, but we are where we are. I'll be honest, I was wrong to want that. I'm pleased you're all on board. Porter would be dead without you. Want to know your collective problem? You are all deliberately ignoring the fact that you've saved each other's lives, worked brilliantly as a team, defeated a once-in-a-thousand-years-evil, and worked tirelessly ever since to find out what happened to Rose."

Namita went to say something, but The Gliss put a supercilious finger in front of his mouth to shush her, something neither Feng nor Porter would ever have risked doing. "You've all been through a lot, physically and mentally, but what I see before me is three friends having breakfast, up with the worm to bring some justice to the world."

"I don't like him either," said Feng. "Too mouthy."

"Yeah, he's a pompous son-of-a-bitch," said Namita.

"And he made me spill my coffee," said Porter, who also lifted off his seat during jump scares at the movies.

They all laughed, a team again. The Gliss drifted over to the corner to sulk. My enemy's enemy is my friend, and all that.

Upstairs, they admired Feng's nascent timeline. He explained the methodology and they got to work supplementing it. This involved cross-checking notes, Dropbox and memory, in a slow process which did indeed show their collective patience and dedication.

Namita confirmed Karin had called Shelly Bland in LA the night before. Bland confirmed Sally Graham's story but didn't want to go into detail. Feng had looked up Valeria Greco. She died of lung cancer two years ago. None of the articles and interviews he read had mentioned anything about casting couches or named any of their director/producer checklist.

Namita asked Porter, "Did you have any luck with those two new directors?"

"There's not much on them. Mayes died in '69. Crowes was still working in film in the 70s but seems to have just faded away."

The trio adjusted the cards, scribbled notes and discussed connections. Two cups of coffee and three hours later, they stood back to admire their handiwork.

> *Cities: Rome, Paris, London, LA, New York, Berlin*
> *Directors/Producers: Buddy Demsky, Clem Rossiter, Bob Crowes, Paolo Agresti, Albert Mayes, Heinrich Becker, Don Lascelles, Morrie Crystal, Oli Caron.*
> *People known to have auditioned but survived: Sally Graham, Lucy Pelling, Susan Wills, Alice Hopper, Ursa Fielding, Valeria Greco, Shelly Bland.*
> *People known to have auditioned and disappeared: Rose Prideaux, Bella Tompkinson, Tonya Hutchins.*

Porter drew attention to the eight red cards in the centre of the timeline.

> *Rose goes missing.*
> *Caron, Demsky, Agresti all die the same day.*
> *Alex Harding is murdered.*
> *Bella and Tonya go missing.*
> *Ursa commits suicide.*

There was a clear split. None of the red cards appeared before January 5th 1967, the day Rose was reported missing.

"Oh my God," said Namita. For once, she spoke for everybody.

"And you know what?" said Feng. "We've uncovered these women's names randomly through research. Odds on there must be more."

"Hopefully not red cards," said Porter.

Namita began filling in autobiographical details for each of the girls. She soon got depressed doing it. "They were all so young, 19-24," she said. The Skelling problem still resonating, she added, "Fucking men."

"Fucking straight men," said Feng.

"Oh, yeah. Gay men are no trouble at all," huffed Namita. "I mean, Joe Orton had no problems with Kenneth Halliwell, did he?"

"Who are they?"

"Orton was a famous playwright, and Halliwell was the jealous lover who bashed his head in," said Porter.

"Charming," said Feng. "Well, no-one's perfect."

It was movie time. Feng had sourced two of the films Rossiter produced in the 60s. As well as being rare, it turned out the only way to watch any of Clem's films was with the fast forward button jammed down.

Forage - zombies invade the Lake District - was one of the most risible films Porter had ever seen. "There's no attempt to differentiate the zombies from the non-zombies, and the acting's so bad, they all come across as dead."

Namita nodded. "Some of them are blinking. Zombies don't blink, do they?"

"All reflex actions cease with the death of the body, so no, they shouldn't," said Feng.

All You Need is Guns was the movie equivalent of swallowing live mice. Its only charm was a few period shots of Soho in all its swinging '66 glory.

"Hip youngsters go on a drug fuelled-rampage," groaned Feng. "What a duff idea."

"It reminds me of Magical Mystery Tour," said Porter. "I saw it as a kid and told Ida it was too weird for me."

"That's cos it's utter crap," said Feng. "And, like this awful film, it was originally shown in black and white, when it clearly had to be in colour to make any sense at all. 1966, the year before the Summer of Love. You could argue it's quite perceptive about what was to come a year later."

"Wait, back up a second," said Namita. She pointed to a group of hip young people laying around the floor of a party, smoking weed. "Is that Rose?"

It bloody well was. Feng grabbed a snap. She was only in the background with no lines, but seeing her move, her eyes blink, her mouth smile, shocked them.

"My God, she really existed," said Feng. "I see what you meant in Berlin now, Porter. I wasn't imagining a real person at all. More like a mannequin with a photo of Rose's face stuck on."

One final surprise. In the credits, the associate producer was listed as Buddy Demsky.

"Holy cow. That links Demsky, Rossiter and Rose too," said Namita. "Flip."

Later that evening, taking a much-needed break in the kitchen, Porter called DCI Dan Crawley.

Crawley laughed. "Porter, are you really calling me this late to ask me to run a non-specific check with Interpol? I haven't got the authority. Do you realise how much work that would be? I could speak to the UK Missing Persons Unit. They might be able to do something?"

Porter, who had Crawley on loudspeaker while fixing more coffee, said, "I know it's a big ask, Dan, but actually the keywords should make it easier - female, 19-24, actress."

"The MPU has a central national database. I think you can search that yourself. Why don't you do that, and I'll put a request in to Interpol, though they'll probably laugh."

"If you could do Interpol, that would be great. You can add some more keywords too: London, Rome, Paris, Berlin, LA, New York."

"Seriously, Porter, I'll try, but I'm pretty sure it'll be a no-go. Too broad. Leave it with me."

After Crawley hung up, the trio called Karin and asked if she would request a similar search from Arnie Flax. She agreed to try, though she too was sceptical about the logistics. "I'm interviewing Susan Wills and Lucy Pelling tomorrow," she said. "Any of you want to come? Johns and Borrison will be there too."

"Would we like to come and meet the most famous British actress alive?" said Porter. "Er. Yes."

"Don't embarrass me," warned Karin.

"Oh my God," said Feng. "What do you think we'll do? Ask for autographs? Grab a selfie? Give her a kiss?"

"If you do any of those things, I'll bop you on the head."

"We wouldn't dream of it," said Porter.

"Fine. Well, get to the British Academy in Carlton House Terrace for 9am," said Karin. "I've borrowed a room there." She hung up.

"Damn," said Porter. "I was going to get her to autograph a poster."

"And I was going to grab a selfie for Facebook," said Feng.

"Humans are very funny. Why does it matter?" said The Gliss. "She's just an old lady."

"An old lady who was in two Bond films, worked with Pacino and De Niro and starred in some of the greatest art house films of the 60s and 70s," said Porter.

"I've been in your head - when you say art house you mean, films where the female leads get their boobs out - right?"

"I think that's over-simplifying it just a tad," said Porter.

"He's got a point though," said Feng. "People weren't so prudish then."

"And of course, the obverse of that culture was the casting couch," said Namita, "so let's not be flippant, all things considered."

Karin would have approved.

Chapter 39

November 13th, 2017
The British Academy, Carlton House Terrace, London

Lucy Pelling looked extremely uncomfortable as her make-up was applied. "I can't believe you talked me into this, Karin," she said. "But you know what? I've seen all these young girls having the courage to open up on TV about the abuse they've had. It would be crap of me to bail out. If you think it'll get people talking, it's worth the embarrassment."

"Thanks, Lucy," said Karin, leaning against a wall, watching the make-up process. She always tried to appear personable but, in professional mode, could come across like a teacher supervising a detention. "I really hope this film does some good. I'll just ask you about your experiences. It's just a conversation, you're not being cross-examined in court, so don't feel intimidated."

"That's about as reassuring as a doctor jumping out the surgery window," Feng whispered to Porter.

Borrison put a lapel mic on Lucy, and Johns touched up the lighting. They were ready to go.

Lucy recapped how she found herself in London just after England's 1966 World Cup victory. "It was really great, honestly. Swinging was the right word for it." She shifted uncomfortably in her seat.

Karin, noting the restlessness, decided to go down a gear. "Where did you grow up?"

"Birmingham. It was very provincial in those days. I remember wearing really drab clothes and getting changed into my Carnaby Street clothing on the train. If I'd worn those clothes in Birmingham, my life would have been hell."

"And you ended up in Soho?" Karin prompted.

"Yes. I hadn't been here 10 minutes when I met Roger Daltrey from The Who. Can you imagine? He bought me a drink, no funny business. Very funny man. I got his autograph on a napkin."

"Where was that?"

"Some bar in Mayfair. I'd heard there were pop stars hanging around. I was only 21 and my head was easily turned. I went with some friends and it was just a fan thing."

"And you were an actress?"

"A struggling actress, yes. But then, aren't we all? I had an agent, Milton Murtagh, whose office was in Berwick Street, surrounded by the red-light industry. It wasn't exactly glamorous. But I felt safe, strangely enough."

"Did you get much work?" asked Karin.

"Bits. I was a looker. I was keen. I had a few cameos - there wasn't much TV in those days - and a few stage parts. Small potatoes but I was just ecstatic to be in the middle of it all - you know, getting direction from Pinter? Wow. I thought I was in Heaven. I met Michael Caine, Paul McCartney, Lew Grade. It was a long way from up the Hagley Road."

"The industry was very different then. Did you have any casting couch moments?"

"I'll come to that. That wasn't my beef. It was the casual sexism that got me. Men joked about my breasts and thought nothing of pinching my arse. Just because it was expected, didn't make it any less annoying or intimidating. 'She's got lovely tits,' one producer said to another. 'Yeah, and kissable lips.' I was standing there, for God's sake."

Karin nodded. Time to go in. "And you met Buddy Demsky? How did that happen?"

There was a slight pause. Lucy took a deep breath and began. "Like I said earlier, this is embarrassing. I met a guy called Clem…"

"Clem Rossiter? The gangster?" Everyone looked at everyone else.

"That's him. I met him and he was incredibly helpful. I picked up a bit of waitressing in one of his clubs - I had to pay the rent - and he introduced me to Buddy when he was in town. Demsky told me he was in London to cast for Omar Sharif's latest. I was so excited, as you can imagine. I still remember running back to my flat to tell my girlfriends."

"Sounds good."

"Well, it was, until I got to the audition."

"What happened?"

"I should have known better. He invited me to his suite at The Hilton. With the benefit of hindsight - why wasn't it taking place in a studio or rehearsal room? Back then, I was just so damned keen. I walked straight into the trap."

"What was Demsky like? I've only seen pictures of him."

Lucy thought for a second. "Well, he was quite attractive, shaven-headed and very charming. I don't think you could work in film without being charming, even then. But it was all surface. You've met those kind of people: nice as pie, but when they blow up, they're psychotic."

Karin thought of her TV commissioners and nodded. "Do you mind telling me what happened?"

Lucy blew her cheeks out, delaying the moment. When she spoke, she was hesitant, but courageous. "I want to make this clear: Demsky didn't rape me. I agreed to everything, but I didn't fancy him that much, and I didn't really want to do it. I admit it, I kept thinking of the film part."

"You slept with him?"

"I had sex with him, yes," corrected Lucy. "It was the bloody 60s. We were young; free love was all the rage. I didn't want to be uncool - whatever that means. God, I was so stupid. I gritted my teeth and accepted it's what you had to do. But I really didn't want to do it. He had to persuade me."

"How?"

"Oh, he was smart. He told me how every actress did it. He was right upfront about it. He boasted about the famous actresses he'd bedded. Their Oscars were down to him and the little favours. That's what he called it: little favours."

"Did you believe him?"

"I was desperate. Yes, I believed him. But it wasn't true, was it? I think they'd call it grooming now."

"But you agreed?"

"I did agree, but it was still abuse. In the old days if someone offered to marry you and pulled out you could sue for breach of contract. What was the difference? None. He had no intention of giving me a part, whatsoever. I'm clear on that. Sordid, true, but he promised me something in bad faith."

"He didn't treat you badly, though?"

"Depends what you mean," said Lucy, cautiously.

"Can you elaborate?"

"I'd rather not. It was painful - then and now. Is that clear enough for you?"

"Yes. Ok. What happened then? When did you realise that you were not going to get the film part?"

"As soon as he got off me, leaving me face down, bleeding and sniffling. He made it very clear I could leave any time I wanted."

"I'm sorry to hear that. And you never heard from him again?"

"The bastard had no shame. He rang in person to tell me I'd failed the audition. He gave some excuse or other but dangled a consolation prize. He offered to fly me to Rome. There was a producer there - I forget his name - who was looking to cast a new film."

"Was that Paolo Agresti?" asked Karin.

"Maybe. Can't remember. What I do remember saying, through tears of rejection, was, 'Do you think I'm stupid?' I wasn't going to be passed around like a cheap prostitute."

"What happened then?"

"What do you think? The work dried up. Clem sat me down and told me to be nice to producers. He made it sound like it was my fault. My feelings? All these years later? It was abuse, simple as that. Demsky held all the cards. It was stupid of me to fall for it, but I honestly felt I had no choice. It was extorted consent. Can we stop now?"

Borrison and Daly went off to get coffee. Karin sat with Lucy, gently patting her back. "Thank you. It was brave of you to be so honest."

"It's ok. I felt I had to do this. And you're very persuasive."

"That's a horrible thought. I don't want to be part of the same lineage as a worm like Demsky," said Karin.

"No!" said Lucy. "You're nothing like him. You're doing good work. I really need to get out of here though."

"Don't go," said Karin. "The next interviewee will be here in a minute. I'd like you to meet her, have a cup of coffee."

"Oh, I don't think that's a good idea," said Lucy.

"It's Dame Susan Wills," said Karin.

"Just a cuppa then," said Lucy.

It was like seeing The Queen in a chip shop. Dame Susan was so famous, her face so ingrained in the minds of everyone in the room, their brains struggled to process her presence.

Even The Gliss was impressed. He'd seen plenty of images in each of the team's heads. "Wow," he said. "She's very small in real life."

"Petite," corrected Feng.

"Who you calling *petite*?" Dame Susan laughed, unwrapping her scarf. "What is this? A morgue?"

"Dame Susan," said Karin, snapping out of it. "How kind of you to come."

"Susan, for God's sake, Karin. Who's everyone?"

Karin did the introductions and arranged tea for all.

"Builder's for me," said Susan. "Wherever I go, they assume I'm going to ask for Lapsang Souchong or something."

Karin took a special effort to introduce Lucy. "Lucy has just done her interview about acting in the 60s. She was very open about what she went through."

"Sit yourself down, love," said Susan, patting the seat next to her. "We veterans have to stick together."

Lucy said she was a big fan. "I saw you and Alan Bates in Odyssey when I was 20," she said. "You were my hero in the late 60s."

"Ah, dear old Alan," said Susan. "A great actor and a total gentleman. It all seems so long ago."

"But not all of it," said Karin. "I presume that's why you're here?"

"Yes, not all of it, sadly. So little has changed."

The team went through their filming prep while Susan and Lucy chatted. Karin hoped Lucy's bravery would inspire Susan to open up, but the plan was in danger of backfiring. The actresses were getting on so well they might run out of time. She had to assert herself. Bark like a pro. "Five minutes to camera, please."

"I think I'm required for my close-up," laughed Dame Susan, putting her hands over her ears. She requested Lucy sit with Karin for the interview.

Camera rolling, they captured Susan's basic account of her 60s' experience, committing the contents of email to tape. Karin was desperate to get to the nitty gritty.

"You mentioned an audition for Clem Rossiter. Can you tell us about that experience, please?"

Susan repeated the story about being introduced to Clem by The Krays. "When I got to the studio in Soho where the audition was being held, I thought, uh-oh, here's trouble. There was an actual couch in the studio. Sure, photographic studios often had them for modelling purposes, but my gut told me it was there for more sinister reasons."

"And you were no stranger to the casting couch?"

"What? I never went on one in my life, you cheeky sod! I told you, I was a fully paid-up wild child and advocate of the Swinging Sixties. I did my bit for advancing women's sexual freedoms, but I never screwed anyone for a job."

Porter, whose post-Quincunx gift was discovering a previously latent empathy for others, winced as he saw Lucy Pelling shrivel slightly in her seat. Everyone else was too gripped to notice.

"That wasn't me, but I knew plenty of people who did. We didn't judge in those days. Did we, Lucy?"

Lucy shook her head, embarrassed.

"It was very odd. They wanted me to audition for a role as a 22-year-old but told me I was too old at 24. No-one could possibly have known what age I was onscreen. There's a reason actors' CVs contain a playing range."

"Why do you think they said that?" asked Karin.

"It's obvious, isn't it? They didn't think I was right for the part. Like I said, Clem and his photographer were very gentlemanly. I was completely wrong about the casting couch. They didn't even make dirty jokes or letch over me, which was much more common."

"You said you fancied him?"

"Yes, I did. I was waiting for him to chuck the photographer out and I was going to jump him, if he didn't jump me. Like I said, I was a wild child."

"But you didn't?"

"I didn't get the chance. The photographer was there the whole time. He offered me some free headshots, but I already had loads of those, so I said no. And that was that. Another failed audition!"

"But the casting couch was a real phenomenon?" said Karin.

"Of course. It's not exactly a secret. I think I had some kind of misguided sense of self-importance at the time. I felt like I was the only one who was going to make it. I knew 100 actresses in London. I'd be surprised if fewer than 10 hadn't been forced onto the couch at some point."

Karin thought, celebrity appeal besides, Dame Susan wasn't that useful an interviewee. Charming as she was, she was also a little sanctimonious and her testimony might actually make other women feel worse. She'd have to be careful in the editing to make sure that didn't happen.

"What happened after you failed the audition?" Karin asked.

"It was good actually. I went with Clem to his club. It was pretty dodgy, and being in a basement, there was no natural light, but it had a real edge to it. Just my thing at the time. He was very considerate all night. I met a few people. He paid for my cab home. Never really had much else to do with him."

"Wait," said Feng, who remembered every detail. "You said the club was in the basement? Kitty, Kitty was at street level, surely? I've seen a few photos."

"Not Kitty, Kitty. The Tutu Club. His private club."

Chapter 40

November 13th, 2017
The British Academy, Carlton House Terrace, London

Porter and Feng forgot the camera and said out loud, "The *what* club?"

"The Tutu Club," said Dame Susan. "It was under a newsagent in Wardour Street. Clem unlocked a little gate, and we went down some steps. You wouldn't have known there was a club there at all from the street. It wasn't a discotheque type place, more like a gentlemen's club."

Karin, annoyed at the filming interruption from Feng and Porter, nonetheless saw they must have done it for a reason. She asked them if this was significant.

"It's the first I've heard of it," said Porter, "but both Clem and Becker had a really ugly statue of a ballet dancer wearing a tutu."

"God, yes! That's right," said Susan. "I remember it. As you came in it was standing by the bar. Hideous thing. I remember it well - the outstretched arm had a couple of ties draped over it. It was ugly and absurd."

"Clem took me there once too," chipped in Lucy Pelling. "I hated it. I was the only woman. Although Clem was very nice to me, it felt creepy."

"Yes, it was a bit sinister," said Susan. "But again, as a woman in the 60s, a lot was. I didn't think much about it at the time. I felt safe with Clem anyway. It would have been a brave man who made a move on me with Clem there."

Porter pulled out his iPad and googled The Tutu Club. Nothing came up. "We need to look into this, right away," he said. "Feng, come on, let's nip out, leave Karin to her filming."

Daly Johns was getting irritable. "Do you want me to keep rolling?"

November 13th, 2017
Namita's flat, Holloway Road, London

Namita stared at her disapproving phone. She was scared to call Skelling. Hammell had accepted her bugging challenge and given her a few tips and words of encouragement.

"Now reel the bastard in," he said.

She hoped to - if she could persuade Martin to meet up one final time in Bristol. Hammell's bugs would hopefully record Martin incriminating himself.

Putting Karin's plan into operation had been simple enough, but rejecting all her professional scruples turned out to be a lot harder. He was still a human being after all. Just. If he was caught on tape blackmailing her, that was his career over - and hers. Mutually assured destruction the only way out.

Sangita jumped in. "You think he's shown you any respect?"

"It's not that - of course he hasn't. But two wrongs don't make a right."

"Law of the jungle. Kill or be killed."

"I know. But it doesn't mean I have to like it."

"That little shit wouldn't think twice. Come on. You know what to do."

Namita seized the phone and dialled before she had time to dither more.

"Hello?"

"It's me."

"You're late," snapped Skelling. "I said I'd give you a week to sort everything out."

"I have sorted things out. We need to meet. Are you around tomorrow?"

"We don't need to meet. A letter will do."

"Forget it. In person or nothing. I'll be at Big Al's tomorrow at 11am. Either be there or the deal's off." Before Skelling could reply, she cut the call.

"Good work," said Sangita.

But Namita frowned. She had betrayed her scruples and if it went wrong...

November 13th, 2017
Starbucks, Regents Street, London

Porter and Feng did their best to find The Tutu Club on Google. Unusually, apart from a mention of a ballet dancers' support group in Switzerland, they found nothing.

"How strange," said Feng. "You'd think it'd have cropped up somewhere. We should call Ronnie Phelps. Maybe he knows about it?"

But Phelps was in the dark too. "I'm sorry, gentlemen, I've never heard of it. Where on Wardour Street was it?"

"Under a newsagents," said Porter.

"There must have been several back in the day," said Phelps. "There's an old vice cop I still know - Larry Jayfield – he was as bent as Uri Geller's spoon. If Rossiter had a place on the side, he'd know about it. Maybe his aging conscience will let him talk to me."

"We'd appreciate you asking," said Porter. "We only just found out about it."

"Word of warning, lads," said Phelps. "Dan's getting a bit ansty about your investigation. Top Brass are asking are all kinds of questions about Shanker's death. Dan's worried he'll get caught up in it too. Shanker would still be alive without you lot poking about in the past. Dan told me the detective leading the investigation has spoken to Shanker's agent - that bloke at the Willesden Chronicle. I guess it's only a matter of time before he calls on you too."

"As suspects?" said Porter, alarmed.

"Probably not. Cops aren't as stupid as we're made out to be. But they'll want to know what you were talking about and if it had any bearing on his murder. Try not to get Dan caught up in it. He's one of the good 'uns."

"What's your view, Ronnie?" asked Feng, straining to hear the old detective's voice on the speakerphone.

"If so many cops in the 60s hadn't taken backhanders, this case would've been sorted then. As far as I'm concerned, you're on the side of the angels."

"There's no such thing as angels," said The Gliss, before Feng shushed him, dismissing the greatest theological discovery ever with a casual wave of the hand.

Feng and Porter returned from the street to Carlton House Terrace, where Borrison and Johns were packing up. Karin, Lucy and Dame Susan were sitting at a table, drinking tea.

"Nothing," said Porter, "but we've asked DCI Phelps to make inquiries."

"That's very strange, isn't it?" said Dame Susan. "I thought everything that happened in the 60s had been raked over 100 times by now."

Karin nodded. "Makes me think this club was important to Rossiter. Isn't the whole point of a club to make money? The way you describe it, it sounds more like a den for little boys to hide in."

"I'm sure everyone who went there was naughty," said Dame Susan. "What they were up to, I don't know. And I disagree: the primary purpose of a club is to make its members feel elite in some way. As I was saying on camera earlier, there was something of the colonial old boys' club about it. Nothing commercial at all. It sounds odd to say it, but I felt sort of privileged to be there."

"Yes, I got the impression that I was being given a treat too," said Lucy. "At least, I think that's what Clem intended. I remember the atmosphere. It was like a spy novel. There were men in suits. One guy was straight out of Graham Greene - buff linen suit, brown shoes, Panama hat."

Karin, wiping some errant tea from her lips, nodded. "Well, we keep hearing that London was filled with spies and Nazis, so that doesn't surprise me."

"Oh yes, spies," said Dame Susan. "I met Philby once. I was never very political - though you can argue that choosing the bohemian life was as political as it gets. When I met Philby he'd been forced to resign from MI5 under a cloud of suspicion, but he hadn't been confirmed as a spy yet. It gave him an air of sexy power."

"Where did you meet him?" asked Karin.

"At a party in Chelsea," Susan replied. "No other actors, just literary types. They always loved to feel like they were living on the edge."

"They did," said Lucy, "but they were all funded by mummy and daddy. They weren't true revolutionaries. I knew plenty of real people from the underground. They couldn't afford soap, let alone champagne."

"Did either of you ever get approached about spying?" said Porter.

"Ah, someone's OD'd on the Christine Keeler," said Susan. "Of course not. We were bloody actresses. What's the defining thing about actors?"

"Acting?" said Feng.

"Gossip," said Susan. "What use would we have been?"

"I don't know as many people as Dame Susan," said Lucy, "but I agree: the last person on earth you'd entrust secrets to would be an actor."

November 13th, 2017
Chartwell House, Surrey.

Karin offered to put up Feng and Porter if they wanted to come back to her pile to review the day's footage. So far, neither had been to the home she shared with her famous-artist grandfather, Arthur Pelenot, The Pel. They jumped at the chance. Namita said she could make it too, but had an early start for Bristol, so she would get her hire car first and drive down.

In the cab on the way to Surrey, Feng uploaded a picture of himself and Dame Susan onto Instagram.

"Trust you," said Karin. "I thought I said no selfies?"

"It's not a selfie," said Feng. "She insisted! Porter took it."

"Under duress," admitted Porter.

"She was interesting," said Karin, moving on. "She seemed quite normal for someone so famous. Did you see the way she just sat down and chatted with Lucy? She poured the tea and did the honours."

"You can take the girl out of Bradford, but ..." said Porter.

"True, but Bradford was a long, long, time ago. It's amazing any of it remains after a life like that."

"I bet you still have boarding school in your veins," said Porter.

"Yes, I do. You're right," said Karin. "I've more porridge than plasma."

Their cab swished through the gravel of Karin's driveway and Porter and Feng did a goggle-eyed impression of Lizzie Bennett seeing Pembury for the first time.

"Good lord," said Porter. "You actually live here? Don't you get lost?"

"I've got GPS on my phone," said Karin.

"That is incredible," said Feng. "And I thought I had money."

"Don't be fooled," said Karin. "It costs a fortune in upkeep. Some of the mice in the west wing go back to the Reformation. We live in about five rooms."

"Why don't you sell it, then?" said Feng.

"What? So it can become a conference centre? Did I ever tell you that Jane Austen slept in the room I use as my study? I'm deeply attached to it.

"I went off the old place a bit after all that stuff with my evil ancestor, Georges Pelenot - for a few weeks. But my mother and father lived here, I grew up here, Arthur still lives here. Even if I wanted to sell, I couldn't till he's gone. It would kill him."

Walking to the portico framing the front door, Karin gestured around. "For better or worse, my family history is wrapped up in this building. It's too big, yes, but it's as much a part of my DNA as that boarding school."

They heard a swish and turned to see Namita's wheels crunching through the gravel. Reunited in a novel location, they were all pleasantly surprised to feel pleasure and comfort in the fact. The Gliss hovered about them, admiring the high ceilings and imposing central staircase.

"Reminds me of that film with Gloria Swanson," said The Gliss.

"Sunset Boulevard?" said Porter. "You're right. Karin, congratulations, this is the most amazing house I've ever been in."

"It's like Downtown Abbey without the frocks," said Feng.

"I do frocks sometimes," smiled Karin.

"Only on award night though, right?" quipped Feng.

"It's certainly a privilege to live here," said Namita.

Karin caught the emphasis on *privilege* with some annoyance. But that was Namita for you. "Thanks everyone. Make yourself at home. I'm just going to check on Arthur, and I'll be right back."

The group and The Gliss shuffled around uncomfortably, like they were waiting for a job interview. Porter and Namita both thought of their modest flats and couldn't comprehend living in this much space. Feng, who had lived big and small, admired the style over the dimensions.

"It's quite marvellous," he concluded. "We should have set the Murder Room up here. My roll of paper could have gone from 1861 to 2017 without going round a corner."

"Don't joke about the dates," said Porter. "My head is already exploding with the timeframe we do have."

Karin returned and took them to her editing room. Her set-up was basic but it allowed her to review footage and do basic cuts to send to her editors for tonal guidance. The others were impressed at the technical knowledge she displayed.

They all agreed the interviews had gone well and been useful. But what now? There was no news from Phelps. They all sensed The Tutu Club must be important, but for now it remained an offline presence.

"Gangster has private drinking rooms. Hardly a surprise," said Porter, "but the fact that the statue connects Clem and Becker yet again. We can't ignore that."

"Did you run it past your Israeli friend?" asked Namita. "He seems to know everything."

The sentence was barely out before Feng was dialling.

"Mr Tian," said Efrayim Davidov, nonchalantly. "How's your investigation going?"

"Good, good," said Feng, filling him in.

"Hmmm. I've never heard of this club of yours. Leave it with me. You think it important?"

"Bit of a coincidence, wouldn't you say?"

"Possibly, most definitely, probably," they all heard the Israeli say over the tinny speaker.

Karin mouthed to Namita, "Does that sentence even make sense?"

"If you come across anything, do let us know. Did you get a chance to check out the photographer, Vince Chambers?"

"Not much. I've got some researchers on it. We have extensive research on Becker/Hartmann. However, at the moment, aside from the headshot, nothing connects him with Becker as far as I can see."

"That's not true," said Namita. "Clem knew Chambers. Clem knew Becker. Becker had one of Chambers' photos. We know Clem sent people to Berlin. We know Chambers took photos of Clem's actresses."

"Yes, but in my opinion it's still more likely than not to be a coincidence - just part of their day-to-day interactions. Same with the headshot in Becker Haus. *Movie director has headshots of actor in study.* It barely qualifies as circumstantial evidence. Also, think about it: Becker was adept at covering his trail. I should know. I've been trying to prove he was Hartmann for years. Yet here is this 'incriminating' photo? Casually pinned to the board? If we go with conspiracy instead of coincidence, that would seem to be a catastrophic failure on Becker's part."

Feng agreed. "If Chambers, Rossiter and Becker knew each other because of film, and Clem liked to help struggling actors, why wouldn't he recommend actresses to his famous filmmaker contact? Besides we know the woman in that shot is alive and well."

Davidov laughed. "I said I hadn't found any obvious connection between Becker and Chambers. I didn't say anything about Rossiter."

They all caught the tease in his voice. Feng was excited. "What have you found?"

"I would have called sooner but have been busy. You'll have to accept my apologies and remember - I'd never come across Rossiter's name before you flagged him up."

The others waited patiently, sensing Davidov might have something big.

"Well, it's not that exciting, just confirmatory. You already know that Becker and Rossiter knew each other. We have found a photograph of them in Berlin in 1976. Let me text you it now." There was a ping.

Feng showed it around.

"Good God," said Karin. "That's not just Rossiter and Becker." She pointed at a third man. "This looks like a surveillance photo," she said. "Where did you get it?"

Davidov, who appeared unfazed by the sudden appearance of yet another woman on the call, said, "Surveillance indeed… Fraulein Pelenot. We had Becker under investigation for many decades. Who is the other man?"

"That," said Karin, "is Don Lascelles, a director in LA we have been investigating. Where did you find this picture?"

"It's been on our files with hundreds of others for decades. We've been playing the long game on Becker. I only found it because I was looking to see if your Rossiter fellow appeared anywhere."

"I wish you'd sent it sooner," said Karin. "Damn it. I can feel my next LA trip coming on."

The doorbell rang.

While Karin went to answer, the others thanked Davidov for his help. He promised to speed up his inquiries.

Karin returned holding an envelope.

"That looks like trouble," said Feng.

"You could say that," said Karin. "That was a courier. This is a cease-and-desist letter from Rossiter's lawyers."

Chapter 41

November 14th, 2017
Big Al's, Bristol.

Martin was extremely late, which bugged the hell out of Namita as she'd arrived extremely early.

Hammell had placed listening devices around a booth he'd chosen for its discretion. Martin was only half an hour late, but every minute she spent in the cubicle was further crushing her confidence. The booth was made of dark, stained wood, and so compact and hard-surfaced that every noise rang back with fluttery echo. She hoped this wouldn't ruin the recordings.

"Relax," said Sangita. "It'll be fine. He's not a drug-runner for a Colombian drugs cartel. He's not going to ask if you're wearing a wire."

"Easy for you to say," hissed Namita. "You're not the one who has to entrap him."

"No, but I've always wanted to do something like this. And so have you. You obey all the rules, but they frustrate you. Indulge your inner Columbo. This guy's a dick. You can sting him, no problem. And, before you ask, I saw your Jiminy Cricket conscience walking around earlier. I stamped on the little pest. Do your worst."

Martin interrupted her thoughts with formality. "Ms Menon, I'm sorry I'm late." He didn't wait to be sat down by a server. He threw off his plastic mac, scrunching it up noisily. The crackles were amplified painfully by the booth's odd acoustics.

"What is that echo?" he winced. "Do you mind if we move? I have sensitive hearing."

"No!" said Namita. "I'm settled here. Sit down please, Martin. We have to talk."

Grudgingly, Skelling sat, throwing his briefcase and mac to the far side of his double seat. The clatter and rustle hurt Namita's ears too. "Well, do you have all the papers? Are we ready to go? I hope you've seen sense on this?"

"I'm not giving in, Martin," revealed Namita. "If you go down this route I will make life just as difficult for you. This is your last chance to accept the original will and its incontrovertible validity. It's time to stop threatening me, blackmailing me into hiding Florence Prideaux's true intentions."

The calmly delivered statement left Skelling frozen. Halfway through taking out papers and pen ready for Namita to sign, he unfroze and dropped the pen. "How dare you," he hissed. "You really are a stupid bitch, aren't you? The complaint is already lodged with the SRA. Any accusations you make now will just sound like pathetic revenge tactics from a desperate woman." He paused while Namita sat pacifically. Martin filled the silence. "And, yeah, you're a pretty desperate woman." He paused. "I could tell that from the way you put your back into it. Been a while, right?"

Namita had agreed with Hammell to stay calm and professional, no matter what Skelling said. Right now, she wanted to jump across the table and stab him through the heart with a fork.

"That's very unprofessional of you," she said, her voice shaking with a controlled rage that Skelling mistook for fear.

"I won't do it. You'll regret this," he said. "I have you fair and square: breaking the Code of Conduct. And now this sad little plead? Forget it."

Sangita whispered in her ear. "It's not enough. He just sounds angry. You need more on tape. Push him."

How? Namita decided to appeal to his vanity. "You know, I wish things hadn't turned out this way. I kinda liked you." That seemed a good enough cliché to get him to slow down.

Skelling was furious. He dropped his voice into a whisper, which echoed around the booth, straight into Hammell's microphones. "Listen, you bitch. For 10 seconds after I met you, I thought you were special. I thought you might make something - with a bit of work. But now? Look at you: a pathetic lonely woman, crawling around in the slime, waiting for the right man to come along so that you can be kept and not have to earn the money yourself. Well, thank you for showing me what you really are… just another pushy, entitled immigrant. I always imagined marrying someone like you, but you've spared me all that crap and the shame of coffee-coloured kids. Fuck you, Namita. You'll pay for this."

Namita was so shocked, she sat in the booth for 15 minutes after he'd gone.

November 14th, 2017
Feng's house, Church Lane, Walthamstow

Porter was still raving about Chartwell House when their cab pulled up outside Feng's.

"I don't have facades or battlements, but I do have a percolator," said Feng.

"I love your place too," said Porter. "How long have you lived here? I remember thinking it's more suburban than I expected of you at the time."

"You should have seen my last place then," laughed Feng. "I had a massive glass and steel monstrosity in Docklands. I bought it in the late 80s for £150,000 cash - I was on £1m annual bonuses at one point - but I sold it five years ago for £4 million and bought this place outright."

"Christ, how much money do you have?" said Porter, suddenly feeling less guilty about Feng's habit of settling every tab they ran up.

"I don't really count it. Somewhere between five and ten million. But there's just me. I have one sister, who I despise. She actively hates me, even though I gave her a million a few years back. My conscience is clear. My other family are all dead. I don't have a partner. What was the point of my huge bachelor flat? I just wanted comfort and homeliness. I love this place."

"Why does she hate you?"

"Can't you guess? She doesn't approve of my openly gay lifestyle. I don't know why it bothers her so much. There are loads of gay British Chinese."

"Why do you despise her then?"

"See the above: it's not very nice being judged just for being who you are."

"I'm sorry."

"What for? I'm the happiest person I know. They say blood is thicker than water but it's not true. Some people are thicker than blood."

Coffee on the go, Porter checked his email to find that Dan Crawley had been in touch. The DCI had come up with a few possible names.

> *CreepyCrawleyDan@hotmail.com Sent: 14.11.17*
> *Hi Porter,*
> *The trawl is ongoing, but I've come up with two people who fit your profile. Both are registered on the Missing Persons database. I urge caution in assuming these are part of your case.*
> *Grace Tilling. Last seen in George Street, Luton, on December 15th, 1969. She was born on August 8th, 1947.*
> *She was a struggling actress, whose bit-part credits included an episode of The Prisoner, Coronation Street and Z Cars. No other information at the moment. Picture enclosed.*
> *Myra McLeod. Last seen in London. Born 6th July 1947. Went missing 5th August 1969. Another actress who went to London to seek fame and fortune. Picture attached.*
> *I'm making enquiries internally to see if there are extant case files on either of these women. Unless you can establish links with Rossiter and co, they're not much use to you. But I will forward on any other names that crop up.*
> *I feel like I have to send this info onto you, but be warned, the detectives looking into Shanker's murder will probably pay a visit at some point. My advice remains to let this go or hand over your files to us.*
> *All the best,*
> *Dan*

They updated the timeline. Two more red cards. Both had a question mark indicating the unproven connection, but the ever-expanding list of the missing gave them both chills.

"This is a strange case," said Porter. "After The Gliss came into my life and I began to accept him, I presumed I'd spend all my time jumping on and off graves. How can I do that this time when there are no bodies? Instead, I've become Inspector bloody Morse."

"And you don't like that because you think it'll all turn out to be nothing?" said Feng.

"No, I don't think that. We know for sure about Rose, Bella and Ursa. Only two missing, but all three were in the same world."

The Gliss piped up. "You wouldn't be investigating unless they died unhappily. I'm sure of that."

November 14th, 2017
Paddington Station, London

Namita jumped into Karin's idling car while a suspicious traffic warden eyed his prey.

"Thanks, Karin," said Namita, buckling up.

"No, problem. The boys insisted we come over as soon as possible. How was Bristol?"

Namita gave in. She told Karin everything as they headed north to Walthamstow.

"What a shit," said Karin. "That's unbelievable. He really said that?"

Namita, who was still coming to terms with the fact she'd slept with a racist, merely nodded.

"I'm so sorry," said Karin. "No wonder he wants to win your case so much. He probably resents someone like Sam getting the money."

"No, he's one of those weirdos whose political views clash with how he actually lives his life. I don't doubt his friends would think it absurd to call him a racist. It's one of those 'all burqa-wearing women look like letterboxes' moments. He dated me and Aysha, remember? He is a racist, but he's in the closet, living openly as a liberal."

"Well, I hope your plan works. It's time to drag him out of the bloody closet and expose him for what he is. This case is really peeing me off about men."

"There's only one way the case can end well," said Namita, shaking her head. "He has to accept he's lost and advise Gary Stormont to drop the case. Then he might as well withdraw his complaint to the SRA. Unless he's more vindictive than practical. Trouble is, if his misdemeanours ever went public, so would how I trapped him. It would ruin my career too."

"It might not even ruin his," said Karin. "You'd be portrayed as a bunny-boiler, he'd probably get a slap on the back down the pub."

"Don't say that. I only went into this reluctantly and, while I'm grateful for your idea to bug him, I'm scared how it'll play out."

As they drove in silence through Archway, Karin dropped one last comment. *"Coffee-coloured kids* - that's worthy of a kick in the pants on its own."

Namita, turning slowly, said, "What did you just say?"

November 14th, 2017
Feng's house, Church Lane, Walthamstow

Porter was making tea when there was a hammering at the door. Remembering the balaclava thugs who turned up last time, he grabbed the largest knife he could find, and ran to the door determined to meet them on the offensive. They weren't going to catch him napping twice.

Yanking the door open, he was confronted by Karin and Namita, who glanced at the knife, ignored it and pushed past him.

"Hello to you too," said Porter.

"Where's Feng?" said Namita.

"Here I am. What's the commotion all about?" said Feng, shocked to see the girls breathless and Porter threatening them with a kitchen knife.

"Becker was a bloody racist," said Namita.

"A throw shit-in-the-face Nazi," said Karin.

"Yes, we know," said Feng.

"And how do you think he reacted when a mixed-race girl like Rose Prideaux turned up on his doorstep?"

"She didn't look mixed race though," said Porter.

"No, it might have been better for her if she had," said Namita. "Come." She led the charge up the stairs to the Murder Room. Unpinning a picture of Rose from the wall, she waved it at them all.

"Imagine. Becker meets this girl. He auditions her but invites her back the next day. What if he forced her onto the casting couch?"

"Sadly, I'm beginning to think that's exactly what happened," said Feng. "Your point?"

Blushing, Namita said, "And what happens after you have sex with someone?"

"Well, I have a fag and call them a taxi," said Feng.

"You talk," said Porter, ignoring Feng's crassness.

"Right," said Namita. "Let's just suppose that Rose, now more confident than ever of getting the part, told some of her life-story?"

"I don't think Becker would appreciate finding out he'd just screwed a girl whose father was black," said Porter.

"You saw him with the nurse, Porter. Phelps told us about the black saxophonist, Persimmons. What do you think an insane Nazi mass-murderer might do in that situation?" said Karin.

The room went quiet as they absorbed Karin's meaning.

The four stared at the timeline. It made Karin feel sick. If their assumption about Rose's fate was correct, then the red cards now took on a sinister new meaning. "They're not just missing, are they?" she said, almost in a whisper. "They're probably all dead."

Rose Prideaux. Bella Tompkinson. Tonya Hutchins. All went to Berlin. The two new cards: Grace Tilling. Myra McLeod.

"My God," said Feng, "Becker got a taste for killing?" Remembering his concentration camp crimes. "Again. Is that what we're saying? Can we assume the other girls weren't mixed race?"

"He already had the taste for sadism," said Porter. "Flossenbürg, remember?"

"Yes, but…" Feng was troubled by something.

"Jesus Christ," said Namita. "Look at that timeline. It's obvious now, isn't it?"

"What is?" said Feng.

"Oli Caron, Buddy Demsky and Paolo Agresti," said the fiercely analytical solicitor. "They all died on the same day, not long after Rose died. January 19th, 1967. Just three days after Alex Harding turned up headless in the Thames, in fact."

"None of them just died then, did they?" said Karin. "They were all murdered. And I think we can guess why."

"They knew about Rose and didn't like it," said Porter.

"Becker had them killed?" said Feng. "But that would have taken some organisation from Becker. Paolo's car went over a cliff. Caron was stabbed by his lover. Demsky was a mob hit."

The Gliss slow-clapped from across the room. "Well done. Good reasoning. Just one thing, and considering the intelligence in this room, I'm surprised you can't see it: Becker could not have done all this by himself. And considering Porter's job is to right wrongs…"

"The perpetrator's still alive?" said Porter.

"Someone with experience of killing people and disposing of dead bodies," said Karin.

Pinned to the timeline was Rossiter's cease and desist letter. "My God," said Porter. "We're in trouble now."

Chapter 42

November 14th, 2017
Feng's house, Church Lane, Walthamstow

The Murder Room was quiet. Feng and Porter were on their iPads. Namita was emailing Hammell, asking him to Dropbox the Bristol audio. Karin was doodling on a bit of paper.
"I think I have something," said Karin. They all looked up.
She walked over to the timeline. "I've been working out the girls' ages."
"I've already done that," said Feng. All aged between 21-24."
"No, that's not right. You need to add in their fate as well."

Rose Prideaux, 22. Missing, presumed dead.
Bella Tompkinson, 22. Missing, presumed dead.
Ursa Fielding, 24. Suicide.
Sally Graham, 21-22. Survived.
Lucy Pelling, 22. Survived.
Dame Susan Wills, 24. Survived.
Shelly Bland, 22. Survived.
Valeria Greco, 22. Survived.
Alice Hopper, 19. Survived.
Grace Tilling, 22. Missing, presumed dead.
Myra McLeod, 22. Missing, presumed dead.
Tonya Hutchins, 22. Missing, presumed dead.

"I stand corrected," said Feng. "All aged 19-24," said Feng.
Karin showed them her doodle. It was the list re-ordered.

Ursa Fielding, 24. Suicide.
Sally Graham, 21-22. Survived.
Lucy Pelling, 22. Survived.
Dame Susan Wills, 24. Survived.
Shelly Bland, 22. Survived.
Valeria Greco, 22. Survived.
Alice Hopper, 19. Survived.
Rose Prideaux, 22. Missing, presumed dead.
Bella Tompkinson, 22. Missing, presumed dead.
Grace Tilling, 22. Missing, presumed dead.
Myra McLeod, 22. Missing, presumed dead.
Tonya Hutchins, 22. Missing, presumed dead.

"Everyone missing, presumed dead was 22," said Porter. He stared at the drawing. "But you're missing a trick."

He pulled up some files, quickly checked something, and scribbled a doodle of his own. "Ursa was 24 when she killed herself but was 22 when she was doing all her travelling. Look at the list again, re-numbered for age at the time of contact with the producers."

Sally Graham, 21-22. Survived.
Lucy Pelling, 22. Survived.
Alice Hopper, 19. Survived.
Dame Susan Wills, 24. Survived.
Shelly Bland, 22. Survived.
Valeria Greco, 22. Survived.
Ursa Fielding, 22. Suicide.
Rose Prideaux, 22. Missing, presumed dead.
Bella Tompkinson, 22. Missing, presumed dead.
Grace Tilling. 22. Missing, presumed dead.
Myra McLeod. 22. Missing, presumed dead.
Tonya Hutchins, 22. Missing, presumed dead.

"That's nine of them aged 22," said Porter.

"You're missing something too," said Namita. "Some of them got away with not being forced onto the couch. Take them out of the list."

They removed Susan Wills and Alice Hopper. "Now put them in the order of their experiences as best we know them," said Namita.

Lucy Pelling, 22. Survived.
Shelly Bland, 22. Survived.
Valeria Greco, 22. Survived.
Ursa Fielding, 22. Survived, but committed suicide at 24.
Rose Prideaux, 22. Missing, presumed dead.
Bella Tompkinson, 22. Missing, presumed dead.
Grace Tilling, 22. Missing, presumed dead.
Myra McLeod 22. Missing, presumed dead.
Tonya Hutchins, 22. Missing, presumed dead.

"Holy crap!" said Feng.

Karin shook her head in disgust. "This is incredible. Let's look at this afresh, then. Our current theory is that Rose marks some kind of turning point. Before Rose, this bunch of film moguls were happy just to screw 22-year-old actresses. And it really does look like they were passing them around. Then Becker kills Rose - let's say for now, in a racism-fuelled rage - and from that point on this same group of men were still picking on 22-year-olds, but then killing them."

"That's why they didn't force themselves on Alice Hopper, Sally Graham and Dame Susan," said Namita. "They were, respectively, 19, 21 and 24."

"And when three of the group decided the death of Rose at Becker's hands was a step too far, they were bumped off," said Feng.

"That is sick," said Porter. "We're saying there was some kind of twisted fraternity dedicated to abusing 22-year-old girls. Why? Why not 21s and 24s? Doesn't make a lot of sense."

"But they had the club. Maybe the club's not on the record because that's what it was for?" said Namita.

"Yes, but why 22-year-olds specifically?"

"We don't know, do we?" said Karin. "But I bet I know someone who does."

"Who?"

"There are only a few people still alive who have any connection to this. Vince the photographer, Clem Rossiter, Don Lascelles and his assistant, the Reverend Morrie Crystal. Lascelles has dementia. Vince Chambers sounds like he's not well either. Clem is not going to talk to us again now he's got lawyers involved. That leaves Morrie Crystal. I've already spoken to him. He's a good man, I think, and the past weighs heavy on him. If I confront him with this list and what we've seen, I think I could persuade him to go on the record. He was Lascelle's PA rather than a producer in his own right."

Karin booked an expensive flight to LA right there and then. "I'll get clothes there," she said. "I've got my passport with me - I'm going straight to Heathrow."

"I'll drive you," said Porter.

"No, that's fine. Uber booked too. I'll call Flax on the way to the airport. I'm sure he'll come with me to see Crystal."

"Don't go see Crystal on your own," said Porter.

"I'm not that stupid," said Karin.

Ten minutes after Karin left, Porter took a call from Dan Crawley.

"Just to warn you, Porter," said Crawley, "the Shanker detectives are coming to see you today. If I were you, I'd call them up front and arrange to meet them - but anywhere other than Feng's house. They will not be happy if they see that Murder Room of yours. If there's one thing cops can't stand is amateur detectives, meddling." Crawley gave Porter, Pesky Kid #1, the number of Gavan, the lead detective and urged him to call immediately.

"Thanks, Dan. Will do," said Porter, gesturing to Feng and Namita to grab their coats. "We need to get out of here, guys. The cops are coming to get us."

November 14th, 2017
Porter's flat, Sylvester Path, Hackney, London

Detective Sam Gavan was so florid, Porter thought his skin might start splitting from the pressure. He was more tightly packed than an elephant in Audrey Hepburn's pantyhose. His demeanour of explosion-ready rolled over into his speech patterns.

"What the hell were you guys doing with Farr?" he barked. "As soon as he talks to you, he winds up dead in The Thames."

Porter and Namita simultaneously gestured, "Leave it to me," their solicitor training asserting itself in both.

But Porter got the first word in. "You're implying we had something to do with his death?"

If Gavan's face had glowed Level 4 on arrival, the flushometer now surged to 11.

"I'm not bloody well implying anything," he blurted. "I'm saying it outright. His manager, that journalist bloke, said you were trying to get him to grass on stuff he did in the 60s."

"We're making a film with Karin Pelenot," said Porter. "Of course, we asked him questions."

"What's the film about?"

"Vice in 60s Soho. Jimmy has done hundreds of TV interviews about that," said Porter, defensively.

"Yes, but apparently none of them were dangerous, were they? Specifically, what were you talking to him about?"

"Nothing unusual," said Porter. "*What was life like as a gangster in the 60s* – that kind of thing. I don't think he said anything he hadn't said before." Porter knew perfectly well it was the context that had caused Shanker's death. The interview had tipped Clem off that the film crew were looking into the deaths of the girls.

"I want to see those interview tapes," said Gavan.

"I bet you do," said Namita. "But we have the right to protect our sources. Do you have a warrant?"

"No, but as good citizens, I'm sure you'll let me see them. Or have I missed something? You're making a programme; everyone will see the bloody thing eventually. No need to be coy now, is there?"

"We are good citizens, but we'd prefer a warrant to keep everything above board," she replied, unmoved.

Small tears appeared in Gavan's scowling face as it tightened. "Are you saying you will not co-operate?"

"I'm putting it on record that we are co-operating, up to and including, allowing you to see the video files, if you do it by the book," she clarified. "I'm recording this conversation for training purposes," she indicated her iPhone, recording audio from the tabletop.

"Put that away, it's not necessary," Gavan said, changing tack. "Let me put it this way - do you think there was a connection between your interview and Shanker's death?"

"We can't know, can we?" said Porter. "We turned up, did a bog-standard interview and he died a few days later. Who knows what he got up to in those days. I can tell you this. No-one else has seen the tapes other than us, so it's more likely to be just a coincidence."

"Did you mention anyone in the interview? Did he reveal any hitherto unknown crimes?"

Namita felt on safer ground. "As far as we can tell, he told us the same stories he's told every other filmmaker over the years. But even if he had revealed anything new, as my colleague has pointed out, we haven't discussed his interview with anyone else. Of course, if Shanker spoke to anyone else after we left, that's a different story. But obviously, if he did, that's nothing to do with us. I really can't see how we're involved."

Namita gestured at the iPhone, still recording. "If that's all, detective? And just to show you that I'm co-operating fully…" She scribbled Karin's address down on a piece of paper. "The camera cards from the interview are stored at Karin Pelenot's edit suite in Surrey. She's in LA at the moment, or on her way at least, but I'm sure if you get the correct warrant, we can organise a viewing for you there."

Gavan was about to say something when Porter cut him off. "Both Ms Menon and I are solicitors. I double confirm for the record that we're co-operating fully, but today's interview has gone as far as it can go without an arrest or a warrant."

Gavan got up and eyed them all suspiciously. "If you think this is over, you're very wrong. Innocent people cough up. You're hiding something and I'm going to find out what - don't you think I won't."

"Well, that was fun," said The Gliss. "I've only seen that kind of thing in Porter's memories of The Sweeney."

"It's nothing to joke about," said Porter. "He's not the sort to give up. It's true the interviews don't show much, but he'll realise we were asking questions about Rossiter. I agree with Crawley and Phelps: he'll join the dots soon enough. Rossiter was one of the lynchpins of 60s' organised crime. Shanker was one of his lieutenants. And he says so on film."

"Is it such a bad thing if the cops arrest Rossiter?" Namita mused.

"It bloody well is for me," said Porter. "I have to find out what happened to the girls. Then the cops can do what they want."

"Then it's a race against time, isn't it," said Feng. "We'd better wrap up our investigation as quickly as we can."

"Let's hope Karin gets new information out of Crystal," said Karin. "If his conscience allows him to spill the beans about Lascelles, we can hand over what we have to the cops at that point."

"That's if Crystal co-operates," said Porter.

November 15th, 2017
Downtown LA

Karin was knackered. The flight was bumpy, and she didn't get much sleep. She'd gone straight to a mall and bought a change of clothing and enough toiletries to get her through a few days.

Sitting in a chic espresso bar, she re-dialled Arnie Flax. His phone went to voicemail again. She put a call into Robbery and Homicide. Flax was on leave. She spoke to one of his colleagues. He remembered Karin but declined to visit Crystal with her. He told her to be patient. Flax was back in tomorrow.

But Karin was used to getting her way. On set, she was no ogre, but everyone who worked with her knew her word was law. Over time, this can-do attitude on set morphed into a will-do approach to life in. She'd met Crystal before; she wasn't scared of him. If anything, he seemed keen to unburden himself. Screw it.

She called him.

"Ms Pelenot, how delightful to hear from you," he said. "I thought you had returned home?"

"I had, but I'm here again," she said. "I've got more interviews to do. A few things came up about the missing girls, and I wondered if you had time to discuss it with me?"

"I'd be delighted. Anything to help," he said.

She pulled into The Mission car park. This time there were no boys hanging around. She clicked her boring rental car shut and rapped on the door.

Morrie Crystal welcomed her warmly. "I was just about to pray," he said. "Did I show you our chapel?"

"Yes. I don't pray myself," said Karin, "but please, don't let me stop you."

November 15th, 2017
Starbucks, Holloway Road, London

Around the same time, Porter and Namita met for coffee. It was the first time they'd ever met socially for no other reason than to just meet up.

"It's funny, isn't it?" said Porter. "All the things we've been through. I never thought we'd just be chatting like this when I first met you."

"Well, that was professional, wasn't it?"

"If you hadn't bent the rules a bit and got Hammell to go into my old boss's servers, it would have ended very differently. Thank you for that. He's damn useful, that PI of yours."

Namita hadn't been feeling that way since Hammell's clumsy intervention with Aysha Miah had gone belly-up. "I don't know about that. He's gotten me into a right mess."

"Why? What on earth happened?" said Porter, concerned by her tone.

Namita sat back in her chair, tightened her scarf against the chill, lit up, and told Porter everything.

"My God," he said. "That's terrible. Is there anything I can do?"

"Like what? Unless you're offering to kick Skelling's butt for me?"

Porter rightly assumed that Namita would outdo him in the butt-kicking stakes. "I don't know. What a shit. I'm sorry this happened to you." Porter patted her arm. Far from being a comfort, it made Namita flinch.

"It's okay," she said. "The tape we made the other day should protect me. I just wish it hadn't happened. I haven't had a boyfriend for two years. And then I go and get mixed up with an idiot like that."

"He played you," said Porter. "Don't think of him as a boyfriend."

"You're saying I'm just as gullible as all those poor actresses, is that it?"

"Not at all. If it feels genuine at the time, that's good enough. Look at me and that psychopath, Tania. I was convinced she was the love of my life. I acted at all times as though she was. I was genuine. It's not my fault she didn't feel the same way. Love confuses."

"I was not in love with Martin Skelling," Namita blurted. "I was just lonely, I guess. I feel like a fool."

"Tania made me feel like a fool too, but that doesn't make either of us actually foolish. We are not in control of other people," said Porter. "We can only interact honestly with them and only time tells us whether we were ill-advised."

"I know, but… well, you know."

"I do."

Porter sipped at his coffee, wondering if they should go inside before his nose started dripping. Namita stared at her packet of fags.

"Do you want one?" she asked.

"I've given up," he lied, but then remembered he'd smoked in front of her a few times. "Oh, alright."

"See, you're easily persuaded too. What a pair."

"I wonder how Karin's getting on?" said Porter, sighing, as he breathed a stack of smoke into the bitter London air.

"We should call her and see how she's getting on, don't you think?"

"Yes, we should. I'm not sure how wise it is going to see Crystal."

"You think she should have waited?" asked Namita.

"If there was a group of directors abusing women, Crystal was awful close to one of its possible members."

"It's risky, I agree," said Namita. "But remember how tough Karin is. Crystal must be in his 80s. If she could knock a Profugus on its arse, she's not going to struggle with an octogenarian priest, is she?"

Porter couldn't disagree with that. There was nothing he could do about it now in any case. He shrugged off his unease.

"I think we should get the rest of our facts together and pass it on to the authorities," said Porter. "Shanker was killed. Yes, he was a gangster and was probably more at risk than we are, but if we keep asking questions, Rossiter and these remnants won't think twice before coming after us. They've already duffed up Feng and me."

Namita's turn to shrug. She wondered if Karin had landed yet, prompting her to say, "Karin knows what she's doing."

November 15th, 2017
The Mission, Los Feliz, LA

"Prayer is central to what we do here," said Morrie Crystal, stroking a large brass crucifix, the centrepiece of the altar. "The boys I work with often come from Godless backgrounds. A daily dose of prayer and TM calms them down."

"You do transcendental meditation here too?" said Karin, surprised.

"Oh yes. I knew a few people who did the hippy trail to India in the wake of The Beatles. I was sceptical at first, but it became all the rage in parties in the late 60s, early 70s. I find it centres people, gives them 15 minutes of calm. Some of the schools here now do it as part of the curriculum, thanks to the David Lynch Foundation."

"You've come a long way since your showbiz days."

"All of life is a journey towards finding God," said Crystal. "Now, if you're not going to join me, would you please excuse me. Take a seat."

Karin, who had no faith whatsoever, sat uncomfortably in the front row of the pews, while Crystal knelt on a black flagstone in front of the altar and quietly prayed.

She wondered how to play this. If she came right out and accused Lascelles of murder, Crystal might clam up for good. After all, Crystal had been Lascelles' PA. Revelations of abuse by his boss were bound to cause him problems too. She was counting on his conversion to the light.

The best approach was probably to talk about the other producers first and only gradually develop the thought – could Lascelles have been involved too? Crystal might volunteer a few tidbits.

She could also ask about Rossiter's club. Both Lascelles and Crystal had been to London. *Surely they would have been treated to a visit?*

His prayers at an end, Crystal stood with an effort and leaned against the altar.

"I'm not as fit as I was," he said. "It's probably selfish but I always tack on a prayer asking God not to let me seize up completely."

"You seem very fit to me," said Karin.

"So, what brings you back to LA so soon, Karin?"

"The missing girls. We think there were a few more now. All of them would-be actresses. We've interviewed people in London and found out that a film producer in London, Clem Rossiter, knew them all." She reached down into her bag, looking for her phone, ready to show Crystal a photo. "It looks like Rossiter had a club…"

The large brass cross hit her in the shoulder and skidded onto her jaw, swung furiously by Crystal. She heard the crack in her jaw but before she could scream, the swinging cross was on her again. It connected with her temple and she collapsed unconscious to the floor. The force flipped her eye patch up, exposing the still healing wound.

"That's enough of that, young lady," said Morrie Crystal, breathing hard.

Chapter 43

November 15th, 2017
Porter's flat, Sylvester Path, Hackney

Porter wound up his old gramophone. He pulled a 78rpm copy of Bing Crosby's Leilani and dropped the heavy needle. Crackle. Spit. Crackle. How he loved that sound. 78s had long since disappeared before he was born, but his gran, Ida, still had an old player in her attic. Growing up, he'd taken a great deal of comfort from her scratchy old music because many of the discs had also been bought and enjoyed by his parents. His mother had died of cancer and his dad, unable to cope, had hanged himself next to his wife's body. In his difficult teenage years, unable to fully process the loss of both parents, he had sought out whatever connections he could to them. The 78s were a key plank of that.

The experience had brought him into two worlds that became precious: music itself and the technology used to reproduce it. When he had time, he created faux stereo mixes from old mono recordings, some of which got limited release through a boutique record label in Portugal. His music systems ranged from the wind-up gramophone to a state-of-the-art MacPro audio-station. His flat was small, but about a third of its floor space was taken up by his passion.

Over time, listening to old music had filled the gap in his life other people needed prayer for. Absorbed in music, he could feel his pulse rate slow, cosy sleepiness washing over him. It wasn't an indulgence; it was his essence. So it was tonight. Leaning back in his chair, a glass of room temperature Mouvédre keeping him company, he mulled over his conversation with Namita.

He hadn't expressed his surprise she had a love life to her directly, but he had been shocked. He assumed she was too cold to have ever had a relationship. Though their friendship had developed since he had been just one of her clients, he still could not imagine her kissing. Balling a lover out; yes. Kissing them; no. He'd never really fancied her, but he did like her as a person.

"Well, that's good to hear, Porter," he said out loud with a tut. "Glad to see she gets your seal of approval. What she does is none of your business." He was always angry at how judgemental his male friends were about women, and equally shocked when he occasionally found himself doing the same thing.

The doorbell rang. He wasn't expecting visitors. The Gliss was nowhere to be seen or he might have asked his spiritual guide to look outside for him. His pulse rate was back up. He couldn't face another beating. He lifted the needle from the record and grabbed a knife.

Taking a deep breath, he walked down the stairs to the door. The bell rang again. "Well, if it's Rossiter's mob, they're being very polite about it," he thought. He opened the door, steak knife at the ready.

"Porter, are you going to greet me with a knife every time we meet now?" It was Tania.

"Tania? What the hell are you doing here? Look, I haven't got time for a therapy session right now…"

"Can I come in?"

"Oh, for God's sake. Come on. Let's get this over with."

"Still listening to Bing Crosby?" she said, seeing the open Gramophone. "It's one of the things I miss about you." Without waiting for an invitation, she poured herself a glass of wine.

"No, it isn't. You hate Bing Crosby. You hate all my bloody music."

"That's not true. I think I've only begun to appreciate it now that I don't hear it anymore, that's all," she said.

"I don't believe you. Your idea of good music is a machine going *boom boom boom boom* at 128bpm, off your tits on MDMA, twirling a glo-stick around your head," said Porter, miffed at the obvious manipulation.

"Whatever." Tania was nothing if not practical. If that tack wasn't working... "I just miss you. I am allowed to miss you?"

"How many times do we have to go over this? Sure, you're allowed to miss me. I missed you too. But when I was hurting the most, you never returned a single call. When we did speak, you made it clear I was a useless sod, and a bar to your freedom. I can't think of anything worse to say to someone. *I need my freedom.* The implication being that life with me was some form of prison or slavery."

"People say things in the heat of the moment," said Tania. "Doesn't make them true."

"You had an awful lot of moments in heat, Tania." He wasn't flirting.

"Whatever you think, I do miss you. Are you really saying you're over me?"

"I am. I'm not just over you, I'm angry with myself that I wasted a year pining for you."

"Which shows how much you loved me."

"I know how much I loved you. But you need to pick up on the past tense, absorb it and get it tattooed on your head. Truth is? I don't love you now. Present tense. In fact, it's me who feels like I've got my freedom back."

"You just said that's a horrible thing to say, and there you are, saying it yourself."

"You think I say it out of revenge? To hurt you? I'm just telling the truth, Tania. I was happy to let things be. I don't see our relationship the way I used to. I would prefer not to discuss it with you, let bygones be bygones etc, but you've forced yourself on me tonight, so let's have it out." Porter took a sip of wine and stared at the woman who'd been main contender for Love of My Life, but who now made him feel slightly sick.

Tania was winding herself up, ready to deliver a barrage. "This is all Pelenot's doing, isn't it?"

Porter jumped, remembering the Profugus in Flanders. *She means Karin Pelenot, you idiot.*

"Why don't you come right out and say it: you're in love with her and you've moved on." Tania spat the words out.

"Listen to yourself. I'm not seeing anyone, least of all Karin. Is that what this is all about? If I can't have you, no-one can? Well, thank you for clarifying that."

This wasn't going to plan. Tania tried to backtrack, but her blood was up. "You really are up yourself, aren't you? You and your stupid music and one-eyed bitch…"

"Right, that's it. Get the hell out of my flat, and don't ever come back. Do you understand? This is it. I'm done with you. Forever. You just can't bear it, can you? That I've moved on. And I don't need Karin Pelenot to do that."

"Are you seeing that solicitor then? A bit exotic for you?"

"Do I have to call the police? Get out. Now."

For one second, Porter thought Tania was going to throw her glass at him. Her eyes seemed darker than he'd ever seen them. He was slightly afraid of her.

"I'm going," she said. "And I won't be back."

The door slammed and Porter lifted the needle back on to Leilani. "Thank fuck for that. Peace at last." He toasted in the general direction of the front door.

November 15th, 2017
Feng's house, Church Lane, Walthamstow

Feng pulled off his lycra workout gear and wiped the sweat from his forehead. The phone rang. It was Peregrine Zouche.

"Oi, Hong Kong Phooey - it's Zouche. Was just wondering if you're coming up to see me this week? I've got a book I want to show you."

"Damn. Peregrine, you old fascist, we're right in the middle of the case at the moment."

"That's an offensive thing to call an old Jew," said Zouche.

"Yeah? And how do you think I like being called Fu Manchu?" said Feng. "The cops are giving us a hard time. I think I'll have to give our meeting a skip, unfortunately. We're up against the clock and need to wrap things up before we get our arses kicked again."

"What happened?"

Feng filled him in on the recent developments.

"You guys do like a good duffing up, don't you? Fair enough, me old China. Call me when you're free."

"Wait," said Feng. "We're a bit stuck at the moment. What would you do?"

"From what you've said, I'd work on the Berlin end. If you can find Rose's grave, Porter will have a good idea of what went down, right? If your Kraut did murder her, the body's almost certainly in Berlin."

"Yes, you're right," said Feng. "We literally don't have a clue where she is though."

"What do you know about him?" said Zouche.

Feng told them about their meeting with Davidov, Fascher and their trip to Becker Haus in Mitte.

"What was the house like? Any vibes?"

"Completely normal," said Feng. "She's not buried there, Zouche. I got no readings. Neither The Gliss nor Porter sensed anything. It was just a normal house, with a normal study and normal grounds."

"You know what serial killers are like," said Zouche. "They nearly all keep trophies."

"Yes, he has an ugly statue of a ballet dancer that Rossiter, the London end of this club, also had. We know this was connected to the Tutu Club that Rossiter owned in London. That's about all we have."

Zouche corrected him. "That's a kind of a trophy - like a poster from a rock concert. They usually have something more personal than that - a necklace, a lock of hair, that kind of thing."

Feng said there was nothing, just lots of pictures and photos and a painting by Picasso.

"What were the pictures of? No portraits of young women?"

"There were a few headshots, but the only person I was able to trace is still alive, according to Google. Other than that, it was just paintings of Berlin etc. He really loved that city."

"Pictures of the Reichstag decked out in swastikas?"

"No, no. Nothing that interesting or incriminating. Just scenic views of parks and streets."

"I see," said Zouche. "Well, stay in touch. I really want to show you this book, Hong Kong Phoo… Feng."

Progress at last, thought Feng, as he put away his phone. "If nothing else this year, I've managed to stop an old racist from issuing an insult. Not a lot to show for so many bruises."

November 15th, 2017
Namita's flat, Holloway Road

There was a voicemail from Martin Skelling and Namita was afraid to pick it up.

She cracked open a can of Pepsi and stared at the phone. Was it too much to hope Skelling had simply caved and decided he'd been beaten? *In your dreams.*

Her mind ran wild with alternatives. He had reported her to the police. A new complaint lodged with the SRA. The threat of violence. Was he likely to get violent? Of course not. But then she remembered Hammell's account of what happened to Aysha Miah. She stared at the play button on Skelling's voicemail.

You have to listen. You have to.

"Listen to you," said Sangita. "I don't understand how you can be such a ball-breaker when you're paid and such a wuss in your personal life."

"It's easy for you to say," said Namita. "If this all goes tits up, he could end my career."

"You haven't got a career. You've got one client: Sam Brownlees. If you don't win this case for him, what does that say about you?"

"I have all the evidence I need to settle Florence's will, but Martin isn't your usual solicitor. He's a by-hook-or-by-crook type."

"Says Wiretap Wilma."

"Don't. I feel bad enough I had to resort to Hammell as it is."

"Kill or be killed. We've already gone through this."

She let the voicemail play out on the speaker.

"Ms Menon. I've withdrawn the complaint and advised Gary Stormont that the will is valid. Please ensure all the paperwork is completed." There was an emphasis on paperwork that Namita took to mean destroy the tapes. "Come to Bristol and we'll wrap it all up."

After a few seconds, it sank in. *He's given up. The bastard has given up.*

"See," said Sangita, "it all turned out for the best."

"Yes, indeed. Thank God for that."

November 15th, 2017
Porter's flat, Sylvester Path, Hackney

Just before midnight, Porter decided it was time for bed. Pulling himself up from his comfy chair, he looked at the empty bottle of wine. When he'd emptied it, he'd tipped the leftovers from Tania's glass into his own. Bar her three or four sips, he'd managed to sink a whole bottle. Perfect.

The Gliss appeared. "Ah, Porter. How was your evening?"

"Great, actually. I sent Tania off with a flea in her ear. It was wonderful."

"So, you know how when I first turned up, it was only you who could see me? The idea was that I'd be your spirit guide through the Quincunx?"

"Yes, you're my own little Clarence." He pinged his wine glass. "Look! A fairy gets its wings."

"Angel. Right. Then you and your friends all mingled blood in Flanders?"

"And now they can all see you and you don't like it," said Porter.

"I don't like it, but at least you're still alive thanks to them."

"Good. It's nice to be alive. No problem." Porter halted a second. "Unless there is a problem." Something struck Porter through the fuzz of the wine. "Why are you asking me so many annoying questions?"

"There's a problem. Remember - they can see me; I can see them."

"Yeah, we've just gone over that. Why's that a problem?"

"Because Karin is currently laying on the floor of a chapel in LA, with a maniac standing over her, wielding a cross, threatening to brain her." This statement seemed to cause The Gliss some distress, not because of the news *per se*, but because he had broken some rule in telling it to Porter.

"What the flip?!" Porter was instantly awake and alert. "What do you mean? Why didn't you just blurt that out instead of twatting about for five minutes?"

"She went to see Morrie Crystal," said The Gliss, sheepishly. "He's smashed her over the head with a giant crucifix. All I can see is blackness at the moment. She's unconscious."

"Not dead?" said Porter, alarmed.

"Not yet," said The Gliss.

"What shall I do?"

"Call the LA police I should imagine. You can't grab a cab to rescue her, she's in LA."

Porter lunged for the phone.

Chapter 44

November 15th, 2017
The Mission, Los Feliz, Los Angeles

When Karin came to, she was minus a shoe, hands tied behind her back, a draught blowing against her exposed eye wound. She tried to sit up, but her head felt like someone had hit it with... well, a large brass crucifix.

"What to do, what to do," said Crystal. He was sitting on a pew, one leg crossed over the other. "I guess I'd better find out what you know, before I decide."

Karin ran through her options. She was a bit muddled, but realised, much too late, that she'd shown too much of her hand. There was no point holding back now. The crack in her jaw was causing her agony. The smallest movement caused white heat pain, but it was talk or die. "This it? Kill me? I have a whole team."

Crystal was unconcerned. "We'll see about that. I've always had an escape route ready. I was hoping I'd never have to use it."

"You're not the person you were, Morrie," said Karin, wincing. "You do good work. Why jeopardise it now? If you accept your punishment you'll go to your maker in better shape than if you run."

Crystal snorted. "What 'maker'? You think my belief is real? God, you're more stupid than you look."

Karin tried again. "The Mission? The boys?"

"Fuck them both. It was the best cover anyone could have. Why do you think there have been so many complaints about priests abusing children over the years?"

"All a lie, then?"

"Mostly. I'm not into boys, if that's what you're thinking. I've never touched any of them. I'm old. The passions have abated somewhat. Something had to take its place, and that's all The Mission has been. It's a pleasant by-product that it has done some good. I've been happy in recent years to put my back into it. I'm glad its legacy will continue after my death. But it was never what drove me."

"How many girls did you abuse?"

"Back in the day? None. They all wanted it. They all thought I could progress their careers. It was transactional. Or, at least, it was until the psycho Becker started killing them."

"So, it's true? Becker killed Rose Prideaux?"

"I don't remember their names."

"They weren't people to you, were they?"

"Actually, they were. But like all people, they were flawed and damaged. Most of them were too greedy for fame. Most were lost long before any of us got near them."

"When you say *us* - you mean, the members of The Tutu Club?"

"Now," said Crystal, "I am curious. How the hell did you find out about the club? It was need-to-know and most of the members are dead - or in the case of Don - *non compos mentis*."

"Detective work," said Karin. "There's no such thing as an iron-clad secret."

"That's true. It looks like I have no choice then."

"You always have a choice. Leave me tied up and make your escape. You're not a killer."

"Aren't I? Am I that good an actor? We all killed in the end. It made it more fun."

"Not for Agresti, Caron and Demsky."

"You *have* done your homework. Yes, they liked 'getting their fill, but no guts to kill' as Rossiter used to say. Becker changed all that. But I confess," he made a mock sign of the cross, "I had much more fun after that."

Karin realised she was going to die after all. She looked at the cross on the chapel floor, laying like a splayed corpse. She said a silent prayer, her first since boarding school.

November 15th, 2017
Porter's flat, Sylvester Path, Hackney, London

Around midnight, Feng paid off his cab and knocked. Porter let him in, thanking him for answering the Bat-Phone.

"Any word from LA?" Feng asked.

"I don't think they took me seriously," said Porter.

"Did you speak to Arnie Flax?"

"He's on leave. I called the cops in Los Feliz and they thought it was a wind-up when I said local hero Morrie Crystal was trying to kill our friend. It didn't help, of course, that I couldn't tell them how I knew. What's that?" Porter pointed at Feng's small holdall on wheels.

"We're going to LA," said Feng. "Tickets booked, we're off at 3pm tomorrow. First flights I could get. I'll crash on your sofa if that's ok. We have something to do in the morning before we go."

November 16th, 2017
Namita's flat, Holloway Road, London

The following morning, Namita sat at her laptop, having a fag. She didn't fancy another visit to Bristol but was relieved it would be the last. She downloaded the audio of Hammell's wiretap to her phone. *If he turns nasty again, I'll give him a blast and remind him of the shit he's in.*

At least she wasn't going to LA like poor Porter and Feng. Her thoughts turned back to Karin. Porter had filled her in.

"I hope you're not too late," she'd told him.

"The Gliss says she's still alive. Maybe Morrie's getting information out of her? Maybe he's got cold feet. But I agree with Feng, we can't leave her to it."

"Ok, I wish I could come with you," she lied, "I've got to seal the deal with Skelling in Bristol. I will try and get hold of Flax while you're in the air."

"Thanks," said Porter. "Good luck in Bristol. I'll call you as soon as we arrive, tomorrow morning your time."

"Do that. Where are you now?"

"Feng wants to see Vince Chambers again - show him pictures of the new names we've picked up, see if he recognises any of them. It's a useful distraction. I'm going mad with worry over here."

"I bet. I'm so shocked. Keep me in the loop."

"Of course. Good luck with your stuff today, Namita."

I'm going to bloody well need it.

November 16th, 2017
The Mission, Los Feliz, Los Angeles

1am. To her amazement, Karin was still alive. Despite confessing his supposed love of killing, Crystal was obviously finding it hard to murder her in cold blood. The caution of old age, perhaps?

He'd spent the night pacing, snorting cocaine from a phial in his pocket. He'd gabbled away all night, talking gibberish, building up courage.

Around 11pm, a couple of his lads turned up, needing help. She had been saved by the doorbell. Furious, Crystal had bound her more tightly, taped her mouth up, and dragged her into a cleaning cupboard, pushing her in with his foot, before slamming the door shut.

She'd spent the last two hours listening to Crystal reluctantly offering advice to the boys. They were being pressured into selling drugs by a local drugs cartel. Crystal was off his mind on cocaine, but his advice was sound enough. She hoped the boys' problems were enough to keep him talking through the night. Her only hope seemed to be time and discovery.

"Karin," said a voice next to her ear. "It's me, The Gliss."

"Mmm fff, hmmm," she muffled through her gag. Just the tiniest of movements, but the largest of pains in her cracked jaw.

"I can hear your thoughts. Listen to me. I saw the trouble you're in and let Porter know. He and Feng should be in LA in about 16 hours. They're trying to get hold of your police friend. You must do everything in your power to stall Crystal until then."

Karin rolled her eyes. *What else would I try and do?*

"Just don't do anything to wind him up," said The Gliss. "Time is your best hope, but you already know that. You know the story of Scheherazade? Use it. I'll check back in. Take care."

The Gliss disappeared. He seemed to take the light with him, except for one tiny spark: a smidgeon of hope blooming in her frightened heart. A rescue mission? But too late, surely? Why hadn't they just tipped the cops off? And then the hope faded a little: what on earth would they tell them if they did? *A ghost had warned them their friend was being attacked?* Fair enough.

Outside, she could hear Crystal telling the boys he was tired and needed to sleep.

"Reverend Crystal," said one of the boys. "Could we stay here tonight? I think they'll kill us if we go home."

There was a longish pause before Crystal replied. "Ok, Leon. You can stay." Karin would have put money on him chucking them out. She was relieved to be wrong. More hope. Was his good side winning out? Or was the coke wearing off? Whatever the cause, the upshot was she had an extra few-hours of safety - if she was lucky.

November 16th, 2017
Old Compton Street, Soho, London

It was odd walking around Soho with suitcases.

"I feel like a tourist," said Feng.

"It's like having a target on your back," said Porter. "You can see all the vultures eyeing you up for prey."

"I've already been given three leaflets. One for massage, one for English as a Foreign Language, and a discount coupon for Subway."

"Are you likely to use any of those?" laughed Porter.

"I'm more likely to get a massage than a Subway, let's put it that way."

Feng gave Vince Chambers' doorbell a stab. Nothing.

"He's probably in then," said Feng, remembering their last visit.

"My nerves are shot worrying about Karin," said Porter. "Last thing I need is to visit this lunatic. Come on, answer!" He gave the buzzer three long and angry pushes.

The door unlocked. Squeezing through the narrow corridor, they found Vince's door ajar.

"Mr Chambers?" called Porter. "It's Porter Norton and Feng Tian. Can we come in?"

Silence.

"Mr Chambers?"

Feng whispered, "Please Goff, don't let us find him in there with his head chopped off or something."

Porter shushed him and tried one more time. "Mr Chambers." Still no reply. Porter pushed open the door and gave a final warning.

Silence. The flat was, if anything, more of a mess than their last visit. Of Chambers, there was no sign, again. Where the hell was he hiding?

Remembering Chambers appearing from the kitchen last time, they poked their heads into the little galley. Nothing. Porter put his hand on the kettle. Warm. They moved to the bedroom. The door was wide open. They could see that was empty too. Feng saw a pot by the bed and gagged. It had a healthy portion of excrement and urine.

"My God," said Porter. "That is old school. I haven't heard of anyone using a po for decades."

"Disgusting," said Feng. "You'd have thought you'd flush that away first thing if you used it. It smells like a gorilla enclosure in there."

"Well, he's not here anyway."

"What do you two want?"

They turned in surprise and saw Chambers standing by the kitchen in soiled flannel pyjamas.

"Where do you keep coming from?" said Feng, astonished.

"What do you want?" repeated Chambers. He seemed a lot calmer than last time. The meds, probably.

"Er... good to see you again," lied Porter. "Can we show you some pictures? Just to see if you recognise anyone?"

Chambers looked suspicious. "Why? Who? What's it got to do with me?"

"Please?" said Feng.

Chambers gave in. "Make me some tea," he said, pointing at Feng.

"My pleasure," said Feng, winking at Porter.

Porter took Chambers into the hurricane-aftermath living room and pulled out an A4 envelope. Feng, standing behind Chambers, pulled his EMF digifier and swept the room for ghostly signals. If any of the girls were killed here.... He couldn't give up on the technology just yet.

Porter shook his head. Feng seemed reluctant to accept that none of his machines actually worked. Anxious to give Feng cover, Porter gave his full attention to Chambers. He fanned out the pictures. "We're trying to track these girls down and wondered if you ever photographed them in the 60s," Porter said.

"Never forget a face," said Chambers, screwing his eyes up to focus. "Show me."

Porter started with shots of Rose, Bella and Ursa.

"Yeah. Saw all of them." He was calm and certain.

"Really? Do you remember anything about them?" asked Porter. Feng was back in the living room, sweeping away behind Chambers' back. Porter gave him a look. Feng shook his head. *Nothing, sorry.*

"Remember their faces, not what they had for breakfast," said Chambers. "Any more?"

He didn't recognise Sally Graham, Lucy Pelling, Shelly Bland or Alice Hopper. Porter laid down a police file photo of Grace Tilling.

"I remember her. She worked at Kitty, Kitty," said Chambers.

"When?"

"I don't know. The 60s."

"What about this one?" said Porter, holding up a shot of Myra McLeod.

"Wait. These are all Clem's girls, aren't they?" It was only bubbling under the surface for now, but the manic Chambers of their previous visit looked like he was on the way back. "Go now. Can't talk about it."

"We didn't know they worked for Clem," lied Porter. "Please, I need to check something. Don't worry, you're not involved in any way."

"No good. He'll find out. Just go."

Porter knew the visit was coming to an end but refused to give up. He touched the photos of Myra and Grace, again.

"We're going, but I just want to doublecheck. You really do recognise them? Grace and Myra?"

But it was too late. Fear had conquered the meds. Chambers brushed the photos onto the floor, desperate to push away his past. "I said, go. Now."

Feng stuffed the EMF digifier into his pocket. "Mr Chambers, may I show you just one more?" said Feng. "Not a girl. I promise." Chambers was agitated, but his silence was taken as a yes, Feng pulled a photo out. "What about this man?"

As soon as Chambers saw the photo of Heinrich Becker his metamorphosis back to the frightened child of their last visit was complete.

"No! No! Take it away, take it away! Leave me be." He cowered in his chair, sniffling. It was time to go.

"It's says something when anyone can breathe in the poisonous fumes of Soho and be grateful for the fresh air," said Porter, who sucked it down like a camel at the oasis. "What a sad case. He really shouldn't be living there on his own."

"True, but it was worth coming. Oh yes, it was worth coming," said Feng, patting his pocket.

November 16th, 2017
Christmas Steps, Bristol

A few hours later, as Feng and Porter boarded their plane to LA, Namita was staring at the cafe at the foot of the Christmas Steps.

She'd had no more luck than the boys in getting anyone in LA to take them seriously. Well, she had other things to attend to now.

She'd chosen the cafe for their meeting because it was so public and teemed with off-duty students playing Dungeons & Dragons. She was 10 minutes early and peered through the glass. Enough room for her and Skelling to sit, but still very full. Any recriminations from Skelling would have to be whispered. *Good.*

She dumped her bag on the last pair of seats available and ordered coffee. Confident he'd be prompt this time, she ordered a latte for Martin too. She was irritated by a pang of regret. Even now, after all that had happened, the thought crossed her mind that real lovers always knew each other's orders. What would it be like to have a lover to be so familiar with? Not Martin. But someone. Someday.

She looked in her cup and the pang was immediately replaced with anger. Staring into the white Americano, she saw the coffee-coloured coffee - what else - and remembered his outrageous sign-off last time they met. *We'll have no more of that, thank you very much.*

At 4pm on the dot, Skelling walked into the cafe, saw her and, without greeting, took off his coat and sat down.

"So," he said. "Let's get this over with."

November 16th, 2017
The Mission, Los Feliz, Los Angeles

It was a physically and psychologically uncomfortable night for Karin. The cupboard was cold, the floor was hard. She had enough pins and needles to make a fakir start a sideshow. Her jaw felt like it needed a splint. She focused on blanking out the pain.

She kept sane by focusing on the gap at the bottom of the door, watching it morph from black to low levels of orange. Morrie had left her alone all night. She hoped the cocaine had worn off and left the elderly man desperate for sleep. The longer he slept, the better. She called out to The Gliss a few times, but he didn't come back.

Loosening her bindings was impossible. She accepted her state and worked up a plan based on The Gliss' Scheherazade comment. What tantalisingly incomplete story could she dangle? She had to delay him. *Where were the bloody police?*

There were three things she knew for certain. Morrie didn't care enough about the victims to remember their names. Sad, but she could turn it to her advantage. She could hint at any number of others. Invent some cock and bull story about the net closing in. Secondly, Crystal didn't know how far they were into their investigation. She could say the LA police were investigating him too. Thirdly, he said he had an escape route. She had no idea what that was, but it could mean he had fake ID and stashed funds, at a minimum. If she told him the cops knew the details, he would need to know how much they knew. No point killing her only to be stopped at passport control with a flagged-up counterfeit.

With a sigh, she realised the only way he could reasonably expect her to give up information was if he tortured it out of her. If she had to put up with a day of torture to delay the inevitable and give Porter a chance to reach her, so be it.

November 15th, 2017
Snakes & Ladders, Christmas Steps, Bristol

"Checkmate, huh?" said Martin.
"I was always going to win," said Namita. "There was no need to be such a dick about it."

"Ah, but were you always going to win? You've broken the Code of Conduct. I won't forget that. Even after this case has wrapped, I'll make sure you live to regret it."

"You really need to stop threatening me, Martin," said Namita. "You know, the entire conversation we had last time was recorded. Listen."

She held her phone to his ear and he winced as he heard the incriminating evidence.

"Put that away, you bitch. I know what I said. Interesting how you spin this. *Don't threaten me* she says. What the fuck are you doing but threatening *me*?"

A long-haired student sitting 3ft away picked up the tone of the exchange and gave Namita a look that asked if she was okay. She smiled and nodded back. Yes. Everything is fine.

Martin pulled his briefcase onto his lap and pulled out a couple of letters and dropped them on the table. "It's all there. Stormont has wisely accepted defeat on this. For your records. I've also let the executors know. It can all go through once they sort out the tax issues with the HMRC."

"Okay, thanks," said Namita. "You may not like my methods, but they were done in self-defence. And it's the morally right outcome."

Namita could see Skelling was boiling with suppressed rage. He really didn't want to let it go. His mouth was pinned shut in a grimace and his left foot tapped repeatedly on the floor. She was sure that if he could have hit her like he had done Aysha, he would have.

Hitting was one thing, fury another. He lost control. He grabbed her shoulder, pulling her ear to his mouth. "You think this is some kind of game, do you? You think I've built up my career just to let some Paki bitch fuck it all up?"

Namita tried to pull back, appalled, but his grip was firm.

"You listen to me. You might have won this, but you'd better be looking over your fucking shoulder for the next 10 years. You won't see me coming, but you're fucking toast - you stupid, pathetic, Paki bitch."

The abuse was heard by the long-haired student.

"Hey! What the fuck, man? Leave her alone."

"You can bugger off too, Shaggy," said Martin.

His attention diverted, Namita pulled free, stood up and punched Martin as hard as she could in the face. His nose snapped and an arc of blood spurted.

"How dare you call me a Paki," she shouted. Everyone heard.

The student jumped up and shouted, "You shitty little racist."

Other customers rose to their feet in outrage. Namita didn't wait. She picked up a board game from the shelf and smashed it over Martin's head.

"You racist, son of a bitch. It's all a game, is it? Well, here's a fucking game for you to play in hospital." And she punched him again. Cheers and claps followed.

Five minutes later, Martin was slinking away, banished from the cafe for life. Namita was comforted by staff and given a free coffee. She let them minister her. But she didn't need it. Her heart was swelling with pride. Sangita told her she was a star. That was a first. She looked at the mess she'd created. The board game was broken beyond repair and several other games had cascaded to the floor, Monopoly, Ludo and a pack of Top Trumps.

Shaggy was impressed. "That was awesome. Hope the bastard's nose is broken," said the student. But she didn't hear him.

She was looking at some of the Top Trumps classic cars laying on the floor. Aston Martin DB5. Horsepower. 10.

My God. It was a game. A sodding game. They were trading the girls like sodding cards.

Chapter 45

November 16th, 2017
The Mission, Los Feliz, Los Angeles

It was another two hours before Crystal came for Karin. She heard him say goodbye to the boys. She felt guilty thanking God for their problems. They had delayed her death, though she was busting for a pee. Those poor sods out there would have another day facing hoodlums and demons. It couldn't be helped. *To be fair, you're in a worse position, Karin, old girl.* She wished the boys silent luck to soothe her conscience. She had her story. Of course, if Crystal came straight in and shot her without removing the gag, she was a goner anyway. Her ears pricked. Another sound. The heavy bolt of The Mission door being drawn.

Great. Here we go.

Crystal didn't shoot her. He dragged her through the chapel and dropped her on the black flagstone in front of the altar. He tore off her gag. He was panting.

"Let's have some fun, shall we?" Karin's eye widened. "Not that," he said, dismissively. "I'm a bit past all that. But I still enjoy the killing. It's been a while. What would you like? Knife, gun or hands? I can make all of them last."

"Whatever suits you," said Karin, with a cheerfulness that unsettled Crystal.

"Oh, a fighter," countered Crystal. "My favourite."

It's now or never. "I'm not a fighter. I don't want to die. It's a shame I won't be here to see you confronted by the faces in the book."

"Book?"

"The book containing the photos of all the girls murdered by The Tutu Club."

"What book? What are you talking about?"

"You don't get it, do you? Why do you think I was in LA? Do you remember Clem Rossiter's photographer, Vince Chambers?"

"Creepy little fag, yeah. So what?"

"He kept a record of every girl murdered. For his protection. I brought a copy over with me. I've been working with LAPD. They have it and a full account of the club's activities. It details everything you, Lascelles, Becker, Caron, Demsky, Rossiter and Agresti got up to. They've been investigating you for months. They know about your accounts. They even found the forger."

"The police here are idiots," said Crystal, confused. "What forger?"

Karin chose this moment to clam up.

"I said *what forger*?" Karin shook her head. "I see, well, you have a choice. Tell me what you know and die cleanly. Or die by knife as slowly as I can make it last."

Karin stared back, mute.

"So be it." Crystal put her gag back on and went to get his knife.

November 16th, 2017
LAX, Los Angeles

Porter and Feng ran for a cab. Roadworks inside LAX made getting out of the airport a cruel and frustrating series of delays. Their driver, left elbow dangling out the window, unloaded his thoughts on the delays.

"Man, you know, why would they seal up two of the car parks, right? Nowhere to go, the cars just go around and around…"

"How long will it take to get to Los Feliz, do you think?" interrupted Porter.

"30-40 minutes at least. Chill out. Rest your jet lag, right?"

"$500 to get us there in 20 minutes," said Feng, waving a wad of cash at the driver.

"Shit man, that'll be tough…but I can afford a ticket with that… alright. Buckle up."

As soon as the cab was clear of the airport jam, Porter and Feng found they had booked Lewis Hamilton. It suited their purpose, but at some cost to their nerves. The cabbie knew all the speed cameras and decelerated alarmingly each time they neared one. He accelerated clear, just as frighteningly, like Apollo Nine on lift-off.

"I feel like I'm getting a facelift," said Feng, gripping his armrest. "These G-forces could turn an elephant into a mouse."

Weaving in and out of the busy traffic on the five-lane freeway, Porter and Feng wobbled about in the back like baby teeth on a toffee apple. Porter had called Flax as soon as they landed. It had gone to voicemail but just as the cab driver undercut a giant Mack truck honking in fury, his phone rang.

"Detective Arnie Flax. You called. How can I help? How's Karin?"

Porter detailed the story as quickly as possible, skipping all the *how I know* stuff relying on Flax's relationship with Karin to make him act. He did.

"Jeez. You sure about this?"

"We're on our way to The Mission right now. We've flown from the UK just to help her. I pray we're not too late."

"Right. I'll grab a squad car to keep me company and we'll be there in 20 minutes. What's your ETA?"

"10-15 minutes," said Porter.

"Don't you even think about going in there without us, capisce?"

"We're unarmed. Of course not."

"Good. You're civilians and don't you forget it. I'm off."

The Gliss appeared. "The good news is that Karin's still alive," he said. "I can see in her head again, so she's conscious."

"Great," said Porter. "Can you tell her we're on our way?"

"I'm not an errand boy," said The Gliss, offended.

"Since the day you came into my life," said Porter angrily, "all you've ever done is state, 'I'm a messenger.' Now go-the-fuck message."

The cab driver gave them a concerned look. "Who you talking to, bud?"

"Some idiot who's dragging their feet," said Porter, gesturing at his phone. The Gliss disappeared like the Genie of the Lamp.

Watching Downtown LA rapidly appear either side of them gave them a little hope. "Not long now," said Feng. "Please Goff, let us be in time."

November 16th, 2017
The Mission, Los Feliz, Los Angeles

The not-so Reverend Morrie Crystal stood in front of Karin holding a steak knife.

"I'll put this in the dishwasher later," he said.

"Do your worst. I'm not telling you what they have on you," said Karin, unable to stop herself from shaking.

"They all say that. Little cuts to the arms and legs hurt and shock, but it's not until you start gouging out eyes that people talk. Of course, you only have one to play with."

He sat down next to her and pressed the point of the blade into her arm. He gave it a little jab. Karin winced and sucked air in through her teeth. "I'm not talking. All the plans are in place, your accounts will be frozen and today they're going into Lascelle's place."

"They won't get anything out of him," said Crystal. "I cleaned his place out years ago and he doesn't speak a lot of sense these days. What do you mean, all the plans are in place?" He turned the blade, still stuck in Karin's arm, a quarter-turn.

Karin made more sucking noises. "You're wasting your time. The forger gave you up. He felt bad about Alison."

"There is no forger. Who is Alison?" said Crystal.

"The one you dumped in the desert," said Karin, making it up as she went.

"I didn't dump anyone in the desert," said Crystal.

"Not you. Lascelles."

"Don? You think that pampered fucker ever disposed of a body? What do you think I did? No, there are no bodies in the desert. You're making it all up. I thought so." He jabbed harder. Karin almost threw up as the tip of the blade struck bone. She felt the warm trickle of blood running down her arm, soaking her blouse.

Drawing deep breaths, she said, "I don't know the details of every case, but Chambers' book lists everything. How the girls were passed from producer to producer, city to city. A couple of the girls who survived before Becker killed Rose told us about your little peccadilloes."

"Yes, we should have killed them all from the start. I told them it was dangerous, as soon as we got going in '64."

Something clicked in Karin's memory. "At the Venice Film Festival."

"Oh, you know about that, do you? Maybe you're not making it all up after all." He paused to consider this.

"I'd love to know exactly what happened there," said Karin. "That's when the club was formed?"

Withdrawing the blade, he jabbed into another part of her arm, so deeply the blade skidded off her bone. Karin convulsed and retched. Just for fun, Crystal slapped her face. It was the final straw for Karin's over-stretched bladder. She felt her groin become warm and wet.

"Don't you be sick, now," he said. "I don't mind cleaning up blood and piss with a mop, but not vomit, okay?" He watched her fighting the pain. "What do you know about the club?"

Her plan meant keeping him talking but Karin, oddly ashamed to have wet herself, was finding it hard to marshal coherent sentences. "Film producers. Abusing women. The old story."

"Oh, it was a bit more interesting than that," said Crystal. "We were collectors."

"Just 22-year-olds." And then, Karin saw it. "The two, two, Club."

"Oh, you do know something. Yes."

"Why?"

"Why not? That was the rules of the game. Of course, girls of all ages were always available to us. Perk of the job. But they were so pathetically easy to seduce. It took the fun out of it. We decided to find as many 22-year-olds as possible and see how long we could keep them fucking in search of a job. It was fun. A couple of them made a home run and fucked us all. All but the most stupid realised something was up after a while."

Karin thought of the cost the women had borne. "You're sick."

Crystal twisted the knife. "Of course. That was clear from the start. I thought I was fairly normal to be honest, but someone like Becker... he had outrageous appetites and missed the freedom of his war years, I think."

"He was a Nazi. You're a Jew. How could you?"

"I'm a Jew so my only choice is to wail and moan like a whinging Rabbi and be stuck in the past? I was born in 1945. By the time I was 10 and thinking for myself, the war was history. To be fair, I didn't like Becker much. But I only met him a handful of times. It was an easy accommodation to make. He was pragmatic about it. He didn't like the fact I was a Jew, but he didn't have to deal with me."

"How did this club work?"

"Ah, that's a bit of a slip: you don't know everything, then. That's good news for me, right? If you don't know, then nor do your so-called investigators. I'm not stupid. I like the fact you're trying to delay me. That's fine. I'm enjoying the process. We won't be disturbed. How's your arm?"

Before Karin could answer, he jabbed her in the thigh. She screamed.

"That's more like it. Scream, all you want, you arrogant, English bitch. I miss that sound. You scream like the Queen on honeymoon."

November 16th, 2017
Trader Joe's car park, Silver Lake, Los Angeles

"Where the flip is he?" said Porter, scuffing the floor with impatience.
"I hope Flax is still coming," said Feng. "Shouldn't we just go in?"
"We're not armed. I'd rather go in with the police."
"Then chill out. I just hope he's here soon."
A car pulled up alongside. "Porter Norton?"
"Thank God! Detective Flax?"
"Jump in. I've got a squad car waiting for us at The Mission. They said it's all quiet there. Are you sure about this?"
"I'm afraid there's no doubt about it. Can't you just tell them to go in?"
"Not till I get there. You're Feng, right? We'll be there in less than five minutes."

Flax pulled up alongside another black and white discreetly parked half a block from The Mission. He greeted the other cops. Plan? *Try the front door. Look in through a window. Kick the door down if they see anything hokey.*

"Any one of those things could tip off Crystal," protested Porter. "He might kill her on the spot."

"How else do you think we should proceed on such flimsy information?" said Flax. "You guys stay here."

Porter held him up. "Wait." And promptly ran into a side street. He called on The Gliss.

"You called, oh master."

"Cut it out. The cops are thinking of going in. Can you tell me where Karin is, assuming she's still alive?"

"She is. She's sitting in front of the altar, tied up, and your man is jabbing at her with a knife."

"Where's the altar in relationship to that building?" said Porter, pointing.

"Diametrically opposite the front door," said The Gliss.

"That's just great. The cops are going in the front. He'll have time to finish her off."

"There's a back door. That's closer."

Flax watched Porter, apparently talking to himself, and asked Feng if Porter was okay.

"Yes, he's fine. Er. He's religious. Probably saying a silent prayer before we go in."

"It doesn't look particularly silent. And you're not going in, remember?"

"Leave it to the pros, definitely," said Feng.

Porter ran back to them.

"Any news from on high?" said Flax, gesturing to the heavens.

Wondering what Feng had said, Porter said, "Er. No. But as far as we know, this Crystal bloke is likely to want to kill her in front of the altar, so start there. And, I bet that's Karin's," he said, pointing at the car with the Hertz logo in the rear window.

"I see," said Flax, wondering if he'd regret taking these two seriously. Ditching the Brits, Flax and his cops swiftly moved into position.

Feng asked what the score was.

"Karin's being tortured with a knife in front of the altar. The Gliss says there's a back door that's closer to the altar. If that lot make a racket, Karin could be dead in seconds."

"We're not supposed to go in," said Feng.

"And you're going to take any notice of that, are you?"

"Of course not. Just putting it on record."

"Let's go then." He called on The Gliss. "You're our eyes and ears."

"It looks like I have been relegated to such a role, yes."

"Let's go."

The cops, some of whom knew Crystal, were taking their time getting organised, still arguing about the likelihood that any of this was true. They took no notice of Feng and Porter running to the back of the building via a side street. When the pair got there, they found the back door was impressively solid and not the kind to budge under a shoulder.

"Great. Anyone have skeleton keys?" said Feng.

"No, but there's a pile of scrap over there. Let's see if we can find a bit of iron to jemmy it open."

There was no iron, but they did find a rusty screwdriver with most of its wooden handle missing. Feng said that would be enough if they could find a brick or something heavy to jam the screwdriver through the lock. They heard shouting from the other side of the building. Recce completed, Flax was yelling through the letterbox, demanding the door be opened.

"Oh yes, that'll work," said Porter. "He'll probably just slit her throat now."

"No, he's still talking to her," said The Gliss, watching on. "I've told her you're all outside."

"This'll do," said Feng, hefting a rounded stone from the garden. Jamming the screwdriver in the lock, he started banging.

"It looks like the cops have arrived," said Crystal. "Maybe you were telling the truth after all. Why they think I might just open the door and let them in, I don't know. The cops here can be very trigger happy. Change of plan then. Get up. You're my shield. I'd rather get out alive than make you another notch on my bedpost."

It was easier said than done. Karin had five deep cuts to her arm and legs. Practiced in drawing out death, Crystal hadn't hit any arteries, but the blood still flowed freely. She was struggling to stay awake and felt nauseous.

Crystal sliced through her leg bindings and made her stand with her back to him, the blade of the knife now held to her throat.

Flax shouted one final warning through the letterbox. "We're coming in, Reverend. Don't do anything stupid."

337

As the police began hitting the front door with a small battering ram, Feng used their noise as cover to hammer away at the backdoor lock. Three heavy smacks and the lock was broken. They turned the handle only to find there was a bolt on the other side too. The bottom of the door shifted a little, but the top stayed firmly in place.

"Shoulders it is after all," said Porter. "Ready?"

"You know, it's quite exciting in its own way," said Crystal, waiting for the cops to come in. "Old age can be extremely dull when your youth and middle-age were so exciting."

"Are you going to kill me?" said Karin, who'd lost any desire to get to the bottom of the case. Just staying awake was hard enough.

"Shhh. Let's see how the cops proceed. If I die, you die." Crystal tightened his grip on the knife. "But I've no desire to die just yet."

On the fifth, bruising shoulder-charge, the backdoor cracked open.

"Jesus, he must have heard that," said Porter.

"He hasn't flinched," said The Gliss. "He's got a knife to Karin's throat, his back to us. He's waiting for the cops to bust in. He told Karin he doesn't want to die."

Karin marshalled every reserve of strength she had left and assessed her situation. Perhaps if Crystal hadn't spent the previous night high on coke, he'd be in better shape to hold her hostage. Despite her own pain, she was aware he was breathing hard, paying the toll of 72 years of excess. Were it not for the wounds she fancied her chances of twisting free and head-butting the bastard, but she knew she was weakened almost to the point of acceptance. She sensed her life ebbing away with her blood.

There was an enormous crack and splintering of wood and Karin opened her heavy lids to see Flax and a handful of LAPD's finest rush into the chapel, revolvers drawn.

"Drop that knife!" screamed Flax, taking in Karin's precarious position. Her shirt was scarlet. She was standing in a pool of blood and urine.

"One step closer and I'll cut her throat," said Crystal. "When you've all put your guns down, one of you can come over here and cuff me."

It was obvious to Karin he actually meant this. He knew he was caught and didn't want to die. The cops couldn't be sure. They firmly rejected the idea of putting their weapons down.

"Stalemate," said Crystal. "If you're going to shoot me, then I might as well enjoy myself and take her with me."

Still no compromise from the police. *For God's sake, put your guns down, you macho arseholes. God, is that going to be your last thought?*

Feng and Porter emerged from behind the screen, peering over the top of the altar table. Whoops. Four cops, guns drawn, pointing in their direction. Karin was held at knifepoint a few feet away. Porter couldn't take his eyes off Karin, but Feng saw they'd been spotted. Fury crossed Flax's face. Feng realised (and hoped) the cops couldn't shoot now even if they wanted to. Any bullets missing Crystal would hit them.

Feng tapped Porter on the shoulder. A large brass crucifix lay on the altar table. Feng mimed bashing the cross over Crystal's head. Porter nodded and made to move. Feng rested a hand on his shoulder and gestured down to his shoes. Take them off. Porter nodded.

Flax, seeing Porter stand, looking like a child creeping around in a game of spies, had no choice but to give Porter cover by stalling. "So, what do you want, Reverend? How does this end?"

"It's very simple. I want you to put your weapons down and then I'll come quietly."

"We can't do that. If I see your hand move, we'll shoot."

"And then her death will be your fault. I should hurry if I were you. She's lost quite a lot of blood already."

Porter, desperate not to be heard, slowly picked up the brass crucifix. He was five feet away from Crystal.

Flax was visibly annoyed. "Look, we won't shoot if you put the knife down. Why would we?"

"It's a question of trust, detective. I've dealt with enough bereaved families who lost someone through police shootings to make me wary."

Karin sighed. *Great. Wind them up.*

Porter edged closer. Four feet away. He lifted the crucifix over his head and looked down at his socks against the chapel floor. As soon as he reached the black flagstone, he would smash the bastard's head in. He had no reservations about that. One more slide should be enough. He held his breath, worried he might alert Crystal at any second.

Flax continued to try and distract Crystal. "That's BS. We don't shoot on sight - only when we need to. No-one's going to shoot an unarmed pensioner. Just put the knife down."

Porter waited for Crystal's reply, hoping the distraction would make him loosen his grip on Karin and the knife. He'd only get one chance to put him down and out.

"Detective, detective. Do I have to go into the history of LAPD at this point? The famous cases?"

Porter nodded to himself. It's now or never. He's about to rant. He took one half-step forward to the flagstone and tensed his muscles, ready to clatter Crystal.

"…I mean, you think the LA Riots just *happened*, do you?"

Porter's foot hovered over the flagstone. He was just about to bring the crucifix down when The Gliss cried out. "Porter!"

Too late. As soon as Porter's foot crossed onto the flagstone, he was plunged into the Quincunx. Dead voices, words of sadness, wails of pain, screams of frustration. Female voices. So many. Overwhelmed, he dropped the crucifix and crumpled.

At the same time Porter's knees hit the floor, so did the crucifix. The clatter and echo rang like a bullet bouncing off Big Ben. Startled, Crystal reflexively turned. With her last ounce of energy, Karin stuck her butt out. Caught off balance and taking an enforced step back, Crystal tripped over Porter's prostrate form, his arms flew up instinctively. His jerking hand sent the knife gashing through the skin of Karin's damaged jaw. She tipped herself to one side, her arms still bound, certain that hitting the floor would hurt like hell. But she saw the cops with their guns drawn and didn't want to be in their way.

Afterwards, Feng would say three things. One, it's amazing how much splatter a police revolver can produce from a headshot. Two, the combination of half a dozen gunshots and a large metal cross hitting the stone floor of a chapel is just about the loudest noise a human can endure. And three, it's no fun watching the muzzle flashes of half a dozen shots going off at once if they're all pointing in your general direction.

Only three of the shots hit Crystal. One whizzed past Feng's head, another shattered a glass jar on the altar table and the third would have hit Feng in the gut if it hadn't deflected off a brass plate showing St Francis of Assisi and his birds.

The running cops all presumed Porter had taken a hit too, because he writhed around on the ground, hands clapped to his head.

But it wasn't a bullet causing Porter's anguish. Not one of the girls buried under the flagstone had died a good death.

Chapter 46

November 16th, 2017
Robbery Homicide Division, West First Street, LA

No-one was particularly happy with the way things turned out. Flax was incandescent, livid at Feng and Porter's *Goddam freak show antics*. Karin was recovering in hospital after emergency surgery and a blood transfusion. Porter was anxious to stay with Karin till she was well again. Feng was desperate to find out who the girls under the flagstone were.

They'd been allowed to ride with Karin and the paramedics to hospital, but Flax insisted they come straight to him as soon as she was comfortable. The ambulance ride allowed Karin, Porter and Feng to get their stories straight. Short version: Crystal confessed to Karin he'd been killing young women since the 60s and burying them in front of the altar. They snatched conversation while the paramedics discussed treatment.

"We can hardly tell him you got a vision, can we?" whispered Feng.

"No," said Porter, who braved the bouncing ambulance to put Karin's eye-patch back in place. It was like being drunk, trying to put the toilet seat down on a cruise ship. "We'll say Karin told us in the ride to the hospital." Porter grimaced. "It was awful. I don't know how many voices there were, but at least six."

"My God," whispered Karin. "Thank you, Porter. I have to sleep now." And she passed out.

"If you want your friend to live, you'd better get out of the way," said one of the paramedics.

"What's the one thing I said to you?" said Flax, slamming a fist on the interview room table. "Don't go in. We could have ended up with four dead people in there. I should charge you."

"With what?" said Porter, not without some risk of a punch in the face. "Besides, everything worked out alright."

"You think so, do you? Do you realise how much paperwork you've created?"

"Yes, but Karin has single-handedly solved half a dozen or more murder cases for you too. That's a pretty good quid pro quo."

"Don't you go all smartass on me, Norton," said Flax. "We've got SOCO down there at the moment, but we don't even know if there are any bodies there yet."

"There will be, I assure you," said Porter.

"How do you know?"

"Everything else Crystal told Karin checks out. He was a bit screwed up about religion, don't you think? A Jew turned pretend-Christian? He probably thought he was making a point burying them in front of the altar."

Flax calmed a little. "We'll see. I should deport your ass, but I guess you'll want to hang around for Karin?"

"If you wouldn't mind," said Feng. "We're all very close friends."

"I gathered that," said Flax. "Screw it. You're free to go, but don't go anywhere. We have a shitload of paperwork to do. I haven't got time to deal with you clowns right now."

November 16th, 2017
10 Green Bottles, Downtown, LA

They both felt depressed walking along South Broadway in search of coffee. It was one of the scuzziest, most run-down streets they'd ever seen. Every other person looked like a point-of-death addict or long-term homeless. Many lost souls pushed homemade carts stuffed with rags and papers.

"We're near Skid Row," said Feng. "This is as far from Beverly Hills as you can get."

"I feel like we're going to be attacked," said Porter. "The vibes here are so bad. This is the first time I've walked down a normal street and heard voices." He stopped and pointed down a dark side lifted straight from the noirest of Film Noir. "There's a voice coming from down there. A Quincunx voice."

"I bet. Sorry, Porter. That's one of those voices you're going to have to ignore. We have enough on our plate as it is."

"I know."

A passing suit told them the best coffee was at 10 Green Bottles. They shuddered with the joy of safety-returned when its door closed on their backs.

They chose window seats and looked out at the dilapidated frontage of an old cinema. It was the Miss Haversham of LA picture houses, rusted and bulb-less. Curious, Porter checked it out on his phone. "It's just the facade. There are a dozen old cinemas from the golden age of Hollywood along this street."

"Facade is right," said Feng. "LA's one of the richest cities in the world, but this is like a favela."

"I feel like someone's been drilling my nostrils. What do you think'll happen to us?"

"What could he charge us with?"

"If he's anything like the Met, he'll at least make things uncomfortable for us."

"We can deal with that. Six women, huh?"

"At least. It was awful, Feng. Don't make me repeat what they were saying."

"Any clues?"

"No, just pain and misery. I don't want to go into the pornography of it."

"Okay, you know best. I won't ask."

They sipped and watched a man in ragged clothes, wide-eyed and gesticulating, standing in the centre of the road, railing against the demons in his head.

"I want to go home," said Porter.

"Homesick, huh?"

"No. Angry. I'm not going to get another day's rest until Rossiter is in jail. This was his club, his idea. He's the last one left. We're going to bring him down."

"Not till we've seen Karin," said Feng.

November 16th, 2017
Bellevue Hospital, LA

Karin was in recovery, and aside from a few stitches, was fine.

"I thought we told you not to go in on your own?" said Porter.

"Not good with orders, am I?" said Karin, squeezing his hand. "I gather I owe my life to you two disobeying the same order. Flax sat there yabbering at me, but I was dopey. I got the gist. Awake now. What happened?"

"Crystal is dead, and the police are digging up the chapel. I heard voices come from under the floor. All girls."

"Damn."

"At least six."

"Did Crystal tell you anything?" asked Feng.

"He was high as a kite most of the time. Rambled. Confirmed The Tutu Club collected 22-year-old girls." She pointed out the obvious in the name. "And yes, they bumped off the other directors when they didn't go along with it."

"The thing is, Karin," said Porter, "we might be in trouble. Flax told us to stay out, but we went in and Crystal's dead as a result. I suspect we're in for some heat."

"Thank you, Feng. Thank you, Porter." Karin slipped back into sleep.

"Time to face the music, Porter."

"Come on then. Let's do it."

November 16th, 2017
The Mission, Los Feliz, LA

Flax took their call and to their surprise, didn't roast them but said to meet him at The Mission. He refused to say anything else.

In the cab, Porter and Feng quickly came to the same conclusion: if they told Flax about their findings in the UK, it would only make more trouble. Unaccredited PIs aren't welcome anywhere. Best to continue with Karin's established story about trying to track down the missing UK girls and leave it at that. The bodies at The Mission would tell their own story and give LAPD plenty to be work on. They were only here to help Karin. Keep it simple.

Flax was in a far better mood than they left him in. "Well, if it isn't Butch Cassidy and the Sundance Kid. How's Karin? She was rattling on about pink slippers when I saw her."

"Recovering. She'll be fine," said Porter.

"Glad to hear it. She sure dumped a ton of crap on my desk. Are you guys squeamish?"

"Not at all," said Feng, speaking for himself, but not Porter, who sometimes closed his eyes frying bacon.

"Good. It's a mess."

Inside the chapel, a team of forensic officers was labelling and photographing. The heads of a few hazard suits were just visible as they stood in the hole where the black flagstone had been.

"You were right. We've taken up six black tiles and found a mass grave. There were seven skeletons in there. Judging from the clothes, they were all women from the 60s through to the 80s. There was no attempt to bury them properly. They were just wrapped in plastic and tumbled in. It's a mess, though the plastic protection will help forensics. I wish the son of a bitch was still here so I could shoot him again."

"Have you identified any of them yet?" said Porter.

"We're in recovery stage. There didn't seem to be any ID on any of them. Dilbert," shouted Flax. "Any ID turn up yet?"

"No, sir. Just bodies. We'll need a full dental and DNA search."

"Thanks, Dilbert." Turning back to Porter and Feng, Flax said, "Tell me what you know. All of it. Your ticket home depends on you playing ball, capisce?"

Feng let Porter handle it. He knew people found him unsettling. They needed Flax to believe their story.

Porter trotted out their cover, some of which Flax already knew: how the search for Rose and Bella in London had thrown up connections between Rossiter and Lascelles and his PA, Crystal. They had no reason to suspect him of murder, and after Flax vouched for Crystal, Karin quizzed him about Rossiter and Hollywood in the 60s. The extent of the crime, and Crystal's complicity, had come as a shock to them all.

"And you think Rose and Bella are in that pit?" said Flax, struggling to get to grips with the labyrinth.

"No. Sadly they're not. We think they died in Berlin. Like I say, we had no reason to suspect any of this in LA. Karin told us in hospital that Crystal seemed to think she was investigating him. He attacked her and fessed up to killing people and burying people in the chapel. He clearly meant to kill her until we all turned up. Caught, he changed his plan to coming quietly. Until we came along and screwed things up."

"You sure did. Still, there's no denying, he got what he deserved." Flax thought for a minute. "The question is, what do I do with you now?"

"Detective Flax," said Feng. "This discovery means our case is a transatlantic one - and a criminal one, which we're not qualified to handle, obviously. We'd already alerted cops in London of our suspicions about Rossiter. Wouldn't the best thing be for us to go home, pass on this new info, and link you up with the cops in London? Obviously, it's gone beyond documentary research now. We need to hand over to the pros."

Flax considered it. "Alright. I want full, independent statements from you both - and Karin when she's well enough."

"Don't worry about her," said Porter. "She's had quite a few stitches and a transfusion, but she's fine otherwise."

"Go on, beat it, before I change my mind. I've got enough paperwork to last a lifetime. Scram."

November 16th, 2017
Bellevue Hospital, LA

They waited until midnight and phoned Namita, who'd slept through most of the drama.

"My God," she said. "Seven?"

"Seven," echoed Porter. "And these will be women we know nothing about yet." He confirmed The Tutu Club was essentially a group of film producers collecting 22-year-old girls, abusing them for sex. After Becker, the abuse turned to murder.

"That makes sense. I was in the cafe at the bottom of the Christmas Steps and I saw some Top Trump cards. I realised then there was some sort of game in play. It's so appalling. What now?"

"I've been thinking about Sam Brownlees," said Porter. "I think I should tell him what we know. We should confirm Rose almost certainly died at the hands of Becker in Berlin."

"It'll kill him," protested Namita. "Don't put him through that. Not yet. Not till we've found her body."

"We might never find it," said Porter. "We have nothing to go on."

"But we haven't exhausted the investigation," countered Namita. "Rossiter was in on all this. He knows where she is, I'm sure of it. We just have to get him to tell us."

"I said the same to Feng an hour ago," agreed Porter. "But it's easier said than done. Unless you have any ideas?"

"I might have," said Feng. "Put her on speakerphone."

Chapter 47

November 17th, 2017
Bellevue Hospital, LA

Karin demanded a discharge lunchtime the following day. "I'm not laying here like an idiot when there's things to do," she said.

Porter and Feng did their best to persuade her to finish her recuperation, but she wouldn't be moved. "I need to give Arnie his statement and then we need to go home. We need to protect Namita too. If news of Crystal's death reaches Rossiter, he'll come after us, for sure."

"Flax and his team went up to Lascelles' mansion last night," said Porter. "They got a warrant to search the place, but Flax said they found nothing and Lascelles can't speak."

"Then I'm right: there's nothing for us here. We need to go home. Feng, do you mind booking tickets for this evening?"

"Right you are," said Feng. "Funny how the more air miles you accrue, the less you want to travel."

November 17th, 2017
Robbery Homicide Division, West First Street, LA

"That's a hell of a cut," said Flax, examining Karin's jawline.
"I'm collecting facial wounds," she said, pointing at her patch.
"You seem in good spirits? All things considered."

"I'm not. Seven girls are dead because of that psycho. For all we know, there were others too. We now think Crystal was part of a gentlemen's club that had sex with young women for kicks. We're sure now though that Rose and Bella both died in Berlin at the hands of a former Nazi-turned-film-director, Heinrich Becker. Crystal said as much. We can't prove it though."

"I guess what happened yesterday helps you, though?"

"It only confirms Crystal and/or Lascelles murdered some women. We don't have Rose or Bella's bodies. It doesn't tell us much else. But it shows our original assumption about the club was wrong. Yes, there was abuse, but they clearly moved on to murder as part of their game. I wouldn't be surprised if more murders are uncovered. But I guess the documentary will have to wait while the case is investigated. How are you going to tackle the IDs?"

Flax grimaced. "Painfully slowly. Remember that big list of missing people? We'll start there."

"I can narrow it a bit. You're looking for actresses who were 22 at the time of their disappearance. That's all those bastards were interested in."

"Thanks, Karin." Flax saw Porter tapping his watch. "Look, I'd better let you go. What time's your flight?"

"6.30pm."

"Will you be back? I'd still like to buy you dinner some time."

"I'd like that. Yes, I'll be back."

"Till then, then." He shook her hand.

Porter, Feng and Karin left West First Street and jumped a cab to LAX.

"I can't believe there are people who do this journey regularly," said Feng. "The jet-lag is atrocious. We're spinning ourselves again going home before I've even recovered from getting here."

"It's worse going east, home," said Porter. "Took me two weeks last time."

"I quite like flying," said The Gliss.

"But you don't get jet lag," said Feng.

"The clouds are so pretty."

"Cut it out, you two," Karin interrupted. "Tell me about your plan for Rossiter. Jet-lagged or not, we have to act as soon as we get home."

November 18th, 2017
Heathrow Airport, London

Namita met them at the airport.

They were tired but pleased to see her. Feng reached out to give her a hug, but Namita was impatient and cut off their greetings.

"No time. Sorry about this, but we've got to shoot. I'm meeting Crawley and Phelps in two hours and you need to be there." They groaned. "I'm sorry. You all look knackered but," and then, registering the walking stick and stitches for the first time, "Jesus, Karin. What the hell happened to you?"

"You didn't tell her?" said Karin, to Porter.

"Didn't want to tell her you'd been in hospital again," said Porter.

"He said Crystal was shot dead and you'd found some of the girls," said Namita.

"Let's catch up in the car," said Karin. "If I don't fall asleep."

November 18th, 2017
Worple Road, Wimbledon, London

DCI Dan Crawley met their car at the curb. He too reacted to Karin's wounds and the walking stick. "What happened? Where's your luggage?"

"I got attacked by one of the producers," said Karin, before calmly stating, "The police shot him. I won't lose any sleep over it."

"We haven't got any luggage," said Feng. "We've been treating our trips to LA like we're nipping to Tesco's for a bag of sugar."

"I couldn't carry anything anyway," said Karin. "Morrie Crystal cut into my arms and leg. I look like a mummy under my clothes."

"You certainly know how to upset people. Come on in. Phelps and Jayfield are waiting for us."

Inside the ramshackle house, they were greeted by Ronnie Phelps. Sitting at a table, looking miserable, another old man in a dark green cardigan, sniffled. Phelps did the introductions. "I'd like you to meet my former colleague, Larry Jayfield."

"You're very welcome," he said, the tone implying the exact opposite.

Crawley poured tea. The gang shuffled about the living room, wondering how to make themselves comfortable in the face of barely-disguised hostility from their host.

Feng sniffed at the decor and Karin wondered how long the hunting scenes prints had been hanging. Every picture was sun-bleached, every frame-top buckling with enough dust to resurface the moon. Eventually, cajoled by an impatient Phelps, they all sat. Karin, Porter and Feng gabbled through an account of how LA had blown up in their faces.

"Seven women? Unbelievable," said Phelps. "And you're sure they were all part of this damn club?"

"What else could they be?" said Karin. "Crystal mouthed off a few things before he died. He got off on it, detailing the abuse of the young actresses. Our suspicions were correct. The Tutu Club morphed from a gang who met for sex into a gang who met for sex and murder - killing 22-year-olds for kicks."

"Well, Larry," said Phelps. "I hope that's loosened your tongue. I know you're not a bad man."

"Aren't I?" said Jayfield, staring down at his lap. "I knew this would all catch up with me one day. I didn't know anything about murders though, you have to believe me."

"I do," said Phelps. "You might have had - ahem - connections to Rossiter, but there's no way they would have involved a cop, even a bent one, in their inner circle."

"You took backhanders from Rossiter, is that right? You can tell us the truth. I'm not judging," said Porter. Both Karin and Namita gave him looks. *Aren't you? We are.*

"Look it was different times," said Jayfield. "Everyone, and I mean everyone, took backhanders." He looked at Phelps. "Alright, not everyone."

"We're not interested in making you pay for your sins," said Crawley. "What's done, is done. But the info you give us could help bring Rossiter to book. Finally. Just tell us what you know."

Jayfield was embarrassed and ashamed. But he managed to get through it. After many interjections and clarifications, this was the story he told.

> *Despite all the Carnaby Street footage you still see on TV, I remember the 60s in black and white. Soho was probably the height of colour, but a flashy dress or pop art poster were still only a fraction of that world.*

There were still bombsites and adverts for Typhoo tea painted on the walls of shops. No-one had central heating. Few had a car. Cockneys still wandered about looking like Alfred Doolittle. Coal men still drove through the streets offloading sacks of coal. The air was gritty, and we still had London fogs, though nothing like the pea-soupers of the 40s.

The only fragments of colour I remember are The Krays, Rossiter and co. Not them as people, you understand, but their worlds. You could wander about Soho and Covent Garden during daylight and it was drab as hell. Grey, grey, grey. Mary Quant was another world to me.

When I was stationed at Savile Row in '65, I was keen and idealistic. I put my back into learning the beat. I felt like the new sheriff had come to town, and I was the one with the tin star. My beat included Soho, which was, appropriately, the Wild West End. Greater London was so dull - nothing like the place I read about now. Any excitement was crammed into my few square miles.

I got moved into Vice and quickly found, to my horror - honestly - that everyone was taking backhanders and turning a blind eye to the seamier stuff. There was prostitution, marijuana, pills, porn, illegal drinking, illegal fighting and gambling - and it was all controlled by a handful of powerful gangsters.

It's not a defence, but I had no choice but to give in. One of our officers - do you remember DS Stanley, Phelps? - no? - well, he was a stick-in-the-mud rule observer. When he refused to take a bribe and pulled in one of The Krays' boys for some petty misdemeanour, a group of thugs turned up at his gaff and kicked the crap out of him. He transferred out of London the next day. Home to Leicester. Couldn't hack it.

I was young and idealistic. I complained about the corruption and intimidation. What are we going to do about it? My boss balled me out. Don't be a Stanley: play nice or get hurt.

In all the time I worked that area, I only ever came across a couple of cops who didn't capitulate. The good ones mostly ended up leaving. I think Phelps was the only one who got away with doing the right thing. I don't know how you did it, Ronnie.

Sure, we carried out raids and arrested people, but there was a tacit rule: only pick at the edge of the scab. Leave the centre alone. If we could get someone for parking or acting drunk and disorderly, the crime bosses all accepted that. After all, if we were seen to do absolutely nothing, questions would be asked. But nothing big: don't do anything to touch the core business of Soho. Let people get their jollies.

And so, yes, I succumbed and, to my eternal shame, became just another bent copper. We weren't well paid, and those little packets of cash helped get my kids through school. I'm not proud of it, but that's how it was. Fat lot of good it did me. My wife ran off with an actor, and my kids ended up as peace protestors and musicians. I haven't seen any of them for 30 years. My right-on kids didn't approve of dad being a pig. My wife yearned for something more than a cop who came home drunk, reeking of fags and booze. But that was my future. At the time, I rolled over and played ball, thinking I was doing right by everyone, if not the law.

Clem Rossiter. Jesus. I'm not surprised by most of what you've told me today. He was a ruthless bastard. Like The Krays, he used violence and fear as weapons. But he was more complicated than them. They were working class through and through and found it hard to look and behave any differently. You see those David Bailey shots of them, black suit and ties, and think this means they were a cut above? But this was before jeans took over: everyone wore suits. Anyone coming for a night up West wore one. Clem would never allow you into his clubs looking like a slob. The Krays looked different because they were twins and psychotic, not because they had a tailor.

Rossiter was a giant. Built like a brick shithouse and with similar appeal. I held my nose and tolerated him. What does surprise me is the club. A villain, yes, but he looked after his girls. And they loved him. All the wannabes fighting for bar work used to dream of working for him. He paid okay, protected them from the arse-grabbers and he helped them fulfill their dreams. I'm sure some of his girls got roles in films.

I'm genuinely shocked he ended up killing some of them. Truthfully, I guess I'm not as shocked he abused them for a game. He was a scary sod, and it makes a kind of sense. Violence is power. And powerful men always express that through sex in the end. But I never heard complaints at the time. I just knew there was this weird contradiction about him: people wanted to be in the safety of his orbit, but everyone was petrified of him at the same time.

He sat with me once, bought me a drink, and told me what his plans were. He wanted to run most of the clubs in Soho. I remember thinking that was a bit of a paradox: a big dream but also a very small one. There was life outside London, let alone a small district like Soho. But he seemed to think that if he ruled Soho, he ruled the world. And I can understand the self-deception. His clubs were crammed with the cream of society; toffs, spies, international financiers, actors, musicians, artists... anyone who thought the mundane life was for suckers. These people wouldn't have been seen dead in an old man's flat-cap pub in Camden but were happy to let their hair down with other thrill-seekers in Soho.

And yes, I knew about The Tutu Club - the building, not the sick game. If Soho was exclusive, then Rossiter's club was next level up. It's important to swear I knew nothing about this game of yours, certainly nothing about murders. The club was just a very quiet exclusive club for the elite. Big stars like Judy Garland used to get drunk in Soho, but Rossiter wouldn't have invited her there. I went 10 times, maybe? Each time felt like an occasion, a confirmation that I was on the inside. It didn't trouble my conscience at the time, but it rankles now. Such a gap between my dreams and how my damn career played out.

There were never more than 20 people in the Tutu, but it had a feel, hard to describe, that made me think it was where only the serious players belonged. It was a place to carry out transactions. I saw The Krays there more than once. I can't imagine anyone ever got out of control there. It would have been inappropriate. And bad for your health.

It was easily the most luxurious club in Soho. No expense spared. I said a lot of his clubs had red cushions, but Tutu was all leather and dark woods. Rossiter had a favourite barman, Alan Shower. He was like Tom Cruise in that film - a total whizz at cocktails - and he was sent there. I remember him well - white shirt, dickie bow, performing tricks to dazzle Rossiter's guests. Slick and professional. That's him and the club summed up right there. It was top-line exclusive.

Yes, there was an ugly statue as you came in. A ballet dancer in a tutu dress. Funny you should bring it up. Once, I walked in with Rossiter and he rubbed his fingertip across the statue's breasts. I remember it as a pathetic schoolboy gesture, but it feels more sinister in the light of what you've told me. Again, although I never heard anything about Rossiter treating women badly - quite the opposite - that small gesture made me uneasy at the time. It was tacky. That I remember it, shows how it stood out. The statue was ugly, but of course, it gave the club its name. And you say he still has it? Incredible. You can believe people survive from the 60s, but the objects, the rooms, you assume they've all gone.

It goes without saying, you couldn't just turn up - you had to be invited. There must have been times when it was completely empty, just Shower twiddling his thumbs. It was halfway down Wardour Street, under the newsagents next to The Ship. I met quite a few interesting people there. No-one seemed to think it strange that a vice cop was there. I guess they knew the score.

I once spoke to Gerry Skye in there. Do you remember him? He directed Albert Finney's film, The Cheetah. He was the biggest director in London at the time. He was telling me about The Oscars. Can you imagine what that was like? London was in black and white and there I was talking to someone who spent half the year in Hollywood? It was completely mad, so different to today when everyone in London has travelled. I didn't ask him what Los Angeles was like, I asked him what the food was like on a plane. The idea of eating in the air was so exotic.

I don't know what happened to the club. I transferred out of Vice in 1974. It was still going then, for sure. You have to believe me. I did nothing more than turn a blind eye to the gambling and prostitution. I'd never have turned my back on murder.

It took an hour to get this out of Jayfield. Feng had taken notes and Crawley had handled the tea.

"So, what now?" said Jayfield.

"What now?" said Porter. "We're going to bang that bastard up."

"For life," said Phelps, "And Larry? You're going to help us."

Chapter 48

November 19th, 2017
The Ship, Wardour Street, Soho, London

"Keith Moon got chucked out of here once," said Porter, reading up on the historic Soho pub. "And David Bowie used to drink here."

It was Play Your Own Vinyl Day, and a spotty young man was annoying them all with a blippy dance track that was all squealing TB303s and thin-sounding drum loops.

"Call that music?" said Phelps, putting a pint down in front of Jayfield, who looked even more miserable today, forced into taking part in their plans.

It was Feng's idea. The old boys should try and get Vince Chambers out of his flat and press him for information. There were two reasons to do it. One, Chambers obviously knew something. He'd been there through those years, had photographed some, if not all the victims, and was still scared stiff of Rossiter. Both Jayfield and Phelps had known him back in the day. He hadn't said much to Porter and Feng, but he might to his elderly peers, in the same way teenagers only share their problems with their friends, not their parents. The power of the conspiracy of peers is much misunderstood. Secondly, Chambers had hinted at having a record of the girls on their first visit.

"He said he'd had to look after himself," recalled Feng. "At the time, I thought it meant he just went along with everything to avoid getting duffed up, but now I think it meant he had insurance. When Karin told me she lied to Crystal that we had books with photos of the missing girls... well, it just clicked. Wasn't there a good chance Chambers did exactly that? He took headshots for Rossiter and was there at some of the casting couch sessions according to Susan Wills and Lucy Pelling. But if we're going to ransack the place looking for anything like that, we need to get him out."

Crawley was reticent. "I know what you think, Phelps, but I really do think it's time to pass this all onto Gavan and his mob. I can't believe you expect me to stand by and let you all break in."

"Come on, Dan," said Phelps. "It's hardly robbing the Bank of England. These guys are so close to getting everything they need to pass on. On what grounds would you get a warrant to search Chambers' place?"

"I shouldn't be here," said Crawley, unhappily.

"Dan, no-one will think the worse of you if you leave," said Phelps. "If they can get something and we'll pass it over after that. I'm retired, I don't care. I can't back out now, but you, well..."

"I'd like to back out," said Jayfield. "I'm still scared of Rossiter."

"Your one shot at redemption," said Phelps, patting his arm. "I won't let you. I've said it before, you're not a bad man."

"I'm sorry people," said Crawley. "I can't do this. It's not just my job, I'd face prosecution. I can pretend I don't know anything up until now, but..."

"Dan, it's okay. We understand," said Porter. "The less you know the better. Go on. Leave us to it."

They all felt a pang of loss as Crawley departed.

"He's a good man, Dan," said Phelps.

They were just getting up to leave when Namita's phone rang. It was the residential home in Atwater. Sam Brownlees was on a respirator after having a heart attack. Namita thanked the nurse for the call.

"That's a shame," she said. "We're so close to finding an answer for him. I hope he hangs on a bit longer."

"It's a good job we didn't tell him the other day," said Porter. "We might have finished him off."

"Poor Sam," said Karin, who'd become very fond of him after their interviews.

Half an hour later, they were all standing in Old Compton Street, looking up the busy road towards the entrance to Chambers' flat. Phelps and Jayfield would visit Chambers alone.

"Our best hope is if Chambers feels comfortable enough to go over old times," said Phelps.

They all agreed this was sensible. It would leave the four of them to go through Chambers' flat.

The gang hid in a diner opposite the photographer's front door and left the retired cops to their end of the mission.

"It won't be easy," said Porter, as they took up their seats. "Chambers is a recluse."

"If anyone can persuade him, it's Phelps," said Karin.

They watched nervously as Phelps and Jayfield went through the usual rigmarole of getting Chambers to answer the door. After a short wait, they were buzzed in, to the gang's collective relief.

Karin, whose arms and leg were healing but sore from the inflammation, was just glad to be seated. She popped an antibiotic pill, washing it down with a bitter espresso. Porter was biting his nails. Feng was sipping his tea, watching eagerly. Namita wondered if they were wasting their time.

Twenty minutes later the door to the flat opened again. Initially, they thought Phelps and Jayfield had failed because they stepped onto the street alone. But the old coppers stood outside patiently until, finally, Chambers emerged too, looking as tentative as a mole on a croquet lawn. The three old men shuffled a few doors down, entering the last greasy spoon left on the touristy street.

"Let's go," said Porter.

Feng used his skeleton keys to get them in.

"Jesus Christ," said Namita, looking at the devastation in the flat. "He should be in a care home."

"Yes, but luckily he isn't," said Feng, giving everyone a knowing look. "Somewhere in this flat are the books containing the details of everyone who was killed by Rossiter, Becker and the rest of The Tutu Club."

They spread out, looking. Unable to ignore the pain, Karin gave up after a few minutes. She put down an old newspaper before daring to sit on the least commode-like chair.

They searched high and low. They were aided by the appalling disorder. Instead of having to put everything back to an exact position, they were able to quickly sift and leave everything still looking a mess. But their searches were fruitless.

"If there is anything here, it'll be well hidden," said Feng. "Rossiter might have been scared of being exposed, but he wouldn't have left that to chance. I bet his goons have been in here several times over the years."

"I'm surprised Rossiter didn't just bump him off if he's as bad as we think he is," said Namita, wincing as she used her foot to move a pile of soiled underwear. "He should have hidden them under this lot," she said. "If I hadn't faced death a few times this year I should never have had the courage to move this lot."

Porter's phone pinged.

"Right, guys, we've got to get out of here," he said. "They're leaving the cafe in five minutes."

Feng was disappointed, but relieved to hear it. He'd had the difficult job of searching the kitchen. As well as the archeologically significant dust covering, the kitchen was greasier than a Teddy Boy's pillow. He checked his watch. They had minutes. "Porter, did you check that cupboard over there?" Feng said, winking. Before Porter could answer, Feng leaned back against the wall. With a genuine cry of surprise, he fell backwards and disappeared.

They pulled him out.

"Well, look at this," said Porter. "No wonder Chambers seemed to appear from nowhere every time." He pushed on a spring-loaded panel leading to a tiny priest-hole space. They examined the inside and saw there was a bolt. It was Chambers' primitive panic room. He could disappear in his own flat anytime and with a bit of luck, not be found.

"That was probably a necessity, working for Rossiter back in the 60s," said Karin. Then she remembered why they were here. "Is there anything in there?"

"My God," said Porter. "There's a cavity. Wait a second…"

The others looked at Porter, expectantly.

"What is it?" said Karin. "Did you find anything?"

"It's the books," said Porter, breathlessly. "A record of every woman Rossiter and his mates killed as part of The Tutu Club." He was about to say more when they all froze.

Gunfire. No doubt about it. At least half a dozen shots coming from the street.

"Phelps!" cried Porter, running for the door.

They emerged onto Old Compton Street to chaos and two dead bodies. Porter, looking around in a panic, saw a man running towards Charing Cross Road. Porter had no doubt it was the gunman. He couldn't go after him, but presumably it meant they were safe. Feng ran to Phelps, who was laying on the ground.

"Phelps, are you ok?"

Phelps' walking stick lay in the road, pointing back down the street. "My leg," he said weakly. A frothy scarlet pool was foaming below Phelps' thigh. Feng took off his jacket and began ripping at the material, using strips to make a tourniquet. Namita was standing over the dead bodies of Chambers and Jayfield.

The ex-cop had a bullet hole through his forehead. The photographer had been hit in the eye. Both men had a chest wound. They were clearly beyond hope. Several of the dozens of passers-by were calling for an ambulance.

Coming out of shock, Porter became aware of a commotion further down the road. He pulled his gaze away from the horror in front of him to see a woman cradling a man 200ft away. A passer-by had taken the sixth bullet.

Now they were in trouble. Gavan and his crew would 100% lay this on them. He didn't have time to worry about it now. Porter tapped the frantic passer-by, letting her know to update the emergency services.

Feng knelt and put Phelps' scarf under his head. Karin watched on helplessly as the folly of their plan revealed itself in the bloody tableau staining the busy Soho street red. She shook her head.

Porter knelt to double-check that Jayfield and Chambers really were dead and, forgetting himself, was immediately plunged into the Quincunx.

He didn't learn much. Jayfield's last thoughts were of his estranged children. Porter realised the first bullet must have hit the corrupt copper in the chest. It gave him a few seconds to have a dying thought. In contrast, he saw a ghostly version of Chambers, almost, but not quite, staring at him. He gave off nothing but sadness, leading Porter to conclude he had been hit in the face with his first bullet and died instantly.

Jayfield's spirit appeared too, looking past Porter. He held out his arms. He could have been waiting for cuffs to be put on, he could have been looking for comfort, but the echo of the dead man gave no further clues. Porter waited for either man to say something, but they were mute, lost even to Porter, their last connection to this world.

Before he could analyse further, Porter was pulled out, back into the chaos of Soho. Feng, spotting the Quincunx at work, had grabbed Porter's arms and pulled him clear of the bodies.

"We have to leave right now," said Feng. "There are enough people here to look after Phelps. We're in enough trouble once this gets back to Gavan. It would be better if we weren't here.

"We can't just leave him," said Porter. "Besides, there must be cameras, we're in this together."

"We'll take the chance. There's a good chance they won't know we've been here. Look how many hundreds of people there are. Let's stay calm and go in different directions," insisted Feng. "Stay amongst groups of people as much as you can. Get cabs to my place as quick as you can."

Chapter 49

November 19th, 2017
Feng's house, Church Lane, Walthamstow, London

Exhausted and shocked, but aware they still had work to do, the four unwrapped fish and chips in Feng's kitchen. The Deliveroo food was bought more from shock than hunger. No-one but Feng did much more than pick at the greasy concoctions in front of them. Feng always had an appetite.

Porter called Dan Crawley for an update, putting him on speakerphone. Dan was furious to hear how things had panned out and rushed to the hospital to be with Phelps.

"Gavan is outraged," said Crawley, from Phelps' bedside. "I knew you guys shouldn't have done this. I'm in deep trouble too. Three people shot in Soho, two of them ex-coppers. He has nothing yet to connect you to the shooting, but he's not stupid. You couldn't have caused more of a mess if you'd tried. It was a stupid idea. I can't believe I went along with it."

"How's Ron?" asked Karin.

"Recovering. The bullet passed through his calf. He'll live, thank God."

"What are you going to do?" said Porter.

"I'm going to maintain the lie I knew nothing, that Phelps and I had hung out recently for a catch-up, but nothing more. But, and I daresay this will happen, if they investigate my involvement, they'll find my emails to you, Porter. If they tie you into this, which it's very likely they will do, the emails shows I'm very much part of it. I'd be facing a disciplinary at best."

"I'm sorry to hear that."

"And you're not out of the woods either," said Crawley. "Gavan already blames you for Shanker's death. No question he'll put two and two together. If they go through any CCTV and see you there… You didn't even wait around for the emergency services."

"I did say that might be a problem," said Porter, giving Feng a reproachful look.

"Indeed." Crawley decided to put the bad news on hold. "But the most important thing is - you got the books?"

The four looked at each other, nodding. Porter said, "Yes, Dan. We have them. As suspected, Chambers pasted a photo of every girl Rossiter and The Tutu Club killed. Every single one. Names, where they'd been, who killed them, where they were disposed of. We should be able to put Rossiter away for life with these."

"Well, hold on to them. I won't be able to get to you today, but I will be with you first thing tomorrow. Sorry, but I'm going to bring Gavan over, telling him you want to see him. You need to give everything over to him now. Your involvement is at an end, the criminal justice system takes over asap. Can you all stay at Feng's tonight?"

Feng said he'd be delighted to put everyone up.

"We'll update the timeline, Dan," said Karin. "We're in trouble, no doubt, but by the time Gavan gets here tomorrow, we'll at least have the whole case written up for him."

"Thanks Karin, I think that's best. Gavan is going to explode. Don't think he won't - whatever you give him. Just don't do anything stupid tonight. He'll bring you all in for questioning. At least you'll be safe there."

"We'll be sensible, Dan," said Porter. "We'll all work together in writing up the case. By the time you get here with Gavan, we'll be able to prove Rossiter and his friends killed many women. That might be enough to divert Gavan's wrath."

Phone conference over, the gang sat back in their chairs, wiping mouths on sleeves, washing the grease down with fresh tea, and looking around at each other, wondering how this would all pan out. But no-one said anything.

The Gliss was the first to break the silence. "You've done great work on this. Porter's job is to put as many souls as possible to rest, to atone for the suicides in his family. This will make a dent."

"But does it mean I'll be free at last?" said Porter.

"I don't know. The Quincunx will end when it ends," said The Gliss.

Namita looked at the clock. "We can't have long," she said. "What do we do now?"

Porter said, "Let's get busy. Let's update the timeline. It's going to be a long night."

By midnight they had written up a long Word doc detailing what they knew of the club, its members and the names and details of the women whose fates they had uncovered.

"This document and the books are some of the most evil things I've ever seen," said Karin. "Man's inhumanity to woman, right there in black and white."

"It doesn't say much for the police - in Europe or the States - that it went on for so long," said Namita.

"Bent coppers like Jayfield didn't help," said Feng.

"But it will all be over soon, hopefully with Rossiter rotting in jail," said Porter.

There was a smash and a tinkle of glass falling. Someone was breaking in downstairs.

"They're here," said The Gliss. "Get ready everyone."

The four of them took up defensive positions, facing the door, waiting for their visitors to charge in.

"I wish you hadn't called this the Murder Room," said Porter.

"Sorry," said Feng. "I'm scared."

"So am I," said Karin.

They heard footsteps on the stairs. Porter was the only one who was armed - with a chair. Not much use against a shotgun.

No shotguns. The door burst open. Not much better: two men in black, wielding machetes. To everyone's surprise, they didn't barge in and start slashing. They stood like sentinels guarding the door. It quickly became clear why. Walking slowly, with the aid of a stick, Clem Rossiter was just behind them.

"Well, well, well, you have been busy little bastards, haven't you?"

"You're wasting your time," said Porter, gulping. "The police know we're onto you. Everything in this room is also on Dropbox, and the cops know about it."

"But they're not coming to see you until tomorrow, are they?" said Rossiter, with a smile. "That gives me the rest of the night to take your fingers off one-by-one until you've told me everything you know. I'm in Spain at the moment."

The group all looked at each other, confused.

"I say that… what I mean is, I will be by the time your cop friends turn up and start sifting through the corpses. My passport shows I've been there a few days already. There's nothing like a secret compartment in a car on Eurotunnel for covering your tracks. Now. Let's have those books."

"What books?" said Namita, playing for time.

"Who asked you to speak?" said Rossiter. "If I want to order a curry, I'll let you know."

"Fuck you," said Namita. "I said, what books?"

"Teach her some manners, Dave," said Rossiter.

One of the sentinels stepped forward and punched Namita in the gut, doubling her up with pain. Karin winced in empathy. Porter gasped. Feng gritted his teeth. He knew they were all facing worse in the minutes to come.

"Stop fucking about. You either all die quickly, or finger-by-finger. Your call."

"There are no books," said Porter.

"I know you found them at Vince's place," said Rossiter. "No point denying it."

"We know all about The Tutu Club," said Feng, bending down to help Namita. "And so do the cops. I guess the club was your idea?"

"Fuck me, the Chinky poof speaks. It wasn't my idea. I just facilitated it."

"And took part," said Porter.

"Of course I took part. I am curious though, how did you find out about it?"

"You and Becker both had the same statue. The dancer in a tutu?"

"What? You think that proves anything? Fucking snowflakes. Ever since Harvey Weinstein made the news, it's like no-one ever fucked someone else in return for a job. Men and women do it all the time. All we did was make it into a bit of fun. Pass around the 22-year-olds. There was nothing wrong with that. Everyone was doing something similar in the 60s. How many people do you think The Beatles shagged? Trying to re-write history now is ridiculous."

"That's disgusting, but it's not the rape and abuse that we're talking about, is it?" said Karin. "It's the fact that after Heinrich Becker murdered Rose Prideaux because she was mixed-race, you started murdering the girls too."

Rossiter looked impressed. "You have done your research. I'd love to know who squealed on that. I have a particularly grim end waiting for them, when I find out."

"There's only you and Lascelles left," said Porter. "You had Caron, Agresti and Demsky murdered, Becker died, Crystal was killed last week in LA, and Lascelles has advanced dementia. And you had Jimmy the Shanker and Vince Chambers murdered. So that just leaves you."

"Here's the thing," said Rossiter, pointing his stick at Porter, "If you know all that and have passed it on to the cops, why haven't I been arrested? Nah mate, I know exactly what you've been up to, and now - the books please. If you don't hand them over, I'm going to cut off the Chinky's hand. Nige, do the honours will you."

The other sentinel took a step towards Feng, when Karin shouted out, "No. Wait. We've got them."

"That's more like it," said Rossiter. "Where are they then?"

"Don't give them to him, Karin," said Porter. "He'll only kill us."

"He's going to do that anyway," said Karin.

The Gliss, who had been patiently watching the confrontation, spoke to the four of them. "Are you ready? You can do it now."

But Porter wasn't ready just yet. "I can't believe you teamed up with a Nazi like Becker. What did you do, help him dispose of the bodies?"

"Someone had to. You know all of our members, that much is clear. They were all namby-pamby film directors. Even someone like Becker, who had a few hundred Yids to his credit, wasn't skilled in the art of peacetime disposal of bodies. I went with an old colleague of mine and we buried the girl in Berlin."

Karin's turn. "You mean Browz, I take it?"

"Yes. I miss him. He'd have had enough fingers from you lot by now to play Jenga with them."

"Where's Rose?" said Porter. "I just need to know. That's what this was all about: trying to find what happened to Rose Prideaux."

"I dunno. Haven't been to Berlin for years, not since Becker died in the 80s. We went to some fucking park in the middle of the night. What difference does it make now? Books. Now. I'm losing patience."

Karin gave a shall-I-do-it? gesture and the others nodded. She walked over to Feng's filing cabinet, pulled open a drawer and yanked out three manilla notebooks.

Walking over to the table, she dropped them down. "Everything Vince had is in there," said Karin. "I presume it's complete. 25 women, right?"

"And the rest," scoffed Rossiter. "No surprise that flake Chambers didn't do his job properly. I was never sure if he'd actually had the fucking balls to do this. He got pissed once and hinted at it. I felt like chopping the fucker's head off, but if he really had possessed the balls, it would mean life if they'd come to light after his death. We looked for them, of course."

Feng said, "So you let him live just in case he'd left the files with his solicitor or something?"

"We let him live. After kicking him about a bit. He was just another washed-up poof. Bit like yourself." Rossiter cracked his knuckles. "Truth was, if he let the files out, we were both dead men, so I assumed, until you lot poked your fuckin' noses in, that they'd never get out. Or, yeah, Chambers would have lost his head years ago. Once he started yapping to you pricks and that pain in the arse, Phelps, well, something had to be done, right? But he's dead because you stuck your fuckin' noses in. Feel good?"

Rossiter didn't seem particularly bothered about the books themselves. He casually flipped open the first book. It was empty. "What the fuck?" He flipped through the others. All empty. He looked up at them and said, "You think this is a fucking game? Right, Nige, take the fucking Chinky's arm off at the elbow. I've had enough of this bullshit."

Nige stepped forward, machete raised, when a voice rang from the doorway. "I'd put that down if I were you."

"Thank God," said Porter. "I thought you'd never come up."

"Oh, we were listening downstairs, taping the whole thing," said Barry Hammell, accompanied by two ex-army buddies holding guns. "We saw they only had machetes. We figured you'd be safe for a bit while you dragged a confession out of him."

"You cut it fine," said Namita, "but thanks, Hammell. I owe you one."

Hammell shrugged it off. "You don't owe me anything after that other balls-up of mine." Turning to Rossiter, Hammell aimed a pistol at his head. "Rossiter, you've been stitched up like a kipper, mate. There are no books. Never have been. Oi! You! Pretty boy. I said - put that fucking thing down…!"

Chapter 50

Three days earlier.
November 16th, 2017

Feng told the others how he found out that he and Chambers were being bugged - almost certainly by Rossiter.

"My EMF digifier might be absolutely crap at picking up ghosts, but it turns out it's pretty good at picking up transmitters," he said. "At first, I wondered what the hell was tripping it when Porter and I were chatting to Chambers. But the reading was consistent with a radio transmission."

"If that's the case," said Porter, "we have to be careful what we're saying from now on."

"No," said Namita. "We should spell it all out."

Feng and Porter, on the other end of the phone in LA, asked her what she meant.

"Karin persuaded me to bug that twat, Martin, to get info out of him that I could use for blackmail," she explained quickly, before Feng and Porter waded in with questions. "Let's do the same and turn the tables on Rossiter. We set up our own surveillance alongside Rossiter's. Hammell can do it. We carry on as if in ignorance, make him think we know everything, provoke a confrontation, and have Crawley's lot monitor and mop-up before we get ourselves killed."

"How would it work?" said Porter. "I don't think Crawley will agree to use us as bait."

"Alright, we get my man Hammell to do the heavy mob stuff as well. It doesn't matter. As long as we catch it on tape."

"And you think Rossiter is going to come out to get us in person?" Karin was intellectually sceptical, but physiologically nervous.

Namita waved all that away. "Who's he going to trust with getting those books back? If he doesn't come in person, he'll send someone he can trust - his daughter probably. But I'm banking on him coming himself. Even a bastard like him might not want his daughter to know he'd raped and murdered women."

"Possibly," said Porter. "How do we get him to think we know everything? We don't."

Namita sighed, as if she were tired of doing all the heavy lifting. "We get Vince Chambers out of his flat, go in, pretend we're looking for something, and make sure that's heard on his bug. We announce loudly we've found a list of all the women they killed. We know enough names to drop in. Bugging Feng and Chambers shows just how paranoid Rossiter is. Let's play on it. He must have wondered over the years whether Chambers had put insurance to one side. If Chambers was a bit brighter, he might have actually done it. But it doesn't matter whether he did or didn't. As long as we never let our roles slip, we should convince Rossiter that his worst fear has come true."

She looked at the gang and saw them weighing up the dangers. She had no doubt they'd say yes. They were all psychos. She added, "Once we're in Chambers' flat, we leave it to the last and then loudly announce that we've found something. After the Soho shootings, I imagine Rossiter has someone listening full-time. I'm sure the message will get to him, and then Rossiter will have to come after us quite quickly."

"So he turns up at mine and then we just get him to spill his guts?" said Feng.

"Right," said Namita. "They probably bugged Feng's when they attacked you and Porter. Let's use their own weapon against them. Are you sure they only bugged your place?"

"Yes, I always sweep at Porter's, I've never picked up a radio signal there."

"Why'd you sweep at mine?" said Porter.

"Well, you know… you're a bit creepy with the visions. I haven't quite given up hope of picking up a traditional headless ghost or white lady just yet."

"Alright, enough you two," said Namita. "Let's set up the confrontation for Feng's, meet there and discuss these incriminating books…"

"It's dangerous," said Porter, "but it could work if Hammell comes on board."

"He won't like it," said Feng.

"He'll do it. He knows some pretty dodgy types for backup," said Namita.

"Well, if we're going to entrap Rossiter, someone need to be there to make sure he doesn't blow our heads off with a shotgun."

"As soon as you guys get back from LA, we'll discuss this with Crawley," said Namita. "It'll only be believable if Rossiter sees and hears us raiding Chambers' flat, supposedly retrieving the fake books. I'm sure it'll get back to Rossiter from one of the two bugs."

"Let's do it," decided Porter. "See you back in London - though I warn you now, I can't see Crawley going along with this."

November 19th, 2017
Feng's house, Church Lane, Walthamstow, London

Nige did not put down the machete. He took a swing at Hammell, but the doorframe stopped it from reaching its target. Hammell stamped hard on Nige's groin. The other thug dropped his machete and put his hands up. Enraged, Rossiter swung his stick at Karin. Despite her weakened state, she grabbed it.

"You're a bit old for this," she said, yanking it from his hands. Rossiter wobbled on the spot. Using his stick against him, she prodded him in the gut. He toppled backwards, landing on his back, yelping with pain.

"My hip! You fuckin' bitch."

Karin took the stick and jammed it against his broken hip. "What did you say?"

"You fuckin' bitch. *Bitch*."

Karin ground the stick into the gangster's breakage. He screamed, and a dark stain appeared around his groin.

"Come on Karin, enough," said Porter, gently taking the stick away from her.

One of Hammell's guys used cable-ties to bind the machete men's hands behind their backs. Hammell approached Rossiter and gestured for him to turn over and put his hands behind his back. He didn't move.

"I can't... it hurts."

Hammell swiftly punched Rossiter in the face and knelt on his hip. "Like hurting little girls, do you?"

"Barry, no," said Namita. "Let the cops deal with it."

"My sister was raped once," said Hammell. "Sorry." And he kneed Rossiter in his piss-soaked groin.

"Enough!" said Namita. "We're better than him."

The thugs tied up, the taped conversation on the table ready for collection, Hammell and his cronies cleared out, leaving Porter and the gang ready to bring the cops in. They called Crawley, who was appalled they'd actually gone through with it all, expressed his reservations, but said he would bring Gavan and be there as quickly as he could.

Gavan's team swapped the cable ties for cuffs on Nige, Dave and Rossiter. A wheelchair rolled through the doorway. It was Ronnie Phelps, pushed by a young copper who was still puffing from the exertions of getting Phelps upstairs.

"I'm not a cop anymore and I should be in hospital, but I had to be here to see you cuffed at long last," Phelps said, jabbing his finger in the direction of Rossiter. "Dan, may I?"

"Be my guest," said Crawley, shushing Gavan, doing his best Etna-ready-to-blow impersonation.

"Clem Rossiter, you're being arrested for the murders of several women from 1964 to the present day, the murders of Jimmy the Shanker, Vince Chambers and Larry Jayfield."

Gavan made it formal. "Clem Rossiter, I'm arresting you. Anything you do say will be taken down in evidence and anything you do say may be used against you in a court of law."

"Fuck off, you'll never make it stick. There are no books. You said so yourself. You have nothing."

"I think you'll find they have plenty," said Feng, gesturing around the Murder Room. "Not least the recording of your confessions just now. You should have saved it for a priest. At least they wouldn't grass." He grinned.

"I can't believe you fell for it, Rossiter," said Namita, rubbing her bruised tummy. "Everything we said at Chambers' flat and here tonight was for your benefit, and you fell for it."

Rossiter, who was no stranger to being arrested, knew it was wiser to say nothing. His glare did the speaking for him.

"I'm so glad I didn't take any backhanders off you," said Phelps. "It's made my retirement worthwhile nabbing you for this. It's a shame we don't have the death penalty. But then, any sentence over five years is a death sentence for someone your age, isn't it? I hope you rot in hell."

November 23rd, 2017
Venetia's Coffee Shop, Chatsworth Road, Hackney

Crawley and Phelps ordered rounds of coffee and lemon cake for all.

The clear-up had gone well so far. Nige and Dave were charged with possession of a machete with intent to endanger life, which carried 14 years. Crawley was sure Hammell's cameras at Feng's were enough to secure a conviction, though both Porter and Namita had doubts about the admissibility of the footage.

Crawley updated them on the police investigation. Rossiter wasn't talking, but Gavan's team were going through the team's research and were preparing a case. Gavan, always one for keeping an eye on his prosecution targets, now had several provable murders on his hands. Even without a conviction for each victim, there was enough to put Rossiter away for the attempted murder of the gang.

Crawley said, "Despite Gavan giddily daydreaming of awards and honours, he was only brought into the loop by me, after all the fun. He's livid, not surprisingly. He's making a complaint against me." Crawley shrugged, remembering the dressing down he got from Gavan. "He shouted, 'Chambers, Shanker and Jayfield would probably still be alive if that bunch of amateurs had left it to the professionals.' Luckily, he still doesn't seem to have worked out you were all on the scene for the Soho shootings."

"Gavan's got a point, really," said Karin, "but we've done good work too - despite the bruises."

Feng and Namita both looked at the stitches on Karin's face and her walking stick and smiled at the understatement.

Porter, recalling Gavan's words on the night - 'You're a right bunch of pillocks and you could all be dead too,' - said, "It sounded like he wouldn't have minded too much if we had been."

Crawley shook his head. When the totals were totted up Gavan had no choice but to accept the group had potentially helped clear up several murders and picked up enough evidence to put away one of London's most notorious gangsters.

"On the negative side, I fear this might be the end of my career," said Crawley, nibbling on his cake. "But if it is, well, what a way to go out."

"We're not finished yet," said Porter. "I can't rest until I've found Rose Prideaux. It's what this was all about. For me, anyway."

Feng's mobile rang. He didn't recognise the number. "Hello?"

"Feng, you stir-fried prawn," said Peregrine Zouche. "Where the hell are you?"

"I'm in a cafe, with the others – not that it's any of your business. Why do you ask?"

"Stop blithering. What cafe? Where?"

"Venetia's on Chatsworth Road, Hackney. Why?"

"I'm at your bloody house. Cab waiting. See you in a minute."

"Oh, my Goff," said Feng, staring at the others. "That was Peregrine Zouche."

"Is he alright?" asked Porter, concerned.

"I guess he must be - he just said he'd see me in a minute."

Crawley asked, "Who's Zouche?"

The others looked at each other sheepishly. Feng decided to take the responsibility.

"He's a sort of friend of mine. A retired author."

"Oh well, that'll be nice," said Crawley.

"Yes, but he's supposed to be in a care home in Oxford. He's *very* retired."

Feng and Porter haltingly tried to explain why they knew Zouche without referring to his supernatural knowledge. Only Feng had met him, the others only knew him from unflattering description. Feng was perfectly prepared to sell Zouche as a madman to Crawley.

But Feng, like Porter, was flustered by the retired detective's presence. Namita tried to change the subject as Porter and Feng glitched more than an Aphex Twin record. They couldn't let Crawley know Zouche was a student of the occult. It would lead to too many embarrassing questions.

To try and distract them, Namita added: "Sam Brownlees is recovering well. I spoke to him today and tried to gee him up, saying we might have some news for him soon."

"Who's Brownlees?" asked Phelps, confused. Namita took some time to explain and Phelps raised an eyebrow. "You only found all this out because of a contested will? You should have been detectives. Well, it's all very complicated... can we stick to the case?"

The door to the garden bashed open and to everyone's surprise, a wizened, white-haired old man in coat and pyjamas, walked towards them, waving a stick.

"Bloody hell, Feng," he blared, "you didn't tell me half of London was here with you."

"Zouche! What on earth are you doing here? They let you out?"

"What? You think they'd have let me out? I'm paying to be there but going out is a no-no. The Clueless idiots. I had to sneak out."

"You're in pyjamas," observed Porter.

"Well done, Sherlock. Let me guess - Porter Norton?"

"That's right. Peregrine, thank you so much for your help on the last case..."

"Sod, the last case. I want to know about this one. Get me some tea then, Feng. Builders. Two sugars. No mugs. And make sure there's some biscuits on the side. Chop-Chop. Haven't got all day."

There was little choice but to accommodate him. Everyone shoved up a bit, and Feng went off to get his drink. After extended introductions and a quick catch-up on where they were, everyone was surprised Zouche took the lead in moving forward.

"What's the plan then? You all off to play Scooby Doo in Berlin, I presume?"

"We do have to go back," admitted Porter, understanding now why Feng found Zouche so irritating. "I've got to find Rose Prideaux's body. To do that, I need to go back over Becker Haus. I can't believe he only kept the statue as a memento. There must be other clues there of some kind."

"We've already examined the house pretty well," said Feng. "Not sure what else we'll find. All Becker's paperwork is in German. Unless you've been at one of those learn-a-language-in-3-days apps, or he hid all the details behind those bloody picture frames, it'll be fruitless."

"You bloody idiots," said Zouche. "Of course, he hid the details in the frames." He tutted, dismissively. "And to think you managed to recite that incantation I gave you and defeated a Profugus with the Saevita? You sound like people who couldn't cut their nails without losing a finger."

Porter, Feng, Karin and Namita, were all a bit embarrassed at Zouche's mention of the Profugus. Phelps looked at Crawley, blew out his cheeks as if to say, "What a nutter."

"Dare I ask what a Profugus with the Saevita is?" asked Crawley.

Zouche's face lit up. "It's..."

Karin jumped in to save their blushes. "When you say he hid the details in the frames...?"

"Oh, my God," said Porter. "I'm so stupid."

"No argument there," muttered Zouche.

"No, seriously," said Porter. "What was it Rossiter said? *They buried her in some park, in the middle of the night.*"

Feng whistled. "My, oh my. We really do need a quick spin in the knife sharpener, don't we?"

Karin asked, "What frames? What's going on?"

"Not frames - pictures," said Porter. "Becker's study has lots of photos and paintings of parks in Berlin."

Feng opened his iPhone and showed them some of the snaps.

"The sick bastard," says Namita. "I hope that's not a grave per picture. If it is, we've completely misunderstood the scale of this."

Feng put his phone away. "I think that's exactly what we've done. I need to speak to Davidov. Update him."

"Davidov?" Phelps and Crawley looked puzzled again. Feng explained.

"Do that," said Porter, downing the last of his latte. "Who's coming to Berlin with me?"

Only Phelps and Crawley made their excuses. "I'd love to, but you know I've got the fight of my life just to save my career now," Dan said, sadly.

"And I'm not fit enough," said Phelps.

"I'm not fit enough either, but I'm bloody well going," said Zouche. "You might need my German. And my ability not to miss the bleedin' obvious."

Feng, who could just about take a tea and cake session with Zouche, but not a trip, dropped open his mouth till it resembled a tunnel bored through a mountain.

"Zouche - you'll need your passport, I'm sorry," said Porter, who clearly wasn't fond of gaining a travel companion either.

"Oh, so not only do you miss all the clues right in front of you, but you think I'm stupid as well," said Zouche, tapping the bag he'd brought with him.

"Oh, that's great," said Porter, ruefully. "That's just great."

"Cheer up, you miserable sods," said Zouche, slurping tea from his saucer. "Let's go wrap this thing up. Anything an old Jew can do to stitch up a Nazi."

November 24th, 2017
Becker Haus, Mitte, Berlin

Max Fascher was mortified at their reappearance and updates but remained surprisingly helpful. He seemed more concerned with the damage to his own reputation than having it confirmed his former mentor was a serial killer and Nazi.

"Tell me everything you know," he said. "I will need to make the preparations."

"Prepare for the worst," said Porter. "May I introduce you to Efrayim Davidov. He represents the interests of victims of the Holocaust. He wants a word with you."

Fascher looked affronted at the physical manifestation of his hateful new reality. But the shock overwhelmed his resistance so far that he meekly strode off with the Israeli for a private conference.

Feng, Porter, Karin, Namita and Zouche surveyed the room. The frames now took on an ominous quality. There were twelve pictures of park scenes - a 6:1 ratio of photos to paintings.

"How will we work out where these are?" said Karin. "They're all tightly framed. I can't see any identifying features."

"You don't live in Berlin," said Porter. "Someone will know. Let's get them down."

It was only after the pictures were stacked on the desk that they noticed each photo and painting had a date pencilled on the back. Namita showed one to Zouche, who grabbed a magnifying glass off Becker's desk to examine it.

"Well, this will help," said Namita. "I think we can guess what these dates are."

"Bullseye to the Goddess Saraswati," bellowed Zouche, bent double, scoping. "This is the mustard, alright."

Namita glared at the old man. The Gliss chipped in before Namita could throttle him. "Porter, you know what this means? Once you know the names of the parks, you're going to have to wander about looking for the hotspots."

"I know," said Porter. "I'm not going home until we've identified all these damn parks."

"I'm parched. Could you get us a cup of tea, love?" Zouche said to Karin.

As Karin walked to the kitchen, she whispered to Porter, "I'm going to kill him, if he doesn't shut up."

"Well, at least he insults us all equally," Porter whispered back.

Fascher returned with Davidov. He looked white. "This is incredible. How could I have been so blind."

"He's suddenly realised his lord and master was a Nazi," said Zouche.

"What's happened?" said Karin, anxious to keep the custodian on-side.

"We are launching a suit against the estate," said Davidov. He looked at the Picasso. "That one painting alone should ensure the well-being of many families."

"Make sure you include the families of the girls. Not just the war victims," said Porter. "Some of their families are still alive."

"Yes, of course. But so are the families of those who died in the camps at the hands of pigs like Becker."

Porter sensed this was only day one of the battle to see justice for all. He decided to park it. "You're a decent man. I'm sure you'll act decently. Assuming these pictures mark the graves of some of Becker's victims, we need to identify the parks. Fascher?"

"Yes, of course." He looked like a punctured football and was fully compliant. Porter suspected this might change as the shock wore off and the full ramifications became clear. The cosy world he had built was dissolving faster than a cake in the rain.

"When do you want to start?" The Gliss asked Porter.

"Today. Immediately. I can't rest until we've found them."

The others nodded. Only Davidov and Fascher wondered how Porter expected to find the graves.

"That's it, Porter, you big girl's blouse," said Zouche. "Get out there and get walking. See what vibes you pick up."

As soon as the first location was identified by Fascher - Humboldthain Park, just down the road - Porter and Feng set off.

According to the pencilled date, 40 years had passed since Becker took the picture. They had no idea which of the girls' final resting place it might signal. Back then, the park was still a mess from extensive Allied bombing. Now it was a joyous sight: beds, woodlands, and extensive landscape gardening. And changes; lots of them. Nothing now matched the photo bar the iron railings that characterised the park. After wandering around the grounds for an hour, the size of the task hit them both.

"This is hopeless. We'd better come up with a strategy," said Feng. "Are you confident that if you just walk over a grave you'll know? You usually have to focus and jump in."

The Gliss answered for Porter. "He will. And if he doesn't, I will. Your job will be to keep him from the public's gaze once Porter does his electric-eel-bites-his-arse impression."

"Like he's been tasered. Well, then there's nothing for it," said Feng. "We have to be methodical. We need to walk up and down on a grid pattern, just like the cops do on the telly."

"I doubt Becker and his accomplices - if he had any - would have dug a grave by the roadside," said Porter. "Perhaps we should begin in the centre of the park and work our way outwards?"

"Either way, but yes, you're right. Let's look for the area that would give a disposal team the most cover at night."

By the time the park closed, Porter had paced the equivalent of 10 miles with nothing to show for it. "We have to come back first thing," he said, crestfallen.

November 24th, 2017
The Adlon Kempinski Hotel, Berlin

Feng booked them all into the famous Hotel Adlon Kempinski and over a lush dinner, everyone but Zouche looked at Porter in sympathy. The walk and the weight of expectations un-met had exhausted him. And he was still dopey from his LA jet lag.

Though he felt despondent and dejected, the others saw what he could not: the aura of righteous determination burning around him. It impressed and inspired them all. But tiredness and disappointment ganged up to put one over on Porter. His colleagues may have been fired-up, but he was silent and meditative over dinner. No-one was surprised when he excused himself. He needed a shower and bed and a spiritual replenish.

Davidov joined the rump of the investigative team later. He quickly filled the void left by Porter.

He said a team was jetting in from Tel Aviv to help pick over Becker Haus - including German speakers. They all celebrated this news as it opened up Becker's written archive to them. Fascher had given Davidov full access. "I asked him if he wanted to join us for dinner," said the Israeli, "but I think he's already preparing words he can publish to distance himself from Becker. He has a feeble mind."

"He's not the first person to be taken in by a demagogue," said Karin. "From what I can tell, Fascher's not complicit, just someone enslaved to the idea of sucking up to someone else's perceived greatness. He was used. He's not so different from all those poor women who thought those vile men could give them a leg up."

"Well, I feel sorrier for the girls," said Namita.

"So do I, Namita. So do I," said Karin.

"Porter is exhausted already," said Feng. "We need to take turns helping him, marking off maps etc. Anyone not in the field with Porter should work with Fascher and Davidov to identify as many of the locations as possible."

"Is it okay if I skip the fieldwork?" asked Karin. "I'm still so sore."

"Me too," said Zouche. "I feel like I tried to take a bath in a tumble dryer. I've been sitting on my arse for far too long."

"I'll do first shift, don't worry," said Namita, patting Karin's arm in a kindly, patronising way.

"I still don't see how he's going to know where the bodies are," said Davidov. The others all shifted uncomfortably. "But, of course, there is something you are not telling me?"

They looked at each other, seeking permission to speak. Several generations of privilege made itself known, and Karin stepped up. "Don't tell anyone, they'll think we're all mad." She sighed. "Porter is... er... psychic. He'll just know. You'll see. And when the police dig up the spot..."

"A psychic? I cannot believe in such things," said Davidov. "That is disappointing to hear, Ms Pelenot. I thought you had more concrete information. Very disappointing."

"Pish and tish," said Zouche. "You've got a kippah on your bonce. If that's not an admission of the supernatural, I don't know what is."

Davidov reacted angrily and turned towards Zouche, before Feng put a restraining arm out.

"No internecine political arguments over dinner, gentlemen. Porter may surprise you yet," said Feng. "Let's just leave it at that."

November 25th, 2017
Becker Haus, Mitte, Berlin

But Davidov's scepticism proved justified. By 5pm the next day, he, Karin, Zouche and Feng had heard nothing from Namita and Porter, who had been pacing Humboldthain Park relentlessly since 8am.

The team were joined at Becker Hause at midday by some of Davidov's people, fresh from the airport. Seeing the new arrivals, Fascher seemed to visibly wake up to his new reality. He finally began the pushback they'd all been expecting.

"Who are all these people?" Fascher demanded. Trying to cut them off from their searches, he snapped, "They look like henchmen from a Bond film."

"The henchmen in Bond are all actors," said Davidov, implying not just that this team weren't actors, but that they were very, very serious people.

Davidov, with a lightness of tone that belied the clear "don't you dare interfere" undertone, said, "They are here to sift through the papers. They are here to help Porter locate Becker's later victims. They are here to do the work of God in bringing SS Obergruphenfuhrer Heinz Hartman to posthumous justice. That is something we all want, I presume?"

"Aren't we fond of our rhetorical flourishes," said Fascher. "What you mean is, they all work for Mossad or the Israelis. I'm sure it's all crap. The SS claims have been rubbished many times over. You haven't shown me any evidence."

"Do you have a problem with Jews?" said Davidov, gesturing menacingly at his own workforce. Before Fascher had a chance to protest, Davidov silenced him. "Try to be patient and we will update you. Thank you for your co-operation."

"Yep, don't mess with us Jews if we're feeling righteous," said Zouche.

Feng watched the confrontation and shook his head. "Davidov and Zouche will get us all thrown out if they keep on needling Fascher. This is not a criminal investigation. We have no authority. Fascher's being a good man in the circumstances."

"Yes, I'll have a word with them," said Karin. She checked her phone. "I feel bad calling to see how Porter's getting on."

"He'll be in touch soon enough."

But by the time the park closed, they'd heard nothing.

Dinner that evening was even more downbeat than the previous night. That had at least been buoyed by the gathering-of-the-clans effect of a first night together in Berlin. Tonight, no-one's mind was on food. Porter looked drained and pale, like he'd accidentally squeezed a tube of baby powder in his face. He had to leave early again. Zouche excused himself too, shuffling off with Porter.

"I think Zouche is going to give poor Porter a grilling," smirked Feng.

"Porter didn't stop walking today," said Namita. "I felt so bad for him. I gave up in the end and sat on a park bench and just watched. I feel like the Little Mermaid, so his feet must look like shredded marmalade." She looked around the posh restaurant to make sure no-one was looking and gently massaged her feet.

"You really are serious about Porter's psychic abilities?" said Davidov. "That is what you are relying on? So very strange of you, Miss Pelenot. I have seen some of your programmes. I find it hard to believe that a person who so admirably employs the strategy and technique of a scientist, would go along with this?"

"It has precedent," said Karin. "I believe in God. The essence of the scientific approach is the constant search for evidence and proof. The downside is that you accept that no theory or evidence is immune from scrutiny. In that tiny gap between the two lies the possibility of belief and agnosticism. While you're searching for proofs, you can suspect and hope a theory is true. As Zouche clumsily pointed out, you're wearing a kippah. Are you religious?"

"I am."

"Well then. I don't think you should comment on Porter's psychic abilities until the day you have proven the truth of your own belief in the supernatural. Which, of course, you'll never be able to do. Scientifically."

Davidov smiled and toasted her. "Touché, Ms Pelenot."

"Efrayim, I can say this: I can't explain Porter's powers, but I have seen him do things other people cannot. I have no proof, true, and I'm still asking questions, but..."

"The proof is in the pudding," said Davidov.

"Talking of which..." said Feng, reaching for the menu, a trencherman to the last.

November 26th, 2017
Humboldthain Park, Mitte, Berlin

Feng and Porter arrived at the park at 8am, following a swift breakfast and a quick check of the park map. "I hope we're right about all this," said Porter. "I can't rest until I find at least one of the girls."

"A year ago, I'd have laughed," said Feng. "But I have seen so many strange things since then. I trust your intuition, Porter."

The Gliss, floating around as usual, said he thought they were on the right track. "I don't have any special power to see ahead, but I can feel something. What about you, Porter?"

"I can't tell the difference between wanting it to be so, and it being so," confessed Porter. "Let's move."

Following World War II, the citizens of Berlin had worked hard to restore the 150-year-old park, not just to former glories, but surpassing them. Today's landscaped gardens and open woodland reflected every era of the park's life. Rubble from the bomb-site craters had been used to create a hill.

Feng, who never went anywhere without researching it first on his phone, looked at the hill suspiciously. "I don't know how long it took to move all that rubble, but if Becker buried anyone under there, we'll never get to them."

"Agreed, but its base is very close to the road," argued Porter. "I'm sure the disposal of remains would have taken place as far away from prying eyes as possible. If Rossiter helped dispose of Rose, he was clued up enough to do it right - no-one has ever found her remains. And we have to assume that Becker learnt from that lesson."

They continued methodically working their way through Feng's grid. They eventually came up against the problem of the stunning, hedge-rimmed flower beds.

"What do we do now?" said Feng. "If you start tramping through the foliage, you'll get arrested."

"The beds are relatively small. We'll just have to wait for windows of opportunity when no-one's around. Are you able to scout for us?" he asked The Gliss.

"If I must."

"You too, Feng. It's only going to take me 20 seconds or so to tiptoe around each bed. Just let me know when I can go."

A strange hour followed, in which Feng and The Gliss repeatedly told Porter when he was in the clear, allowing him to hop over the hedges and dance like a fairy through the flower beds. He did his best not to damage the layouts.

Waiting for safe slots of inconspicuousness slowed the day's searches down immensely. After two hours, Porter had only managed to get through six. He was getting very impatient.

"Porter, this is no different from training in St John-at-Hackney's cemetery," said The Gliss. "Be patient."

Feng picked up supplies from a supermarket and they had an impromptu picnic at 1pm.

"You must be knackered, Porter," said Feng, a mouthful of egg mayonnaise cycling around his mouth like porridge in a tombola. "Fizzy?" He offered Porter a swig of Coca-Cola from a bottle.

Porter saw crumbs of egg around the rim and shook his head. "I'm okay. I want to get going again. Besides, it's not the warmest day to have a picnic."

Soon, they were loitering beside another flower bed, waiting for the all-clear.

"Ok, Porter. Be quick - now!" said The Gliss.

The second Porter's feet hit the earth, he felt himself plunging out of this world.

November 26th, 2017
Becker Haus, Mitte, Berlin

Davidov was consulting with one of his crew in a conspiratorial huddle. Karin, who was resting her injuries, studied him from across the room.

He was tall, handsome, well-dressed, but she sensed a coldness - no, wait - ruthlessness, emanating from him. It was like nothing she'd ever experienced before. The others all suspected he was Special Forces, but Karin *knew* he was. Most people's arms fill their sleeves in a nondescript way. She saw perfectly formed biceps appear whenever the black cloth of his polo neck connected with his. She noticed buttocks made of stainless steel, perfectly formed and hard. Real arses were weirdly shaped and flabby. He had the air of an elite athlete. *Special Forces. Definitely.*

Looking at his team, she saw they were all similarly toned, including the women. *Taut. That's the word. They're all so bloody taut. They make me feel like Bella Emberg.* Ruefully accepting the reference to the chubby 70s comic actress dated her, she also realised the Israelis were all incredibly young. None seemed older than 35 - the more junior members, maybe 10 years younger than that.

As she studied them, one of the females hurried excitedly over to her boss. Davidov broke off his conversation, and the group of three pored over her find.

"Anything interesting, Efrayim?" Karin projected across the room.

Davidov, nodding to his colleagues, brought the document over to her. Zouche dragged himself over to muscle in too.

"Ms Pelenot, this is quite a find," he said, showing her the papers.

"You'll have to excuse my schoolgirl German," she said. "What is it?"

"It's a letter in code," said Zouche.

"Yes," said Davidov. "It must have been important to Becker for him to have kept it at all, let alone hidden. Lisa found it tucked inside a sliding drawer on that old clock."

"Will you be able to crack the code?" Karin asked, knowing full well the team in the room were part of a well-funded operation, Israeli government or not.

"Of course," he said. "But the content's not why I think it's important. Time will tell on that score. No, for a man who was so careful to erase his past, this is a big mistake. Can you not see?"

Karin examined the foxed, handwritten letter and envelope. It had no addressee, just an address. Kirchweg 49, Stulln. The postmark wasn't fully legible, but Karin thought it might have been sent in 1942. The coded content was unsigned.

"Unless you can break the code… honestly, I get nothing from this."

"Stulln," said Zouche. "You… crafty little sod."

Davidov smiled. "It is, as they say, a dead giveaway, nein?"

"Is it important?" Karin guessed anything in code might contain secrets, but how could they know before they broke the code?

"Stulln was the site of a concentration camp for a short time during the war," said Davidov.

"1942, if my memory serves," said Zouche.

"Correct, Herr Zouche," said Davidov. "You are a student of these things, like me, nein?"

"Nine, ten, eleven... but I lost my mother, father and brother and countless aunts and uncles in the camps."

"I'm sorry," said Davidov.

"Ancient history," dismissed Zouche.

Karin understood at last. It wasn't what was in the letter - it was where it had been sent to. "Do we know if Hartmann served at Stulln?"

Davidov smiled. "I don't think so, Miss Pelenot. But it was no ordinary concentration camp," Davidov picked up. "Stulln, was a sub-camp. One of a few, dotted around the main camps, to handle overflow etc."

Karin was a fast-thinker. "And I guess you're going to tell me that Stulln was a sub-camp for Flossenbürg?"

"Just so," said Davidov. "I cannot tell at the moment whether the letter was sent to Becker - aka Heinz Hartman - or whether Becker sent it to someone else. We shall soon know."

Namita, butted in. "I see. Only a Nazi could have sent or received it. If you can prove that – even better if you break the code and it mentions Hartmann - it would seal the fate of the estate nicely."

"I think so," said Davidov. "I truly think so. It may just contain trivial information or not, but it goes a long way to proving Becker was Hartmann. If we're to wrest control of his estate for reparations, that's our first task. It all happened before this Tutu Club of yours."

And with that comment, Karin knew the families of the murdered girls would not be benefitting from any future break-up of Becker's estate.

Chapter 51

November 26th, 2017
Humboldthain Park, Mitte, Berlin

Porter slumped to the ground, squashing a great number of flowers in the process. "Leave him!" shouted The Gliss as Feng darted forward to help. "He has to see first."

The bright and nippy 2017 morning dissolved into another time. Porter recognised the vintage of the clothes on the floor instantly. The 80s: the fashions he hated the most. He barely had a second to register this before he registered Becker throttling the life out of a naked young woman on a bed. Porter wanted to throw-up but knew he couldn't or wouldn't until he came back to reality. For now, his eyelids were pinned open by the Quincunx.

The young woman dragged her nails across Becker's arms and face, but he was way bigger than her. He exhibited all the signs of mania - the twisted passion of a zealot, the ruthlessness of a screen monster. Disgusted, Porter realised Becker was still erect, still inside the woman. He was getting off on killing her, mid-rape. The neatly piled clothes by the bed suggested this murder may have begun as a consensual, if reluctant, transaction.

He didn't recognise the woman but was shocked it was happening so late - way past their projected timeline. The last victim they'd heard of was in the early 70s. My God, how long did this go on for?

Breathless, Becker said nothing, concentrating on the strangle. The woman's eyes bulged, and her struggle weakened. Becker began grunting, orgasming as he tightened his stranglehold and the girl's eyes closed for the final time.

The loop began again, but Porter couldn't face watching. With a mighty effort, he pulled his mind from the Quincunx quicksand.

November 26th, 2017
Hotel Adlon Kempinksi, Berlin

The previous few days of disappointment morphed within hours into dilemma.

The group were gathered to watch the evening news. The police phoned to say Porter and Feng had been arrested but would be released shortly. The German police had quickly realised the strange Englishmen really had just *discovered a body*. He would probably have been under-10 at the time of the murder, ruling him out as a suspect. One look at the skeletal remains, an orange leather jacket, and a decayed trainer told them that.

A live news report featured footage of Feng and Porter leaving the police station, covering their faces. Zouche translated for everyone. They all gasped: the reporter named them both. That wasn't the problem. The reporter had good enough police sources to reveal that Porter had claimed to be psychic and had been drawn to the grave.

The gasps turned to groans. They all knew it was his only defence, but knew it must have pained him to tell the police how he'd found the body in the absence of any other plausible reason.

"Now we're in trouble," said Karin, whose first selfish thought was she might get dragged down with Porter. It was well-known in the UK that she and Porter were working together on their World War I doc. Angela Bluebottle would be creaming herself over this news. Karin could almost hear the commissioner gloating: *I told you so - we can dump him now.*

"It is incredible," said Davidov. "Are you sure he did not have inside information?"

"As we've already told you," Namita said, "Porter was drawn there. As you also know, he's been wandering around the park for days. He just needed to stand over a grave."

The German reporter said the Englishman - who'd been in the news in the UK for having made errors that lead to a young girl's death - had implicated the famous German film director, Heinrich Becker, in the murder. The reporter was defensive, and her tone radiated *typical English arrogance and misguided sense of superiority.* Nothing could be less true in Porter's case, but he wasn't writing the report: he was its supremely reluctant subject.

Namita's phone rang. She gestured to the group. It was Porter. After talking for a few minutes, she turned to them. "That was Porter calling from the station," said Namita. "They're free again. He says he doesn't know who the woman is. She was murdered in the 80s."

"The 80s?" groaned Karin. "The last case we had was Tonya Hutchins in 1973?"

"That's right," confirmed Namita. "Maybe The Tutu Club went on much later than we thought. Please God, it's not still going."

"Becker died in 1986," said Davidov. "He was a very old man then."

"Yes, but Crystal, Lascelles and Rossiter weren't dead in the 80s. I feel sick," said Karin.

"They should be back here shortly," Namita was able to confirm, reading a new text from Feng.

When Porter and Feng arrived, there was no sense of jubilation, no display of vindication. Everyone shared Porter's depressing thought that more women died than they had ever imagined. There was still much to be investigated.

"I'm going back to the park tomorrow," said Porter. "I sense we haven't found all the bodies there yet."

"The park's super-close to Becker Haus," said Davidov. "It makes sense he used it for more than one disposal."

No-one could face eating that night.

November 27th, 2017
Humboldthain Park, Mitte, Berlin

They hadn't really thought it through. When they turned up mob-handed the next day to support Porter, the park was still filled with police and cameras.

Marcus Stein, a young reporter from Tagesschau, NDR's evening news show, recognised Porter from yesterday's coverage. Stein grabbed his crew and ran off in pursuit of Porter.

Karin and Namita did their best to ward off the reporter, but the situation spoke for itself: the man who claimed to have found a body through psychic means, was now pacing the same park, methodically.

"He thinks there's another body, ja?" said Stein, excitedly. "Stellen Sie sicher, dass Sie ihn filmen!" he barked at his crew.

"Can't you leave him alone?" said Namita, trying to find words of discouragement. "He's just tired and emotional from yesterday."

"Nein. He's searching, I can tell. Are you his girlfriend?"

"No, I'm not!" said Namita.

"And nor am I, before you ask," said Karin.

"Are you psychics too?" asked Stein.

"Look, just leave him alone," said Karin, accepting no journalist worthy of the name would do so. Stein was worthy of the name and refused to budge.

Later that day, Karin, Namita and Feng, watched in horror as Porter again collapsed to the ground. Each time he fell into the Quincunx, Porter spasmed and squirmed about on the floor. His friends were used to it, but to an outsider it looked like Satanic possession at a Southern Baptist meeting.

"Oh God," whispered Karin, "they're still filming."

The candid footage didn't have quite the impact Karin expected. Tagesschau ended up with two priceless assets: the footage of Porter writhing, as well as fly-on-the-wall footage obtained during the dig, when cops emerged from the tent to say they'd found another skeleton. Cops later confirmed at a press conference that fragments of rag left on the skeleton showed the woman had worn a type of dress common in the 70s.

"Was it her? Was it Rose?" said Namita.

"Perversely, I wish it had been," said Porter. "Sadly, it's another one we don't know about. I've not seen her before. Same MO: she was strangled, while he raped her."

November 28th, 2017
Hotel Adlon Kempinski, Berlin

The next morning, they awoke to find they were splashed all over the German front pages. Every paper carried a screen grab of Porter writhing, accompanied by aggressive headlines.

The Gliss was appalled. "The mission is not supposed to be carried out in public!"

"What can he do about that?" said Feng. "It is what it is."

Davidov, who had turned his *I-can't-believe-it!* knob up a notch since yesterday, gave them some cheer. "Whatever's going on here, the impact is positive. A woman representing Germany's sex workers has praised Porter for doing the work the police did not."

"They weren't sex workers," said Namita. "They were innocent young women sacrificed over a sick man's lust."

"The question is," said Feng, "What now? Surely, you don't intend to go out again? At least try a different park."

"Yes, they won't look for you in those," said Davidov, handing over a copy of one of Becker's photos. "We think this is Schlosspark, Charlottenburg. Also very near to Becker Haus."

"Ok, let's do it," said Porter.

This time they all left together, an incongruous ensemble looking like the world's worst walking tour group. Three hours later, the gang watched as Porter once again collapsed to the floor of a park.

This time, as soon as Porter fell through the worlds, he knew he had found what he was looking for.

It was the snow. He couldn't see it yet, but he sensed it was freezing. He passed through the glass of a window like an Orson Welles' tracking shot, ironically, only to see a bare film studio floor.

In the middle of it, a much younger Becker was sitting naked on the floor. Tied to a post in front of him, naked, eyes wide-open with fear, Rose Prideaux sat shivering in the cold. Porter would have done anything to break into the room to kill Becker, but these were only shadows of the past - Rose's last unchangeable moments. She was screaming. Becker did not care. He knew he was the only other person in the building.

"Why don't you call for your nigger father," said Becker. "You filthy piece of shit."

Whatever happened next, Porter vowed never to speak the details to anyone else. It was the only dignity he could give her back, the privacy of death. Porter could only make out the one word amongst the animal howls. "Mum." He felt sick.

Bored, Becker produced a pistol from the floor. Porter's heart pounded. He tried to look away. But Porter was gifted, and cursed, with a wide-angle view and there was no way for him to avert his eyes.

Becker used his left hand to point the gun at Rose's head and his right hand to masturbate. Grunting as he came, he chose that moment to pull the trigger. Rose's pain stopped instantly, just as Porter's began.

Feng pulled Porter clear and they were all shocked to see him sobbing more deeply than ever before, his hands covering his face. He retched and sat, his arms around his legs. Rocking, Porter said, over and over, "I'm so sorry, Rose. I'm so sorry."

Chapter 52

December 14th, 2017
Chartwell House, Surrey

The gang were trying to de-compress and Karin was hosting them.

They had a lot to think about. The German media had dubbed them The Irrationals. By the time Porter had found 11 bodies, newspapers all over the world were covering the mounting death toll in Berlin. Agency photos had shown an exhausted Porter tirelessly pacing the parks of Berlin. On the days he found a corpse, he'd often been pictured wriggling about on the ground. Reporters picked up The Irrationals moniker, and the gang all knew they were now stuck with it.

Aside from the painful ridicule, his ability to find bodies opened him and the gang up to suspicion and curiosity. Neither had been welcome. However, despite extensive police interviews, the ages of Porter, Feng, Karin and Namita conclusively ruled them out of any involvement in the murders. Zouche could have been a problem, but the German cops were quick to establish Zouche had never travelled to Germany - not many Jews did in the years after the war. Under questioning, none of them had felt able to explain how they knew about the bodies, so they'd been forced to tell the truth: Porter had psychic abilities. It opened them up to ridicule, but they'd seen no other way. LA's Cold Case team had fed the story further by revealing Porter had alerted them to seven bodies in Morrie Crystal's Mission.

At the age of 47, after a year of mishaps and misfortune, Porter unexpectedly found himself a celebrity. Twitter and social media platforms were full of comment. Most saw him and his fellow Irrationals as outrageous frauds. Just as many others were delighted their own beliefs in psychic ability appeared to be confirmed by this diffident Englishman, who refused to do any interviews.

Netflix, Amazon, the BBC and Fox, approached Porter to offer TV series. The offers were all basically the same: "Let's do Time Team for dead people." Porter turned them all down. He knew they would be joke shows, designed to make them all look stupid.

Karin was mortified. She had the most to lose, career-wise, being seen as an advocate of someone who believed in the supernatural. Yet, she fought to overcome her embarrassment because she believed in the work they were doing. And she realised the gang were also her friends.

Once Gavan approached Interpol, various Cold Case teams in Italy, France, Germany, America and Britain pooled resources. They examined the methods and scope of The Tutu Club. Once news of the club became public, other women came forward. They were the "lucky" ones - abused before Rose Prideaux's murder changed Tutu's remit.

Eventually, the authorities identified 35 women. This included survivors, including the first, Susan Lucero, an escort gang-raped by the directors at the Venice Film Festival, and the last-known murder, Darlene Gore, who turned up on Arnie Flax's list.

Questioned by Gavan, Rossiter had refused to say a word and no relevant remains had ever been found in London. Neither Crystal nor Lascelles were able to make confessions, but the LA police assumed all the bodies they found in The Mission were the work of either/both men. The German cops' working hypothesis was that all 11 Berlin bodies were the work of Becker.

Eventually, by examining travel records for 22-year-old actresses who'd visited more than two of the key cities, Porter's team were appalled to read the final (though not definitive) international count.

The list of women, their home cities and fates, made for grim reading.

Name	City	Fate
Susan Lucero	LA	Venice Film Festival 1964.
Chiara Marino	Italy	
Valentina Ricci	Rome	
Petra Schafer	Dusseldorf	
Sandra O'Connell	NYC	
Cate Arnaud	Paris	
Anita Kendrick	NYC	
Shelly Bland	LA	
Sally Graham	Leicester	
Anja Braun	Munich	
Regina Kruger	Berlin	
Lucy Pelling	London	
Dana Schulman	NYC	
Mel Hart	LA	
Jules Aubert	Dijon	
Kerstin Schmitz	Berlin	
Valeria Greco	Rome	
Ursa Fielding	Bristol	
Cathy Galvan	NYC	
Sherri Meeks	LA	
Bettina Kaiser	Cologne	
Rose Prideaux	Bristol	Murdered by Becker
Beate Lang	Berlin	Murdered by Becker
Tamara Helms	LA	Murdered by Lascelles/Crystal?
Bella Tompkinson.	Bristol	Murdered by Lascelles/Crystal?
Monika Vogel	Munich	Murdered by Rossiter?
Grace Tilling	Luton	Murdered by Rossiter?

It appeared the Club was suspended while Rossiter served two years in prison for tax evasion, Jan 4th, 1970 - Jan 3rd, 1972.

Heidi Ludwig	Berlin	Murdered by Becker
Angie Dell	London	Murdered by Lascelles/Crystal?
Myra McLeod	Aberdeen	Murdered by Rossiter?
Tonya Hutchins	LA	Murdered by Lascelles/Crystal?
Tammy Lake	LA	Murdered by Lascelles/Crystal?
Nicole Kramer	Berlin	Murdered by Becker
Lori Hatcher	Anaheim	Murdered by Rossiter
Ruth Shelby	Ipswich	Murdered by Becker
Tina Dye	LA	Murdered by Lascelles/Crystal?
Amy Lockhart	Tucson	Murdered by Becker
Astrid Gross	Malmo	Murdered by Becker
Rhonda Tatum	LA	Murdered by Lascelles/Crystal?
Brigitte Busch	Berlin	Murdered by Rossiter
Molly Patrick	London	Murdered by Becker
Denise Redhead	Brighton	Murdered by Lascelles/Crystal?
Unidentified	Berlin?	Murdered by Becker
Robin Blanton	Monterey	Murdered by Lascelles/Crystal?
Wanda Simms	LA	Murdered by Becker
Polly-Laura Helt	London	Murdered by Rossiter
Justine Dale	London	Murdered by Lascelles/Crystal?
Penny Morrison	NYC	Murdered by Lascelles/Crystal?
Darlene Gore	LA	Murdered by Becker

Feng, who was chronicling the results of their investigation, whistled as he typed the last name up. He thought for a second and added a note.

At the time of writing, one of the bodies found in Berlin remains unidentified. Likewise, while LA police believe Lascelles/Crystal were responsible for at least 11 murders, only seven sets of remains have been found. The search for Tamara Helms, Angie Dell, Tonya Hutchins and Rose's friend, Bella - whose disappearances all pre-dated Crystal's purchase of The Mission - will continue. We can't rule out further names coming to light as the various police investigations roll forward.

Feng wandered into the living room of Karin's house. Porter was sitting alone on the veranda of Chartwell House looking at the Ashbright Tree which had played such an important role in their previous case. Porter had grown very quiet and introverted over the past few weeks. Namita, Feng and Karin watched him from inside the house with a mixture of love and pity.

The Gliss appeared.

"Look who it is. Porter's outside," said Feng.

"I'm not here to talk to Porter. I want to talk with you three," said The Gliss.

"Oh, we exist now, do we?" said Namita.

"Yes, you exist. I've been in his head. He's not in a good place. He's seen an awful lot of death recently."

"Yes, we know," said Karin. "What can we do for him?"

"You get him back on his feet and help him. You haven't finished yet," said The Gliss. "Porter has to speak to Sam Brownlees. It will be painful, but it will help him recover."

"Sam or Porter?" said Feng.

"Both," said The Gliss.

"Oh no," said Namita. "Not LA again?"

"You can't do it by phone. You must all do it in person," said The Gliss.

"I've been wondering how to break the news to Sam," admitted Namita. "He hasn't called me, so I suspect he hasn't read about it in the papers. What do you think, Feng? Karin?"

They groaned. Feng said, "I'll book the tickets."

Chapter 53

December 14th, 2017
Atwater Village, LA

For any Brit, Christmas in Los Angeles is a strange experience. The sun is out and people are wearing t-shirts, yet White Christmas and Jingle Bells are playing over every Tannoy. The four friends sat in a coffee shop on Los Feliz Boulevard, steeling themselves for what would be a difficult conversation.

"I'll do it, if you like," volunteered Namita. "He is my client after all."

"I've spent more time with him, but I'm happy for you to do it," said Karin.

"Porter, don't you think it should be you?" said Feng.

"Let's all do it together," said Porter. "I could do with the support."

Sam Brownlees was clearly nervous to see them. Had he already heard? He looked smaller than when they last saw him. "Well, I guess the doctors are here to deliver a gippy diagnosis," was all he said.

Porter, flooded with empathy, turned to the others. "It's ok. I got this. I can see it's my job after all."

The others peering through a window, saw Porter go down on his knees, take Sam's hand and hand him a tissue as the old man cried for the daughter he'd never met.

Twenty minutes later, Porter re-appeared. "He wants to see you all."

"I'm so sorry, Sam," said Karin. "I wish there was more we could have done."

"You think this news is bad? I already knew. Knew since 1968 at least. But I didn't *know*. And that can kill a man as surely as a gun, Miss. No, you've released me. For the first time in 50 years, I feel free. Sad to my corns, but free."

No-one knew what to say. Sam broke his own silence. "I've been thinking hard about this for a week, ever since you told me you were coming over. I know what to do. I haven't got but days left now. It was only the pain keeping me awake, I see that now.

"There's a church round the corner, Christ's Church at Griffiths Park. You need to take me there one last time. I've spoken to my carers. They understand. They're finding a wheelchair for me."

Namita, remembering their first conversation, asked Sam if they could take him to his wife's grave, so he could lay a rose on it.

"I think I'll be giving her the next rose in person, Miss, but thank you for the offer. Thank you for the offer."

Within half an hour, they were approaching the pink church. When they were just a block away, Sam asked them to halt. "Would it be okay if Porter pushes me the final block? Join us inside in 10 minutes. I got something to say to this young man."

As Porter took control of the wheelchair, watched on by the others hanging back, Sam thanked him again. "I saw the newspaper stories, son. I know what you did. Do you know how important it was for me, for Flo, for poor Rose, to get some justice?"

"I tried my best," said Porter, embarrassed.

"No, that's not good enough. Are you religious?"

"No, Sam. I'm not."

"But you're doing God's work."

Porter had no idea whose work he was doing. "I don't know about that. There's been tragedy in my family too. Finding justice for others is me atoning for their tragedy."

"When we get back to the home, we'll be met by my solicitor and the head of the care home. I'll be dead within the week, Porter. I can feel the life flowing out from me. All the pain did was plug me up. Now you've cleared it, I haven't got long."

"I'm sure you'll be fine, Sam," lied Porter.

"Sssshh, son. I'm going to make over my entire estate to you and your friends. You must continue this work."

"But Sam! I can't take your money!"

"You can and you will. It's already drawn up. We just need to witness it when we get back. Sometime, somewhere, look at a church and think of me and my Rose. Do good, son."

Porter wanted to cry, but instead wheeled Sam to the front of the church and put the brakes on.

"I'm fine here. You sit at the back and wait for your friends. Don't tell them about the will. I want it to be a surprise. Don't want the witnesses thinking you've forced me into it. Thank you, Porter."

The will was signed, dated and witnessed, to the amazement of the others. Sam asked if there was any cake in the home. His nurse, tearing up, went to find some.

"I don't know what to say, Sam," said Karin. "Sam, I promise we'll put the money to good use. But hopefully we won't get it for some time to come."

"Karin, I wouldn't bet your breeches on that," said Sam.

Sam Brownlees died that night. The nurse called Porter at their hotel. No-one said anything. Even The Gliss was on mute. Feng fumbled in his case and brought out a flask of whiskey. He poured each of them a small nip into white plastic cups.

"To Sam, Florence and Rose," said Feng.

"God bless you," said Karin.

"Rest in Peace," said Namita.

Porter downed his whisky in one go. "The question is: What now?"

The silence was deafening.

THE END

Postscript

Dalisay was rescued from her life as a modern-day slave and given a place in a women's refuge in Holloway. Namita took on her case, ensuring she was well treated.

Rossiter was sentenced to life in prison. He is expected to die there. During the criminal investigation, various financial irregularities emerged, and his daughter was prosecuted for tax evasion.

Zouche was given a ticking off by his care home but shocked everyone when he announced he'd had enough and was moving out. With his remaining savings he was able to rent a small flat and employ a part-time carer. Once the gang received Sam's bequest, they helped Zouche furnish it in payment for his help on both cases.

Karin's wounds healed well, and she brought in some specialist researchers from SOAS to help her finish the documentary on slavery, angled towards Sam's story. The British Library and The Smithsonian both asked Karin if she would deposit the interview tapes with them. Her film, Un-making of a Slave, would eventually win a BAFTA for her and Channel 4.

Feng spent a few thousand quid turning the Murder Room into a state-of-the-art office on the assumption there would be more cases. He installed secret cameras to ensure the room was safe from interference next time. He also began writing up their first two cases. Now that they were in the public eye, people ought to know what really happened.

Tim and Sophie did a special from their sofa claiming credit for kickstarting Karin's appeal. Dame Susan Wills appeared as a guest to talk about her 60s' experiences.

Skelling attempted to apologise to Namita, but she blocked his number. Karin had given her some much-needed work, but Namita realised she might have a full-time job just keeping an eye on the others now that they were official (and funded) thanks to Sam's bequest.

Dan Crawley remains suspended. The inquiry into his involvement in the Soho shooting continues. Phelps recovered from his injury and submitted a witness statement on Crawley's behalf.

Porter bought a batch of 78rpms from eBay and set about restoring them.

Karin, however, did something sneaky. She entered into secret negotiations with Netflix. They had made her another very tempting offer after their first crass attempt: would she and Porter look into the murder of JFK? A psychic investigation of the most famous political assassination of the 20th century?

On balance, if she could persuade Porter, Karin thought, "Why not?"

Porter and the gang will return.

If you enjoyed this book, please consider leaving a review.
The more people who review a book, the better chance it has to find more readers.

Book 3 in this series will be out in 2021.

To stay up to date and to find out more about my other work, please visit desburkinshaw.com

You can also email me:
info@magnificent.tv

Or find me on Facebook and Twitter.

Acknowledgements

In my first job as a journalist in east London, I interviewed many criminals from the 60s, sometimes going for drinks or breakfasts with them: Ray the Cat, Mad Frankie Fraser, Charlie Kray. Drawing on those chats and the many books I've read, I've done my best to capture some of that world in this story. If you find their words offensive – you should. But believe me, I heard worse back in the 90s.

Just in case you are curious: this book was plotted in November-December 2019 and drafted between January and March 2020. The BLM protests and lockdown were not even on the horizon during the principal plotting and writing.

Quite a lot of people helped me get this book over the line, and I want to thank them for their encouragement, their time, their offers of accommodation, and their feedback. A special thanks go to Debi Alper, my editor, for her feedback and suggestions - virtually all of which I took on board.

Without my LA posse, James and Dana Childs, Tania Saylor-Godard and Paul Saylor, Keith Barrows, Kerry Michelle, I wouldn't have been able to research in person.

I'm so grateful to my UK friends, Sofia Ullah Khatun, Michelle Tuft-Smith, Bethan Cole, John Armstrong, Simon Lawrence, Christopher Travers, Vicky Cepel, Mark Powley, Melinda Waugh, Gill Hall, Gilly Hewer, Chris and Cheryl Wood, Josh Davis, Astrid Keogh, Jo Daykin, Nazli Alizadeh-Shepperd, and many others who fed back, bought me coffee, and blew enough smoke up my backside to get me over the line.

Thanks to Canan from Venetia's coffee shop on Chatsworth Road for the writing space - until lockdown forced me back home.

Most of all, I have to thank my family who literally sat for hours listening to me talk about plotting, plots and plotters without hitting me once. Terry and Wendy Yea were incredibly generous. My siblings, Tim, Beck, Chris, Mum and Phill - all helped me with words, money, and/or kindness. And my long-suffering wife, Shazna, and my daughter, Zizi, have given me space, time, permissions and encouragement that can never be repaid.

Des Burkinshaw

A final thanks to Anna Bazyl for the sleeve design. www.fiverr.com/annabazyl

Printed in Great Britain
by Amazon

THE
OF
THE HEART
(Kuntres Maarat Ha-Lev)

A Treatise on Jewish Contemplative Prayer

Nachman Davies
Tzfat
2022

Copyright © 2022 NachmanDavies

All rights reserved.

ISBN: 9798837112690

בס"ד

DEDICATION

To my Friends and Teachers
and for the aliyah of the soul of
R'Aryeh ben Tzvi zt"l
who was both.

CONTENTS

Acknowledgments	i
Preface	p1
Frontispiece	p2
The Invitation	p14
The Shema	p15
The Internet	p21
The Contemplatives	p24
Receptive Prayer	p31
The Voice	p36
Standing before G-d	p48
Prophecy	p56
Glossary	p61
About the Author	p65

ACKNOWLEDGMENTS

My thanks are due to
R'David Sears in New York,
to **Mr. Solomon Garson** in London,
and to **Mr. Prosper Edery** in Torremolinos
without whose support this book could not have been published.

PREFACE

Judaism is a religion of action. It is highly communal and it places great importance on shared community worship. It values the family unit with passionate zeal, and it is fundamentally devoted to the nurturing and education of children.

So what do you do if you are single, without a partner or family? What do you do if you are old and without known living relatives? What do you do if you live far away from any Jewish community centre? What do you do if you want to be as observant as possible in your love of G-d but experience alienation in social interaction through unavoidable circumstances, disability, or illness? What do you do if you are Jewish but feel called to solitary living and want to live in constant intimacy with G-d?

The Cave of the Heart (Kuntres Maarat Ha-Lev) was written in 2005 to address some of those questions. It generated the author's personal experiment in intentionally solitary contemplative living, three *Jewish Contemplatives* websites, and it also became the basis of a much longer book entitled *The Mitkarevim: Jewish Contemplatives and the Return of Prophecy*.

Much of the original 2005 *kuntres* was concerned with promoting community outreach *via* the internet, an activity that has since emerged and is now flourishing. This publication is an attempt to restate the core of that *Kuntres Maarat Ha-Lev* without those elements that are now redundant or obsolete. It describes a very simple method of contemplative receptive prayer and outlines the reasons why the author believes such prayer to be both timely and crucial. It was written especially for intentionally dedicated Jewish Contemplatives—*Mitkarevim* (those who would 'draw near' to G-d in intimate service)— but it speaks to all those who wish to encounter the Divine in their contemplative prayer.

The Kuntres Maarat Ha-Lev Frontispiece

This graphic was drawn by the author in 1992 and later became the frontispiece to the original kuntres in 2005

The Supernal Torah cries out:

"Happy is the man who listens to me, eagerly at my gates every day, waiting at the posts of my doors, For he who finds me finds life, and finds favour before G-d" *(Proverbs 8:34)*

The 'point' of the Maarat Ha-Lev is at the threshold of the arch. It is a point of focus in the distance (the transcendent) and simultaneously it is a point of focus inside us (the immanent).

-That point inside us is represented by the star-light inside the Magen David...

-The same point appears as the Larger Light present at the heart of the graphic, between the outstretched wings.

-Whether it is behind or infront of the arch is ambiguous: it represents the threshold of the expanded consciousness which is everywhere...

-The two angelic Elyonim are guardians, witnesses, silent worshipers.

-They are symbols of the event taking place, marking the point of intersection.

-They are the keruvim of the ark and the lights of Shabbat.

-Lights who are also called Shamor and Zachor, Yachin and Boaz.

וְהָיוּ
הַדְּבָרִים הָאֵלֶּה
אֲשֶׁר אָנֹכִי מְצַוְּךָ הַיּוֹם
עַל־לְבָבֶךָ

And these words which
I command you today
shall be upon your heart.
(Deuteronomy 6:6)

The Cave of the Heart (Maarat Ha-Lev) is the 'place' or 'state of meeting' in which the contemplative Jew encounters the Divine. Our sages tell us that

"G-d is the place (Makom) of the world but the world is not His place."
Bereshit Rabbah 68:10

Every created thing is *in* Him, and yet His Essential Being could not possibly be contained by creation. He cannot be grasped, delineated, or limited and yet He is *in* every thing and sustains all created life moment by moment. *Ein od milvado*— There is nothing but G-d. He is everywhere.

The *Cave of the Heart* is a 'place' which is beyond time and space yet we can feel momentarily drawn into it when we experience a wonder of Nature, or when we are drawn into the gaze of a *tzaddik*. When we see the light of heaven in the eyes, or the face, or the actions of such a righteous person— we are standing at the mouth of that cave looking in.

When we attempt to meet G-d in private, on a one-to-one basis, so to speak, we are being drawn into that cave. When we enter it in the contemplative prayer of attentiveness, we can become vehicles for the Presence of G-d. The *Shekhinah* then prays through us and thereby, each of us can attain a close intimacy with the Divine; with the rest of *Knesset Yisrael* (the Community of Israel); and with *Kol ha-Olam* (all creation).

-Why do I call it a cave *of the Heart*?

The heart of something is its essential core, its deepest generative impulse, the source of its vitality. It is the spiritual faculty—the *spiritual organ,* as it were—of intimate knowledge and intuition. Its manner of understanding is both supernatural and supra-rational yet it is not divorced from either intellect or common sense.

It is a spiritual cave in the heart of each individual soul, and simultaneously in the Heart of our G-d.

-Why do I call it a *Cave*?

A cave is a place of shelter and security. It is also a home base. It is a place of quiet and intimate retreat. It has two highly significant elements: *the interior* of the Cave which is enclosed and introverted, and *the threshold* which opens out onto another world.

The Cave of which I speak is to be found in our own deepest soul-chamber within the Heart of our G-d.

For this reason it is also possible to experience it, simultaneously, in its unlimited and polarised forms: We can find a second threshold to an interior world inside G-d from the deepest part of the interior of the cave itself and, with our backs turned (as it were) to the cave's opening, and with our senses totally in the dark, find ourselves somehow lifted into *His World*.

The *Cave of the Heart* thus has a threshold which stands between contemplation and the created and temporal world, and another hidden threshold (between the *olam hazeh* and the *olam haba)*[1] which is where the individual soul can 'know' G-d intimately. The more we allow our ego to dissolve into the Divine, the more these two states/thresholds blur into one.

---

[1] The *Olam Hazeh* is the plane of our mundane daily existence, the *Olam Habah* is the plane of Eternity, the world of Heaven.

The *Cave of the Heart* is the place in which we stand during the *Amidah* [2] when we daven formally; the state into which we enter when we are sitting in silent focussed *hitbonenut (meditation/contemplation)*; and it is the secret place in our minds when we are walking in the midst of crowds or going about automatic tasks with our minds on G-d.

It is the state of consciousness in which Eliyahu haNavi heard the 'still small voice'—with his senses shielded by his mantle and standing on the threshold between the worlds.[3] Paradoxically, it is often only when we retire deep into the Divine shelter in solitary prayer that we can view things as they really are.

It is the state of awareness which strips away the veil that hides other worlds from our everyday vision. It is the state of *mochin d'gadlut* (expanded consciousness) in which we can hear the hidden melody of a true reality that suddenly emerges from within the mundane— momentarily but long enough for us to have been given the profound (if obscure) certainty that what we have seen or heard is not illusion but truth. It is a reflection of the Holy of Holies in the Heavenly Jerusalem, and an archetypal descendent of the Tent of Meeting. It may even be the generator of the Third Temple.

This all sounds very grand. It is. And what is more: the miracle of the *Cave of the Heart* is that it is open-all-hours; it is open to everyone and not just to an elite few—and it is much more

---

[2] The *Amidah* is the central prayer of the daily services, performed standing, it contains eighteen/nineteen blessings.

[3] I Kings 19:12: "And after the fire there came a still small voice. And when Eliyahu heard it, he wrapped his face in his mantle and went out, and stood at the mouth of the cave."

easily encountered than one might think.

The 'World which is to come' is not in the future. It is the moment which is now.

The day on which 'G-d is one and His Name shall be one' is here right now— if we would only *listen*.

How can anyone listen to G-d personally?

How can anyone meet Him in prayer?

Nobody can see Him and live.

Any perception we may have of Him comes heavily screened.

In Jewish texts, the Name of G-d—the *Shem Havayah*— is composed of the four letters Y-H and V-H. This name is never pronounced but is read as '*Ado-nai' (Lord)*. It was pronounced the way it is written but once a year by the High Priest in the Temple of Jerusalem at the most solemn moment of the liturgy on Yom Kippur, the Day of Atonement. The fact that it is a mysterious and 'unpronounceable' Name emphasises our acceptance that we can never comprehend the Divine Essence.

However much we might try to philosophise, there is always a feeling of utter helplessness in delineating or accurately expressing *any* concept of G-d's nature.

The unfolding revelation of the Name from the midst of the burning bush *(*Exodus:2*)*; at the Giving of the Torah on Sinai (Exodus:20*)*; and the inner vision of HaShem's[4] glory from the cleft in the rock (Exodus:33*)* are personal as well as ancestral

---

[4] *HaShem* means 'The Name" and is also a way of referring to G-d.

or community revelations of the Divine – and they are given to us as models of our relationship with G-d in prayer.

We are invited to remember that, simultaneously, we are standing *before* G-d and also that we are *in* G-d. He is the Existence which fills all Creation. At Sinai we are commanded to hear His Voice daily and at every moment. In the Cleft of the Rock we are told of His Attributes so that we may emulate them, but we are also being shown a reflection of His perpetually creative activity in this world. The Attributes are there for us to feel with our intuitive hearts as much as to philosophise about, despite the cloud of unknowing thrown about any attempt to grasp His Name cognitively. They are a revelation but their enigmatic and elusive form is their beauty.

Our kabbalistic tradition has formulated many beautiful and complex prayers and meditations composed around the *Shem Havayah* and around the permutations of this and other 'Names' of G-d. They are all above my pay-grade, as it were. I have similarly been dazzled and gripped by lines extracted from the *Zohar* but almost all the classical forms, analyses, and systems of kabbalistic meditation are just too complex and intellectual for me. They may well be so for you too. If you are reading this book hoping for some insight into such meditational techniques you will be disappointed— what I am sharing in this book is extremely simple.

There is presumption here.

I'm convinced that there is a simple way for those needing a kind of spiritual minimalism. It is a path I have been walking for many decades and, having given it a good try and found it to be meaningful, I simply want to share it. I have the trepidation of a Bar-Mitzvah boy in making it public here but my instinct tells me there are others out there who may actually need to read these words. It is a method for those who are fired by what can only be described as an ache to be connected to G-d and to be of use to Him, but whose psychological or intellectual inadequacies make the ascent of Mount Carmel or Mount Horeb necessary by a less travelled side-path. It is a simple path, but in no sense is it an easy short cut—and travelling on it can often be boringly uneventful.

The kabbalists refer to G-d as *'Ein Sof'*—This term is sometimes translated as 'the Infinite' or 'The Endless' and it also indicates that the Essence of the Divine is beyond description. Ultimately we can never understand or grasp even this concept, let alone the Supreme Being/Necessary Existent that it attempts to describe—but contemplative prayer is a way of developing our awareness of being in It, part of It, and crucially with respect to our role in creation— a receptacle and channel of It. Individually.

This awareness can arise in highly charged moments, come and gone as swiftly as the brief appearance of light on a cloud-darkened sea. It can also grow imperceptibly at an agonizingly slow and apparently uneventful pace, to emerge like a crystal, revealing something which was actually there all along. Like the breath of a breeze it may come as a once in a lifetime momentary shift in perspective after which our memory of it is our only *manna*. Or it may not be 'felt' at all and only be sensed in its results.

Anyone who approaches G-d in contemplation becomes painfully aware of the dynamic tension caused by His distance while simultaneously feeling His immanent personal action ever more deeply in the heart. The unpronouncable *Shem Havayah* is, as it were, the embodiment of this dynamic tension—not on parchment, not in a devotional *shiviti* graphic,[5] but in a part of our soul which is made pregnant by contemplative awareness. As indicated in the *Aleinu*, it is a Name that we are required to 'make One'.[6]

There is a sense in which we can enter into this state of contemplative awareness every time we pray with *kavanah* (intentional focus) and there is a sense in which we need to enter into some form of solitary retreat if we are to feel its true depth and if we are to listen with the profound attentiveness asked of us in the *Sh'ma*.[7] In the paragraphs that follow I will suggest a way to do this.

The term *Olam/Alam* comes from a root implying concealment and hiddenness. It also signifies 'the World', 'all Creation', 'Eternity', and 'Time'.

G-d is often referred to as *Ribono shel Olam*, as the Master of '*Olam*', with all the shades of meaning I have just described. G-d is the Master of All Time.

Since early childhood I have never been quite convinced that time was anything but an illusion. As I age, the relativity and flexibility of time and space seems to have become more fact than theory. I am not sure if this is because I have

---

[5] *Shiviti*: The *shiviti* is a popular meditational text that may appear at the top of a siddur page or on a calligraphic plaque. It almost always bears the Divine Name.

[6] *Aleinu:* Concluding prayer of formal services whose last line reads: Then the L-rd shall be king over all the earth,on that day the L-rd shall be One and His name One.' (Zechariah:14)

[7] *Sh'ma:* A prayerful statement found inside the *tefilin* and also recited daily in public and private. Texts are from: Deuteronomy 6, Deuteronomy 11,and Numbers 15. The word *'sh'ma'* can be translated as 'listen', 'hear', or 'understand'.

accumulated experience of the 'hidden' supernatural world over the years, or whether it is simply because I am ageing and thus, as it were, nearer to death—a state in which personal time and space becomes irrelevant.

When one undertakes a period of extended solitary retreat in silence, it is not long before time starts bending, slowing down, and sometimes, to all intents and purposes: stopping.

In a contemplative retreat, the moment which is the present becomes, as it were, slower or even suspended — while the progress of the minutes in an hour, the hours in a day, and of the days in a week, seems to accelerate. This phenomenon is also familiar to those whose observance of Shabbat is so complete that its twenty-five hours can seem to have been almost momentary when one reaches *Havdalah* time.[8]

Being able to wallow in this kind of time transcendence is a precious luxury denied to all save the solitary contemplative. Most readers will have babies to feed, businesses to maintain, agendas to prepare and deadlines to meet. But I have an unproven theory (unproven save in my personal experience) that once you have experienced even a short moment of such time transcendence—others follow. Just one really deep period of such an experience can somehow be recalled in the midst of everyday bustle, though it might need a periodic topping-up.

It can not only be recalled, it can sometimes break in to our consciousness unannounced. Revelation often comes as an unexpected surprise when G-d descends upon us without an appointment to catch us off-guard, in what often seems to be

---

[8] *Havdalah*: the ritual concluding ceremony at the end of each Shabbat.

an act undertaken with a sort of Divine sense of humour.

This is one of the reasons I claim that encountering the Cave of the Heart is easier than one might have expected, and it is not necessarily the exclusive experience of those who enjoy periods of extended retreat.

These moments of epiphany might come out of the blue, but they can be so momentous that they are generators of a relationship that lasts a lifetime, and beyond. They are to a person's life as Shabbat is to the other days in a week—They are a foretaste of the *Olam Haba*—the beyond life which is ever present though concealed.

They are the appointed times in our spiritual life that the world of G-d's immanence can somehow receive some element of His transcendence.

I should mention here that I have written of 'moments'. The reader should understand that such moments may last a second, minutes, and even hours when reckoned in chronological time. This will have implications later when you see that the method of prayer which I am about to outline takes place at a still-point in time which is immeasurable.

The Invitation

It begins as a gentle but insistent sense that He is giving us an invitation to meet Him.

So simple, and yet so easily ignored or discounted as being merely our imagination— hence His insistence.

It is not a special gift for the chosen—it is an invitation for everyone— It just embarrasses us to admit that we sense it. Possibly out of personal reticence, or maybe and quite justifiably, we are simply rather afraid of it and its implications.

We can find many excuses to ignore the invitation, or postpone its acceptance, or face its momentous consequences— It is however, an invitation to share in the kind of listening and attentiveness which is the most essential part of the *tikkun* process: the process of personal and universal redemption that all Israel is commanded to proclaim each day when we recite the *Sh'ma*.[9]

The first verse of the *Sh'ma* is perhaps our most fundamental and cherished commandment, and it is a command that we should listen, be attentive, and understand:

---

[9] In *Mishneh Torah 1:2*, the Rambam instructs us that the commandment refers to the Unity of G-d: 'a fundamental principal on which everything else is based.'

שְׁמַע יִשְׂרָאֵל יְיָ אֱלֹהֵינוּ יְיָ אֶחָד

LISTEN ISRAEL, Y-H&V-H IS OUR G-D, Y-H&V-H IS ONE

In the congregational recitation of the *Sh'ma*, focus on performing this type of hearing/listening can be rather difficult but by no means impossible. From within the Cave of the Heart in individual prayer it can become a contemplative event in itself. There it becomes more of an action or a process than a text to be recited.

Responding to the invitation to 'know before Whom we stand' and to listen to what He might have to say can best be done in solitude.[10] It feels very personal, even though the One inviting is not a person. All very paradoxical—but less so if you let Him take the lead.

To do this, one has to clear an internal space and make oneself ready to be receptive: One can do this best in solitude of one form or another. Solitary contemplative and meditative prayer is well documented in the Hebrew Bible, and has been practised in all stages of Jewish history.

Perhaps the most typically Jewish use of solitude as a religious discipline is when it is used in regular periods of secluded meditation whose duration is measured in just hours, or even minutes.

---

[10] *Know before Whom you stand:*— "Be careful of the honour of your colleagues; restrain your children from superficial recitation, and seat them between the knees of the disciples of the wise; *and when you pray, know before Whom you stand ;* and by doing so you will be worthy of the life of the World Beyond." *(Berachot 28b)*

R' Avraham Abulafia (1240-1291) writes:

> Choose a special place for yourself where your voice will not be heard. Meditate alone with no-one else present. If you engage in this by day do so in a darkened room. It is best if you do this at night.[11]

The same practice is recommended by R' Chayim Vital (1542-1620):

> You should be in a room by yourself ... It should be a place where you will not be distracted by the sound of human voices or the chirping of birds. The best time to do this is shortly after midnight.[12]

The practice of such solitary prayer is especially dear to the followers of R' Nachman of Breslov (1772-1810) who used the word *hitbodedut* to denote a form of informal prayer in solitude to be practiced on a daily basis by Jews of every type and spiritual capability. Here are two short examples of his advice on this:

> It is also necessary that you should meditate in an isolated place. It should be outside the city, or on a lonely street, or some other place where other people are not found ... You must therefore be alone, at night on an isolated path where people are not usually found. Go there and meditate...[13]

> Hitbodedut meditation is the best and the highest level of worship. Set aside an hour or more each day to

---

[11] *Chayei Olom HaBah*, trans. R' Aryeh Kaplan in *'Meditation and Kabbalah'*, page 107, (*Samuel Weiser, York Beach, Maine, 1982*)

[12] *Shaarei Kedushah*, trans. R' Aryeh Kaplan in *'Meditation and Kabbalah,'* page 197.

[13] *Likutey Moharan I:52*, trans. R' Aryeh Kaplan in *'Meditation and Kabbalah,'* page 310.

meditate, in the fields or in a room, pouring out your thoughts to G-d ... Every person can express his own thoughts, each according to his own level. You should be very careful with this practice, accustoming yourself to do it at a set time each day.[14]

However, I use the term *hitbodedut* according to its more ancient and classical usage by Jewish Mystics. In that context, the word has two meanings: (i) an act of physical seclusion in a solitary retreat or (ii) meditation or contemplation by an individual in private.

In common modern usage the term *hitbodedut* is most often used to describe the specific kind of solitary devotion practiced by the Breslover Hasidim. That form of *hitbodedut* is also an act founded on the desire for an intimate connection with the Divine, but its focus is usually upon acts of joyous praise or upon the sharing and elevation of the troubled thoughts and difficult experiences of the one praying. As such, it is more a matter of informal and spontaneous petition and expression than a form of contemplative prayer, and it is very often highly vocal.

The kind of contemplative prayer that I am advocating in this book is a much more *receptive* activity, and it comes somewhere between the discursive *hitbodedut* of the Breslover and the *hitbonenut* (silent meditation) of one seeking spiritual illumination. Consequently the focus is not on the outpouring of one's soul before G-d, but on developing a kind of attentiveness of the mind that (as it were) opens a window or door in the soul for the Divine Breath to enter.

---

[14] *Likutey Moharan II:25*, trans. R'Aryeh Kaplan in '*Meditation and Kabbalah*,' p. 309.

This can involve preliminary and preparatory verbal prayer, vocalised or silent, and it may involve music and dance or meditation on a text or a particular thought. But ultimately it is a case of the soul making itself *attentively available*, in patient, silent, and solitary contemplation. It is a form of quietening the soul in hopeful expectation that some form of Divine influx and intimate activity might take place. Often it will seem that this has not occurred (hence the need for patience and humility) but if G-d wills, it can lead to an awareness that a direct input has occurred and may even lead to an experience that resembles a two-way conversation.

This particular kind of *hitbodedut/hitbonenut* is a way of inviting G-d to make use of us as a channel of His Presence. It is not about us and our individual needs or condition. It is an attempt to invite G-d to 'speak' to us or to show us something we need to see. To reveal to each individual soul the way in which it can best be a channel for the activity of the *Shekhinah* in our world.

The esoteric systems and complex meditation practices of the kabbalists, the deeply intellectual forms of *hitbonenut* proposed by the Chabad hasidim, and the frequently cathartic expressions of *hitbodedut* practiced by Breslover hasidim are beyond the scope of this little book. There are several reasons for this. As I have indicated, I am neither a scholar nor a rabbi. I am not qualified or experienced enough to make deep analytical comment on these jewels in Judaism's contemplative crown. You can find shelves full of books which deal with these subjects by many gifted authors without too much effort.

But the main reason you will not find them, or theosophy, or theurgy, or self improvement methods discussed here is because I am presenting a somewhat simpler path—a path for those whose primary focus is to seek intimacy with G-d, and maybe to become a selfless channel for His activity in this world.

This is the aim of anyone who would draw near to G-d hoping to receive the spirit of *ruach hakodesh* that approaches prophecy, and I believe this to be the core *tachlit* (aim/goal) of all prayer in the Cave of the Heart.

באחרית הימים
ושבת עד
יי אלקיך
ושמעת בקלו

In the latter days,
you will return
to HaShem your G-d
and listen to His Voice.
Deuteronomy 4:30

In our day, we are witnessing an ever increasing and often hyperactive pace of life that has frequently become coupled with a decreasing attention span. Pauses for thought are snatched rather than savoured and we seem to collect and share trivia more than we value focus and depth in our interior reflections. Online and offline, we are a generation that is hungry for spiritual satisfactions as much as for spiritual duties, and it is possible to lose ourselves in an endless peripheral playing around with mystical studies whilst overlooking (and avoiding) authentic solitary communion with our G-d.

I do not carry a phone around with me habitually— its use being reserved for essential business, or for those times when I need to use its speech-to-text technology due to my severe deafness—but I often ask myself how many hours have I spent browsing 'religious/spiritual' websites at home when I should have been standing in receptive prayer?

The technological advances of the present era have been both a blessing and curse. The development of the internet, and development in communicative information technology generally, have brought the isolated Jew into real contact with other Jews in ways which would scarcely have been imagined just a few years ago. The shared liturgy and group-conference study sessions which I called for in the original 2005 version of this book are now a valued and ever expanding resource. Texts from classical and contemporary Jewish sources are readily available through websites such as *Sefaria*, and they can even be automatically translated online in seconds. All this is certainly a blessing of the highest order.

So far, however, no computer app or electronic communication accessory has developed a means of communicating directly with G-d Himself.

The internet and the ubiquitous hand-phone can also have a negative impact on the Jewish Contemplative's life of prayer and study. The tendency to be permanently and actively attached to an *iphone* or a *tablet* (or whichever new media-toy is in vogue by the time you read this) means that we may be more easily side-tracked into peripheral chatting or doodling or socializing on the media-toy and thus completely forget that we were searching for a particular Talmudic reference, or some specific halachic detail, or an exact citation from a Tzaddik's sefer when we first picked it up. Furthermore, it encourages us to think and feel at a speed that makes considered reflection a rarity.

How often have I put off the hour of prayer by extending time spent on some less viscerally-exposed and stoic activity so that when the time came for davening[15] or *hitbonenut*: all I had the energy for was a brief liturgical recitation and a few passing words in the Divine Ear?

I would be the first person to echo the Kotzker Rebbe's dictum that the hour of prayer should be delayed until sufficient preparation had been made. He declared that there were no clocks in his community, only souls. He reminded us that the woodcutter is engaged in his trade even while sharpening his tools.

But I still think that, for the aspiring and the experienced contemplative alike, the number one distraction is to be excessively engaged in reading, talking, (or writing!) about spirituality and contemplation when the task at hand is meant

---

[15] **Davening**: to daven is to recite the formal and liturgical prayer services

to be action not theory.

Praying is the *principal* task of the dedicated Jewish Contemplative—but because it can often be demanding, we put it off, we skimp on it, and we allow our energies to be spent elsewhere.

Studying the thoughts and discoveries of others is one of the ways in which we learn. For Jews, the thoughts of our predecessors in mysticism can often be a safeguard and (almost but not quite) a route-map. It is true that we can be temporarily carried away into the world of deep prayer whilst engaged in such religious study. Sometimes this can be the very deepest prayer for we are only truly in contemplative prayer when we are no longer aware that we are praying.

Similarly, the thoughts of our contemplative contemporaries, both in print and online, are often an exciting and refreshing stimulus to our own development. Quite obviously and laudably, we need to be faithful to our tradition and study the works of those who have gone before us and those who walk with us today in our living community. But we can overdo this: In the end, the Contemplative Path to G-d is one on which we travel alone.

Our unquenchable thirst for stimulation and gratification can often become addictive, and we may mistake the accumulation of religious, intellectual, or liturgical bric a brac for knowledge—when our Sages insist that the only true knowledge is that we know nothing. In the forest of distraction whose paths frequently lead nowhere, we are in danger of turning something that is pure and simple into something that is more complex than it need be.

And yet, there are those among us who sense a force that pulls us away from such noise and distraction and who search for a way to turn their somewhat introverted natures or their spirituality into a practical form of service that frees one from egocentricity.

Such people may be a minority but they have always been active on the fringes of Judaism and their number has been growing through our contemporary interest in spirituality, mindfulness, and meditational practice. They are often Hidden Contemplatives. They are the *mitkarevim* (those who would draw near to G-d).

Within the Jewish Community there are people who know from the start that they are called to live an intimate life of prayer. Such people will sometimes be pursuing this vocation in varying degrees of isolation, and sometimes they will be following personalised versions of the 'Intimate Path', of R' Avraham ben Ha Rambam[16] in the midst of busy social, cultural, or educational, careers.

For others, their potential as contemplatives emerges gradually. It is often more fragile, and it can be encouraged enthusiastically or squashed by negative criticism. Though our modern age has seen something of a renaissance in meditational activity there are still many in contemporary Judaism who are unaware of the eremitical tradition within our religion and who actually belittle its relevance.[17]

---

[16] In his Jewish-Sufi compendium, the *Kifaya al-Abadin*, R'Avraham ben HaRambam (1186–1237) proposed a 'special path' (suluk al-khass) for dedicated contemplatives, it is this path which the present author aspires to follow. The work is translated into English: see '*Sefer HaMaspik*' *Chapter 13*, R'.Avraham ben HaRambam, trans R' Yaakov Wincelberg in '*The Guide to Serving G-d*', (Feldheim, Jerusalem/New York, 2008).

[17] I have attempted to redress the balance of that sad situation in my book *The Mitkarevim*.

So, who are these potential contemplatives in our midst and how can their apparent loneliness be transformed into a happy and fruitful solitude?

I'll start my answer to these questions by asking you to consider this list for a moment:

- Some isolated Jews may have found themselves made redundant or incapacitated through illness or other circumstances.

- Some of them will have been disabled all their lives and thus prevented from engaging in many forms of social activity or communication.

- Some people may be living and working in unavoidable isolation from Jewish community centres or even in situations of restriction or oppression.

- Some may have lost a life-partner, who in many cases was the only practically functioning community they had.

- Some may be people for whom family life has not been possible—sometimes they are people whose attempts at partnership formation have simply not worked out, or they may have emotional or other issues that prevent them from marrying and creating a family.

- Some people may be both single and desperately lonely, and thus feel excluded/exclude themselves from the world of 'family life'. Their isolation can be physical or internal or both.

- Some may simply be people in isolation who for one reason or another have found themselves with more time on their hands and fewer opportunities for a social expression of their religious feelings and aspirations than they had expected. Within this group there will be Jews who are in prison, or who are medically quarantined or terminally ill.

o Some isolated Jews may be retired people, with or without dispersed families, who have found themselves unexpectedly confronted with questions which they had been cushioned from in the bustle of their previous working lives. In our day, as we witness the expansion of artificial intelligence and robotics and also the many life-extending medical discoveries, this group is almost certain to swell in number dramatically.

o And—I have to add—Some may feel called to solitary life both naturally and supernaturally, and they may well have no idea how to go about it. As Jews, they will very possibly feel marginalised and embarrassed.

If you go back through that list of life situations you will see that the people I have described are by no means an insignificant minority. They are diverse, hidden, dispersed, and very probably in need of spiritual support. Judaism is not a 'one size fits all' religion and a certain distribution of labour keeps it strong and healthy. We wave the *arba minim* at the festival of Sukkot: fruit and bound-together plants which represent the variation and diversity which individual Jews bring to the community of Israel as a whole. Some commentators view the *arba minim* as a symbol of a diversity in which the strong support the weak. Others, myself included, view it as a non-judgemental and positive statement about diversity being celebrated for its particular beauty *per se*. It was a diversity accepted and expressed by the arrangement that was made between Yisachar and Zebulun without any taint of elitism or conflict of interest, for in *Bereshit Raba 99:9* we read that the tribe of Zebulun financed the Torah study of the tribe of Yisachar as a way of sharing in the *mitzvah*.

There are those who are forced to snatch whatever time they can away from family duties or business responsibilities in order to pray the daily obligatatory services, and for whom *extended* periods of contemplative solitude are virtually impossible. There are those with more free time on their hands. Each has their place in the execution of the shared vocational task of *Knesset Yisrael*.

Might it not be possible to accept that some people have what might be termed a natural gift or predisposition for the contemplative life which could be acknowledged, and maybe developed, for the good of the whole? And here, I mean the good of *kol ha-Olam* as much as for *kol Yisrael*: for the community of all Creation and not just the Jewish community.

We hear the Voice of Sinai as *Knesset Yisrael* in our individual hearts. Each individual has their own unique perspective according to personality and potential, and yet the revelation is actually experienced communally.

The covenantal relationship between *Knesset Yisrael* and G-d is manifested in the inner and outer life of each individual Jew. This is what makes Judaism a religion and not a club, not just a grouping of people with a common nationality or shared ideals. It is that *individual* communication with G-d which paradoxically produces the 'We' of all Jewish prayer— and all Jewish activity— and it is a paradox which is at the heart of specifically Jewish mysticism. The revelation at Sinai was unique as it was simultaneously communal and personal, and that is its nature to this day.

If one accepts that there is a *Knesset Yisrael*, an eternal

Community of Israel which is not bound by the limitations of time, space, or number—and if one accepts that there is a Universal Soul of Humanity of which we are the re-uniting fragments—it should be a small matter to see that neither can be contained by synagogues, by denominations, by movements, or by sectarian units.

The best they can do is to facilitate points of focus for some of the fragments. The only real point of focus is the spiritual one they hope to represent.

The worst they can do is to allow themselves to think that they embody that Point of Focus exclusively, making themselves feel stronger by denigrating those whose perspective doesn't match their own.

The Task of the Contemplative Jew

The thought is often expressed that we are G-d's only hands in the world. There is a sense in which G-d is more present in 'our' world when we make Him so. Following the image through— might the spiritual activity of the *Mitkarevim* be an expression of His Mind or Heart in the world?

R' Levi Yitzchak of Berditchev assures that the contribution of contemplatives is absolutely indispensable:

> When man nullifies himself completely and attaches his thoughts to Nothingness, then a new sustenance flows into all the universes. This is a sustenance that did not exist previously.[18]

---
[18] *The Chassidic Masters*, R'Aryeh Kaplan, page 73,
(Moznaim Publishing Corporation,New York/Jerusalem, 1984)

A person living a contemplative lifestyle (whether by choice or circumstance) can transform isolation into living community action by consciously turning their focus in prayer to the healing or *tikkun* process. By making this intentional transformation, such a person brings a new sustenance into all the universes. If such a person does not intend to effect this transformation, especially when it may well be their personal vocation to bring it about—then the *tikkun*, willed by G-d, will either not happen, or be delayed.

This process is active in the individual's never-ending journey in and to G-d—and it is simultaneously active in the process of the evolution of all Creation. From the position of the former we hope to influence the latter.

In my personal prayers, I find it easier to do this on an individual level by joining my thoughts to those of friends, especially when they are in periods of distress. Attempting to give such spiritual support on a wider scale, perhaps even a global scale might have highly significant consequences, and it may be something that you alone can do in G-d's Name.

Yes—You alone.

Maybe you need to see these words to realise that.

The method of contemplative prayer I am recommending in this *kuntres* is very simple. All we need to do is sit down in solitude and silence, put ourselves in G-d's Presence, and attempt to relate to Him in some focussed way. It may involve the words of a set prayer or not. It may involve reflection on a text or a concept—or not. It may involve a search for meaning in a particular life-situation—or not.

But whatever form that *hitbonenut/hitbodedut* might take there are two things that make the method I am promoting special. Firstly: It is not about us, but about Him. It is an attempt to be present *before* G-d and *in* G-d for its own sake. Secondly: It is an attempt to be so intentionally and **profoundly attentive** that our contemplation becomes an opportunity to listen for, and maybe even hear, the Divine Voice itself.

It requires that the contemplative simply makes time and space for G-d to get a word in edgeways.

A set time of solitary intimacy.

A short period, or a long period of simple and silent availability to G-d in the Prayer of Nearness.

The attentive gaze of one in love with the Divine.

In order to assist those unused to this kind of contemplative practice, and for those who have been baffled or confused by complex meditation methods — here is an example format I would like to propose as a guide to get one started.

It is a form of contemplative prayer that I have used daily in some years and occasionally in other years. These days it's a format I rarely use at all, but I am recommending it strongly, and will explain why as this *kuntres* unfolds.

Here it is:

In order to meet G-d in private contemplation,
we really only need to do one simple thing:
We need to make some time to be with Him Alone
and give Him our undivided and loving attention.
Contemplative Prayer is giving G-d a chance to speak to us/do something to us.
It is not about us, it's about Him.

הרפו
ודעו כי־אנכי אלקים

BE STILL

And know that I AM G-D
(Psalm 46:10)

The method is simply:

Stand or sit in His Presence;

Make space inside yourself for Him to act;

Then <u>listen</u> with focus to whatever He may have to say to you, personally and individually.

That's it.

Yes….

That's *all* of it

The listening/attentive/receptive form of meditation I am presenting here might be practiced at the conclusion of a regular meditation period; perhaps within the framework of a more verbal Breslover-style of *hitbodedut*; or as a feature of one's private recitation of the *Amidah*. It might also be a form of contemplative prayer that one practices extremely rarely and which stands completely on its own as a focussed exercise aimed at making oneself available to G-d and open to receive Divine inspiration.

If you were expecting this *kuntres* to offer you a contemplative method replete with manipulations of Hebrew letters and numbers, or guided meditations, or ascetic practices you will be very disappointed by that. If you are a scholar of Jewish mysticism you might be irritated by my impertinence. If you are somebody who feels relief or excitement (and perhaps a sense of recognition) on reading those last few statements but need a little bit more help to make those words make sense: then read on.

There are countless methods of contemplative prayer which take the practitioner through various stages of meditation by suggesting things that one might do— often in a progressive and hierarchic order or scheme. The specific exercise I am describing and promoting here is a supplement to such activities.

It is not being promoted here as the only or somehow superior meditational method to be practiced by a contemplative — though for some people it may prove to be their principal form of contemplative activity. Rather, it is presented as an activity that all Jews could practice (in some form or other) if they want to 'meet' G-d and reach their full potential in prayer. As a main-course contemplative activity, it is a path of intimacy that leads to focussed service, but it may also prove to be a sort of sourdough to kick-start a person's introduction to contemplative/prophetic practice.

There is nothing new in the three-point method I have just outlined. The method is ancient. It consists of nothing more than periods of attentiveness and receptivity in prayer, and such periods—or something very like them—must have been part of the core curriculum of the Schools of the Prophets of Biblical Judaism. Prophecy in Biblical times was something that sometimes required training and those students of the Prophets *per se* were educated in the equivalent of residential yeshivas. They were the **bnei ha-nevi'im** –the Sons of the Prophets (Amos 7:14), and the *Talmud* numbers them in excess of a million.[19] References to the prophetic schools may be found in the time of Shmuel Ha Navi (I Samuel:19) and most especially, under the tutelage of Eliyahu and Elisha. (I Kings 19:18 and II Kings 4:38–41)

Furthermore, I believe that there is an echo of the practice of

---

[19] Though there are fifty-five *Biblical* prophets, the Gemara in *Megillah 14a* estimates that the number of Israel's prophets was around 1,200,000. The Midrash in *Shir Ha-Shirim Rabbah 4:11* numbers Israel's male prophets at 'sixty myriads' with a further 'sixty myriads' of female prophets.

such a receptive, focussed, and attentive form of contemplation in the *Talmud* itself. In *Berachot 32b* we are told that the Sages of old spent an hour before and after reciting the formal *tefilla* in some form of meditation—and the word used for their activity is 'waiting'. It is apparent (from *Berachot 32b:24*) that this waiting was neither inactivity nor study, and it is significant that they were said to 'wait' both before and after reciting formal prayers. The term must therefore refer to some form of private contemplation made in *preparation for* worship, or in *reflection on it* after its formal (and usually communal) enactment.

The sort of attentive contemplation I am recommending is certainly a form of expectant and reflective 'waiting'.

It also resembles the kind of prayer that must have been made by those standing at the entrance of their tents while Moshe Rabeinu entered the (second) Tent of meeting in Exodus 33:7-10.[20]

The simple contemplative practice I am promoting may however be 'new' for many Jews who will not have considered that prayer could (or should) include a time for G-d's response. Jews are very familiar with the idea that listening to G-d takes place whenever the Torah scrolls are read, studied, or discussed — but that same Torah is to be found in the heart of each individual Jew.

The **heart** is our intuitive intellect. The **soul** is our very life-force. The **Torah of the Heart** is eternally given and when we

---

[20] This tent of meeting outside the camp (*ohel mo-ed asher michutz lamachaneh*) is especially significant as it had a resident "Dedicated Jewish Contemplative", namely Yehoshua, who was permanently on contemplative retreat there in his youth as a sort of custodian. (see Exodus 33:11)

receive it intentionally, it produces a connecting link between our intellect and our life-force. Our tangible experiences and our spiritual perceptions are thus bound up with our essential soul root, and from there, bound up with our G-d.

When we open up this channel we deepen our relationship with the Supernal Torah, because our obedience to the commands of the Torah would be incomplete if love and true internalisation were absent.

G-d speaks to all of us through the *Torah She-bi'chtav (Written Torah)* and the *Torah She-ba'al Peh (Oral Torah)*. He also speaks to us in our own prayers and in our own private study and meditation. When we read the scriptures with pauses for meditation or when we meditate in silent prayer, we are hoping to access the Torah of the Heart.

We know how and when we are called to action as a nation and as individuals through the words of the written and oral Torah—but we each receive that Torah according to our own abilities and character, and for this reason we also need to receive and digest those 'words' *personally,* in the Cave of the Heart, alone with our G-d.

This Torah of the Heart is rarely accessed, but it really ought to be—for how else can we begin to hear the Voice which goes out daily from Sinai in our own times? [21]

Is anyone listening? Truly listening?

What I have suggested is extremely simple: During private prayer, ask G-d to speak to you and then wait in humble silence to let Him respond. It is possible that you may only be able to hold your attention on listening out for Him to 'speak' for a

---

[21] In *Pirkei Avot 6:2* we read that a voice goes out from Sinai everyday, admonishing the Jewish people to return to the Torah.

minute or so before you lose concentration. But it is also possible (sometimes after years of making this effort) that you may find yourself standing there waiting for many minutes—or even hours—and cannot account for the time passing. But believe me, the Voice of Sinai is calling—if only we would listen. Our effort to do so may often seem to fail but we are commanded in the *Sh'ma* we recite daily to at least try. And try again.

In the *Zohar* we read:

> The acts of G-d are eternal and continue for ever. Every day the one who is worthy receives the Torah standing at Sinai. He hears the Torah from the mouth of the Lord as Israel did….Every Jew is able to attain that level, the level of standing at Sinai.[22]

And the midrash in *Shemot Rabbah 5:9* confirms this by pointing out that all members of the Community of Israel heard the Voice of Sinai "according to each individual's capabilities and strengths". It is a miracle of miracles, but this kind of inspired listening is potentially attainable every day.

THE VOICE

The reader will be familiar with the biblical concept of prophecy where Divinely appointed leaders encourage or admonish the community as channels of the Divine Will. But in Jewish mysticism, the term "prophet" is also used to describe one who is in a state of intimate and communicative

---

[22] *Zohar* 1:90a

union with the Divine. Such a "prophet" is one who has attained their highest potential level of perfection, each one according to their individual capabilities and perspectives. As such, they are in receipt of various levels and forms of inspiration, intuition, and insight (though, obviously, of a lesser degree than that of the biblical prophets). The return of prophecy to Israel is the belief that a time will come when prophecy is attainable by all, a time when "the knowledge of the Glory of G-d will fill all the earth as the waters cover the seabed" (Habbakuk 2:14) [23]

I believe that we are all capable of hearing G-d's voice. Not in the way Moshe Rabeinu did, for sure, but in the way that all Israel did at the foot of Sinai. I mean that literally.

It comes to us, in its purest form, as a voice during contemplative prayer itself or out of the blue when least expected. We hear it in our hearts and not through our ears. It is not our own voice (though part of it is). It seems to have a tone all of its own and does not speak often—There may be years between perceived occurrences.

The Voice seems to respond to questions, and its answers are often unexpectedly mundane, brief and brutally to the point, or just plain odd. In the latter case, we may have a crossed-wire in our imagination that has simply short-circuited the brain's ability to decipher input. The meaning or significance of apparently unintelligible answers that we have 'heard' can often emerge long after the event—maybe in another prayer session or when something happens in our lives to explain it. When one is dealing with a 'world' that is free of time and space, such

---

[23] This topic is discussed in much greater detail in *The Mitkarevim*. (by the same author)

temporal re-organisation of past present and future experience is par for the course.

The Voice sometimes answers us before the first word of such a question has even been expressed. Sometimes we have just begun to frame a question and we hear the answer rocketted out at us.

Sometimes 'answers' are delayed to give us an opportunity to re-think or re-phrase any request or petition that we might have made. This often happens when we realise that the question we thought we needed to ask had been masking a different question that we were originally afraid to ask.

Sometimes we are given an 'answer' which seems to bear no relation to any question we may have asked, in such cases it is what we really needed to hear.

Often, we are the ones being asked a question.

Frequently, we are left to our own devices to find our own answers. Once we have struggled and found our own answers or made our own decision we then hear or sense a 'Voice of Approval' which comes as an unexpected blessing on what we have ourselves obtained.

This confirming approval can come in the form of signs or words or events immediately following our own decision making, either from the actions of the people we meet, in a passage in a book we pick up, or an email we receive, or through something we chance upon in a moment of *déjà vu*. Such approval really feels like it has come from a parent who congratulates a child on developing its independence, and when it happens it comes with a unique scent of authenticity that tells us that it is not a mere illusion.

The Voice can be commanding, but it never makes our decisions for us. Sometimes we may even be invited to challenge its demands. It seems to enjoy the tussle of a good fight.

The Voice may be heard synesthesically. It may be in the form of verbal communication, it may present a visual image, it may cause a movement in our body, or it may not be sensed at all save by the heart— by a spiritual, intuitive faculty which is neither intellectual, emotional, nor purely imaginative.

On the many occasions when absolutely nothing seems to have happened and no answers given, this part of our consciousness often seems to be aware that something has been done to us even though it is not necessary for us to know what or why.

There is some similarity between the type of awareness I have just described and the dream state and, perhaps not surprisingly, the Voice sometimes speaks in dreams themselves.[24] Some deliberately seek information in dreams through *she'elat chalom*—dream questions (Moshe Chayim Vital and Ibn Ezra for example), and many say that a hasidic rebbe who is apparently dozing at a communal meal-table is not dozing but 'visiting the academy on high'.

In such special dreams (special because we recognize they are in a class of their own, not that we are) it has the same synesthesic quality— The dreamer perceives a dream-message which appears before the 'eyes' of the mind as a kind of

---

[24] See *Derech HaShem 3:1,6*. also *Berachot 9*

written banner whose word or words are simultaneously recited by a voice heard by the mind's 'ears'.

Many times such dream-messages are delivered in a way that allows for multiple interpretations. This can present us with a knotty paradox to unpack, or with a conflicting set of instructions for action— thus confirming the adage that the significance of a dream is in the control of the dreamer. This is a core concept in Jungian theories of dream interpretation, but it predated Jung's reveries and has a considerable following amongst classical Jewish thinkers.

In *Berachot 55b* we read "all dreams follow the mouth of the interpreter," and in *Berachot 57a* we are given a detailed description of the meaning of various dream omens and 'encounters' with Biblical personages or with Scriptural passages themselves; and in R'Moshe Chayim Luzatto's *Derech HaShem,* we read of the interrelation of the individual soul's imaginative faculty and the (indirect) Divine inspiration couched in dream encounters:

> It emerges that dreams in general are images that are formed by the imagination, either on its own—or as a result of what the soul arouses within [the imagination] in accordance with what the soul perceives in the spiritual realms.[25]

Sometimes, in the midst of such dream-visions, we wake suddenly with a flash of intuitive recognition or have it on our lips as we arise in the first waking moments of the morning so that we should not forget (or try to minimalise) the importance

---

[25] '*The Elucidated Derech Hashem*', R' Abba Zvi Naiman, page 363, (Feldheim, Jerusalem, 2012) A discussion of specifically prophetic dreams follows on page 453.

of what we have been told.[26] I think that sometimes such special dreams act as a channel of information because we were somehow not sufficiently receptive to hear such a 'message' in a recent prayer session.

The Voice sometimes seems to make use of synchronous events—inexplicable chains of coincidences which seem to come in proximate bursts (often in threes for some reason) to ensure that we get the intended message.

These answering events often resemble those occasions when we sense that something is wrong with someone we are close to in thought but miles away from in space—only to find that a split second later, a phone call confirms our apprehension.

They resemble those moments when we think of someone, only to have them turn up out of the blue at the door, in our path, or in our email in-boxes. Often they come as a sort of underlining of something we have just experienced in contemplative prayer. Sometimes we may have 'heard' something in prayer only to find someone saying almost exactly the same thing to us in a conversation, or in a phrase we read—often within seconds or minutes of the original prayer experience. Their rapidly consecutive appearance convinces me that, as the Baal Shem Tov said: "there are no accidents" wherever this little miracle occurs.[27]

My use of the terms Voice, hear, see etc. can be taken

---

[26] In *Berachot 57b* we are told that one who wakes in the morning with a verse of Scripture on his lips is a recipient of minor prophecy. My experience is that apparently mundane or enigmatic 'textual messages' can also serve a similar purpose.

[27] *Shiv'chei Baal Shem Tov 150* : 'Nothing is accidental. I know that everything, however great or small, is overseen by Heaven. Therefore one must think about the meaning of everything that happens'. (quoted in *'The Path of the Baal Shem Tov'*, R' David Sears, page 43 *(Rowman & Littlefield publishers INC., New York, 1997)*

(almost) literally or metaphorically. They are used in an attempt to describe an experience which will differ from person to person, and which takes many different forms in the various periods of an individual's life. The common denominator is that they describe a process of a kind of spiritual intuition (and maybe of inspiration or revelation) which operates on a level beyond the superficial, emotional or intellectual.

However it is perceived, it is a process which produces insight, learning experiences, and attentiveness to G-d in our deepest self and in the world about us.

I believe that the Voice I have described can be G-d's Voice and ours simultaneously. The extent to which it is His Voice, I cannot say.   If you are brave enough, ask it!

How much of it is our own voice can often (but surprisingly, not always) depend on the level to which we have removed our self-centredness, our insatiable desire for material and spiritual things we don't really need, our prejudices, and our totems— or had them removed for us.

That is an ongoing process, and as it is a work in progress we may mishear the Voice by hearing only the frequencies we want to hear, or simply be filtering it in inaccurate language.

But if our intention is truly to listen to G-d alone with the motivation of service overriding all others, then our misinterpretations are short lived. Other presentations of the same 'word' are made till we get the message. This way, we get as near to understanding it as we can.

Certain things in those last few paragraphs will not make a lot of sense to some readers, but my hope is that they will strike a chord in the hearts of those readers who are intended to see these words—possibly as confirmation of their own intuitions—and that for such readers it will give both peace and encouragement.

Secular psychologists reading these paragraphs may also be having a field-day examining the mental processes described in those last few paragraphs from a purely natural view-point—superimposing whatever diagnostic or therapeutic model they prefer when analysing them.

I am not at all embarrassed when writing about the experiences of those who 'hear voices' because I actually expect G-d to operate using natural human processes when communicating with humans. There is a world of difference between psychic sensitivity and psychopathy, and reticence about the former is out of place here, in a document which is being written to encourage others to come out of the contemplative/prophetic closet.

Generally speaking, individuals are best advised to discuss their spiritual experiences with their spiritual guide or mentor and none other. In our era, religious people who journey on a mystical path are often ridiculed and even despised —and they are often fearful of exposing their spiritual activity, even when amongst their own religious fellows. Some might even find it impossible to discuss such matters with their own rabbi.

For this reason, in these paragraphs I have attempted to give some circumspect description of the processes one might experience, a few hints without full detail. I have done this because my aim is to support and encourage such people at a time when support may well be lacking. Being a Contemplative in the tradition of the Sons of the Prophets takes guts, and I know there are people out there who need such encouragement.

Challenges to the authenticity of our experiences and perceptions are not to be avoided or shied away from. They may themselves be a part of the process of purification that the contemplative is initiating and working through.

Hearing The Voice—that is to say, being able to practice a level of intuition that may sometimes approach inspiration — does not produce rock-solid faith in G-d, nor does it produce an unwavering confidence in one's interpretations of His Word. If anything, such experiences are more often accompanied by an increase of doubt and periods of self-questioning that are part of the sort of intellectual and spiritual struggle that gives us the name *Yisrael*.[28]

These periods of struggle are sometimes agonisingly empty and desert-like. Sometimes they are times of storm, wind and fire. The Voice may be a still, small voice[29] but its stillness resembles the apparent stasis of a surgical laser beam coming sometimes with anaesthetic, sometimes without. Our delusions and our false securities are burnt out. One way or the other.

It also has to be said here that those delusions sometimes come temptingly gift-wrapped in self-promoting misconception, and are thus hard to differentiate from the real thing. There are also times when we are excited by emotional or ecstatic episodes in prayer.

Sometimes the mere sensation that we are engaged in a

---

[28] Genesis 32:29
[29] *Kol dimamah dakah* : (I Kings 19:12)

Spiritual Quest can itself create excitement or produce spiritual self-gratification. If we are not on our guard we may be tempted to elevate ourselves beyond our proper place.

Such delusions are often hard to self-identify, but that task is not impossible: People who 'hear voices' may be suffering from illness; they may feel commanded to perform selfish or hateful acts; they may feel driven by a compulsion which leaves no room for argument or discussion.

The Voice I am referring to **never** causes any of these.

If you 'hear' a voice in prayer and doubt its origin, test it. If hearing such a voice produces an increase in practical acts of compassion and kindness, of *tzedakah* and *chasadut*, and if it removes or diminishes self-absorption or ego-focus, then it is likely to be both safe and healthy. If it is clearly and demonstrably making you a better person, then trust it.

The method of attentive and receptive prayer that I am promoting is based on the following premise: That if we place ourselves regularly in the Presence of G-d, silently or sometimes not so silently, sooner or later He will do something—and it is my belief that putting ourselves in that situation is somehow of great use to Him.

It all takes place in clouded internal worlds of fleeting half awarenesses, but it changes us and makes the world we return to after such prayer different. If it is not too presumptuous to claim it, I would suggest that by engaging in receptive contemplative prayer, we begin to perceive things a little more in the way G-d sees them.

This book's simple method assumes that G-d is perfectly

capable of revealing His Presence and activity in our dimension if He wants to, but for that to happen, He seems to prefer us to invite Him to do so. It is principally a profound acknowledgement of that belief.

The proposed form of receptive prayer that I have presented here is not as passive as it may seem at first glance. We are by no means exempt from putting considerable effort into the process ourselves. Preparation before standing in His Presence involves intensive care and effort, and during the prayer session itself we will often have to work quite hard to clear away the mental clutter that blocks our path.

Making an internal space, a personal void that G-d can fill needs our time, our effort, and our persistence. Neither is it so passive a method that it consists solely of the exercise itself. It is also an intentional method for the development of the soul's intuitional faculties, both during and after prayer.

The point of standing in attentive contemplation is to be open to inspiration. That is inspiration for action— both spiritual and material action. We do the work it inspires.

The follow-up activity that our prayer session often generates (by demand or by suggestion) is often even more arduous than the prayer itself, and it can be much more physical, temporal, spatial—and social— than we bargained for.

We also have to be prepared to accept that our effort may rarely produce any lasting sense of fulfillment at all. Similarly, it may not be completed in our (current) lifetime—but 'neither should we desist from the task of trying.' [30]

---

[30] *Pirkei Avot 2:21*

One who begins such a contemplative practice needs determination and perseverance—I have known many years when, despite standing in receptive silent prayer regularly (sometimes for hours) most days of each week, I have felt/heard/seen absolutely nothing that I could identify as being a response of any kind whatsoever.

Please read that last sentence again—it is really important.

STANDING BEFORE G-D

It is possible to engage in contemplative prayer when sitting, standing, reclining, or strolling. My own preference is sitting or standing with my eyes closed. I recommend using a standing posture, most of all, because I first started using this method when in the midst of the personal and solitary recitation of the *Amidah* prayer. a term which itself refers to a standing position. But I also chose it in reference to two scriptural verses in which I see a hint at the sort of contemplative prayer I am describing:

עמד והתבונן נפלאות אל

Stand still
and consider the wondrous works of G-d [31]

and

התיצבו וראו את־ישועת יי
אשר־יעשה לבם היום

Stand still
and see the salvation of HaShem
which He will show you today [32]

In order to be aware and begin to appreciate that everything created exists solely by the breath of G-d, we need to pause and focus. In order to see that *today* means *every* day and *every*

---
[31] Job 37:14.
[32] Exodus 14:13.

moment we need to develop a consciousness of timeless eternity, however partial that altered state might be for most of us.

In the eighteen blessings of the liturgical *Amidah,* many prayerbooks contain an inserted or additional invitation to make certain *personal* requests and prayers. The place for these is usually in the middle blessings or after the words: *'May the words of my mouth and the meditations of my Heart find favour before You'.* [33]

In fact, the prayer which begins *Elokai netzor l'shoni meira (My G-d, guard my tongue)* was inserted into the *Amidah* as a formalised example of the sort of personal additional requests that one might make at this point.[34] As such, it is an ideal place for one to insert one's *silent attentive prayer* when davening privately and alone.

When davening during public worship, it is quite likely that, out of concern for the waiting fast-daveners, the community will leave insufficient time for such expanded personal prayer. Weekday communal worship also has to make allowances for the work-schedules of the congregants, which can often leave little or no time for extended prayer. Assuming that one habitually davens with a minyan[35] and wants to make a unit of receptive contemplative prayer at a separate time altogether, here is a suggested format that readers might like to try:

---

[33] *Berachot 34a*

[34] *Berachot 17a.* It was a prayer composed by the Amora, Mar Bar Ravina (Fourth century CE) in the tradition of the sages who used to improvise similar prayers at the conclusion of the *Amidah.*

[35] *Davening with a minyan*: performing the daily liturgical services in a congregational quorum of ten.

In a room where you are not seen or heard,
find a spot where you are not likely to bump into anything.

Stand straight with your arms relaxed at your side.
Close your eyes and keep them closed
After a few moments of vocal or mental prayer

Ask G-d to permit you to draw near and enter into His Presence
When you feel ready and with eyes still closed

Slowly take three steps back,
Wait a moment,
Then very slowly take three steps forward
(through earthquake, wind and fire)
to draw near and to come into His Presence.

Then say:
LORD, if there is something You would say to me,
Or something that You would show me,
Or something that you want me to do

HINEINI
[I AM HERE AT YOUR SERVICE]

After which you should stand in profoundly attentive silence
For as long as you feel you are being asked to.
[Retiring with deep respect in three steps as before.]

A brief word of clarification is called for here in this second edition. The aim of this method is to 'create a space' that can be filled with the awareness/ immanence/ inspiration of the Divine. Consequently when one has silenced the activity of the mind (as far as possible) and declared "HINEINI" one needs to be totally silent and free of verbal or representational thoughts for the inspiration to enter.

Jewish mystics have understood that this is extremely difficult to do and have most often advised the practitioner to distract the brain with word permutations or the recitation of repetitive mantras or the visualisation of letters. These can all help, but I want to stress that my intention is that one should (at least) strive to empty the mind of any distracting thought *in totally silent attentiveness* for as long as is possible.

Having said this, I will share the following. I have found that it can help to reach this 'vacated silence' if one mentally repeats the phrase *"You not me"* or simply *"You"*, or perhaps *"Ad-nai"* (as one breathes in) and *"Ani"* or *"Hu"* (as one breathes out) with closed eyes—and with intense visual focus on what appears in the 'darkness'. More than this I should not say. You must follow your own instinct/inspiration not mine.

The sort of contemplative 'standing before G-d' that I am recommending as a method can be taken figuratively rather than posturally. I have simply and respectfully borrowed the posture and approach choreography from the *Amidah* as I have found it really helps me to prepare to enter into attentive receptivity with all my body and soul. It may help you to do that as well. Prostration and kneeling with the head between the knees also have a noble heritage, but sitting may work better for you.³⁶

The *Amidah* choreography of taking three steps forward at its start has many nuances. Foremost of these is the kabbalistic one in which the steps reflect Moshe Rabbeinu's passage through *choshech* (darkness), *anan* (the cloud), and *arafel* (impenetrable darkness) to approach the Divine. I take them also in reference to the experience of Eliyahu HaNavi in passing through *ra'ash* (earthquake), *ruach* (wind), and *eysh* (fire) before encountering the Voice.

Silent and still attentiveness may often be very hard to achieve or maintain but it can be developed by the repetition, over time, of the exercise I have suggested here.

Distracting thoughts can either be gently dismissed or followed, they might themselves be an intended route to lead you to the same moment of encounter. According to R' Yaakov Yosef of Polonoye in his *Toldos Yaakov Yosef (Vayakhel)*, the Baal Shem Tov taught that these *machshavot zorot* should not be ignored or cause the meditator to cease praying, but that they should be elevated by being woven into the meditation itself as their redemptive *tikkun*.

What counts is that you are trying not to be concerned about yourself or what you are doing so much as trying to be prayerfully available to G-d, even though it may be for a very short space of time, and despite being plagued by distractions.

What counts is your attempt to be attentive to Him.

In presenting this model, I have to leave the reader at the

---

³⁶ *Kneeling with the head between the knees* is referred to as "the prophetic" or "Elijan" posture in many works of Jewish mysticism. See I Kings 18:42

'hineini' point. Each individual needs to grapple with their own 'creation of the empty space' using their own experience and creativity. Everyone is unique and needs to find their own ways to do this. In a sense I am hoping to lead you to water but only you can decide when and how to drink.

There are a million religious and secular meditation books dealing with ways to promote 'stillness', 'mindfulness', or 'attentive silence'. They may help, or they may confuse and distract the religious contemplative. Reading about prayer can be a good way to avoid doing it. Nothing beats the 'suck it and see' approach because in the end—you are your own Teacher and Tzaddik.

The important thing is your attentiveness to Him.

The *Maarat Ha-Lev* is not a *metzar (*a confined space) and a place of *mochin d'katnut* (small mindedness)— It is the *Merchav-Kah* (G-d's wide open expanse)[37] and a vehicle for transporting us into the Courts of the Divine. Should you feel like singing or dancing or moving or whatever after some time being still and silent, let it happen. That may actually give you what you are meant to hear or receive.

If nothing happens, or it *seems* that nothing is happening, remember that 'No' and 'Not yet' are also answers to prayer and that they do not necessarily imply a rejection.

Again: The important thing is your attentiveness to Him.

If you have never done anything like this before or if you feel awkwardly self-conscious despite really wanting to do it—my suggestion is that you persist in making the experiment for a

---

[37] *Psalm 118:5*

reasonable period of time on a regular basis before giving up. The fact that contemplative prayer or meditation is a lot less glamorous than your hopes or expectations may have led you to expect should not be allowed to put you off. You are doing it for Him more than for yourself after all.

As to how often you should perhaps do this kind of meditation: My advice to someone unfamiliar with this kind of prayer is to do it every day, or every few days, or once a week, or whenever you feel called to—but, if possible, more or less regularly and for a reasonable length of time. I'll leave the definition of what that might be to you but ask you to remember, if you'll pardon the anthropomorphism, G-d seems to enjoy an old fashioned lengthy courtship.

If you find it produces no results in your life—then leave it. It might not be the right time— but you may feel unexpectedly called back to it at a later date.

Or perhaps it's just not a way meant for you, in which case, He will surely offer you another one.

The primary task of the contemplative is a prophetic one. To be fully effective as channels of the Light of *Ein Sof,* we have one principal task: To be still and to be attentive to the Divine Voice. That *stillness* is not a lack of activity. It is a change of mode that consists in opening the spiritual airwaves and keeping them open, and that can take considerable effort on our part. That *attentiveness* can be developed but whether or not we may actually perceive some aspect of the Divine is utterly dependent on the Divine Will.

The intimate service of the *Mitkarevim* is not something that can be adopted part-time as some sort of spiritual hobby or diversion. It is dedicated, intentional, and focused. It involves the whole heart and the whole soul and it is not something to be played around with. Those who would walk this path must be prepared to streamline things and avoid diversions if they are to be truly useful to G-d.

The practice of extended retreat has sound roots in Jewish Tradition, and if living an intentionally dedicated contemplative lifestyle really *is* a valuable minority option for modern Jews—then the *Mitkarevim* should be encouraged, or else they might not otherwise emerge. Their prophetic potential might go to waste.

These students of the Torah of the Heart are deserving of the same support and encouragement that is given to students of the Written and Oral Torah.

If one truly believes in the power and efficacy of prayer—scripted and unscripted, public and private, petitional and contemplative— then it should be reflected in our Nation's priorities in our move towards the final Redemption.

Furthermore, if the Torah which is written on our hearts is ever to be properly understood, and if the spirit of prophecy is to return to us in its fullness: the individually-tailored personal communication, and the spiritually receptive attentiveness which they require is not only desirable, it is crucial— *For all Jews*— and not just for a pietist minority.

It was Israel's wish at Sinai that Moshe Rabeinu did the listening for us though this does not seem to have been the Divine intention. Moshe Rabeinu himself wished that all Israel were in receipt of the prophetic spirit and the subsequent institution of the prophetic role was perhaps a kind of compromise. We were rightly in awe of the terrible Presence of HaShem at the giving of the Law, and our humility in seeking that Moshe Rabeinu be our spokesman is laudable. But was there an element of cowardice present there also? Were we also a little afraid of the responsibility that continued intimacy with HaShem would produce?

Ultimately we are destined to become a nation of prophets. If that is to become an imminent reality, there has to be somebody listening.

The parallel development of contemplative lifestyles and contemplative prayer in the life of all Jews might go some way towards making sure that those 'listeners' are in place.

The old, or isolated, or disadvantaged, and those forgotten on the fringes of community are frequently the very Jewish souls who have the spiritual credentials in hard-won authenticity and in wholehearted 'searching for G-d' which might qualify them to develop the prophetic spirit anew.

The isolated, the elderly, and the infirm are also often the ones with the time to focus on the prayerful task of drawing down the light and the strength of Heaven with intensity and perseverance.

Can we afford to neglect their contemplative potential any longer?

-Contemplation is not about possessing or attaining.
- It is about receiving.
-It cannot be taught or studied-
We only learn by doing it ourselves.

-Contemplation is not about 'me', or 'them',
or even 'Us'-
It is about G-d.

Israel's compunction to 'keep working' and indeed 'keep talking' can sometimes be as counterproductive as it can be dynamic. We *really do* need to give G-d the chance to get a word in edge-ways. Prayer is a two-way conversation, not a monologue.

Israel's response at Sinai was, and is: "We will do and we will hear." That is most often interpreted with the meaning: Israel *hears* G-d's voice by *observing* the commandments—that the practical action of observing the *mitzvot* leads to spiritual understanding. That is most certainly true. But a complementary interpretation occurs to me. I'm absolutely certain that there are no accidents:

It surely must be of primary significance
that the first commandment
in the principal text of Judaism,
is Sh'ma!

— **Listen!** —

Judaism has been focussed for centuries on 'doing'. But the time is coming when the significance of 'listening' will grow in importance. We read in the prophet Joel:

והיה אחרי־כן
אשפוך את־רוחי על־כל־בשר
ונבאו בניכם ובנתיכם
זקניכם חלמות יחלמון
בחוריכם חזינות יראו:

And it shall come to pass afterwards
that I will pour out My spirit upon all flesh,
and your sons and daughters shall prophesy;
your elders shall dream dreams, your young men shall see visions.[38]

In a letter of Maimonides to the Jews of Yemen we read that shortly before the coming of Mashiach, prophecy will return to the Jewish people. It is my belief that the 'coming of Eliyahu haNavi' in the days before the start of the Messianic era refers to the re-emergence of the spirit of that prophet in the souls of those contemplatives who are being truly attentive and receptive in their prayer.

It would seem that R' Yitzhak ben Shmuel of Akko (13th-14th century) also believed this:

---

[38] Joel 3:1

So ponder and envision with your mind, that the evil inclination… will be turned on its head… and because of this *the number of recluses (mitbodedim) and ascetic hermits (perushim) will increase* so that, before the end of the six thousand year period, the physical and animal aspects of mankind will cease to exist in this world.[39]

It is time for us to 'listen' in contemplative prayer because it is only by paying attention in receptive contemplation that we can become the prophets, or *Sons of the Prophets* that we are all destined to be. Dedicated Jewish Contemplatives—the *Mitkarevim*— may well be in the vanguard of those who hasten the coming of that emerging consciousness.

May HaShem open the minds and hearts of all those who would hear His Voice.

May He bring us near to serve Him.

May His Name be blessed in all the worlds.

אהרון-נחמן דייויס

©Nachman Davies
Shavuot 5782

First edition…Spain 2005
Second edition…Tzfat 2022

---

[39] Isaac of Akko, *Meirat Einayim* ed. H. Erlanger, Jerusalem 1975 pp. 307-8 (pericope nissabim.)- I discovered this remarkable quotation in November 2021 and then inserted it into this edition of the *Kuntres*. (Thanks to R'David Sears and R'Menachem Weinberg for assistance with translation.)

The Cave of the Heart ✡ Kuntres Maarat Ha-Lev

Glossary of Hebrew Terms

Aleinu—the concluding prayer of formal services

Am Yisrael—the Jewish People

Amidah—"Standing before G-d"— The central prayer of the daily services. It is also called the **Shemoneh Esreh** (the Eighteen Blessings) in reference to the original number of constituent blessings—there are now nineteen.

Arba minim—The four plant species used during the festival of Sukkot

Chassadim/gemilut chasadim—Loving Kindness/ acts of charity.

Daven—to recite the formal services of the prayer book

Ein Sof—sometimes translated as 'the Infinite' or 'The Endless', the term indicates that the Essence of the Divine is beyond description.

Halacha—The legal rulings and customs of the Oral Torah

HaShem—A term used in referring to G-d. It refers to the *Shem Havayah*—the four letters Y-H and V-H.

Havdalah— the ritual concluding ceremony at the end of each Shabbat.

Hineini—"Here I am" (also implies one is offering one's services to the one addressed)

Hitbodedut—*(i)* solitary retreat/reclusion or *(ii)* solitary personal prayer/meditation

Hitbonenut—silent contemplation

Kabbalah—The principal body of Jewish esoteric mysticism.

Kol d'mamah dakah—a still (fragile), small (almost imperceptible) voice. IKings 19:12

Kuntres—A booklet or ethical/spiritual letter

Maarat Ha-Lev—A spiritual 'cave': a place of meeting and revelation in the heart of each individual soul, and simultaneously in the Heart of our G-d.

Machshavot zorot—distracting 'foreign thoughts'

Minyan—Prayer quorum of ten adult males

Mitkarevim—Dedicated Jewish Contemplatives. Jews who seek to draw as close to G-d in as intimate a way as they possibly can. Jews who experience their contemplative practice as a vocation to a particular Divine Service.

Mitzvah—A practical commandment of the Torah

Mochin d'gadlut—expanded consciousness

Mochin d'katnut—restricted awareness

Olam Haba—the beyond life which is ever present though concealed

Ruah ha-kodesh—Divine Inspiration/prophecy

Shem Havayah— The Divine Name composed of the four hebrew letters Yod-Heh and Vav-Heh.

Shiviti — The *shiviti* text is a popular meditational text that may appear at the top of a siddur page: or on a calligraphic plaque (often) just above Psalm 67 in the form of a menorah. It bears the *Shem Hamevorash* and usually the text "I will set HASHEM always before me always." (Psalm 16:8).

Sh'ma—The three Scriptural texts recited by observant Jews each day. The first word means 'Listen!' or 'Understand!'

Siddur—Jewish prayer book

Tachlit—*the ultimate goal or purpose.*

Tefillah—formal liturgical prayer

Tefillin— leather boxes containing scriptural texts worn on rhe head and arm.

Tikkun/Tikkun Olam—Spiritual restoration/the healing or repair of Creation.

Tzaddikim—Thoroughly holy and righteous Jews who are often regarded as spiritual leaders or exemplars.

About the Author

Nachman Davies is an Orthodox Jew, but in his youth he had been a Discalced Carmelite monk. He converted to *Progressive* Judaism in Jakarta under the auspices of the RSGB in 1992. In 2016 he completed an *Orthodox* Jewish conversion process in Madrid under the auspices of the Israeli (Sephardi) Chief Rabbinate.

For most of his life he was a school music teacher and Javanese Gamelan musician, working in schools in the United Kingdom and then as the Director of Music in large International schools based in Jakarta and in Singapore.

He became deaf in 2000 as a result of senso-neural illness, and he accepted that apparent tragedy as a call to return to the intentionally contemplative life of his youth. He spent twelve years as a Jewish Contemplative (a *mitkarev*) in a cave-house in Salobrena, Southern Spain, and then in Torremolinos as a devoted member of its warm and supportive Spanish-Moroccan Jewish Community.

With the help of Heaven, he made aliyah to Israel in 2019 and has since returned to life as a full time dedicated contemplative, currently living in a hermitage in Tzfat, Israel.

The Cave of the Heart ✡ Kuntres Maarat Ha-Lev

The Cave of the Heart ✡ Kuntres Maarat Ha-Lev

Printed in Great Britain
by Amazon

Savage Mafia Prince

Copyright ©2016 by Annika Martin
Print Edition

All rights reserved. Except as permitted under the U.S. Copyright Act of 1976, no part of this publication may be reproduced, distributed, or transmitted in any form or by any means, or stored in a database or retrieval system, without the prior written permission of the author.

This is a work of fiction. Names, characters, places, and incidents are either the products of the author's imagination or used fictitiously, and any resemblance to actual persons, living or dead, or business establishments, organizations or locales is completely coincidental.

www.annikamartinbooks.com
Cover art: Bookbeautiful

Savage Mafia Prince/ Annika Martin.—1st ed.
ISBN-10: 1539345068
ISBN-13: 978-1539345060

Where is Kiro?
He's the lost Dragusha brother, heir to a vast mafia empire—brilliant, violent, and utterly savage…and he's been missing for years.

Ann
I'm supposed to be doing simple undercover research at the Fancher Institute for the Mentally Ill & Dangerous, but I can't keep my mind off Patient 34. He's startlingly young and gorgeous, but it's not just that. He's strapped way too tightly to that bed. And there's no name or criminal history on his chart. What are these people hiding? My reporter's instincts are screaming.

Here's the other thing: the staffers here believe he's so sedated that there's not a thought in his head, but I catch him watching me when nobody's looking. Our connection sizzles when I enter the room. When our eyes meet, I know he understands me in a way nobody else ever has.

I'm supposed to follow my editor's orders—I have secrets, too—but everything about Patient 34 is suspicious. How can I not investigate?

Don't miss a release. Get on my private release alert list for book releases and special deals! It's at
www.annikamartinbooks.com

"I LOVE this book. One of my absolute favorite reads of 2016. I want...no, I NEED my own savage!!!"

~USA Today bestselling author Natasha Knight

Savage Mafia Prince

A DANGEROUS ROYALS ROMANCE

BOOK 3

Annika Martin

CHAPTER ONE

Ann

R*ANDALL IS A rosy-cheeked man with a long gray beard and kind eyes. He sits on a bolted-down bench at the corner of his room in the Fancher Institute, formerly known as Fancher Institute for the Criminally Insane.*

Thirty years ago, Randall killed three people on a city bus, then tried to poison a group of office workers with arsenic-laced cookies, gravely sickening five.

Today he is heavily medicated and confined to the small room twenty-two hours a day. To his right, there is a large window where you can see the face of an orderly peering in, one of two orderlies whose entire job it is to sit in the hall and watch Randall during his waking hours. Randall's one burning goal in life is to behave well enough to reduce it to twenty-one hours.

I decide that's how I'd start the story if I were writing it as a human interest feature on the patients in the mentally ill and dangerous (MI&D) wing of the Fancher Institute. You always hook a story up to one person's drama and try to find one killer detail. The ever-present watching face is a killer detail.

Stories about people have power. They humanize people, connect people. But I'm not here to do a story about a person.

I'm here to do research on a story about *things*. A supply-chain story. The most boring type of story.

A supply-chain story in the middle of nowheresville Minnesota is what you get for kneeling in the rubble in Kabul crying and holding a kitten while you miss the most important meeting of your career.

Everyone called it a breakdown. It's as good a word as any.

Just complete the assignment, I tell myself. *Put your head down and do the work.*

Because I was lucky to get this assignment at all. No reputable editor will touch me these days. This assignment was set up by an editor at *Stormline*, which is not a reputable publication.

A nurse named Zara is introducing me to the patients I'll be monitoring. She thinks I'm a nurse, and in fact I am. I was a nurse before I decided I really just wanted to be a journalist.

I wear a plastic face shield and gloves, and I'm doing a little something with each patient so that Zara can ensure none will react poorly to me. She also wants to make sure that I can handle these MI&D guys.

The MI&D guys won't be a problem. The antiseptic smell might be, though. It's so overpowering, I feel like I'm swimming in it. I don't do well with antiseptic smells these days.

Nurse Zara doesn't want me here, and she's not trying to hide it. "Nurse Ann is going to take your blood pressure now, Randall," Zara says. "You'll be seeing a lot of her."

The HR guy warned me that the staff would resist my presence. Nurse Zara's friend was supposed to be promoted to this job. Everybody on the team thought she'd get it. Then I swooped in and stole it. So I'm a little bit of a pariah.

I've handled worse.

"Hello, Randall," I say softly. Randall's face is flat affect—that's psych-ward talk for no expression. His eyes are vacant as I fit the blood pressure cuff around his flabby bicep. Randall is on a cocktail of drugs they call B-52, which does exactly what you'd imagine it would do—sedating him and slowing his thoughts so much that he's more garden plant than human. He gets extra medication at night. That's the only time an orderly doesn't need to watch him.

I note his progress in a tablet, clicking boxes and entering in the numbers. "Great job! Looks like if you behave well for the rest of the week, you'll get three hours out in the general room," I say to him.

Randall grunts and mumbles something that sounds like agreement.

Zara grumbles. I'd put her age at around twice mine—twenty-nine—so nearly sixty. She has short dyed-blonde hair held back in a bright polka-dot hair band. She told me the guys like when she switches around the pops of color like that. She cares about the guys, but she wants me gone.

In addition to the hostility, I'm starting to sense that Zara smells my lie, or maybe she just senses my unease. Nurses can be really attuned to people's mental states like that, and Zara's good. Spend three decades in a mental ward, and you grow some pretty fierce antennae. She doesn't know about my breakdown, of course.

But Zara's not going to be my biggest problem.

My biggest problem will be Donny, the hulking head of the orderlies. The man has "twisted motherfucker" written all over his face. As far as I can see, the only thing separating Donny from the men strapped to these beds is a conviction in a court of law and a commitment order.

The next patient is a schizophrenic in his early twenties. As a college student, he blew up a highway rest station, killing three. He's in a two-point restraint, which means his wrists are bound to a strap around his waist. He, too, gets the B-52 cocktail, and he has those same flat B-52 eyes.

Zara stands at the door texting on her phone and half watching me as I take his blood pressure and do a blood draw. The skin prick doesn't even seem to register with him. I wonder whether he knows I'm here. I pull up his progress chart. He's working toward having his hands loose for sleeping. "If you behave this well the rest of the week, you'll have a hands-free sleep," I tell him brightly.

"Thank you," he mumbles.

We pause in the hall between each stop to discuss patients. Zara watches my eyes a little too closely during these discussions.

"You can't do this job if you let these guys scare you," she barks.

She's picking up on all the ways I don't belong, or maybe my fragile, fucked-up state of mind. She's picking up on something.

I try for a serene smile. "These guys are fine. I'm good."

What with all of the sedation and restraint, not to mention the watchful orderlies at my beck and call, I couldn't be safer from these men, especially compared with a lot of the subjects I interviewed out in the field in my long-ago days as a reputable journalist.

A lot of those interview subjects were just as imbalanced as these men, except they usually had assault weapons. And the only meds they were on was coffee and maybe alcohol, not the greatest combo when you're a dangerous madman.

And yes, Donny, twisted king of the orderlies, will probably try to push me as far as possible.

But it's the antiseptic smell that's my kryptonite.

Six months ago, I would've laughed if anybody had tried to hand me an assignment like this. I was the intrepid girl reporter you sent to Bhutan or Somalia or Syria. I was the one riding around in Jeeps and Hummers, sitting with fixers in shitty little cafés waiting to meet some of the most interesting people in the world, chasing that fucking story. I lived for the story.

And if it involved the underdog, or the crazy militia leader, or somebody going for the impossible? Sign me up!

Now I'm counting supplies for an editor with a conspiracy theory he thinks the cops are ignoring. I was lucky *Stormline* needed somebody with a nursing degree.

But this is how I'll dig myself out of the burnt and blackened crater of my career. I'll investigate the shit out of this supply-chain thing. I'll do it like it's the best, most important assignment I ever got. The *Stormline* editor will vouch for me on the next one. Then I'll investigate and write the shit out of that one, and so on.

I'll focus on the story in front of me like it's the most important one ever—that's how I'll dig out.

I close my eyes, heart pounding. The antiseptic smell is still getting to me, six months later. I thought I was ready.

I knew the smell would be here, but I thought it wouldn't be a problem. This hospital is not under attack. Nobody will be getting trapped in here. It's a world away from any war zone.

Worse, the smell is making me think about that kitten. I shake it out of my mind. I remind myself the kitten is fine. *You stepped up and saved the kitten. You are a badass.*

Well, I used to be a badass.

I don't feel like a badass. The antiseptic smell is seriously fucking me up. I'll be smelling it all night—I know it already. I won't be able to sleep.

You don't have to tell me how sexy a good downward spiral story is—I'm a journalist. I know.

There is nothing more delicious than the rich Ponzi-scheme guy in handcuffs. The arrogant rock star sliding into drug addiction. The high school heartthrob who was cruel to you who's now cleaning your toilet.

I never thought I'd star in a downward spiral story of my own. I guess nobody does.

We head farther down the hall. I meet a hippie orderly who monitors four guys from a hub. I can tell that he would make an interesting subject, but I'm not writing that kind of piece. Meth. Supply chain. *Stormline.*

Donny, twisted king of the orderlies, comes up. Donny has neon running shoes, several empty ear piercings, and a strategy of showing you who's boss by looking really hard at your tits. His eyes are small and frontally placed. Predator eyes.

"They're ready for 34," Donny says.

"Come on," Zara says.

"What's 34?"

"Patient 34," Zara says. "Come on."

He doesn't get a name? I grab the cart and push it down the hall to where three orderlies are assembled, talking in low tones. They all have stun guns.

"What's up?"

"We go three on standby for hellbeast," Donny says, looking at me a little too hard. He's the kind of guy who's always up to something and who therefore can sense when you're up to something.

I ratchet him up from problem to definite danger. And I see how things will play out, like a perfect storm—

dangerously lechy Donny sensing a chink in my armor, Zara's antagonism toward me, the indifference of the few other staff members I've met, the fact I'm on probation and, worse, not who I say I am.

Handle it.

Donny opens the door. The antiseptic smell is always worse in the rooms. I'm feeling hot, suddenly.

I thought I was ready.

Donny unhelpfully guides me in, hand at the small of my back, except a little too low. I stop and spin. "I got it."

He puts his hands up, like I'm being unduly aggressive.

I turn and push the cart into the tiny room. The door clicks shut, closing us all in.

Donny takes up a post at the corner.

"We got it," Zara says. She doesn't want him in here, either. Donny just stares at her with his scary, frontally placed eyes.

Fuck it all, I think. And I turn to the patient.

And the breath goes out of me.

Patient 34 has a violent halo of dark curls and a short, unruly beard. Sooty lashes line his amber eyes. His energy is…intense, wild, like he was created in some brilliant hellfire. Something about him pulls at me. He's gorgeous in a furious way. He's gorgeous in a stunning, suck-you-in-and-spit-you-out way.

The highest level of restraint is typically a four-point restraint, but Patient 34 is in more like eight points, arms to waist, waist to bed, wrists to bed, ankles to bed, neck to bed.

He stares at a fixed point on the ceiling like the other B-52 patients, gaze blank, but he *feels* utterly different to me. He feels truly alive.

I look up to find Zara watching me sternly, like she caught me doing something wrong. Did I stare at Patient 34 too long?

I lower my face shield and take my place next to his bedside, ready to take his vitals, though I have half a mind to look around for a camera crew, like this is one of those elaborate joke shows where they play tricks and see what people do. He's just...not at all like the others.

Not like any man I've ever seen.

According to 34's chart, he's on B-52 plus a few muscle relaxants and something extra I don't recognize. Enough medication to take down an elephant.

I wrap the BP cuff around his shockingly muscular arm. Shocking, because this is the kind of guy who'll be unhitched from that bed exactly twice a day—to use the restroom and eat. And he's so heavily sedated. When and how is he working out? And what did he do to get himself this level of restraint?

I scroll to the history section of his chart. Blank. I really want to know what he did to get in here. There's no age, though I'd put him younger than me—twenty or twenty-one. I can't even find his goals program chart. "Where's his goals?"

Donny laughs from the corner. "He doesn't get goals. He will never have his meds reduced, he will never have his restraints reduced, and the only way 34's getting out of this room is feet first." *If I have anything to do with it* is the unspoken part of it.

Donny returns his attention to his iPhone.

This guy—so heavily sedated and restrained with a man like Donny hating on him. How does he endure it? I lay a hand on his arm and feel the warmth of him through my latex glove.

"Escape artist," Zara mumbles, not looking up from her phone. The people working on the wing aren't supposed to have their phones, but they all do. They know how to avoid the cameras when they're on them.

"What's his escape technique?" I ask. "Does he turn into The Incredible Hulk?"

Neither of them responds. Well, I thought it was funny.

I slip the cuff around 34's arm, rest my gloved hand on his forearm, and start pumping it. The patients here all wear blue pajama-style shirts and pants. The shirts are short-sleeved and snap at the sides for access.

I glance at his face again.

And the world stops.

Because 34 is there—really there. He's watching me with intelligence, lips quirked like he thought my Hulk comment was funny.

My heart pounds madly. "Hey, I'm going to take your BP, and we'll draw a little blood, okay?"

"He doesn't know what you're saying," Zara snaps from the corner, like I'm this huge idiot. "He's not going to answer. Read his chart."

I read the fucking chart, I think at her. *Why don't you look at his fucking face?* But when I look back down, 34's eyes are blank again, and the shadow of a smile is gone. Was I hallucinating? "It seemed like he was there for a second."

"He hasn't had a coherent thought in his head for months," Donny says. "And he never will again." And again, that unspoken end to the sentence: *If I have anything to do with it.*

Asshole, I think.

I look back down. His eyes are fixed on the ceiling. Back to being a heavily sedated lion. Was I imagining it? I do his BP. It's high for how much he's medicated. "One-twenty over eighty."

Zara pushes off the wall now, annoyed. "That can't be right. Move."

I retreat back to where Donny stands while she takes 34's BP. I'm starting to feel sweaty and a little bit wrong.

Zara calls out the BP results, which are lower—right where it should be for a man on all those drugs. I note it down on his electronic medical record. She thinks I fucked it up out of nervousness.

"Don't worry, we gotcha," Donny says. As you can imagine, he makes it sound like a threat.

I just nod. No words, just a nod. You never give a creep like Donny energy.

Zara puts the blood pressure assembly back in the cart, looking at me hard. "You up for doing the draw?"

"Of course," I say, moving away from creepmeister Donny. I take my place at 34's bedside, and Zara goes back to her phone, safely out of camera range.

Patient 34's eyes are blank as sheetrock. Did I imagine that silent interaction? If I did, that's bad.

If I didn't imagine it, it means he's faking. I suppose it doesn't really matter, considering they have him tied up like he's King Kong crossed with Hannibal Lecter.

I draw his blood. They probably had a dedicated phlebotomist on this at one point, but budget cuts have hit this sector hard. The phlebotomist would've been cut. I try not to watch his face at all.

I think about Donny's crowing words—*Never a coherent thought ever again.* Like Donny is a victor over 34 in some imagined and unfair contest between them. That is so Donny, to have vendettas with the patients he's supposed to be caring for. What did 34 do?

When I'm done, I press a cotton ball to the draw site and set a gloved hand on 34's arm, which really is startlingly thick with muscle. I know I'm not imagining it.

I look into his golden eyes that gaze at nothing and everything. It's likely he did horrible things—you don't end up like Patient 34 because you've been a Boy Scout. But there's a sliver of humanity in everyone. Hopes, dreams, things that unexpectedly touch their hearts.

This is something you learn from telling people's stories.

"All done." I squeeze his arm reassuringly, because everybody deserves compassion, and Zara and Donny can fuck themselves.

CHAPTER TWO

Kiro

"ALL DONE," SHE says softly. She squeezes my arm. Heat floods my body. My heart pounds out of control.

She has piercing green eyes and hair the color of peanuts. She tries to hide it by pulling it back, but her hair is big and curly and will not be hidden. She purses her pink lips. I love watching her lips. She's the most beautiful woman I've ever seen.

Again she squeezes my arm. She seems like a dream with her gentle touch and her talk of The Hulk, like she reached back into another life.

Is it a trick? Another one of their endless tortures? I fight for control, willing her to leave. I can't concentrate with her here.

I should've let the drugs take me under today—that would have dulled the power of her. I sometimes let the drugs take me under as a break from the crushing boredom of this dead place with its buzzers and alarms and the ticking clock that never stops.

And the grating loneliness.

And now her, destroying my concentration. You can never show life in here, or they drug you even more.

She works for them. She's just another one. I'll kill her if I have to. I'll kill them all if I have to. All that matters is getting home. Back where I belong.

How do they even know about The Hulk? I haven't thought about him since I was a kid, locked up in that root cellar.

She moves out of my periphery. The distance makes it easier for me to get myself under control.

I need three conditions to escape. One—a clear head. I have that. Two—the ability to break out of my restraints. The small pair of clippers I have hidden in the mattress is that. Three—some sort of chaos or diversion to take out the guards around the perimeter. I need a disaster, somebody else escaping, a power failure—something. The perimeter guards were my downfall last time.

I don't make the same mistake twice.

So I wait. I'll get my chance. It's a matter of time.

They can never know I have the clippers. They can never know I'm able to work the drugs through my system. The professor who kept me in that cage said I had a high metabolism. Maybe it's true. The exercises help me stay clear, though. I know that. "Isometrics," the professor called them when I'd do them in my cage.

I thought the year that the professor kept me in a cage was bad. Wrong.

The professor would at least read to me, trying to educate me. I would pretend not to hear, not to understand, but the things he read and said were always interesting. I would listen hard, and think things over when he slept.

He hope to educate me and get me to understand supposedly important concepts, so that we could have discussions about how I survived in the wilderness, and mostly, how I got a pack of wild wolves to trust me. He'd guessed—rightly—that they'd let me live in their den.

I would not confirm it. I would tell him nothing.

I felt so lonely, caged up like a savage. Missing the pack. My only friends.

Here is far worse.

They drug me every twelve hours. I strain against my bonds whenever they leave—hard enough to get my blood pumping, to break a sweat. Hard enough to stay clear in the head, ready to kill everyone.

She draws her finger along the shiny front of her computer pad. The screen flashes. Then her fingers are back, a whisper on my arm. I fight to keep my expression dull and lifeless.

She squeezes my arm. Nobody ever touches me like this. I think my heart might explode.

Nurse Zara: "Come on."

She's gone. I follow her footsteps down the hall. I track the squeak of the cart wheels.

You develop strong hearing in the wilderness. It's a form of paying attention, of disciplining the mind. That's something the professor would say, and I always felt he was right, even though I never said so.

Back when he had me in that cage, he would give me sneaky tests on my sense of hearing and my sense of smell, too. Once I caught on that it was what he was doing, and that overdeveloped senses made me different from people who hadn't grown up wild, I pretended not to hear or smell things so well.

You can never give people anything. They only hurt you with it.

If I listen hard enough, I can hear birds singing beyond these walls. Bird songs can be the most lonely thing of all in here. But on some days, on the good days, those songs help me to get back there in my mind, and I can almost convince myself I'm running through fields and forests with the sun on my face.

Wheels squeak. Her heartbeat grows fainter. Room 39.

Mitchell DesArmo is in that room. A dangerous man. I follow their conversation. I stay with her all the way through the rest of her rounds.

The farther away she gets with the power of her beauty and her gentle touch, the more control I feel.

It's a trick—it has to be.

Everything has a rhythm, a pulse. This hospital is a system, just like the forest. Things move. Holes appear. I'll be ready. Nobody else will be ready, but I'll be ready. Stillness is an effective way to hunt.

Stillness is how I killed the professor. He thought he could write a book on me. He thought he could make a sideshow out of me. He thought he was educating Savage Adonis—he told me that was the name the reporters gave me when I was pulled out of the wilderness.

The professor thought that if he got the Savage Adonis's head filled full enough with words and concepts, that I would be his loyal helper.

The professor wanted Savage Adonis's secrets. Instead he got Savage Adonis's hands around his neck.

I waited for my moment just like I'm waiting here.

Soon.

The squeak of the wheels.

Nurse Ann leaving the wing. A door. Another door. Gone.

I should feel relief. Misery gnaws at my gut instead.

If I can endure the boredom and pain of this place, I can endure her gentle touch.

I shut my eyes to close out the feelings. Three things to escape. The path I cut back home will run with the blood of anybody who tries to stop me.

Does he escape by turning into The Incredible Hulk?

It's coincidence that she talked about The Hulk. It's been so long since I thought of my boyhood before the forest. The piano wire. The tree. The root cellar.

She's a new torment, that's all.

A new torment that hurts more than Donny's stun gun.

CHAPTER THREE

Ann

AFTER WE FINISH our rounds, Zara and I head to the general room, which is a type of rec room with bolted-down chairs and tables and a TV on the wall that only staff—meaning Donny—controls. Two dozen patients are in here, coloring and watching TV. Zara tells me about where the different groups sit, who doesn't get along with whom.

These are the most well-behaved patients, but still, orderlies hover all around, watching, tracking things on tablets. This is a place of immense bureaucracy and paper trails denoting every action of every patient right down to when they take a piss, and I mean that literally.

We head to the staff room, where it's a little easier to breathe thanks to the cooking smells overpowering the antiseptic smell. In a way, though, it's worse, because I'm in a room full of people who don't want me here.

I hold up my head. Stay pleasant. This isn't my life, right?

There are more than a dozen nurses and nurse aides: a few guys out of the army, some older women from the float pool—substitute nurses, basically. There are full-timing young mothers—the sister hospital across town has a great free day-care program they get to take advantage of.

Sometimes in a strange group of mostly women, I'll try to get the talk around to kids and get people pulling out pictures. It's nice as an icebreaker. And the truth is, I really do love seeing the kids. I love the way women's faces look when they show you. I love to hear the little stories they tell about pictures. Stories bond people, humanize people to each other.

When I first entered journalism, I believed that understanding each other's stories could solve all of the world's problems.

It takes strength to believe big things like that, and I don't have that kind of strength anymore.

And I have a feeling that, in this group, my questions will be seen as nosy.

When they ask me whether I have kids, I tell them no, I don't have kids. The truth. I tell them I'm from Idaho and that I did a ton of travelling and volunteer work around the world, which is close to the truth. I know my story doesn't make sense to them, to go from worldwide travel to a notorious MI&D facility in an impoverished rural northern Minnesota town, a place where I have no friends or relatives. They may not acknowledge it consciously, but deep down, they know I don't add up.

The best lie would be to say that I'm really into camping and that I want to be at the edge of the Boundary Waters Canoe Area and Quetico, the massive swath of pristine wilderness between Minnesota and Canada. But I can't talk outdoors talk, so I tell them instead that I think it's gorgeous, and that I want to buy a canoe and explore this beautiful area. Zara warns me about winter. It's early October and already cold as fuck. She asks me whether I'm ready for the true cold.

"So far, so good," I say.

She proceeds to tell me the horror stories about six-foot snowdrifts and stretches of subzero temps. The group joins in; they seem to enjoy telling me how bad it's going to be, like, *you made your bed, now lie in it.*

Will this be their attitude if I have trouble with Donny?

Somebody has brought cake along with bright paper plates and plastic forks in celebration of a young nurse's birthday, and I find I'm hugely conflicted about taking a piece. Will they dislike me even more if I pass up this offering or if I take one? I decide it won't matter either way, so I take one.

Talk ceases as we eat our cake. Back in the magazine office where I worked in New York, we would celebrate birthdays just like this, except nobody would actually eat the cake.

The cake is delicious, and in spite of their vague hostility, I'm seriously hoping that if there is a meth supply pipeline running through here, it's all Donny.

If there's a pipeline at all.

Murray Moliter, my editor at *Stormline*, could be smoking crack with the whole thing. He got a tip he felt was credible for whatever reason, and the tipster suggested the cops weren't investigating because they're in on it.

Fine by me. I'm getting double pay here—my nursing wage along with a per diem from *Stormline*. I'll get Murray the facts he needs on what's going in and out of here. I'll do a good job. Work my way back.

Each of the ten nurses under Zara oversees the medical care of ten patients. They all seem to know I have Patient 34. I suspect I got him because I'm new, and he's the dangerous one nobody wants.

I was surprised when Zara called him an escape artist. The layers of security here are insane—how could anyone escape? "So how many times has Patient 34 tried to break out?" I ask. "Has he actually gotten close?"

They glance at each other the way people do when there's juicy gossip. Soon the stories are flying.

It seems Patient 34 once used a ballpoint pen to wear down his canvas wrist restraint. Another time he got free and tied up orderlies and nurses. He has smashed through the supply closet door and two walls. He has jumped through safety glass. He once beat up five stun-gun-wielding orderlies.

Twice Patient 34 has made it to the parking lot. The electrified fence stopped him once. For the most recent attempt, he created his own rubber mitts with art materials. He smashed Donny's head on a wall, knocking him out, and almost made it, but the guards around the perimeter took him down with tranquilizer guns.

It seems the Fancher Institute has implemented quite a number of new features thanks to Patient 34. The general consensus is that he won't be trying to escape anymore, but people are a little voodoo about him.

"Why doesn't he have a name?" I ask.

"Because he's a John Doe," one of them says, like I'm stupid.

"But surely he knows his own name," I say. "He could've told you it before he was so sedated."

"Patient 34 cooperates with nobody."

"What was his original conviction?"

"We don't have that," Nurse Zara snaps, like it's an outrageous question, which it definitely isn't.

It's important to know whether a patient is a firebug, whether they have women issues, various triggers, all of that. All they know about Patient 34 is that it was some sort of violent assault around a year ago. "A year and some change" is how Zara had put it.

"The rumor is that he's in WITSEC," one of the guys says. "That the stuff is sealed for his own protection."

I nod like this sounds reasonable. It's not. If he was in witness protection, he'd have a fake name and a fake history. "Who handles his board hearings?"

"Fancher," one of the nurses says. "You could ask him about it," she adds with an innocent shrug. People's faces are carefully blank. Which tells me that going all the way to the top of the Fancher Institute—to Dr. Fancher himself—is a bad idea.

Still, I think about it. I pass Fancher's office on my way to HR to drop off my insurance forms. His door is cracked. I pause. I tell myself not to get curious. I tell myself Patient 34's story is irrelevant.

And I knock. And then I think, *fuck fuck fuck.*

A booming voice: "Come in."

Dr. Fancher is a man of about fifty with a military haircut, strangely wet lips, and frontally placed eyes just like Donny. In fact he looks a lot like Donny. Possibly a relative. Great.

"I wanted to introduce myself. I'm Ann Saybrook—I just joined the team on the MI&D wing."

"Welcome." He taps his pen. He doesn't get up.

"Are you and Donny—"

"He's my nephew," Dr. Fancher says. "So far, so good?" He asks this in a way where you know the only answers he wants to hear is "yup-thanks-bye!"

"Yup." I smile. I should go away. I'm not here to draw attention to myself. At least that's what I'm repeating over and over in my head. But I keep picturing Patient 34 in his crazy restraints, and Donny's hatred of him, and the way he looked at me.

The way he *felt*. So intense. So alive.

I suck in a breath. "Patient 34 is one of my cases, and I noticed there's not much on him in terms of family history or incident history. The more I know, the better care I can deliver."

Fancher levels his gaze at me. "If we were at liberty to add that information to his chart, we'd add that to his chart, don't you think?" He says it as though I'm just a little slow-witted. "I don't imagine you could have any issues with him already..."

"Everything's going great." I give him my best "no-threat-here!" smile. "I just want to deliver the best care possible."

Fancher rocks back in his chair, relaxing. "He's an extremely troubled and dangerous John Doe. Of course we do everything we can to locate family and get family members involved in the patients' care, but they're not always out there, Ms. Saybrook."

I nod like I'm swallowing his utter bullshit. "Of course."

"You let me know if you have trouble with him."

Smile smile smile. "I will! Thank you!"

I leave, telling myself I'm here to count supplies, not draw attention. *Supply chain!*

That afternoon, I learn that there are two places medications are kept. Pharma One is controlled by a staff pharmacist during the day and locked at night. Pharma Two is where we get medications that don't require a pharmacist's sign-off—the kind of stuff you'd find in a drugstore, including ephedrine, which is one of the substances I need to keep an eye on. I'll figure out who's doing the ordering and set up a ghost system for tracking it.

Over the next few days, I work on being the invisible observer.

Randall earns his three hours in the general room. Zara and I set a new goal for him: behave well enough in there to earn a drop in meds.

The rewards for the guys here are always either a reduction in the level of restraint and medication or an increase in freedom. It is up to me to suggest rewards for my men to work toward.

But when the patient behaves poorly, Donny and Zara decide on what happens—increase in restraint, increase in meds, reduction of free time out in the coveted general room. And then it's a climb back up.

I'm like these guys in a way. I fucked up and now I'm digging myself out, trying to regain a few privileges. Win back some professional respect.

I monitor Pharma Two like a hawk. I take my own personal inventory and find out shipment days before the week is up.

On the downside, the smell doesn't get better. Some days I feel like I'm drenched in antiseptic.

The antiseptic smell brings me back to being trapped in that rubble with those kids. Singing. Maybe a vat of it spilled during the bombing, I don't know. The smell clings to me at night. More and more, I wake up in the middle of the night gasping for breath, reliving the kitten incident, my sleep broken into useless bits.

Patient 34 is a complete zombie when I visit him the first time on my own—or as much on my own as you can be with three stun-gun-wielding orderlies in the hall. They're supposed to be watching through the window, but as usual, they're all on their phones—mostly Facebook and YouTube, from what I've noticed.

I carry around two phones—one dummy one, and one in a knee sock holder under my pants. It's an old habit from the field. You always have a little bit of money and the phone you're willing to let them steal out and visible, and you hide the stuff you need to protect—the important phone, the real money.

I'm struck again by his beauty. There's something utterly powerful yet totally vulnerable about him. Somehow, this man hits me right in the gut.

It's not just about his moment of seeming consciousness; it's because of how he calls to me. How something in me answers. Just lying there, he calls to me.

I find myself reaching for my important phone—my secret cell—to get the shot.

Taking photos like this is second nature. A shot like this isn't just about recording a subject, it's about seeing from a new perspective, seeing more deeply. Honoring something amazing.

I photograph him close up and full body, then I slip the phone away.

I pull out the blood pressure and blood draw stuff. Not even the crinkling paper seems to attract 34's attention. His face is a perfect blank.

I should be relieved that I'm seeing the blankness everyone else is seeing. Ask most people who fucked up in a big way and they'll tell you their first goal is simple normalcy.

In truth, I'm disappointed 34 is so blank.

I made that joke, and he smiled yesterday. It was a nice moment. I want that consciousness back, if only just for a moment.

It's probably a bad sign that the warmest human connection I've felt all week is with a guy strapped to a bed in an institute for the mentally ill and dangerous. Because he's in *an institute for the mentally ill and dangerous.*

I fit the cuff around his arm and press the Velcro pieces together. "You should at least have a name. A fucking name."

He doesn't answer. Not that I expected it.

It offends my sense of fair play that he only gets a number. Fancher's stonewalling offends me even more. "*But the family is not always there, Ms. Saybrook,*" I repeat under my breath. "*Ms. Saybrook.* What an asshole. You wanna patronize me? Really?"

Patient 34's blood pressure is way up yet again. The last thing I want to do is call Zara in again and have her get a normal reading, as though I'm fucking it up.

But I can't ignore it.

I step away and lean against the door to give him space, just in case my talking did it. He could be picking up on my anger at Fancher and this whole situation. Unbalanced people can be extraordinarily sensitive.

I go back for a redo, trying to use Zara's super low-touch style. His BP is down a little on the second try. At least in normal range. I jot down that reading and do his blood and the rest of my check.

The rest of the week is uneventful, aside from my not being able to sleep, thanks to the antiseptic scent clinging to my skin and nose. It feels like it's inside me sometimes, which I know is crazy.

On the upside, with every visit, 34's blood pressure drops a bit more. At the end of the week, it's right where it was for Zara.

He always exhibits that flat affect, but there are times, as I go about my business, that I could swear he's almost glowering at me, or at least staring at me intensely, but then when I look directly at him, his face is blank…though sometimes it's more like *furiously blank.*

Which sounds a little odd, I know. It's just that, even when he's staring blankly at the ceiling, he *feels* aware. Sometimes I have this weird sense that he doesn't want me there.

But I'm not sleeping, so I'm a mess. I could be imagining things. Projecting.

I keep talking to him. It's not like anybody else there wants to talk to me. I say little things at first, like, "It's me again. What do you think about that? Not much, huh?" Or I report on the ever-evolving cake and treat activity in the staff room. I tell him I'm thinking about bringing cookies. "Maybe the way to their hearts is through their stomachs," I say. "Wow, that kind of makes me sound like a termite, doesn't it?"

A muscle in his cheek twitches at that. I tell myself it was a shadow.

I come to look forward to seeing him. Strange that the most engaging person in this place would be a John Doe on so many drugs that he probably has the consciousness of a cantaloupe, but there you have it.

Still, there are these moments when I'm sure he's fucking with me.

It's exactly ten days into my brilliant career as a Fancher Institute team member and secret tracker of ephedrine supplies that I catch him.

I'm sitting at 34's bedside updating patient charts on the Fancher-issued tablet. He's his usual blank self, and as usual, I'm talking to him like he's there.

"I know what you're doing. You want to lull us into complacency and make your big break. I've heard the tales of your last attempts. They sound brilliant, for what it's worth." I flick through screens while I talk. "And I hear you smashed Donny's head into a wall. I don't know why they have you strapped up here. Between you and me, you'd have to be insane *not* to want to smash Donny's head into a wall."

I look up and our gazes meet, or, more accurately, his eyes are momentarily riveted to mine. He quickly looks away, all blank, but it's too late—I caught him.

I stand, shocked.

I know what I saw. He's only pretending to be out of it. Fooling everybody.

I don't know what to do. I'm inclined to keep his secret, because I feel this strange connection with him, but he could be really dangerous.

Who am I kidding? Of course he's dangerous. Everybody in here killed at least one person. And he's also an escape artist.

I think of the innocent children beyond these walls. I think about the nice girl at my coffee shop. The cops. My fellow nurses.

I have a responsibility here.

I walk out and tell the orderlies to stay put. I go down the hall to find Zara at her computer. I tell her that I suspect Patient 34 has found a way to skip his meds. "He is highly aware, and his thoughts are as fast as yours or mine." I say. That's one of the main effects of the drugs they give the patients—slow thoughts.

"They do move and twitch," she replies, like I'm stupid.

"It wasn't that, Zara. This man is acting. He tracks speech and responds."

She heaves out of her chair, annoyed. "He's ingesting every bit of his medication."

We head down the hall. "I know it sounds improbable," I say.

"He's on B-52 with zyzitol. It's not improbable, it's impossible. What exactly happened?"

"I was…kind of talking as I went about my protocol. I, um…think the sound of a voice can soothe, you know, and I made this joke, and—"

"What was the joke?"

"Just some dumb joke."

"What?" she asks.

"Oh, I was talking about his escape attempts, and I said…a joke about how he knocked Donny's head into a wall…"

She stops and turns to me. "Do you think it's appropriate to joke about violence toward the staff?"

I suppose I could say that he's supposedly on so many drugs that it shouldn't matter what I say to him, but seeing as how I've been saying all along that I think he's alert, I decide to go for a simple answer—"No."

She leads the way into his room. Patient 34 has his perfect flat affect. She checks his pupils, his pulse, his blood pressure. She runs through a few low-tech tests, poking his foot and so forth. Patient 34 passes with flying colors…if your goal is to appear barely conscious.

"Do you need me to have one of the other staff members take him over?" she asks.

Fuck.

"Of course not." I'm on probation here. Why couldn't I keep my big mouth shut? And it's not like he's going to ever get out of his huge amounts of restraints. "It must have been a twitch," I say obediently.

She turns on her heel and heads out. Angrily. The guys in the hall return to their social media empires. I go back in and sit down on the side of 34's bed with my back to the hall window so they can't see my face—not that they're watching. Still. I fight back the tears.

Maybe I really am losing it. What if the whole world is right about me and I'm wrong? That I really am messed up?

"Happy now?" I ask him.

He stares vacantly at the ceiling.

"Oh, fuck you, you fucking faker." I take a deep breath, trying to center myself. I have to collect myself. I can't go back out into the hall like this.

It's my lack of sleep, that's all.

Patient 34 just stares on and on, eyes fixed on a point on the ceiling, godlike features perfectly fucking arranged. I decide it's the contrast that makes his golden eyes pop, because his lashes are so dark and inky.

"Fuck you for that, too," I say. "For those lashes. Oh my God, I've officially sunk to a new low. A guy in a loony bin has gotten the best of me without saying a word. Oh, I'm sorry, mentally ill and dangerous ward. Is that better? Do you prefer that?"

I'm feeling all emotional, like I did with the kitten.

"Fucking kitten, I should've left it trapped." I rub my eyes. "What was I doing?"

Still he stares vacantly. His lips are lush and full for a man's. They don't shave a lot of these guys; they just clip their beards and hair, and not really well, but somehow the slightly choppy look is awesome on 34. Like a hot post-apocalyptic warrior youth. On goes the stare. The somewhat mechanical blinking.

"Don't even," I say. "I know you're there. You don't have to playact anymore. Just don't even."

Nothing.

I need to get myself under control.

"If I wasn't sleeping so shittily, maybe I wouldn't be obsessing about the kitten," I whisper. "Or do you think it's the other way around? If I wasn't obsessing about the kitten, maybe I wouldn't be sleeping so poorly. What do you think? Or is this just like that movie. *One Flew Over the Cuckoo's Nest,* right? Will I end up in here? Damn."

I focus down on the tablet.

"It was so tiny." I bite back the tears. I will not cry. "I never talk about the kitten, and now I'm telling you. That's not messed up." I take a deep breath here. "Except you don't talk back. That would really make me look crazy! Wouldn't Nurse Zara love me then? You should try to squeeze out a few words. That would really be some badass gaslighting."

I feel that awareness from him, and when I look, I think I catch a flick of his eyes. Or do I? *B-52 with zyzitol. It's not improbable, it's impossible.*

I suck in a breath. "I remember once in driver's ed, they showed this movie where it simulated if you tried to drive while on drugs. They showed this windshield, and everything was blurry except a bug that splattered there. They said, 'If you are on drugs, you might focus on something like a bug instead of the road.' Maybe that's what I did back in Kabul. But it's not like I endangered anybody." I look at the time. I need to get to my rounds. "I couldn't pass it by. Its little screams. I couldn't not hear them."

He says nothing, of course.

Myself, I laugh-cry a little. "It cost me everything. So yeah, I guess there's that. No, that's a good point. But I had to save it, you know? It was like I hit a wall, and I couldn't let my fixer drive on by any more than I could've swallowed my own tongue. It was a physical impossibility."

I grab a tissue just to rip it up.

"That little paw sticking out of that gap in the rubble." My voice is hoarse. "I felt like I wouldn't be able to breathe if I didn't get that kitten out of there. Literally couldn't breathe, you know what I mean?"

His chest rises more abruptly than usual. Just twitches. I won't let him fuck me up again.

"I know what you're thinking—the kitten was Freudian projection."

I pause, surprised. I actually never thought of that before. How did I not think of that before?

"Yeah, you're right. It seems so obvious—no, you're right. I walk out of that hospital collapse like it's nothing. All that time like it's nothing. But then a few weeks later, we pass a tiny kitten trapped in rubble, and I lose my shit. Pretty suspicious, right?"

I focus on his strong hand, mind racing. *Could* it be projection?

"Yeah, you think the kitten is me. Crying. And I rescue myself, and then I just sit there holding it, crying. But why would I sit in the road and cry if I rescued myself? That's a flaw in your theory, 34, clever as it is."

My blood races. Strangely, I feel better.

I straighten up. Do I honestly feel better, having talked about it? I pack up the cart. "Should we meet here tomorrow? Yes? Tomorrow's good for you? Awesome."

CHAPTER FOUR

Aleksio

THE BACK DOOR of the storage warehouse is secured with a chain and padlock.

I smash the fuck out of it with a sledgehammer. This is the seedy part of Chicago. Nobody's around—nobody that will care, anyway.

I slip in with Tito at my side. We've worked together, bled together, killed together for years, me and Tito. We don't even have to signal, we just slip in, weapons out, and start clearing rooms. Five guys slip in behind us, quiet as night.

The choreography of crime has sunk deep into our bones.

Gunfire sounds from the front. Tito raises his brows. The point was for us to handle the fighting part, being that my brother Viktor is still injured.

We head up to find Viktor standing over ten men. They're all on their bellies, arms outstretched. Viktor's girlfriend, Tanechka, walks up and down the row of them. Tanechka and Viktor came out of the Russian *mafiya*. They know how to hold a room.

"So much for the intel about them being in back of the warehouse," Tito mumbles, holstering his Luger.

I catch Tanechka's eye and put my hand out, palm down. It's our sign for Kiro, our lost baby brother, like patting a little boy's head. Of course Kiro would be a grown man by now—twenty-one years old. My heart twists at the thought.

Kiro was just a baby in a crib, fat little arms waving, when they ripped him away. Sold him into a shady adoption ring, we later learned.

Tanechka nods and places a boot on one of the men's heads. I never met him, but apparently she has. "Hello, Charles."

"I'll tell you where the cash is," Charles says. "You can have it."

"Is not enough." Her Russian accent sounds extra harsh, and I wonder whether she's doing it for effect. "You remember me?"

Charles says nothing. The correct answer would be *yes*. Nobody forgets Tanechka.

"You kept me in a little room. Prisoner, auctioning me off like eBay. You kept all those girls. You made them cry. You think all I want is cash? Cash is where we start. Can you guess where we end?"

The man says nothing.

My brother Viktor grins, stupidly, madly in love with Tanechka. Tito just leans against a wall, enjoying the show.

Tanechka demands cash, records, and communications equipment. She's not going to kill Charles, but he thinks she will.

Any one of us could threaten him, but it feels good to leave it to Tanechka. He wronged her and a lot of other women. He probably has a thing against women.

He starts spilling. Tanechka smiles over at Viktor. The information he's giving up will help us destroy our enemy, Lazarus, aka Bloody Lazarus, and take back what's ours—namely, the kingdom he stole from us when we were too young to understand.

But our real goal is Kiro. We've heard rumors that Lazarus has a lead on finding Kiro.

Lazarus wants to kill Kiro. He *needs* to kill Kiro.

It might seem strange that Lazarus, a powerful Albanian mafia kingpin, would need to kill a man he hasn't seen for twenty years, but that's the power of a prophecy for you.

I know, it's the twenty-first century, but the Albanians are a superstitious bunch, and the prophecy holds that we brothers together will rule—me, Viktor, and our baby brother, Kiro. Enough people believe the prophecy that it matters—a lot.

It's bad. We have to get to Kiro first.

Unfortunately, Lazarus has ten times the men we do, and ten times the resources.

The prophecy was given by an elderly crone who supposedly had the evil eye. She had blood-red fingernails that transfixed me as a child, and I can remember her pointing to baby Kiro in his crib and saying that nobody could beat the three of us. That together, we brothers would rule.

It was the week after Kiro was born. I was eight or nine, and Viktor was maybe two.

People have been trying to tear us apart ever since. Or, barring that, to kill at least one of us.

That would be Lazarus's goal. He can never truly rule if all three of the Dragusha brothers are alive with the potential of uniting.

Viktor and I are hard as hell to kill. I doubt there are any guys left who are willing to try anymore. But where's

Kiro? He has no idea of any of this. No awareness of the firestorm with his name on it. He could be easy to kill.

A sitting duck.

Viktor and I found each other last year. Now we just need Kiro. Kiro's more important than ruling or being invincible. But short of finding him, the fastest way to protect him is to take down Lazarus. Keep him hurting. Rattle every cage.

It's about family.

A few months after the prophecy came down, Lazarus and his mentor slaughtered our parents in the nursery where we used to play. They carried off Viktor and Kiro, both screaming and crying.

I saw it all.

A family friend grabbed me and hid me before all this went down, but he wasn't quite fast enough to get me out of the house. The best he could do was to pull me into a dark nursery nook and hold me tight while the bloodbath raged. While my brothers were taken. His arms were iron bands around me, his hand a cigar-scented seal over my mouth.

That was the last time I saw Kiro. A baby with big, bright eyes.

I make the sign again. Little boy. Ask about Kiro.

"What is this about Kiro Dragusha I hear?" Tanechka asks Charles. "Is it true Bloody Lazarus has found him? Perhaps if you tell me, perhaps I won't make you a pincushion for my *pika*." She moves her blade in a figure-eight, silver flashing in the light.

"Kiro Dragusha is dead," Charles says. "Everyone knows."

Viktor shoots me a glance. I shake my head grimly. Not true. I'd feel it if Kiro were dead.

"You have seen the body?" Tanechka asks.

"Not me, but people have."

"Who?"

"Sabri, I think…"

I shake my head at Viktor. It's bullshit. This guy doesn't know.

We start pulling them out.

Tito comes up beside me. "It's bad that everyone thinks he's dead."

"He's not dead," I bite out.

"I get it," Tito says. "But the more guys think Kiro is dead, the more they want to go over to Lazarus. Be on the winning team. And the more powerful he gets. Perception is reality, man."

"Fuck that," I say. "The reality is that we just took down Bloody Lazarus's most profitable operation and took ten of his guys off the street. The reality is that we'll just keep hitting and hitting until Laz is ended and Kiro is back." I turn to Viktor. "Get that C-4. I want this place rubble."

Tito eyes me. "You sure? This warehouse is a nice fucking asset."

"Now it's a fucking message," I growl.

CHAPTER FIVE

Kiro

WAIT FOR MY chance to escape. Destroy anybody who tries to stop me. A simple strategy. It was always so simple here.

Until her.

Morning. I catch her clean, spicy scent in the hall. Starting her rounds for the day. My body floods with heat.

I try to calm myself. I listen to her with Randall. She rips the Velcro. Pumps the pumps.

The cart squeaks nearer. My heart pounds. Lightness in my chest.

Her kindness is the most dangerous weapon they've brought out because it screws me up and makes me forget she's one of them. Makes me forget she's the enemy.

I recite my three conditions of escape: a clear head, bonds broken, gate guards distracted or incapacitated.

Three conditions. Ann is irrelevant. She's just one of them. An enemy.

The cart wheels squeak, then stop. Four stops before she gets to me.

She doesn't ever sit and talk with the other patients, but she almost always sits and talks to me these days.

I turn her words over in my mind in the hours after she leaves. I don't know half the things she talks about. I don't know what Freudian projection is. I don't know what *One Flew Over the Cuckoo's Nest* means or what Kabul is.

I don't understand her story about the kitten or the rubble. I can't tell if it's one story or many stories, or what any of it has to do with being a nurse.

The professor tried to stuff a lot of words and concepts into my head over the year he held me and studied me, but there's a lot he didn't teach me. I understand nothing about the pads and phones they all have. Always touching the glass to light it up.

The professor was studying me, but really I was studying him. Absorbing his language. Learning how to act like him so that he could forget what I was. So that he could forget I was dangerous. It worked.

I killed him.

And ended up in this place—a far worse place. Never mind; I'll get out of this place, too.

Nurse Ann found herself holding the kitten in the middle of the street. Drawn by its cries. I understand that part.

The squeaky cart wheels. Another door. Another patient. Soon it will be me.

I love it and hate it when she talks to me.

It's the worst when she sounds sad. I want to break my bonds and grab her, hold her, speak to her in soft tones like she does with me. It's stupid to blow my one chance at escape just to comfort her.

She's one of them.

Nurse Ann has already tried to hurt me—she ran to get Nurse Zara when she caught me staring at her.

If they understood my head was clear, they'd give me more drugs, and my chance to escape would be gone. Everything in me needs to be pointed at getting back home—not at Nurse Ann with her sad stories and pretty green eyes and the unbearable torment of her touch.

Never again.

I have to get away from them all, back to the wilderness where nobody can find me.

Home.

Ann thinks I'm playing games. She couldn't be more wrong. I'm in a struggle for my life.

Voices. The orderlies gathering outside. Waiting for Ann.

I resolve to keep my face and eyes perfectly blank this time.

I was angry when she raised the alarm, but I still felt sorry for her when Nurse Zara made her feel stupid for thinking I was alert.

Do you need me to have one of the other staff members take him over? Nurse Ann was so upset, so distressed. God, I could feel her pain like a blade.

The impulse to break away was nearly overwhelming. I wanted to rip Nurse Zara's throat out. I wanted to hold Nurse Ann in my arms.

My heart was racing so wildly, it was a miracle nobody noticed.

I loved the angry way she spoke after Nurse Zara scolded her, though. *Fuck you, you fucking faker.* I felt so proud of her for the way she refused to collapse.

I stare at the water-stained tiles above me, getting myself under control. They're waiting for the third orderly, following the rules. They like three out there. They think three could stop me.

Three would not stop me.

I'm not good with words or technology or knowing TV or movies or the names of faraway places, but I'm good with my hands. Good at killing. I just need the perimeter guards handled—that's the lesson I learned the last time I tried to get out. There will be a storm. A disaster. Any day now, a hole in the security will appear.

And I'll be ready to take advantage of it.

Squeaky cart wheels. She talks with the orderlies in low tones.

I shake the thoughts from my head.

The door opens. She walks into the room. Heat floods my veins.

"Hi, 34." The pain in her voice cuts me.

She sits so near my right hand, I can feel her warmth.

She folds her hands and rests them near my hand. So near.

I stare at the ceiling, fighting the urge to look into her eyes and show her she's not alone here. She sighs. The sensation of her crashes into me.

"Another shit day at Casa Fancher." No, it's not sadness; it's distress. My muscles buzz with energy. I stare at the ceiling, faking blankness.

It's here I smell Donny on her. My pulse spikes. My blood races with the need to go crazy.

Donny touched her.

Every nerve ending in my body goes on wild alert. I ball my fists before I can stop myself. I force myself to relax them. Luckily, she doesn't see.

I remind myself that Donny touches people all the time. He touches Nurse Zara. He slaps guys on the shoulder. It doesn't mean anything.

Still my blood races.

She's rustling wrappers. Something's wrong—I can tell by her face, and even if I couldn't see her, I would know from the way she rustles wrappers. Wildly, recklessly, I study her profile for clues to her state of mind—sadness, desperation, fear? I study the swoop of her nose, the way her lips plump out in silent concentration. I love her lips.

When she's upset, pink spots mark the skin under her cheekbones. When she's embarrassed, pink creeps up her neck. Her emotions live at the surface of her pale skin.

She's so pale, but her spirit is rich and wild. Her heart beats strong and true.

It's hard not to stare at her. Hard not to imagine touching her. Feeling her warmth. Kissing her.

She takes out the computer tablet and studies the screen, tapping it now and then. I'm grateful she's not looking at me—my eyes are anything but vacant. I imagine pulling her to me and burying my nose in her neck—that's where her clean spicy scent comes from. Mostly from the left side of her neck. I imagine putting my nose there and sucking in her scent, of taking just that one thing for myself. Like everything might be worth that one moment of holding her.

I want to do it so badly, spots appear before my eyes.

I haven't felt sunlight on my skin since that brief race for freedom some months back. If I ever want to feel sunshine on my skin again, I need to ignore her. I tell this to myself over and over.

I manage dull eyes just in time for her to look over at me.

"We're going to do blood pressure first. What do you think?" *Rrrrip.* Velcro. "Please be low," she whispers. "Please just be low."

Desperation. Weariness. What happened?

My blood pressure won't be low. Her distress is ruining my calm.

Ignore her!

It would be better if Nurse Zara sent a different nurse to manage me, but I think I would die if I couldn't see Ann again.

Electricity slides over my skin as she takes hold of my arm. With gentle movements, she fits the cuff around my arm. The sweetness of her touch kills me, even through the gloves. What would it be like if she touched me skin to skin?

She sighs the way she sometimes does before she speaks.

Every fiber in me strains toward her. She mumbles something unintelligible about counting, then, "Fucking antiseptic." More mumbling. Then, "If I just didn't smell it at home. If I could go an hour without it in my nose. Like particles of smell are stuck in there. Or is it some hallucination? Fuck. Sorry."

She rips off the cuff and repositions it. My mouth goes dry.

"Maybe I should wear that stuff mortuary workers wear, you know? Under their noses? To mask the smell? That menthol. What do you think? That menthol. A little menthol…lotta menthol." She sighs.

Her sad sigh makes me want to rip the clouds down. She repositions the cuff and pumps. She won't like the number.

"I should do that, huh? Anything's better. If I could go a few days without the smell, I could sleep. It's just the smell. It's the smell. Of course it's bothering me. Who wouldn't be bothered?" She checks the numbers. "Fuck."

You get a lot of self-control living wild. I could stay hungry for days. I could catch and kill prey with my bare hands. I could sit in a snowy glen for hours and melt the snow around my skin long before I felt cold. I used to be able to control my blood pressure here, once I'd realized that a higher number meant more attention, sometimes more drugs.

Try harder. Fight for the sunshine. Fight for your life.

She sighs. Everything about her is beautiful.

My desire to touch her twists my heart.

CHAPTER SIX

Ann

THE PROBLEM WITH being sleep-deprived is that you lose your center, your ballast. I feel like I'm drifting in a boat at the mercy of wind and waves.

I tell myself that people go without sleep for days on end all the time. I tell myself it's fine.

It's not fine, though.

I'm tired. Mentally fragile as a tissue. I cried on the way driving here because of a Tom Petty song on the radio. Fucking Tom Petty, right?

It doesn't help that Donny was out in the parking lot when I arrived. He popped up out of nowhere and scared the shit out of me.

It was pretty clear that he was waiting for me. Thank goodness I had my keychain in my hand with a mini-canister of mace attached. I smiled and twirled it on my finger, then clasped it, making sure he saw it. A silent threat.

A man like Donny, he's had mace in his face before.

We went into the facility together with its fog of antiseptic smell. Of course I had to ditch my mace with my keys in my locker before I passed through security. Mace and keys are on the list of things you're not supposed to bring in. Can't have the patients get hold of anything they could use as a weapon.

Donny smiled and headed through security ahead of me. I let him get some distance, then I went through.

Without the mace, my self-defense skills amount to what places to kick a guy. A guy like Donny would be ready for those kicks.

I said hi to the other staffers in the hall. Most grudgingly said hi back. It's better to force people to pretend to act civil—that's the decision I've come to.

The antiseptic smell is strong today. Sometimes I have this feeling that the smell will cling to me and chase me even after I quit here. Maybe it was already there. Maybe it seeped into my soul after the hospital bombing. It never bothered me before that.

A lot of soldiers who see action end up with tinnitus, a permanent ringing in the ears, from exposure to explosions or loud gunfire. Maybe the antiseptic smell is my tinnitus. The smell. The screams. The songs that didn't work to cover the screams.

Just do the job and get out, I remind myself for the zillionth time. *And no more thinking about Patient 34. No more wondering about his history, no more wondering whether he's faking his stupor. No more.*

Yet an hour later I'm sitting at his bedside, studying his eyes.

He stares at the ceiling with his hellfire beauty. He feels...unusually alert.

His blood pressure is going to be up this time, I just know it. I fit the cuff around his arm. I get it crooked and redo it. "Calm and steady," I say, kind of to both of us.

I watch the numbers stabilize. Too high. This is the kind of number I'd need to report.

"Fuck!"

I have this feeling that if I report it, Zara will come and get a normal reading like the past two times, and it will be another demerit. I could enter a fake number, but what if something is really wrong? It's a huge load of toxic chemicals they're giving this guy.

"I'm going to try this again in a minute. We'll pause and rest."

I take a deep breath, modeling restfulness. I glance over at the backs of two orderlies' heads through the window that looks out into the hall. On their phones.

"Yup." I turn back to 34. I study the proud line of his nose, the curve of his cheekbone. He's beautiful in a stormy way, a statue hewn in hell, hair black as night. Short downy beard. He has a very Mediterranean look—as though he has Italian or Greek or maybe Middle Eastern heritage. I shouldn't think he's hot. He's in his early twenties and I'm almost thirty. I'm his nurse. He's supposedly criminally insane. Or is he?

"I would give anything for your story," I say. "And seriously—no name? No history? It's like putting a lit sign over your door saying, 'We're hiding something about this guy.'"

He keeps up his blank stare, eyes the color of fire. Occasional blink. He doesn't look aware, but he *feels* aware.

And what if he is? But if he was sane and aware, the boredom and immobility would drive anybody out of their mind. I rest a gloved hand on his arm, so solid under my fingers.

"We're going to go again. We're going to sit here, and then do the BP again. I could do the blood draw first. But I'm not going to poke your arm and then squeeze it with the cuff like an asshole. Unless I did it on the other side. Hmmm. What do you think?"

I decide it's not a bad idea. I move the chair to the other side of him and do the draw. He doesn't react to the prick at all. I fill the tiny vial and drop it into the marked tube.

One thing down. I take a centering breath, filling my lungs with the antiseptic smell.

"Okay." I set my hand on the bed next to his muscular arm. It's ironic that my presence seems to shoot his BP. I find his presence calming.

Another deep breath. "We're okay. And you know what? The kitten is okay. And I'm not there."

I scratch my finger back and forth on the sheet, so cheap and coarse I can feel the grain through the glove. Sometimes this thing happens where I forget about it momentarily, but then I get this feeling of dread, and then I think, *What bad thing am I forgetting?* And then I remember the kitten.

"It's okay. I fucking saved it, right? But in my mind, it's still in trouble. Trapped there."

I sigh.

"It could be worse. I could be talking to a whiskey bottle, right? I know what you're thinking. Many kittens die in the world. Why did that one kitten take me down? Yeah, that is definitely the question of the day. You hit it right on the nose, 34. Nobody asked me, but that's what they all wonder. It's like death or cancer or something. Nobody wants to ask. They think you want to forget. They don't know you're still in it. Really, I don't want to talk about it."

So why am I talking to him? This completely inanimate man who burns with intensity.

"It's so much suffering over there, you learn to tune it out. The hungry kids chasing the car, the bombed-out shells of homes that were once places where happy families lived. You remind yourself you're there to make a difference. It's a matter of relative weight, right? So much is a matter of weight. Things need to not weigh the same, you know? You can't just react to every tiny thing, or you can never do anything big. And then I went and reacted to the tiniest thing."

I pinch the bridge of my nose. One good night's sleep, that's all I need.

The kitten incident happened while I was on my way to the assignment of a lifetime—to interview a female warlord. It was going to be amazing. She was going to let me spend the day with her. A female warlord in the hills of Afghanistan.

"You can't even imagine what a coup that would've been," I say to 34. "This was somebody you couldn't get to—like ever. And like a fucking miracle, she agreed to this meeting. The one meeting she'd do—ever. Everyone wanted that meeting, but I got it."

I scratch against the grain of the sheet, throat too thick to talk, remembering the way my fixer looked at me when I got out of that Jeep. He was being paid by the magazine to take me around and translate for me and protect me to a limited extent, but in that Jeep, I was boss. We stalled out in this ruined intersection. The engine cut, and that's when I heard the tiny mewl.

My voice is a whisper. "And then I see the paw poking out of that hole. I couldn't leave it, crying like that. At first I thought, 'I just have to see what's up,' you know? I got out and I go over, and I could see it in there. It was under a bunch of steel and mesh under this stone slab. And once I saw it, I had to get it out, you know?"

The clock on the wall clicks away. One second. Another.

I'm back there a little bit. "I made my fixer pay a few guys to move the slab. It took two fucking hours to round up enough guys to move that stone slab. They thought I was insane. Maybe a little like you do right now."

His pulse is a drum in his neck—even I can see it. I smooth down his sleeve, wondering who cuts his beard. I hope it's not Donny. Fucking Donny.

"Fuck fuck fuck, you have to calm down," I say, and I don't know who I'm talking to—him or me. "They freed it, though. Put it in my arms. It was every kind of selfish, I guess. I passed by so much suffering there. You pick your battles. Until you don't. And mine was the kitten. What was I doing?" I close my eyes, and it's like I can feel the grit on my knees and the kitten's tiny ribs. I'm back there breathing in the dust, with my fixer looming above me, unsure whether to watch me or look away.

"I'm holding that little thing, crying. I'm sure the mother was long gone. Probably dead. I couldn't stop crying. So yeah, that was impressive. And then like an asshole I get in the Jeep with the kitten in my shirt, and he's driving like hell to make time to get to the meeting, but we both knew she'd be gone. I kind of didn't care. I got it to drink water. It was so scared, but it liked being in my shirt. That's all it needed, you know? It just needed somebody to hold it. To give a fuck."

Am I really pouring my guts out to 34? Suddenly I can't stop.

"We got to the market where the meet was supposed to happen, and the warlord had already left. I would've spent a day with her. It would've been amazing."

I think back, remembering how excited I was to land that interview. When you get to spend a whole day with a subject like that, they start to forget you're there, and you get really genuine stuff. Unguarded truth. The stuff they don't know not to tell you. Of course she was gone by the time we arrived. I just felt numb about it. I was all about the kitten. I had my fixer drive us to this small village at the edge of a relatively lush area. Just this random area I'd seen pictures of."

I sigh, remembering.

"I was basically Caligula at that point," I add. "Caligula with a kitten. I dropped it off. It seemed like a nice place for a kitten. A good food supply. And then I went out and got so fucking drunk. God." I tip my head back and gaze at the stained tiles on the ceiling. This is 34's view forever. "You'd at least think saving the kitten would make me feel better. But it didn't. It made the kitten feel better. I hope."

Those next couple weeks I drank and drank. Fixers gossip like old women. The world of journalism is not a large place, and there's always somebody hungrier. With every sweating bottle of beer, I felt my career crumble a little more. I'd found the one thing that was worse than getting emotionally involved. Worse than fucking an interview subject. I missed a career-making interview to save a trapped kitten.

"It was just so helpless and scared, though," I say to him. "And so thin. It weighed nothing and its little claws...its little fucking claws. It needed me. It just needed..." I gust out the last word—"something."

The room starts to look wavy through my tears. They trail down my cheeks like hot, wet fingers.

"Okay! See? Happy now?" I sniffle, thankful my back is to the window. "This is why I don't talk about the fucking kitten. This—"

My throat thickens up, like a band, tightening around it.

"This—" I whisper as the sobs take on chest-convulsing lives of their own, like too many got trapped inside my heart that day, and now they're all trying to punch out at once.

Everything inside me is a chaos of heat and pain. The room is wavy. I can't see. I can't think.

I grab hold of the sheet, telling myself I'm in Minnesota, but really I'm in that collapsing hospital. I'm on the dusty street. I'm in the half-crushed cooler, I'm swimming in antiseptic, I'm in a Jeep, I'm holding the kitten crying against my belly, sobs like a fist inside me.

Something crushes my hand. Hard grip.

Warm skin.

My eyes fly open.

Patient 34 is holding my hand.

He pins me with a torn expression.

My mouth hangs open. My heart thunders.

He just watches me, fierce and true, holding me in the strong container of his hand.

"Oh my God," I whisper. I'm suspended in his grip, a stunned rabbit, caught in a cloud of shivers.

Patient 34. Really with me.

My gaze falls to his steely, sinewy hand gripping my latex-covered one. Our hands form a defiant knot against everything normal.

My chest softens. My sobs calm. Suddenly I can breathe again.

I look back up at him. "You're here."

He just watches me. I have this sense we're the only two people in the universe. I have this sense that his hand holding mine is the only true thing in this place. The only thing that has weight in a world that's spinning off its axis.

He shifts his hand, gripping stronger, harder, conflict raging in the fire of his eyes.

Some wild part of me doesn't want him to let go—ever.

Don't let go.

"You're here," I repeat.

Silence. Again I get that crazy sense he's angry, somehow. Or maybe "anger" isn't the word. He's a dangerous fire, flames licking my core.

I could call out. I could hit the cart alarm. It's the last thing on my mind.

"You've been here all this time."

"No," he whispers. "I'm not here."

Breath whooshes through me. This really is happening. I wait, but he says nothing more. I simply dwell in his harsh, strong hand. He has me.

I shouldn't need that, but I do.

Suddenly the fire goes out of his gaze. He lets go of my hand. He turns back up to the ceiling.

"Wait! 34!" I whisper. I want him to come back. "It's okay. I won't—" *Won't what?*

A scrape behind me. The door opens. It's Raimie, one of the nurses. "I'm out of kits. You mind?" She grabs a few of the draw kits I put together. "God, you're behind." With that, she swoops out.

I look down again at 34. He's got the zombie act going again. "She's gone," I say softly.

He doesn't react.

"It's cool now."

Nothing.

"Seriously?" I wait, wanting him to come back. But why would he? My blood races. I don't want to leave.

I have to leave.

With trembling fingers, I punch in a fake number for his blood pressure.

I turn back to him. Staring at the ceiling. "Thank you," I say. The thank you comes from my heart—I hope he hears that.

I straighten my stuff and push out.

CHAPTER SEVEN

Ann

I GO THROUGH the rest of my rounds in a daze, speaking softly to the tormented men with their goals and their glassy gazes.

The whole time my thoughts are on Patient 34—a man without a name. Without goals. Without a story.

The only one who has ever shown me compassion in this place.

I don't tell on him.

It's a decision I make from the gut.

Tuesday. Delivery day. I collect myself enough to time my supply refill visit to Pharma Two to happen around the time the delivery truck arrives. I make myself look busy refilling my cart with pads and cotton and sterile setups while one of the pharma staffers checks things in.

Donny wanders in, which is interesting. He squeezes past me, mumbling something about aspirin and touching my ass in a pseudo-accidental way. He heads to the rack on the end.

I watch how the staffer logs the shipment and puts the stuff away. The invoices go into a three-ring binder stored in a cabinet that isn't locked. It's stunningly low-tech. I try to think how I'd get extra ephedrine going through here. I could think of a few ways for sure. It's a soft operation.

I turn and leave, much as I want to stay and see what happens. I'll come back and tally the ephedrine supply and study the sheets. With an investigation like this, a clear and detailed picture of current reality is always where you start.

Needless to say, my mind is not on the supplies; it's on Patient 34 and the gravitational pull of his story. His lack of story.

I tell myself there are rational reasons to get his story; if he's a serial killer, for example, people have a right to know he's not sedated like they think he is.

Deep down, though, I know he's not a serial killer. I've met serial killers. I've met every kind of person. Until 34.

I skip lunch in favor of hitting up Fancher's administrative assistant, Pam, while Fancher is out of his office—exactly the kind of attention-getting activity I shouldn't be doing.

Pam has frosted hair, a friendly face, and lot of owl collectibles. She's the one who tracks the institute's calendar.

I tell her I'm looking to put in a good word for one of the patients in time for his next commitment hearing. This is actually true—it's a kid named Jamaica. His official sentence ran out two years ago, but like so many here, he continues to be kept, and this guy has been really conscientious and helpful around the general room. I ask her to walk me through how to find out when a patient's hearing is coming up.

She lets me come around the back of her desk, and she goes into her spreadsheet. She explains the procedure. There are two lawyers at every commitment hearing—one for the state and one for the patient—plus a psychiatrist. She shows me where their names are, shows me the notes function, and how the group emails get sent when there's a change. I'm supposed to email her with notes.

I know all of this stuff already, but I act clueless because I want her to explain it, and most of all, I want to see her screens. I'm scanning for 34. If I can see his schedule of hearings, I can figure out the date he was committed. It's amazing how much intel you can draw from a date. Zara had said "a year and some change," but that's not good enough.

I finally find his row, and it's not just blank—it's grayed out. Nothing can be input. *What. The. Fuck.*

"Huh. No hearings for 34," I say neutrally.

"Fancher handles 34. Patient 34 is in a separate category."

"Huh." I quickly point to something else. I can't look too interested in 34. That's a reporter trick. You always look like you're going for something else, not the thing you're actually going for.

I can still feel his hand around mine, the connection between us buzzing with life.

I scan around the office while she talks. His commitment papers have to be here somewhere. Those papers would tell me a lot. And if there aren't commitment papers for him, that's even more of a story. It means he's in here illegally.

"Would you need the note of support for transition to a halfway house in a hard copy with a signature, too?" I ask. "Where I worked before, they signed the notes and kept them together in the commitment files. We'd just add them in."

"Staff had access to commitment files?"

"Oh yeah." Actually this is something that would never ever happen.

I wait for her to show me where the commitment files are kept. Sure enough, her gaze flicks to Fancher's door. So that's where they are.

Fuck.

"But of course it was overseas," I add.

"Oh." She smiles. "I was gonna say."

I straighten up. "I'll get you the note by the end of the month. Thanks for all your great help!"

CHAPTER EIGHT

Ann

PATIENT 34 GIVES no sign of awareness when I walk into his room the next day.

"Hey," I say softly.

Nothing.

I look down at his hand. I get it in my head to grab it. I force my gaze back to his gorgeous eyes, rimmed in darkness, fixed on a spot on the ceiling. Water stains. Shitty old tiles. Pure 1950s institutional architecture. I pull out my phone and take a picture of the ceiling. It's a way of connecting with him, grabbing that ceiling shot. I quickly put my phone aside.

Stop it.

I look back at his hand. I really want to touch him.

I compromise. I press two latex-gloved fingers to his throat, to feel the slow, steady thrust of blood through his veins. It's a clinical touch. His neck is warm. Solid.

I force myself to remove my hand—I'm practically ravishing a tied-up patient. "I didn't say anything. Just in case you're wondering."

His empty eyes are fixed on the ceiling. It's weird how he can stay utterly still. He's like a fucking yogi, being able to control himself like that. Or a sniper. Snipers can get really still. Some of them can slow their heartbeats.

I wait, really wanting to touch him again, but I feel suddenly too shy to. Touching the other patients is routine and robotic. "Give me your name. I know you can talk."

Zilch.

I was reporting in Colombia once, staying in a beautiful mountainside village that was fogged in every morning, but then the sun would burn off some of the fog, and just the tips of the mountains would appear, as if out of the clouds—massive, menacing, and dark.

That mountain appearing out of the fog would fill me with a sense of awe.

It's the way I feel at 34's bedside. Shrouded majesty. The tip of something important. "Come on, tell me your name," I whisper. "Tell me your story. Let me help you."

Nothing.

"Fine, I'll talk. Something's going on with you. You don't get hearings. You know you're entitled to a hearing every six months, right? But you don't get them. Or do you? But then why aren't they listed? Why is Dr. Fancher handling your case personally? What's up with that?"

I glance over my shoulder at the guys out there. Still the backs of their heads. I rest a hand on his chest, soaking in the massive thump of it.

"Come on. Can you bring down your pulse? Do you put yourself in this state, or are you muscling it?"

I wait.

"Fuck you! Come on, answer me, dammit! Just a name. If you're being unlawfully held, maybe I can help you. The jig is up, I already know you can hear me."

His stonewall act is more than frustrating. When he took my hand yesterday, it was the first time since the hospital bombing that I didn't feel so fucking alone. And now it's as if he, too, has abandoned me.

I get the cuff out. "Don't worry, 34. I won't give up on you. There are other ways to get your story."

If he hears me, he doesn't show it. Not that he would. I take his blood pressure. It's up there—it's not in the danger zone for a normal person, but this cocktail should have it seriously depressed. I'm getting the feeling I affect him. He definitely affects me.

"I'm going to take a past reading. Because here's what I'm thinking—I'm thinking you don't want to draw any extra attention to yourself. Amirite?" I've stopped expecting him to answer.

***

THE FREELANCE JOURNALIST life is incredibly transitory. You create fierce friendships for short bursts of time in faraway places, and then you all get sent somewhere else, and the friendships are over. I kept in vague email touch with a few fellow journalists, but that ended after my kitten breakdown.

If I did have any friends left, they'd definitely be telling me to turn back. They'd be telling me I'm officially crossing deep into the land of bad ideas.

Hell, I'm telling it to myself, but I don't care. I need this guy's story. I won't pretend I don't.

Thus I set my sights on Fancher's office.

I let my evening and night counterparts know I'm willing to trade shifts. One of them bites right away, asking me to cover his graveyard shift for the next two days.

I come in around dinnertime. The people in the admin wing are gone by six. Donny is there doing a training session, which I'm not entirely thrilled about, but at least it keeps him occupied.

Fancher Institute is slightly lazier at night. The night nurses don't take blood, but they do everything else, plus some side work.

I've brought my lock pick kit shoved into my knee sock with my secret cellphone. The pick set is highly fucking illegal due to the fact that it's kind of a weapon, but this is a private contract institute, so security is a bit lax.

I take up a position at the bulletin board outside the door to the admin area. I pretend to study the leaflets and notices, getting a feel for the hall and what sounds mean somebody's coming around the corner. When the coast seems clear, I go at the lock. I get it open on the first try and let myself in. I close the door quietly behind me.

The computer monitor on Pam's desk pulses an eerie blue glow that lights her owl collectibles.

I take a picture just because.

The ambient light is enough for me to see my way to the door to Fancher's office, opposite her desk. I pull out my pick kit and get at the knob. I find it's always best to just do these things without thinking—especially now, with my sleep-deprived mind prone to paranoid thoughts. Still, I'm trembling by the time I get in there.

Moonlight streams in from a high window. Heart pounding, I move to the cabinets, checking them to see which are locked. This shit's going to be under lock and key. I work open the locked drawer and riffle through. Finally I get what I want—the file on 34.

Too easy, I think. Then, *Shut up. Go forward.*

I open it on Fancher's desk. He's listed as John Doe. Assault on a police officer. Is that why he got deep-sixed? Cop vendetta? There's a lot of info I don't take the time to read. I take pictures of each page and fumble the file back, buzzing with adrenaline. I close up Fancher's office and go back to the outer office.

Pam's desk. Her cats stare out at me from their photos, little faces glowing blue. Owls standing by.

I put my ear to the outer door, listening for footsteps in the hall. Nothing.

Unless somebody is standing there. Could somebody be standing out there?

I take a deep breath, say a little prayer, and slip out...just as Donny rounds the corner.

"What are you doing?"

"Looking for Pam," I say. "Nobody's in there. When do they leave?"

"You're not supposed to be in there." He comes to me. The hall is empty, dammit. "That door should be locked."

"It was open."

He crowds me. "No, it wasn't."

"Yes, it was. I wanted my wellness survey, and..."

He closes an iron grip on my wrist, looking hard into my eyes. I don't want to call out unless I have to. I think he knows. Fuck.

"You need to let me go."

In a maniacally quick move, he pushes me into the office and shuts the door with his foot.

We're alone.

"You know how much trouble you can get in for being in here?"

"Let me go."

"Or what?"

"Or I'll scream."

He yanks me to him. "Will you?"

With that one utterance, my worst fear is confirmed—my fear that Donny, with whatever built-in dirtball radar he possesses, has detected that I don't want to draw attention to myself, that I'm maybe even up to something.

It's not implausible that a newbie would peek in the office thinking somebody was there, not implausible the door would be left unlocked, but Donny smells the lie.

I wrench my hand from his and stomp on his foot, grabbing for the knob.

"Oh no, you don't." He pulls me back.

My belly coils with panic. I try to twist free. I knee him, hitting his thigh, and twist away from him.

He grabs my shirt as I pull out, ripping it before I get the door open.

I go out and run like hell, slowing only at the corner, nearly colliding with a trio of orderlies coming around.

I smile, pulse pounding. "Whoops!" I mumble something about being late.

I'm within sight of the secure admittance desk. I head toward it, like an oasis of safety. I plaster on a smile for the night guard as he lets me into the secure wing.

I sweep in and get to the general room. Donny comes in right behind me, but he won't try anything here. His uncle might not care what he does—that's probably the reason he's even still here. But in this room there are cameras. People.

He comes up next to me, talking at me with his fish lips. "What are you hiding, Ms. Saybrook?"

"What the fuck would I be hiding? I'm looking to get through probation without making waves, buddy, but I'll lodge a complaint if I have to."

He cracks his knuckles. "I'm watching you." He has letters tattooed on his fingers that say F-U-C-K T-H-I-S. That's nice. A real top-quality guy.

I get the fuck away. Donny is going to be a problem and a half, but if I stick to patient rooms and public spaces, I should be okay. The pharma rooms could be a problem.

I go through my duties. Patient 34 doesn't break character. I can't tell whether he's surprised to see me in the place at night. Mitchell has the flu, so I spend extra time with him. When I get a moment alone, I move out of camera range and pull out my second cell. I send the images to myself on two accounts and delete them from the obvious areas.

I get home at seven in the morning and start digging.

I'm not turning up much. No surprise there—I need access to official records that won't be on the web, but I do get the name of the psychiatrist who testified at 34's initial commitment—one Dr. Roland Baker III. He's around sixty years old, attached to a large regional health center in Duluth.

His office opens at eight. I make a quick call, posing as a court clerk, asking for confirmation on the dates of the original hearing, mumbling something about lost data. Really, I just want to make sure he really was there. Because what if the whole hearing never happened? His admin tells me he was present.

I'm disappointed.

I imagine hopping in my car after my shift and driving to Duluth to question the man, but no psychiatrist is going to divulge anything to a stranger. They don't even have to talk to the cops in most cases.

I have a better route, anyway—contacts from years of reporting.

I wait until nine to call in a favor from a colleague who owes me—he's done some public beat investigations and knows the Health and Human Services scene. I'm not sure what kind of record I need.

I get him on the phone. When he realizes it's me, he's cagey. I have this reputation now for spinning out.

"Dude," I say. "Come on. Who put you together with the Iranian Consulate? I'm doing a thing inside of a place, and I really do need this."

"For who?"

"*Stormline.*"

He's polite and doesn't say anything like, "Oh, how the mighty have fallen!" *Stormline* really is the lowest. "What you need is the 24A from the case."

"So you can get it?" Silence. "Is this a HIPAA problem?" That regulation makes getting health-related info hard.

"No, it's not that..." He pauses, and right then I know he could get it if he tried.

"Please," I say. "You owe me. We'll be even." Sometimes you have to be shameless.

"I'm calling in a favor of my own here for you," he tells me, just to show he's really sacrificing. He doesn't want me coming back to the well a second time.

"I appreciate it. This closes our accounts until I fucking claw my way back up and you need me again."

He laughs. He likes that I'm sounding like the old Ann Saybrook, the pre-spinout Ann Saybrook. A.E. Saybrook— that's my byline. I send him the photo of the commitment certificate.

While I wait for him to call back, I make a sandwich and scan old *Duluth Tribune* news stories from the year before 34's commitment. The paper appears to cover all of northern Minnesota. I make a list of all assault and murder cases from fourteen to eighteen months back. After that I expand my search geographically, out through all of Minnesota and then northern Wisconsin.

I show up the next night early as a way of Donny-proofing my arrival. I do my rounds, stopping for an extended one-sided conversation with Patient 34. "I'm looking into your case, pal," I say. "What do you think?"

For just a moment, I think I catch a hint of agony in his unfathomable eyes. Physical pain? Mental pain? Anguish?

"Do you not want me to find out? It'd be fine for you to tell me that, too." Not that it could keep me from it at this point. But he's free to tell me. I really just want him to say anything to me.

"You're good. You can almost make me think it never happened. Like maybe I dreamed it. *Almost.* But I know it happened. You should tell me your name and save me time."

I fit the cuff and pump it up.

"I always find out in the end." Usually I get the subject to tell me, though.

People like to talk to somebody who gives a shit—that's basic human nature. Sometimes easy questions get you the best stuff. Like if I'm talking to a cook, I get her to explain something about dicing vegetables. Or with a mercenary, maybe I ask about how he decides what to put in each pocket.

"Mercenaries have a lot of pockets, did you know that?" I rest my hand on his forearm, just above the band that traps his wrist. I can't imagine how alone he must feel.

The night shift is lax, so I stay a bit longer than usual. I tell him about my childhood idol, Harriet the Spy. I tell him about the trailer where I grew up in Idaho, and how Greyhound buses would pass by three times a day. My sister would dream of being one of the people on the bus going somewhere glamorous, like L.A. I'd just want to know their stories. It seemed like the buses were forever passing us by. "I wonder if you feel like that. You have to. Oh, and newsflash—did you know Donny has 'FUCK THIS' tattooed on his fingers?"

Something flickers in his eyes.

"Right? Fuck. I'm going to get to the bottom of this." Without thinking, I slide my fingers under his. Loosely grasping his hand. It feels natural. Like the two of us alone against the world. Then I drop it, because what am I doing?

I get the fuck out of there.

My guy calls me a few hours later. There's no record of the hearing even happening.

"But you saw the certificate. The hearing happened. The psychiatrist's office confirms it."

"But I sent the image to my guy, and the file isn't there. Here's what he found interesting—the data is kept in a database, and he noticed a blank row on the batch for that date. The formatting was weird. It was kind of a flag to him."

"What does it mean?"

"He said the blank row could possibly have happened because somebody entered something by mistake and they deleted it and didn't take out the row. But he thinks it's more likely that there was a deliberate deletion at some point. Looks like you're on to something."

There was a time when I would have been thrilled about this. But not now. I'm worried about 34.

"Does your guy have any next-step thoughts?"

My guy reads me off his notes. There are things I could file for. Another name who could chase the paperwork deeper, but I'd have to give him some serious juice, meaning serious money. Which I have none of.

And then there's the option of fingerprinting the patient. Yeah, I can get his prints, but getting them run on IAFIS—the FBI's national database—would take more juice.

I thank him for his time. Favor burned.

CHAPTER NINE

Lazarus

THERE ARE A lot of really idiotic martial arts systems out there. Karate, for instance. Do you really see people squaring off like that out in a street fight? No. It's not at all functional. Yet one of my toughest motherfucking soldiers came up in karate.

My point is, it's not the system that makes the man, it's the man that makes the system. It's about what the man brings, not what the system brings.

This is especially true with Valerie, my executive coach. Valerie has never met a motivational saying she doesn't like. The more idiotic and trite the saying, the more she likes it and uses it.

But she makes those fucking sayings work—that's the thing about Valerie. That's what sets her apart. In Valerie's hands, the sayings aren't trite.

So I'm talking on the phone with her in one of our coaching calls, enjoying her, enjoying the way she laughs—she's smart, and it's easy to make her laugh. I'm even enjoying her lame-ass motivational sayings.

And then we come around to the Kiro account. "Have you found your way into the Kiro account yet?"

I tell her no. "We've been researching the hell out of it. It's just always out of our reach."

"Your competitor isn't anywhere nearer, though, right?"

"I think our competitor might be getting inroads," I say. "They've been making business trips that look like they're related to Kiro."

Needless to say, she doesn't know Kiro's a guy I'm trying to find and kill. She thinks I'm running an accounting firm.

Gotta keep it clean with Valerie, being that she's an executive coach.

"But they don't have the account yet," she says. "So it's still in play. Are you thinking positive? Are you encouraging your people to view it as already a done deal? Already yours? Letting the universe know that Kiro account belongs to you?"

This sounds hokey, but it's actually been good advice. People thinking Kiro is dead has made us more powerful. Everyone wants to be on the winning team. Especially when it comes to criminal organizations.

"But it's not truly a done deal. I don't know what they'll say if we *don't* get the account."

"Keep your eyes on the prize, Lazarus. When one door closes, another opens."

It was a two motivational-saying call. Three if you count "Think Positive."

Anyway, when one door closes, another opens. Right?

The very next day I get a phone call from one Dr. Roland Baker, a psychiatrist up in some hospital in northern Minnesota. I almost don't take it. I don't know the guy. He said he had some business with Aldo, my late boss. What do I care?

I take the call.

"This is about the boy," the shrink says. "Aldo wanted me to alert him if anybody started poking around about the boy. He said it was vital. I know that Aldo's passed, but..."

"Yes, he's passed," I say. *Due to the fact that I killed him.*

"I thought if this information was important to Aldo, it might be important to you, too," the shrink says, clearly looking for a payday.

"I don't know that it's my business if somebody's poking around about a boy," I say. "I can't say I condone it, exactly..."

"No, no, not like that. The *wild* boy. I'm talking about the wild boy, Lazarus. The wild Dragusha."

Needless to say, this gets me sitting up straight. "Kiro Dragusha?"

"Yes. Kiro. It took a lot of doing to get that boy under wraps. Aldo didn't want people poking around, asking questions, undoing all of our work."

"Aldo knew where Kiro was all this time?"

"Of course. He gave explicit instructions to be alerted the moment anybody started asking about him."

I grin. I imagine telling Valerie how fucking wide the Kiro account door just opened.

"It's very much worth my while, Dr. Baker," I say. "I don't know the specifics of Aldo's arrangements, but I'm very invested in the Kiro situation."

I always said Aldo should've killed the babies when he killed their parents, but he never could quite bring himself to. This is the result. The babies grow up and become problems.

The doctor and I proceed to have a fascinating conversation where I learn all about the travels of Kiro, with Aldo paying for one stopgap measure after another, culminating in his paying for Kiro to be committed to an asylum for the criminally insane.

It seems we have people on payroll in the asylum. He doesn't know who. It doesn't matter. Kiro's there.

I thank him and get a funds transfer going.

Kiro, strapped to a bed in a nuthouse.

Thank you, universe.

CHAPTER TEN

I GET BACK on the day shift and start running my rounds, but the usual trio of orderlies isn't in the hall outside Patient 34's room at the agreed-upon time, which is strange. I text one of the guys. He says they're doing a simulation.

This puts me in a bind, because the guys on highly toxic cocktails need periodic checks according to state rules. If I break state rules, Nurse Zara could write me up.

But if I go in, I'd be breaking the institute rule about the three orderlies.

I decide to go in. State rules trump institute rules, that will be my defense. And it's not like 34's going to attack me.

I head in with my cart. "Hey," I say softly, wanting anything—just a glance, even. To see that warmth in his eyes again. To know I didn't dream our connection.

Nothing.

"The thousand-mile stare again. There's a shocker."

I feel such intense fondness for him. I've always admired people who decide on a direction and go for it against all odds. The rebels, the heretics, the true believers, the doomed warriors. Those are the people I love the most. The female warlord in Afghanistan. Unbelievable.

But with 34, it's something deeper.

I start setting up the kit. "You're tenacious, I'll give you that. You're the kind of guy who, when he commits, he really commits, aren't you?"

I tick off the boxes on my tablet and pull on my gloves.

His dusky whiskers almost qualify as a beard at this point. I rest my hand against his cheek, thinking I should find out who cuts his beard and hair and try to take over the job.

"Update, 34: the plot thickens. Massively. Congratulations, you're more of an enigma than Easter Island."

The sound of footsteps out in the hallway. I drop my hand and crane my neck around. Donny. *Fuck.*

"Why are you in here without proper guard, Nurse Saybrook?" He closes the door.

I sit up. "He needs his vitals checked on a regular schedule. State regs."

Donny comes up next to me, too close.

"What are you doing?"

He flicks a finger onto 34's cheek. "Diagnosis—vegetable."

"What the fuck!" I push his arm away. "Stop it!" I say protectively.

And Donny sees it. *Shit.*

He grins and flicks 34's cheekbone this time—hard—leaving a mark above the line of his beard.

I shove Donny away from the bedside. "You're going to stop that."

"Or what, Nurse Ann? Will you arrest me?" He goes to do it again, and I grab his arm. He breaks my hold like it's child's play and grabs my wrists, yanking me away from my cart...where my panic alarm is.

Out of camera range, too.

The smile widens. It's here I comprehend the implications of the closed door. The door isn't supposed to be closed except when complete soundproofing is required. Some of the patients are screamers, and it upsets the other patients.

Door closed. Complete soundproofing. Fear shoots down to my belly. I was worried about 34. Stupid. I should've been worried about myself.

"Fuck off!" I twist. Totally futile. Donny's a fucking linebacker, twice my size. His grip is so tight, I think he might crack my bones, and he's backing me into the bathroom, which will really hide us. From the cameras, from the window.

"Please," I say.

My ass hits the sink. My blood runs cold as he squishes me in with his tree-trunk legs.

I bring a knee into his groin, but he's ready for that.

He gets both my wrists in one hand. His breath is hot and slightly antiseptic, like minty, mediciney mouthwash, and that adds to my panic. He's going to rape me, and I'll have to smell that smell the whole time.

"Don't," I say.

"Don't what?" He stares at me with those predator eyes.

An unholy growl sounds from somewhere behind him. There's a *pop*.

Donny twists around just as 34 bounds in through the doorway, huge and brutal and furious, gaze afire. He pulls Donny off me and drives him face first into the wall with wild force. Donny crumples.

And then 34 comes to me.

I shrink back as he touches my cheek, gaze afire.

Donny was dangerous, but 34 seems...wild. Something deep and instinctive inside me prompts me to slide away into the corner of the bathroom. He's so much bigger now that he's standing. And free. How did he get free?

"Are you okay?" he rasps.

"Yeah."

He cups my cheek, then he runs his thumb over my lips. So strangely gentle and sensual after such violence.

"Thank you," I say.

His hard face softens.

Movement from the corner of my eye. Donny's coming for him with a Taser.

Patient 34 seems to sense this. He grabs Donny's arm and twists. There's a sickening crack as the Taser clatters to the floor. Patient 34 pulls him right out of the bathroom and smashes him into another wall.

And then his fist goes, pounding Donny's face over and over. He's a blur, destroying Donny's face. Donny fights back, gets in a few hits, but 34 is fighting with a vicious abandon I've never before seen.

The door bangs open. Did Donny get to his panic alarm?

A trio of orderlies bursts in. Patient 34 takes them down like three rag dolls, carefully and expertly avoiding the Tasers. I crouch against the wall. More arrive, coming at 34. I crouch in the corner.

Another orderly comes and shoves me aside so hard I smash my head on a shelf. I cry out.

That's when 34 stops fighting. His gaze is fixed on me. The world seems to stop, and for a moment, it's like we're the only two people who ever existed. Alone together. Doomed.

I shake my head. *Ignore me,* I want to say. *Keep fighting. Save yourself.*

Too late. The orderlies are on him—giant guys shooting 34 with enough electricity to light a city. His big body jerks. He collapses. They keep shooting current into him.

"Fuck!" I go right into the thick of it. I pull one off. I hit another on the back. "Hey!" I kick. "That's enough! You're gonna kill him!" I finally get them all off and kneel beside 34. He's out cold.

I press my trembling fingers to his throat. His pulse is thready. Weak.

Donny comes up on the other side of him, lip bleeding down his neck and onto his shirt front. He kicks 34 viciously in the ribs.

"Enough!" I stand and shove him away. "This patient is out cold. You do not attack an unconscious patient, or I will report that shit to the board. Any of you, I don't care who it is." I spin around, address the group of them. "If any of you do anything more to this patient, it's actionable in a court of law."

Donny wipes the blood from the side of his fish lips, hard gaze fixed on me.

Nurse Zara arrives, demanding to know what happened.

Donny jerks a thumb at me and tells her that I was stupid enough to go in there without the trio of orderlies standing by. He says it seems to have excited Patient 34, and he went in there just in time to save me from Patient 34.

"Are you fucking kidding me? You attacked me—you! Patient 34 was protecting me."

Nurse Zara purses her lips and gives me a stern, scolding glare. My mouth literally hangs open when I realize she believes Donny. Or worse, maybe she doesn't. Maybe she just wants me gone that bad.

My heart pounds. I kneel down next to 34. He's really out. I check his pupils. I don't care that much about what happens to me—I'll be fine. But Patient 34 is screwed. It wouldn't matter if he was fighting for world peace. He got out of his restraints—that's the bottom line.

If he was dosed up enough to put out an elephant before, he's going to get dosed up enough to put out two elephants. I try to keep my touch clinical.

One of the orderlies finds a pair of clippers on the floor. "He had this hidden."

My head spins. Patient 34 had an escape plan, and he blew it for me.

To protect me.

"Heads are going to roll." Donny turns to Nurse Zara. "And the meds—I don't care about the guidelines—the guidelines don't apply to this one. He's got some kind of hellbeast metabolism. His meds need to be severely adjusted." He straightens his shirt. "Severely. It's high gravity pudding time for this guy."

I kneel back down at 34's side, feeling sick. High gravity pudding is what you feed to stroke victims whose muscles are too slack to swallow. One step away from a catheter and a feeding tube. Dosage at that level starts affecting the brain. Like a chemical lobotomy.

I shouldn't have gone in there without a trio out there.

And right then, I wonder whether it was a trap. Like maybe Donny planned it.

He clearly didn't count on 34 getting free.

He's half on his side, one muscled arm out straight, one arm flung over his chest, legs akimbo, eyes shut. Downy curls dark and a bit too long.

I'm not here.

For once I know it's true.

Nurse Zara is full of angry questions. I give my defense—I was just following state regs.

They put Patient 34 back onto his bed, back into restraints. Ignoring protocols about the possibility of spinal injury. Maybe it's something they're hoping for.

"I'm going to have to write this up," Nurse Zara says. "This is number two."

"Number two?" I protest. "What was my first?"

"Inability to get a correct BP."

She wrote me up for that? One more write-up and I'm out. And then what happens to 34?

CHAPTER ELEVEN

Kiro

I'M FLOATING FOR what seems like days. Maybe it is. Then her scent comes to me, like the sun through clouds.

I open my eyes. Her ponytail flops over her shoulder as she peers down. Eyes the color of grass. Pink lips in a frown.

"Fuck," she whispers. "Tell me you're not as out as all that, dammit."

She's silent after that. It's a minute, or maybe an hour, before she speaks again.

"Can you hear me?"

I say nothing. You never give them anything, or they hurt you. Even her. She hurt me worst of all, but my heart still sings when she lays a hand on my cheek.

"Fuck."

I fight to open my eyes, or maybe they are open.

"Fuck, 34." She strokes my beard. It feels like heaven. "34, 34, 34." She pats my cheek.

My heart pounds.

"Thank you for what you did. I know what you did. I know what you gave up. I'm going to take a look at you now." She's unsnapping my shirt. "If he fucking broke anything..." She's talking, but I'm not hearing words. Only the tone of her voice. I soak in her tone the way the wolves would soak in mine. The way I would soak in theirs.

I dream of home. The pack. My head on Red's warm, furry belly rising up and down. The one place I wasn't a savage beast.

Something settles onto my chest where the pain is sharpest. Gentle. It's a cloud. It's a whisper. No—it's her hand. She's whispering fast words. Ann's upset—it's in her tone. In the distance, I hear the birds. That's what she took from me. Any chance at freedom.

Her hand is gone. She swears again—*Fuck it!*

A softness settles back onto my chest. Different from the glove. Warm. Alive. Nourishing, somehow. Her skin on my skin. She's touching me without her glove!

Am I dreaming?

She's touching me with her bare hand. She's my enemy, my beautiful enemy, and I drink up her touch. I drink it like sunshine.

Fuck, 34, fuck. Fuck! And then other things. *X-ray. Where's the doctor. Did he even fucking see you yet?*

More words. Her skin on my skin. My breath shakes with the power of her touch.

Shhh. Here we go. Suddenly her hand is gone. She's snapping my shirt back up, quick, furtive movements.

She takes my hand and holds it open, palm up. She's crouching over me, as if to hide me. She's brushing something wet onto my fingers, touching my fingers. She presses my thumb onto something dry. Then she presses my finger onto something, rolling it. She keeps doing it, one after another, a strange caress on each of my fingers.

"We need this, 34," she says. "I'm going to help you...get us the truth."

Alarm bells go off in my head. We. Us. Help you. That's the way the professor talked when he pretended to be my friend. The way the medics spoke when they pulled me out of the forest, when I was too weak to run. It's how my adoptive father would talk when he was trying to trick me.

I always fell for it. I always wanted to think things would be different. Especially with my father. But as soon as I appeared, he'd grab me and make me sorry out in the woods or in the root cellar, trying to beat the savage out of me.

I was savage and feral from the first moment I can remember, a creature of blood and violence and hell with a fever inside me. My father told me so.

He tried very hard to beat the savage out of me, but he never could.

It was the cries of my adoptive sister Glenda that brought the savage out of me most. Kids down the road would tease her and make her cry because of her deformed lip. Sometimes they'd hurt her. The sound of her crying would take over my mind and turn me wild with rage. I would hurt a lot of kids trying to protect Glenda.

Things would be calm for a while, but then the boys would gather an even larger group, sometimes even a few older boys, and they'd make Glenda cry again, and I would get angry again and want to hurt them.

They always thought a bigger group or larger boys would help, but it never did. I'd hurt them all. Then the beatings. The root cellar.

The very last time I fought the neighborhood boys, the police came. Afterwards I got tied to a tree and beaten with a piano wire.

My family got the money to fix Glenda's lip that winter. She was pretty after the operation, and she didn't want me around anymore. My family adopted kids who had things wrong with them and tried to fix them up, but there's no operation to fix you when you're savage inside.

That spring, my father took me and the other kids camping far, far up north. It was just after my eighth birthday. He took me aside and told me the police were going to lock me up forever when we got back. I hadn't hurt anybody for weeks, but I knew it was true. People always said I'd be locked up in the end. He said they were afraid I'd get away, deep into the wilderness where they'd never find me.

My adoptive father never did anything nice for me, so it meant a lot that he told me this secret. I took the canoe when he and Glenda and the other kids went on a hike. I took it deep, deep, deep into the wilderness where they'd never find me.

The police sent helicopters and crews to look for me, but my father had given me a long head start.

It was the nicest thing anybody ever did for me.

The wilderness was good at first. I felt lonely, but I was free, and there were no rules to break, nobody to beat you or confine you. Campers trekked through sometimes, but they rarely saw me. I would steal food from them before I figured out how to get it for myself.

Years later there were the campers who wanted to party and fuck. They, too, saw me as a savage. They wanted to fuck the savage. Or rather, for the savage to fuck them. That's how they would say it.

My fingertips feel funny. I remember I'm in the hospital. Tied to my bed. She's here. She's scrubbing my fingertips. Are my fingertips dirty?

She tucks something cool around my fist. Other voices. *Shit. Shit shit shit.* A chemical sweet flower smell. Nurse Zara.

Nurse Zara's tone is angry. *Not your patient anymore...not supposed to be on this wing.* Nurse Ann stands—I can tell by the location of her voice. *Unconscious...state protocols...needed to see...Hippocratic oath...*

Nurse Ann leaves with Nurse Zara, leaves my fingers wet, my hands covered with something. And this feeling of bliss where she touched me.

I don't strain to hear the bird songs now, trying to let them take me back. Instead, I go back to the moment of her touch, skin on skin. I'm drifting, lost.

Nurse Ann took her glove off and touched me. She wanted her skin to touch mine.

Everybody who has ever been nice to me has actually wanted to hurt me, and she's part of this place. I shouldn't trust her.

Still, her touch felt like heaven.

When Donny went after her, I had to stop him. I couldn't let him hurt her.

I replay her visit in my mind—the sound of her pulling off the glove. Her hand on my chest. On my heart, rising and falling with my breath. Distant doors. Bells. Buzzers. *Fuck fuck fuck, 34,* she said.

Sparkling green eyes. Fingertips the weight of a cloud. Curly hair the color of peanuts. Eyelashes to match.

Something wet on my fingertips. I wake with a jerk. It's Nurse Ann. She has my hand. She scrubbing my fingers again ...*have to get this off...sorry...not supposed to be here...fuck fuck fuck...*

When she's done with my fingers, she scrubs the sheet around my hand.

"I'm going to get this story if it's the last thing I do. You watch, 34. I am going to investigate the shit out of this. I'm going to get answers for you even if I have to rip them right out of somebody." She scrubs some more, and then she's gone.

There's just the endless ticking of the clock.

Her touch is what I think about when Donny comes back. He stands where Nurse Ann did, to block the camera, but instead of scrubbing my fingertips he hits me in the ribs. The pain spikes through me, but it's not enough to erase her touch. *Feel good? You like this, motherfucker?* He fits his hands around my throat. I can't move my arms. I gasp for air. *You like this? Who's the big man now?*

I'm spinning. Darkness creeps into my vision, my brain. ...need...air.

You wanna see what I do to her next? You wanna know what I'm gonna give her?

I jerk at my bonds just as the darkness starts to consume me.

I wake up gasping and coughing, alone again with the ticking clock.

CHAPTER TWELVE

Ann

I'M CAREFUL NOW. I stop off at a gas station near the institute every day on my way to work and wait for somebody who doesn't hate me too much to drive by, so that I can pull out and follow them into the parking lots so that I'm always walking in with somebody. Like a buddy system I force on them.

They've got me on the ass-crack-of-dawn shift, but I don't trust that Donny won't make a special trip to intercept me.

The only problem is the supply room. I make sure to head in when Donny's good and busy.

They won't let me in to see 34 anymore. I'm assigned to a different wing. I think about sneaking over, but with that third write-up hanging over my head, I can't risk it. I ask the doc about 34's condition when I see him in the hall, and all he says is "rough."

My mouth goes dry. "What do you mean, *rough*? Did you X-ray him? Is it his ribs? His breathing seemed okay when I checked…"

Suddenly Nurse Zara is there. "Patient 34 isn't your business anymore," she says it like I'm way out of bounds for even asking. "Is he?"

I want to say something smart, but I know where that'll get me. So I put my head down. I work. I take my meth supplies inventory. With luck, there'll be some major shake-up here, and everybody will go down.

Meanwhile, I wait for 34's fingerprint results. It took every cent I had, an advance on my paycheck, plus borrowing a lot of money from a truly scary guy in Duluth, who I found through one of my reporter colleagues. I don't know how I'll pay this guy back. It's a textbook example of exactly what you should never do.

The actual process of running the fingerprints will take my FBI contact, Agent Hancock, a half hour, but in addition to taking every cent I have, she's taking her own sweet time. I steal an uneaten dinner roll off a tray here and there. Swipe yogurts. Stocking up. It's not pretty. It'll be worse when rent comes due.

I could get 34's fingerprints run more cheaply by a cop, but if there's a coverup, this woman can actually dig. She can jump into other databases—restricted ones—if she has to. In reporting, you learn to go with the Cadillac when it comes to facts. Shitty facts ruin everything.

In addition to being utterly expensive, the fingerprints are a gamble. I could've done the other option and paid my guy's guy to chase the paper deeper into the system, but the fingerprints are my best bet for a name. Why conceal his identity? The name is the key.

Secrets have power. Sometimes secrets are the only power you have. Once I know his secrets, I'll know how to fight for him.

The call from my FBI agent is a buzz on my calf where I keep my secret cell. I steal into the fourth-floor bathroom and lock the door. I've been trying to stay out of the private bathrooms due to Donny—it's a perfect place for an ambush. But I can't wait until I'm off work.

"Where'd the prints come from?" she asks. "How'd you come by them?"

"That wasn't part of our deal. Telling you that." I close my eyes and say a little prayer that she doesn't get pissed off and hang up. She could keep my money and not deliver.

"They appear twice. He first surfaces as a John Doe in a psych unit in East Webster, Minnesota. Two years back. Are you near a computer?"

"No."

"Well, I took the liberty. This was the fucking kid who came out the woods up north. Come on, East Webster? All those camera crews? Where were you two years ago?"

"Um...Libya." I'm wary. Agent Hancock usually doesn't go beyond the prints.

"Yeah, well, they pulled a kid out of the Boundary Waters Canoe Area. It's huge—hundreds of square miles of primitive wilderness, millions of acres—"

"I know the place," I say, heart pounding. It's not far from Fancher. East Webster is in the next county. "What about the kid? A lost kid?"

"Not just lost. A kid who grew up wild there. A wild boy. You know? Raised-by-wolves shit?"

"That actually happens?"

"Oh, yeah. Bottoms of his feet like shoe leather. Two years back. Savage Adonis. Google it."

"Savage Adonis?"

"That's the name the media gave to him. He got on our radar for a number of reasons. Border control shit with Canada. Nobody was thrilled to hear some kid was living completely wild up there, because the terrorists start looking at that and getting ideas about what they could do undetected."

"What happened to the kid?"

"That's the strange part. When they pulled him out, he was half-dead from a wound, an infection, something like that. He was conscious, and he could speak, but he wouldn't give up his name or anything. Once they got him to the hospital, they figured out he'd been living utterly wild, possibly for most of his life. Doctors can tell that on a physiological and behavioral level. It seems this kid was violent. Extremely unhappy to be closed up between four walls. And apparently quite the looker. The story of this stunningly beautiful kid got leaked. A wild kid with movie-star looks, raised by wolves. The paparazzi went insane. Prices for a clear photo of him went into the six figures."

Right then there's a knock at the door. "Just a sec," I call out, eyeing a shadow under the door. The shadow moves away. I close my eyes. *Please don't be Donny.*

"Are you in touch with the subject?"

"I can't say," I whisper breathlessly. Telling her that is not part of our agreement, and she knows it. "I need the rest of the story. I don't have a lot of time."

"You had legions of paparazzi up in this nothing town up on the Minnesota Iron Range. A gorgeous, mysterious wild boy…the way things were headed, his image would've been on every computer screen, every supermarket rag, every news show…his own reality show. Teen idol shit. It was human interest but also scientific interest. Some of the experts had this idea he'd become some kind of superalpha, kind of like domesticating wild wolves, because you're not out there surviving those winters without wolves. There were a few kids in Siberia who survived like that. Everybody wanted a piece of the supposedly beautiful wild boy. Well, you can imagine."

"Whoa."

"It's a miracle no decent photos got out. But the director of the medical center was ex-military, and he ran security like a World War II general. One staffer lured Savage Adonis out a side entrance while he was coming out of anesthetic from some procedure, and we got one shit picture out of that. It was a feeding frenzy for the poor kid, and a few people went to jail off it—I'm forwarding you a shot that never got out. A while later, just when Savage Adonis mania was at its peak, it all got shut down."

"Shut down?"

"East Webster authorities came out and did a press conference and said it was a hoax. The identities of the people involved in the hoax were under wraps because the person or persons were underage. Something else broke that week, and paparazzi cleared out, and that was that. We dropped it then, too. Better for us that it turned out to be a hoax, in terms of border security image."

"But you're not convinced."

"It always smelled funny. We all thought it. We heard rumors he'd broken out. He had hair down past his shoulders, a beard. Did somebody decide to clean him up and get him out of there for his own sanity? Did he run back to the wilderness? Why wouldn't anybody talk? Was there money involved? There were a lot of questions."

"Christ." I drop to my knees and peer under the door. I'm completely paranoid Donny is out there, waiting to do a push in.

"Here's what's interesting. The fingerprints turn up a second time. A year ago, right around Halloween. Rhone County, Minnesota. But the case number is behind a wall. Classified. I wouldn't have seen it if I hadn't run it for the gaps and seen the number skip. It's a glitch. Unfortunately, you need clearance to crack in."

I have no idea what she's talking about with the gaps and the number skip, but I hear the word "classified" loud and clear. "Tell me you cracked in."

"It's classified, Ann. Classified information," she says. "National security."

"What does the wild boy have to do with national security?"

"You know what a...broad umbrella that is. Broad." There's a pause, as if she's choosing her words carefully. "Things get classified for a lot of reasons. It's possible things get classified just because somebody is playing keepaway. Still. I can't give you that number or any details."

"I see," I whisper, head spinning. Her message between the lines is that I'm not paying her enough for that level of risk.

My blood races. What the hell did 34 do to be deep-sixed like he is? "Thank you."

"So you're not going to tell me where you lifted the prints from? I wouldn't mind knowing. Be grateful to get the end of that saga."

An investigator to the last. Her message is loud and clear—she wants to know, and she'd owe me one if I told her. But I have to think about 34. "Let me sleep on it," I say. "I appreciate this."

"Wish I could help you more."

"I understand," I say. "Thank you for trying."

I take a quick look at my email for the image, and there it is. It's a blurry shot taken from the shoulders up, and it's definitely Patient 34. He glares at the camera, beautiful and feral and even a little otherworldly with long beautiful curls half in his face. Scruffy beard. He's like an angry mystic, pulled down off the mountaintop. So alone. So beautifully, intensely alive.

And actually, she helped me a whole lot, giving everything she could between the lines. She gave me a place—Rhone County. A date—around Halloween a year ago. The fact that she thinks somebody paid to get it classified, which means it's likely not about national security. Pay-to-classify is a something agents hate almost as much as journalists.

Rhone fucking County. A place where parking-lot fender-benders make headlines. I don't need a case number, and she knows it.

My beautiful, feral boy. What did he do?

I hold the phone to my chest, staring at the crack of shiny tile outside the door. My gut says Donny's out there. Fourth floor. What was I thinking coming up here in the afternoon? There's nothing scheduled up here until dinner. I grab a plunger and press it into the toilet and flush once. Again. Then I call maintenance and report an actively overflowing toilet. I shove a toilet paper roll into there.

And wait, hoping they'll hurry. I'm missing rounds.

Ten minutes later, Jerry the janitor is at the door. I let him in and speed the other way. Donny's nowhere, but he was there. I know it in my bones. When you're a journalist, you learn to trust your instincts.

I get on my rounds and start making up time, but my mind is on 34. I do a quick search of the *Rhone River Tribune* on my phone while I'm between tasks. I'm unhappy to see there was nothing written about it. Or maybe there was, and it got deleted.

The rest of my shift seems to take forever. I get out of there with a group, make it home by five, and go right online.

There's plenty about the Savage Adonis, and all of it is based on speculation and interviews with the campers who found him, mostly descriptions of his injury and his incredible beauty, his huge muscles, his bare feet like shoe leather.

One of them gave him water, and the wild boy whispered "thank you."

The breathless descriptions from unnamed sources go on and on. The wild boy's amazing beauty. The wild boy's strength. Speculation about his age—about twenty seems to have been the consensus—and how he would have survived. Background on other wild kids—the ones from Siberia, two from France, another from Africa. Anonymous interviews from medical staff that he can talk, that he wants to get out. A few anonymous campers come forward with tales about fucking the wild boy.

Just like Agent Hancock said, the paparazzi feeding frenzy exploded overnight, and half the story was coverage about the coverage. Everybody waiting for the first pictures of the wild boy like he was the royal baby. There were bounties for those pictures until it was declared a hoax.

I hit the *Rhone River Tribune* a little harder. I pay my two bucks to get behind the paywall and into the archives. Nothing. I try other area papers. Same. Nothing.

Screw that. I grew up in small-town Idaho. I worked summers on the local paper. Something happened out there. They erased the coverage, but people know. I scroll to the bylines of the townie stories from a year ago. Reporter Maxwell Barnes was the main guy covering the area.

I flip to the paper today. He's still there. Still writing.

I pull up a map. An hour away. My head is spinning. It might be hunger. I have no money and nothing but rice in the kitchen. Rice takes forty minutes. And I need 34's story now. I remember a pack of Gummi Bears in the bottom of my airline bag. I grab it and get out.

Second problem: I have enough gas to get to Rhone River, but not back.

I run back into my ugly 1970s piece-of-shit building and head into the boiler room, which is full of tools and junk. I find a bunch of tubing. I pull my car to a shaded corner of the lot and siphon some extra gas from the neighbor below me. It's an asshole move, but he plays his stereo loud in the middle of the night. So now we're both assholes.

I twist the cap closed, spitting to get the taste out of my mouth. I throw the tube in my trunk and take off.

The only person at the *Rhone River Tribune* office is the production person. I tell her I'm doing a *Stormline* story that relates to an area incident. She gives me Maxwell Barnes's cellphone number without too much trouble. We journalists help each other out. He agrees to meet. He gives me his address and tells me to come on over.

Barnes is raking leaves in front of a small bungalow that sits on a road that runs like a zipper through the forest. He's thickset, maybe forty, with a genuine smile and wire-rimmed glasses. I like him instantly.

I thank him for meeting me.

"*Stormline*," he says with a squint. He knows it, and he's not judgmental about it. "Is this off something I reported on?"

"It's more something you didn't report on," I say. "Halloween weekend last year."

His eyes twinkle. He knows exactly what I'm talking about.

I do him the courtesy of giving him what I have. "There was an incident. There was a police report filed, but it went classified. I looked to the *Rhone River Trib*, and nothing's there. I came up on the *Beckerton County Reporter* just a ways out of Boise. A house gets egged, and we'd do a story. Someone sneezes, and we'd do the story."

He smiles wistfully. The smile of somebody who's been stymied.

"This is just between us, but in the course of working one story, I've run into an institutionalized John Doe. Heavily sedated. Things feel off."

Maxwell nods.

I'm taking a risk giving him this much, but sometimes you give a story to get a story. "I'm supposed to be researching something completely different, but everything about how this guy is being held is wrong."

"He's institutionalized."

"Yeah."

He grunts. "We had something happen...this is off the record, okay? But you can get it from other people around here as easy as you can from me."

Meaning he's prevented from talking about it, but if I need a source, I can go find one. "Sure."

"I signed something," he says. He's trusting me here.

"Got it," I say. "Absolutely never talked to you."

"Southwest of here, you have part of the reservation, and then a lot of hunting land. There was this guy, Pinder, who's got a no-trespassing posted parcel, or had one. But it was odd, because he wasn't using it for hunting. He seemed to live in his cabin. He came into town. He said he was a researcher. Kept to himself."

Maxwell shrugs and continues, "He was in and out for years. Then one day, some hunters hear yelling. Some guy, yelling for help. They follow the voice, and it's like something out of one of those shows—there's a man in a cage in there, and from the looks of things, he's been in there a while. Kept like a wild animal. Metal bars, plexiglas panels—for soundproofing, the cops thought. There's a body on the ground. Dead. It's Pinder. Holding a guy in a cage and nobody knew. You know how much I wanted to tell that story?"

"I can only imagine," I say.

He goes on with the story. The man apparently strangled Pinder through the bars and called for help. The cops torched the lock open and got him out, but he attacked them.

"What was this guy like? Violent? Crazy? Did you meet him?"

"I interviewed one of the hunters who found him. He said the guy seemed normal at first, carrying on conversation like a regular guy. The cops got the lock open, and he slips out and heads for the door. One of the cops tried to keep him from leaving, and that's when this guy went wild. Well, he'd been in a fucking cage for a year. Guy broke a cop's arm and hit another in the face on his way out, and that man lost use of an eye. It was a hard hit." He goes through the rest. The manhunt through the woods. A vet finally brings him down with a tranquilizer gun.

"Did you ever get a name on the captive?"

"No. They had him out at the station," Maxwell says. "I get there to find things shut down. I can't interview him. The cops aren't talking. Next I hear, the feds have the case, and the guy's gone. And the owner of the paper didn't even want us calling it 'resisting arrest' in our police blotter. This was a hostage situation with a murder, and it got covered up. You know what kind of juice covers that up?"

"It would've been a national story," I say.

"Easily." He gives me everything else he can. He can't do the story or be a source, but he really, really wants me to do it.

A few minutes later I'm driving off, heart pounding, because this is a story and a half. I sketch out a timeline while I drive. I figure there were two weeks between his capture and the commitment testimony of the psychiatrist in Duluth. So where was the hearing? It's like he bypassed the entire legal system.

I speed on down the wooded road.

Patient 34 has powerful enemies who have gone to great lengths to hide him. This thing is bigger than me. I have to work safe and smart.

And I realize that my best ally is actually *Stormline*.

Stormline is disreputable, but it has a hell of a bank account and a great legal team, and they'd do anything to help me...if they could have this story.

A "Where is the Savage Adonis Now?" story where Savage Adonis turns out to be criminally insane is a sad story. A tragic story. But a "Where is the Savage Adonis Now?" story where he only ever tried to be free and now he's been stripped of his identity and deep-sixed inside an institution for the criminally insane, deprived of due process?

That's a unicorn of a story.

But it's also tricky. Patient 34 is vulnerable and possibly quite dangerous.

The light of the media is really 34's best hope right now.

I hesitate a moment before calling Murray, my editor.

The light of the media is probably not something Patient 34 would choose, considering he was sent into a shark tank of paparazzi while he was weak from surgery. It would have felt like a vicious attack. Publicity will bring them back again.

Still.

I put in the call. My editor is there, of course, because nobody in New York ever leaves the office.

As soon as I utter the words "Savage Adonis," he sucks in a breath. He had people on-site the first time around—of course. He's all about Savage Adonis. He tells me he wants to send his top guy, Garrick, a total slimeball.

I tell him it's me alone or nothing. He wants proof. Pictures. I want money. I want the resources required to get the story right. He wires a few thousand dollars into my account to get things started.

I hang up and drive in silence. This is how 34 gets free—the bright light of the media. An exposure of what was done to him. It's the best I can do for him.

And I feel like total shit.

CHAPTER THIRTEEN

Lazarus

MY EXECUTIVE COACH Valerie says there is a new lesson to be learned every day. That the world is full of knowledge. Here's my lesson for today: a home for the criminally insane? Not hard to break into.

We put a team on the underground cables around five in the morning, taking out the alarm system.

The perimeter guards are the only heavy guns here. We bribed one to fake an illness and leave early. We wait for the other to get the call from his wife about an intruder. As soon as he's out of there, we ice the other two. We turn off the electrified fence. We pull our stockings over our faces and roll in.

We take out a few guards inside. The middle-aged woman behind the window in the wall screams.

"Touch anything and you die, too," I growl, kicking in the door and getting into her small space. I spot the panic button and caress the side of her face with the gun. "Did you touch that?"

She shakes her head no. Violently no.

It wouldn't have helped, but I like to feel obedience.

Everything is brown or beige tile. Is that calming to the nutjobs? Valerie would probably know. She has opinions on colors. She once told me to wear a blue tie—she said it was more executive than all black. I told her it was a long-standing tradition to wear all black in my "accounting firm"—black shirt, black jacket, black tie. She seemed surprised, but she wanted me to try the blue. "The brightness is going to look more modern to people. You're setting a tone for your regime. You're your own man."

I think people responded well to the blue tie.

My main man Mercal crowds in, and we study the feeds, count the staff. Like taking candy from a baby.

But then, nobody is interested in breaking a person out of an institute for the criminally insane, not like with a real prison. A real prison is full of angry guys who can be useful to an organization. The criminally insane tend to be a bit more dubious.

I send one crew member to lock down the office wing.

"You got a list of names?" I ask the woman. "I'm looking for a Kiro Dragusha."

"I don't believe we have such a person." She gets on her computer and with shaking fingers brings a spreadsheet up. Names, room numbers. "No Kiro."

"How about a Keith. You got a Keith?" That was another name Kiro had. The name his adoptive parents gave him.

She stares at me. Deer in the headlights. After a prompt to the side of the head, she finds no Keiths.

I nod at Mercal, who takes her away.

No Kiro. No Keith. I figured he'd be under a different name, but it was worth a try. It's okay. We know Kiro's about 20. We know he's been in one year. That'll narrow it down, and I know a Dragusha when I see one.

I make the call, and fifteen more of my guys slip in. We've rehearsed this. It's simple stuff—a violent takeover, four guys to a wing. Paint the walls with blood if we have to. I adjust my stocking mask.

"Fast and furious," I tell my guys. "Ten minutes in and out. You call me when you find him."

Killing Kiro is something I need to personally oversee and film, and I'm getting DNA. No fucking around.

We go in and disperse. My own team and I take the most likely floor—the top. We start by rounding up staff. That's the key to this operation, controlling the staff. Taking the phones.

We put the three guys face down on the floor—we're not expecting heroes, but you never know. We let the females sit against the wall.

I press my piece to an older nurse's forehead. She has a polka-dot headband. "You in charge?"

She nods. She's crying and shaking. Her powdered face is garish in the fluorescent lights.

"You should apply your makeup when you get here—not beforehand at home. It's all about the lighting." A little chitchat. Valerie would be proud. She looks at me with terror. "Are you hearing me?"

A hot younger nurse is fumbling with something. Mercal turns his piece on her. "That better not have been a phone."

She opens her hands, wide green eyes. "I gave you my phone. It's my..." She shows us her stethoscope. "Nervous habit."

I turn back to the older nurse. "We're looking for Kiro. He may be going by Keith. Got anyone like that?"

Her lips move. Trying to speak.

"No such person," the hot young one says.

I turn my attention to her, because at least she can fucking talk. "What are you?"

"Attending nurse. This was my floor until a week or so—"

"You're our tour guide now. We'll meet each patient, and you'll tell us how long they've been here."

She gets up slow and sure. Her hair's up in some kind of braided style. "Can you give me a clue? I want to help. I don't want trouble."

Something about her is off. She's not fucked-up enough. She pretty much volunteered, didn't she? You can't trust a volunteer. I walk up to her, peer into her eyes. "You a cop?"

Her eyes widen. "Fuck no."

Truth. Still, my gut says she's hiding something. Valerie says to listen to my gut. Then again, if I kill this one, I have one of the guys as a tour guide—or the puddle of an old lady nurse. My gut doesn't like that any better.

"I'll help. Just don't hurt anyone."

"Oh, we're gonna hurt someone, sister. But if you play nice, we'll keep the body count down. Now we're going to start at the end of the hall, and you're going to introduce me around." I pull open a slim door. Storage closet. "Get the rest of the guests in here, Mercal."

We start the tour—me and the hot one, flanked by two of my best. One of the guys cries out. Mercal. He's playing games. A fucking psycho. Is this how people used to see me?

We head in the first room.

She says, "This is Wendell, he's—"

"No oldsters," I say. "Kiro is in his early twenties. He's been in here for a year. Anyone who meets that criteria—"

"S-so you don't want to meet the guys who have been here forever?"

I shove the barrel of my Glock to her throat. "Does the term 'a year' have meaning for you or not?"

She leads us down the hall. She waves at a door. "Ronald's fifty years old."

I look in. Old guy. I look back, catch her monitoring me. I shove her.

We pass another. "Pearson's been in two years. He might be little old…"

I go in. Blond. Wiry. "Stop wasting my fucking time."

We go on. She's nervous. We pass another room. The hair color's right. I can't see his face. "Him?"

"He's forty. Been in twenty years. But this next guy could be it—the next guy could be your Kiro for sure." She speeds up, like she really wants us to come and see this next guy.

We follow her in, but the next guy is a redhead. Clearly not a Dragusha. Fuck. We keep going, checking the guys. Nobody fits the description. We head back, and that's when I happen to look into the dark-haired guy's room. All that dark hair. The large frame. I slow.

She gives me a panicked look.

I grab her hair, drag her into the room.

He's a fucking Dragusha if I ever saw one.

Kiro Dragusha.

I jerk her and shove the gun into her eye. "You trying to fuck with us? This guy's not forty."

"He's not your guy!"

I twist her arm and use the torque to slam her face into the wall. "Wrong answer. Get the cameras rolling and get a lock of his hair," I call over my shoulder.

"Leave him!"

"Trussed up and drugged. Thank you, Fitcher, or whatever this place is."

It's right then that the nurse decides it's a good time to raise holy hell, screaming like a banshee, calling out the number 34.

She's going crazy. I cock my gun. I'm about to pop her when I hear the crash. I spin around to find myself face to face with Kiro, a pair of scissors flashing in his bloody hands. He's breathing hard. Coming at me.

All three of my guys are down. I don't look directly at them. I don't need to. They're lying wrong on the floor. Broken dolls.

The fucking nurse is screaming her head off. "No killing. No killing!"

I pull off my stocking mask and level my piece at him. "Stop right there." A barrel in the face is enough for most guys. But this guy isn't most guys. He's drugged up, that's clear. Unsteady on his feet.

But it's more than that.

This guy isn't quite human. What the fuck?

He's bigger than his brothers. Panting, bloody. But it's his eyes—something more animal than human in his eyes.

I've seen all kinds of guys, seen them when they're out of their minds with fear, with anger.

This guy is in a class all his own. Like words don't get through, and in that moment that we're facing off, I'm wishing I'd brought something bigger. More of a cannon. But this guy isn't even seeing my gun. Like having a .45 against a bear who's looking to fly at you. You'll get a shot off, but will it matter?

"No more killing, 34," she gasps from behind me.

Kiro's gaze shifts. Words don't get through—unless the hot nurse says them. But then she starts sobbing—maybe she's seen the bodies.

My heart pounds. "Listen to the lady," I say. "No killing." Like I'm talking to the wind. This guy's gone.

I manage to get off a shot as he lunges for me. Flies, like a fucking madman, going for my throat, fingers grabbing my face. I hit him, but he's pure rage. Kiro doesn't like his nurse being messed with.

He hits me. I play dead, but he has me up. You don't fool a killer like this. He has me by the neck. I'm clawing at his fingers, and right then my life flashes before my eyes. Spots form in my vision. I feel my legs start to go.

I think about that old bitch's prophecy. The brothers together. He's a fucking nuclear arsenal. I should've dynamited the whole place.

"No, 34! Don't kill him."

CHAPTER FOURTEEN

Ann

HE'S CHOKING THE life out of the man. Right before my eyes.

"No!" I sob. I don't know what I'm saying "no" to. The rubble. The smell of blood. The antiseptic. Donny. The kitten crying. The insomnia.

Patient 34 slams the man against the wall like a rag doll. The sound is sickening. The man slumps to the floor, out cold. Maybe dead.

Patient 34 turns to me then. I whimper and scramble sideways, but that just seems to draw him. In a fluid motion, he has my arm.

My mouth goes dry. His hair is wild, amber eyes fiery. I freeze, unable to move. His nostrils expand and contract, and I can feel him tremble—with murderous energy, I think. He's scary, yeah. Like a beast of a warrior.

But the main word that comes to my mind is "majestic."

There might be a little bit of awe as well.

He reaches up to my cheek. I jerk away, not wanting him to hurt me, but he tightens his hold on my arm. "Don't be afraid, Ann."

I reel at the force of my name on his lips. Again he reaches up his hand and lays gentle fingers on my face. Sticky. Blood. Am I bleeding? Is he going to kill me, too?

"Please let me go," I whisper. "Please, 34."

He doesn't listen, or maybe he's just beyond hearing. Wildly I look around at the dead and unconscious men. I've never seen anything like this. Not even in the war zones.

He seems mesmerized by my forehead. I squeeze my eyes shut, shaking in fear as he touches my hair. He holds me in place with a grip of stone. I try again to pull away.

"No."

He touches my cheek, and I open my eyes. Emotions have a size, and this man's anger is huge, like a force of its own. I can feel myself fraying—it's the exhaustion, the fear, the kitten, the antiseptic. Tears roll down my cheeks.

"You want to get out," I sob. "I know you do. This is your chance. Go." I don't give a fuck about my story anymore. I just want him to survive. I want him to be free.

"You're hurt," he pants.

"It's just a cut. You won't get another chance, 34!"

He won't stop checking my head. I try to push him away—it's like trying to push the wind away. He keeps touching me, fingers on my forehead and head like I'm an inanimate object, his to control.

"Th-they came up from the north stairwell. You can get out the other way."

"Hurt," he says.

"Listen to me, 34! There's a back way out on the far side of the craft room. You know the craft room?"

He brushes the hair out of my eyes. My heart pounds. Savage Adonis.

"Go!"

He looks in the direction of the craft room, and I think he's going for it. The wild boy, sensing freedom.

"You understand, right?"

He kneels and sweeps me up into his arms.

"No!" I cry as we bang out the door. "You can't!"

But he can. He is. He's tearing down the hall, down to the craft room, like I said.

Carrying me.

It's here I realize that he's not entirely steady. Is the adrenaline of the fight wearing off? There was a shot. Was he hit? His blue PJs have blood on them.

"Let me down," I beg. "I'll be fine."

No answer. He takes another flight of stairs.

I struggle in his arms. He tightens his grip, face beautifully brutal, dark curls wild, eyes distant and feral.

We reach the emergency exit door. He kicks it open.

It falls out—*face first.*

It's a cloudy morning, just past seven. The guard towers are eerily dark. Where are the guards? The spotlights are all off.

He stills, sucks in a breath. It comes to me that this is the first time he's breathed outdoor air in months.

"You're out now." I push on his chest. He's ignoring me, carrying me around to the front, to the parking lot and the gates.

I start to say something, but he seals my mouth with his hand. He's panting, carrying me along the side of the facility.

Like being in the arms of King Kong.

We round a corner.

"Hey! Hey you!"

A few men are coming at us with military-style weaponry.

These are not institute guys.

I feel 34 stiffen.

"Stop! On the ground! Both of you!"

He crouches behind a car and sets me carefully on the pavement. "34!"

Again he touches my hair, my cheek. I feel strangely like a doll he's decided to care for. And then I see he's bleeding from the shoulder.

I gasp.

In flash he's gone.

"There he is!"

A shot goes off. There are more shots. I crouch, terrified. I hear a smack, a groan, a sickening crunch.

I hug my knees to my chest as the sounds spin on, then I crawl to the side of the car. What I should really do is pull out my phone and get some footage. I was getting footage when they first attacked. When they first sat us in the hall. The guys almost caught me, but I made up that thing about my stethoscope.

Now I just want to survive.

I inch out in time to see Patient 34 shaking a man by the neck a few times before he whips the man's face into the side of the shiny black SUV. The man crumples to the ground next to two other bodies.

And 34 stands over them, hands dripping with blood. I suck in a breath.

He killed the armed men with his bare hands.

And then he turns to me. Our gazes lock. A bolt of fear goes through me.

He's a force of nature. Pure aliveness. Pure power. He's the most ferociously hot thing I've ever seen. The most dangerous thing I've ever seen.

Barely human.

Savage Adonis.

Is he even seeing me? Or is he seeing prey? Heat goes into his eyes as he stalks toward me. There's a strange inevitability to everything now, as if he's been coming for me forever.

I'm trembling deeply. All the death. I can't handle any more death, any more horror. Strong arms lift me. The earth tilts.

"I'll protect you, Nurse Ann." He carries me back to where the bodies are.

"Y-you killed them."

He settles me gently into the front seat of the SUV. Says nothing.

"What are you doing?"

He pulls out the seatbelt and puts the buckle in my hand, like he wants me to finish buckling it.

"You're wounded. You need medical attention," I say.

He grabs my face. "Seatbelt." He slams my door and starts around the front of the car, sticking out a hand to support himself on the hood as he rounds the front. He gets in and starts the thing up. Did he take the keys off the guys he killed or were they in here?

"You can drive?"

"I've driven." He studies the dashboard, fits his hand uncertainly over the shifter. Then he shifts to drive and pulls out with a lurch.

"Jesus!" I scream.

He races out, crashing the gate. He's going fast. He's shit at driving.

"Get on the right side of the road! Jesus, 34!"

He looks at me uncertainly.

I gesture frantically. "Stay on this side of the line! You see it? See the line?"

He jerks the vehicle into the proper lane. He drives like a newbie, pressing the gas in pulses.

"Driven isn't the same as *can drive*," I say.

He doesn't answer. He's swaying in his seat. He swerves. I scream and grab the wheel. That jerks him back to attention.

"You're going to pass out and kill us! Come on! Let me drive."

He pushes my hand off. He's pale. Is he losing blood? Is it the drugs?

"You're half passed out!" He doesn't even have his seatbelt on.

He glowers at the road. It's a two-lane nowhere highway. We pass a Pine Cone Motel billboard. Free WiFi. Spotlight beams shine up from below it. The ambient light kisses his full lips, his powerful cheekbones.

I grip the door handle and quietly unbuckle my seatbelt, hold it in place, ready to run.

"Buckle it."

"No!"

He sucks in a breath. "...won't get far."

"I won't get far dead!"

He doesn't reply; he just tightens his grip on the wheel.

"Talk to me. Have you ever driven on a road before?"

"Cars at campsites."

"You're going to kill us. Do you even know traffic signals? Pull over."

He barrels on. Too fast for me to jump out. Or should I try it?

"I'm not dying in a car, 34."

He drives on, concentrating. I grip the handle, riding helplessly.

"You're going to pass out."

"I won't."

Keep him awake, I think. "They were trying to kill you. Why did they want to kill you?"

"People always want to kill me."

"No. These were hitters. Organized crime guys."

A car comes from the other way. Light on his face.

"Fuck!" Our headlights aren't even on. They should be on in this gloomy weather. "Stay on this side of the line. God!" I squeeze my eyes shut and duck as the car passes, horn blaring. "Let me drive."

"No."

"Slow down at least."

He squints. Woozy. *Don't pass out.*

"They called you Kiro. Is that your name? You seem like a Kiro."

He's weaving.

"Stay awake, dammit!" I poke him. "There has to be a reason they want to kill you. Right?"

"I'm different," he growls like it's so obvious.

"You're not that different," I say. "You won't let the woman drive even when it's the best choice."

He looks at me strangely, then swerves. "Pull over!" I scream.

My scream seems to have gotten him alert again. But for how long?

"Where are we going?"

He looks up at the sky. "This way."

What's in the sky? Then I realize he's navigating by the sky. Back to the forest. Back home. And…taking me with him?

"You're in no shape to drive. Let me drive."

"You'll run."

"I won't. I promise I won't. Kiro—"

He thinks I'll run. Why not? Everyone has probably always either run from him or tried to hurt him. Kill him. Drug him. Imprison him. He starts looking groggy again. He swerves.

I grab his arm, screaming. "Slow the fuck down!" He doesn't slow down. I shake him. I start to cry. He's losing blood. He trusts nobody. He's going to crash. "Kiro!" I sob, deeply, deeply frightened now.

"Stop crying, Nurse Ann. Stop. Please."

He really hates my crying. It gets through to him more than my screams. Yeah, I'm not above turning it on a bit. "You're scaring me!" I sob.

"Stop it!"

I keep it going, begging him to rest his eyes a bit, telling him how scared I feel. "You want to go north? I'll take you north. Please!"

He grits his teeth.

"Look at me!"

He turns and regards me with a pained expression. "We're on the same side. You saved me. Pull over. We help each other."

"You'll..." He doesn't finish the sentence.

I put a hand on his arm.

"Slow," I say. "Slow."

The speedometer ticks down. He slows. Or maybe he's just losing strength.

"Good."

He sways forward. Losing consciousness. The truck heads for the shoulder.

I grab the wheel. Still slowing. I crawl over him, sitting partly on his lap. I kick around, trying to find the brake, jamming it on as I navigate to the shoulder.

I heave out a breath once it's finally in park, sitting there on this unconscious feral man's lap. Then he wraps his arms around me, whispering something that sounds like "mine."

I push and coax him over into the passenger seat. Luckily, he cooperates, climbing over. I rip off his shirt. Still bleeding. I use my phone light to inspect the wound. I rip strips of his shirt and bandage the wound as best as I can. It's a gash in his shoulder. Not so bad. His pulse seems okay. I think the drugs are pulling him back under, like he used all the adrenaline he had. I put my hand on his neck, his cheek. "Kiro," I say.

He mumbles.

I get behind the wheel, jerk the thing into drive, and pull out, hands shaking. What am I doing? I should run. Save myself. But then I look over at him, slumped in the seat, and I feel this surge of crazy affection.

He just wants to go home. He wants to get back to the woods. And then there's the matter of his story. Who is he? Why are they trying to kill him?

"Kiro!"

No response.

I shove at his arm. He's out cold. I reach over in the dark and take his wrist. His pulse feels strong. It's no wonder he's out. What with the drugs and two fights to the death.

I try not to think of that.

I drive at exactly the speed limit and quietly pull out my phone and text my editor, Murray. I send him the photos I got of the men who attacked Fancher Institute. A few minutes later I make the call.

"Ann!" That's the sum total of Murray's breathless answer. "Ann Ann Ann! The Fancher attack is just now hitting the wire. Talk. Go."

I give him the story down and dirty, pyramid style. His pleasure knows no bounds when I inform him the attack was connected to 34—that what appeared to be professional criminals were specifically hunting for Patient 34.

"Fuck yes. Thank you, Jesus," he says. "Savage Adonis, hunted by Albanian mafia."

"Excuse me?"

"The lion tattoo in one of the images you got. One of your nylon-stocking guys? Have you looked at these pictures?"

"I was busy staying alive, dude."

"Research just identified it as Albanian mob. What did 34 say about the attack?"

"He doesn't seem to know who they are. But they definitely knew him."

"Are you sure he doesn't know? You sure he wasn't shitting you?"

I touch his hair. "He wasn't shitting me." I don't know much about 34—Kiro—but he's not a bullshitter. He really didn't seem to know them.

I'm different. They all see it.

I don't tell Murray that part. Is it possible he truly thinks they want to kill him just because he's some sort of abomination? It breaks my heart a little that he would think it, but he's never had a reason to trust anyone. Of course he'd think it.

"It could be a blood feud, I don't know," Murray says. "I mean, maybe. The Albanian mob definitely gets into that shit. Did you know when one family member is killed, vengeance extends to *all* the male members of the of the killer's family? Those fucking Albanian mobsters are psychos."

"Wait, send a team into a high-security psych ward just to carry out a blood feud?" I say. "Risking a dozen guys like that? Even a psychotic organization doesn't do that. No. There's something else going on. It's all connected. Savage Adonis. This hit. There're more pieces out there. Something bigger's going on."

"What's going on is this story just got twice as dangerous. Sure you don't want me to send Garrick?" He really wants to send slimy Garrick.

"I got this."

"Okay. Dump that vehicle. I'll send a rental car."

I give him my location; we talk plans. He gives me an update on the Fancher attack from the wire. Rumors of escaped prisoners. Some staff unaccounted for. "They don't know a lot at this point in time," he says.

I smile. Not knowing a lot at this point in time means you don't know shit. Or that you're not being allowed to report it.

"I'll call in. I'll say I got freaked out and escaped when Kiro did," I tell him. People do that during shootings—just run for the hills. "In the meantime, I need to get us somewhere. I need medical supplies. Kiro needs medical attention. I've got ID, but…"

"Don't use it." He tells me there's a Holiday Superstore ten miles up where I can get basic medical supplies. He gives me directions to a small motel well beyond that—he'll get a room under his own name. "Don't bother giving your ID or license plate. They'll take mine."

Of course they will. Leave it to a muckraking rag to know these things are even options for purchase.

"Stay safe. I'm having cash and ID couriered up there. They'll knock and tell you it's a package from *Stormline*."

"Got it."

"How long is his hair?" Murray asks.

"What?"

"How long?"

"It's long. I'm going to need to clean him up."

"Don't cut it."

"What?"

"Look, I've got a courier heading out there with ten thousand dollars. You know why? Because I'm buying a story on Savage Adonis. When I buy a story on Savage Adonis, I want Savage Adonis, not a frat boy."

I run my fingers through his hair. "All he wants to do is to go north. I think he wants to go home."

"And you're going with him. You'll help him. You'll take photos along the way."

"The Albanian mafia..." I whisper, half to him, half to myself.

"Your boy dealt them a serious setback. Just stay off the grid and you'll be fine."

Riiiight, I say under my breath.

He continues. "Savage Adonis wants to head into the woods? Good. That's the safest place you can be. If anybody can get lost in the woods, it's him. Tell me you have a charger for that phone of yours."

"I'll grab a charger pack."

"Good girl. Stay with him. Don't stop taking pictures."

CHAPTER FIFTEEN

Aleksio

I STROLL INTO Agronika with my brother Viktor and Tito and Yuri and a few of our guys. We move through the front dining room, all dark wood paneling and candlelight illuminating the heavy red curtains and tapestries all over the walls.

There's a hush all across the place.

Yeah, we're the Dragusha brothers walking through Agronika, famous for roasted lamb, stuffed peppers, and being the stronghold of our greatest enemy, Bloody Lazarus Morina.

People bolt up from feast-laden tables and walk out—quickly and quietly. Some even as they're still chewing.

I catch Viktor's eye. He's determined. Ready to get bloody. His black suit has a bit of a shine to it, as though even his suit is ready to get bloody.

The images on the tapestries that cover the walls are nothing but a lot of strange animals and soldiers on horseback, unless you give a shit about Albanian history. Then you know it's the traditional tales. Love and war, tragedy and redemption. Fantastically powerful families like mythical beasts woven all through. The lions are the Dragushas more often than not.

The Dragushas are an old family.

Viktor and I know the stories and the customs and all of that. We know who we are. Our enemies tried to prevent exactly that—they sent Viktor to an orphanage in Moscow, sent Kiro to be adopted, and hunted me. Put a price on my head.

But Dragushas are tough.

My old mentor, the man who saved me that bloody day in the nursery when they took my family, instilled appreciation for the Albanian customs in me. The honor of the Black Lion clan, the criminal empire we will be taking back for our own. And I taught Viktor once I found him.

"Showtime," my guy Tito mumbles, adjusting his cuffs as we approach the end of the civilian dining area. Or maybe he's touching the slim hilt of the blade he has under there. He likes to do that before a fight the way some people like to touch the hull of a plane before they climb on board.

Around the corner the light will grow dimmer, and the thieves will be thicker. Lazarus's thieves. Lazarus's hitters, all his made guys.

But we happen to know Lazarus is injured, laid up somewhere in a private facility with a lot of his guys protecting him.

We got word of his attack on some institute up north just an hour ago—the Fancher Institute. He fucking went after Kiro—we're sure of it. We knew Kiro was in the system but not *where* in the system. How did Lazarus find Kiro first?

The important thing, though, is that he didn't get him. We've got a cop inside who described the scene, did some interviews, sent images. A lot of casualties, but none of them are Kiro. And if Kiro was dead, word would be out. Lazarus would see to it.

It's bad, but not like it would be if Kiro was dead.

We're heading up there. This is a pit stop. We're here to mess up some guys and take some others for intel. We need to know what Lazarus knows.

We turn the corner, and there they are—a handful of tough guys from Lazarus's crew drinking grappa and smoking cigarettes. Health laws don't apply at Agronika.

They start shooting, but not fast enough. We gun down a few. Take the rest to shake down.

CHAPTER SIXTEEN

Ann

MURRAY HAS GOTTEN us a room at the very end of a 1970s-era motorist motel, a small, low building with alternating doors and windows. I sit in the truck staring at Kiro, who's utterly out. I look back and forth between him and the door of our room.

And sigh.

I like to think of myself as a capable woman. I definitely was before the kitten incident, but carrying a 200-pound unconscious man even ten feet isn't—has never been—in my wheelhouse.

I shake Kiro.

I think of him as Kiro now. It's a strong, fabulous, awesome, totally unique name, which suits him perfectly.

I shouldn't be getting attached to him like this. I really shouldn't.

I pat his cheeks. Nothing. I don't like that he's so deeply out. I grab the bag from the Holiday store and drink one of the waters while I think.

I get out and go into the room and look at what I've got to work with. Luck comes in the form of a chair with wheels. Can I get him into that?

As it turns out, yes—with his help. I pinch his cheek, and he wakes up enough for me to get him into the chair.

Ten minutes later he's out cold on the bed, and I'm a frazzled, exhausted mess, running on fumes and no rest. It's entirely possible I'm not making the greatest choices.

Kiro deserves somebody better to protect him. Somebody better than me.

But I'm what he has.

One foot in front of the other, I think. Just concentrate on that next step, which in this case is handling the vehicle. The Albanian mob is out there, probably with a network of cops on the lookout for the vehicle Kiro stole—probably one of theirs.

The SUV has to go.

I go out and take the license plates off of it and drive it to a vacant lot behind a shed in back of a 7-Eleven store a half mile down the street.

Then I jog back to the room, thankful to find him sprawled out on the bed. I didn't think he had it in him to run, but you never know with Kiro.

I stand there for a moment in awe of how kinetic and wild he feels, even in sleep. It's amazing to me that he even fits inside the four corners of a bed. He blows me away. I want to fight for his wildness. I want to fight for *him*.

I nab my phone, get a quick photo, and tuck it away.

I shred his shirt with the scissors I picked up, baring his massive chest—dirty, bloody, sweaty. It's the wound I'm worried about. I remove the makeshift bandage I created and start cleaning it with the rubbing alcohol from the Holiday.

Kiro was stabbed with something in the shoulder. It's not as bad as I thought. Back in my field nursing days, I worked on a lot of wounds like this. Assisted with a lot worse.

Not infected. He'll be okay, though he won't be enjoying jumping jacks anytime soon. How did he even carry me?

He's shaking, but I think that's him detoxing. He's coming off of a lot of heavy psychotropic drugs.

The bite of rubbing alcohol rouses him. I pull away, wary, but he just moves his arms as if to make sure he's free.

"It's okay," I say. "I'm here to help you."

He squints at me.

"You probably feel how I look," I say. "Or is it the other way around?" It feels good to talk to him the way I used to. Like something regular in this insane situation. Not that the previous situation was all that sane.

He swallows. Eying me. I wonder how fucked up he feels.

I grab a fresh cloth and approach him slowly, gently. "Didn't I tell you I'd stay?"

He's forming a word. "Where..."

I kneel to be level with his golden eyes, feeling this surge of fondness for him. I can't help it.

Stay objective.

"You're safe. Hiding. You're safe with me." I offer him water, and he drinks greedily, massive throat undulating.

I shake out three aspirins for him. He bats them away.

"I'm not trying to drug you, okay? You were shot." Does he even understand me?

"I'm going to sew this thing up. Are you with me?" He opens his eyes again. I touch his cheek, stroking gently to show I'm not a threat. He closes his eyes, seeming to enjoy my touch.

Stay objective, I say, even as I fall into his beauty, this trembling, fucked-up, feral lost boy who's eight, nine, maybe even ten years younger than I am. I stroke his cheek again, and he seems to relax more deeply. And I wish I didn't have to stitch him and hurt him. I wish I had all the money in the world to help him and get him free without having to write a story about him in exchange. But this deal with the publicity devil is part of how he keeps safe. He doesn't know it, but I do.

Murray will want this story ASAP—Savage Adonis in all his hot savagery. Kiro deserves better than that. He deserves a beautiful, thoughtful piece.

Kiro has been treated as something less than human by the system and the media, but when I look at him, I see a man who is achingly, intensely human.

He's scary and violent, yes. But what choice did he have? Hit men were after him. He didn't kill the people when I told him not to. Hell, he didn't kill Donny during his first few escape attempts—that shows real restraint, if not downright sainthood.

And he did carry me off in spite of my asking him to put me down, but it felt...protective. Which would go along with what I know about him. Kiro gave up his chance to escape from a living hell to help me when Donny attacked, after all. That shows a lot. It shows that Kiro's force of will and sense of right and wrong didn't crumble even in the most degrading, demoralizing circumstances.

So that's where I'm heading with my fucking piece.

Murray can fuck himself if he doesn't like it.

I don't know what happens once I get Kiro to his home. Does Murray imagine sending camera crews at that point? I can make sure Kiro can't be found by Murray, but what about these hit men?

I can't fight for Kiro if I don't know the full story.

I look down at Kiro. It might be best to get away from him before the sedatives work themselves out of his bloodstream—I know that for a fact. But all I want to do is to curl myself around him and hold him.

"It's going to hurt, but this is how I help you."

I mean the stitches, but I guess it applies to doing his story, too.

Slowly he opens his amber eyes.

"Okay?" I say.

He blinks, fighting sleep. As if he wants to keep looking at me as long as possible.

I pull out the kit I put together, sterilizing everything. I grab the fishing line and a small pair of pliers and get to work. His eyes fly open when I pierce his skin the first time. But he doesn't pull away, he just watches me work. It's a little unnerving, feeling his gaze on me as I stitch his shoulder—he just lets me do it. I numbed the area with a little bit of ice, that's all. He's calm. Watching me.

Is he out of his mind from the drugs? Or simply accustomed to pain? My heart breaks a little bit for him.

I talk to him softly as I tie each stitch, telling him how we're going back to the forest, just as soon as we get him nice and strong. He seems to drift off…until the *rrrrip* of tape wakes him. His hand flies to the clean, dry bandage, then he looks at me.

Gratitude in his eyes.

"You're safe for now. I'll do my best to help you, but what you need now is rest."

He eyes the window where the noontime sun bleeds out the edges of the blinds.

"Rest for me, okay? Go back to sleep."

He reaches out and grabs me around the waist.

I pull away, but he won't let me go. With a surge of unexpected strength, he pulls me onto the bed with him, holding me flush to his big body. He curls around me, like I'm his teddy bear.

I try to move, and he tightens his powerful arms.

Fuck.

"Sleep," he whispers into my hair.

My pulse pounds. I wait a bit, then try to pull out all at once.

No go. It's like trying to break through rock.

It hits me that I'm alone in a motel room with a man from an institution for the criminally insane. And yeah, I feel this crazy affection for him. And he's gorgeous. And I have good reason to believe that he's not criminally insane, but then again, he did kill a few people with his bare hands. My editor thinks hanging out with him is a grand idea, but he really just wants the story.

It doesn't look good on paper.

And now Kiro's acting like he's in charge. I'm supposed to be in charge here.

"Kiro, let me up."

His breath evens out. Is he sleeping? He won't let me go even in his sleep?

I sigh and tell myself to relax. Not like there's anything else to do. I won't be able to get up from this bed until he lets me up. It should be scary, but I find I'm not scared.

In fact, there's this nice silence in my mind. I've been living with an unnerving buzz of anxiety for months. Like static on the radio, but harsher, more jagged.

And now this silence. My mind feels strangely clear. I'm weightless.

I'm a creature in his arms. A heartbeat. Held. Trapped. This feeling is so strange, so new.

Just as I drift off, I realize that this strange, new feeling is peace.

***

I WAKE UP with a start, disoriented by the weight around me, the massive arms entrapping me. The warm, rhythmic heave behind me.

Patient 34—Kiro. I remember my plan—waiting for his sleep breath to start so I can extricate myself.

I lift my head and squint at the red numbers on the digital clock, shocked to see it's the middle of the night. I slept? I blink, unable to believe it. I slept for how many hours? Eight? Ten?

I shift, and he moves too, pulling me tight. My heart pounds. I haven't slept this long in ages. Since I can remember. Since the hospital collapse. The children. The kitten.

I stiffen, waiting for the fear to close back in. That's always how it happens—I wake up feeling good, and then the memories tumble back, and fear closes around me, poisoning everything.

I lie there, waiting for the fear. But I feel...okay.

So much of being a journalist is about recognizing the relative weight of details. You want to pull out that one little detail that has significance for people, the detail that helps tell the story in a way that words can't. Maybe it's something somebody said, or an image. Somebody's hands. A broken doll in the street.

The detail that takes everything over.

The kitten became that detail for me in a negative way. It haunted everything, blocked everything. I couldn't see past it. The kitten, the antiseptic smell.

And suddenly, lying in this strange, savage man's arms in the middle of nowhere in the middle of the night, the kitten has the weight of...a kitten.

And when I breathe in through my nose, the smell is gone. The smell that would cling to me for days on end, even through long weekends off, even when I wasn't there at the hospital.

And I slept. Did I sleep because the smell wasn't there? Or did the smell go away because I was able to sleep?

He pulls me tighter, breath steady. And I think that I can't go anywhere even if I wanted to. And then I think that I don't want to.

And I let my eyes drift closed again. And I wonder if we're saving each other.

CHAPTER SEVENTEEN

Kiro

I SHOULD HATE her. I should walk out of this room and leave her. Lock her up so she can't follow. Kill her if she takes yet another photo of me. I should kill her for how she's fooled me.

Instead I breathe in the scent of her hair.

All these long, grueling months, I've wanted one thing—home. To be back with my pack, the one place in the world I ever belonged. The only ones who ever wanted me.

Ann acts like she wants me, but she just wants my story. I know that now.

I should kill her for being so kind to me. For making me think she cared.

I should kill her. Except I can't. And I want her.

My head is still foggy from the drugs, but better than I can remember for a long time. My shoulder burns, but no feeling is quite so powerful as the feeling of her in my arms.

I want her with a fever that burns so brightly I can think of nothing else.

Morning. Birds nearby. Not nearby like at Fancher Institute but right outside the door. The sun is just rising; I can hear it in the bird songs. I need water. Sun. Food. Air. To run.

But my desire for her overpowers all that.

She's nothing but a reporter, hungry for my story. I heard her on the phone. I heard what that man on the other end said.

She wants my story because I'm different, savage, wrong.

Still I want her. Need her.

I knew she had secrets, with that strange kitten story. I knew she wasn't like other nurses. I never expected she was one of *them*.

Those reporters.

I still remember the way they went at me when I was so weak, unable to defend myself.

I faced lots of deadly predators out in the forest, but it was always the natural order of things. They were after me because they were hungry. Trying to protect their young.

The reporters came at me because I'm different. Bad. Wrong. Savage. It was personal.

I still remember holding the wall by the side door of the hospital where that man led me. Holding myself up, swaying, still sedated from the operation, trapped between the mob of them and the locked door.

I was in a lot of pain, but it was the despair that twisted my heart. Somehow, after being accepted by the wolves in every way, I'd come to think I wasn't an abomination.

The pack of reporters showed me I still was. Their shouts and pictures and questions. Calling me Savage Adonis.

I only ever wanted to belong.

I thought Ann was different. I would've done anything for her.

Then I heard Ann talking to the man called Murray, talking so casually about photos and stories about me.

When I buy a story on Savage Adonis, I want Savage Adonis.

I trusted Ann. Dreamed about her. We were a pack of two, there in the hospital. We helped each other. We fought for each other.

She's one of them.

The betrayal cuts hard.

At least the other people at the Fancher Institute didn't pretend to care, to be pack with me.

She wants to come home with me and take pictures—I understand that now. That's why she's here.

I stare at the sun's glow coming from the edges of the curtain. She tried to cover up the window just like she tried to cover her true nature, but it's there all the same.

I close my eyes, hating that she's one of them.

I should knock her out. I should tie her up and leave. But I can't let her go. I pull her to me. I stroke her soft brown curls. Waves like the edges of a peanut.

Mine.

I imagined her with me out there. It made me so happy to think of it.

And I realize that I don't have to let her go.

The place we're going is so remote, so deep in the woods, she'll never find her way out. Not without me.

I could take her for my mate. Out in the wilderness, I don't need to trust her. She would be mine to keep. To care for.

Fully and completely mine.

My heart begins to pound as images of taking her crowd my mind. The fierceness with which I want her makes it hard to think.

She would struggle, and I would chase her, and then I would catch her—and I wouldn't let her go.

Something amazing happens out in the woods when a predator catches its prey. When a wolf has a squirrel in its jaws—not just the tail, but when the wolf fully has a squirrel's warm body trapped in its jaws—teeth, pressing into warm flesh. No way out.

The squirrel will stop struggling and go limp. Just relax into it.

Heart beating furiously, it submits to the superior force of the wolf.

It always fascinated and compelled me, ever since I witnessed it as a boy, cold and hungry and alone. The flop of the body, like a dance of death and life.

It felt ancient and cruel and beautiful.

I nuzzle her hair, cock hard as steel. She could be my mate. I'll bathe her and wrap her in furs and keep her safe from the Donnys of the world. I'll find food for her. There's a hilltop I would bring her to where you can watch the sunrise light the trees and paint the water pink. I'll hold her down and fuck her and care for her. I would never let her go.

She groans and shifts against my cock, sleepy and sweet. I put my mouth to the back of her neck and taste her and breathe her in, letting her sweetness flood my senses.

She was different at the hospital. Wary. On edge. Here she's soft. I move my lips to her ear, taste her skin there, cock pressed to her back.

I move my hands over her hair. She's so warm, body so soft and sweet. She's betraying me, yet I can't stop liking her.

I want her affection, too. Not fake affection but real affection.

That's something I can't have.

I tell myself I don't need it. I'll take her either way.

I reach around to her belly, push my hands under her shirt and touch her skin. Her belly isn't hard and rough like mine; it's smooth and soft. I spread my hand and pull her ass to me. I nearly lose it right there, separated from her warmth by mere layers of fabric. I imagine bending her over the bed, her ass pale and bare, her pussy open to me.

Right then, I catch the scent of her arousal, and everything in me surges to life. I've woken up her body, but not her mind.

I imagine tasting her. She'd struggle, but I wouldn't let her. I'd plunge my tongue into her warmth. My tongue and my fingers.

I imagine her out in a sunny field, naked, rolling on her back, looking up at me, baring herself to me, waiting for me.

I stroke her soft belly. She hisses out a sleepy breath and moves with me.

Slowly, gently, I push my hand down and graze her waistband.

Her breath is like the water, slow and deep. I pull her closer.

Her rhythmic breathing tells me she's still sleeping.

Still I touch her.

Savage, the drugged campers said, laughing. *You fuck like a savage.* I didn't fully understand what they were saying until I saw the TV and all the gentle people.

I was a sideshow to them, too. A freak. A savage fuck. I didn't know.

I stroke her belly, making her breath speed up.

She sighs in her sleep.

The camping girls would joke that I was raised by wolves. They didn't understand that I actually was, in a way. They walked around naked and drugged with their glowing necklaces and bracelets. They would touch my hair.

They would rip their clothes off and run from me, laughing. They liked me to chase them and fuck them. The drugs made them crazy to touch and be chased. Eventually, I didn't care that they saw me as an oddity. I was a teenager by then, and all I wanted to do was to fuck.

At least they weren't keeping me in a cage. At least they didn't pretend to be my ally when they just wanted to use me for my story.

We move together, animated by lust. Her body responds to me, moving against me.

A jolt moves through her. She spins in my arms with fear in her eyes. She pushes me away and clambers off the bed and onto the floor. She stands there, shocked. "What are you doing?"

I rise out of the bed, swaying on my feet.

In a flash, she turns and bolts for the bathroom—not fast enough.

I follow her and trap her against the wall next to the bathroom door. She's shaking, frightened. I'm a savage to her.

I shouldn't care what she thinks. My heart thunders with the need to bend her over and take her. The feel of her is overpowering. Her scent, her softness.

But this is Ann. I protect Ann—even from myself.

I slide my hand over her cheek, breathing in the potent scent of her arousal. She sucks in a breath as I press her to the wall, cover her with my body.

With a wild effort, I push off the wall, stagger back. "Go in. Lock the door."

She widens her eyes, then she goes into the bathroom. There's a click. Not that it could stop me.

I press my hand to the door, and then I press my face to it.

I focus on the sounds of the birds out there. It's dawn. The first morning bird songs. The bird songs mean almost nothing with her in there. I want her so badly.

But she's mine now. I care for her. It means not scaring her.

"Wash yourself," I say.

"Wh-what?"

"I can smell you," I pant.

The water goes on. I feel more in control.

I force my attention outside. The cracks of light around the curtain. Sunshine.

Her voice from inside. "Kiro? You okay?"

I bring my fist down on the door. I'm not good with words like Ann is. I bring my fist to the door again.

I turn and focus on the light coming from around the curtains. Freedom. It's what I always longed for. I force myself across the small room, away from Ann. I pull open the door, expecting green, but the sky is gray. The street is gray. Cars and colorful lights swirl around. Giant stores line the street like sleeping lions, guarding their parking lots.

But the air smells fresh. And then, on the other side of the motel's small driveway, I see a small patch of green. Grass. Nature.

I'm naked aside from the bandage on my shoulder, but that patch of aliveness calls to me. The earth—I have to touch it. I close the door, and like a sleepwalker, I go. The pavement is harsh on my feet. Like when I first arrived in the forest. They'll toughen up. It'll be like normal again.

There's a tree, a picnic table with dirt around it...my steps speed up. When I get there, I fall to my knees, palms pressed to the ground. I breathe in, feeling almost normal.

Home. I need to go home.

I curl up on my side with my cheek to the grass. It's stubby, prickly, not like the grass I love, but it's grass. It's alive.

I breathe in, feeling everything. The sky above is brightening at the edges. The earth feels vast underneath me. I gaze up at the fading stars.

I want her so badly it hurts.

I close my eyes, and I'm back on the bed, holding her, soft in my arms, given over to me, and the powerful smell of her arousal.

As if I called to her with my thoughts, the door to our room opens with a slash of light. I don't see her, but I hear her. I no longer smell her arousal. I track her. She won't get away. Will she try?

Footsteps across the pavement.

A dark figure above me.

"Kiro." She kneels beside me and lays something soft over my waist. A towel. "Dude, our best bet right now is to be inconspicuous. Lying naked on the motel picnic area at six in the morning? Um…"

Her care isn't genuine. She doesn't want us to get caught, that's all. She wants my story to herself. It stings me. I growl.

She puts her hand on my shoulder. "We're together in this."

Together. I wish with everything in me that it was true. I've been so alone for so long.

She touches my cheek. I close my eyes, soaking up the goodness of her touch.

When she touches my cheek, I can pretend I'm not alone.

CHAPTER EIGHTEEN

Ann

HE CLOSES HIS eyes when I stroke his beard.

His head is clearing of drugs. He's not suffering from blood loss. Things are getting real. Maybe even dangerous.

Still, I had to go to him.

This little fucking patch of nature out in the freezing cold morning. He's lying there like it's heaven. People have taken so much from Kiro.

He's dangerous. I know that.

But he's amazing, too. Fierce and vulnerable and beautiful. And honest in a way other men I've known aren't.

I'd never slept so deeply as when I was in his arms. And I've never felt so turned on until I woke up with his hands on my belly and his teeth two faint wicked indents on the back of my neck. It was…dangerously hot.

And when he had me against the wall, I knew he was out of control. It scared the fuck out of me, but I also liked it.

The electricity surging between us felt forbidden and good.

I move my hand over his beard. Lord, how I slept. For the first time in ages, I slept. The anxiety is coming back now—so stupid to think it wouldn't come back. For a while, I felt clear and happy. Free. Normal.

He doesn't take his cheek from the grass. His dark hair is splayed out around him. There is something so primal about how he is right now.

Again he takes in a ragged breath, as though my touch burns him. Why would my touch pain him?

"How does it feel? The grass—how does it feel?"

"It smells of chemicals."

Yeah, I suppose it does. "Exhaust. Probably pesticides."

Does he know what those things are? Maybe. He would've been exposed to a lot of TV at Fancher—at least before he was confined to his room. He has some familiarity with cars.

"Your sense of smell is amazing."

His soulful amber eyes never stray from mine. Is he thinking about the scent of my arousal…that he could smell *through the fucking door?*

My face feels hot. "The smells at the hospital must have driven you out of your mind."

Warily he observes me. The streetlights cut through the gloomy morning, lending rich drama to his cheekbones, his eyes. His kissable lips.

"It feels good," he says, and I realize he's talking about the grass.

I smile. "This grimy little scrub patch?"

"I haven't been outside more than minutes at a time in…two years."

Fuck.

"Do you remember anything from your life before the wilderness?" I ask.

"No."

"Do you know why somebody would want to keep you in there? In Fancher? Hide you, keep you out of the way...I don't know. The more information we have, the stronger we are. They called you Kiro."

"That was never my name. I never heard it before."

"What is your name?"

"Keith," he says. "Keith Knutson."

"I'll call you Keith, then."

"No, don't," he says. "The family who gave it to me never wanted me. It wasn't my real family."

"Where is your real family?"

He just gazes sadly at me.

"What do you want me to call you? You don't want me to call you 34, do you?"

"They called me Kiro? The ones trying to kill me?"

"Yeah."

"Maybe that's my real name."

"Do you like the name Kiro?"

He grunts. It seems like a yes.

"It's a cool name. I'll call you Kiro for now, but it's a decision you can make yourself. I want you to be able to make a lot of decisions. That's your right." I slide my hand over his dark whiskers. "I'm going to get you back into the woods, back home, Kiro. And we're going to be smart about it."

He says nothing.

"I know people have been horrible to you. I know about the man who kept you in a cage. That professor."

He shows no sign of hearing me. I know he does, though.

"I'll help you. I've been in all kinds of places. I'm very resourceful. Not to mention I know how to drive."

He turns his gaze to the sky.

"We're going to get you back there, okay?"

He rests a finger on my knee, traces a lazy line across it, one light touch, wild with intensity. I think about how he pressed me to the wall, so out of control. A gorgeous force of nature.

"We have to be smart, though. There's probably a manhunt after you involving the cops. Not to mention some really dangerous people trying to kill you."

He turns his pained gaze to me.

Doesn't he want my help? Well, it doesn't matter. He needs an ally, considering his attempt to get home so far has involved carrying me out of a firefight while wounded and now lying naked in a patch of motel picnic area grass.

I have a nice fat expense account. I can help him get back to where nobody can find him.

There's power in a good story. And for him, there's also money. I can make sure he gets money without being wildly exploited. I can stand between him and the public. Get the story and the photos, but keep his location secret. I can use my power as a journalist to make sure things are run in a way where he can live free. Maybe I can make sure he's paid and we can buy him tons of land. A place of his own. Land is cheap in northern Minnesota.

Most of all, I can figure out who is after him and why—that's the only real way for him to be safe. Mob guys are hunting him. Cops are hunting him. And quasi-paparazzi sent by *Stormline*. My money might be on the paparazzi finding him first, frankly.

But he might have allies out there. A real family. I have to figure this out.

"Here's my plan, Kiro. We're going to clean you up so that you don't look like an escapee from an institute for the criminally insane. Then we buy supplies and get a car. Use the car to get as far north as they'll let us go with vehicles. Can you get us the rest of the way?"

He seems…upset.

"Say something."

He studies my eyes.

"Can you control yourself from my amazing womanly charms enough so we can cut your hair and re-bandage your wound and get you some proper clothes? Can we just do that much?"

"Yes, Nurse Ann." He says it in a way that makes it sound as if it might be a struggle for him.

That shouldn't be hot.

Not hot, I tell myself.

"How long will it take if we drive in and then take a canoe?"

"Not long," he says.

"We'll get a canoe and supplies. After we eat a ton of food. Are you hungry?"

One word in a gust: "Yes."

"Do you like…eggs? Meat? Hot buttery rolls? What do you like to eat?"

"All of it." He watches me in a way that's not just about food. My heart skips a beat.

Not hot, I remind myself.

The fastest way to ruin this whole thing is to get emotionally involved with him. For one thing, all my credibility and my power to help him as a journalist would go out the window if I fucked him.

I look around nervously. More cars. "Let's go then. We don't want somebody calling the cops." I want to tuck the towel around him a little better, but that's a bit…intimate.

I feel like we're both on the knife edge of control.

I get up. "Hold the towel around yourself and come on. We'll do this right and get you to some real grass. Not this pathetic stinky grass."

CHAPTER NINETEEN

Ann

I'VE NEVER SEEN anybody eat so much. I'd expected it, for sure. I ordered five steak-and-egg breakfasts from the nearest delivery place in preparation for it. And he ate four of them, and the steak part of mine, sitting there on the hotel bed in the dorky University of Minnesota Golden Gophers sweatpants I got him at the gas station. Somehow they don't look dorky on him.

I pull out my phone. I feel weird doing so many secret photos, so I do one above board. "Smile," I say.

He glares.

"Oh, come on," I say playfully. I take his picture, then I do a selfie of us. I want less and less to be taking his picture. Less and less to be doing this story.

He drinks glass after glass of water, like he's trying to get the drugs out of his system.

The white of his bandage is stark against his massive chest, muscles marred with scars and dirt, the chest of a beast of battle.

There's even something about the way he tears into the meat that's hot. He transforms everything around him. He makes the world glitter darkly. He makes me feel alive.

I get hold of myself and pull a chair into the bathroom. "We need to cut your hair and trim your beard."

He stiffens, and I think about what they'd done to him at the institute in terms of grooming—probably lopping off his locks in the minimum number of snips and snipping his beard before shoving him into the shower to be basically hosed off—by people who fear and hate him.

I go to him. "Let me, Kiro. Please?" I take his wrist and pull him in, and make him sit on the chair I brought in there. I drape a towel around his bare shoulders and start to comb out his dark curls. I go slowly, getting out the knots, careful not to pull.

"You don't like my hair," he says.

"Oh, I like it. You're rocking kind of a Renaissance king look right now. I'm thinking we should go for more urban beardsman. You'll blend." *But still look wild. Like my editor wants.*

I pull out my camera. "We'll get a before picture." I say it like it's some kind of favor, ignoring the sick feeling in my gut as I snap the photo. The Savage Adonis makeover images will sell like nothing else. The public loves before and after. I tell myself these images have potential value, which gives Kiro power.

"I don't care about blending," he growls as I pocket my phone.

"You should. There are people after you for whatever reason—deadly people."

"I'll kill anyone who tries to stop me," he says casually.

My mouth goes dry. The atmosphere feels too charged, too full of dark possibility.

I continue to comb out his hair. This is a man who was caged, imprisoned, strapped to a bed by people. Maybe it's foolish to get so comfortable with him.

"I frightened you," he says.

How does he know? Does he hear my fucking heartbeat? Does he scent my fear in some way? "I'll tell you if there's a problem with us."

He nods.

"We just have to make sure they don't find us. We need to not be obvious. The best offense is a defense, which means we get proper clothes and camping gear. Without turning it into a circus."

He scowls.

I arrange his rich dark locks over his shoulder. Did I hurt his feelings? I realize suddenly that it was probably the circus reference. A place to display animals. Strange acts. "I didn't mean it like that."

He meets my eyes. Since his escape—since I realized just how *there* he was—I've started to think sometimes that he hates me.

I swallow and continue to comb out his hair, and then I start on his beard. I snip slowly, carefully, heart pounding. I try to keep my touch clinical, the way they train you to do in nursing school.

The heat that comes off him is dizzying, though. Sometimes I'm not sure whether it's heat—maybe it's just sensation. Awareness.

Every time I brush his neck or his bare shoulders, this wild electricity blooms up, as if the surfaces of our skin carry opposite charges. From the way his breathing changes, I think he feels it, too.

I can even feel the sweep of his gaze on my skin. This wild, wrong thing between us has too much energy for this tiny space. His lips are inches from my breasts.

Finally he speaks. "The best offense is a *defense?*"

I straighten. "You don't agree?"

He gazes over at the tub, handsome face dark with disdain. "The best offense is a better offense," he growls.

I stifle a smile, loving that he said that. How oddly smart it is. I move around him, stroking and snipping.

Eventually he closes his eyes, and I think maybe he's finally relaxing. Has anybody in his miserable life ever tended to him out of affection?

I trim the underside of his beard, trying to avoid touching his thick, corded neck. The neck of a beast.

Hellbeast, Donny called him.

I flash on the way he carried me out of that place. The way he saved me from Donny. The way he pinned me to the wall. My heart feels thundery.

You can't have him.

I concentrate on getting his beard trimmed evenly.

Sometimes he watches my throat. I feel weirdly vulnerable to him when he watches my throat like that. Like he could have anything from me.

Stroke. Clip. Don't meet his eyes.

I channel my wrong, wrong lust into caring for him. Giving him this. Wanting this nice look for him. Still a wild boy, but superhot.

When his beard is trimmed to perfection, I unwrap one of the razors from the pack I got. I suds up his neck with soap and clean it up with careful razor strokes. I'm gentle. Slow.

He's one of the most powerful men I've ever encountered, and he's letting me put a razor to his neck. It means something.

I have to touch him a lot for this part and he seems to like it. He seems to like touch. I suppose he hasn't had much touch in his life. Not of the caring kind, anyway.

I step back. Perfect.

He just stares off to the side.

"It's very good," I say. Understatement of the year.

He doesn't seem to like being made much of. So I just move on.

I rinse his neck, patting it dry, trying not to adore him too much, but he's starting to look way too fucking amazing.

I move on to his hair. I take off length. I give him soft layers just over the shoulder. He never once looks at the mirror. His big body heaves in a sigh at one point. There's still that edge of wariness to him.

It means a lot that he's making himself vulnerable to me like this, considering who he is and what he's been through.

Considering that he's completely feral.

I think I never understood the concept of feral until Kiro gripped my arms and pressed me to the wall, trembling on the knife edge of control. I felt utterly held. Utterly open. Utterly powerless.

When I'm done, I stand behind him in the mirror. He keeps that faraway stare, just off to the side, seemingly lost in thought. Or maybe just enduring my attentions. I brush aside a sooty curl and then force myself to stop touching him.

God, the way he looks now…he was hot with the long hair, but now he's pure and utter madness… "Shit," I say. "Kiro."

He keeps his gaze fixed on the tub spigots.

He's a dark, scowly angel. Hard and gorgeous. The neatly trimmed beard brings out his cheekbones and the sharp, confident line of his jaw. I really want to touch his beard again. "Shit," I say, because apparently that's all my vocabulary has left. "Take a look, dude."

He finally turns his gaze to the mirror, but not at his reflection. At mine. My eyes. "You don't think it's good?"

"No," I say, mouth dry. "I think it's a little thing called *un-fucking-believable.*"

His gaze doesn't stray from my eyes. This so Kiro. One-pointed. Committed.

"Take a look for yourself."

"No thanks."

Something seizes up in my heart.

"Look," I say.

He keeps his gaze fixed stubbornly on mine.

"Fine." I go around to the front of him, my back to the sink, the mirror. "Then look into the mirror of my eyes," I say. "Not only are you the most fucking brave, fierce man I've ever met, but you're officially the hottest."

He stays hard and wary. The air between us seems to tremble. He seems to take up more space than he ever did. He's mostly clear of the drugs, now. He's so there, so alive, so...male.

"Do you seriously not believe me? Do you think I'm a liar?"

His gaze tells me he does.

"We need to wash you up, now—without getting that bandage or your stitches wet. Maybe you could bend over the side of the tub and hold a towel to your shoulder while I wash your hair with the sprayer and then you take a bath after, carefully avoiding..."

He stands, crowding me in that small space. He takes the towel from my hand. "Leave me."

"You'll do it?"

He glowers.

"Just don't get the bandage wet."

His glower intensifies, or maybe it's the atmosphere in that small space that intensifies. Nervously, I back out of the bathroom and shut the door. I listen to the water crashing, leaning in that spot where he had me, remembering the way he pressed me against the wall. Feeling his arms around me as he held me in the bed. I squeeze my legs together, imagining it's his fingers between my legs.

I listen to him swish the water, testing it.

In the tub now.

I grab my phone and call Murray, talking in low tones. He's sending over a rental car and a burner phone—any minute now, he tells me.

Good. I give him an update. There's a rural shopping mall twenty minutes out. I'm going to get him decent clothes and shoes. Outdoor supplies. I cut his hair.

"Savage Adonis getting a makeover. Tell me you're getting this."

"This isn't *Pretty Woman*," I say.

"No, it's better than *Pretty Woman*," Murray growls.

"I got a before shot, don't worry."

"And notes?"

I lie and say yes, even though I hardly need to take notes. I tell him about the meal he ate. There's a lot I leave out.

"Listen, I looked into the mob angle from here. The lion tattoo is probably the Black Lion clan, headed by Lazarus Morina, aka Bloody Lazarus. They're powerful, but they don't seem to have any active blood feud that would merit this kind of hunt. Another clan family, the Valcheks, were enemies at one time, but they wiped them out some twenty years back. All the males."

"Could Kiro be a Valchek? Maybe hidden? At the time of the war?"

"The timing is right, but I put a researcher on it, and there is no Kiro Valchek. There's a deceased Kiro here and there. A few back in Albania that are connected to the organization, so we're checking on them to make sure they're still there. But I think you're right—that kind of firepower doesn't come out for a vendetta. These mob guys aren't idiots. They're not going to expend the resources like what we saw at the Fancher Institute for a blood vendetta. They have fucking criminal businesses to run, bottom lines to think about. It doesn't make sense."

"Keep me updated. Look for any missing twenty-something Kiros. I need that side of the story."

"What about his life in the woods? I need the wolfy stuff. Cutting his hair and a meal, that's not front-page-feature stuff."

"You're going front page?"

Murray goes on. This will be a front-page feature, multiple days running. It'll get picked up all over. He wants to hold some sexy images back to sell to *BMZ Confidential*, the ultimate sleazy Hollywood gossip site. "Get his buy-in. Does he want to be independently wealthy? Would you keep him from that? He plays this right, he can write his own checks."

"I'm not doing a *BMZ* kind of article."

It's then that he utters the worst two words he possibly can: Garrick Price. "I think I'm going to send him. He'll be a lot of help to you."

"I don't need Garrick."

"I think you do. I'll have him on a plane in an hour—"

"I got this," I say softly, listening to make sure the shower's still running. "And I'll tell you something else—Kiro would not take well to Garrick."

"Garrick gets along with everyone."

It's true in a way. Garrick can play anybody. He gets people under a spell, and then he twists the knife. He leaves people in ruins. Could he do it to Kiro?

My heart pounds. Garrick will either spook Kiro or make him his big buddy. It would be bad either way. "I have mojo going that Garrick would fuck up."

"How much mojo?"

"More than Garrick ever could have." I'll say anything to keep him from sending Garrick. "I got this," I whisper loudly. Maybe too loudly.

"You sure?"

"Who found Savage Adonis? After all these years, who is the badass reporter who found this fucking story? Who? Me, that's who," I say, hating myself, but I can't let Garrick come around. "I am going to deliver the shit out of this story."

"Prove it."

"You watch." I click off. I have to send him something decent. Some good images. I have to keep Garrick out. If I can do that, I stay in control of the story.

Just then Kiro comes out of the bathroom in the sweats, damp hair tousled around the angry planes of his face.

"What's wrong?"

His fierce attention is on the door. He looks like he wants to bang down the door. "Somebody's here."

"What do you mean?"

Just then, a knock sounds.

"Oh." I stand. "I got it. A friend. Sending stuff."

He watches me.

I call through the door. "Who's there?"

"Package from *Stormline*."

"A friend." The car, the money, the phone. I crack the door, sign the paper with the fake name Murray gave me, and thank the guy.

Then I close it and turn. Kiro has put on a shirt.

"Let's go, let's stay on the move." I grab the hoodie I got at the Holiday. "We're going to a mall."

CHAPTER TWENTY

Ann

ONE THING ABOUT northern Minnesota, they have a lot of really comprehensive rugged-guy stores. I go for the priciest outdoor hiker-hunter clothes in the biggest mall.

I can feel eyes on us as we walk in. The store is mostly empty, but that's not the reason. Kiro is the reason. Two shop girls come around. One smiles. One of them discreetly checks his hand. Not married.

They're checking me out, too. I'm a few years older, and only medium pretty. I'm in an oversized hoodie over nurse scrubs.

Not his girlfriend.

I smile through the queasiness that rolls through me. "We need everything for him. The best, most rugged outdoor stuff you have—layers, something that will work for every season. He's going to be…" I look up at him and find his eyes glued to me. I'm so used to him as the drugged-up wild boy that it's hard to get used to him so alert. Sensing everything before I do. "Um…camping and hunting for long stretches of time. He got separated from his old stuff.

The best of everything, but portable." We're near the shoes area. "I'm thinking winter boots and rugged sandals."

"I don't need foot coverings," he says.

"Yes you do."

He glowers, and I soak it up. Again I'm back in our motel room, pinned to the wall. I could bask in that glower of his forever. I like all of his looks.

"You need them. Gas station flip-flops fall apart. And they kick you out of places without shoes..." His glower changes, and I get it right then—any place that would kick him out for no shoes isn't a place he wants to go. He's going back to the wilderness. I move in close to him. "It would just make me feel better."

He grunts softly. Annoyed assent. A slight edge of anger.

I nod, wondering distantly when I got to be able to read his grunts and glowers.

The girls keep smiling at him.

They're zeroing in, and the skin on my back is definitely up. Yeah, Kiro isn't the only one with instincts on the rampage here.

I can't have him, I tell myself. *No—just no.*

"Are you good if I leave and get my own stuff?" I ask.

He gives me a wary look. He doesn't like this, but he'll tolerate it for now.

I force myself to go to the women's department and get a few basics—underwear, jeans, boots, shirt layers. I check the forecast for the next few days. It'll be warmish, but the nights will be in the 40s.

I make my purchases and change into the new clothes. Then I head back to the men's department.

I spot him across the showroom floor being attended to by the two women. He looks miserable. Restless.

I don't have a good view of him, but I think they've gotten him to change into a new outfit. One of them puts a hat on his head. He rips it off.

I think to intervene, but he needs proper clothes.

I go to a rack of rain slickers. He'll want something waterproof, too. I go through them, then I stop and watch across the store with a gnawing pressure in my gut as one of the saleswomen adjusts the buttons on his shirt.

He allows it. Barely.

The two of them back away to get a look.

The air seems to still. The sounds of the store fade. The racks and lights seem to dim. All I can see is Kiro.

Shivers go over me. He's stunning—fashion runway stunning.

Back when he was tied to a bed in grubby PJs and a crude haircut, he was the most beautiful thing I ever saw. Now he's beyond gorgeous.

I drink him in from behind the rack.

I force myself to pull out my phone and take a few discreet photos, holding the phone casually, like I'm not really taking them. You get good at taking discreet shots when you're me.

And these I have to get. Wild boy makeover at the clothes store—these are more money shots. His bargaining chips. These photos will satisfy Murray enough to keep people like Garrick away. They get Kiro the fuck-you money that gets the world to leave him alone.

I check the shots. Kiro is madly photogenic. Ironic for a guy who hates to see himself in the mirror.

Another sales clerk brings over sunglasses.

Sunglasses. Fuck. I suck in a breath.

Our eyes meet. It's as if he heard me suck in that breath.

He accepts the sunglasses and, eyes never leaving mine, he puts them on. He watches me from behind the dark lenses, towering above the clerks like a movie star.

I know two things right then—one, that he hates those sunglasses. And two, he put them on for me. He heard me, and he knew.

My heart pounds as he watches me—for an inappropriately long time. He looks at me openly, taking what he wants, crashing through the rules. Kiro makes the world over in his own way.

He makes the world beautiful.

Another of the women loops a men's scarf around his neck. They're dressing him like their own personal runway model. Paul Bunyan meets GQ. Still he doesn't look away from me.

My heart whooshes in my ears. *Kiro.*

Again they stand back.

My mouth goes dry. He's always had a powerful presence, but dressed in these beautiful clothes with his hair unfairly awesome, even mussed from trying on clothes, he feels larger than life. He charges the air. He steals the air.

One of them is talking now, making him decide on colors. He glances down.

I take a few more photos and forward one to my editor. It's low-res—nothing he can use for much, like tossing out a bit of meat to keep the shark busy. I'll make Murray pay through the nose for the high-res version, and the money goes to Kiro.

Quickly I pocket it.

The sunglasses are off him now. Another clerk comes up with two shirts for him to choose between. He takes them, eyes again boring into mine—invasive, unapologetic.

Angry. Why?

I think about going over, but they're almost done.

I busy myself at the rack of rain slickers. I hold up a large one. What did Kiro do in the rain all those years out there?

A male clerk comes up and slips a thick card into the frame on the top of the rack that shows the price. Fifty percent off. "Fall outerwear sale starts up today," he says.

I finger the sleeve of one. "These are probably too heavy. He might need more of a layer than a coat."

"We have shells along the wall."

Motion from the corner of my eye. I turn and see Kiro strolling over in his hot new outfit. The jacket is plaid, the insulation is the latest in heat-reflective fabric, but the gaze is pure barbarian. He walks up and stands between me and the male clerk, invading his space.

"Kiro—"

The guy is already backing off. "Let us know if you can't find something." He walks off.

I turn to Kiro. "He was just giving me some sales information."

"That's not what it was."

"Of course that's what it was."

He glowers at the guy's back. The atmosphere is full of testosterone and heat. "We need to go," he grumbles.

"We have to finish this."

Kiro continues to glower, but this time it's kind of at everything.

"Please, Kiro. We'll finish it and go. And you'll never have to come back here." The saleswoman who seems most in charge comes and holds a jacket up to Kiro's back.

"Let's wrap this up," I say to her.

"He needs a shell. This is an XXXL. I could go a size larger, but we'd have to order it."

"We need it now."

A low rumble. I give him a pleading look. He needs to last a bit longer. We need clothes and outdoors supplies. We can't be stupid. "We're almost done."

He sighs.

I trace the line of his dark gaze. There are a few other shoppers in here now, and I notice that they're all stealing glances at Kiro. It doesn't really surprise me; Kiro's not just hot, he has a brutally commanding personal presence.

They're really looking at him a lot. It occurs to me they think he's somebody famous.

Is that what he's noticing? Is that what he's grumbling about?

More sunglasses appear.

"No sunglasses," I say. "He likes the sun in his eyes." I don't know how I know; I just know.

Kiro gazes down at me, expression haunted. Something's wrong—very wrong. What happened?

The youngest woman brings over an oversized plaid shirt for him to try. The black-brown matches his hair, the blue contrasts with the gold of his eyes. "Try this one," she says.

He fingers the fabric, still with that haunted look.

I hand over the sunglasses. "I'd love if you'd all double-check on some of those large sizes for the jackets and shirts," I say, but my real meaning is *give us a moment*. "What is it?" I ask after they're gone.

"You don't see it?" he asks.

"No. What?"

"Me. On display as a savage. Dressed as a circus animal."

I clamp my hand on his arm before he can walk off. "That's not what they're thinking."

"They all know what I am. Everyone here. The way they stare—"

"That's not why they're staring at you! They think you're hot. Gorgeous. Kiro—you're not a savage."

His faraway gaze is directed over my head now, not meeting my eyes. He sounds so vulnerable, so angry. *They want to kill me because I'm different.*

That's what he thinks. It's what he really, really thinks. "I swear to you, that's not what's happening here."

He shakes his head.

"You spent time lost in the wilderness. It doesn't make you savage."

"So you say."

"I know that of all the people in the Fancher Institute, you showed me the most humanity."

His lips twist. He doesn't believe me. "The professor who caged me up had a theory. He said my primitive brain, my lizard brain, was in the driver's seat. He thought it was because I'd lived with wolves. He didn't understand I was born that way."

"What? No kid is born that way."

He takes hold of *my* arm now, eyes boring into mine. "Ask me how it felt to choke him. To feel him die in my hands. Ask me."

"You need to let go," I whisper.

His gaze burns into mine, stripping me bare, stripping us bare. "I loved it. I loved to feel the life draining out of him."

"He kept you in a cage."

He lowers his voice to a growl. "Ask what I want to do to you."

Energy pulses between my legs as I try to pull from his grip. His eyes sparkle as he tightens his fingers. I'm back in that hotel room with him pressing me against the wall. My belly feels melty.

His voice rumbles with emotion. "Ask me."

"Kiro—"

"You can dress me up and cut my hair, but you can never cover up the savage."

He lets me go and storms toward the men's dressing room.

I watch him, feeling his pain so acutely...and his isolation.

I can't let him be alone. I head in after him. He's not hard to find. There's only one door closed.

I knock.

He's grunting. Something rips. Buttons bounce along the floor.

"Let me in."

"Leave."

I grip the knob. "I'm coming in." Still I hesitate. He's in a dangerous mood. But fuck it, he needs me. I pull the door open.

He's standing, in a state, giant hands tearing at the buttons. He pauses, gaze unreadable. I'm reminded of the way cats look sometimes, how you can never tell what's in their minds, like it might be affection or maybe they're thinking about killing you. He goes back to the buttons.

"Keep that stuff on."

He eyes the sweats on the floor. Is he thinking about putting those back on? Yes. "The flannel and jeans are practical," I say.

"I don't need practical."

"Do it for me."

His expression is torn, chest heaving. He's so goddamn beautiful, it breaks my mind. I'm hyperconscious of his warmth, his power.

"A few supplies and we're out of here. Keep the new stuff on and let's go."

"I'm tired of shopping."

"Just a little more."

"You were so beautiful, standing there across the store," he pants. "I loved looking at you. And then that male—talking to you like that. I wanted to rip his face off, and then fuck you in front of everyone. Hold you in place...fuck you and feel you and have you." He balls his fists. "I could barely keep myself still."

I'm unsure what to do with his strange mixture of possessiveness and vulnerability. "Well," I try, voice wavering, "being that we're trying not to attract attention, it's probably a good thing you didn't go with that plan."

He just watches me with that amber gaze. "I can scent you, Ann. Your scent is beautiful to me."

I swallow. Is he scenting arousal?

He closes his eyes. "It's better than anything I know."

I've never had a man so focused on me. I squeeze my legs together. "Let's grab the camping stuff and go then, okay?" I go to him and redo a button. My fingers shake. I can barely do it. They have him wearing a black T-shirt under the quilted flannel shirt. "This will be warm and good. You'll be glad."

He grabs my hands, electricity in his eyes.

"What?"

His gaze drops to my crotch.

"What?"

"Your scent."

I swallow. "Um..."

He turns his gaze back up to mine, and I get the feeling now that he can read my "um's" as easily as I can read his grunts. He stands, crowding me in the small space.

Heat rolls through me.

He lets me go. His hands are at my jeans now. He's fumbling with the snaps, the zipper, holding my gaze the way he does.

"Kiro!" I whisper. I try to stop him, but it's like his hands are carved from steel and stone. Make that warm steel and stone, because they're on my hips, my ass, pushing my jeans to my ankles.

"Oh my God, Kiro, you can't just..."

The heat in his eyes matches mine. He grunts. *He can. He is.* He yanks down my panties and pushes me down onto the dressing room bench.

"Kiro!"

He has me bare from the waist down, and he's kneeling in front of me. He grips both my wrists with one hand on my arm, pinning them to the wall.

Gently he takes hold of my thigh with the other hand, pressing it wide, spreading me open there in the dressing room. I'm speechless, panting.

He simply holds me open to him there on the dressing room bench.

His body thrums with savage power. I don't know whether to be frightened or desperately turned on. I'm both, I suppose.

The air is cool, a wild sensation on my sex.

I twist and tremble, caught in his grip. "We're in a public place. Come on, Kiro. You can't—"

He tightens his grip in response. *He can.*

He leans in and puts himself face to face with my pussy, still holding me open. He doesn't even touch me, he's just looking. Scenting. I've never felt more vulnerable, never more exposed.

My pussy shivers with sensation.

I'm pinned. Helpless. Desperately aroused.

Holding me with that heated gaze, dark hair curling around his cheekbones, he draws his lips even nearer and sucks in a breath.

I gasp, utterly sensitive. It's as if my folds are scattered with nerve endings, feeling the cool in-rush of air molecules.

I still, frozen with anticipation.

And then he exhales. Breath hot. Stoking my libido. He draws in yet another breath, scenting me.

I melt in his grip. My entire body a well of need. He's just smelling me, and I'm about to come.

From him smelling me.

"Kiro—we're in a dressing room. On the run. We can't…"

"You don't like it?"

Now I'm the one with no answer.

He raises his gaze to mine. "I think you like being made helpless by a savage. Held open wide so that you feel everything, here where anybody could discover us. Tell me."

"Kiro…"

He sucks in another breath and pushes his nose closer—close enough that the tip of it hits my sensitized bud.

"Omigod!"

He draws his fat, warm tongue through my folds. I start to cry out, and he claps his hand over my mouth.

I feel his breath rush out in a gust. He drags his tongue up the seam of my pussy. He licks again, a long, wicked stroke, and then he sucks what feels like pretty much every available fold and flap into his mouth.

My brain melts.

He sucks me. The force of it pulls me down into a quicksand of sensation. His beard scratches the tender insides of my thighs. He moves his tongue around while he's sucking, in a merciless, mind-melting movement around my hole.

I cry out behind his hand, shaking my head. He removes his hand from my mouth, seeming annoyed at my interruption. "What?"

"We're in a dressing room," I pant.

His look says, *You fucking interrupted me for that?*

He simply smashes his powerful hand back over my mouth and returns to his wicked and ravenous sucking and stroking.

And then licking. His tongue seems to lift the sensation right out of my core. Lift, lick, lift, up, in…I protest from behind his hand.

My protests are irrelevant. My objections are gnats to a bull. My pussy is his.

He's taking his time with long and leisurely licks, using the flat part of his tongue now.

I'm helpless in his hold. He takes me. He enjoys me. He moves mercilessly on me with the pointy part of his tongue now. My heart pounds as I realize he's chasing my orgasm, like it's prey or something.

The sparkly sensation peeks up and hides. He finds it, chasing, bearing down. I whimper behind his hand. I squirm.

My squirming makes his chase turn ruthless.

I swallow, face hot, body electric. He's holding me still, licking me, pushing me onto the knife edge of feeling. There's nowhere to hide, suddenly.

I'm trying to hide, trying to draw back, as if on instinct.

He grunts and jerks my hands, as if to shake me into submission. It feels so good, I don't know what to do. All I can do is go still.

He licks again, and it's as if he knows I'm close, because he's flicking his tongue across my bud, evilly, mercilessly. He knows he has me. He knows.

He goes for the kill.

I break apart under his power. He grunts softly as I come. He changes his grip. He's cradling me through the tremors that rack my body.

Still he won't stop licking me. It's gentle. It's harsh. It's un-fucking-believable.

I'm dizzy, panting.

He slows and grunts. He takes his hand from my mouth and slides two fingers into me, nearly sending me into the stratosphere. My hips undulate as if of their own volition.

He brings his slickened fingers to my lips. "Suck."

"Wh-what?"

He gives me a dark look and squeezes my cheeks with his other hand, forcing my mouth open. "This is mine, too." He pushes in his fingers. "Suck."

I suck, trembling.

"This is how beautiful you are," he says. "How you taste. How I know."

Know what?

He pulls his fingers from my mouth and pushes them into his own mouth.

I watch him dazedly.

He shoves my legs wider and slides his giant fingers into me. I try to snap my knees closed. He pushes them wider.

"Again." He resumes licking, this time with his fingers lodged thickly inside me.

"I can't take it! I'm too—"

He presses his hand back over my mouth and continues to lick and fuck me with his massive fingers. It feels amazing, but my clit is so sensitive—too sensitive.

I writhe and beg him to stop, which eventually takes the form of moaning behind his hand. I try to push his head away with both hands.

He removes his hand with a sigh that seems to travel all the way into me.

"What?"

Put your fingers back in me is the only thought I can form. "Um…" I say.

He presses my hands to my belly. "I will always find you, I will always take you."

"Uh," I breathe.

He smiles wickedly, then he pushes his fat tongue into my hole. I whimper. He draws it up over my clit. Down and up. I shudder with every pass. I'm raw, exposed.

He chases, and I retreat—bewildered, breathless. I don't care about anything. Are people walking past? I don't even care.

He's chasing down that silvery feeling. I can't hide. I'm shaking my head, ragged and weary. This is what it's like to be at the mercy of a true predator, I think vaguely. He feels everything, uses everything. He doesn't give me a chance.

At some point, my cries and protests turn to whispered begging. He claps his hand over my mouth again.

He has me. He will always take me. He's toying with me, mastering me.

He seems utterly aware of this fact, just the way he seems to know everything.

He pushes his tongue into my hole. It feels giant and alive. He curls it, licking inside me. I imagine it's his cock. I want him to stretch me, fill me, take me, use me, have me.

He pulls it out and drags it along my clit again—harshly.

I shudder ecstatically.

He has me, and he's going to make me come again.

I can run, but I can't hide. It seems unfair. Maybe it is. It doesn't matter—he's dragging his tongue over me yet again.

I can no longer take it, but I have to, over and over. I'm a creature dwelling in pure potential. I'm stranded at the tip of his tongue.

He stills and pulls away, turning his golden eyes to me.

He looks almost smug.

He sees everything. He sees that I'm right there, waiting for him, open and helpless as any being can be. I try to pull my wrists from his grip, wanting to grab his hair, make him come back. I need him. I'm crazy without him. I can't beg him with my words or my hands, so I beg him with my eyes.

He seems satisfied with this. He lowers his face to me, applies his tongue back to my madly sensitive nub—knowingly, wickedly.

Pleasure erupts over me. He keeps me going, spinning. I'm crying behind his hand. He's crossed so many lines. I can't count how many. I don't care.

I come, shattered and spinning.

He's broken me somehow. And I like it. I want to be broken by him over and over. He rises up and kisses my neck, my cheek.

Eventually he untangles himself from me and stands, towering over me, darkly. "Everything about you is so beautiful to me," he grates out.

I sit sprawled below him, barely comprehending his words. I don't know what anything means; I just have this nameless surge of affection for him. My affection for him feels a little bit like madness.

It's out of this that I reach up to him. Both hands, reaching to him.

I need him back with me. Touching me.

He regards me in the strangest way. He doesn't take my hands; instead he bends down and lifts me in his arms.

I feel weightless, treasured.

He puts his nose to my hair, breathing me in. I'm a thing in his arms in the middle of some rural mall in Minnesota at the edge of a great primeval wilderness under the vast spray of stars and planets and solar systems. And everything is different.

He puts me down and smoothes my hair. Points at my clothes. "We have to go."

My gaze falls to his pants, the massive bulge in his pants. "Don't you want..." I reach out to his cock. He catches my hand before I make contact, sliding his thumb along the inside of my wrist, along where the blood runs, like he's checking my pulse.

Like I'm his pet or something. Like I'm his.

"I want to go," he says.

I look up into that ineffable gaze, so full of harshness and affection. It's here I dare to think it—that maybe he is different. Wilder, somehow.

I can still feel his massive hands on me, the way he held me down and smelled me, as though he was animated by some primeval force.

This is a man who can fight like he has eyes in the back of his head. I've seen men fight. I've looked out of slits in tanks and seen the most deadly men in the world in full battle mode. I've seen even more than that on videos that will never be released to the public in a zillion years.

But never have I seen anyone fight like Kiro does. It's possible he literally *did* want to rip apart the store. Guys hate shopping, but they usually don't have the urge to destroy the store. And the way he just took me over...

I'm different, Nurse Ann. He's said it to me enough times. I feel the truth of it in the way that I suppose he feels seasons, predators. The implications seem huge, ancient.

He gazes down at me. My heart pounds. What *does* he think when he sees me? What does he think any of this is?

I try to pull on my wrecked jeans, feeling wrecked myself. And unaccountably sad.

He scowls. "What's wrong?"

I don't know what to say. Everything feels so tragic suddenly. The way he sees the world, the way the world wants to use him. "We can't hang round in this town this long, but we can't go without getting you supplies."

I fold over the top of my wrecked jeans. It's the best I can do now that the metal buttons are off. This is how Kiro takes off a girl's clothes.

"You have to pick out the stuff you'll need to live up there," I say.

"You'll help me."

"I'll help." Though I don't see why he needs help. Who'd know better what he needs than him?

I buy an extra pair of jeans on the way out and quickly change into them at the camping and hunting supply store. When I come out of the dressing room, I find him at the knife counter.

I come up behind him, knowing he knows I'm there. He inspects a series of hunting knives, evaluating and discarding one after another, superpredator that he is. What is he imagining as he turns them over in his fingers? I should get pictures of this, too. People will want to know what he chooses.

Fuck, the endorsement money off just a shot like this could buy him a thousand acres of wild land to have as his own. Because who wouldn't want the knife Savage Adonis chooses?

I pull out my phone as if to check my mail and discreetly take a few photos. I'm starting to question this whole process, but the thing about photos is that once the moment's gone, you've lost the shot.

He settles on one large knife and one with a small grip. The small one seems too small for his hand. What's the small one for?

While they're boxing up the blades, he inspects the contents of a box on the counter. Keychains in the form of different animals.

Suddenly he yanks one out and holds it in his massive palm, staring at it with a mixture of shock and reverence, like he's discovered a rare and precious jewel.

I draw near and see that it's just some howling wolf figurine attached to a keychain. Just some cheap molded plastic thing from China. Practically worthless.

But apparently not to Kiro.

It's the one thing he's shown true interest in on this whole shopping trip.

Wolves. Family.

All this time wanting to get home. The realization dawns on me that it's not about the wilderness—it's about the wolves. They'd said he'd been raised by wolves. Could it be true? The way he holds the stupid little keychain tells me it is. Like Kiro's version of coming upon a photograph of your long-lost mother.

I nod at it. "Let's get that."

"What for?" he asks, not letting it go. "It's for keys. I have no use for keys."

"Liking it is reason enough to buy it. Welcome to shopping."

He closes his massive fingers around it. It makes me feel every kind of feeling, watching him hold onto that thing.

This is the killer detail I'd hang the story around. Kiro, ripped from the only place he was ever happy. Caged, imprisoned, drugged.

He just wants to go home—to the only true family he ever knew. The one place he felt loved.

And he latches on to this fucking keychain.

"We should definitely get it," I say casually.

We move on to the sleeping bag section. He feels inside each one, asking my opinions, finally choosing the largest, softest one of them. I smile, amused that Kiro likes a little comfort after all.

He looks at me and catches me smiling.

And he smiles.

CHAPTER TWENTY-ONE

Kiro

I'VE SEEN MANY beautiful things. Unexpected, startling beauty on misty mornings. In the deepest nights. Inside the bloodiest of battles. Sunny, lazy autumn days.

Nothing like Ann, half-naked back in that dressing room. Reaching up to me like she thinks I'm someone good.

I run my fingers over the fabric of the sleeping bag Ann chose, as if to check its softness, but really I'm living back in that dressing room with Ann below me, reaching up to me.

I remind myself I can't trust her. That she's only with me for my story.

Still I had to take her in my arms.

Even fake things can make you feel good.

Like Ann, reaching up to me.

Like the wolf in my hand.

It's just a plastic thing, but it looks like Red, one of the best friends I ever had. My heart twists when I hold it. I'll see Red again. I can almost feel his warm, coarse scruff.

And Sally, with her pointy black muzzle. Fierce eyes. The rest of them, all so distinct.

I used to lie in that bed imagining the moment of scenting my old friends, seeing them, feeling the happiness shiver through them. I never imagined it would come true.

Ann walks through the store with me, pointing out all the things she imagines I might need. "What about rope? A camping water purifier? That would be good, right?"

I say yes to them all because these are the things she thinks *she'll* need.

A woman like Ann is fragile and unused to the wilderness. Having these things will make her more comfortable.

The wolf toy is the only thing I want from the store. And a canoe, because a canoe will get us home faster. She chooses a Kevlar canoe.

Our cart is full to the brim before we get to the tents. She'll come to see that we need only the den, or maybe the cave if we want a fire. But the wolves are better for warming cold fingers and toes than any fire. Still, we pick one up.

She'll be frightened at first, but the wolves will remember me, and if I carry her to them, they'll accept her as mine.

Eventually she'll feel happy there the way I did.

"We'll go there in a canoe, drop all this stuff at your home for you, and you'll canoe me back to the car," she says.

I understand from the way she says this that she's imagining our trip will take a day, maybe two. She has no sense of the vastness of this wilderness. She has no sense we'll be travelling for many days.

I touch the hem of her shirt, thinking about the way she tasted. I smile.

She enjoys when I smile. People have always wanted me to smile, told me to smile. I never would. But Ann is different. I want to smile around Ann.

We unwrap the things we've purchased, which are in maddening plastic containers, and load them into the backpacks right there in the store. We sling them on and carry the canoe over our heads. We're only a few steps out the door before I stop.

They're here.

"What?"

"Back in the store. *Now*." I turn us, canoe and all, back into the store, as though we forgot something. We put the canoe down.

"What?" she asks.

"They're here," I say.

She widens her eyes. "Who?"

"The ones who attacked the Fancher Institute."

"The canoe was over your head…how did you see them?"

"I didn't see them, I smelled their chemical scent. They're out there waiting for us near our car."

"The rental car? How could they have found us?"

Ann cares about details. I don't. "You wait here while I kill them—"

"No." She puts a hand on my arm. "They're waiting for us at our rental car. Let's let them wait."

"Go on foot?"

She looks around. "We'll borrow a car."

"Borrow?"

"We'll go out the back and find something…to steal-slash-borrow," she says.

"You need keys."

"I don't," she says. "We just have to be fast. I'll get one started while you get the canoe fastened to the top with the bungees. Will you be able to tell if anybody is back there?"

"Of course." I leave her and go to the back door. I take a whiff and return to her. "They're not out back. Only in the front."

She smiles as though I've performed a trick. Collecting facts for her article. I pick up the canoe and carry it myself this time. It's what I wanted to do before, but Ann insisted on helping. I allowed it because it seemed important to her, but now the men who attacked us are here.

She leads me to a blue truck parked at the far end of the lot, hidden behind a larger truck. She breaks the window and an alarm sounds out, piercing my ears. Quickly she slips in and gets to work, doing something next to the wheel—pulling, prying. The alarm stops.

She moves with confidence.

Her confidence makes her even more beautiful to me. It makes me feel sad, too, because she really isn't with me. She really isn't on my side. She's my natural enemy. A reporter.

For a second, though, I allow myself to imagine her coming home with me as a true partner, wanting to be there.

The engine starts.

I tie the canoe onto the top. Ann sits behind the wheel, taking apart her phone.

"What are you doing?"

"Just in case," she says mysteriously. Soon we're on the road.

"You can start a car without the key," I say. "How do you know to do that?"

She hesitates, and my heart darkens because I know she'll lie, or at least tell me a half-truth.

It's good to remember she's lying and that she doesn't want to be with me, that she only wants me for the story.

"I learned while spending time overseas," she says finally.

I nod.

"Working in conflict zones," she adds. "Some of these areas, half the cars don't have keys to them anymore."

"You were a nurse in conflict zones?" I ask, smoothing my finger over the side of the plastic wolf that looks so much like my old friend. A true ally. I'll see them soon. It's beyond imagining.

I'm sure they'll love Ann. I hope she'll come to love them.

"You worked as a nurse in war zones," I say, wanting her to lie more, to remind me what she really is. The professor read me a famous book about a war hospital once. The man was injured in a hospital, and a nurse loved him. The nurse in the book really did love the man, though.

"I took on nursing roles," she says.

It comes to me that this is what she does everywhere—she pretends to be a nurse when she's not.

Pretending to care. It shouldn't feel like a blade in my belly—she does it with everyone.

Still, I keep going back to that moment when she reached up to me. It felt so real and good.

I tell myself it doesn't matter. She'll submit to me just as prey submits to the superior force of the predator.

"Have you thought any more about the Kiro thing?" she asks. "Have any more memories come?"

I study her lips. I love watching her lips. "No."

"What were the people who raised you like? Were they Albanian by any chance? The people after us had the tattoos of the Albanian mob." She pauses. "You know Albania? It's a tiny country…"

My face flushes with shame. "I don't know that country."

"A lot of people don't know Albania. It's an Eastern European country near Greece. Crime organizations out of that part of the world can be very deadly. Very vicious. Could the people who raised you have any ties at all…"

"The people who raised me were interested in church and riverboats and fixing their adopted children. My father owned a hardware store. My mother was a teacher."

"Hmm. Even so, could they have…I don't know, taken a loan from the wrong people? Though that's really a stretch. Plus the men who attacked you called you Kiro," she says. "Do you remember anything from before your adoptive family?"

"You certainly are eager for my story."

"These people are hunting you for a reason, and it's a big one," she says.

"Does it really matter so much?"

"They're desperate to kill you. Don't you want to know why? If you've truly had no interaction with the Albanian mob growing up and don't know anything that could hurt them, then it means they want to kill you because of who you are. You represent something…a threat. Or maybe you have some sort of power or possession you don't know about, and they mean to prevent you from seizing it. Maybe you're important to somebody they want to hurt. Maybe you're a relative of an enemy. You have a story, Kiro. Don't you want to know it?"

"My story," I spit. "It was because of my story that the reporters mobbed the hospital when I was first taken. It was because of my story that the professor kept me in a cage. Because of my story they're trying to kill me. I want nothing to do with my story."

"What the professor did, what those reporters did, what happened to you at Fancher—all of that was wrong. It disgusts and offends me."

Her emotion feels real.

"But that's not an argument for ignorance," she continues. "If you don't know your own story, it controls you. The ignorance of your story is hurting us."

Us. I tell myself not to trust it.

I thought the professor was on my side. I wanted to believe it so badly I let him trick me.

I close my eyes, so tired of being alone.

CHAPTER TWENTY-TWO

Ann

HE SAYS NOTHING for miles; he just gazes out at the passing forest land. We're entering serious wilderness now. The path will be dirt in about fifteen miles, according to the maps.

He seems so troubled. So sad.

He sets the little wolf keychain on the dashboard. "They'll be in their winter place by now."

"They have different places?"

"Nearer to civilization as winter nears."

"And they'll remember you?"

"They're family."

My gut twists. Going home to his family. That's what my editor will want images of. Kiro approaching the wolf's den or whatever it is for the first time would be like gold to Murray Moliter. Nobody could touch that.

I look away from him and his little keychain, feeling utterly ill, and grateful I have the driving to concentrate on. I don't want him to see my eyes. I feel like he can read me sometimes. Like he doesn't trust me sometimes.

I should tell him what I am, what my plan is.

But if he knew I was a reporter, he'd hate me. I'd be like all the rest of the people who used him.

The headlights make splotches of light on the dirt grooves ahead of us. The road is just two tire grooves now. It's not even a road anymore.

He stiffens. "There'll be a chance to go left up ahead. Take it."

"Okay." Sure enough, there's a fork. I take the left. We're getting deep into the parkland now.

Kiro takes over the wheel soon after, and we drive through the night. It's slow going—we're on the uncleared back trails, and this truck isn't the best for that.

Sleep starts to dull and disorganize my mind. I close my eyes.

The next thing I know, I'm stretched out alone in the front seat alone. It's 3 a.m., judging from the dashboard clock. I sit up and rub my eyes. He's out in front of the truck, clearing branches by the light of the headlights.

Nobody's passed through here in a vehicle for months, maybe even years.

I reinsert my SIM card and check my phone. Still have reception. A miracle. There are texts from my editor loving the picture I sent.

He's sent me back promos for the series—it's a series now—the photo of Kiro with the caption: *You won't believe where we found Savage Adonis.* There's another promo that's more hypey—*Caged by a madman. Strapped to a bed in a mental hospital, Savage Adonis emerges and you wouldn't believe how.* He has another that's the mystery angle: *Why was the public lied to? Why was Savage Adonis being hidden? Get a front seat to his reunion with the pack. The wolf boy bares all, exclusively to* Stormline.

I put in a call.

"Like them?" he says. "I was going to work in the mob and a hail of bullets, but nobody would believe it then. This fucking story has everything. I need the high-res versions. You need to send those."

"Look—I'm not going for the kill here. This is going to be a serious profile. And *bares all*? No."

"He's practically a caveman. Don't tell me you can't get him to strip down and sign a piece of paper."

"That's not how I'm working this story," I say. "This is not an exploitation piece."

There's a silence. It was the wrong thing to say. From Murray's point of view, this is all about exploitation.

"You need to trust me," I add. "You need to trust me to do the right thing *and* to deliver."

"No, actually I just need you to deliver," he says. "I'm paying you to deliver, got it?"

Anger rises up in me. "No, actually, you're paying me to deliver research and up to a thousand words if needed on a meth supply line at the Fancher Institute," I say. "Instead you're getting Savage fucking Adonis. Even though we don't have so much as a contract on it."

"I've sent you money."

"I'll send it back."

There's an uncomfortable silence where Murray wants me sweating. I do, a little. I don't want him sending a team of people up to scour the wilderness area. Though the mob and the police may be doing that soon enough.

"This is going to be a good story, and it's going to leave him with dignity and money. Do you want it? Because I'll get you your meth story instead—"

"Of course I want Savage Adonis. I'll send a contract—"

"I'll save you some time and send you language to insert about me approving final edit," I say. He grumbles as I tell him what I want to see in terms of money. "And don't even think about lowballing me." I tell him to hurry—I might not have reception for long. Once I have the protections in place, I'll send him high-res images for the promo. We spend a little time going back and forth until I have the best deal for Kiro that I can negotiate.

I shove the phone into the recharger.

Kiro's still out there, toiling with a massive tree trunk now, his huge, sweaty bulk illuminated by the headlights. He's trying to push it off the road. When he turns and puts his back to it, I catch sight of blood blooming red on the white of his shoulder bandage. Fuck!

I open the door and scramble out. "Hey! You're bleeding!"

He stops, back pressed against the huge thing, but he's just leaning on it now. He pants, face framed in sweat-drenched curls.

"It's nothing," he says. A droplet of sweat hovers on the tip of his nose. I really want to touch it, swipe it off of there.

"Can I just check it?"

"After this is clear."

"I'll help clear, then."

He snorts.

"Concept of two people better than one? Women's lib? Ever hear of it?"

He glowers, radiating a kind of angry, wild brutality that no camera could ever capture. I want to tell him he's beautiful. I want to stroke his beard the way he likes.

Instead I put my shoulder against the thing and heave. "Uh." I look up and find him watching me. "What?"

"You think you can move it," he observes.

"I think I can try."

There's a strange light in his eyes. It might be lust. It might be hate. Maybe it's both.

It's like he's zeroing in on me, locking in on me. I've never had somebody watch me so intently as Kiro does; even as I stand before him, it's as if he's tracking me. I was always the tracker, the observer. It's strange to be on the other end.

"Take a picture, it might last longer," I joke, nerves skittering. I'm just so acutely aware of his heat and testosterone. Of us alone out here.

His nostrils flare.

Instinctively, I back up. One step. Another, backing along the tree trunk.

He follows. It's as if there's a string between us, and my retreat draws him, steadily, inexorably, eyes glued to mine.

My ass hits something—part of the downed tree. My pulse races as he continues toward me, closing in.

"Are you frightened of me, Nurse Ann?"

"A little. I don't know, I just woke up."

He slides two fingers down my cheek, down my neck. He reaches around and takes my hair in a fist.

Tightly.

"Ow," I breathe.

His burning eyes fall to my lips. "Now?" he asks.

He's manhandling me and it's heating me up. I can't seem to answer; all I can do is stare at his lips, his cheekbones, his wild, ferocious beauty.

He pulls me closer. "Now?"

"What are you doing?"

His lips hover over mine, air electric. My heart pounds, and I know that he hears it. I'm utterly fucking aroused, and I know that he smells it. It's unfair that he has this inside knowledge. "What do you *think* I'm doing?" he grates out, breath hot, gaze fixed on my lips. "Tell me."

The whole conversation is utter nonsense. He doesn't care what I think he's doing; he just wants to see my lips move. He enjoys seeing my lips move.

It's so crazy. I work with words, and this guy, this hot caveman, he doesn't give a fuck about words. I throw the sentence back at him, enunciating for maximum lip movement: "*What* do I think you're—"

He devours my mouth before I can finish, twisting my hair, forcing me up against him in a bruising kiss.

He holds me flush to him, chest to chest, the bulge of his erection between my legs.

I want him suddenly. I want him all over me. In me.

He pulls away.

"Kiro," I whisper.

He kisses me again, hauling me up, this time—clear up off the dirt path.

I make a quick, unromantic calculation: I happen to know I'm clean. I've had a birth control shot. And Kiro's clean. I saw his chart, his tests.

He breaks the kiss and sets me on a log on the side of the road. "You'll watch." He goes back to his exertions.

"What?"

"We have to make more progress than this."

"Did you kiss me just to distract me from helping?"

"I kissed you because I wanted to." He grunts and heaves against the downed tree.

I spring back up and push alongside him. He glares.

"Seriously?" I say. Suddenly it's budging. Moving. Together we get it out of the way.

He gazes at me like that was something so amazing, us working together to move that thing. The moment feels poignant, somehow.

I raise my hand. "High-five."

He stares at my hand.

"We're supposed to slap hands together. It's a thing you do with somebody at a moment like this. Like, job well done, dude! High-five!"

"Let's go."

I leave my hand up there, waiting. I don't know why. I'm all turned around, and I want one thing to feel regular. "Come on, Kiro."

He grabs my hand and closes his fingers around mine.

"We'll work on it." I nod at his shoulder. "Now you're going to let me re-dress that wound, and we'll be off."

He grumbles, but I can tell by the tone of it that he'll consent.

Back in the vehicle, I pull the old dressing off and clean the fuck out of the wound. He doesn't react to the pain, as usual.

"You need to pay attention to this shoulder. It's not bad, but it could get bad. There's a big bottle of rubbing alcohol in the packs, plus sealed packets of anti-bac stuff and more tape and bandages. It's a really nice kit I put together for you."

"You'll care for my shoulder."

"I'm talking about when I'm no longer with you. After we get you home."

He grunts. For once I can't read his grunt.

Soon enough, we're back on the road. I try to go back to sleep, but I can't. A while later, Kiro stops the truck again. The terrain ahead looks extra wild and rough.

I watch him through slit eyes. His nostrils move in a way that tells me he's experiencing intense emotion. He eases the door open quietly, slowly, as if not to wake me.

I stay, letting him have this moment alone.

Kiro goes to a tree, touches it. Even in the darkness, away from the shine of the headlights, I can see his huge frame rise and fall.

He falls to his knees.

Sobbing or laughing or maybe just breathing really hard—it makes no difference. It's happiness.

He's home.

How long did he dream of this? Strapped to a bed in that horrible place.

I think, vaguely, that this could be the hook. On instinct I shove the battery back into the phone, fit the back on, and fire it up. Then I pause.

I can't do it.

I don't have to document every moment. I shouldn't even be watching.

I force myself to look down at my phone. This is Kiro's moment. His alone.

I take it off airplane mode, just to check, and I'm surprised I still have a signal. Barely, but I have it.

Texts begin to ping through. Murray. He wants me to send him more images—all the images I have so far. We have the contract, now he wants me to deliver.

I start going through the images, making sure they're backed up into the cloud, emailing a few to myself just to be redundant. There's the shot from the store where they'd dressed him up with that scarf and glasses, but I see his wild heart shining through in spite of it all. And the before and after haircut pictures. I pause on one of the motel images. Kiro on the bed, back against the headboard, glowering, steak bone in each hand, surrounded by empty to-go cartons, hair still wild and long.

I spread it large and study his face. I smile, even though he's glowering. I'll never get sick of looking at Kiro.

I decide not to send the photos yet. I'll deal with it all later. I shut it off and pull the thing apart.

I store the battery in one baggie and the body in another baggie—it keeps better that way. I tuck the baggies into a pocket in my purse and look out at Kiro, kneeling there, so still. Loving that he's back.

How can anybody blame him for wanting to get lost in the wilderness after the way the world treated him?

I grab the stupid little wolf keychain off the dashboard and turn it around and around in my hand.

I've never known anybody like Kiro. I'll never know anybody like him ever again.

It makes my heart ache.

CHAPTER TWENTY-THREE

Lazarus

MY EXECUTIVE COACH, Valerie, has a bias for the carrot over the stick. If you asked her, she'd try to tell you that fear doesn't inspire excellence.

It's possible she has that right vis-a-vis the corporate world; people fearing for their jobs may not be as creative as they could be. But people fearing for their lives—that's a whole different level of creativity. The human animal longs to stay alive. Will do nearly anything, even the seemingly impossible, to stay alive.

So when my team loses Kiro and the girl outside the mall, I send my pet hitter, Tarik, to take out the leader. Because this was a balls-to-the-wall fuckup. Kiro and the girl were in the store. They were sitting ducks. It was a miracle we'd picked up their trail at all.

And what did my guys do? They set up on the vehicle instead of the people they were following. A team of five lethal killers and they were all standing around that parking lot in sight of one another. It was fucking lazy.

And such a simple hit—a bullet in the brain in parking lot. Easy to film.

Somehow, the girl and Kiro made my guys and slipped out the back.

Lazy. Sloppy.

I get the second in command, a man named Dirk, on the phone. I tell him I want him and his men to come up with three strategies for locating the pair of them again. I have more guys on their way up. He needs to handle the manhunt. I don't threaten to kill him if he doesn't succeed. But he gets that I will kill him if he doesn't give 110 percent.

Kiro needs to die. Hell, he needed to die before he knocked me out and dislocated my shoulder. Things aren't looking great.

Until seven hours later.

That's when I get the call from some editor from out east telling me he has a way to get the location of Kiro and the girl, who turns out to be a reporter—in exchange for a generous finder's fee and a favor. He wants to embed his own reporter. He actually uses the word "embed." Like this is a troop situation.

"How'd you get my number?"

"I have sources everywhere," he says. "A journalist never reveals his sources. It goes for you, too. You want my info or not?"

"You know where they are right now?" I ask him.

"I know where they were two hours ago. And as soon as my freelancer puts her battery back into her phone, I'll have her location."

"They're heading into a wilderness area the size of a small state. You think you can run GPS off her phone?"

"No, I've got a tracker on her. Runs behind the scenes off the lithium battery," he says. "The phone doesn't need to connect to a tower to give me her location. She just needs to assemble the thing to take a picture. It's only a matter of time."

"And I want a reporter telling the world what my people do...why?"

"My guy, Garrick, is interested in getting a few pictures of Savage Adonis in his home and, if possible, to have a word or two with him. After that, Garrick walks away. A quick interview, a few images of Kiro in his natural habitat. Keeping you strictly out of it."

"I don't understand—this freelancer that's with him now is yours, didn't you say?"

"She's...off-roading. Not really doing the story anymore."

"Huh." I'm thinking maybe this guy could use a few sessions with Valerie on leadership.

"I'm assuming you have people up there. Probably a helicopter at your disposal, but it's a lot of tundra. We could deliver the coordinates."

It's strange but creative. I don't have to think about it long. One of the top things that distinguishes a successful leader is quick decision making, according to Valerie. That's one of the few things I don't have trouble with. I need that location.

"Put your guy on a plane to Duluth. If he's cool, we're cool."

I put down the phone. When one door closes, another opens.

We'll gun down Savage Adonis. See whether we can deal with this embedded reporter. My guys have a sense of people. They'll suss out whether we can play ball with this Garrick. If we can't, we'll kill him, too.

CHAPTER TWENTY-FOUR

Kiro

I SUCK IN the night air, palms flat against the cool dirt, feeling the wilderness come alive around me.

I should be happy, but everything hurts.

My shoulder wound throbs. My muscles ache. Ann said that might happen—that it's the drugs working through my system.

But none of that compares to the pain of Ann betraying me over and over. Just a reporter, out for my story.

I heard the phone sounds—more pictures? I squeeze my eyes shut, remembering how it felt to be trapped outside that hospital with those reporters taking their photos, hounding me while I could barely stand. Shouting their questions, reminding me that I'm different. Wrong.

I'm a story and a savage to Ann, too.

The knife of it twists in my heart because for a moment there, back when we worked to move the branches, I felt like we were really together.

Well, I'm nearly home now. My pack is out there somewhere. That's my family.

I breathe in the scent of the soil. Wet leaves under dry. A nearby stream. This area was on the edge of where I used to roam. I recognize the types of trees. The air. The look of the rocks.

This wilderness area has lots of official entrances across northern Minnesota and Canada. This is not one of those official entrances. We probably won't see any people from here on in.

I brush the dirt from my hands and wipe my eyes on my sleeve. I don't want her to see my tears.

More phone sounds. Pain rages through me.

She wants to learn about the savage. Well, she'll have her savage.

People love to hold their phones, love to look at them when they're upset. I hate the phones, and I hate Ann's most of all. I would love to take her phone and smash it, but I won't.

Yet.

I'll wait until we're deep in. I need her to go with me voluntarily.

It's one hundred fifty miles back to where my pack is. I can make thirty miles a day by canoe and foot. Carrying her, while she struggles? More like fifteen miles a day.

I try not to think about her struggling. I don't want her distressed and I don't want her to struggle, but even if she struggles, I'll take her with me.

I have to take her with me. I get this crushing feeling in my chest when I imagine letting her go.

She climbs down from the truck. She smiles, and my heart swells in spite of everything.

She helped me. She really did seem to care for a while.

She looks up at the dawn sky above the tiptops of the pines. I follow the line of her gaze, wanting her to see the beauty here. Her gaze lowers, then.

"You're not going to..."

She eyes a downed tree, then turns to me with a kind of wonder. She thinks I'll move it. I suppress a smile. Even I have limits.

"No," I say simply. "We're here. Near."

She looks happy.

My heart swells to see her happy. "We'll leave the truck here," I say.

She watches me a little bit longer, and I think she's going to sneak a photo like she does, but instead she goes over to the downed tree and begins to crawl up. I hop up and pull her up and steady her. We stand there together, face to face. She looks into my eyes, and I wonder what she's looking for, what she hopes to see.

I slide my fingers over her curls. She shudders a little. I think it's me, then I realize it's the cold. Early fall. There's a chill in the air. I pull off my jacket and put it around her, over her smaller coat.

She resists. "Kiro, just a shirt can't keep you warm. You need this, come on." She begins to pull it off, but I still her arms.

"You'll wear it."

"You can't just make me wear it."

"Can't I?"

Her pulse jumps—I see it in her throat. How well does she understand the situation she's in?

"You'll freeze."

"I won't freeze. You just have no tolerance for temperature variation."

Yet.

She pulls the jacket around her, as if it's so strange, as if she's unused to...this. Has no male ever cared for her? I find it shocking, but at the same time, the idea of any other male warming her or feeding her or fucking her makes me feel crazy.

"So it's near here?"

I jump down. Not only is it one hundred fifty miles away, but deep into Canada. I know only because the professor would show me maps on his computer, trying to get me to show him where I had lived. The summer and winter ranges. He figured out a good amount about me and the wolves. "The walk will warm you," I say simply.

We pull the packs out of the back. Pull the canoe off the top. Ann puts plastic over the broken window—so the seats don't get moldy.

I nod like I think it matters.

She brought a lot of energy bars and dried food. She'll soon see she has no need of them. I'll provide everything she needs. She's also brought the wolf keychain. I won't need that, either. I'll have the real thing.

"There's a river this way," I say. "Maybe an hour's walk from here."

"You really know this place."

We begin to trudge. I carry the canoe on my head. The canoe slows us, but not as much as she does. She asks me questions now and then, points out birds. "Stop!" she says after a while.

I halt, thinking there's something wrong. She points out a doe on the ridge above us.

Has she never seen a deer? I put down the canoe, and we watch it together.

"It's magical," she says.

She won't like it when I kill one. I decide I'll kill things away from her and bring her the parts, not let her see the whole animal. "Have you never been in the wild?"

"Not like this. The trailer park where we lived, it was more suburban, I guess. And when I worked in war zones, well, the animals were usually mostly gone by then. This is real wilderness. Deep, wild wilderness."

I nod, amused she thinks this is deep or wild.

It takes us two hours to reach the river. It's midday by the time we set the canoe in the water. I take the paddle. She wants to help, but I tell her it's faster for me to do it alone.

She gets in, sits sideways, and we set off. I paddle upstream—north. The water is low, but not so low that we can't take the best way. She watches the trees go by. Now and then, Canadian geese fly overhead, honking, heading south for the winter. The opposite direction from us.

She shivers. Is it the geese flying south? Do they make her think of winter?

"You sure you don't want my help? There's another paddle. I mean, I'm here to help you."

"I don't need your help."

She furrows her brow. The forest around us grows darker, deeper. "So you have this kind of handled? You don't really need me?"

"Not at the moment."

"But you might later? To help carry the things?"

"I'll let you know."

"Oh. I kind of thought you needed help."

Maybe she imagined it was all about the supplies. She was helping me bring back supplies. And I would walk her back to the vehicle. Like a date, like on the television at the Fancher Institute.

"Can a wolf pack ever move?"

"The pack moves all the time. Different places for different seasons."

"Oh. So there's not just one place…one cave?"

"Wolves are hunters. Hunters always move around."

"Would the pack ever relocate entirely, like to a whole different wilderness area? Like if there was a better place to live?"

"There is no better place to live."

"That may have been true before, but you understand, you're living on federal land, which is illegal."

"It's never been a problem."

"You've never had the mob and U.S. law enforcement after you before. A manhunt. They didn't know you were living up here before," she continues, looking all around, "but now they do. The police will track you here because they know this is where you're from."

"They won't be able to track me."

"It's not like you're on the moon, Kiro. They'll get the forest rangers involved. And then there's the Albanian mob..."

"This is a big place," I say. "My place."

"But you don't own it," she says. "It's a park. What if there was a place you owned? What if you had land of your own where nobody could touch you? Even campers couldn't go there without your okay. All yours—your home. Miles of land."

"That's what I have now. I own this in every way that matters. It's not a park; it's a world."

She watches the clouds. "Seriously, don't you want to know why they're hunting you?"

This again. "I know why they're hunting me."

"Uh. Wrong. You *so* don't know."

I love when she's so confident and capable. She's wrong, of course, but I love it, and it makes me want to kiss her.

"What?"

"Nothing," I say. We round a bend. The waterway opens up into a large lake walled in by trees and massive rock formations.

"Omigod," she whispers.

"What?"

"What? Um, hello! The whole thing! It's beautiful."

My heart swells with pride.

"Look how the lake is a perfect mirror for the trees. All the yellows and oranges. The mist rising up at the end. It's like a magical glen or something."

She spots an eagle. A moose up on the ridge.

"How long?" she asks an hour later, when we're going up one of the smaller rivers.

"We won't get there today," I say simply. "We'll stop for the night."

She goes still, eyes the color of moss in the waning light. The unfocused look tells me she's thinking complicated thoughts.

She bites the side of her lower lip. She knows why she wants to come along with me—to get my story. Is she's finally wondering why I want her along?

"You see the black rocks around the water's edge? Those are slippery as ice."

She brightens. "Is that personal experience talking?"

"Yes. I learned very much the hard way." I tell her about slipping into the icy water as a kid. How long it took me to put even the simplest things together. The details of my story seem to calm her.

The details for the article she imagines she'll be able to write about me. The dirty savage.

"Weren't you hungry?"

"The loneliness was worse than the hunger."

"It must have been so hard."

She has no idea. How the loneliness wore at me.

I've only ever wanted companionship. Affection. The affection of the wolves meant everything—even the slightest scrap of it.

Ann's affection in the institute was even more powerful to me than the affection of the wolves. The realization shakes me. Her affection meant more.

And now I'm bringing her home.

CHAPTER TWENTY-FIVE

Aleksio

WE SET UP at the Sky Slope Hotel, just outside of Duluth. My luxury suite becomes a command center, and my guys and I are generals, plotting our incursion into the giant wilderness area northwest of here. We're assembling guides, getting ears on local law enforcement, developing teams, hiring copters.

My brother Viktor's working on getting ears inside Bloody Lazarus's organization. Lazarus has some kind of intel that's keeping him a step ahead of us.

My girlfriend Mira comes in. She has her lawyer outfit on—the suit, the skirt. She looks so fuckable, I want to die.

"Baby," I say.

She shoves Viktor's feet off the coffee table. He grins at her.

She slams down the paper. Kiro's commitment order. Vacated. "Your brother is never going back to that place," she says. "Ever."

An unfortunate choice of words. I'd love him to go back there. I'd love him to be anywhere I could find him, rather than out in the vast wilderness, unaware of the danger he's in.

"They're already moving against the committing officer," she says. "I think the director's dirty, too. Dr. Fancher."

"Good work," I say. She's amazing. She just started her own solo practice down in Chicago and already she's kicking ass.

"You're going to find him." She eyes the camping shit all over the floor and then Viktor. "That's what you're going to wear out there? A wise-guy suit and necktie? Shiny shoes? You know it's wilderness, right?"

"He's not going," I say. "He's still recovering."

"What's your excuse?" she asks Yuri.

"This is what I fight best in," Yuri says.

I snort. The Russians love their suits.

She picks up a Tavor with holographic sights, the latest in semiautomatic weaponry. "You're bringing this to the wilderness? It weighs a ton. You think you'll hike with this?"

"When you need one, you need one," I say.

She puts it down. She hates guns. Once we get Kiro back, things are going to change.

"Everyone in the world is chasing your brother. How will he know you're the good guys? His brothers?"

"Our *bratik* will know us by the path of blood we paint on our way to rescue him," Viktor says.

I smile. I can't wait to meet him.

CHAPTER TWENTY-SIX

Kiro

WE MAKE GOOD time, moving over land and water. At times we're so hemmed in by the trees that you can't see the dusky sky. Other times the vista opens so wide, you feel like you're on top of the earth.

We cross a lake.

"You're not breathing," I say, slipping the paddle into the dark water, stroking us onward.

She sighs.

"You smell it? The leaves? The moss?"

"I smell...no smell."

I frown.

"No, it's a good thing," she says. "A relief."

"Because of the Fancher smell?"

"Yeah. For a while there I thought I'd never escape it. That antiseptic smell. I sometimes almost felt like it chased me. Like it went everywhere I did." She gets a haunted expression, like she used to in the institution. "I hope I never smell it again. That smell, it's just so…" She seems lost, suddenly.

Getting lost in my head was a way of surviving. I would lose myself in memories of running with the pack. Of lying on the forest floor. The trees. When she gets lost, it's not good.

"Hey." I grab the extra paddle and pat the space next to me. "Come here."

She furrows her brow.

"Come here."

"You want me to help paddle now?"

"Yeah."

"I thought I would just slow you down."

"Now I want you to help."

She accepts my hand and sits next to me, takes up the paddle. We paddle side by side. The breeze shakes the treetops. A loon's cry pierces the quiet.

"A little faster," I say.

She puts her muscle into it. We get up speed; not the kind of speed I had alone, but it gets her out of her thoughts.

"You can smell the leaves? The moss?"

"Yup."

"Both of them? Right now? All the different notes?" she asks. "Like a wine connoisseur or something?"

"I don't know about a wine connoisseur, but…it's right there in the air for anybody to smell."

She smiles. She's happy to be with me, I suppose. For the moment, anyway.

"The institute smell must have driven you crazy."

"More than you can imagine."

"The antiseptic. Oh my God. You know, that cleaner they used?"

"Right," I say. "The floor smell was the worst. But really every person and surface had their sharp smells."

"You have such a sense of smell. It must have been hell."

"Not when I caught your scent."

Her face goes red.

"I mean your everyday scent. Clean and spicy. I could be in a place with dozens of people and hundreds of smells and pick it out. I could tell when you would enter the building."

"Wow." She paddles on, swishing the water.

"It's nothing special. Just a skill I developed."

She perks up. "For hunting?"

My heart sinks. That's the sort of stuff the professor wanted to know. Would I practice smelling? Did hunger make my smell better? Would I scent and track my prey? Kill it with my bare hands? Feel the life go out of it? Even one of her beautiful deer? Yes. Absolutely.

Her boss Murray called me a caveman during one of their conversations. My face glows hot to think of it. They had a caveman cartoon on the TV at the institute. A figure of ridicule. Dragging women by their hair.

"A skill for hunting?" she asks again.

"Smell is a good skill for hunting," I bite out.

She purses her lips.

We paddle in silence. I can see the trouble in her eyes. I hate when she looks like that. It's how she always looked when she thought about the kitten—that mysterious kitten. She's growing more and more upset now. More upset with each stroke of the paddle.

I pull her out the only way I know how—by giving her a piece of me.

"It always stunned me nobody else could smell things as I did. At first, anyway."

She's interested. Alert. "You mean back wh pulled you out of the woods?"

"Yes."

"You thought everybody had a grea then they didn't, and you were surprised?

"Yes."

"Wow," she says. "It must have been like entering another world."

"It was." It's working. She's back with me. I tell myself it's for the best—that the more I can string her along, the less distance I'll have to carry her.

But really I just don't like to see her distressed.

"Of course they hadn't used smell to survive. I understood it when I remembered back to what it was like when I was a boy. I had only to sit at the table and food would appear, or toward the end, in the root cellar."

"The root cellar?"

"A small room set into the ground on the side of a house—"

"Dude, I know what a root cellar is."

"So yes, I would hunt by smell out here. It was especially important in winter, but harder then, too, because cold animals have a fainter scent. It was worst of all when there was no snow and cold out. I would have to use my sense of hearing."

She stills. "Would you say your sense of hearing is as good as your sense of smell?"

"Maybe."

"Huh."

"Most often I'd hunt through stillness. Pretending to be part of the scenery. When the rabbit hops by, you snatch it. If you wait long enough, something will scamper by." I lower my voice. "It was a trick I used at my most desperate. Even a starving kid can wait."

We're moving faster now, getting down a rhythm. She's moving. Focusing on me, on the task of paddling together.

"Why didn't you just ask for help? Couldn't you have found campers to help you?"

"Why would I ask for help? The police wanted to arrest me."

"Wait—I thought you were eight."

"Yeah, and the police were after me."

"The police don't arrest eight-year-old boys."

"They wanted to lock me up even then," I tell her. "Just like now."

"That's not how it works. A kid out alone? So many people would have helped you."

"No thank you."

"What do you mean, *no thank you*? People would've wanted to *help*—"

"Help me get locked up or killed," I growl. "Or paraded in front of cameras like a sideshow beast at the circus. Wanting my story."

"I'm sorry that happened to you." She looks like she really is sorry, like she really cares.

I grunt.

"It must have been...horrible."

Anger fills me. I want to believe she cares. "I dealt with a lot of predators out here. I've been at the mercy of some of the worst ones. But the way those reporters came at me...I was weak from my injury, weak from the drugs. I didn't understand."

"I read about the orderly when I was researching your case. The one they paid to get you to come out of the hospital."

"I thought he wanted to help me," I say. "He said he would get me outside. I wanted to touch the grass." *Eat the grass.* But I don't say that. "I was so weak and dizzy. The infection made me hallucinate, or maybe it was the drugs. I wanted to go home so badly. It's all I wanted." I look at the passing scenery. It's still like a dream to be home.

"Kiro," she whispers.

"He took the tubes from my arm and got me a winter jacket and boots. He made me wear a hat—a ski mask—and shoved it over my face. He told me to walk normally. He told me they didn't want me to leave, but he'd help me get home. He got me out a side entrance. Instead of nature, there was pavement and a mob of reporters, flashing camera lights at me, shouting. I was...bewildered. The orderly tried to take the ski mask off my face, and that's when I started fighting. I hit him. I hit everyone I could. The flashes blinded me. I could barely stand. I was so weak. Thrashing around." *Like a wild animal.* She probably knows. There were lots of witnesses to it.

"I heard about it."

"I finally braced myself against the wall, fighting just to stand, unable to get away. They kept asking about the wolves—did the wolves raise me? Did they feed me? Where did I live? And the flashes from the cameras..." I breathe in, trying to stay calm. The terrain is changing. I concentrate on that.

"The kind of work those sorts of reporters do dehumanizes people. It's wrong. But not all reporters are predatory like that."

I close my eyes, remembering their dark hunger, wishing I could trust her. Wishing she wasn't one of them.

CHAPTER TWENTY-SEVEN

Ann

I FEEL SHITTY and stop asking questions.

We hit shore and trudge on. It's farther than I imagined.

And it really seems far just for him to turn around and bring me back to the truck.

At first I had this idea that I could visit him again. I imagined mapping his coordinates on the phone. I would drive up and hike in.

The longer we go, the more I realize how silly that was.

And little by little I have this sense of journeying into something deep, not just in terms of geography, but something more—like sinking into shifting sands.

It makes me uncomfortable.

I used to say that the story begins where the comfort zone ends, but this feels different. Dangerous. But then I look at him, and he's so beautiful and wild. And I think how he's been treated—he's never met anybody who doesn't want to hurt him.

Most of all, I'm starting to question any story about him.

I don't want to use him like those other reporters did—I won't fucking do that. But what does that leave me with? The idea of doing his story for his own good? To help him gain economic independence?

This guy doesn't need economic independence any more than the wind needs it.

I could figure out why he's being pursued like he is, though. I could arm him with the information about who his enemies are and why. That's still important. Or is it?

I own this, he said.

This wilderness area is as large as a small state. Maybe he really can get lost in it. Maybe he doesn't have to literally own land. Maybe I don't know jack shit about anything.

We head down a river that's bounded by massive rock formations like a giant baby's blocks, piled haphazardly. Pines along the sides stretch heavenward, as if to create a cathedral ceiling.

Times when I've been deep in the tropics I had this feeling of being somewhere exotic and otherworldly. I never thought about the far north as being exotic and otherworldly, but the wildness of this place is every bit as intense.

What the fuck am I doing out here?

But then I look at Kiro, and I know what I'm doing here. This is the man who reached his hand out to me, who protected me from Donny. And our connection sizzles. It sizzled every time I walked into his room, and it sizzles now.

And I'm seeing him home. It's just a longer trip than I thought.

He carries the canoe from one waterway to another like it weighs nothing. When I ask to stop, tired, he humors me. I eat a few energy bars. I'll need to make the food stretch out a day or two longer than I'd originally thought.

I want to take pictures, but I decide to wait. Conserve my battery. We end up back in another stream at dusk. He pushes us off. So much water up here. The stars overhead are bright.

"Can't we stop? I'm so sleepy."

"Sleep."

I resist at first, but finally I give in and curl up with my head against a pack, telling myself I'll just close my eyes. I drift off to the soft sound of the paddle.

When I wake up, he's carrying me in his arms.

"Kiro?" I whisper.

"You don't have to whisper, Ann." He lays me down on something soft. The sleeping bag. He zips me in and stretches out beside me.

A strange shriek echoes through the dark forest, sending a shiver down my spine. "What is that?"

"Predator and prey," he rumbles. He draws a finger down my cheek. "You're safe here. Nothing can get you here."

"Is this your place? Are you home?"

"It's an island. Sleep."

***

I PULL OUT four slim packets of Starbucks instant coffee the next morning and set them on a log near the fire. Four slim packets from Starbucks. "I need to heat water. You're lucky I brought extra of these. I'd be a monster without my coffee."

"You need coffee every day?"

"Hell yeah. Don't worry. I have four."

He looks concerned.

"I'm a total addict. What can I say?"

"What happens when you don't have your coffee?"

"You don't want to know."

"You would survive it, right?"

"No."

He draws nearer and takes a strand of my hair. "Tell me what happens." It's kind of a command.

"Why?"

"I just need to know."

I narrow my eyes. "Exactly how far is your place?"

He winds a curl around his rough, sinewy finger. "It's far."

"How far?"

"I can make thirty miles a day." He watches my face, all-seeing eyes rimmed in rich, chocolatey lashes. "Four more days, I would say," he adds casually, unwinding the curl now.

"Wait—what?" The air goes out of me. I'm sure he's joking...except Kiro doesn't joke. "Four days? You mean two days in and two days out?"

"No, I mean four days in."

"A hundred twenty miles into the wilderness? That's where we're going? We'll be in Canada."

He shrugs.

"And then you're going to bring me back? All that way?"

He observes me curiously, as though he's waiting for something.

I get this sense that the shifting sands I've been feeling really *are* shifting sands. That things are no longer solid. That I've sunk into a different world.

"It's a long way just to...bring me to your place..."

The birds sing around me. Water laps at nearby rocks.

"It's a long way just to turn around," I add.

The way he watches me now, I have this crazy flash of insight—that he's the predator and I'm prey.

"A long way..."

He drops his voice. "You're not going back."

"Seriously, Kiro. Come on."

"You're coming home with me."

"And then I'm going back. I have to go back. You know I do."

"You won't go back."

Something flips upside down in my belly. *You won't go back.* He's serious. Dead serious.

Even so I smile, because it's so preposterous. "No, Kiro. That's not going to happen."

He studies my eyes. We're awash inside a moment of truth, a strange pivot point between two universes. It's not a question for him. Maybe it never was. "You'll be my mate."

My mouth goes dry. "You can't just make me come with you and be your mate."

He observes me with those fathomless golden eyes, waiting to see what I'll do, thinking maybe I'll try to get away. Knowing he can stop me.

Because he's the king out here.

My heart pounds. Is it possible he imagines us growing old together in some cave or something? I hang out the wash on a tree branch? Woodland animals frolicking in the background?

Why not? Kiro's in control here.

How stupid I was! So blinded by this man's heartbreaking beauty, so consumed with affection for him, with getting his story, that I let him lead me miles into his world. So deep that I have no way of finding my way back.

Yes, he melts my panties. Who am I kidding? He inspires confusing, aching feelings in me that run way deeper than lust. But I've also seen him kill men with his bare hands as easy another man might open a jar of pickles.

"It's not happening," I say.

"It already happened."

"What, you'll just drag me by my hair?"

A flicker of pain in his eyes tells me the comment stung. "I would never drag you by the hair, Ann," he says softly, touching my hair again. Watching my lips. "I'd carry you, though. If you forced me to."

"Are you fucking serious? Listen to yourself." I push him away. "You would deprive me of my freedom? After the hell of your confinement and the way we fought out of that place, you'd seriously turn around and do the same thing to me?"

He crouches by the small blackened pile of wood and starts working on making a fire by twirling a stick. Because he's fucking Kiro. "We'll start out soon."

"And you don't tell me until now?"

"I knew you wouldn't like it."

"I can't even believe you. You would trick me and take my freedom? Can you get how fucked up that is? How fucked up on every level? You of all people should understand how wrong that is."

The fire springs to life. "Yes, it would be wrong, wouldn't it? To deceive a person. To trek with them for miles, never revealing their true purpose."

I stiffen. *He knows.*

He glowers up at me, all brutal beauty, wilder and hotter than the fire he made with his bare fucking hands.

My heart pounds as I think about that phone conversation I had in the motel room with my editor. Is his hearing as advanced as his smell? Of course it is! And oh my God, the way I talked to my editor in the truck…

"To trick them," he continues. "To make them think you just want to help."

My blood races as he rises, as he comes to me. "All you ever wanted was to have the savage's story. To get the pictures of him that nobody else could get. For your news story."

"You're misunderstanding this, Kiro. I'm not one of them—I swear."

He fingers the collar of my jacket. "Then why didn't you tell me your true purpose? Your true identity?"

Fuck. "So this is my punishment? To be your conquered woman?"

Another flicker of hurt behind his eyes. I feel like shit.

"Kiro, listen—it was an accident that I figured out who you were. I was there for a different story. And I did want to help you—I still do."

"Like those other reporters?"

"I'm not like them."

His eyes are beautiful and golden and totally feral—how did I never see it? He uses the collar of my jacket to pull me to him. He slides a hand down the lapel, and I think he's going to strip it off—strip me.

I pull the sides together. But instead, he reaches into my pocket and draws out the baggies that hold my phone parts. My lifeline. He pockets them.

I grab for it, but he takes my wrists.

"I thought we were friends."

His voice is a velvety rumble. "We're not friends."

"Why would you want somebody not your friend as your mate?"

He brings his lips to the crown of my head. "You don't need to be my friend to be my mate."

"Kiro, think. I'm on your side. You're being hunted. Why? You need to understand what's happening out there. You live in the world, and whether you like it or not, you need means, you need knowledge of your situation—I can help you with all of that…"

"I have all I need."

The gravel in his tone makes me think about the dressing room. He's thinking about it, too—I can feel it.

Four or five days of travel.

The deeper we go in, the more helpless I'll become. And he has my phone, though it's not like I'd have a signal out here anyway.

I really am alone—with Kiro. He's utterly in charge of my destiny now.

I look over at the canoe. What if I jumped in and just paddled away? I could backtrack...maybe.

He seems to read my mind. "You think you can paddle faster than I can swim? You think you can run faster than I can? And even if you could somehow disable me or lose me, which would not happen, but even if...do you think you could find your way back?" He slides a knuckle under my chin, lifts my head.

He touches me now because he can. Because I'm his. Heat fills me.

He lowers his voice. "Even if you knew your way back, do you think you could make it? I'm not the only predator in these woods. There are bears, bobcats, wolves, of course. Massive ground-wasp nests. Unstable cliffs. A hundred ways to injure yourself."

"I'd survive until I found a camper."

"This isn't an area campers like to come to, even in the high season. The maps warn them away. That's something I learned in the professor's cage. This is the wildest territory. And not a season for campers."

"It's not happening," I whisper hoarsely.

He lets me go and turns his back, digs around in the pack. It's almost like a taunt—run, go ahead. Try it.

He takes the tin cup from the pack and goes to the shoreline. He dips it in and drinks. If I run, he'll catch me.

We both know it. He dips it in again and brings it to the fire, extending the retractable handle.

"What are you doing?"

"You like your coffee hot." He holds the thing over the fire.

Coffee. How could I forget? Being a prisoner of a feral man is a lot to comprehend before I've even had my coffee.

"It's one thing I can't provide you with indefinitely. Would you prefer to drink it all up or try to make it last?"

"How about neither? How about a nice big cup of *not in your dreams is this happening*?"

"Out here, you want to make things last," he says thoughtfully. "I'm going to make you a small amount. I want you to have it for a long time, but then you'll be without it. You won't die, I don't think. I'll find new things for you to enjoy."

"I don't want new things to enjoy."

"I'll find them anyway. I'll care for you, Ann. I'll give you everything." He looks up. "I'll protect you. I'll even die for you if I have to."

My pulse whooshes. Kiro only ever says what he means.

"You're mine now," he explains. Like that clears it all up.

You're mine now.

He splashes a bit of the water onto his finger. "It's ready."

I look over at the canoe. "I think you won't like swimming after me in the icy water. This water is coming down from the glaciers or something, isn't it?"

"The human body can adjust to a far wider range of temperatures than seventy to seventy-five degrees, Nurse Ann."

His calling me Nurse Ann has this edge now. Like he's calling attention to my deception.

"I didn't tell you about what I was doing because I knew you'd hate it. I didn't have evil motives. I only ever wanted to help."

He waits with my heated water.

"You can't keep me."

"I think I can." He puts down the tin cup and grabs one of the slim foil packets that contains my coffee, one of four. Four servings left.

"Go ahead, then, put it all in," I say. "Because this shit that you have in mind? It's not happening."

He puts it all in.

I grab a trail bar and rip into it. "And I'm eating as many of these as I want, because there is no fucking way I'm doing *Clan of the Cave Bear* with you." I stir my coffee. It's stronger than it needs to be.

I gulp a bit down and instantly start feeling more rational.

He rolls up the sleeping bag. *My* sleeping bag. He didn't use his sleeping bag. I guess that one was for me, too. All of this camping stuff is for me, I realize.

Kiro's like one of those wilderness guys who can be airlifted into the middle of nowhere naked and survive, no problem. And there I was in that camping store, picking things out like a fool. No wonder he was so interested in my opinions.

I wander to the shore, savoring my coffee, trying to think. What if I did disable him? He might be right about how hard it would be to get back. But surely if I trekked far enough south, I'd get a signal with my phone or run into somebody. And if I had the canoe? It's not like I'm in a desert with no water or food surrounded by scorpions and rattlesnakes. I need the canoe and a head start, I decide. And my phone.

It's foolish to try to run—he's probably right about that. But isn't it foolish just to go with him? The foolish ledger seems pretty evenly balanced between my two options.

I sip, looking out at the craggy, rocky shores. I spot one of the slick black rocks Kiro warned me about. I'll avoid those.

He comes up next to me. "I missed this so much. This beauty. The sun. The silence. The scent of live things. You can't know what it is to be home."

"And I don't get the same consideration? I don't get to go home?"

"You said you didn't have a home."

"I'm between homes. It doesn't matter. The point is, I like to pick my home."

He goes to pack up the canoe. I watch him, mind racing in circles from one option to another. He kind of has me checkmated. Even if I knocked him out with a boulder and took the canoe and phone, I don't really think I could get back. I need a map. Campers. Something.

I spot a deer grazing on the shore, and all I can think is, *fuck*.

"Are you enjoying your coffee?"

"I always do."

"Finish it. We have to set off."

"Aren't we having breakfast?"

"Later."

His hair catches the light as he puts our stuff into the canoe. His plaid shirt looks soft, tightening over his huge muscles. His canvas shorts cup his ass as he bends to bungee cord the stuff in.

He's my captor. He shouldn't seem hot anymore.

I turn away and take another sip. I'm not stupid. I know I can't make my move now—this is exactly when he'll be expecting it.

"Ready?"

"Part of having coffee in the morning is enjoying it."

He comes up behind me and smoothes my curls. My pulse races as he touches me with that strange mix of tenderness and domination. "I like your hair like this."

I stare into the last bit of my coffee, cooling in the tin camping cup with its fancy retractable handle. The coffee doesn't help much with my ability to wrap my mind around the fact that beautiful, savage Kiro has me in the middle of the wilderness under his total control.

Because you're my mate. The words make my belly feel melty.

He pushes his lips to my neck. "You can finish it in the canoe."

I stay there. It seems foolish to consent to going even deeper into the wilderness now.

"If I carry you to the canoe, do you think you'll spill your precious coffee? I think you might."

Pick your battles.

"Fine." I go over. He stabilizes it as I get in. He has the packs arranged differently now, so that the only place for me is a little nest right in front of where he sits to paddle.

"You want me to sit between your legs now?"

"I don't know what you might do."

"I liked where I sat before. When I was in the front. Like the Queen of Sheba."

"And now you'll sit in a different place." He urges me forward.

Pick your battles, I think again. Though it occurs to me he's winning every one.

"Fine." I settle in and stretch out my legs over the plank of the canoe bottom, back against the bedroll. He shoves us off, and we begin to move. His long, powerful strokes move us silently up the stream.

I sip my coffee and watch the scenery go by, thinking about where we are, where the sun is. I need to pay attention now.

"What are you thinking about?" he asks.

"How I'm going to escape."

"Mmm-hmm."

It's common for freelance journalists to wade too far into danger in the course of digging up the real story on something. You just keep going further and further, because that truth you need, that nugget you need, is just up ahead—you're sure of it. And you need it so bad for this story that you're going to write, this story that will make some fucking difference in this twisted-up, tangled-up world.

You see a lot of us dying to get a story. You see a lot of us quitting once we get married and definitely once we have families. The last thing you ever want is for your kids to see your beheading video. Or for your partner to get a hundred pieces of you in a body bag.

I always figured I'd quit.

This isn't what I had in mind, though. I was thinking more along the lines of writing a book or a blog. Not being a captive in the wilderness.

I lean back, bracketed by his thick, muscular shins, which are lightly covered with hair. His muscles flex with every stroke, thick and powerful. I tear my eyes from them, force them down to the boots we bought him.

"How are the boots?"

"Fine for now. Once I get my feet used to rough ground again, I won't need them. You won't need shoes eventually, either."

I snort. "And if you look out the tour bus window to your right, folks, you'll see a massive rock formation as we enter utter and complete motherfucking fantasyland."

"Tour bus? What?"

"Nothing. Never mind."

"Don't you want to be strong?" he asks. "How can it be a bad thing for your feet to be so tough and strong that you never need shoes? To be so free and wild you don't need anything, and this is your home, and all of this beauty is yours? Out here, you're richer than the richest person in the world."

My heart pounds like it does whenever I feel the edge of another person's reality. We all see the world so differently from one another, but every once in a while, you see through the eyes of another. And it never ceases to blow me away.

Kiro definitely blows me away.

Abused and lied to all his life. So he makes his own damn life out here—fuck all the people and phones and cars and insurance plans. The sky is his. The river is his. With everything he tells me, I want more, more, more. Not for the story, but just...to know him.

"King of the forest."

He says nothing. He is king of the forest. Master of everything he sees. It's madness.

And way hot.

I crane my head back to look up at him. Our eyes meet. "King of the wolves."

He glares down. Massive pines stretch up into the blue, blue sky behind him. The ever-changing cathedral ceiling. And Kiro, the high priest.

"Not like I'm going to run off and tell it, right?"

He paddles steadily, all scowly at me. It's quiet out here. The only sounds are the wet swish of the paddle and the whisper of breezes high above.

"Did you really run with the wolves?"

"A man can't run as fast as a wolf."

"But you were leader of them?"

He snorts.

"It's cool. I know why you won't tell me—because you know I'll get away. I'm so out of here, and you know it."

"You won't get away."

"Yes, I will. That's why you won't tell."

A long silence goes by. "I know what you're doing," he says.

"You took over a wolf pack. King of the wolves."

"It's not how it was."

"Tell me how it was. Please. I so want to know."

He glances down at me, and my reporter's antennae zing to attention. He's thinking about it—I can tell. Kiro very much doesn't want me to think he was king of the wolves. He wants to set me straight.

"The professor always used the term 'superalpha,'" he begins. "About me and the pack. He thought I took over the pack in some feat of strength, but he had it wrong. It wasn't a feat of strength. It was bribery. Desperation."

"Who wouldn't be desperate? An adult would be desperate. You were eight."

He seems to consider this. "When I was first out here, I was frightened of people, because of the threat of police."

Which didn't exist, but I don't argue. "Right," I say.

"But I was lonely. I spent a lot of time in trees, and I'd watch the wolves below. They looked like dogs to me. I'd had a dog I loved. I thought maybe the wolves could be friends with me like my dog was. So I made a plan of winning their friendship. That's how it started."

He dips the paddle into the velvety-looking water and pulls it back with strength and skill.

"I started by robbing campers. I'd take their meat and bring it to the wolves and scramble up a tree while they ate it. I didn't want to lead them or take them over. I wanted them to be my friends."

"Like with your dog back home."

He nods.

"Did you have other friends back home?"

"I had adopted siblings. None liked me, except my little sister—for a while, anyway. She came to hate me eventually, too, but at least I wasn't alone. Alone *and* lonely is harder."

"So you fed the wolves."

"Yeah. I stole meat mostly. Those bars and dried things for myself, but the meat was always for the wolves. I wasn't even thinking ahead to winter," he says. "There was this tent that I stole, and I figured the tent would be enough. I was a kid, what did I know? Minnesota winters never seemed like a big deal. When campers started getting scarce, I'd lure and trap rabbits for something to give to the wolves. It was hard to kill those rabbits at first, but I got better. Eventually a few of the wolves would let me feed them by hand. It was such a small victory, but it was okay. My life was so simple. Just survival. These small victories. I felt...happy. I thought, 'As long as I keep going, they'll let me be a friend.' I wanted...just one friend."

"And it worked?"

"Two of them began to approach me when I didn't have food, sniffing. Nipping. But not the rest. The leader, who I called Brutus, was always growling at me. Teeth bared, fur puffed up. Wolves are like people. Different ones have different ideas about things."

We've gotten to a shallow part of the river. Kiro uses the paddle to shove us out of a muddy patch and back into clear water.

"Then came the first cold snap of winter. It was so cold—far below freezing after being warm for all those months. And there was no snow for tracks—just the bone-chilling cold. I tried and tried to catch anything, but it was too cold and windy for me to move around outside. I knew where the wolves stayed—it was this dry place near a rock under a mammoth fallen tree, but I didn't dare go there. I'd moved to a cave by then, so I would sit in there and wait out the night, shivering, covered by the coats and sleeping bags I'd stolen. I'd make fires, but they kept being blown out by the howling wind—it had shifted for the winter. At one point, the cinders burnt my warmest blanket. All of the lighters I'd stolen were out of fuel. No more campers came around."

I'm stunned that an eight-year-old boy could keep himself alive even that long. He'd been out there for months by then.

"Two of the wolves came by. They were used to me feeding them, and I thought for sure that when I didn't have food for them, they would kill me. And I was curled up, so cold, I almost didn't care. They sniffed around for food, and I just cried, ashamed." He pauses, and I wonder whether he's feeling shame now. "And then the brownish one who was the first to let me feed him from my hand came to me and sniffed me. I thought he would bite my hand—I really did. I was willing to let him. I was pretty fucked up by then."

He pauses for a long time. I can tell by Kiro's eyes that he's back there, thinking.

"I waited. He smelled my hand, and I saw this flash of teeth. Then he curled up next to me with his big warm body partly on me..." His voice drops to a whisper. "It might sound like a fairy tale, but it's what he did—he kept me warm. And the other one curled up next to him. They were just so warm. I shivered there, crying and talking to them. Petting them. They were kind to me even though I had nothing to offer them. It was the most amazing experience of my life."

Shivers come over me.

"I never told this to anybody."

"It means a lot that you would tell me." Does he believe me? I want badly for him to believe me.

"You're my mate now. You should know these things."

I don't reply.

"Snow came, and it aided in my hunting. I would play with the brown wolf—Brownie, I called him. My first friend. The other, Beardy, would play, too. I would get wounded a lot—wolves aren't like dogs; they are really rough. But I got strong fast. There were seven in the pack, and they would disappear sometimes, and I'd feel so sad, thinking they wouldn't come back, but they always would. Off hunting—that's where they were. I worked harder on being a help to them after that. It was getting colder, and it wasn't even winter. I understood then that I'd die if they wouldn't let me stay into their den. I started making traps—mostly pit traps. That's what the professor called them. He'd show me pictures, trying to get me to talk. Wanting us to share a vocabulary about the wilderness—that's what he always said."

"But you didn't talk to him."

"No. I only ever wanted to kill him," he says. "I would wait so silently at my pit traps. I was so small then, but I knew how to wait. One night I had five rabbits, and I made my move—I brought them to the den. The wolves ate the meat. And I stayed the night, curled up at the edge, right up against the rock, making myself as small as I could. Brutus, would snap at me when I'd get near the group, so I shivered by myself. It wasn't so cold as that one night I almost died. The next night I did the same thing—I brought two rabbits and stayed. But I was so cold in the middle of the night, I approached the group. I knew it was dangerous, but I figured that if I was dead, at least I wouldn't be cold anymore. Brutus was on me immediately. He had me on my back, snarling, jaws on my throat. I whimpered. I thought he would kill me. And then he licked my face." Kiro looks down at me with a happy light in his eyes. He looks so young. "That was the first time I really felt...like I belonged."

"It must have been amazing."

"It was the best feeling in the world. Brutus never liked me, I think. But he didn't kill me. But with the other wolves, things were good. It was...amazing."

Amazing. He's using my language, trying not to be the savage.

He looks out at the trees like he sometimes does. "I'd always been fast and clever, strong for my age. Active. Energetic. It was something the family that adopted me hated about me. It saved my life with the wolves, though. They saw me as a fellow hunter."

"Your family hated that you were strong and energetic?"

"They liked to sit and watch TV, and I had so much wildness and savagery in me—I never liked to sit still."

"That's normal boy behavior—not *savagery.*"

He gives me a look. "You say it because you don't know."

I do know—I know he's wrong, but it's not an argument to start now. "So they didn't like your...energy."

"Out in the wilderness, nobody hated me for being what I was. The wolves never let me actually hunt with them—they were too fast. Too good. But they would bring me food. You can't imagine how it made me feel. They moved for summer. I didn't understand that's what they were doing. I thought they'd abandoned me. But I followed their voices and found them. They accepted me right away."

"So that's what you'd eat? Just...flesh?"

"There's a lot to eat out here. Raspberries, seeds. Walnuts. Some plants have sweet leaves. Fish. I started growing things in our summer place—potatoes and beets. Those I got from the campers. It got even easier as the pups came. The pups saw me as one of their own from the start. I was there for over two generations. Sometimes when the wolves left for hunting and I sensed it would be a long, lonely time before they were back, I'd trek out to the camping areas and take clothes. Or food. I'd talk to the campers sometimes and make up stories that my family was nearby. I'd steal comic books. I still remembered how to read. As I grew older, I took books. Sometimes they'd invite me to smoke and drink and fuck, and I would happily do that."

An unpleasant feeling fires up my spine. "Yeah?"

"I stole radios sometimes. When I started roaming farther, I'd steal cars. ATVs sometimes."

"From the campers?"

He nods.

"That explains the driving skills."

He gives me a look. "I enjoy driving."

His paddle strokes become hypnotic—stroke, stroke. I watch the tree canopy move by overhead. It's strangely relaxing. I have to remind myself I'm being kidnapped. "It means a lot that you trusted me enough to tell me."

"I don't trust you at all," he says. "You're a reporter. You want to show the world I'm a savage."

"God, Kiro, I'm *not* like those reporters. That's not at all my interest."

"It makes no difference now."

"It makes a difference to me. Telling your story the way I would? It isn't about you as a savage. It's about you as a human. That's what I'm interested in. I don't make people into objects. That's the opposite of what I do."

He watches my lips. My words mean nothing to him. Just more lies, like everyone who's lied to him. He points out a tall peak. He tells me how to spot where a bear hibernates.

"I could use all of this information to get away."

A rich brown lock of hair falls over his slash of a cheekbone as he looks down at me. There's a brutality to his beauty that sometimes renders me breathless. Like now, riding below him like this, on a cushion of packs between his legs. "You won't get away," he says casually.

Shivers go over me. I'm angry, of course. Offended. But I'm a little turned on, and it's this fact that scares me the most.

I was turned on in the dressing room by his caveman treatment. Now he's gazing down at me, lord and master of the wilderness, and I'm feeling that same heat. What is happening to me?

"Well, you're wrong," I say, mouth dry. "I'm so out of here."

He stops paddling and smoothes my hair. It's a tender movement at first; he seems to like to touch my hair almost as much as he likes to stare at my lips. After a while, he clenches his fist around it, as though suddenly remembering he should probably be harsh when I say such things. He jerks it, making me turn my face up to him. "I suggest you don't try."

He's all savage fierceness on a dizzying background of blue, blue sky.

He slides his other hand up my exposed throat, then cups my chin, keeping my head turned up to him. Blood thrums through my jugular, and I know he's feeling it with his fingers.

It's like we're communicating on some primal level.

Like he's figured out about my caveman kink.

It's so fucking wrong. But we're drifting under the blue, blue sky, and he has his massive hand on my throat, and he's vowed to care for me and protect me with his life.

It's strangely powerful that he said that.

Kiro doesn't lie.

It's kind of amazing considering how people have lied to him and let him down, but Kiro won't let me down. It's a strange thing to think about your kidnapper.

My pulse drums under his huge hand...his huge hand that I don't want him to move.

I wanted the savage story.

Now I'm in it.

CHAPTER TWENTY-EIGHT

Kiro

I LET GO of her hair, but she doesn't snap her head forward right away.

She lets me have her neck a little while longer. I slide my hand along it again, so smooth and soft. She lets me touch her freely, unaware of what she's telling me by exposing her neck like this, like a submissive wolf.

Sometimes I can't believe she's mine. Not that I don't think she wants to get away. I know she does. But if she stays long enough, I can help her come to love it here. And she'll see I can be a good mate to her. She'll see that I'll protect her, that I'll do anything to make her happy.

Except let her go.

All night on the island, I watched her sleep, dozing only now and then. I enjoyed the feeling of watching over her. I didn't want it to stop. I didn't want to miss any of it.

I would watch over the pups now and then, but it's nothing like watching over Ann. Pups have teeth and claws for fighting, and fur to keep them warm. Left alone, they could find food and fight off most predators. But not Ann. She needs me out here.

I let her go and resume paddling. There's a stretch of land ahead. "We'll walk soon."

I can feel her come to attention with this. Will she really try to run?

I land us on shore and pull the canoe up. I pull out the pack and sling it over my shoulders, then I hoist the canoe. "I'll walk in front of you. You'll step where I do."

Her attention is elsewhere. She's looking around, weighing her options. My heart sinks. It shouldn't be a surprise, that she wants to run—I knew she would.

It makes me feel sad, though.

Telling her my story made me feel close to her. I want her to feel the same way about me.

I put down the canoe and shake off the huge pack and unzip it and dig around. I pull out the rope.

"What the fuck? What are you doing?"

"You want to run." I advance on her.

"What are you doing?" She takes a few steps back, but I lunge and grab her, quickly binding her wrists. Trying to be gentle. I hate that I have to tie her. Maybe if I'd been less pushy with her...less savage with her.

She tries to pull and twist. I grasp her hands in mine. "Don't. It just makes the knots tighter."

She stills, eyes glowing with shock and anger.

Please, I think.

I loop the other end of the rope around my wrist and put the pack back on, then hoist the canoe on my back. "The rope will tighten the more you pull."

I begin to walk.

"Are you fucking kidding me? Like I'm a pet now?" She grabs the rope and pulls back, but she's not strong enough to do much.

I pull and let her stumble along. I'm trying not to be too hard on her, but we need to make a certain spot by nightfall.

I cross a stream, balancing precariously on a rock.

"Fuck this!" She digs in and jerks back, putting me off balance, nearly putting me in the water.

I stop and turn.

Her eyes widen, but she stands her ground.

I put down the canoe and go to her, stalking slowly. She backs up, but I have her leash. I reel her in as I approach. "I should let you get away just so you see how dangerous it is. But I'm not that kind of man."

"No? Call the neighbors and wake the kids."

I don't know what she means by that, but I know it's not the time to ask. I wish I understood her better.

I kneel and tie her ankles with the length of rope I'd hoped not to have to use.

"Hey! What the—" She kicks.

"I'm sorry."

"I don't think you're sorry at all."

I'm sorry to be distressing her. I'm sorry she doesn't want to go with me.

I can't live without her. The slide of my hand over her bared throat was the most powerful thing I've felt in ages. Or maybe it was the feel of her writhing in the dressing room under my hands and tongue. I've told her my secrets. I've vowed to protect her. I can't let her go.

I hoist her over my shoulder.

She squirms, and I tighten my grip. With one arm, I get the pack back on and then I get the canoe over my head, much as she attempts to prevent me. I nestle it on my shoulders and partly against her, using her to balance it. This will not be easy going.

"Ow! It's cutting into my leg."

"We have to make this crossing."

She kicks. "Come on. It's cutting off my circulation."

"You'll live."

She does her best to make the walk hard. It is hard. Walking like this is the last thing I want to do. Going up hills is especially hard.

"I'll walk on my own."

"You've shown you won't," I say, hoping to hide how thankful I am to hear that she wants to walk. I'm not good at hiding the truth of things from her. Maybe she can tell; I don't know.

"This hurts. It's stupid."

"That I'll agree with."

"Fuck you. Come on."

"How can I trust you?"

"I've never lied. Have I? Have I ever lied?"

I grunt. It's true, she's never lied. She's left things out, but she's never lied.

"I'm telling you. I won't run. For *now*."

"You'll walk with me? And you won't jerk the rope?"

"For now."

I put her down.

She holds out her wrists. "Untie me."

"You'll prove yourself first."

"You want a relationship with me? This is not a good start."

A relationship.

Relationships are for the shiny people on the TV at the Fancher Institute. They're for people who went to school and have jobs and families that loved them. "What do I want with a relationship?" I growl. "Show me you can walk, or I'll carry you again."

I unbind her ankles, but not her wrists, and I go on, carrying the pack and the canoe. She follows.

It's wrong to tie her, but it's my job to protect her.

We trace along a ridge above a stream. From here you can see the streams split off and flow, and then split off again, like veins in leaves. I spent a lot of time pulling apart leaves as a kid. Not like I had much else to do out here.

I point it out to her. She grits her teeth and averts her eyes, but I know she's listening.

With horror, I remember how I was with the professor, how I'd soak up his words, how I'd love when he read to me because it cut the boredom, but I'd never let him know it.

A sick feeling comes over me as I think again of her bitter words—*You would trick me and take my freedom? Can you get how fucked up that is? You of all people should understand how wrong that is.*

I tell myself I'm not like the professor. I remind myself how she betrayed me, how she wants to use me. But the sick feeling just grows.

CHAPTER TWENTY-NINE

Ann

*S*AVAGE ADONIS LEADS *me by my tied wrists, deeper and deeper into uncharted wilderness. He carries a canoe on his head. He'll carry me, too, if I misbehave. Yesterday morning he pinned me down and made me come in a shopping mall dressing room. Today he informed me that I'm to be his mate. He pauses and points out how the streams fork and split apart. He tells me rivers are the same as blood veins, and that blood veins are the same as veins in leaves. He seems to see the forest as a body, a system. Needless to say, leaves and streams and forest systems are the furthest things from my mind.*

Would that be a fuck of a hook or what? It sounds like an honest hook, but it hides what's really going on for me. Sure, we're journeying deeper and deeper into the wilderness where I may never find my way out. But I feel like I'm moving deeper and deeper into a kind of forbidden craving for him, with his king stuff and the way he handles me. The way he makes me come with impunity. There's the rush of pleasure I get when I think about him holding me down and fucking me.

Kiro is beautiful and powerful, and he takes what he wants. And I'm the one he wants. It's wrong. It's scary. It's intoxicating.

I tell myself I'm just weak right now, that's all. I've been tired for so long and so fucked up about the kitten. So the peace of this place and his hot dominance and his intelligence and beautiful inner strength, of course it's powerful. Of course I feel conflicted.

We stop at midday. Maybe it's later. I suppose it doesn't matter. Another reason I seriously have to get away.

This man could suck away my soul.

"I'm going to catch some fish," he says.

"Okay."

He looks down at the stream, maybe ten feet down a rocky gulley. "Trout down there."

"Knock yourself out."

He grabs the rope that binds my wrists. "Are you going to run, then?"

My pulse races. "That's for me to know you and you to find out." In truth I don't plan to. Him being down at the stream doesn't give me that big of a head start. He would catch me. And my hands are bound. Bound hands will slow me down and mess up my balance. I don't want to go deeper, but I don't want to be stupid.

But I smile at him just to make him nervous. I like it, even as I realize what I'm doing—taking the power of the powerless. Meaningless little rebellions.

He pulls me to him. "It would be foolish, even without your hands bound."

I put on my most defiant smile, just to make him feel out of control. Because he makes *me* feel out of control. "Maybe you should've thought of that before you decided to adopt me as your forced mate."

The air between us seems to crackle as he shoves me down, making me sit on a boulder next to a tree. He backs up and lays my leash along the ground in a line some seven feet long, eyes on mine the whole time.

"The ol' leash doesn't quite reach down to the trout stream, does it?"

He twists his lips.

"Whatever will he do?" I ask playfully.

His lips twitch. Sooner or later he has to see this whole scheme of his is crazy. He crouches down and grasps either side of a boulder.

What is he doing? He'll never lift that thing. It's so caveman.

I snort. "It's called lever and fulcrum. Look into it, dude."

He looks up at me, eyes crinkled, lip quirked. He grasps the sides of it. The veins in his neck bulge. His face hardens into a grimace. He lifts it, heaves it over a yard, and drops it onto the end of my leash with a thud that shakes the ground.

I shoot up, tugging at it. Trapped. "What the hell?"

He looks up at me. And he smiles.

Smiles.

And I forget to breathe. His smile lights his features, softens everything. Something flops in my belly.

"What the hell," I say, pulling on my rope. He's laughing.

I should be mad, but I'm having...fun. It's the weirdest realization. When was the last time I had fun? Maybe before the kitten. Fuck, I forgot about the kitten.

I forgot about the kitten?

I yank on my rope. "This is so crazy."

"I can't let you run off. It's too dangerous."

"Don't you see how ridiculous this is?"

"You're my mate. I care for you. You don't like it now, but you will."

"I very much doubt that."

He brings me closer. "Do you? Do you really doubt that?"

"Really," I say, belly melting. *Fucking caveman,* I tell myself. *Not into cavemen.*

Softly, gently, he takes hold of my hair. He pulls down, as if he wants my throat fully exposed. I shiver as he presses rough lips to my tender neck. The entire surface of my body lights up with nerve endings, fanned by the brush of his lips, up, up toward the edge of my jaw.

Heat simmers in my belly.

Not...into...cavemen.

I tell myself it's the crisp outdoor air. The exercise. The fact I forgot about the kitten.

He slides his lips over my pulse point and up, then whispers all rumbly into my ear, "Here's what's going to happen. I'm going to catch a nice fat fish for us down there."

"How?"

"With my hands."

"What are you? A bear? You can't catch a fish with your hands."

"I can, Ann. Then I'll make a fire."

"By rubbing sticks together again?" I ask inanely. Because the rumble of his voice is doing something to my mind.

He lets my hair go. "I'll use the lighter." His tone is a dirty promise. "But if we didn't have that, I'd rub sticks together. I'm home now. This place is mine. Everything here is mine."

I swallow.

"Then I'll cook it. It'll be delicious and juicy, and you'll eat it."

"O-kay," I say sarcastically.

A glint appears in eyes. I'm paranoid that he's smelling my arousal right on my skin, like it's misting out of my pores.

"I'm going to feed you." My heart pounds as he slides his hands over my arms, looking down at me, feral and hot with those kissable lips. "Then I'm going to bend you over and fuck you."

My belly drops through my shoes. "Um, excuse me?"

"You heard what I said. It'll be best if you make yourself ready for me."

"What? That's what you think will happen here?"

The savage light in his gaze makes my skin heat more. "It's what I know will happen."

"And I'm going to make myself ready for you. That's how you think this will work."

His voice lowers. "You're aroused already. I feel it in your throat. See it in your eyes. And your scent..."

Shivers slide over me. "You're dreaming."

He puts a hand to the center of my chest and backs me up to the tree. He takes my hand and guides it toward my crotch. I pull, trying to reroute us, but he's too strong. He grabs two of my fingers and moves them for me. I hiss out a breath as everything between my legs comes alive.

A few strokes, and I could totally get off.

"Don't resist me."

"I get the idea. Make myself ready. I don't need your demo."

He keeps on, guiding my fingers between my legs. "Shit," I breathe, closing my eyes.

"Open your eyes. Open them."

I keep my eyes closed. There's not much he can do about it, being that he doesn't have a third arm and hand.

He growls and bites my cheek. My eyes fly open. "Better." He continues on, getting me off. Slowly, surely, I'm about to come.

"Feel it," he says. "This is how you'll make yourself ready for me."

"For somebody who's so sensitive about being as a savage," I gasp, "you're acting like one."

"I think you like it." He presses me more firmly to the tree. Bark gouges into my back as the pleasure rises between my legs. "This is how I want you. Ready for me to take you when and where I choose."

I'm moving my hand on my own now, angling into all the best parts, because fuck it feels good. My breath heats up.

His breath tickles my ear. "This is how I want you getting ready for me, for when I bend you over."

I'm angling to hit a certain spot, panting, mad with the buildup of pleasure. This is not me, turned on by a caveman like this. Mind and body taken over by a possessive brute.

His breath is velvet on my cheek. "There's nowhere you can hide from me. No part of you can hide from me."

Suddenly he's off me. I'm 98 percent of the way to an orgasm, and he lowers me onto the forest floor, onto a bed of sticks and pine needles. I lie trembling at his feet like a piece of meat for the savage, a virgin sacrifice for the beast.

He stalks away in a wake of power and glory and man.

My face goes hot with shock. "What the hell?" I call after him. This was a power play—Kiro, showing how he can take over my body and mind. He's going to feed me. Then he'll bend me over and fuck me. And the worst thing is that

I'll like it. And then we'll go deeper into this wilderness, into this insanity.

Caveman and captive is a good role-play fantasy, but this role-play is moving into reality with alarming speed, and cavewoman is not my preferred lifestyle. Lying at his feet, I would've given him anything. Everything.

It's as if he's predator and I'm prey on some deep soul level.

I lost myself once already.

I have to get away.

He has his knife with him, but I realize he didn't bring the lighter. I eye the pack, just out of my reach. The lighter's in the pack.

I don't see him, but I hear the babbling water. I know he's down there...catching fish with his bare hands—supposedly. Is he messing with me? People can't do that.

But I know he thinks I'm trapped. The leash under the boulder is effective—or would be if I were a four-legged pet.

Luckily I'm a human woman with opposable thumbs.

I rip a branch from a young tree and use it to snag the pack. Soon enough, I have the lighter. I hold the flame under the rope, grateful the breeze is flowing away from the stream where he's down fishing, so that he can't smell it so easily.

Or maybe he can smell it. He basically has superpowers out here. Still, I have to try.

He's master of the forest, that's for sure, but it's his superpowers over me that really have me worried. The dark pull of belonging to him tugs at my belly. The sensation of being at his mercy is as intoxicating as any drug.

The rope blackens and fries.

I use my teeth to rip it the rest of the way, spitting out the charred, bitter threads.

Freedom.

I can do this. I'm resourceful. I've survived in all kinds of dangerous places. If an eight-year-old boy can handle this wilderness, I sure as hell can.

I pocket the lighter and nab my phone, which is still in two parts in the baggies.

Quiet as a mouse, I creep off the other way—the direction from which we came. We've been heading pretty steadily north and northwest. I'll go south and southeast. I'll keep going until I get a signal.

Guilt twists my belly as I move through the trees. I'm surprised by how bad I feel, leaving the man who's depriving me of my freedom.

But then, beneath the captive thing we have going, there's a friendship. Maybe even something deeper than that.

I care about him. I don't want him to be lonely.

But taking a woman captive isn't the answer.

I move at a steady pace. I make good time. I'm not a complete idiot about moving with stealth; I've been in contested areas. Hot zones. I avoid sticks that might crack. Piles of leaves. I veer off the path and break random branches to fool him. Or at least try.

I come to a fork and take the wrong direction, thinking to circle back. Hopefully he won't expect it.

I go for maybe twenty minutes. Up ahead, I see a thicket of pine trees. I'm thinking I could get into there and climb one. He won't expect that, either. People don't look up. I'm really doing it. Part of me wonders whether it's a little foolish, but I have water, fire, and enough clothes to keep warm. A person can go two months without food. I grab a pine frond and rub the needles between my fingers, releasing the pungent juices. Like perfume to cover my scent. I rub it on my pulse points.

I step it up. I crunch over some leaves, and then I crunch over something that gives weirdly. I think I've stepped into a hole. Until I feel the rush of tickles on my ankle.

Up my pant leg.

And then the stinging, like needles, jabbing bone-deep.

My leg is covered with black wasps.

I scream.

Mud wasps are swarming my pants. I shake my leg, screaming, flailing, but keep stinging me through my pants, my jacket.

With wild motions, I brush them from my face and hair, whirling, trying to get them off of me. Then I just start to run, waving my arms.

My leg feels like it's on fire. I feel pricks on my back, my arms.

I run like crazy, batting them from my face. They're in my hair, everywhere.

I crash through the forest. I trip and fall. I bound up and keep going.

I run for what seems like forever, hysterical. They don't let up.

Hands grip me, stilling me, batting off the bugs. I'm crying. Screaming. I'm lifted up off the ground. Something goes around me. A coat, a blanket.

Kiro.

He's carrying me, running hard. I cling to him as the world jolts and shakes. His cheek is dotted with black bugs, all along the strong ridge of his cheekbone.

He's moving fast, not trying to be gentle. He himself is wriggling around. Fuck—the wasps must be stinging the hell out of him.

"Don't look at me," he says through his teeth as he wipes them away by rubbing his cheek against the blanket around me. "Put your face to my chest. Take in a deep breath—through my shirt! Now!"

The last thing I see is his beautiful face, dotted with a new round of black wasps, before I press mine to his shirt and suck in a breath.

"Another breath," he commands, speaking through his teeth. "Hold it."

I'm barely able to comply before I feel us flying through the air.

And then a rush of cold as we plunge into icy water.

I cling more tightly to him. I wait for us to come up, but we don't.

I feel him pulsing us through the water—underwater—using his powerful legs to propel us. The ice cold feels good on my stings, but I need air. I pull my head away from his chest. I need air!

He holds me tightly.

I try to push away. Through the blur of the water I see light up above, but he's moving us to the bottom. I panic, fighting him. He grabs a few rocks and suddenly we're going up, up, up to the surface.

He's going too slowly! I need to breathe! I need to get up there!

I struggle as I see the light above, pushing, pulling. I feel like I might pass out. Like my lungs might collapse. Or maybe explode.

He squeezes my shoulder, as if to urge me to calm. I try—I really do. He grabs my hair and pushes my head down, keeps me down while he's above the surface. Why won't he let me breathe? Is he trying to kill me?

I kick and fight. I can see him breaking the surface. He's doing something up there—throwing rocks? Suddenly we're heading down again.

No! I need to get back up there! My lungs burn!

He drags me down, down to the rocky lake floor again. I fight him as if my life depends on it. It feels like it does.

He has me tight against him. Black spots crowd the edges of my vision.

I'm no longer paying attention to what he's doing. All I know is that I need to get away from him, to breathe. When I see the light above, I thrash more wildly.

Air.

He palms my head, keeping me under while he breaks the surface. Then, finally, he guides me up—slowly. He seems to be communicating something to me. What, I don't know, don't care. I need air.

I break the surface and gulp in great mouthfuls of air, sputtering, coughing.

"Quiet," Kiro whispers. "*Do not* splash!"

I can't stop sucking in air—loudly. I push away from him and tread water. My boots are heavy, weighing me down. I try desperately to focus.

"Shhh!" He points at a dark cloud at the far end of the lake not a hundred yards away.

A chill comes over me when I realize it's the wasps, swarming out there. "Oh my God," I breathe.

"Shhh. Stay still."

Quietly, and with balletic grace, Kiro somehow heaves the bulk of his body up out of the water, throwing a rock high into the sky. He sinks back down and pulls me next to him.

We're two heads, bobbing at the surface, watching the rock he threw sail up past the trees into the blue dome above us. It make its lazy arc down, plummeting down, down toward the dark swarm. It splashes.

The swarm darkens, pulsing furiously near where the rock went in, seeming to attack the water itself.

A chill comes over me. That would be us.

They were waiting for us, searching for us.

If we'd come up for air near where we went in, without being sneaky and smart, they would've killed us.

Fuck.

I turn to meet his golden gaze. Giant welts glow red on his cheekbone.

And then he smiles. I can't believe he's smiling at a time like this. "They're dangerous," he whispers. "But so stupid."

And suddenly I smile back. We're in this horribly freezing water hunted by angry wasps, and I just grin like a fool. I can't stop smiling at him. I can't believe how badass he is. How young. How beautiful.

His beauty rips at me.

"I'm going down again," he says then. "Okay?"

"We can't stay in here," I say. My limbs feel heavy, and it's not just because I have hiking boots on—the water is freezing. My fingers feel numb. So do my lips. We're at risk for hypothermia.

"Keep moving," he commands.

"This cold is dangerous, too."

He says nothing. He knows it's dangerous. "I'm happy to see that my mate can swim."

"I'm not your mate."

He smiles. He's fucking with me. Keeping my mind off them. "They're stupid, but they hunt well," he breathes. "I'm going down again."

An unspoken question—*Can I last?*

I nod, teeth chattering.

He studies my eyes, and then he disappears below the surface.

I tread water, keeping a watch on the swarm, ready for them. My bones feel brittle, like the cold is turning them to threads of steel. My breath comes in gasps, an effect of the cold. Everything constricts. It's not good.

After a ridiculously long time where I start to worry, Kiro breaks the surface soundlessly.

My heart does this flip as our eyes meet. He hurls a series of rocks, one after another, seeming almost to defy gravity, the way he can get his body out of the water to make his throw.

He's directing the swarm away from us, moving them away.

"I'm cold," I whisper. "This isn't good." Does he understand how vulnerable we are to hypothermia right now?

"Soon," he says softly, watching the swarm. "Once we're out, believe me, we won't want to jump back in."

I try for a smile, unsure whether my lips actually form it. "Voice of…" My lips feel too cold to form the word "experience."

"Yes." He dives under and comes back up with more rocks, throwing them farther away. He's landing them in the forest at the far end of the lake now. He's getting a lot of fucking distance. I think he could've been a baseball player. He could have been so many things.

"They're gone," he says.

We swim toward the rocky shore. He helps me out.

I'm shaking like a leaf. I curl up on the ground, pulling my knees to my chest. It's a cool day, maybe in the fifties, hazy sun sparkling in the treetops. "We have to get warm," I say through violently chattering teeth.

He wrings out the blanket I discarded—I can't believe he had the presence of mind to grab our only blanket. He thinks of everything, knows everything that's happening at any given time. He wrings the fuck out of it.

"I'll get you warm." He picks me up and wraps us both tightly in the damp blanket. I don't know how he's walking; I don't know that I could walk on my frozen limbs. I just cling to him, arms around his neck.

He watches my eyes as he carries me, looking so fierce and strong. He's like nobody I've ever known. Not even close.

"Thank you, Kiro. I'm so sorry. If you hadn't found me..." I can't even finish the sentence. No words can capture the horror of death by stinging wasps.

This softness moves over his features—more than softness; a kind of sweetness comes over him. "I'll always come for you," he says. "Always, as long as my heart beats, I'll come for you. Protect you."

I know right then that it's true. I hold on to him tightly as something inside me unwinds, unclenches. It's something so deep, so hidden, that I wasn't even aware of it.

I'm so tired of fighting. I think I haven't relaxed since the Fancher Institute. Or maybe before that. Kabul. The hospital collapse. When did I last relax?

I'm thinking about that kitten. I'm remembering it on the street. The need to save it. The way saving it fucked everything up. The way my world crashed down. It's a familiar treadmill of thoughts that always ends in me condemning myself and hating myself for grabbing it and fucking everything up.

My life imploded the day I saved the kitten.

But a new thought creeps in. Not everything imploded. The kitten's world didn't implode. It was scared and dying. I rescued it, and I made it safe.

I hated myself for saving that kitten. Like it was the wrong thing to do. But was it so wrong? Something loosens inside me. Like maybe I forgive myself a little bit.

I catch Kiro looking down at me. "Don't worry, Ann. I will always protect you."

I stare up at him in a kind of shock. I'm like the kitten. Somebody out there cared enough to come for me. Not just anybody—this guy.

"Move your toes around."

I move my toes around.

We trek forever. Every time I go still, he chastises me to move.

Before I know it, I'm on the cold, hard ground surrounded by our stuff. He gets a fire going. He's untying my boots, big fingers moving clumsily; he's not unaffected by the cold, either. I don't want my clothes off, but I know he's right. I help him, wriggling out of my coat and stripping off my layers.

"You should, too," I say, lips still clumsy.

"I'm fine," he growls, undoing the snap of my jeans.

"I got it." I stand and wriggle out of them, stripping off my bra and panties. I sit near the fire, utterly naked, holding out my hands and feet, barely covering myself.

He's fussing with the tin cooking pot over on the other side of the fire. Is he going to make something warm to drink? It seems like a low priority. He's stirring something with a stick.

The day has become overcast, not that it matters under the thick forest canopy. "You need to get out of your clothes, too, dude."

He grunts. Well, some things are back to normal.

After a bit, he rises and walks around to my side, holding the little tin pot. He gazes down at me. I don't know what he's thinking or if he's angry or what. I suppose he should be.

"Are you getting feeling back in your toes?"

"Yeah," I say. "I'm okay. What about you?"

He crouches, stirring the pot with the stick. "I'm fine." He puts the stirring stick aside, shoves two large fingers into the tin, and dabs something cold onto the large, angry welts that cover my calf.

"Aagh!" I pull away my leg.

He clamps a hand around my ankle. "Be still!"

"What are you doing? What is that?"

"Mud," he says. "It'll draw the poison out. Soothe the pain."

The mud feels cooling, and medically speaking, he's probably right—it's a form of poultice. Probably especially effective if there's a lot of clay in there. "That's smart."

His motions are slow, big fingers gentle. How did he learn to do this? Is this what animals do when wasps sting the fuck out of them? They go into the clay?

"So many stings right here. Your calves will feel stiff for a day or two."

"My muscles already feel weird."

"Stand," he says after my calves are half-caked with mud.

I stand, and he dabs the mud onto my thighs, my ass. I'm freezing and I almost died a horrible death, but there's something weirdly sensual about him painting me like this. He stands, holding the tin. "Raise your arms."

I comply and he paints my midsection with the cooling mud, strokes slow and sure. He gets every sting. I can feel his hands trembling. He says he's fine, but he has to be freezing.

"Get those clothes off, Kiro. I can finish."

He ignores me and moves around to my back, pushing aside my hair. His touch is strangely nourishing. He dabs mud on my neck, lastly my cheek. Then he gets the dry sleeping bag and wraps it around me.

Only then does he peel off his own shirt.

I sit, covered in the sleeping bag, but keeping my toes and fingers exposed to the fire.

"Don't let it catch fire," he warns.

"I won't."

He strips off his pants. His body is shockingly covered in red. More stings than not.

"You must feel like you're on fire."

He says nothing. Yeah, he's on fire. Because of me.

He grabs the stick and stalks back over to make more of his mud stuff, his thighs and ass pale curves in the firelight, dotted with red.

He dabs the new mud stuff all over himself, smearing it on his neck and chest in the firelight. He's a warrior, ancient and fierce in the fire glow.

This shit is way beyond competence porn. It's no wonder he could beat the Fancher Institute system.

"Let me get your back."

He squints, like he doesn't entirely trust me in this.

"I *am* a nurse."

Our hands brush as he gives me the small pot. He turns.

I loop the sleeping bag around my shoulders in the chilly air, shivering as I paint the thick, cold mud over the lumps that cover his muscular back.

I finish and he turns to me. Kiro has a way of staring shamelessly into my eyes long past the point where civilized men would look away.

"What?" I ask.

He wraps the sleeping bag around me. "Sit."

"You need to be in here with me!"

His lips quirk.

"For body heat. Come on—you need to be in here. It's dangerous for you to be exposed to the air after being in that water."

And I want him with me. I want to huddle together. To hold him. To care for him the way he cared for me.

He kneels in front of me. "I'm not like you."

I don't know what he means. Is it a warning? A sad fact? He smoothes my hair, gets some tangles out, and then he sets his fingers on my chin, light as butterflies under the towering pines.

How can a man so fierce be so tender?

It's all just so surreal, us out here alone in this utterly wild place. And then a horrible thought comes to me. "My phone!"

He pulls away. This expression I can read—it's unhappiness. He hates my phone. But it's my only lifeline to…everything. Precisely why he hates it, I suppose.

"It's in my jacket pocket. I have to…" I start to peel out of the sleeping bag. The chilly air stings.

He grabs my shoulders and forces me back down. "No."

"I need it, I just need it. I need to know it works, that's all." Emotion seizes me, like a fist around my chest at the thought of losing it, this one link I have to my life. "If I could just see that it works…that's all. If it got wet, I could set it out to drain. I just need to know." Fuck, am I going to start crying about my phone?

"You no longer need your phone."

"My life is on it. Pictures. My family. My whole…" Tears heat my eyes. I feel like an idiot, but it represents everything. Not just my past, but not giving up getting away from him. Not giving up who I am.

He holds the ends of the sleeping bag tight around me. "I'll do it."

"You will?"

His brow is furrowed. It seems his need to keep me from crying is stronger than his hatred of my phone. He stands. "In the pocket?"

"Yes."

He retrieves the wet jacket.

"Carefully."

He unzips the pocket and pulls out the baggies. One piece of my phone in each.

"Is there water?"

He holds them up. There's a tiny bit of water in the bottom of one. "I should throw it in the fire."

"Please. No."

He regards it darkly. Of course he would've heard me talking to my editor. How could he not have? This is a man who knows everything that happens all around him. Fuck, he probably heard it every time I snapped a picture.

I wouldn't blame him if he stomped on it and threw it into the fire. Considering what he went through with that pack of rabid reporters.

My phone is the thing I would use to destroy him. He knows it.

"Please?"

It's such a sight, him naked with mud smeared on him like war paint. Hair tangled with it. His muscles huge, cock half-hard, or maybe that's just the size of it. He's brutally gorgeous—that's the only way to put it. Holding this phone of mine, a greater foe than the wasps.

"At least don't tip it anymore."

His scowl darkens his face and makes him look all the hotter. A man shouldn't look so beautiful when he's scowling. "Do I look like I'm tipping it?"

"No. Just...be careful."

"You want me to piece it together and turn it on?"

"No—we'll make sure it's fully dry first. Take the pieces out carefully, let the water run out of them, and set them out on rocks with the plastic housing up. You know what I mean?"

He gives me a dark look that tells me he does. He takes the pieces out like they're precious jewels and sets them on the rock, not too near the fire, but not so far. Because I want him to. Need him to.

"Your precious phone. You want to make sure it's dry and warm even before you are."

"I just need it."

He grunts as he wipes the battery and sets it out. My only connection. My only lifeline.

In a weird way, I think this phone thing is more painful to him than the wasp incident. It makes me love him a little.

"Thank you, Kiro."

He comes and stands over me, fierce and fucking glorious. "I'll always take care of you, whether you like it or not."

My blood races as he reaches down to where I hold the sleeping bag around my chest. He fits the sides together even more snugly. His abs are face level, lightly furred, but it's his cock that's consuming my attention. His cock is beautiful like him—dusky and rough, but probably soft to the touch.

He takes my hair in his fingers. He grows harder as he touches me. Harder and huger. "You should make yourself ready for me."

"Wh-what?"

"I want you to spend this time touching yourself and making yourself ready for me to fuck you instead of running this time. You understand?"

"We're back to that plan? The feeding and fucking bit?"

He regards me as if I've lost my mind. Like, what else are we going to do?

He disappears. I pull the sleeping bag around me. Is he fishing again? Were the wasps just another day at the office?

I shiver in front of the fire, surrounded by our wet things draped over trees, covered in wasp-sting-curing mud, and Kiro is down there fishing naked with his bare hands.

I'm a journalist who started life as a nurse. Not a lot of things surprise me. But Kiro does. No, scratch that—he doesn't surprise me. He fills me with awe.

I've never truly respected what he is—actually wild.

A few minutes later, he stalks back with a fish in each hand. He'll feed me, and then he'll fuck me. That's the plan here.

He crouches in front of the fire, working the fish with his knife, chopping off the head and tail and carefully slicing it in half. He places it on the grate I'd made him buy, and then he turns to me with his usual dark scowl. And I get butterflies in my stomach.

Butterflies.

"You like it cooked a great deal, I suppose," he grumbles.

"Don't you? Aren't you glad we got that grate?" I say inanely.

He crouches there, naked and powerful and gorgeous, arranging the fish over the fire.

"Right? How would you cook it otherwise?"

Casually, he shifts the fish, poking at it. He pulls up the whole network of bones and tosses it aside, then does the same for the other.

"I wouldn't cook it," he says finally.

"What?" I ask. "You'd just rip into it like a bear? Like *rarr-rarr* with your teeth?" I'm joking around.

He frowns. It's here I realize that it's precisely what he would do.

"I don't mean that like—"

There's no sound but the sizzling of the fish. "Yes, I rip into it like a bear. Very much like a bear."

I hurt his feelings. Fuck.

He twists some weedy leafs between his fingers. Seasoning the fish.

I realize the bandage I put on his shoulder gash is long gone. "I should look at your shoulder wound."

He gazes up at me like, *really?*

"I'm just saying."

"You should be making yourself ready for me under there."

"What if I don't? You can't just be like, 'I fed you, now I fuck you.'"

He studies my face, expressionless and savage. "You're mine now, Nurse Ann." He says it like this all is a concept I'm not grasping.

"Kiro—"

He turns back to his task. "If you don't make yourself ready, then I'll make you ready."

He concentrates on the fish. I can smell it cooking. It smells good. I suppose I'm hungry, somewhere deep down, but all I can do is look at his cock. Big and wild and beautiful like him.

And he's painted in mud. This beautiful, feral youth. I look at him, and I feel awe. Gratitude. Heat.

I look at him and I think, *mine*. Like he's mine.

He sets two chunks of fish to the side to cool while he cooks another two.

He goes through the same process with this piece of fish.

When he deems the fish done, he stacks the pieces on the pie-sized tin that goes in the set with the drinking tin. And stalks to me, gaze hot, massive chest rising and falling.

The fish smells unbelievably good.

"Stand."

I stand, wrapped up tightly in my sleeping bag.

He sits down on the rock I was on and simply pulls me down onto his lap, nestling me into him. My arms are pinned inside the sleeping bag. But mostly I'm aware of the stone of his cock at my ass. I squeeze my thighs together, feeling it…really a lot.

"I need my arms."

He puts his mouth to my ear. "I'll feed you."

"I can hold the fish and feed myself."

He tightens his arm around me, keeping me cocooned in. "All you have to do is stay warm."

He holds the fish with one hand and rips off a morsel. "Open."

I turn my head. "I can feed myself."

He holds the piece in midair.

"Dude, I'm not a giant doll. I can feed myself."

He puts a morsel nearer to my lips. "Open."

I hesitate, then I open. He puts it in.

I chew. It's delicious. And suddenly I want to cry. It's crazy, but I just do. Nobody ever cared for me like this. Not for years, anyway.

"What is it?" he asks softly.

"I don't know," I sniffle. "I guess I always did want to try the paleo diet."

"You joke when you're upset. Another."

He feeds me another.

"Aren't you eating?"

"I will."

I open my mouth. He feeds me.

It's most delicious fish I've ever tasted, and suddenly I'm starving. I want more, and he feeds me more, his arm an iron band around my torso. "Is it good?"

"Yes," I gasp.

He eats some himself. Grunts. He doesn't give a fuck about the food.

He feeds me more. "Nothing will hurt you as long as I'm alive."

I'm about to say he can't make that promise, but he can. He almost died saving me today. Because I belong to him, a savage in the woods.

The word "surreal" comes from French, meaning "beyond real." I never understood the full weight of the word until now. With Kiro. So surreal.

I'm a captive wrapped in a sleeping bag on the lap of a naked, half-wild man who's covered in mud. He won't let me go. He says I belong to him. He risked his life saving me today. He hunted for me, and now he's feeding me. His cock is a stone at my ass crack. It feels good. I'm thinking about the French derivation of the word surreal.

Fuck. Where am I even going with that?

He brings his lips close to my hair. His voice is deep and rumbly. "Open," he commands.

I open my mouth, and he feeds me another morsel. He watches me chew, arranging my hair around my shoulder. Because he wants to watch me eat the food he made for me. Because I belong to him.

The next piece is done. We eat it. Or more, he feeds it to me and himself. Eventually I feel full. "No more," I say when he tries to feed me another.

He continues to eat. "Are you making yourself ready for me under there?"

"Excuse me? No."

"Why not?" He sounds annoyed. "I told you I would fuck you, didn't I?"

"That's not how it works."

"You know nothing of how it works." He puts down the fish and presses a finger to my lips. I turn my head.

He grabs my hair and forces my head to turn back to him. "Suck it," he says. "Make it clean."

"I'm not your finger cleaning crew," I say.

He touches my bottom lip with his pointer finger, holding me tightly. My belly feels animated with energy. Fuck—this is not turning me on. It can't be.

He traces a finger around my lips. "Open."

I stare into his amber gaze. His dark curls are caked with mud. It's a fabulous look on him. Of course, everything's a fabulous look on Kiro. He waits patiently, fingers at my lips. He's willing to wait. He knows he's in charge here.

I keep my lips zipped, heart pounding. It's not that I don't want to let his fingers invade me. It's not that I don't want him.

I want him too much. He's too much—he's too much man, too sexy. I'm too grateful. He's too much in charge here. The balance of power is way too skewed.

He brings his face to my cheek. I stiffen. Will he bite me again? He can do anything he wants to me out here.

But instead, he presses his lips to my cheek. He kisses me softly. I didn't even think he knew how to do that—to kiss not in a bruising, wild-man way.

His voice feathers my ear with heat. "I know when you're aroused. I hear it in the tone of your voice. I see it in the way your gaze changes, as if you see everything and nothing. The taste of your skin. And your scent…"

I let out a shuddery breath.

He presses his fingers along my lips, asking for entry. "Take me, Nurse Ann."

It's the need in his voice that gets me. The need tells me he's a little out of control, too. I open.

He pushes his fingers in. "Suck."

I comply. His finger tastes mostly of…some spice. Thyme, I think. Maybe it grows wild. Maybe that's what he used to season the fish. For me. He'd eat it raw, of course. And not in that sushi way.

I feel controlled, invaded. Wildly turned on.

"Take two." He pushes in two, sliding them in, invading my mouth, exploring it, breath speeding. Then he puts in three. It's a dress rehearsal to sucking his cock—we both know it.

I imagine him holding me down and shoving his thick, dusky cock into my mouth, taking his pleasure. And I would get a hand free and squeeze him at the root and make it feel really good. Has anybody ever sucked him really nicely and made him feel good like that?

Panting, he pulls out his fingers and slides them down my neck, leaving a cool, wet trail.

He pulls the sleeping bag sides from my grasp, exposing my naked body to the cold air.

"Hey!"

He ignores my protest and explores my body tenderly, pausing at my right breast. He traces a finger around the bottom of it, lifting it slightly as he goes.

I'm quivering, a naked captive on a half shell, pulse banging like a jackhammer. His fingers are magic on me. He plays me like a strange instrument, but instead of sound, he's creating wild electricity.

The feeling is so intense, my skin feels tight. I think I can't take any more of him touching me, but I don't want him to stop.

"I smell your arousal already." He hooks his feet inside my ankles, nudging my legs apart, exposing my bare sex to the cool late-afternoon air.

My heart pounds even harder.

One hand has reached my belly. "You like when the air is on your pussy. I remember from the store. You came alive when I held you open. Do you remember?"

"Um..."

"You see that flat limestone slab over there?" he asks, touching my nipple worshipfully, reverently. The way he touches me isn't just about turning me on, though it's definitely turning me on. It's as if he needs to be touching me, sliding his hand over me, skin to skin.

"I didn't know you'd be so soft here," he says. "Your breasts are the softest things I've ever touched. And right here..." He scissors two fingers over a nipple, squeezing—hard.

I gasp at the sting of it, and he stops.

I'm panting.

"Too much?"

"Just enough!"

"Put your head back. Show your neck."

I put my head back, unsure about this move. He puts his mouth over my jugular vein, kisses me there, utterly dominating me, enjoying me.

He traces his rough fingers down my belly, lingers there.

I squirm, but he doesn't let me go. My pussy is bare to the endless wild, dark around us. Somewhere up above, the sun has come out. The forest floor is dappled with splashes of light.

"I asked you a question—the flat limestone slab, lighter than the rest. You see?"

"What about it?"

"It's a little bit warm from the fire, but not too hot. I'll hold your hair and press your cheek to that rock while I fuck you. It'll feel good on your cheek. A little rough, but it won't mark you."

I swallow.

He slides his hand to the top of my mound. My entire soul curls and unfurls from sheer anticipation. I want him in me—his fingers, his cock, his tongue, whatever he'll give me.

He slides his hand down, hitting my drippingly wet core. "You're ready for me," he whispers as he slides my juices around with two fingers.

His fingers are blunt and thick, like finger-sized caveman clubs, but he plays me like a maestro. He's a master hunter, this guy, with superhuman physical skills.

"I'm going to have to fuck you hard," he says. "I can't help it. We almost died, and something gets in me when that happens." His breath sounds a little ragged. "I'm making you very ready, though." He applies two fingers to the job of getting me off now.

The more I twist, the more tightly he holds me.

He's like one of those Japanese finger traps, tightening the more you try to escape—except in addition to tightening his hold on me, he strokes my core with more concentration, more keen resolve. More wicked technique. I twist on purpose now, enjoying his harsh hold.

"I want to enter you, Ann, and feel you tight around me." He's stroking me, panting. I'm fighting not to come, clenching my pussy, but really, that just makes the feeling more intense.

"I'm going to hold you by the hips. I'm going to hold you hard."

He's moving his fingers. Or maybe I'm moving around them.

"We almost died, and it makes me need you so much."

He removes his hand from my sex and returns to my nipples, anointing them with my juices—gently this time.

My pussy throbs with need in the cold air. "Kiro! Touch me there again," I beg. "Or let go of my hands and I'll...I make myself ready."

"*Now* you'll make yourself ready? You're already ready."

"God, yes," I gasp. "So ready."

He hauls me up by the wrists and drags me to the flat rock he'd pointed out to me.

He lowers me down to my knees, standing behind me. I'm naked in the cool air—a naked, mud-covered warrior princess, kneeling in front of Kiro.

"Put your cheek to the place I showed you. Ass in the air for me."

He doesn't wait for my compliance, or maybe he's just as crazy into the caveman thing as I am right now. He grabs my hair and forces me facedown, presses my cheek to the rock. Then he caresses my butt cheeks, like this is a new thing he wants to get into exploring. "You are so beautiful."

He holds open my butt cheeks and drags a finger up my seam. My asshole jumps and quivers as he brushes his wicked finger over it.

I nearly implode from arousal. "Kirooo..."

This pleasurable feeling spreads through me as he presses a hand to the small of my back, pressing me down. It so turns me on, I feel crazy.

Fingers of sensation move all over my skin now, even where he's not touching. My body is a topographical map of craving. I almost died today, too. And now I've never been more alive.

He jabs his fingers into my hips, positioning me for his pleasure.

I'm completely debased, this animal for him to fuck. I've never wanted it more.

I feel him position the head of his cock at my entrance, and all I can think is, *yes.* I want him to fuck me. Not just fuck me, but like this.

I feel him at my entrance, rough fingers positioning his head for me. They hit my clit, and I squeeze my pussy, trying to stave off coming. But that just makes it hotter. The feeling of him effervesces through me and he's not even inside me.

"Relax for me. Open for me," he grunts, working himself in.

My sex throbs, needing, wanting whatever he'll give me. He starts out slow, pushing, filling. Then he shoves in, slamming mercilessly into me, filling me, filling my body, filling my mind.

I can feel him all up to my eyes.

He stays deep inside me, pressed flush to me. Then he reaches around and touches me, finding my pleasure, taking it like prey.

I come, shattering in a thousand pieces. A sound tears from his throat, and he begins to move, stoking me higher, taking me higher, taking everything from me.

He comes with something between a groan and a cry. He comes forever, sliding his hands around my lower back, coming down raggedly.

CHAPTER THIRTY

Kiro

WE SET BACK out and make excellent time. I allow Ann to go without her hands bound now. I carry the canoe, and she follows me without objection.

She seems…different. I ask her what's wrong, and she says nothing's wrong. Still, she looks at me differently now. Like she's seeing new things in my face that she didn't see there before. She's a little wary of me, I think.

Having her bend in front of me and beg was the most amazing thing I ever experienced. No, being inside her was the most amazing thing. Or maybe it was just touching her. Listening to her breathe. Or having her on my lap and listening to her enjoy the way I learned her and touched her. Maybe that was the best.

It was all the best.

Several hours and many miles later, I set the canoe into the fast-moving water. I want her again already. If we didn't need to make good time, I'd stop to fuck again.

Instead we go. We're heading west for a time. The current will be with us. The water is nice and high for this time of year, thanks to a rainy summer. It's good; the trek was tiring. I still feel the poison of the wasp stings in my body, though the mud I found was good. Light in color, best for stings.

In the boat I ask her about her life growing up. I want to know everything about her.

She tells me about walking to school. 'A shitty little school,' she calls it. Her face softens. Stories relax her.

She went to high school, which I didn't do—I stopped in third grade. She tells me about high school. She studied subjects I don't even recognize.

She assures me that I'm as smart as anyone who attended high school, but I know my knowledge isn't the same.

I ask her about one thing I've really been wondering about—the kitten.

"I don't talk about the kitten," she says.

The kitten experience wounded her somehow. She doesn't trust me enough to tell me. I wait, but she doesn't relent.

I die a little to realize she doesn't trust me, still. But why should she? I'm her captor. I tied her up and carried her. It was wrong to do that—so wrong. I always hated when it was done to me. I can't do it again—I won't. I'll find other ways to make her come with me.

I ask her about her sister and her parents. She enjoyed family dinners instead of dreading them like I did. She told her parents things that were important to her instead of hiding them like I did, for fear they'd be somehow destroyed or taken away. She loves her sister, too. She talks about how proud she is of her sister, the actress in Hollywood.

I listen, seized with so many emotions, I can barely paddle. This is what the people on TV have—their families love them, and they love them back. They want to see each other and tell each other things. Help each other.

I would have loved such a family.

Is this what I'm taking away from Ann?

I try not to think about it. I'll make her happy—I know I can.

Sometimes she pauses and stares up at the trees, and I know she thinks it's beautiful. It gives me hope that I can make her happy. I have to make her happy. I don't want to be without her.

We make good time. We stay overnight on another island. I bend her over and fuck her after she's good and ready, which means begging. I decide to only fuck her if she begs me. She seems to like that best.

We share the sleeping bag. I want to be near her, but I also need to know if she gets up.

The next morning, we push off the shore, under the shadow of towering rocks. She sits on the seat in front of me, facing forward—away from me. She seems to want her own space at times.

I allow it.

She won't jump out because of the icy water—I'm sure she had more than enough of swimming out here, and the water is even colder now, being that we're getting farther north.

I imagine her paddling around on her own someday and coming back to me—not because she can't survive or doesn't know her way home, but because she wants to be by my side. It's a dangerous thought, yet I can't help but have it. I want so badly to trust her, to think she's my partner, my ally, my pack, like when we were back at the institute.

Back then she felt like a true ally. A true friend. So much more.

I paddle us forward, under soaring rocks and trees. With the current behind us, it feels like we're flying.

Three days until we get there. On my own I could make it in two.

My heart pounds when I think about seeing my pack again. They're not the original ones I met: they're more. These are the wolves I grew up with. I describe each one to Ann and tell her their names. I tell her exactly how they'll greet me in exactly what order.

First Red will leap on me, nip at me. My closest friend, like a brother. Pack leader by the time I left. I'll grab his scruff, gray and black, a slash of reddish fur along his back. And Snowy. Wild and playful. She'll come next.

I tell Ann about the different things they do. Like snapping—they're not trying to bite you; it's just about making that sound with their teeth to warn you off. Or when they bow, chin near the ground, eyes up. It means they want to play.

Red and Snowy and I were a unit in the pack. They stayed with me when I was injured and couldn't move. They slept with me and protected me from unfriendly wolves. They only ran when the campers came with guns. My heart pounds to think of seeing them again.

Now and then I hear other wolves howling. Not mine—we're deep into another pack's area. But soon. Every smell feels like home. Like family.

I can almost feel Red's rough scruff in my fingers, the cool wetness of his nose.

They'll accept Ann if she's with me. I'll keep a close watch until I know things are right.

"Wait," she says. "Where's that keychain? Wait." She pulls it out of the pack and examines it. "This is like your friend. Red. The reddish back. Is that why you like it? Because it looks like him?"

"Yeah. But I don't need that thing anymore."

She beams at me. "You're going home to your family. You so can't wait to see them."

"I so can't wait," I say.

She smiles. She smiles when I say things the way she does.

She wears her brown hair in a braid, exposing her pale neck. I think she's more beautiful than anything out here. More beautiful and still more painful.

She could have died so easily. She would only have had to swallow one wasp.

She's paying attention to her surroundings, memorizing the way back. I hate that she's doing it.

"Until you're really used to this wilderness, all the trees and rocks look the same."

"We'll see."

I put extra muscle into my strokes, as though I can glide over her words, hating her, hating this. I'm in utter control of her out here, so why do I feel so helpless? I want to fuck her again so badly, I can't think straight.

"Don't worry, I'm not planning on running off and stepping in another wasp nest if that's what you're worried about."

In truth, I'm worried about everything.

"But I am going to leave. And I'm going to find out your story—not your forest story—that's yours, and I won't invade it. But Kiro, your story with the mafia. What the fuck. I can't stop thinking about it. No matter how deep we go, I feel like it's dangerous. Have you ever heard the saying 'you can't run forever'?"

I sigh, weary of the story talk.

"I get it, you don't trust me quite yet. But you should trust my journalistic instincts. I wish you knew I only ever wanted to help you."

The emotion in her hits me. She really wants me to believe it.

"Anyways, the point is, you don't have your power until you know your story. More knowledge is always best. More light is always safer. If I were you, I'd do anything to understand what the fuck was happening."

"Knowing my story won't stop them from hunting me. My story isn't the reason—"

"Yeah, yeah, yeah. They hunt you because you're different." Her eyes shine. "It's such total fucking *bullshit*."

Her ferocity takes my breath away.

"You are being hunted, and you have no idea why. I know you think it's because you're different, but trust me—you're wrong."

She sounds so sure of herself. I love her like this. "So you say."

"So I know! They know your name from before you were adopted—this name of yours. Kiro. Why do they need to kill you so badly? I can't believe it's not driving you crazy. Because it's definitely driving me crazy."

The moon has risen, a circle in the sky, a pale, shimmering splotch on the water.

"I get that you hate that I'm a journalist, but guess what? I know when there's something big. I have instincts. I can't recognize one pile of rocks from another—it's true. But you don't know shit about stories. Light is better than darkness. Knowledge is better than ignorance. It's true for you just like it's true for everyone else. You think you're so fucking different."

"You don't understand. You can't understand unless you're me."

"Ugh!" She flops back, frustrated. I want to kiss her, but I think she wouldn't like it right now.

We enter a narrow stretch of river. Familiar bird sounds echo in the trees—night birds, starting to hunt. The terrain rolls out like a map in my heart.

I close my eyes and imagine the howls of my pack, each voice utterly distinct. I imagine the relief of hearing them and calling back. I imagine falling into them.

My heart hammers. Even Ann wants to get away from me, but Red never wanted to get away. Snowy never wanted to get away.

"Why did the wasps go after me?" she asks after a while.

"Because you stepped on their hive. You became a threat," I explain, surprised she doesn't understand something so obvious.

"Maybe they attacked me because I'm a human."

"They would only bother to attack you if they saw you as a threat."

"Maybe they didn't like me because I'm different."

I growl. The professor used to do what she's doing—questions and answers designed to teach me things. "Talk to me normal, or don't talk to me at all."

"You need to ask the question, Kiro. Why are you a threat to the mob? You're clearly not after them, so why is your very existence a threat?"

I push us on forward. There was an island near here. Always so much better to stop on an island for the night. I'm hard already thinking about her.

"You have to ask the right questions to get the story."

"The professor used to say, 'If all you have is a hammer, everything looks like a nail.' You're a reporter. All you think about is a story. Everything is the story. Let them come after me. If they get too close, I'll rip their throats out."

She continues on, undeterred. "It costs thousands of dollars a day for a mob boss to have soldiers after somebody. And to send them on trips like what they did? There's a big reason they want you dead. I've been thinking about it. You have either power or people."

The island comes into view. I point. "We'll stop up there."

We pull up the canoe. She unpacks while I make a fire.

"You could have assets of some sort that you don't know about. I wonder if that's it," she says.

"I'm tired of this talk."

"I'm not. The more I ponder, the more my money is on family. You have a family. A true family. Maybe your enemies want to hurt this family or usurp some territory…"

"I have a true family. The wolves are my family."

She sits and warms her hands near the fire. "You're not a wolf."

Not a wolf. Not a man.

I take her hair in my hand and pull her up. I put my lips to her ear. "The wolves are my true family. And you're my mate, so they're officially your family now, too."

"Repeating it a lot doesn't make it true."

I jerk her softly, to remind her who is in control. Her pulse begins to hammer in her throat. "You're mine to feed. Mine to care for." I'll smell her arousal soon. "Mine to fuck," I breathe into her ear.

The moon catches her hair, giving it a soft glow.

"Mine to make come."

"You can make me come," she says breathlessly. "Congratulations. You think that makes us mates? A relationship is mutual. It's about mutual trust and respect of what the other one knows and says."

Miserably, I twist her hair, wondering if there is some man out there she has that with. Mutual trust and respect. Love. A man who's not a savage.

"Like a fucking caveman. You don't even know—"

I jerk her hair to stop her from talking, feeling so hopeless. She wants to leave and figure out my story. I know how to make her stay, but I don't know how to make her *want* to stay.

She looks up at me, all fire and defiance. I don't know how to behave like one of the civilized men she prefers, but I know how to make her beg.

So I do it—I make her beg, and then I put her on her hands and knees and fuck her, lose myself in her warmth and softness.

Afterward, she collapses on her back and stares at the sky, sated. "Kiro. Fuck."

"What is it?"

She says nothing.

"Maybe you're hungry. I'll get us food."

"Yeah, that must be it. Great sex and food. That's all I need."

I go to catch fish.

When I get back, she's riffled through our things. Looking for her phone. She didn't find it; it's in my pocket, along with the wolf keychain.

I cook the fish, and we eat in silence.

The meal is good, and there are roasted hickory nuts and berries, too. "You're still unhappy," I say.

"There's a shocker. You fed me, and I'm not happy. Maybe I'm not a pet hamster."

I frown. Everything with her hurts.

"Can I have my phone?"

"No."

"I'm not going to call anybody. It's not like I can get a signal out here. I just want to see if it still works."

"Something tells me not to," I say.

"You can watch me. You'll see the little bars not firing up."

I don't know how the phones work. What if she signals somebody? But the phone would make her happy—I know that. I can't let her go, but I can give her the phone.

"I promise," she says.

She's a reporter, my natural enemy, as much as she says she isn't. I can't see how it can be otherwise. She doesn't trust me—not even enough to tell me the secret of the kitten.

But then she turns her pleading eyes to me and my heart melts.

I want to make her happy.

I force myself to hand the plastic bag to her.

"Thank you."

My pulse drums in my ears as she takes the parts out of the baggies and fits them together. She moves over on the log and pats it. "Come here. You can see."

I sit. The thing is just a black rectangle. She presses something. Nothing happens. "Please, please, please," she whispers to her phone.

A white apple appears. "Yaasssss." She turns to me. "Thank you. Thank you for trusting me."

Something warms in my heart.

"I know it wasn't easy," she says.

"It was worth it." I catch a brown curl in my finger. I watch her watch her phone. I enjoy making her happy.

"Look," she says. "There's my dog. Bernard."

I look down at a large black and brown and white dog with a boxy nose. He has a stick in his mouth.

"Bernard?"

"He was a St. Bernard dog. Big. Friendly. He was…such a good dog."

She flicks the photos by, one by one. She stops on another one with her and Bernard. Bernard's licking her face. She's smiling, laughing.

She flips on and stops at an image of her with an older couple. "My mom and dad. That's our porch. Ten years ago. And here's me and my sister, Maya."

She shows me the house where she grew up. She shows me herself standing next to a dusty Jeep in front of a sign that has strange squiggly writing on it. Then her and four smiling men crowded around a table, all holding tall glasses with leaves stuffed into them. "That's a café in Beirut," she says. "We drank a lot of mint tea there." The men are all journalists like her, doing pieces, she says. She shows me a picture of the desert. She stands next to a camel.

I sneak glances at her face as she moves through the photos. She seems so alive when she looks back on this life of hers.

This is how she looks when she's happy, I think with a start. A way she's never been with me. A way she might never be again. Because I've taken her away from her life.

I bite back the despair.

CHAPTER THIRTY-ONE

Tanechka

VIKTOR GLANCES OVER at me from the front seat of the car. He's not used to me dressing as a nun. I'm sure he hoped I never would again. But this outfit will help us get close to the man who can give us information on Kiro. We hope.

It is very much like old times in Moscow when we worked as assassins together. Waiting outside a man's home. Two hours we have been out here, but the man will come now—we both have the sense of that. We share the sense of it.

It feels good.

"Soon," I say.

He doesn't smile, but small dimples appear on his cheeks. Something that comes before a smile. A flash of happiness, I suppose you would call it.

I feel it too.

We're together again. Dangerous like old times. We'll find his brother.

This man we pursue—this Gregor—is a Russian mob techie who defected to Lazarus, and he's quite religious. I know how to move like a nun. How to speak like a nun. He'll be easy to fool.

We have to take him off the street and make him help us get ears on Lazarus—that's how Viktor's brother Aleksio likes to put it. Get ears on a man. Hack into his communications.

Somehow, they're tracking Kiro. We need to know everything.

Lazarus isn't a stupid man. Kiro beat him once at the insane asylum. The next time Lazarus goes at Kiro, it will be with an army. Aleksio thinks he's already chasing him.

I feel as fierce about finding Kiro as Viktor does. As Aleksio does. I want to find him as if he's my own brother. He will be once Viktor and I are married.

Viktor passes me a pear. "If he comes with more than one, I'm going out with you."

"There will be no killing, *pryanichek*." I slice off the fat side of the fruit. "If there are more than one, I'll handle them all, and if you come out with me when I don't need you, I'll put you back in the hospital, perhaps right next to them."

"I've never wanted to fuck you more than right now, Tanechka."

I hand him over a slice and smile. I will very much like him to fuck me.

"I'm not letting you fight a group," he says.

"I tire of this discussion." The plan is for me to separate Gregor from the herd. "This one respects nuns. His friends too." I slice off another bit of pear. I hold his eyes and slip it into my mouth. With this I make him think many things.

I no longer strive to be a nun. I can't be true to Jesus in my body like a nun should. And there were my years of being an assassin; it was easier to aspire to be a nun when I didn't remember those years. But still Jesus is in my heart. Viktor doesn't understand, but it's okay.

My love of Viktor is deeper than it ever was. My concentration is deeper. Even my aim is better. Things are better now that I have this peace.

Viktor and I have made a new home together. The home Viktor made for us before was very much a museum of our old life. I'm glad it burned. Our new home has things from our new life in America, like a giant painting of a fish from IKEA. We have named it "Guppy."

They let him out of the hospital four weeks back. Gunshot wounds to his midsection. It was mostly his spleen. He hides his pain. He's not supposed to move around violently. A difficult thing to enforce.

A car slides by—too slowly. Our intelligence is that Gregor will walk home from his dinner at the restaurant, but the car doesn't move right. We both mark it. A minute later we both ignore it. Texting.

"I should shoot his phone from his hand," he says.

I slide my gaze to the side mirror. A group of three men. One of them Gregor. "Hey."

"Gotcha."

I shoot Viktor a warning look. "No killing." He puts up his hands in pretend self-defense as I slide out, prayer rope in one hand, switchblade in the other.

I wander up the street, appearing lost.

Gregor needs to approach me. This is the hard part, what to do if one of the others approaches me instead.

I make eye contact with Gregor, willing him.

He addresses me in Russian. "Sister? Can I help you?"

I clutch my rope, so humble. I move in a way that he recognizes, a way that is deeply familiar to his bones. He reads me as real. This is something the sisters gave me when I had amnesia.

"It's okay," he says in Russian to the other guys. He flicks his fingers, an order to stay back. "It's okay."

I go to him and show him my map.

"Let's see now," he says.

Out comes the blade. "My pika is two inches from your beating heart. It is not good."

He stares at me, mouth agape. He thought I was real.

I am real. Not in the way he thinks, perhaps. "You will tell them to leave you. You're troubled. You want to talk to the mother alone. You will walk me back alone. Tell them this."

He complies, telling the men he'd like to walk me to the address I seek. "Go on without me."

The men amble away. There is no trickery—they really are leaving.

"That is good. Maybe you will live."

"Did Dmitri send you?"

I smile a small smile. "I'm with Viktor." My heart swells as I say this.

Gregor, however, goes white. As he should. Viktor Dragusha is crazy—everyone knows it.

"Help us and you won't die," I tell him. We walk down the street and around the corner, and then another. Viktor drives up, and I shove Gregor in and get in.

We'll get a lot out of this one, I can tell. I pray he can lead us to Lazarus, to Kiro.

Kiro has no idea what's coming at him.

CHAPTER THIRTY-TWO

Ann

WE SHARE A sleeping bag again. I wake up first and watch him sleep. It's nice. I feel safe next to his big, warm body and I wish he was awake. I want to talk with him and hang out with him. Joke with him. Fuck him.

Not that I don't want to get away. I have to get away—there's no other rational choice, right? But still...

I don't just feel safe with him, I feel relaxed in a way I haven't for a long time, and I'm finally caught up on my sleep. Trapped out here with Kiro, exactly where I don't want to be, I feel...almost human.

And I don't have nightmares of the kitten anymore. I still have nightmares, but they're of the collapsed hospital. Which actually *was* nightmarish. It always seemed suspicious that I freaked about the kitten and not about being trapped in that hospital.

Like maybe my mind has decided it's strong and safe enough now to freak out about something that was actually scary. Out here in the peace and quiet.

With Kiro.

I reach out and smooth a beard hair, getting it into place alongside the others. He's a beautiful study in browns. His wasp stings are still visible as lumps along one cheekbone, but they only seem to accentuate his rugged hot-guy looks.

Him giving me the phone was huge. He doesn't trust technology, but he trusted me. I wish he'd trust me about his story. He needs to know what's going on out there.

Little furrows appear on the insides of his eyebrows, then they disappear.

Softly I whisper, "Are you awake?"

The side of his mouth quirks.

I press my finger to his lips. "Freak."

He keeps his eyes closed.

I touch his chin.

He grabs my wrist.

I laugh, surprised, and something softens in his face, as though he likes the sound. Hearing is everything to him. He opens his eyes.

"Take a picture, it might last longer," I joke.

He furrows his brow, like he does when he doesn't quite understand something.

Suddenly everything that was soft and beautiful in him goes hard and feral. He tightens his hold on my wrist. His gaze shifts to the side.

He hears something.

All I hear is the wind in the treetops. "What—"

"Shhh." He sniffs the air.

"Ow."

"They're here."

"Who?"

He glares at me.

"What?"

"You alerted somebody. With your phone."

"I didn't alert anybody! There was no signal. We're not near anything—"

"There's no way anyone could've tracked us. It had to be your phone."

"I didn't alert anyone. I swear—"

He sucks in a breath. "They're the ones from before. They'd kill you as easily as they'd kill me. Why would you signal them?"

"I didn't! I wouldn't—I don't even have anyone to alert."

He studies my eyes. He wants to believe me. Finally he takes my hand and pulls me up and away from the small encampment. Maybe he half-believes me.

"You won't call out to them if you know what's good for you."

"Why would I? What's happening?"

He regards me warily. "We have to get off the island." He pulls me across to the far, swampy edge. We're surrounded by cattails and scrubby willows.

He listens. I still don't hear anything, but from the way he moves his head, I can tell he hears and smells things. Maybe he's even zeroing in on the location. Because Kiro is fucking magic.

"Take off your boots."

"Excuse me? Should we get the canoe?"

"So they can see where we are?" He points across the channel to the woods.

He wants us to muck out there and swim for it.

"No," I say. "Fuck no."

He turns to me, glowering. "Do I need to drag you?"

I swallow, knowing he would. I gather myself. If he says they're here, they're here. I untie my boots and step out of them, sinking even deeper into the freezing muck. "Let's go."

He points. "My footsteps."

I follow him out, sinking knee-deep in the cold, slimy muck, holding my boots above my head until we hit clear water. Kiro's in bare feet, of course. He's been going more and more without his boots, like he's reverting back to his wild self the deeper we go.

I swim quietly after him through the painfully freezing water, copying his movements, staying quiet, aware. There's more muck on the other side. I'm chattering my teeth off.

We trudge up to the shore. I follow him in. The terrain hurts my feet. "Wait. Let me put on my boots."

"No time." He picks me up, carrying me through the woods—fast. He doesn't quite follow a straight line; he seems to choose his course by the terrain, and he gets some serious loft as he goes, his movements more animal than human.

He slows at the base of a huge pine tree, looks up, then goes to another and another, and then he stops.

"What the hell, Kiro?"

He puts me down. "You'll climb."

"What?"

"There's no time."

I feel the blood drain from my face. He senses danger. Whether he trusts me or no, he senses that the danger extends to me.

"Maybe I can help you."

"I'll fight better if I know you're safe. I won't have to listen for you."

"How do you know I can't help?"

"I know. Please," he grates.

It's so unusual for him not to simply issue a command that I'm taken off guard.

"Let me see you get up there. High up. You're safe up there—nobody will look up there, nobody will shoot up there. Wait for me to call to you. If I don't call…don't trust the silence. Stay. Wait it out."

I rest my palm on his beard. "Okay." I mean the touch as a comforting gesture, but there's a tightness in his brow; it seems almost to hurt him more than anything. Like my kindness hurts him.

And I realize something about him: This is a man who doesn't know what to do with kindness.

Kiro knows what do when people hate him. He knows about being hunted and trapped and confined and beaten. But he's never known kindness.

He's never thought to expect anything like that from me. Why should he?

It makes me want to put my arms around him and pull him to me. I want to tell him he's amazing and fierce and brave, and surprising all the time. I want to tell him he deserves kindness. That he's worthy of love.

Very worthy of love. My heart pounds. "Kiro."

"Please." He hoists me up to the lowest branch. Kiro needs me to do this now. I catch the branch and scramble up, shivering, channeling my inner monkey, making sure not to look at the ground.

Up, up I climb. My hand slips at one point, but I catch myself on my arm and keep going. I find a place that's good and high. I cling to a branch, waiting, hoping he doesn't think it's me who alerted them.

I peer down through the branches. My vision of the forest floor is mostly obstructed by tree limbs, but I can see stretches here and there. I don't see Kiro. But I'm thinking he's made himself invisible, hunting in the shadows.

Kiro. Caring for me. Feeding me. Protecting me. I tell him that's not how it works, but it's more than anyone else has done for me for a long time.

He suspects I signalled for them to come, but he protects me anyway. He made a vow.

I wait for forever, thinking about what it must have been like for him, a boy, really and truly alone. Maybe hiding in trees just like this, frightened of what roamed below. Trying to make sense of the world. Always on the outside looking in.

Kind of like me—alone, always watching. Peering in from the outside at other people's stories, but never a part of them. Living life, really, in service to other people's stories.

And when you fall apart, nobody is there.

I try to think how anybody could track us so deep into the forest. Kiro thinks the phone is the only way, but...

A sick feeling comes over me. My editor, Murray, sent over that phone.

Fuck.

Did he put something in there? He'd know I'd disable the GPS if I didn't want to be found, but could there be a tracker? Fuck. Of course. Activated by firing up the battery, I'm guessing. It would have to be, way out here. A small enough one to fit into the phone, anyway.

Fuck!

How could I be so stupid? Murray's motivated by money. Once I took control of the story, it was less scintillating. Less exploitative. Much less valuable to him. The Albanian mob would pay way better.

Kiro's right—I alerted them. He knows it was me, and still he tries to keep me safe.

I need to explain, but not now.

I track the shadows of the branches on the forest floor, watching them move. I suppose it would be a way of marking time if I knew anything whatsoever.

The shadows move a good long while before I hear the vehicle. No—two vehicles. Maybe more. ATVs? How did they get them here—choppers? Motorized boats? Motorized vehicles aren't legal in this wilderness area, but then again, neither is the hunting of humans.

The faint timbre of male voices carries through on the breeze.

I make myself small. Still. The canoe is back at the island—that's where they'll look for us. I suppose it gives Kiro the opportunity to observe them.

The breeze shifts, and the talking fades. How many?

Shouts, then nothing.

I wait a while longer. I hear rustles now and then, but that may be animals. Or Kiro.

A voice is raised. They're calling a name. There's confusion. Something's happening. I squeeze my eyes shut.

Kiro. Please be okay.

A sharp blast rips the silence. A gunshot. Another.

Craaack-craaack-craaack.

I smash my palms over my ears, a vice grip that does nothing to muffle the blasts of semiautomatic weaponry. The firing intensifies. I imagine them strafing the woods.

I hold on to my head, like if I cringe hard enough, I'll keep out the guns, keep Kiro safe.

My legs are looped around the branch so hard, I think I'll never pry them off. The shooting seems to go on forever.

And then it stops.

I grip the branch and listen. The wind shifts.

Nothing.

I press my forehead to the rough bark, willing for Kiro to be okay. The idea of a world without Kiro seems...unbearable.

The shooting starts up again. I clap my hands around my ears again. I tell myself it's good they're still shooting—it means Kiro's alive. A threat to them. But then, one bullet could end him, so how is that good?

Footsteps underneath me. I stiffen as I see guys in camo with South African street sweepers pass below. You get to know the makes of assault weapons out in the hot zones. You need those details for your pieces. The men down there are being stealthy, which I suppose is a good sign. It means they're scared. Another group goes past.

One man follows them from a distance; he turns now and then to walk backwards. There's a slight movement to his side—I see a flash. Hear a soft *oof*.

Rustling. *Snap*. That's a bone breaking.

I stretch to the side and catch sight of Kiro, face bloody, rising from the broken heap that was the man. Kiro wipes his eyes again and again. A cut on his brow is bleeding into his eyes.

Head wounds bleed like a motherfucker, even when they're not serious. A head wound. Does he have a concussion? At the very least, it's fucking up his vision.

He can't fight if he can't see!

He's gone in a flash. I hear more commotion. Somebody goes down. There's a shot. Yelling. The guttural cry of a man dying. Frightened voices.

Kiro's out there, hunting and killing them one by one. One unarmed guy against dozens of armed men.

Awe shudders through me. Kiro.

I want to help him, but I need to trust what he told me—that I'm more of a help if he doesn't have to worry about me. I rub my thumb over a little rough patch of bark.

More of the men pass under me. They're talking about his bloody face. They sound confused, like there's something they don't understand.

I hear the words "Savage hearing...how he's doing it?...fucker doesn't need to see..."

Of course. Kiro's tracking them through sound and probably scent.

His words trail off. Suddenly a shrieking alarm pierces the air. A key fob alarm.

No! He won't hear them coming now.

I panic, clinging to my branch. There are more shots. Yelling. I'm really torn about going down there, now. Suddenly it all stops.

Utter silence.

Movement below. "Ann."

"Kiro?"

"It's okay."

I scramble down into his arms. His shirt is off, tied around his head to stanch the flow of blood.

"Are you okay?"

He touches his forehead. "A scratch."

"You're bleeding. You might need stitches."

"I'm fine. Unlike your friends."

"I didn't signal them. I figured it out, Kiro—I got played."

Warily, he searches my eyes. "You put your phone on, and it brought them."

"But I didn't mean to. I thought it was okay, but my editor who sent my phone put something on it that I didn't know about. I swear I didn't know. I was fooled..."

I trail off. The hopelessness in his face is fucking killing me.

It's all just words, and Kiro doesn't care about words. My actions make me a liar. I brought them. I said it wouldn't happen, but it did. "Kiro," I plead.

"We should get the canoe and go." He takes my arm and leads me to a tree at the shoreline. The canoe is still there, across the stream. "I'll get it. You'll wait here."

"I don't get it. You don't trust me, you think I'd send people after us like that, but you want me to stay with you?"

"You're my mate." He reaches out to take my hair in two bunches, like two ponytails, and pulls me to his chest. He kisses the top of my head. I think he's relieved I'm okay. He pulls away. "We have to go."

Fuck.

He never expected anything better from me. He doesn't think to ask for more for himself. Not trust, not affection. Certainly not love.

I look up into his beautiful, bloody, bee-stung face. The world sees a savage, but I see a man so achingly alone that he'll have me even if he can't trust me.

It breaks my heart.

I slide my thumb along his cheekbone. "You have blood here," I whisper. I urge him to the water's edge. "Come here."

He comes with me. I pull the shirt from his head and bend over to dip a corner of it in the water and clean his face. He stands still as I do it, eyes shut. It's as if he doesn't want to scare me off from this small act of caring.

I inspect the cut on his forehead. It's small. Only an overzealous doctor would stitch it.

"It looks okay," I say.

I wet the cloth in the river and use it to clean his face a bit more. He sucks in a breath as I swipe a bit of mud off his chest. So many scars. I find I want to kiss the scars of this beautiful, wounded, savage boy who thinks he's not worth loving.

I scrub a little harder. I can feel the enjoyment in him. I love the enjoyment in him. I love caring for him like this. Being a team.

"We have rubbing alcohol in the first-aid kit. That would be good for your head."

He nods.

Words mean nothing to him; he said as much before. But my caring for him means something. My giving a shit that he has blood and mud on him means something.

Nobody ever gave a shit about him. Maybe that's why he felt so fiercely toward me in the institute. It probably seemed like I was acting as his mate.

"Close your eyes." I wet the cloth again and clean a streak of mud from his temple. A warm glow spreads in my chest, lighting dark corners, like tendrils of warmth and light, connecting the disconnected cold, dark bits that I had hidden away.

I press my other hand to his cheek, but this isn't a clinical touch at all. It's affection. It's me not getting enough of Kiro. It's me maybe never getting enough of Kiro.

He opens his eyes.

"Didn't I tell you to close your eyes?"

He closes his eyes. "Yes, Nurse Ann."

I slide my hand across his whiskers. The warmth spreads deeper, hotter.

My wild affection for him exists the way a mountain does—it's just there, damn everything else.

"We should move on," he rasps.

I touch the spot next to his eye. And then I get up on tiptoes and kiss his nose.

His eyes fly open, a bolt into my soul. I slide my palms over his arms and chest, dirty and sweaty.

I kneel and dip the cloth into the water and clean him some more. I want to clean him. I want to do everything for him. This is Kiro's language. His pulse thrums in his neck. I slide my hand over his neck, feeling the way desire builds in him. In me.

I want to do everything for him.

My eyes rest on his cock, hard through his pants. I press my palm over him. He hisses out a breath. Maybe he's hard from the fight, maybe from the way I'm caring for him, or just the kiss.

I kneel before him and put my face to the place where the bulge strains most tightly against the rough canvas of his pants. His cock jumps under the fabric.

I turn my eyes up to him. He's watching me, half-wild. Words mean nothing, but actions mean everything to him. I set aside the shirt and hold his gaze as I unsnap his pants. I shove them down, partway down his legs.

His chest heaves.

Panting.

I'm stricken with awe at the sheer wildness of him, hair tangled and dirty from battle, breath heaving in and out. He's like a medieval warlord, nostrils flaring with every breath.

"Ann," he grates out.

I wrap my hand around his cock, wild and beautiful and foreboding as he is. His hand goes to my hair. I hold him around the root, barely fitting my fingers around his massive girth. I set my lips on his head, licking off the gleaming droplet at the end.

He strokes my hair, breathing ragged. His clumsy movements tell me he's as turned on as I am.

I wet him with my lips, take in more of him, sucking, squeezing. He tastes of salt and sweat and man. He tightens his hand in my hair and begins to move, fucking my mouth gently.

I squeeze him and jack him off as I suck. I know the hand feels good, but it's also a little bit of self-preservation—a stopper from him shoving his crazy Kiro hugeness all the way down my throat.

His hand snags on my hair. He's covered in sweat and the dirt of battle. I love him like this. I want him to make me dirty.

I look up into his face as I suck him. I show him by my actions that I'm with him. It makes no sense to my brain, but utter sense to my heart. The affection I have for him is strange and real and true. Does he feel it?

He makes a little sound, eyes glued to mine, fixed on mine.

He's all I see. All I hear. Until the explosion rips out from behind me. I pull my lips off him and turn.

A man on the ground. With a gun—pointed up at Kiro.

Hands clap down on my shoulders. A heavy weight. I turn and meet Kiro's eyes. My first thought is that he's unhappy I disengaged.

Then I see it—his eyes awash in pain. Shock. Accusation. Blood drips down the side of his neck.

"No!" I burst up to steady him.

Blood flows from the side of his head—a wound in the side of his head. That man just shot him.

"Oh my God! No!" I get him to the ground. I kneel at his side. There's so much blood. "Kiro!" My hands shake as I wipe away the blood. Shot in the head.

A noise right behind us. I look around. The bloody man is on his belly, gun shaking in his hand. He's going to shoot Kiro again, or at least try.

I go to him and slam my boot down onto his wrist. There's *craaaack* as he releases the gun. He's pale. Sweating. Respiration failing. Lots of blood on his shirt.

He's alive but bleeding out. "Help me," he says.

He has the look of a man beyond help. It would probably be best to kill him.

I take his gun instead and rush back to Kiro.

"Kiro, stay with me!" I brush his hair back with shaking hands, trying to assess the wound, keeping the man's gun by my side, alert for any movement, any sound.

He's losing consciousness.

I dab at it and determine that the bullet didn't go through. It grazed his head. I heave a sigh of relief, though a bullet doesn't have to go in to do a hell of a lot of damage. It's a blow to the head, just like a baseball bat could do.

He's mumbling.

"Stay still." I tie a makeshift bandage around his head like a headband, then I tear off my jacket and tuck it around him. I pull his pants back up and tuck his cock back in and button him up.

A rustling sound. I grab the gun and stand. The one who shot us stares sightlessly at the sky. I watch him for a while, just to make sure he's not faking it. I'll shoot him if I have to.

More rustling—from another direction.

I back up to the shadow side of the tree.

A squirrel.

Deep breath.

I go back to Kiro. He tries to get up, then sits back down. Dizzy.

"You're okay, you just need to keep still."

Except this is a dangerous place to stay. Dead men all around. Are they all even dead? More could just be injured.

I examine the gun in my hand. I've had firearms training, but I've never shot anybody who wasn't made of paper. That'll change if anyone else goes after Kiro.

Think, think.

I turn my senses to our surroundings. Handle immediate danger first—that's the rule at times like this. I creep around, find another body. Another. One that looks alive until I toe him and see the amount of blood that's run out of his mouth.

I spot a pack near a tree and go to it, carefully, like something might jump out.

There's some kind of radio walkie-talkie device in the outer pocket. Inside a small Styrofoam pack are several baggies of dried food and beef jerky. Money, first aid, two guns. I hear the voice—faint. *Hello? Come in.*

It's coming from the radio walkie-talkie thing. The connection is open.

I put down the pack and take it out, holding it like it's alive, like it might bite me.

Come in, motherfuckers, the voice says.

Nothing.

Who's out there? We're fifteen minutes out. Keep your lines open—we have your location. You copy? You out there?

I stare at the thing.

Last time I send boys to do a man's job, another voice snarls.

Fifteen minutes. Keep the line open. Can I get to the canoe and get us out of here in under fifteen minutes?

Then I get an idea. I open the pack and take out the Styrofoam. I break it up and shove the walkie-talkie in a baggie and wrap the thing up with medical tape. I run to the nearby river and set it off.

I collect a few other walkie-talkies and quickly do the same thing. Then I set my phone off in its own Styrofoam raft. My whole fucking life.

I hear the drone of engines in the distance, but it could be my imagination.

I check Kiro again. Groggy. "You can't fall asleep."

He grumbles. He's really dazed.

I take off my boots and jump into the freezing water, cursing and swimming madly for the canoe. I stuff our things into it, but I don't even get into it, I just turn and swim it back. I pull it up onto shore and urge Kiro in.

I should really be keeping him still, but we have to get the fuck out.

This might be a shit plan, but it's my plan, and I'm not second-guessing it. I get in and shove us off.

I take a quick look downstream—none of my Styrofoam vessels are around, none caught on the rocks or reeds. Hopefully that's what's making the signal. Hopefully the mob guys will follow it and not us.

Okay.

I start paddling upstream, keeping to the shady west side of the shore. It will be dark soon.

Kiro's watching me. He's trying to focus. "Ann," he says. "Was I out?"

"A little. How do you feel?"

He doesn't answer. Just squints around.

"Kiro? Tell me how you feel."

"Dizzy," he says. "Like a hammer is inside my brain."

A bullet graze can be a serious head trauma. "What else? How's your eyesight? Move your feet."

He complies.

"Looks like systems online. But you probably have a hell of a concussion."

He grasps the sides of the canoe, squinting around. "Where are we?"

"I don't know. But being that I'm a way faster paddler than you are, we may be all the way to Canada. Possibly Alaska. What do you think?"

Nothing. I need to get him talking, get a sense of how he is.

"What do you think?" I ask.

"I think you're a good mate."

I keep us going, around one bend and then another. I go for an hour, getting him to answer stupid little questions. He's not sitting up and not insisting on paddling. Not great signs.

An hour into our trip, he growls.

"What?"

"They're coming. Hunting. Helicopters." I don't hear anything, but it doesn't mean they're not there. Kiro sits up and grabs the other paddle. "Hurry—" He points at a swath of brown way off across the waterway.

"What?"

"We can hide there."

We paddle like hell for the spot. He maneuvers the canoe under a fallen tree at the river's edge and ties it up between the branches. It's great cover.

"What are you going to do?"

He climbs out, using the rotting branches as a bridge to the shore. He slips a few times—I can't tell whether it's the instability of the branches or his dizziness. When he gets to shore, he straightens, sways a bit, and then reaches out to hold onto a tree. Definitely dizzy. It's not good—it could be something with his inner ear. But then he withdraws his hand from the tree and takes a few more steps. He's stable. Or maybe it's willpower.

He comes back to the canoe. "We'll sleep here until light," he says.

I snuggle him into the blankets and stretch out by him. I poke his ribs. "Hey."

He stirs.

"You hear that?"

He gives me a look. Stupid question. Of course he hears it. The *chop-chop-chop* of a helicopter. A spotlight slides around the landscape. Luckily, the Kevlar of the canoe isn't reflective like metal would be.

Kiro closes his eyes and traces my lips. We're two peas in a pod in the slim canoe and he's feeling my lips.

The moon comes out from behind a cloud, lighting his features. "Look at me," I whisper.

He opens his eyes. "I've been looking at you for days, Ann. I'll never be tired of looking at you."

"I mean look at my eyes. I want to see your pupils."

I place my hand on his beard and pull up his right eyelid, then the left. The left pupil is bigger, but only slightly.

"Does your head still hurt?"

"No."

"Liar."

His pause tells me everything. "I'm feeling better. I'm almost home."

I slide my thumb along his unwelted cheekbone. "Almost home."

"I can't wait for you to meet them. Especially Red and Snowy. They'll be older now, but they'll remember."

Home is all he ever wanted. "I'm looking forward to meeting them."

"I'm surprised they're not here already. They'd be here if the helicopters weren't up there."

"What if they never give up on finding you?"

"They always give up on finding me," he whispers.

There's this silence where my mind spins with all of the sadness of that statement.

He pulls me to him more tightly. "I can hear you thinking."

"No you can't."

"Your breathing changes when you're thinking in dark pictures. It always has."

He's right, of course. "You think you can read minds now?"

"No. I can read your body. Even at the institute. All I had was to watch you. Think about you. You know when I first knew you were special?"

"When?"

"It was The Hulk. When you made a joke about The Hulk."

"Oh my God. I knew you tracked it. Your lips moved, and your eyes were like, so *there* for a second."

"You surprised me."

"Yeah, and you pretty much gaslighted me. I *knew* you were aware. God, everyone made me think I was crazy. Including you."

The helicopter comes over again, flashing its light down the shore. We still; we don't even speak, like the helicopter might hear us.

"The Hulk and I go way back," he says after a spell. "When my dad would lock me in the root cellar, The Hulk kind of saved me. The villains would hurt Bruce Banner and put him down so much, and then when he'd get mad enough, angry enough, he'd turn invincible. It was a powerful tale to a young boy in a root cellar."

I know he's probably only telling me more of his story because he knows that hearing stories calms me, but I listen eagerly.

He talks about how he'd imagine scenarios of himself as The Hulk, bursting out of there.

"It came true a little bit," I say sleepily, nestled into his chest.

"I'm nowhere near The Hulk."

"In comparison to others, you are."

A rumble in his chest. He's not like The Hulk right now. He's badly concussed. Probably dizzy, judging from the way he looked on shore. He takes a curl in his finger, the way he loves to. "And then you came like a beautiful angel, and you asked if I turned into The Hulk to escape. And I wanted you more than anything."

More than his freedom, even.

The drone of the helicopter fades away, and it's just the soft waves lapping at the bottom of the canoe, and us alone under the stars.

CHAPTER THIRTY-THREE

Kiro

THE NEXT MORNING, we trek through the forest. Midmorning. I should feel happy. Every turn is familiar. Every view. I'm nearly home. But everything's wrong.

I told her the helicopter scared off my pack. But if Red or Snowy or the others were anywhere near, they'd scent me. They'd come.

"Our den was just over that hill," I say, with a mixture of excitement and dread. "It's possible they're not here for the winter yet, and that's why they're not out to greet me."

A lie. They should be here. They would be here.

My heart pounds as we get to the peak of a hill overlooking a valley that's lush with reds and oranges. A stand of green pines pointing up to the sky like feathers.

"It's beautiful," she says.

It is. And it's all wrong.

My eyes aren't on the panorama. They're on an outcrop of rock and two huge downed trees midway down the hill. You wouldn't mark it as a home by looking. But it's a home.

Or was.

I feel her eyes on me. "Kiro?"

The world sways. It's not my head.

I start down toward the den, then break out in a run, not wanting to get there, yet needing to get there with every fiber of my being. I stumble once but keep going. I round the boulder and duck in under the massive downed trunk like I did so often, so deeply familiar.

I move into the cool shade and protection of the den. A wide space. Not so tall. Not tall enough to stand.

I scent him before I find him. I go cold. No.

With shaking hands I slide aside the leaves and decay, and there it is—a slash of white that shouldn't be there. A half-buried skull. Red—I know it's Red by the scent. Bones still carry the scent of the animal.

I unearth it a bit more and press my hand against what would have been the side of Red's head, breathing hard, unable to believe that this bump of bone was once my friend.

I press my forehead to the side of his head, like I used to when he was alive. When we would sleep side by side. Red. So loyal. All the misery and loneliness of those years of being trapped crashes through me.

It's then I scent Snowy. I'm heaving in gulps of air. I scent Ghost, another of the older ones.

I scrabble around in the dried leaves and dirt, finding the bones.

Three dead. Shot in the den. Or maybe outside of it, and they crawled in. Were pursued. Two years of dirt layered over them. It would have happened soon after I left.

My family. My only true family.

I collapse in the gloom of the enclosure feeling as dead as the dirt. These wolves weren't just my family, they were my anchor, my sanity. Bright spirits in a dark world.

I lie there drifting, lost in a sea of misery, pulled under by it, unable to breathe, to see, to think beyond this moment.

I'm only dimly aware of Ann's hand on my back.

When did she come in?

She stretches out next to me, rubbing my back.

I'm not sure how much time passes. It's possible that I sleep. Maybe I pass out. That has happened since I hit my head. The next thing I hear is Ann's voice. "Tell me about them, Kiro. Tell me another story about Red."

I turn to her, there in the den, in the bed of dry leaves next to the half-buried bones. Something wells up in my chest, like a bubble made of stone, filling me, choking me. I can't speak. I don't want to speak. I rise up and heave myself against the side of the enclosure. Years of debris falls onto our faces. I kick open the side.

"Hey!" She scrambles out as I smash the den apart, pushing the accumulated branches and leaves and debris this way and that. I go up on the top and stomp on it, smashing it. The years of stuff trapped and cemented in by snow and moisture and sun breaks apart. I destroy it all, flattening it, crushing it into a heap.

When it's utterly destroyed, I collapse on top of the rock outcrop next to it, face wet in the sunshine.

Again Ann is there.

She doesn't fool me. I'm her captor. She'd leave if she thought she could. She only truly wants to be with me when I make her beg, or when there's danger.

My pulse races. The world seems to spin. "He was family. They were my family. Even at the darkest in the Fancher Institute, they were there with me."

"You loved them," she says.

I reach up and touch her cheek.

She searches my eyes like she does when she's trying to understand things about me.

And right then I think, *I love you.* It fills me with even more despair. She, too, will leave.

"Tell me about him."

I tell her one thing, simple and small. About how upset Red would get when I'd climb a tree. He'd be at the bottom, jumping.

She soaks up the story. It's always stories with her. I'm a story. It seems dangerous to love her when I remember that.

"The other," she says. "Tell me about the other one. The female. What was her name?"

"Snowy."

She makes me tell stories. She urges me to move away from the den and up onto the sunny part of the bluff. We sit in the sunshine in the tall grass. She has some sort of dried meat that she shares with me. "What about the rest of the pack? Are you so sure they won't come back?"

"The three strongest, oldest wolves were shot," I say. "It would have left the younger members vulnerable, in disarray. They would've scattered. They could be dead. They're probably dead. If the hunters got the older wolves, they would gotten the pups. Red's pup…" I close my eyes, remembering him, a nipping ball of fur. "Those pups would've been too vulnerable to survive being hunted after something like this."

I imagine the pups out there alone without the elder wolves. A few were almost a year old, but still. "If we looked hard enough, we'd find the bones of the younger ones."

The idea fills me with despair.

"Hey," she says softly, sliding a finger over my beard the way she likes to.

The sun has been climbing. It's afternoon.

"I imagined them so fiercely when I was lying there in bed. They felt alive. I can't believe they were dead all that time."

"You kept them alive," she says. "You're keeping them alive now."

"Just words." I shove my hand in my pocket and pull out the wolf keychain. Something flip-flops in my stomach. The little wolf looks so much like Red.

I tighten my fist around it, like it's my last link to my old friend. But it's just plastic. Not real. I throw it into the grass.

"Hey!" She starts after it, but I grab her arm. I don't want her to leave me.

She stays half standing, searching my eyes. "They're not gone, Kiro. They still live inside you."

Words. I hold her arm, feeling so alone. I need to not be alone.

I know what I am to her—I'm her captor, her enemy. Still she feels like life to me, and I hold on to her.

She gives me a strange look. Gazes into my eyes. She kneels on the grass and pushes me back, coaxing me to lie back on the rough warm grass. "Just lie there. Stay like that."

I allow it, keeping hold of her.

She climbs on top of me, sits on top of me. Her peanut butter-colored hair hangs down on either side of her head. The brilliant blue sky behind her is dotted with cotton-ball clouds.

But nothing's so beautiful as Ann.

She places her hands on the grass on either side of my head. I let her go, unsure what she's up to. Then she lowers herself down and she kisses me.

Her kiss is tender. Her tenderness breaks something in me.

She sits upright and moves backward down my legs so that she's sitting on my thighs. I watch with amazement as she presses a hand over my cock, making it harder. She leans over and kisses it through my pants.

I shove my hands into her soft hair. I'm her captor, her enemy. Her actions make no sense. "You want me to fuck you?" I ask incredulously.

"No." She stands over me and takes off her shirt, unbuttons her pants, and pulls them down. I watch in wonder as she steps out of them, out of her boots. Naked. She looks like a goddess.

She kneels back down and frees my cock, bares my groin, eyes holding mine.

I can barely breathe.

She crawls back up over me. She takes hold of my cock and guides me to her hole.

"What are you doing?" I ask. It's obvious, but I don't mean it that way, and she knows it.

"You're mine," she says.

I clutch onto her and still her. I don't want her like this if she doesn't mean it. I don't mind words that are lies, but I can't take this if it's a lie.

She grabs my hands and threads her fingers into mine, holding my hands and my eyes as she lowers herself down over me, guiding me into her. It seems like a dream. Another reality. She's fucking me, fucking all of me. I hiss out a breath as she takes me into her, warm and tight.

Ann is with me. I grab her hips and begin to move, needing her like I've never needed anything.

I look into her eyes as she fucks me. Because she wants me. Because I'm hers.

She says something I don't get. I don't care. This is everything—her coming to me.

I'm lost inside her. The whole world is spinning wrong. But she's right. She's the still point at the center.

"I'm here," she says.

And I know that she is. I fuck her and watch myself inside her, watch the way her eyes change as we move.

I get enough of her on top. I roll us over, roll on top of her. I push into her, fucking her, kissing her sun-warmed face.

She rolls off me afterwards. We lie in the sun, watching the sky.

"You're a good mate," she says.

"I didn't even feed you."

"You don't always have to feed me."

"I should feed you. I should fish before dark."

"That would be good. Can I come along?"

"I'm faster without distraction."

"I want to go with you," she says. "And I still kind of can't believe you catch fish with your bare hands."

"You'd question me at a time like this?"

"Who catches fish with their bare hands?"

"What do you think I use?"

"I don't know. Sticks? A net made from a sock? I'd believe almost anything before your hands."

I frown and rub my face. "Come on, then."

She trails along behind me to the stream, a speck of light at the edge of my dark world.

CHAPTER THIRTY-FOUR

Ann

THE RIVER FLOWS through a bed of rocks and boulders in the shade of a huge limestone ridge, which stands like a dark sentry above us. Kiro leads the way, picking along stones and spots of dry ground until we hit a downed tree whose fat limbs stretch out over the river like a giant's hand.

"This was always the best place. This tree. This shade."

"It's beautiful," I say.

He regards the mighty downed tree for some time.

Kiro has a powerful imagination for putting himself in the past—he told me that he'd lie in that institution bed imagining himself free and wild. I know he's thinking about his pack.

I don't want him to stop thinking about his pack, to stop honoring them with memory, but I hate seeing him in pain. "What now?"

"I catch the fish. This is going to be boring for you to watch."

"Oh, I don't think so," I say. "Considering it's pretty much an impossible feat."

He climbs out onto the tree over the water and stretches out on his belly. Then he sticks a hand in the water. And waits.

And waits.

"That's what you do?"

"Shhh," he scolds.

"Are you shitting me?"

"They think my hand is part of the tree. I grab them."

I cross my arms. "You wait for them to come to you. Like the rabbit."

He turns his gaze to me. Yes. He doesn't have the speed or claws of other animals. But he has stealth.

I see a silvery flash go by. I point. "Kiro!"

He gives me a look. "You scared it."

There's another. It's kind of exciting.

He pulls his hand out of the water and comes back to shore. "I'll teach you. Come on."

Part of me wants to say no—I won't learn. I won't live here—surely he's not imagining it anymore. But he's teaching me things, starting to trust me. It means something. "You think you can teach me to fish with my hands?"

"It takes patience, that's all."

He leads me out, helping me balance on the massive trunk as we go a ways over the rushing water. He shows me where to stretch out, shows me a limb to hold on to. I go onto my belly and lower my hand in. It's cold.

He goes farther out on the same limb and lies in the opposite direction, so that we're facing each other, our hands dangling in the cool flow of water. "If your fingers get too cold, pull them out—slowly. Or switch hands."

You can see all the way to the gloomy depths. Fish flash by. Sometimes big ones—trout, maybe? I have no idea.

"Is this how bears catch fish?" I whisper.

"They more scoop. They have speed and claws."

"How are you doing?" I ask.

His hand is a sinewy blur in the water. "The dizziness is gone."

"I don't mean that."

He's silent for a while. Then, "I can't stop thinking about them."

"I know," I say. "It's hard to stop thinking about a thing."

His gaze meets mine. "Like the kitten."

The cold water gurgles by, flowing through my fingers like cool velvet. "Yeah."

"I spent a long time puzzling about the kitten," he says. "When I was lying there."

I actually stopped thinking about the kitten for a while. Free of the fucking kitten. I don't want the kitten back on my mind.

"You said it cost you everything. I spent a lot of time staring at the ceiling, wondering what it meant."

"The kitten isn't important."

"Did it die?"

"No."

"You always said you lost everything because of it."

He remembers. Of course.

"Why did the kitten cost you everything?"

I'm about to remind him I don't talk about it, but I look up and meet his gaze.

Kiro. He acts like such a brute, such a savage, but at this moment, he's more achingly human than anyone I've even known. Needing to connect. Like his life depends on it.

"What did you lose?"

Am I really going to do this? To tell him? "Just my career," I say. "I guess it shouldn't be that big of a deal—"

"Your career is a big deal for you."

"It is. Was." I swish my hand in the water, and suddenly I'm telling him how I used to be so badass. I tell him how I was on top of my game in the journalism trenches. "It's different from the kinds of reporters you met. You know what long-form journalism is? It's where you write articles that are way longer than…they're just long and hopefully thoughtful. Anyway, I'd pitch stories to good publications, and they'd bite, sending me to far-off locations. They'd know I'd get the story I promised or a better one. I have a nose for a story."

"Like with me."

"I was right, wasn't I?"

I feel the quicksilver slide of a fish against my fingertips, and I grab for it. I have its tail for a split second, then it slips through.

"Hard to keep hold of the tail," he says. "You learn that pretty fast."

"Yow." I switch arms. My right hand needs to thaw.

"As a woman, I gained access to realms that guys couldn't get into. I also had nursing skills, which made me valuable in a crisis. I could sometimes stay long after they were shooing the civilians out. War zones. Or refugee situations. Disasters."

"You're also resourceful, Ann. I saw you at the hospital, the way you were. You never gave up. You kept fighting no matter what."

I rest my chin on my non-fishing arm and look into his eyes. Some men, when they look at you, it's like they're taking from you. But Kiro gives. He looks with his heart.

It makes it easy to tell him the hard things. I tell him about the hospital bombing. "I was working alongside Worldcorps Medicale, doing this long, in-depth NGO story, when the hospital we were in was shelled. I'd been shelled before, though I'd always been in bomb shelters. This was like nothing I'd ever been through. The building groaning like a monster. Metal girders screaming. I pulled four kids from the unit into a stainless steel meds cooler just as everything collapsed around us. We were trapped, the five of us. In near darkness—just a tiny sliver of light. The smallest boy was badly injured on the way in, and by the time the chaos quieted, I knew he was dead. The other kids were hysterical from the collapse alone. I couldn't let them know, so I pulled the dead kid into my lap. I said he was sleeping. Sometimes I pretended he was moving around. We were in there for thirty-nine hours, trapped, listening to people—"

"You held a dead child for nearly two days?"

"The other kids would've freaked out. The kids and I sang a lot of songs. When we got out, everybody was really amazed at how I kept my famous cool."

He just lies there. Fishing. Listening.

"My editor at the time wanted that story instead; obviously it was better than the NGO story I'd gone to cover. That means nongovernmental organization. Like an aid group. It was a coup to have an actual journalist trapped in rubble with kids. But every time I tried to write about it, it was chaos in my mind. I couldn't find the story. I couldn't find my way in. I couldn't find the right detail."

I describe how she held a feature space open for me and I blew two deadlines and they had to run something from the can. I couldn't handle even a Q&A with another reporter. I wasn't sleeping anymore.

"I felt so numb in those days after, and there was this sense I had suddenly that every single detail from those thirty-nine hours weighed exactly the same. That maybe doesn't sound important, but it really is. When you're a reporter, you're always sifting through the pebbles of a story, looking for the one detail that weighs the most, that means the most. I couldn't find it. And every time I'd go near a hospital, the antiseptic smell would seriously fuck me up."

"Oh," he says.

"Right." I tell him how I had another gig lined up after that, also in Afghanistan. "It was a glorious story—an interview with a notorious and nearly mythical female warlord from out of the Hindu Kush mountain range."

"The one you missed. You were two hours late."

"You were listening."

"Every word."

"Everyone was jealous I landed it. A career-making story. And the kitten incident made me miss the only chance at this interview. Made me trash months of legwork by a very major publication."

"You saw the little paw. You got men to move the rock slabs," he says. "That's what you said. You talked about your…fixer. I wondered what that was."

"A fixer is a helper, often in places where the order has broken down. Sometimes just a driver." I swish my hand around. "So yada yada yada, I'm supposed to be this pro, and I'm kneeling in a road with a kitten. I suppose you remember that part."

"I do," he says, listening intently, chin on the rough bark.

"That's when you held my hand, Kiro." I grin. "Fuck, do you know how much that shocked me? You nearly sent me through the ceiling."

"I'm sorry."

"No, it was beautiful…I felt…not alone."

There's a beat where he just watches my eyes. "Me too."

I feel so close to him right then. Us lying on the logs. Fishing with our hands.

"Tell me the rest, Ann."

"Well, fixers talk, journalists talk. I suddenly had myself a reputation for zero objectivity. Overly emotionally involved, the kiss of death. There are plenty of other hungry journalists to send for a story. I was also out of money, so I couldn't even freelance it, which means going out and doing a story on your own dime in hopes of selling it to somebody. And the biggest thing was that I couldn't think straight. It was like, the kitten was the biggest detail. A detail as big as the sun."

I go on. Me coming home career-less and more or less friendless.

"You saved the kitten."

"I got it to this mountain village."

"Did it make you feel better?"

"No," I say.

"Does telling it make you feel better?" he asks.

"Not really," I say. "You listening makes me feel better, though. The way you look when I tell you. Everyone in the world thought it was sad and fucked up, including me. But you don't."

"I don't," he says softly.

Something cool brushes between my thumb and forefinger. I grip and pull. A fish wriggles in my hand. I'm so startled I let it go. It splashes back out, back into the water.

Kiro is laughing.

"It's not funny!"

"You caught a fish with your bare hands, Ann." He grins. "Who's the savage now?"

I dangle my hand back in the water.

Kiro stretches back out in front of me, facing me.

Birds sing above—long, elaborate calls. Animals rustle in the leaves up and down the bank.

It's peaceful. I pull my hand out of the water now and then when it feels too cold. I flex my fingers. Shake it out.

And it comes to me that that's probably what hurt him the most with the reporters at the hospital—not their aggressiveness or the lights and flashes, but the way they made him less than human. A bizarre object for the consumption of the nation.

I don't know what to say. I want to apologize on behalf of all journalists, to tell him he's amazing, but I know it won't mean much to him. Words never do.

So I reach out to him. I hook my pointer finger to his.

He looks into my eyes in that honest, unselfconscious way he has. Something wild and good sparkles through me.

The connection of our gazes feels more intimate than fucking. More dangerous than the mob. We lie there like that, fingers hooked, hands trailing in the water.

He smiles. "You remember when I was lying there and you said, 'oh fuck you, you fucking faker'?"

"Oh my God. That was such a jerky thing to say."

He stares at my knuckle where our fingers hook. He stares with that fierce intensity of his, then he leans forward and brushes a kiss onto it.

Shivers go over me. He looks up into my eyes. Kiro needs no words.

CHAPTER THIRTY-FIVE

Kiro

I CATCH THREE fish. She manages to touch another one.

I bring her to the cave. The place where I nearly died. Where I would've died if it hadn't been for those first wolves. I picture Red and Snowy. It feels like there's a hole in the world.

"It's...nice," she says, walking into it.

It's not nice, not when I look at it through the eyes of a woman who's used to furniture and a dry bed with sheets and blankets. I kick aside the dirt and leaves, showing how it can be made clean. I point. "That's the good side for sleeping. We'll make a fire here on this side."

She looks out at the hillside. Her eyes are a dazzling green in the setting sun. I start the fire, but we need more wood.

"Go on," she says. "I'll be fine. I'll unpack."

I go to her and kiss her, then I grab the small hatchet. "This is good. It's good that we brought it."

She smiles, but it's not a real smile.

I set off toward an area of downed trees just over the next hill. They'll be nice and dry for a fire. I slam at the largest log, hacking and hacking. It feels good to slam the hatchet against something, to do this violent thing, to stop myself from thinking. If I tire myself out enough, maybe I'll stop thinking about those wolves suffering and dying out here at the hands of hunters.

And maybe I'll be able to stop thinking about how much I love having her out here, like a window into a life I'll never have.

Because I know now I have to bring her back. It was wrong to take her the way I did. It was wrong to tie her up. Wrong to make her beg just because I could. Wrong to keep her.

She belongs to me. It's the best thing in the world to feel like she belongs to me, that she's mine. Mine to care for.

Ironically, that means I have to let her go.

We'll set back out tomorrow, back to the truck.

I'll say goodbye.

I'll let her go.

CHAPTER THIRTY-SIX

Lazarus

I'VE ALWAYS HATED nature.

Especially the shrubberies. Are they even called shrubberies when you're in the wild? Or would that be bramble? In any case, they're annoying, and they block your way from every direction.

Nature.

Like they say, you don't have to taste much to know it's cottage cheese.

My wilderness guide finishes tying down the canoes and scolding my guys to stay silent. He's extremely eager for us to catch Kiro unawares.

He's a rugged specimen of a man in hiking boots and purple Gore-Tex and the kind of sunglasses that have a leather band keeping them attached to your head so that they stay on no matter what peril you encounter—with the possible exception of a beheading, one would suppose.

I got him at a resort at the edge of this wilderness. I asked for the best guide money can buy, and he was it. He was booked up until I paid a few thousand bucks to his handler.

We got here by helicopter. Our Gore-Tex-clad guide put together an idea of where Kiro's home might be from the anecdotal intel we provided him and from reports that filtered down through the years.

We landed six miles away from where our guide thinks Kiro is. *Out of hearing range,* he explained. "Who are we hunting here? The Bionic Woman?" I joked.

"You never know," he said simply.

We went with it. He's a real high-performance type and highly motivated, thanks to the live feed of my men sitting in his living room, threatening his wife and kid.

We went by foot and boat after that. He climbed a peak not an hour ago—scrambled up there just like a monkey with binoculars. He saw smoke. He thinks he knows where they are.

An hour later, we're stepping out of our canoes.

My guys and I have sprayed ourselves with deer piss. This is something you get in a bottle when you're a wilderness guide. It's a way a hunter masks his scent. If Kiro is out here somewhere and really did live wild all those years, our rugged leader theorizes, it could help mask our approach.

My guys gear up their rifles and adjust their night-vision goggles. We'll be underestimating Kiro exactly zero more times. An orderly named Donny out at Fancher Institute gave us a lot of good intel on the man.

Sir Gore-Tex-a-Lot finishes tying down the canoes with a bungee cord. I stand over him, watching while the men spray more deer piss on themselves.

"What time is it when your favorite hobby involves spraying yourself with deer piss?" I ask him.

He looks up at me, confused. "Are you asking me the time?"

"No, I'm asking you, *what time is it* when your favorite hobby involves spraying yourself with deer piss?"

He gives me a stony look.

"Time to get a new hobby."

He doesn't find it funny.

Garrick the journalist snickers.

Garrick and his clipped British accent accused me earlier of not holding up my end of the bargain with his editor, Murray. He informed me that the idea of an embed is to be where the action is, where Kiro is, not hanging back with the man directing the action. He'd accused me of scuttling the deal.

"You still feel like I scuttled that deal, Garrick?" I asked when we found the bodies of my forward team, buzzing with flies. "This the kind of story you were looking to be embedded in? Would certainly give new meaning to the term 'embedded.'"

He had little to say to that. In fact, I wasn't entirely sure he got the joke, though admittedly it was a stretch. Our guide wanted to radio back about the bodies, but I put him off of that idea easily enough.

Garrick took a few photos. He even shifted a body to get a better shot, much to the disgust of our guide.

"They're dead," Garrick informed him clippedly.

We make our way through the forest and around a bluff. Our guide has a topographical GPS that tells us there's a cave system to the south, and between that and some sort of triangulation involving the wind and the smoke, he has their location.

I find it dubious until we actually get the cave in view and see the smoke puffing out the entrance.

We trudge nearer. When we're quite near, he steals up and scopes it out with a mirror on a retractable rod, then returns to inform us that there is one person in there—a woman.

"No man?"

"I'm sure."

"Thank you, Santa," I say.

It's the girl—it has to be. Orderly Donny has informed us that Kiro would do anything to protect her. That's the mistake my first group made. Not going for the weakness.

We tie up our guide with his precious bungee cords and head up to the cave, picking around the trees and boulders.

"Kiro?" she calls.

It's not the smartest for me to head in first; she could be armed, after all. Garrick has a passing acquaintance with the girl, and he assures me that she'd know perfectly well how to shoot. But a leader who stops taking risks becomes brittle; that's something that Valerie likes to say.

And I really, really want to see her face when I pop in.

I whip on a tie for the occasion. You never get a second chance to make a first impression. I walk in casually. "Why, hello," I say. "Haven't we met someplace?"

It's every bit as rewarding as I imagined it would be. The color literally drains from her cheeks.

I snap my fingers. "Oh, don't tell me, I have it—the insane asylum. You were trying to keep us from finding Kiro."

She stands, eyes wide, as my guys crowd in. Her eyes go even wider when she sees Garrick. "What the fuck?"

"You didn't want to do the job." Garrick takes a few pictures. "Is this where he lived?"

"Garrick!"

"Where is he?" I ask.

She turns to me. "He's gone. He's not coming back."

"Not buying it, sister." I press the business end of my Ruger to her forehead and back her up to the cave wall.

"No need to hurt Ann," Garrick says.

He couldn't be more wrong. There is a great deal of need to hurt Ann. "Hands knit on your head, Ann."

She complies, eyes wide.

My guys crowd in. They'll have left a few in the bushes. Sharpshooters, but we want Kiro walking in alive. Walking out, not so much.

"Kiro's not here."

"No, but he'll come for you. I've learned the Dragusha boys tend to come for their mates. I've learned that the hard way."

"I'm not his mate."

"Should we test that? Garrick, are you rolling?"

"I'm just here to get the Savage Adonis story. Ann should be kept out of this."

I nod, and my guy puts his piece on Garrick.

I say, "The answer I was looking for, Garrick, is, 'Yes, I'm rolling.' You're going to get this on film, and most of all, you're going to get when Kiro comes through that opening. You are going to keep filming no matter what happens. We're going to kill Kiro, and you're going to record it."

Garrick stiffens, looking affronted. "That's not something I'm willing to do."

"No? Do you want to guess what happens if you don't get the footage I need? Do you want to take a guess on that?" I wait. Only serious footage will put the prophecy to rest once and for all. I need serious proof.

"Kiro! It's a trap!" she calls.

One of my guys puts a light on her. Garrick apologizes to her and films.

"What the fuck, Garrick?"

"Call out to Kiro again," I tell her.

"Fuck you," she spits,

I slide a glance at Garrick, who's holding his camera on her with a resigned look. He was a war correspondent. He knows how to film fucked-up things. Probably already running through his defense, too. Under duress and all that. It'll hold up in a court of law. The legal system gives you a lot of leeway when your life is in danger.

I'll edit myself out of it later.

"We can do this so many ways," I say to her, backing up. "You call to him, or I kill you and guess what? He'd still come. When these brothers get emotional, they get stupid. It runs in the family."

"He has a family?"

I narrow my eyes. She doesn't know who he is?

Interesting.

She glares. "What's his family?"

I can't believe she's still going for the story.

Garrick regards her wistfully. "The Dragushas. Albanian mafia. There was some kind of coup when the boys were babies."

"He has a family," she whispers.

"Does that mean you're going for the killing option? Because I haven't heard you call out." I pull out my piece and aim for her belly.

The look of a woman who thinks you'll shoot her is radically different from the look of a woman who thinks you're bluffing. Ann thinks I'm bluffing.

Garrick knows I'm not. He's spent a bit more time with me.

"Come on, man," Garrick says.

I back up a bit, leaving her standing against the cave wall, and I level the piece at her kneecap. "You'd think it's the kneecap that would produce the loudest scream," I say to Garrick. "In fact you'd be wrong. It's the foot. You want to know why?"

He's not answering.

I sigh.

Ann tries to make a run for it.

I aim. Squeeze the trigger.

Crrrrack! I shoot her foot.

The blast echoes through the cave like a motherfucker. It's almost as loud as Ann's scream.

"Fuck! Fuck!" Garrick calls out. "Fuck!" He's still filming, through. He gets that his life depends on it.

Ann's down, though much to her credit, she doesn't scream again.

"Come on. That's all you got?"

It's surprising. Admirable, even. She needs another hole in her. Nothing that will kill her right away. The last thing we want is a beast like Kiro with nothing to lose.

Crrrrack! I get her in the gut. She crumples. That does it—she screams. Nice and loud.

It's then we hear the roar. It's loud and anguished, echoing through the hills.

I exchange glances with Garrick. I point, meaning, *tell me you fucking got that audio*. He gives me a grim look, camera steady. That's a *yes*.

I signal my guys to drop back into the shadows. "We let him get to her, got it? He's not coming for us, he's coming for her."

They get way the fuck back in the shadows. They're all feeling pretty fucking nervous. I can hear the chopper now. My guy moving closer, ready for the evacuation.

"I probably don't need to tell you, Garrick, to concentrate your camera on the shootees instead of the shooters. I don't want a lot of footage I can't use. You understand what I'm saying?"

He looks like he might throw up.

"Watch out, Kiro! It's a trap!" she yells. "You can't do anything!"

You can almost feel him coming. Even the air seems to change.

"This tension is unbelievable," I say to nobody in particular. I go up next to Garrick and check the little window in his camera that shows what he's filming. "The theme I'm going for here is straightforward and unambiguous."

"Kiro," she calls, holding her belly. "Don't fall for it! Stay out there!"

Oh, this is good. Better than I imagined. Death, like porn, needs a bit of a story. Not a lot of story, but a bit, and these two are going to deliver.

Kiro in his last moments holding his dying beloved in his arms before they're both gunned down. Nobody will doubt his death with this kind of performance.

Aleksio and Viktor will go wild.

I'll get this footage to them and put every resource out looking for them. Killing them after they see footage of their brother dying like this will be like taking candy from a baby. They'll be fucking stumbling around on the streets like drunks.

I turn to my men, motion with my gun. It means *weapons up*. I'm taking the shot. Not them—*me*. It's not just that I want to be the one to kill Kiro, but also, I don't want to cut the scene too fast. I want this shit to spin as long as possible.

"You sure?" my number one says. He thinks I'm getting greedy.

I have only to raise my brows. He, too, puts up his weapon.

CHAPTER THIRTY-SEVEN

Ann

I'M ON THE rough, cold cave floor on my side, holding my belly, legs drawn up. I can't imagine moving.

Still, I yell.

"Don't fall for it, Kiro! Leave! Run!" I take a momentary break, then: "They won't kill me if you stay away!"

It's a lie. No way will they leave me alive.

The pain is blinding. I press my palm to my belly, sucking in the smoke-tinged air, thinking about this last day with Kiro, and the way we connected.

I thought I was helping him feel less alone by reaching out, but he was helping me.

All my life, I've looked in from the outside. Kiro showed me what it was to be on the inside. To live my own story. Those moments when I looked into his eyes made me feel like we've been together forever.

I think to yell, to warn him off again, but I know it's pointless.

Kiro will come.

Kiro has wanted one thing his whole life—to belong.

Kiro would rather die belonging than remain alive and alone.

And there's that vow.

"Kiro, please…no." It's barely a whisper. He'll come to die with me.

I hear the men talking. They know it. That leader knows it.

I hold my side, trying to keep my mind clear and objective as long as possible. I need to stay awake for him.

A wave of pain. Trauma to the liver, I'm thinking. Not good. The liver is the most regenerative organ. It can be 95 percent destroyed and regenerate itself. It's more the internal bleeding that's the problem.

I grit my teeth against the pain.

I think of the eyes of people I've treated with injuries like this. It's like they can see you, but there is so much going on behind the eyes. I always thought it was a sense of the body, the animal taking over, slowly shutting down, preserving blood flow to the core. I'm thinking now it's just fear.

I pull my legs in more tightly. I can't imagine stretching my legs ever again.

I suppose I won't.

The light they shine on me is bright, but not so much that I don't see him burst through the opening to the cave.

Even knowing he's doomed—that I've doomed him—my heart lifts. I feel him. He feels like happiness.

He stalks to me. There's this wild look in his eyes, and I think he smells all the blood, and he knows I won't make it. He knows he's going to die by coming to me.

He doesn't give a fuck.

He kneels in front of me.

"Kiro," I whisper.

"I'm here." Strong, warm arms circle around me. He puts his body over mine. His forehead to my cheek. "I'm here, Ann," he whispers.

I wish more than anything that I could hold him, but I can't move, clenched around my wound like a fist. But Kiro is here.

The man's trying to get Kiro's attention. He's calling out to him. He wants him to turn to the camera, but Kiro is nobody's bitch.

Kiro is wild and beautiful and utterly his own man. And we'll never let go of each other now.

"Mine," he whispers into my hair. His arms feel strong and good around me. I feel like the whole universe is around me, protecting me in Kiro's embrace.

I can hear the sociopath saying mocking things in the distance.

His words don't matter to us.

I turn up my head and kiss Kiro's soft beard. Kiro is what's real.

Kiro grunts softly. It's a comforting sound that goes to my heart. We're both more animal than human now, but our humanity has never been stronger. Clinging together like this.

Somebody approaches and tries to kick us apart.

Kiro snarls and throws the man into the cave wall with a horrible crack, and then he's back.

Maybe they wanted to film Kiro's face. Well, they got his face. I feel like I'm floating out of my body—like it's all happening, yes, but to somebody else.

"Kiro," I whisper.

Kiro grunts again, sounding more anguished. He feels like he's losing me.

I tell myself to hold on. They'll start shooting soon. They'll have to kill him soon. He has to know that.

"Well, 34, what should we do now?"

He presses his forehead to mine. It hurts to remove even one hand from my belly, but I do. I don't need to stanch the bleeding anymore. We won't be getting any help out here, and anyway, I need to touch him. "I love you," I say.

I stroke his beard the way he likes.

He holds me more tightly. Words never did mean anything to him. But they mean something to me.

There's a yell just then.

Followed by a snarl. Not just any snarl, but an unholy snarl.

More than one snarl. Growls rip through the cave, savage and guttural.

Then the screaming starts. The place thunders with snarling and screaming. Kiro gasps. I can feel the shock and surprise in his body, in the way he tightens his arms around me.

Gunshots sound out, but that only seems to increase the snarling. The agonized cries of men echo off the walls.

I look past his arm and see the blur of fur and teeth.

Wolves!

There's blood everywhere. The roaring in the cave is deafening. People are dying, being ripped apart.

I feel Kiro lifting me. My belly is on fire. I'm bouncing in his arms.

No! I want to say. But I know we have to get out of there.

He's running. I'm gasping for air. My face feels wet—I have no idea whether it's sweat or tears. Maybe blood.

I hear Garrick's voice. *The copter. Get in—get in, goddammit! Get her in...do it.*

Kiro growls.

I clutch onto him. "Do it," I manage to say.

Because fucking Garrick knows how to fly. Most of us covering the hot zones know the basics of flying, but he's a high-performance asshole, and if he's saying "get in," he's confident about getting us out of here.

I feel us getting in. I'm hanging on one moment to the next, powering through the pain.

I concentrate on keeping myself together.

I black out, or maybe time is moving at a different speed, because suddenly we're aloft. Garrick's giving Kiro directions. Battlefield bandage for my foot. I smell the first-aid kit.

Two clumsy fingers at my neck.

"You with us?" Garrick.

I force my eyes open. I focus on Kiro.

"We're doing this," Garrick says. "I've radioed ahead."

We're flying. I'm still conscious. My insides feel ripped apart, but consciousness is a good sign.

I grunt.

"Ann—I didn't know what that guy was," Garrick says. "I didn't know."

Fingers on my forehead. Gentle. Strong. Kiro.

"The wolves…" I say. "They came."

"The younger ones came," Kiro says. "They didn't die after all. They stayed together. Red's pup. They saved us."

"The wolves."

"Yes," he says.

"Did they…get out…"

"Did the wolves get out of that alive? Is that what you're asking?" Garrick says. "Did you *hear* the screaming in there?"

"They came out of it," Kiro says. He's saying something about guns. They don't like anyone with guns.

I close my eyes.

"Stay awake," Kiro says.

I stay awake. He talks to me. I hang on to his voice.

CHAPTER THIRTY-EIGHT

Kiro

DULUTH MEMORIAL MEDICAL Center is a place that I hate. It's where they took me two years ago. I was on a different floor, but the smells are the same. The colors are the same. The sounds are the same, too. Worse, there are beeping sounds that are exactly like beeping sounds at the Fancher Institute, and they make me want to destroy something.

I stand in the waiting room just to the side of the double doors that they won't let me through.

I could go through if I wanted to. I did it before, but the nurse, a man named Chris, pushed me out and told me that if I go through the doors again, they'll stop helping Ann because they'll have to concentrate on me. "Is that what you want?" he asked me. "Do you want the medical staff to have to deal with you instead of helping your girlfriend?"

I'm not good with words. I didn't know how to tell him how badly I need them to help her, and how badly it hurts to be away from her. I don't know how to tell him that she's everything in the world to me.

And I need to protect her. Those men from the cave could still be alive. The wolves were there to protect us, not to slaughter our attackers. The wolves would have left as soon as we were gone.

The man named Lazarus could be coming. Garrick explained the situation to me—or as much as he knows, which is that Lazarus wants to kill me, and he thinks going through Ann is the best way.

It drives me crazy. So many entrances I can't guard.

So I stand next to the doors, making sure not to block them. They've scolded me for that, too. I stand, fists balled, waiting for them to tell me when I can go to her.

Garrick comes to me. "Murray spoke with her family." Murray. The editor. The boss of Ann and Garrick. "He's keeping them updated."

I can see a window. If I go to it, I'll be able to look down to the edge of the parking lot far below. That parking lot was filled with reporters the last time I was here. "You were one of them," I say. "Out there when I was here last."

"Yeah," he says.

"Not Ann."

"Fuck no," he says. "Ann would've never been down there. That's not her style. She doesn't do the money stories."

"She looks for the humanity."

"Exactly."

The buzzing in my ears is so loud, it's deafening. My woman. My mate. "You will not make a story of Ann."

"I'm not making a story of her," he says.

Is he lying? I don't trust this one. "If you anger me in any way, I will rip your throat out."

"How about you tell me what exactly will anger you so I can avoid that then."

"I'll know what angers me when I become angry."

"Hey." He nods at the pair of men in blue at the desk on the far side of the waiting room. "Cops," he says under his breath. "You ready?"

Garrick warned me that they'd be coming. He told me to "act cool." He had me memorize a fake name and phone number.

"I'm ready," I say.

The pair of them come to us. An officer with a young, square face draws me away from the door and asks me questions.

I don't trust Garrick, but he seems to hate and fear the police as much as I do, so I follow his instructions. I act cool, or at least I try. I give them the information Garrick told me to give. I suppress the urge to fight, to get away. Twice I tell the officer that I didn't witness the shooting.

They're much more interested in Garrick when they learn that he witnessed the shooting and has video footage of it. Garrick told me this would happen.

He talks with them for a long time while I wait. Then he sits in the chairs. He does things on his phone. He goes for food and comes back with burgers—one for him and one for me.

"I won't eat," I say. "Not until Ann eats."

He brings his food back to the seats and does more things on his phone.

After another hour, Nurse Chris comes up and tells me I can visit Ann.

I follow him in, impatient for him to walk faster, to show me where she is. It's not so easy to smell her with all of the smells coming off every surface and object, but as we near, I catch her scent. He tells me Ann's okay, and that she needs rest now. I can barely hear it.

I burst in and fly to her side. They've put a tube into her arm. Her eyes are halfway open. She looks fragile. I take her hand.

"Kiro," she mouths.

I put my finger to her lips. "They say you'll be okay. You need rest."

"You have to get out of here," she whispers. "Everyone in the world is after you."

I put my finger to her lips again, like a kiss. "I gave a fake name."

"Kiro." Her eyes drift closed. "That won't work for long."

I talk to her a little bit, even as she sleeps. I tell her things about the waiting room, the helicopter ride. I tell her how Murray has spoken to her family.

And then the door bangs open, and Garrick stalks in holding his phone, looking upset. He's followed by Nurse Chris.

"You need to leave, sir," Chris says. Chris is big and burly enough to throw Garrick out.

"Just a minute," Garrick says. The look he fixes me with says everything. *Trouble.*

I stand.

He gets right into my face and speaks in low tones. "I'm still on a loop from when I was embedded. Lazarus and some others got out. He's injured—I don't know how bad. But they're in the air."

"They got away?"

"They scared the wolves off. Smoke bomb, I think. I don't know all their lingo, but it sounds like a smoke bomb. They're in the air."

Smoke. Fire. That would throw the animals into chaos.

Nurse Chris informs us that he's getting security.

"So the wolves got out?"

"It sounds like they did, which is kind of a miracle, considering they attacked *armed men*."

"Men with guns freeze in the face of animal rage," I say vacantly. "When they know the animal will stop at nothing."

"Lazarus knows you're here. He's coming, or at least he's sending people. Count on it. He wants you dead."

"Go back," Ann grates out. "Get out while you still can, Kiro."

I turn to her. "It's okay."

"It's not. It's you he wants. Go back to your pack."

I take her hand. Does she understand nothing? "You're my pack," I tell her.

She smiles faintly through the pain.

I squeeze her hand. I want to throw myself over her and never leave.

"You're *my* pack," she says.

Garrick swears in the background. Men fill the room.

"We're leaving, we're leaving," Garrick says.

"I'm not leaving," I say.

"You prefer to be arrested?" one of the guards says. "Noncompliance with staff wishes—"

"He's coming." Garrick takes my arm, gives me a significant look. "Ann needs you to leave."

I don't want to leave Ann, but I can't allow myself to be arrested—she'll be in even more danger then. What I really want to do is destroy this room. That helps nobody.

I allow Garrick to drag me down the hall, away from Ann.

"Lazarus will never stop going after her," I say. "He knows now that she's my weak link."

"Why the fuck does he want to kill you so bad?" Garrick asks once we're dumped back in the waiting area. "What did you do?"

"I don't know."

"You don't know?"

"No. I just know she'll always be in danger as long as we both breathe. He knows I'll always come for her."

"If you knew why they're chasing you, that would be helpful."

I go to the windows. So many roads in, so many entrances to the large facility. I can't guard them all. I can't guard Ann without getting arrested.

I don't know how to give her the safety she needs. I have to hunt and kill Lazarus, but I don't know where to start.

I stare down at the parking lot, remembering the flashes. The news vans. The fear and bewilderment I felt.

It reminds me of what Ann said, about light making things safer. Better. More knowledge and less secrets is always safer.

I realize with a deep shudder what I have to do. And it goes against everything in me.

Garrick comes to me. "You can't take her out of here, if that's what you're thinking. She's too sick to move."

"You remember how it was the first time? How many of you were out there?"

"Well. Savage Adonis," he says, like just that name explains it. "Feral teen idol," he adds. "Everyone wanted a look."

"How long would it take to everyone back here to see me? To take all the pictures they want. Ask all their questions."

"Wait—I thought that's exactly what you didn't want."

"I don't want it," I say darkly. "But it's all I have left."

"Making yourself a target? Is that what this is about?"

"No. Getting answers." I turn to him. "You're right to ask why they hunt me. Ann asked, too. I never cared, but I do now. If I had that answer, maybe I'd know how to stop them. Ann says there's safety in light over darkness. Truth instead of secrets."

"I see Ann's been filling your head with ideas." I don't like the twinkle in his eyes, but I have to trust my mate now. I'm out of ideas that will work.

"More light is what Ann believes in."

"Oh, I know," Garrick says.

"She thinks I'll get the answers that way."

"You sure the fuck will. A story like this and everyone comes out of the woodwork. We'd have to leak out some of those pictures of you. Have you sign a blanket consent. We have the pictures." He says something about her phone being cloned.

"I'll do it," I say, knowing what the world will see. Me on that patch of grass. Me eating like a savage. None of it matters anymore.

His fingers fly over his phone. "If I say I'm delivering Savage Adonis, I need to deliver Savage Adonis." He lowers his voice, his tone very nearly sexual. "I'm talking about you turning on that growly thing. Giving the juicy stuff. You'll hold back some details for my story, though. Deal?"

"Deal," I say through gritted teeth.

He reaches up and messes up my hair. It's all I can do not to break his hand. "We'll let your shirt hang open so they can see the scars. And make that stormy face you do. Where you look like you're lost and you want to kill somebody."

My pulse races as he messes up my hair some more.

"That's it, Kiro—that's the look! Fuck—yes. Do that up there and you'll be trending on Twitter and showing up on half the phones in America. Nothing held back. Paraded up there with that angry lost hot guy look…you have to have that look."

"I'll have the look," I say.

"I'm calling *BMZ Confidential* right now. You sure you're serious? You gonna fuck me?"

"I'm not going to fuck you," I spit out.

CHAPTER THIRTY-NINE

Aleksio

THE DESK IN our suite at the Sky Slope Hotel overlooks the endless pine forest. But I'm not looking at the view; I'm examining the images from the cave again. A few of the bodies are impossible to ID.

Our guy got DNA, and he's flying back. We're hoping Kiro isn't among the dead.

We got there just a few hours after the attack. So fucking close. We could've been there. We could've helped him. Instead it was just carnage.

Is Kiro among the dead? Is he wounded? Was he taken? He had a journalist, A.E. Saybrook, with him. Are they still together? Or is she dead, too? Some of the bodies are badly mauled.

I sent Viktor to his room to cool down. I'm hoping he doesn't break anything. Mira's on the bed, fucking around online.

I zoom in on a tattoo on one of the dead. I can't imagine Kiro would have tattoos. And honestly, I can't imagine that

Kiro, a man who lived more than half his life in the wilderness, would be ripped apart by wolves.

There's a tip that a gunshot wound went into Duluth Memorial Medical Center—something out of the wilderness area. I sent a guy to check it out. They're saying it's a hunting accident.

Probably is.

"Aleksio!" Mira screams. "Oh my God! Oh my God!"

"What?"

She's off the bed. She's shoving the phone at me. "Look!"

I take a look and the world drops out from under me. I'm staring into the face of Kiro. My brother.

His lips are moving. Talking. It's a gossip website of some kind. Underneath him in a blaring red rectangle, it says, "LIVE REPORT: Savage Adonis is alive and well, and you won't believe where we found him."

"What the fuck? This is live? Where is this?" I fumble on the sound.

Mira grabs the laptop. The shot switches to a reporter asking a question about his feet. Something about bare feet in the snow. There's a mob of reporters out in front of him.

The feed switches to a still shot of him with long hair in some sort of gloomy hotel room. Another of him in a store wearing glasses. All these weeks of searching for him, and now this firehose of information.

I grab my shit. "Get Viktor. Tell him to meet me at the car. Then you get the rest of everyone you can round up—"

"I got it," she says. "Go!"

Five minutes later I have the SUV in front of the hotel. Viktor jumps in, and we peel out. There's a load of automatic weaponry in the back, and I have half a mind to use it on the mob of reporters taking apart our brother.

Viktor has Mischa and some of his other guys on the phone. They're on the road, too.

"Tell me they're nearer to the hospital than we are."

"No. They were at one of the park entrances."

I gun the fucker. Nothing matters except getting to Kiro. "If we're seeing him out there online, it means Lazarus is seeing him, too."

"*Bladny*," Viktor says. "All they need is a clear shot."

"Not if we kill them first."

CHAPTER FORTY

Kiro

THE LIGHTS ARE blinding. The questions don't stop. How did I get the wolves to accept me? Is it true I went in bare feet even in winter? When I caught animals, would I simply eat them right then and there? Still warm and bloody? The reporters ask more about this. They want me to say that the animals would still be alive when I ate them.

"Sometimes," I growl. "Sometimes they would still be alive, and I would rip out their throats with my teeth."

Garrick tries to hold his mouth in a neutral line, but I see the smile in his eyes. They begin to ask about the professor. They want me to talk about killing him.

Now and then Garrick takes the microphone. "We'll get the deeper details on this in the *Stormline* article—we want to get to as many questions as possible here today."

Garrick wants me to show my scars.

I rip off my shirt. Nothing matters. I'm baring all. Allowing myself to be made into a thing. Their savage. Their circus spectacle. Blindly following her advice.

There's a squeal of tires. Voices yelling to get out of the way. A commotion. The reporters part for whoever is coming through.

Garrick puts a hand on my shoulder, thinking about getting me out of there, maybe.

Uniforms. Somebody official.

The police.

I exchange glances with Garrick. We knew this could happen, that this is how it might end. Garrick has a lawyer. He says the lawyer will keep me free.

My heart pounds as they come. Reporters are getting footage of them now, though I'm sure they're capturing my expression, too. Fear, despair—I don't try to hide how I feel. This is like after the professor—a moment of freedom, then the police come.

Garrick's lawyer tries to stop the cops, but they push him aside. Guns come out. Two familiar faces appear alongside the police. One is Dr. Fancher, head of the Fancher Institute. He would walk around with Nurse Zara every week, peering into the room.

The other is Donny. Donny grins at me.

I freeze.

The lawyer comes up to Garrick, says something about a commitment order.

Panic rises in my chest. I'm beyond hearing.

The instinct to fight surges through me. I imagine hurling myself at Donny. I could rip his throat out—possibly before I die of the bullets they pump into me. But cameras are rolling. And Ann's out there. She'd say to trust the story. She'd say light is better than darkness.

I let the cops cuff me.

Garrick protests loudly. He wants to stay with me, keep a film crew on me.

Donny comes at me. Grinning. Something flashes in his hand. A needle. The police push me away as the Fancher director takes the microphone. The Fancher director makes an apology to the gathered press. As the police push me away, under instructions from Donny, it seems, I hear the Fancher director using words like "unstable." And "mentally ill and dangerous."

Yelling. Garrick is being cuffed and taken away, yelling about lawyers.

Reporters trail us as we head to the Fancher van. Cops bar the way.

The van.

I know that van. It's more than a cage on wheels. It's a fortress on wheels. Seeing it nearly breaks my spirit, and I think maybe I should've fought, that maybe Ann is wrong about trust and light.

A sharp bite on my arm. The needle. I feel Donny's breath on the back of my neck as the numbness spreads.

I meet his eyes. He smiles as spots cloud my vision, as I'm pulled along.

I stumble, limbs sluggish. I'm unused to the drugs. Or maybe he's increased my dose.

Probably both.

Donny oversees the orderlies who shove me down onto the padded bench. They chain my ankles to the ring on the floor. They chain my handcuffed wrists to the bar that runs along the side.

I yank in fury, desperately trying to free myself. They close the cage and then the outer door.

Darkness. Confusion.

We're on the move. I focus on sounds. There's a siren behind us, and one in front of us.

Taking no chances with me. The savage. Drugged and bound once again.

My limbs feel dead. It makes me want to give up. I try to remember the feeling of sunshine. I try to remember the feeling of Ann.

I remember about working against the drug. Vigorous activity.

I yank and struggle, clanking the cuffs and chains. My lips begin to feel fat. My thoughts slow. I fight on with everything I have.

I tell myself that if I don't stop, the drugs will take over. It's a big dose, maybe too big, but I fight like crazy, thinking about Ann. I have to get back there. I pull and pull, feeling the cuffs cut into my skin. My wrists feel warm. Blood.

I don't care. Nothing matters except getting out. I have to get back to Ann.

I rail and bellow as we speed down the highway to the Fancher Institute. It's where we'll go.

Or somewhere worse.

I yank and yank. I know I'm wearing myself out. I just need my alertness back.

I think the hopelessness I feel makes the drugs worse. The hopelessness makes my limbs feel heavy. I tell myself to keep fighting.

I fight to exhaustion, and then I collapse. It's just me in the darkness, breath heavy. The sirens have stopped. There's only the hum of tires. The engine.

The van takes a violent turn.

Or maybe it's my equilibrium.

I fold forward, head over the floor, arms stretched out behind me, shoulders nearly out of their sockets. It's here I realize one good thing: Ann's finally safe. My enemies surely know I'm away from her, that I can't get to her. They have no more reason to go after her.

I press my forehead to my knees, hanging, swaying.

It's me they want. So her plan worked, at least for her. It's enough.

The other thing I realize, chained up back there, is that I probably won't make it to the institute alive. My enemies need me to die. Donny needs me to die.

I hang there alone in the van, thinking about fishing with Ann. I'm back there on the downed tree with her, a pack of two. More than a pack. Back there with Ann was the first time I'd stopped being an outsider to people. It was the first time I belonged with another human being.

You're not a wolf, she said once, and she was right.

She showed me I was human.

Complete with a heart that's breaking. But for one shining moment, I belonged. I had somebody.

The tires hum.

The ride seems to last forever.

Alone.

The loneliness hurts more than ever. Because I know what it is to belong, I suppose.

In my mind, I'm back with her.

The van turns again—careens. I feel a little ill. It's the drugs, the fatigue. The hopelessness is making things worse. The hopelessness can be worse than the drugs. Its fingers spread through me, deadening my soul.

And then a gunshot blasts out. There's a pop below.

Tire. I sit up.

Lazarus—it has to be.

The ride's bumpy, and it comes to me that the tire's blown. The van turns and speeds up. The bumping is more pronounced. I'm bumping off the bench.

Donny's up there—he's either driving or directing the driver. What is happening?

More gunshots.

I can't imagine why he'd try to get away from a man who's trying to kill me. I'd think he'd be happy to see me gunned down and not have to answer for it. He'd fling open the doors himself.

For whatever reason, though, he's running. We take another turn. The going is rougher. I grab the bar behind the seat. We're off the road, maybe. Or maybe it's the tires being shot out.

More bumps.

A crash jolts me forward, nearly pulls my shoulders from my body. It's as if the whole planet comes to a stop.

Silence.

My pulse races. They'll come now. I yank at my chains. I hear keys in the door. Bolts slide open, the cage mechanism unlocks.

I may be chained up for them, ready to be gunned down, but I sit up straight. I'll meet my death head on.

I squint as daylight fills the space. Dark forms jump in.

"*Bratik*," one says, coming to me.

He puts his hands on my cheeks.

More strange words—urgent, emotional. A language I don't know. I cringe. Is he going to snap my neck? Gouge out my eyes? I could take him with just my legs if only they weren't chained.

He pulls me into an embrace. "*Bratik!*"

Another voice behind him. "Fuck. Kiro. Fuck." This one knows my name. He's working at my chains, unlocking my bloody shackles while the first one hugs me like a madman, speaking that strange language.

Suddenly I'm free. I push the first one off.

The other grabs my shirt. "We're your brothers, Kiro." He pulls me up. "Can you stand?"

"Brothers?" I whisper, swaying, hardly grasping the meaning of the word.

He watches my eyes. "We're your brothers."

I blink, eyes adjusting to the light, lips still numb. "Brothers?"

The American's eyes shine. He holds my shoulders, steadying me. His eyes are darker than mine, but his hair is the same, his face is the same. "We've been looking for you forever."

My pulse races.

He pulls me to him, chest to chest. "Fuck, Kiro. We're here now. We have your back."

I feel numb. It's not the drugs this time; it's too much emotion. I pull him to me, bloody hands digging into him. A brother. My eyes feel hot. *Brothers.*

"Out of the way, *brat!*" the other one growls. The music of his growl connects to something inside me. There's something so familiar in his voice. Then I realize it's like my own. These are my brothers.

The other one claps a hand onto the top of my head, ruffling my hair. "Baby brother!"

The American one lets me go and nods at the other. "This is Viktor. I'm Aleksio. Fuck, we've been searching for you. They said you were dead, but I knew you weren't."

My heart thunders.

"We have to get out of here," Viktor says.

"The reporter said they shot you up with something. Is it true? Can you walk? Run?"

"Can you shoot?" Viktor asks.

I scrub my face and take a deep breath. I have brothers.

Viktor is on the phone, telling somebody to hurry. A dark thought comes to me. "The hospital," I say. "Ann. He'll go after her now."

"The gunshot wound victim?" Viktor asks.

"Yes, she has a gunshot wound. Room 363."

Viktor instructs somebody on the other end of the phone to go to the hospital. "Tanechka," he says. "Whatever it takes."

"She'll be safe," Aleksio says. "We're sending people."

"Brothers," I say him.

He grins. "For better or worse."

"Worse right now," Viktor says. "Our vehicle is toasted. This one, too. We have to get out of here. We're vulnerable."

My mind is beginning to clear. I feel happy. Then I spot movement outside the open van doors—out in the field, behind my brothers.

They turn.

Donny's face is bloody. He holds a gun. "Lazarus is coming," he says, swaying. "You're not going anywhere until he gets here. One step out of this van and I'll shoot you."

Lazarus survived? I stiffen, wanting to fly at Donny. Aleksio seems to know it. He presses a hand onto my shoulder, holding me in place.

"Go ahead, Patient 34, make my day," Donny says. "Come at me."

"Fucking seriously?" Aleksio says. "Make my *day*?" He laughs and points at the road beyond the field. Way off far to the right. "And what about that? Does that make your day, too?"

Donny turns to look.

I look, too.

A blast to my left. I swing my gaze to Viktor. He lowers a weapon, grinning.

Donny's down, crumpled in the weeds, a hole in his face.

"Do not threaten our *bratik*," Viktor says.

A shiver slides over me. These are my brothers.

Aleksio squints at the road. "Goddamnit." He pulls Viktor and me in. "They're coming. It's a fucking caravan." He checks his phone. "Tito and Yuri and the guys are twenty minutes out. Fuck."

Viktor speaks in his strange language. He's not happy.

"Who's coming?" I ask.

"Lazarus," Aleksio says.

"Him again," I growl. "He shot Ann. He's been after us."

"Oh, he's definitely been after you," Aleksio says. "He needs you dead. Well, any of us."

"Now he thinks he can get all three of us," Viktor adds.

Viktor pulls one gun after another from his pack. He sets them on the padded bench. "Lazarus helped to kill our father and mother. He helped send you away and split us up. He is our greatest enemy."

My head swims. This man who shot Ann—twice—is also why I never had a family? Why I never knew these brothers? And now he wants to kill us?

I begin to feel wild.

"Fucking surround us…" Aleksio tells us what he thinks Lazarus will do now. Fish in a barrel, he calls us.

Viktor pulls the one side of the back door closed. I watch him with a mixture of pride and anguish. *My own brothers.* They came for me. Now they're willing to die for me.

My pack is larger than I ever dreamed.

Aleksio has unbolted the bench. He tips it on its side. Preparing for a shootout. "If they have C-4 with them, we're fucked," Aleksio says. "A van in the middle of a field. Fucked."

"I have C-4." Viktor pulls a small metal container from his pack.

Aleksio snorts. "That would be perfect—if *they* were the ones in a van trapped in a field."

"I can hear them coming," I say. "Two vehicles more. A lot of men, all coming across now."

My brothers look at me. "You can hear all that?"

"Two different engines just now turned off. Boots crunching dried weeds. All sides. Trying to be quiet."

Viktor hands me a gun. "You know how to handle one of these?"

I give it back. "No."

"Oh. Okay."

"It's cool," Aleksio says. "We have your back, Kiro."

My heart pounds as I breathe in the scent of Lazarus. Our greatest enemy. I look out at the rectangle of sky and field in the back. "He's out there. Hiding. Waiting for us to look." I point to where he is.

"This is bad," Aleksio says. "They're going to storm this van if they don't blow it up."

Viktor says, "Some old crone once said that together we rule. Together we cannot be defeated."

I'm barely listening anymore. I've just found my brothers, and now he'd take them away? Rage boils in my heart.

"We need a plan," Aleksio says. "The prophecy is not a plan. Holding out is not a plan. They have no cover. Let's get creative. Can we get up front through this panel? Drive this thing?"

"I'm ready to get bloody," Viktor says.

"How many, Kiro?" Aleksio asks.

"Twelve, fifteen. All sides. Except—" I motion at the part where we can see.

Aleksio goes on. Tactics.

I'm no longer listening. I smell them. I hear their heartbeats. Frightened. They want to kill my brothers. Something deep and primal animates me.

"Come on, can we shoot through this panel, you think?" Aleksio wants to change things in the van. He has complicated plans.

All I hear is the fury of my own heartbeat.

All I smell is blood. All I feel is love for these brothers who would mock Donny and then kill him for me. It was something I'd always dreamed of doing, and my brothers did it for me.

My brothers.

They came for me.

The heartbeats of our enemies grow stronger as they close in. Wildness fills me with the power of sunshine, huge as the sky. Thoughts fall from my mind. I see only pictures—me flying at the men. Flying through the air.

I leap out the back of the van, spinning at the men. I'm faster than wind. I'm grabbing and crushing their throats and faces, more airborne than not. Snarling, bloody.

They'll have to shoot off my arms and legs to stop me, and they know it. It makes them hesitate. It makes them afraid.

My brothers yell something.

Their words mean nothing. I fly at our attackers, ripping, kicking.

My brothers are behind me, shooting, taking out those who recover from their shock long enough to fight back.

Time slows. I close my hand a throat and yank, breaking a neck. Warmth in my fingers. I break a face with my foot. I spin and throw. I kill. Some bodies I lift against me. I allow them to absorb the endless bullets shooting from the endless guns.

My brothers fight beside me so beautifully. I feel as if we've been together always.

Men fall.

I feel invincible as I meet another set of stunned eyes, as I close my grip around another throat.

Men with guns freeze in the face of animal rage—even if that animal rage is coming from a human.

Nobody will take my brothers from me. Never again.

I feel Viktor come up next to me. "*Bratik*, hold!" He grips my arm, pulling me. There are bodies all around. We jump into the front of the van.

Aleksio's driving. He guns it across the field toward a big, blocky tanklike truck up on the road. Bumpy going.

"You sure Lazarus is in that Hummer?" Viktor says.

"Hiding in there like a little girl," Aleksio says. We bump onto the road, wheels barely intact—you can feel it through the bottom. Viktor hurls something out the window. "Go!"

Aleksio guns the engine. "Goodbye, fucker." There's a massive explosion behind us.

Sirens sound in the distance.

"Yuri's five minutes up the road. We've got this!"

"Baby brother. The way you flew at them!" Viktor laughs and slings an arm around my shoulder. "It's good to get bloody with you, brother. You're a great warrior. More fierce than I ever imagined."

I look into his eyes. My heart swells bigger than the sky.

CHAPTER FORTY-ONE

Ann

"THAT CONVICTION ORDER was invalidated a week ago. It was invalidated, overturned. There are records of that on file if your men had bothered to check. No—right, overturned by a judge in a court of law…no, that's bullshit—your men didn't follow procedure. That's right, you know how I know? Because I'm the one who got it overturned. I'm the one who saw that it was on file."

I fight to open my eyes. They feel gluey, gravelly.

"…no, you listen to me. If you interfere with Mr. Dragusha's rights one more time, deprive him of one more instant of his freedom, I will bring a suit against your department so fast…kidnapping…accessory to attempted murder…collusion with a criminal organization…"

I blink. The light is so bright.

A woman with bright blonde ponytails sits at my bedside. "Good morning!" She has an accent. Slavic. Russian.

The woman speaking legalese is across the room, pacing, phone glued to the side of her head. She has dark hair and an air of authority.

"She's not as scary as she sounds," the woman with ponytails says. She wears a red T-shirt with the iconic Rolling Stones lips. Russian.

"Okay," I breathe.

"My name is Tatiana, but my friends call me Tanechka. Kiro sent us." She smiles. "Nobody will bother you."

"Okay," I say again, unsure what's going on. "Where's Kiro?"

"He's okay. He's coming."

"What happened."

"Did you miss the whole press conference?" The dark-haired woman comes up to the other side of my bed. "It was quite the thing. I'll let him tell you. He's on his way with his brothers. I don't think we'll have any more trouble."

Tanechka grins. "Let them give us trouble. I will fuck them up."

"A press conference? His brothers?"

"Kiro pretty much called his own press conference. It's how his brothers found him. I'm Mira. Hi." She gestures at the tubes in my arm. "I won't make you shake my hand."

"He found his family by holding a press conference?" I imagine him up there, standing in front of cameras. The one thing he never wanted.

"Two brothers. Very fierce," Tanechka says.

Mira grins. "He got himself brothers and a third of a massive criminal empire called the Black Lion clan, but we won't go into that."

"What? Black Lion clan?" Things start to make sense. "That's why they were after him."

"So you know it," Mira says. "He's a Dragusha. Don't worry, the Black Lion clan...it'll evolve once things settle."

Tanechka grins. "We all fell out of our chairs to see Kiro on the internet."

"Does he know they wanted to find him?" I ask. "Does he know he had brothers out there who loved him all that time?"

Kiro bursts into the room. He comes to my side. He takes my hands.

His face is bloody, and his clothes are torn. He looks every inch the savage, and so do his brothers. And they're all smiling. All so happy.

CHAPTER FORTY-TWO

Ann

Two months later

I START UP a fire using a starter log, something Kiro would laugh at, but he's spending a rare night out with his brothers.

Kiro and I bought a big old apartment near Washington Park in Chicago. It cost a fortune, but it turns out the Dragushas are fabulously wealthy.

Kiro's gotten used to the city surprisingly well. He says it's just another forest, just another system. He's kind of amazing.

He's starting to trust people and fill the gaps in his education. He's learning new things and falling into step with his brothers like they were never apart. I'm not so sure how I love his newfound delight in drinking vodka with them, and the way they like to sit around throwing knives at targets…well, I guess he missed a lot of little-brother time.

Still, I know he's looking forward to getting land up north once I'm fully recovered. A place of our own for the warm months. Lots of wilderness. We spend a lot of time these days dreaming up a life for ourselves. Part time in Chicago, to be with his brothers. Part in the wild.

Aleksio's girlfriend, Mira, found a great lawyer who got him off on all the charges against him. The six of us go out to restaurants a lot—Kiro and his two brothers and Mira and Tanechka. Like an instant family—for both of us.

At first he wanted us to go overseas together, so I could chase my stories, but chasing those dangerous stories was never something I meant to do all my life. There are stories here. We're talking about writing a book on the wolves. I've always wanted to write a book.

I arrange the presents under our tree and find a new one for me from Kiro. It's a large box. Hat-sized. Did Kiro go on a secret shopping trip?

He's been trying to make up for kidnapping me and tying me up. He's apologized a zillion times. I've forgiven him just as many times. But words still don't mean much to Kiro. He gives me lots of presents. He's been by my side nearly nonstop while I recover from my injuries.

He's a good mate. I tell him that sometimes. Understatement of the year. I love being with him. I love him.

Viktor and Tanechka want us to go to Ukraine with them when they visit there this spring. They're planning on rebuilding the bombed-out convent where Tanechka spent time, but Kiro's not quite ready for flying. It's a little suspicious—rebuilding the convent sounds like it might involve a few armed battles.

Maybe someday.

I shake the box. Nothing rattles. It's heavy, though.

I hear a growl at the doorway. Kiro. He stalks toward me. "What are you doing?"

"Snooping."

He comes to me and kneels and takes the box from my hands, puts it back under. Then he kisses me. "I love you," he says. Words mean nothing to Kiro, but he knows they mean everything to me. "But you don't get to see what's in the box until Christmas morning."

"I love you, too, but that doesn't mean I won't snoop."

He twists one of my curls around his finger. He's always doing that. Still.

"Where were you guys? Out being royal?"

He snorts. The second he was back with his brothers, an entire mafia empire coalesced around them. Apparently everyone was waiting for the return of Kiro. It kind of stunned us, like walking into a royal court and finding a throne waiting for you.

The men who worked for their enemy, Lazarus, either fled or came over to beg for forgiveness. People regard the three of them like...well, royalty.

They never found Lazarus's body, but it barely matters. Even if he were alive, even if he came back, he would be neutralized so fast.

I'm not so keen on the criminal empire. Luckily, Mira and Tanechka aren't either. And, while Viktor and Aleksio are pretty damn badass, they've been getting into more wholesome things. Aleksio is opening a restaurant.

They're going legit little by little. Handing off some of the supercriminal parts to their underbosses.

It suits Kiro. He loves fighting, loves playing the tough guy with his brothers, but he's no fucking criminal.

"Were you out on the docks?"

"Not exactly." He peels off his shirt. I gasp. His arm is covered in plastic and underneath, an intricate tattoo of a battle scene, covering a huge swath of his arm. "What did you do, Kiro?"

"Viktor and Aleksio and I got tattoos today. It's a depiction of the prophecy."

"Uh. That stupid prophecy. Why would you want that on your arm?" The prophecy is why Lazarus and his mentor tore them apart all those years ago.

"The tattoo shows our own version of the prophecy. Everyone thought 'together the brothers rule' meant us ruling the Black Lion clan," he says. "But the old woman who gave the prophecy never said *what* we would rule. So we decided it meant we would rule our destinies. This is of us finding each other and ruling our own lives."

"Oh my God. I love that."

"I got the idea from you. The story is important, that's what you always say. I said we needed to think of a different story."

"The tattoos were your idea?"

Kiro grins. He's been fascinated by tattoos since we got back. "Yes." He shows the battle flag and the fanciful swirls and scrolls, all meaning something. They put a lot of thought into it. But there's a part of his that's different. My name is there. And there's a wolf. I trace it through the plastic. I know he misses those wolves. He still mourns his dead friends.

"Wait." I go and grab a small gift. "I want you to open this."

"It's not Christmas."

"I want you to have it now," I say, heart pounding.

He tears off the paper and lifts the lid of the little box. He goes still, holding it in his shaking hands. "It's...." He swallows back the emotion.

It's the keychain with the wolf figurine, the one that reminded him so much of Red. The one he got at the outdoor store. The one he threw into the grass on the hillside.

"You grabbed it," he says.

"Yeah. I grabbed it. You can keep your keys on it. Keep it with you always."

He pulls it out of the box and holds it in his palm, reverently. Like it's precious. He touches its little scruff the way he used to when we first had it.

I look away, thinking to give him a private moment.

"No, you can look, Ann." He looks up, my beautiful, clear-eyed Kiro. Unflinchingly honest. Utterly there. "I want this with me always."

"That's the great thing about a keychain."

"I want you to be with me always," he says.

"I want to be with you always," I say.

"No, I mean..." He crawls under the tree and pulls out a small box I hadn't noticed. "I want you to be with me always."

My pulse hammers in my ears as I take it.

A small box. A jewelry box. I hold it to my heart and meet his amber gaze. And smile.

And he smiles. We don't need words.

The End

Thanks for reading! I hope you enjoyed your time with the Dragusha brothers as much as I did!

I love hearing from you and hanging out!

- ❖ Email me at annika@annikamartinbooks.com
- ❖ Visit annikamartinbooks.com to find out about the latest news and to get on my newsletter.
- ❖ You are warmly invited to join my facebook group, the fabulous gang at: facebook.com/groups/AnnikaMartinFabulousGang
- ❖ My facebook page is: facebook.com/AnnikaMartinBooks
- ❖ And twitter! twitter.com/Annika_Martin

Acknowledgements

Kiro's story has always felt so important to me, and I'm grateful to my critique partners who brought him such love and tenderness – Joanna Chambers, Katie Reus, and Skye Warren all read the story at its earliest and roughest and helped me see it clearly. Thanks also to Editor Deb Nemeth, who provided amazing developmental editing and copy editing. Beta readers Hannah Orenich and Denise Coffee helped ensure the book could stand alone and had helpful insights, and lovely Heather Roberts of Social Butterfly came through with great beta reader feedback and PR hand-holding. Sadye of Fussy Librarian did an incredible job of proofreading and so far beyond. (Any mistakes are my own last minute changes.) Sparkles to BookBeautiful for the gorgeous cover and BB eBooks for the wonderful formatting. I'm so grateful for all the bloggers and facebook book-lovers for helping to promote my series—you are beautiful! Tacklehugs to my Annika Martin Fabulous Gang peeps!

About Annika

I love writing dirty stories about dangerous criminals, hanging out with my man and my two cats, and kicking snow clumps off the bottom of cars around Minneapolis. I've had tons of jobs: factory worker, waitress at a zillion different places, shop clerk, advertising writer. Animals are a huge passion of mine, especially whales and lost dogs. I like to run and read books in bed, and I spend way too much time in coffee shops. In my spare time I write as the RITA award-winning author Carolyn Crane.

Books by Annika Martin

Dangerous Royals
Dark Mafia Prince
Wicked Mafia Prince
Savage Mafia Prince

Taken Hostage by Kinky Bank Robbers
The Hostage Bargain
(Book 1 of Taken Hostage by Kinky Bank Robbers)
The Wrong Turn
(Book #2 of Taken Hostage by Kinky Bank Robbers)
The Deeper Game
(Book #3 of Taken Hostage by Kinky Bank Robbers)
Taken Hostage by Kinky Bank Robbers: the 3-book set
The Most Wanted
(Book #4 of Taken Hostage by Kinky Bank Robbers)

Criminals & Captives
PRISONER (book 1)
by Annika Martin & Skye Warren

Writing as Carolyn Crane

Sexy, gritty romantic suspense
Against the Dark (Book #1 of the Associates)
Off the Edge (Book #2 of the Associates)
Into the Shadows (Book #3 of the Associates)
Behind the Mask (Book #4 of the Associates)

Plotty, twisty-turny urban fantasy
Mind Games (Book 1 of the Disillusionists)
Double Cross (Book 2 of the Disillusionists)
Head Rush (Book 3 of the Disillusionists)
Plus assorted shorts and single titles

More about Carolyn's books:
authorcarolyncrane.com